Jonathan Franzen is also the author of the novels *Strong Motion* and *The Corrections*. His fiction and non-fiction appear frequently in *The New Yorker* and *Harper's*, and he was named one of the best novelists under forty by *Granta* and *The New Yorker*. He lives in New York City.

The
TWENTY-
SEVENTH
CITY

Jonathan Franzen

FOURTH ESTATE • *London* and *New York*

First published in the United States by Farrar, Straus and Giroux
First published in Great Britain in 2003 by
Fourth Estate
A Division of HarperCollins*Publishers*
77–85 Fulham Palace Road
London W6 8JB
www.4thestate.com

10 9 8 7 6 5 4 3 2 1

The author is grateful for permission to quote the following copyrighted works:
"The Red Wheel-Barrow" from *William Carlos Williams: Collected Poems
1909–1939*, Volume I, copyright 1938 by New Directions Publishing
Corporation. Reprinted by permission of New Directions.
The "Chicken of the Sea" jingle, reprinted by permission of the
Ralston Purina Company.

The author wishes to thank the Artists Foundation of Boston and the
Massachusetts Council for the Arts and Humanities for their support in 1986.

A catalogue record for this book is available from the British Library

ISBN 1-84115-748-1

Printed in Great Britain by
Clays Ltd, St Ives plc

To my parents

THE
TWENTY-SEVENTH
CITY

1

In early June Chief William O'Connell of the St. Louis Police Department announced his retirement, and the Board of Police Commissioners, passing over the favored candidates of the city political establishment, the black community, the press, the Officers Association and the Missouri governor, selected a woman, formerly with the police in Bombay, India, to begin a five-year term as chief. The city was appalled, but the woman—one S. Jammu—assumed the post before anyone could stop her.

This was on August 1. On August 4, the Subcontinent again made the local news when the most eligible bachelor in St. Louis married a princess from Bombay. The groom was Sidney Hammaker, president of the Hammaker Brewing Company, the city's flagship industry. The bride was rumored to be fabulously wealthy. Newspaper accounts of the wedding confirmed reports that she owned a diamond pendant insured for $11 million, and that she had brought a retinue of eighteen servants to staff the Hammaker estate in suburban Ladue. A fireworks display at the wedding reception rained cinders on lawns up to a mile away.

A week later the sightings began. An Indian family of ten was seen standing on a traffic island one block east of the Cervantes Convention Center. The women wore saris, the men dark business suits, the children gym shorts and T-shirts. All of them wore expressions of controlled annoyance.

By the beginning of September, scenes like this had become a fixture of daily life in the city. Indians were noticed lounging with no evident purpose on the skybridge between Dillard's and the St. Louis Centre. They were observed spreading blankets in the art museum parking lot and preparing a hot lunch on a Primus stove, playing card games on the sidewalk in front of the National Bowling Hall of Fame, viewing houses for sale in Kirkwood and Sunset Hills, taking snapshots outside the Amtrak station downtown, and clustering around the raised hood of a Delta 88 stalled on the Forest Park Parkway. The children invariably appeared well behaved.

Early autumn was also the season of another, more familiar Eastern visitor to St. Louis, the Veiled Prophet of Khorassan. A group of businessmen had conjured up the Prophet in the nineteenth century to help raise funds for worthy causes. Each year He returned and incarnated Himself in a different leading citizen whose identity was always a closely guarded secret, and with His nondenominational mysteries He brought a playful glamour to the city. It had been written:

> *There on that throne, to which the blind belief*
> *Of millions rais'd him, sat the Prophet-Chief,*
> *The Great Mokanna. O'er his features hung*
> *The Veil, the Silver Veil, which he had flung*
> *In mercy there, to hide from mortal sight*
> *His dazzling brow, till man could bear its light.*

It rained only once in September, on the day of the Veiled Prophet Parade. Water streamed down the tuba bells in the marching bands, and trumpeters experienced difficulties with their embouchure. Pom-poms wilted, staining the girls' hands with dye, which they smeared on their foreheads when they pushed back their hair. Several of the floats sank.

On the night of the Veiled Prophet Ball, the year's premier society event, high winds knocked down power lines all over the city. In the Khorassan Room of the Chase-Park Plaza Hotel, the debbing had just concluded when the lights went out. Waiters rushed in with candelabras, and when the first of them were lit the ballroom filled with murmurs of surprise and consternation: the Prophet's throne was empty.

On Kingshighway a black Ferrari 275 was speeding past the windowless supermarkets and fortified churches of the city's north side. Observers might have glimpsed a snow-white robe behind the windshield, a crown on the passenger seat. The Prophet was driving to the airport. Parking in a fire lane, He dashed into the lobby of the Marriott Hotel.

"You got some kind of problem there?" a bellhop said.

"I'm the Veiled Prophet, twit."

On the top floor of the hotel He stopped outside a door and knocked. The door was opened by a tall dark woman in a jogging suit. She was very pretty. She burst out laughing.

.

When the sky began to lighten, low in the east over southern Illinois, the birds were the first to know it. Along the riverfront and in all the downtown parks and plazas, the trees began to chirp and rustle. It was the first Monday morning in October. The birds downtown were waking up.

North of the business district, where the poorest people lived, an early morning breeze carried smells of used liquor and unnatural perspiration out of alleyways where nothing moved; a slamming door was heard for blocks around. In the railyards of the city's central basin, amid the buzzing of faulty chargers and the sudden ghostly shiverings of Cyclone fences, men with flattops dozed in square-headed towers while rolling stock regrouped below them. Three-star hotels and private hospitals with an abject visibility occupied the higher ground. Farther west, the land grew hilly and healthier trees knit the settlements together, but this was not St. Louis anymore, it was suburb. On the south side there were rows upon rows of cubical brick houses where widows and widowers lay in beds and the blinds in the windows, lowered in a different era, would not be raised all day.

But no part of the city was deader than downtown. Here in the heart of St. Louis, in the lee of the whining all-night traffic on four expressways, was a wealth of parking spaces. Here sparrows bickered and pigeons ate. Here City Hall, a hip-roofed copy of the Hôtel de Ville in Paris, rose in two-dimensional splendor from a flat, vacant block. The air on Market Street, the central thoroughfare, was wholesome. On either side of it you could hear the birds both singly and in chorus—it was like a meadow. It was like a back yard.

The keeper of this peace had been awake all night on Clark Avenue, just south of City Hall. Chief Jammu, on the fifth floor of police headquarters, was opening the morning paper and spreading it out beneath her desk lamp. It was still dark in her office, and from the neck down, with her hunched, narrow shoulders and her bony knees in knee socks and her restless feet, the Chief looked for all the world like a schoolgirl who'd been cramming.

Her head was older. As she leaned over the newspaper, the lamplight picked out white strands in the silky black hair above her left ear. Like Indira Gandhi, who on this October morning was still alive and the prime minister of India, Jammu showed signs of asymmetric graying. She kept her hair just long enough to pin it up in back. She had a large forehead, a hooked and narrow nose, and wide lips that looked blood-starved, bluish. When she was rested, her dark eyes dominated her face, but this morning they were cloudy and crowded by pouches. Wrinkles cut the smooth skin around her mouth.

Turning a page of the *Post-Dispatch* she found what she wanted, a picture of her taken on a good day. She was smiling, her eyes engaging. The caption—*Jammu: an eye to the personal*—brought the same smile back. The accompanying article, by Joseph Feig, had run under the headline A NEW LEASE ON LIFE. She began to read.

> Few people remember it now, but the name Jammu first appeared in American newspapers nearly a decade ago. The year was 1975. The Indian subcontinent was in turmoil following Prime Minister Indira Gandhi's suspension of civil rights and her crackdown on her political foes.
>
> Amid conflicting, heavily censored reports, a strange story from the city of Bombay began to unfold in the Western press. The reports con-

cerned an operation known as Project Poori, implemented by a police official named Jammu. In Bombay, it seemed, the police department had gone into the wholesale food business.

The operation sounded crazy then; it sounds hardly less crazy today. But now that a twist of fate has brought Jammu to St. Louis in the role of police chief, people here are asking themselves whether Project Poori was really so crazy after all.

In a recent interview in her spacious Clark Avenue office, Jammu spoke of the circumstances that led up to the project.

"Before Mrs. Gandhi dispensed with the constitution the country was like Gertrude's Denmark—rotten to the core. But with the imposition of President's Rule, we in law enforcement had our chance to do something about it. In Bombay alone we were locking up 1,500 lawbreakers a week and impounding 30 million rupees in illegal goods and cash. When we evaluated our efforts after two months, we realized we'd hardly made one speck of progress," Jammu recalled.

President's Rule devolves from a clause in the Indian constitution giving the central government sweeping powers in times of emergency. For this reason, the 19 months of such rule were referred to as the Emergency.

In 1975 a rupee was worth about ten U.S. cents.

"I was an assistant commissioner at the time," Jammu said. "I suggested a different approach. Since threats and arrests weren't working, why not try defeating corruption on its own terms?

"Why not enter a business ourselves and use our resources and influence to achieve a freer market? We chose an essential commodity: food," she said.

It was thus that Project Poori was conceived. A *poori* is a deep-fried puff-bread, popular in India. By the end of 1975, Bombay was known to Western journalists as the one city in India where groceries were plentiful and the prices uninflated.

Naturally, attention centered on Jammu. Her handling of the operation, as detailed in the dailies and in *Time* and *Newsweek*, caught the imagination of police forces in this country. But certainly no one would have guessed that one day she would be in St. Louis wearing the Chief's badge on her blouse and a department revolver on her hip.

Colonel Jammu, however, entering her third month in office, would have it seem the most natural thing in the world. "A good chief stresses personal involvement at all levels of the organization," she said. "Carrying a revolver is one symbol of my commitment.

"Of course, it's also an instrument of lethal force," she continued, leaning back in her office chair.

Jammu's frank, gutsy style of law-enforcement management has earned a reputation that is literally world-wide. When the search for a replacement for former Chief William O'Connell ended in its deadlock of opposing factions, Jammu's name was among the first mentioned as a compromise candidate. And despite the fact that she had no previous law-enforcement experience in the U.S., the Police Board confirmed her appointment less than a week after she arrived in St. Louis for interviews.

To many here, it came as a surprise that this Indian woman met the citizenship requirements necessary for her job. But Jammu, who was born in Los Angeles and whose father was American, says she went to great lengths to preserve her citizenship. Since she was a child she has dreamed of settling in America.

"I'm terribly patriotic," she said with a smile. "New residents, like myself, often are. I'm looking forward to spending many years in St. Louis. I'm here to stay."

Jammu speaks with slightly British intonations and striking clarity of thought. With her fine features and delicate build, she could hardly be less like the stereotype of the gruff, male American police chief. But her record gives an altogether different impression.

Within five years of entering the Indian Police Service in 1969, she became a deputy to the Inspector-General of Police in Maharashtra Province. Five years later, at the astonishing age of 31, she was named Commissioner of the Bombay police. At 35, she is both the youngest police chief in modern St. Louis history and the first woman to hold the post.

Before joining the Indian police she received a B.A. in electrical science from the University of Srinagar in Kashmir. She also did three semesters of postgraduate work in economics at the University of Chicago.

"I've worked hard," she said. "I've had plenty of luck, too. I doubt I'd have this job had I not received good press from Project Poori. But of course the real problem was always my sex. It wasn't easy to buck five millennia of sexual discrimination.

"Until I became a superintendent I routinely dressed as a man," Jammu reminisced.

Apparently, experiences like this played a key role in the Commissioners' selection of Jammu. In a city still struggling to overcome its image as a "loser," the Board's unorthodox choice makes good public-relations sense. St. Louis is now the largest U.S. city to have a female police chief.

Nelson A. Nelson, president of the Board, believes St. Louis should take credit for its leading role in making city government accessible to women. "It's affirmative action in the truest sense of the word," he commented.

Jammu, however, appeared to discount the issue. "Yes, I'm a woman, all right," she said with a smile.

As one of her primary goals, she names making city streets safer. While not offering to comment on the performances of past chiefs in this area, she did say that she was working closely with City Hall to devise a comprehensive plan for fighting street crime.

"The city needs a new lease on life, a fundamental shake-up. If we can get the business community and citizens' groups to aid us—if we can make people see that this is a *regional* problem— I'm convinced that in a very short time we can make the streets safe again," she said.

Chief Jammu is not afraid of making her ambitions known. One might venture to guess that she will meet with jealous opposition in whatever she attempts. But her accomplishments in India show her to be a formidable adversary, and a political figure well worth keeping an eye on.

"Project Poori is a good illustration," she pointed out. "We applied a new set of terms to a situation that appeared hopeless. We set up bazaars outside every station house. It improved our public image, and it improved morale. For the first time in decades we had no trouble attracting well-qualified recruits. Indian police have a reputation for corruption and brutality which is largely due to the inability to recruit responsible, well-educated constables. Project Poori began to change things."

Some of Jammu's critics have voiced fears that a police chief accustomed to the more authoritarian atmosphere of India might be insensitive to civil-rights issues in St. Louis. Charles Grady, spokesman for the local chapter of the American Civil Liberties Union, has gone even further, urging that Jammu be dismissed before a "constitutional disaster" occurs.

Jammu strenuously rejects these criticisms. "I've been quite surprised by the reactions of the liberal community here," she said.

"Their concern arises, I believe, from an abiding distrust of the Third World in general. They overlook the fact that India's system of government has been deeply influenced by Western ideals, particularly, of course, by the British. They fail to distinguish between the Indian police rank-and-file, and the national officer corps, of which I was a member.

"We were trained in the British tradition of civil service. Standards were extremely high. We were continually torn between sticking up for our troops and sticking up for our ideals. My critics overlook the fact that it was this very conflict which made a position in the United States attractive to me.

"In fact, what strikes me now about Project

Poori is how American our approach was. Into a clogged and bankrupt economy we injected a harsh dose of free enterprise. Soon hoarders found their goods worth half of what they'd paid for them. Profiteers went begging for customers. On a small scale, we achieved a genuine *Wirtschaftswunder*," Jammu recalled, referring to postwar Germany's "economic miracle."

Can she work similar wonders in St. Louis? Upon taking office, other chiefs in recent memory have stressed loyalty, training, and technical advances. Jammu sees the crucial factors as innovation, hard work, and confidence.

"For too long," she said, "our officers have accepted the idea that their mission is merely to ensure that St. Louis deteriorates in the most orderly possible way.

"This has done wonders for morale," she said sarcastically.

It was perhaps inevitable that many of the officers here, especially the older ones, would react to Jammu's appointment with skepticism. But attitudes have already begun to change. The sentiment most often voiced in the precinct houses these days seems to be: "She's OK."

Five minutes into Joseph Feig's interview, Jammu had smelled sweat from her underarms, a mildewy feral stink. Feig had a nose; he didn't need a polygraph.

"Isn't Jammu the name of a city in Kashmir?" he asked.

"It's the capital during the winter."

"I see." He looked at her fixedly for several long seconds. Then he asked: "What's it like switching countries like this in the middle of your life?"

"I'm terribly patriotic," she said, with a smile. She was surprised he hadn't pursued the question of her past. These profiles were a rite of passage in St. Louis, and Feig, a senior editor, was generally acknowledged to be the dean of local feature writing. When he first walked in the door, in his wrinkled tweed jacket and his week-old beard, fierce and gray, he'd looked so investigative that Jammu had actually blushed. She'd imagined the worst:

FEIG: Colonel Jammu, you claim you wanted to escape the violence of Indian society, the personal and caste conflicts, but the fact remains that you did spend fifteen years in the leadership of a force whose brutality is notorious. We aren't stupid, Colonel. We've heard about India. The hammered elbows, the tooth extractions, the rifle rapes. The candles, the acid, the lathis, the cattle prods—

JAMMU: The mess was generally cleaned up before I got there.

FEIG: Colonel Jammu, given Mrs. Gandhi's almost obsessive distrust of her subordinates and given your own central involvement in Project Poori, I have to wonder if you're at all related to the Prime Minister. I don't see how else a woman could have made commissioner, especially a woman with an American father—

JAMMU: It isn't clear to me what difference it makes to St. Louis if I'm related to certain people in India.

But the article was in print now, definitive and unretractable. The windows of Jammu's office were beginning to fill with light. She rested her chin on her hands and let the print below her wander out of focus. She was happy with the article but worried about Feig. How could someone so obviously intelligent be a mere transcriber of platitudes? It seemed impossible. Perhaps he was just paying out the rope, "giving" her an interview like a final cigarette at dawn, while behind her back he marshalled his facts into an efficient, deadly squad . . .

Her head was sinking towards her desk. She reached for the lamp switch and slumped, with a dry splash, onto the newspaper. She closed her eyes and immediately began to dream. In the dream, Joseph Feig was her father. He was interviewing her. He smiled as she spoke of her triumphs, the delicious aftertaste of lies that people fell for, the escape from airless India. In his eyes she read a sad, shared awareness of the world's credulity. "You're a scrappy girl," he said. She leaned over her desk and nestled her head in the crook of her elbow, thinking: scrappy girl. Then she heard her interviewer tiptoe around behind her chair. She reached around to feel his leg, but her hands swung through empty air. His bristly face pushed aside her hair and brushed her neck. His tongue fell out of his mouth. Heavy, warm, doughlike, it lay against her skin.

She woke up with a shudder.

Jammu's father had been killed in 1974 when a helicopter carrying foreign journalists and some South Vietnamese military personnel was downed near the Cambodian border by a communist rocket. A second helicopter captured the crash on film before escaping to Saigon. Jammu and her mother had learned the news from the Paris edition of the *Herald Tribune*, their sole link with the man. It was from a week-old *Herald Tribune* that Jammu, more than a decade earlier, had first learned his name. Ever since she'd been old enough to ask, her mother had evaded her questions, dismissing the subject brusquely whenever Jammu tried to bring it up. Then, in the spring before she entered the university, her mother spoke. They were at the breakfast table on the veranda, Maman with her *Herald Tribune* and Jammu with her algebra book. Her mother nudged the paper across the table and scraped a long fingernail across an article at the bottom of the front page:

TENSION MOUNTS ON
SINO-INDIAN BORDER
Peter B. Clancy

Jammu read a few paragraphs, but she didn't know why. She looked up for an explanation.

"That's your father."

The tone was typically matter-of-fact. Maman spoke only English to Jammu, and spoke it with a perverse disdain, as if she didn't accept the language's word for anything. Jammu scanned the article again. Countercharges. Secessionist. Bleak vistas. Peter B. Clancy. "A reporter?" she said.

"Mm."

Her mother wouldn't say what he was like. Having acknowledged his existence, she proceeded to ridicule her daughter's curiosity. There was no story to tell, she said. They'd met in Kashmir. They'd left the country and spent two years in Los Angeles, where Clancy took a degree of some sort. Then Maman had returned, alone, to Bombay, not Srinagar, with her baby, and had lived there ever since. Nowhere in this obituary narrative did she suggest that

Clancy was anything more than a second set of luggage. Jammu got the idea—things hadn't worked out. It didn't matter, either. The city was full of bastards, and Maman, in any case, was oblivious to public opinion. The newspapers called her the "laughing jackal of real estate." Laughing all the way to the bank, they meant. She was a speculator and slumlord, one of the more successful in a town of speculation and slums.

Jammu selected two Tylenols and a Dexedrine from her top drawer and swallowed them with coffee dregs. She'd finished the night's reading sooner than she'd planned. It was only 6:30. In Bombay it was 5:00 in the evening—Indian time was a quaint half hour out of step with the rest of the world—and Maman was probably at home, upstairs, pouring her first drink. Jammu reached for the phone, got the international operator, and gave her the numbers.

The connection hissed with the difficult spanning of half a world. Of course in India even local calls hissed this way. Maman answered.

"It's me," Jammu said.

"Oh, hello."

"Hello. Are there any messages?"

"No. The town seems empty without your friends." Her mother laughed. "Homesick?"

"Not especially."

"Apropos—has the Enlightened Despot called you?"

"Ha ha."

"Seriously. She's in New York. The U.N. General Session opened."

"That's a thousand miles from here."

"Oh, she could afford to call. She chooses not to. Yes. She simply chooses not to. I read this morning—do you still read the papers?"

"When I have time."

"That's right. When you have time. I read about her mini-summit with American intellectuals is what I was going to say. Front page, column one. Asimov, Sagan—futurists. She's a wonder. Study her and you can learn. Not that she's infallible. I noticed Asimov was eating ribs in the picture they ran. But anyway— How is St. Louis?"

"Temperate. Very dry."

"And you with your sinuses. How is Singh?"

"Singh is Singh. I'm expecting him any minute."

"Just don't let him handle your accounts."

"He's handling my accounts."

"Willful child. I'll have to send Bhandari over later this month to check the arrangements. Singh is not—"

"Here? You're sending Karam here?"

"Only for a few days. Expect him on the twenty-ninth or so."

"Don't send Karam. I don't like him."

"And I don't like Singh." There was a faint sound that Jammu recognized as the rattle of ice in a tumbler. "Listen dear, I'll talk to you tomorrow."

"All right. Good-bye."

Maman and Indira were blood relations, Kashmiri Brahmans, sharing a great-grandfather on the Nehru side. It was no coincidence that Jammu had been admitted to the Indian Police Service less than a year after Indira became prime minister. Once she was in the Service, no one had been ordered to promote her; of course, but occasional phone calls from the Ministry would let the pertinent officials know that her career was being watched "with interest." Over the years she herself had received hundreds of calls similar in their vagueness, though more immediate in their concerns. A Maharashtra state legislator would express great interest in a particular prosecution, a Congress Party boss would express great distress over a particular opponent's business dealings. Very seldom did a call originate from higher up than the governor's office; Indira was a great student of detail, but only in curricular subjects. Like any entrenched leader, she made sure to place plenty of buffers between herself and questionable operations, and Jammu's political operations had been questionable at best. The two of them had spoken privately only once—just after Jammu and her mother concocted Project Poori. Jammu flew to Delhi and spent seventy minutes in the garden of Madam's residence on Safdarjang Road. Madam, in a canvas chair, watched Jammu closely, her brown eyes protuberant and her head turned slightly to one side, her lips curled in a smile that now and then made her gums click, a smile in which Jammu saw nothing but machinery. Shifting her gaze a quarter turn, towards a hedge of rosebushes behind which machine-gun muzzles sauntered, Madam spoke. "Please understand that this wholesaling project won't work. You do understand that, you're a sensible young woman. But we're going to fund it anyway."

A shoe squeaked in Jammu's outer office. She sat up straight. "Who's—" She cleared her throat. "Who's there?"

Balwan Singh walked in. He was wearing pleated gray pants, a fitted white shirt, and an azure necktie with fine yellow stripes. His air was so competent and trustworthy that he scarcely needed to show his clearance papers to get upstairs. "It's me," he said. He set a white paper bag on Jammu's desk.

"You were eavesdropping."

"Me? Eavesdropping?" Singh walked to the windows. He was tall and broad-shouldered, and his light skin had received additional sunniness from some Middle Eastern ancestor. Only an old friend and ex-lover like Jammu could detect the moments when the grace of his movements passed over into swishiness. She still admired him as an ornament. For a man who up until July had been living in Dharavi squalor, he would have seemed remarkably—suspiciously—dapper if he hadn't dressed exactly the same way among his so-called comrades in Bombay, whose tastes ran to velour and Dacron and sleazy knits. Singh was a marxist of the aesthetic variety, attracted to the notion of exportable revolution at least partly because Continental stylishness was exported along with it. His haberdasher was located on Marine Drive. Jammu had long suspected he'd forsaken Sikhism as a youth because he considered a beard disfiguring.

Singh nodded at the paper bag on her desk. "There's some breakfast if you want it."

She placed the bag on her lap and opened it. Inside were two chocolate doughnuts and a cup of coffee. "I was listening to some tapes," she said. "Who put the mikes in the St. Louis Club bathrooms?"

"I did."

"That's what I thought. Baxti's mikes sound like they're wrapped in chewing gum. Yours do pretty well. I heard some useful exchanges. General Norris, Buzz Wismer—"

"His wife is a terrible bitch," Singh said absently.

"Wismer's?"

"Yes. 'Bev' is the name. Of all the women here who will never forgive Asha for marrying Sidney Hammaker, or Hammaker for marrying Asha—and there are a great many of these women—Bev is the nastiest."

"I've been hearing the same complaints on all the tapes," Jammu said. "At least from the women. The men are more likely to say they're 'ambivalent' about Asha. They keep referring to her intelligence."

"Meaning her bewitching beauty."

"And her fabulous wealth."

"Wismer, at any rate, is one of the ambivalent ones. Bev can't stand it. She taunts him constantly."

Jammu dropped the lid from her coffee cup into the waste-basket. "Why does he put up with it?"

"He's strange. A shy genius." Singh frowned and sat down on the windowsill. "I started hearing about Wismer jets twenty years ago. Nobody makes a better one."

"So?"

"So he isn't the man I expected. The voice is all wrong."

"You've been doing a lot of listening."

"A hundred fifty hours maybe. What do you think I do all day?"

Jammu shrugged. She could be certain Singh wasn't exaggerating the amount of time he'd spent on the job. He was studiously beyond reproach. With no distractions (except for an occasional blond boy) and no responsibilities (except to her), he had time to lead an ordered life. A precious life. She, who had a pair of jobs that each took sixty hours a week to perform, was no match for Singh when it came to details. Her foot began to tap of its own accord, which meant the Dexedrine was working. "I'm taking you off the Wismer case," she said.

"Oh yes?"

"I'm putting you in charge of Martin Probst."

"All right."

"So you're going to have to start all over. You can forget Wismer, forget your hundred fifty hours."

"That was just the tapes. Try three hundred."

"Baxti handed in Probst's file. You start immediately."

"Is this something you only just decided?"

"No, it is not. I already *spoke* to Baxti, he already handed *in* his file, that's what you're *here* for. To pick it up."

"Fine."

"So pick it up." She nodded at a tea-stained folder by her desk lamp.

Singh walked to the desk and picked it up. "Anything else?"

"Yes. Put the file down."

He put it down.

"Go get me a glass of water and turn up the heat in here."

He left the room.

Martin Probst was the general contractor whose company had built the Gateway Arch. He was also chairman of Municipal Growth Inc., a benevolent organization consisting of the chief executives of the St. Louis area's major corporations and financial institutions. Municipal Growth was a model of efficacy and an object of almost universal reverence. If someone needed sponsors for an urban renewal project, Municipal Growth found them. If a neighborhood opposed the construction of a highway, Municipal Growth paid for an impact study. If Jammu wanted to alter the power structure of metropolitan St. Louis, she had to contend with Municipal Growth.

Singh returned with a Dixie cup. "Baxti is looking for new worlds to conquer?"

"Get a chair and sit down."

He did so.

"Baxti's obviously only marginally competent, so why make an issue of it?"

He shook a clove cigarette from a caramel-colored pack and struck a match, shielding the flame from a hypothetical breeze. "Because I don't see why we're switching."

"I guess you'll just have to trust me."

"Guess so."

"I assume you know the basics already—Probst's charming wife Barbara, their charming eighteen-year-old daughter Luisa. They live in Webster Groves, which is interesting. It's wealthy but hardly the wealthiest of the suburbs. There's a gardener who lives on the property, though . . . Baxti terms their home life 'very tranquil.' "

"Mikes?"

"Kitchen and dining room."

"The bedroom would have been more telling."

"We don't have that many frequencies. And there's a TV in the bedroom."

"Fine. What else?"

Jammu opened the Probst file. Baxti's Hindi scrawl made her blink. "First of all, he only uses non-union labor. There was a big legal fight back in the sixties. His chief attorney was Charles Wilson, Barbara's father, now his father-in-law. That's how they met. Probst's employees have never been on strike. Union wages or better. Company insurance, disability, unemployment and retirement plans, some of which are unique in the business. It's paternalism at its best. Probst isn't any Vashni Lal. In fact he has a quote reputation unquote for personal involvement at all levels of the business."

"An eye to the personal."

"Ha ha. He's currently chairman of Municipal Growth, term to run through next June. That's important. Beyond that—Zoo Board member '76 through present. Board member Botanical Gardens, East-West Gateway Coordinating Council. Sustaining membership in Channel 9. That isn't so important. Splits his ticket, as they say. Baxti did some interesting fieldwork. Went through old newspapers, spoke with the man in the street—"

"I wish I'd seen it."

"His English is improving. It seems the Globe-Democrat sees Probst as a saint of the American Way, rags to riches, a nobody in 1950, built the Arch in the sixties, along with the structural work on the stadium, and then quite a list of things. That's also very significant."

"He spreads himself thin."

"Don't we all."

Singh yawned. "And he's really that important."

"Yes." Jammu squinted in the clove smoke. "Don't yawn at me. He's first among equals at Municipal Growth, and they're the people we're working on if we want capital moving downtown.

· 21 ·

He's nonpartisan and Christ-like in his incorruptibility. He's a symbol. Have you been noticing how this city likes symbols?"

"You mean the Arch?"

"The Arch, the Veiled Prophet, the whole Spirit of St. Louis mythos. And Probst too, apparently. If only for the votes he'll bring, we need him."

"When did you decide all this?"

Jammu shrugged. "I hadn't given him much thought until I spoke with Baxti last week. He'd just eliminated Probst's dog, a first step towards putting Probst in the State—"

"The State, yes."

"—although at this point it's little more than bald terrorism. For what it's worth, the operation was very neat."

"Yes?" Singh removed a speck of cigarette paper from his tongue, looked it over, and flicked it away.

"Probst was out walking the dog. Baxti drove by in a van, and the dog chased him. He'd found a medical supply company that sold him the essence of a bitch in heat. He soaked a rag in the stuff and tied the rag in front of his rear axle."

"Probst wasn't suspicious?"

"Apparently not."

"What's to stop him from buying another dog?"

"Presumably Baxti would have arranged something for the next one too. You'll have to rethink the theory here. One reason I'm giving you Probst is he didn't seem to respond to the accident."

The phone rang. It was Randy Fitch, the mayor's budget director, calling because he'd be late for his eight o'clock appointment, due to his having overslept. In a sweet, patient tone, Jammu assured him that she wasn't inconvenienced. She hung up and said, "I wish you wouldn't smoke those things in here."

Singh went to the window, opened it, and tossed the butt into the void. Faint river smells entered the room, and down below on Tucker Boulevard a bus roared into the Spruce Street intersection. Singh was orange in the sunlight. He seemed to be viewing a titanic explosion, coldly. "You know," he said, "I was almost enjoying the work with Buzzy and Bevy."

"I'm sure you were."

"Buzz considers Probst and his wife good friends of his."

"Oh?"

"The Probsts put up with Bev. I have the impression they're 'nice' people. Loyal."

"Good. A pretty challenge for you." Jammu placed the file in Singh's hands. "But nothing fancy, you understand?"

Singh nodded. "I understand."

In 1870 St. Louis was America's Fourth City. It was a booming rail center, the country's leading inland port, a wholesaler for half a continent. Only New York, Philadelphia and Brooklyn had larger populations. Granted, there were newspapers in Chicago, a close Fifth, that claimed the 1870 census had counted as many as 90,000 nonexistent St. Louisans, and granted, they were right. But all cities are ideas, ultimately. They create themselves, and the rest of the world apprehends them or ignores them as it chooses.

In 1875, with local prophets casting it as the nation's natural capital, the eventual First City, St. Louis undertook to remove a major obstacle from its path. The obstacle was St. Louis County, the portion of Missouri to which the city nominally belonged. Without the city, St. Louis County was nothing—a broad stretch of farmland and forest in the crook of two rivers. But for decades the county had dominated city affairs by means of an archaic administrative body called the County Court. The Court's seven "judges" were notoriously corrupt and insensitive to urban needs. A county farmer who wanted a new road built to his farm could buy one cheap for cash or votes. But if parks or streetlights were needed for the city's common good, the Court had nothing to offer. To a young frontier town the Court's parochialism had been frustrating; to the Fourth City, it was intolerable.

A group of prominent local businessmen and lawyers persuaded the framers of a new Missouri state constitution to include provisions for civic reform. Despite harassment by the County Court, the group then drafted a scheme for the secession of St. Louis from St. Louis County, to be voted on by all county residents in August 1876.

Pre-election criticism focussed on one element of the scheme in particular: the expansion of the city's landholdings, in a kind of severance payment, from the current twenty-one square miles to sixty-one square miles. Countyites objected to the city's proposed "theft" of county property. The *Globe-Democrat* denounced the unfairness of annexing "divers and sundry cornfields and melon patches and taxing them as city property." But the scheme's proponents insisted that the city needed the extra room for tomorrow's parks and industry.

In an election run by the County Court, voters narrowly rejected the secession scheme. There were cries of fraud. Activists had no trouble convincing a Circuit Court judge (one Louis Gottschalk, who had personally drafted the reform provisions for the 1875 constitution) to appoint a commission to investigate the election. In late December the commissioners reported their findings. The scheme had passed after all, by 1,253 votes. Immediately the city claimed its new land and adopted a new charter, and five months later the County Court, its appeals exhausted, dissolved itself.

Time passed. Sixty-one square miles of land soon proved to be less ample than the secessionists had supposed. As early as 1900 the city was running out of space, and the county refused to give it more. Old industry fled the messes it had made. New industry settled in the county. In the thirties, poor black families arrived from the rural South, hastening the migration of whites to the suburbs. By 1940 the city's population had begun to plummet, and its tax base to shrink. Stately old neighborhoods became simply old. New housing projects like Pruit-Igoe, begun in the fifties, failed spectacularly in the sixties. Efforts at urban renewal succeeded in attracting affluent county residents to a few select zones but did little to cure the city's ills. Everyone worried about the city's schools, but it was an exercise in hand wringing. The seventies became the Era of the Parking Lot, as acres of asphalt replaced half-vacant office buildings downtown.

By now, of course, most American cities were in trouble. But compared with St. Louis, even Detroit looked like a teeming metropolis, even Cleveland like a safe place to raise a family. Other cities had options, good neighbors, a fighting chance. Philadelphia had land to work with. Pittsburgh could count on help from Allegheny County. Insular and constricted, St. Louis had by 1980 dwindled to America's Twenty-Seventh City. Its population was 450,000, hardly half the 1930 figure.

The local prophets were defensive. Where once they'd expected supremacy, they now took heart at any sign of survival. For forty years they'd been chanting: "St. Louis is going to make it." They pointed to the Gateway Arch. (It was 630 feet tall; you couldn't miss it.) They pointed to the new convention center, to three tall new buildings and two massive shopping complexes. To slum-clearance projects, to beautification programs, to plans for a Gateway Mall that would rival the mall in Washington.

But cities are ideas. Imagine readers of *The New York Times* trying in 1984 to get a sense of St. Louis from afar. They might have seen the story about a new municipal ordinance that prohibited scavenging in garbage cans in residential neighborhoods. Or the story about the imminent shutdown of the ailing *Globe-Democrat*. Or the one about thieves dismantling old buildings at a rate of one a day, and selling the used bricks to out-of-state builders.

Why us?

Never conceding defeat, the prophets never asked. Nor did the old guiding spirits, whose good intentions had doomed the city; they'd moved their homes and operations to the county long ago. The question, if it arose at all, arose in silence, in the silence of the city's empty streets and, more insistently, in the silence of the century separating a young St. Louis from a dead one. What becomes of a city no living person can remember, of an age whose passing no one survives to regret? Only St. Louis knew. Its fate was sealed within it, its special tragedy special nowhere else.

After his meeting with Jammu, Singh took the heavy Probst file to his West End apartment, read the file's contents, called Baxti eight times for clarifications, and then, the following morning, drove out to Webster Groves for a visit to the scene of future crimes.

The Probsts lived in a three-story stucco house on a long, broad street called Sherwood Drive. Barbara Probst had driven off punctually. Tuesdays, like Thursdays, she worked in the acquisitions department of the St. Louis University Library, returning home at 5:30. Tuesday was also the gardener's day off. When the beeping in Singh's earphone had faded into static (Baxti had equipped Barbara's BMW with a transmitter that had a range of one kilometer) he checked the two channels from the mikes inside the house and, finding everything quiet, approached on foot. During school hours pedestrians were as scarce on Sherwood Drive as in a cemetery.

Singh was dressed approximately like a gas-meter reader. He carried a black leather shoulder bag. Ready in his pocket were surgical latex gloves for fingerprint protection. He descended the rear stairs and entered the basement with the key Baxti had given him. Looking around, he was impressed by the great quantity of junk. In particular, by the many bald tires, the many plastic flower pots, and the many coffee cans. He went upstairs to the kitchen. Here the air had the smell of recent redecoration, the composite aroma of new wallpaper, new fabrics, new caulking and new paint. A dishwasher throbbed in its drying cycle. Singh removed the screen from the heating register above the stove, replaced the battery in the transmitter, adjusted the gain of the mike (Baxti never failed not to do so), replaced the screen, and repeated the procedure for the transmitter in the dining room.

Baxti had already gone through Probst's study and Barbara's desk and closets, the address books and cancelled checks and old correspondences, so Singh concentrated on the girl's—Luisa's—bedroom. He shot up six feet of microfilm, recording every document of interest. It was noon by the time he finished. He mopped his forehead with his shirtsleeve and opened a bag of M&M's (they didn't leave crumbs). He was chewing the last of them, two yellow ones, when he heard a familiar voice outside the house.

He moved to a front window. Luisa was walking up the driveway with a female friend. Singh entered the nearest spare bedroom, pushed his shoulder bag under the bed, and slid in after it, stilling the dust ruffle just as the girls entered the kitchen below him. He switched channels on his receiver and listened to their movements. Without speaking, they were opening the refrigerator and cabinets, pouring liquids into glasses and handling plastic bags. "Don't eat those," Luisa said.

"Why not?"

"My mother notices things."

"What about these?"

"We'd better not."

They came upstairs, passed the spare bedroom, and settled in Luisa's room. Singh lay very still. Three hours later the girls tired of television and went outside with binoculars. Back at the front window, Singh watched them until they were a block away. Then he returned to the basement and came up the outside stairs jotting on his meter-reader's pad.

In his second apartment, in Brentwood, he developed and printed the film. He stayed inside this apartment for three nights and two days, reading the documents and working through some of the hundred-odd hours of Probst conversations recorded thus far. He warmed up frozen preprepared dinners. He drank tap water and took occasional naps.

When Luisa went out on Friday night he was waiting on Lockwood Avenue in the green two-door LeSabre he'd leased two months ago. To himself, willfully, he gave the name its French pronunciation: LeSob. Luisa picked up four friends from four houses and drove to Forest Park, where they sat on—and rolled down, and scampered up, and trampled the grass of—a hill called Art. Art Hill. The museum overlooked it. When darkness fell, the youths drove ten miles southwest to a miniature golf course on Highway 366 called Mini-Links. Singh parked the LeSob across the road and studied the youths with his binoculars as they knocked colored balls through the base of a totem pole. The faces of the two boys were as soft and downy as those of the three girls. All of them giggled and swaggered in that happy ascendancy, repellent in any land, of teens on their turf.

The next night, Saturday, Luisa and her school-skipping friend Stacy shared marijuana in a dark park and went to a soft-core pornographic movie, the pleasures of which Singh opted to forgo. On Sunday morning Luisa and a different girl loaded birdwatching equipment into the BMW and drove west. Singh followed no farther than the county limits. He'd seen enough.

On the no man's land bounded by the sinuous freeway access ramps of East St. Louis, Illinois, stood the storage warehouse in which Singh had a loft, his third and favorite apartment. Princess Asha had found it for him—the building numbered among the Hammaker Corporation's real-estate holdings—and she had paid for the green carpeting in the three rooms, for the kitchen appliances and for the shower added to the bathroom. The loft had no windows, only skylights of frosted glass. The doors were made of steel. The walls were eleven feet high, fireproof and soundproof. Locked in the innermost room, Singh could be anywhere on earth. In other words, not in St. Louis. Hence the attraction of the place.

A dim shadow of a pigeon fell on the skylight, and a second shadow joined it. Singh opened the Probst file, which lay near him on the floor. All week Jammu had been calling him, pressuring him to set in motion a plan to bring Probst into her camp. She was in a terrible hurry. Already, with the help of the mayor and a corrupted alderman, she was designing changes in the city tax laws, changes which the city could not afford to enact unless, in the meantime, some of the county's wealth and population had been lured east again. But the county guarded its resources jealously. Nothing short of reunification with the city could induce it to help the city out. And since voters in the county were adamantly opposed to any form of cooperation, Singh and Jammu agreed that the only way to catalyze a reunification was to focus on the private individuals who did the shaping of policy in the region, who determined the location and tenor of investment. No more than a dozen catalysts were needed, according to Jammu, if they could all be made to act in unwitting concert. And if her research was to be trusted, she'd identified all twelve. Not surprisingly, all were male, all attended Municipal Growth meetings, and most were chief executives with a strong hold on their stockholders. These were the men she "had to have."

What she would do when she "had" them, when she had cured the city's ills and risen above her role in the police department to become the Madam of the Mound City, she wouldn't say. Right now she was concerned only with the means.

Fighting her enemies in Bombay and furthering the interests

of her relatives, Jammu had developed the idea of a "State" in which a subject's everyday consciousness became severely limited. The mildest version of the State, the one most readily managed in Bombay, exploited income-tax anxiety. To the lives of dozens of citizens whose thinking she wished to alter, Jammu had had the Bureau of Revenue bring horribly protracted tax audits. And when the subject had reached a state in which he lived and breathed and dreamed only taxes, she'd move in for the kill. She'd ask a favor the subject would ordinarily never dream of granting, force a blunder the subject six months earlier would not have committed, elicit an investment the subject should have had a hundred reasons not to make . . . The method couldn't work miracles, of course. Jammu needed some sort of leverage initially. But often the leverage consisted of little more than the subject's susceptibility to her charm.

The State had two advantages over more conventional forms of coercion. First, it was oblique. It arose in a quarter of the subject's life unrelated to Jammu, to the police, and, often, to the public sphere in general. Second, it was flexible. Any situation could be developed, any weakness on the subject's part. Jammu had transformed the dangerous Jehangir Kumar, a man who liked to drink, into an incorrigible alcoholic. When Mr. Vashni Lal, a man with recurring difficulties with his underpaid welders in Poona, had attempted to have Jammu unseated as commissioner, she'd given him a labor crisis, a bloody uprising which her own forces were called in to help quell. She'd taken liberals and made them guilt-stricken, taken bigots and turned them paranoid. She'd preyed on the worst fears of energetic businessmen by preventing them from sleeping, and on the gluttonous tendencies of one of her rival inspectors by sending him a zealous Bengali chef who cooked up a gallbladder operation and an early retirement. Singh personally had entered the life of a philanderer, a Surat millionaire who died not long after, and rendered him impotent in the service of Jammu's Project Poori.

Given the interchangeability of corporate executives, Jammu insisted that her subjects in St. Louis remain functional. They had to stay in power, but with their faculties impaired. And it was here—looking for a path to the State, for a means of impairment—that Singh ran into the problem of Martin Probst.

Probst had no weaknesses.

He was viceless, honest, capable, and calm to the point of complacency. For a building contractor, his business record was unbelievably spotless. He bid only on projects for which there was a clear-cut need. He hired independent consultants to review his work. Every July he sent his employees an itemized accounting of company expenditures. The only enemies he had today were the labor unions he'd thwarted back in 1962—and the unions were no longer a factor in St. Louis politics.

Probst's home life also seemed to be in order. Singh had overheard a few domestic tiffs, but they were nothing more than weeds, shallow-rooted, sprouting from seams in solid pavement. The tranquil image of Probst's family was, in fact, what St. Louis seemed to admire most about him. Singh had gleaned an assortment of citations from the library of tapes that R. Gopal had been cataloguing for Jammu. In one, Mayor Pete Wesley was speaking with the treasurer of the East-West Gateway Coordinating Council.

WESLEY (+ R. Crawford, Sat 9/10, 10:15, City Hall)

PW: No, I haven't talked to him yet. But I did see Barbara at the ball game on Thursday and I asked her if he'd given it any thought.

RC: At the ball game.

PW: Isn't that something? If she was any other lady, you'd think she was nuts.

RC: Going alone, you mean.

PW: I don't see how she pulls it off. Anybody else . . . Can you imagine seeing somebody like Betty Norris sitting by herself in the box seats?

RC: What did Barbara say?

PW: We talked for quite a while. I never actually found out how Martin feels, but she certainly had *her* mind made up.

RC: Which way?

PW: Oh, for. Definitely for. She's a great little lady. And you know, for a small family, isn't it amazing how often you run into them?

Ripley (Rolf, Audrey, Mon 9/5, 22:15)

AR: Doesn't Luisa seem like one of those children that something could happen to? She was so sweet today. Everything's so perfect about her, isn't it hard not to think something terrible will happen? (*Pause.*) Like a doll you could break. (*Pause.*) Don't you think?

RR: No.

Meisner (Chuck, Bea, Sat 9/10, 01:30)

CM: That was Martin. He wanted to make sure we made it home all right. (*Pause.*) I'm sure he couldn't sleep till he'd called. (*Pause.*) Did I really look that drunk?

BM: We all did, Chuck.

CM: It's funny how you don't notice it so much with them. I mean, they make you comfortable.

BM: They're a very special couple.

CM: They are. A very special couple.

It was unfortunate, Singh thought, that R. Gopal would no longer have time to sort these recorded conversations and put them into such a usable form. "I think we're past that phase," Jammu had said. "I have something else for Gopal."

Murphy (Chester, Jane, Alvin, 9/19, 18:45)

JANE: Know who I saw today, Alvin? Luisa Probst. Remember her?

ALVN: (*chewing*) Sort of.

JANE: She's turned into a very pretty girl.

ALVN: (*chewing*)

JANE: I thought it'd be nice if you called her up sometime. I'm sure she'd be thrilled to hear from you.

ALVN: (*chewing*)

JANE: I'm just saying, it might be a nice thing to do.

ALVN: (*chewing*)

JANE: I remembered her as being a little chubby. I hadn't seen her in, oh, three years. I never get to Webster Groves anymore. I see her mother all the time, though. (*Pause.*) I think it would be very, very nice if you gave her a call.

CHES: Drop it, Jane.

A very pretty girl. A special couple. Singh was careful not to infer that Probst's lovely family contributed to his actual power in the city, but the family was obviously a source of unusual strength. Strength like this could amount to a weakness. Even Baxti had recognized this. In his summary he'd written:

UnCorrupted in 72, and worse.

(In 1972 someone on the Slum Removal Board had requested a kickback and Probst had gone to the press with the story.)

He is haveing no sins but morality. He will die: every man is moral. This is the key to this. *Death in air*. Step one: dogg. Step two: doghter. Step Three: wife. Patterne of loss. And standing a lone. He loving his dogge. Calling it petname. And no doge . . . ? ? ?

This was Baxti's inspirational mode. His informational, in Hindi, was somewhat easier to follow.

Singh closed the folder and glanced at the blurry pigeons on the skylight. Baxti was clumsy, but he wasn't stupid. He'd started in the right direction. As a citizen of the West, Probst was *a priori* sentimental. In order to induce the State in him, it might be necessary only to accelerate the process of bereavement, to compress into three or four months the losses of twenty years. The events would be unconnected accidents, a "fatal streak," as Baxti put it elsewhere. And the process could occur in increments, lasting only as long as it took Probst to endorse Jammu publicly and direct Municipal Growth to do likewise.

Very well then. The daughter was the next step. Filling in the last gap in Baxti's research, Singh had read Luisa's letters and diaries and notebooks, he'd heard the testimony of her possessions, and though he was no expert on American youth he judged her to be quite typical. Her teeth were orthodontically corrected. She had no diseases or parasites. She was blond, more or less, and five and a half feet tall, and she wore her affluence to good effect. She'd attracted boyfriends and had dropped the most recent one. She owned a TEAC stereo set, 175 phonograph records, no car, no computer, an insect net and cyanide jar, a diaphragm in its original box with a tiny tube of Gynol II, a small television set, 40+ sweaters, 20+ pairs of shoes. She had $3,700 in her personal savings account and, though it didn't matter, nearly $250,000 in joint accounts and trust funds. This ratio—2,500 to 37—was a mathematical expression of her distance from adulthood. She cut school and used intoxicants; she was a sneak.

Singh had to decide how to detach her from the family. "Nothing fancy," Jammu insisted. The least fancy technique was violence. But while it was one thing for Baxti to kill Probst's dog, it was quite another to apply trauma to the family as a first resort. Trauma induced grief, cathartic convulsions. Very nice. But it did not induce the State.

Few of the other standard techniques fit Luisa either. Singh couldn't abduct her; abduction involved too much terror and grief. He couldn't use blandishments, couldn't persuade her that she had great talent in some particular field, because she didn't, and she was too sarcastic to be conned. Bribery was also out. Jammu had a Talstrasse banker who'd be happy to open an account, but Luisa hadn't learned the meaning of cash. She was also too young to be persuaded, à la *Mission Impossible*, that a close associate or relative was plotting against her. She wasn't too young for narcotics, of course, and Singh was an excellent pusher, but drugs were just another form of trauma. Political indoctrination might conceivably have worked, but it took too much time.

He was left with little choice but to seduce the girl. Though a rather fancy technique, seduction was ideal for lusty young targets, targets at the age where they were sneaky and looking for fun or trouble. The only real problem was access. Luisa was never alone except at home, or in the car or in stores or birdwatching or at the library (and Singh already knew enough not to make acquaintances in American public libraries). Where was the opportunity for a strange man to get to know her?

The man would have to be Singh, of course. There was no one else. Imagine Baxti: she'd sooner do it with an alligator. But Singh was clean. He'd modeled neckties in harder times. He projected Clean. People told him it was his teeth. Maybe so. In any event, he was clean. Clean and—not to overstate the point—

irresistible. He was an old pro with Americans. Why, just last week . . .

The problem was access. No matter how he lured her out—mailing her free passes to a bar, free tickets to a concert—she'd bring a friend. Sometimes, it was true, she did go birdwatching by herself, but Singh knew nothing of birds. It would take him weeks to learn the "lore," and the idea of wasting his time on willful squirters of liquid excrement (Singh did not love Nature) was wholly repugnant to him. It was a shame Luisa's hobby wasn't knives. He had some items that seasoned collectors would sell their sisters for. The Burmese Flayer . . .

The problem was access. One hour alone with the girl would suffice. The Mystique of the East would take care of the rest. Jade figurines, Moët, a dozen roses. Then debauch; take to New Orleans; feed cocaine.

Singh reclined on the soft green carpeting.

1. An out-of-state friend, for example a pen pal, comes unexpectedly to town. Calls Luisa, asks her to a bar. Is gone when Luisa arrives. She gets to know a courteous stranger.

2. A representative of a popular teen magazine, an intriguing man with good teeth, gives her a call. Would like to interview her. In depth. Would like her to be a stringer for the magazine. Invites her to closed-door editorial sessions.

3. A Nature-lover with some very appealing physical attributes meets her in the field one day when she is alone. Following some innocent badinage, they go for a walk in dense woods.

Singh lay isolated on the floor, in a room that brought him to his senses. His stomach gurgled softly, a hungry sound track for the silent pigeon shadows on the skylight. Of the people he'd come of age with, his comrades in Srinagar, the People's Reading Group, at least ten were in jail. A dozen were dead and another ten were organizers in Madras, Sri Lanka, Bombay. Several lived comfortably in West Bengal. There was one in Angola, three in South Africa, one in Ethiopia, half a dozen still in Moscow, and at least two in Central America, while Balwan Singh, the brains of the group, the kid who'd bayoneted the vice-governor, had gone farther than anyone else. All the way to East St. Louis, Illinois, where now, on his back, he plotted the most decadent of subversions. The only other member of the old cadre even in the U.S.A. was Jammu. Jammuji, mountain flower, unlikely perfume. And she didn't have to plot. She amassed power and left the soiling details to subordinates, her dignity untarnished. Singh wanted to be in action, in action he'd forget this planning. He wanted Luisa Probst, too, with sudden criminal force. Wanted to break her. He removed a shoe and winged it fiercely at the skylight. The shadows dispersed.

.

Martin Probst had grown up in St. Louis proper, in an old German neighborhood on the south side. When he was eighteen he started a demolition business, and two years later he began to expand it into a general contracting company. At twenty-seven he shook up the local building establishment by winning the contracts to erect the Gateway Arch. Soon he was the busiest contractor in St. Louis, his low bids preferred by local governments, his high standards of workmanship much in demand among private groups. Newspapers often listed him as a potential candidate for state and local offices—not because he ever showed any inclination to run, but because observers couldn't see him working all his life within the somewhat shabby confines of the contracting world. Unlike many contractors, he was not a "character," not a bony and drawling daredevil, not a red-faced cigar-smoking operator. He was six feet tall, a good speaker, a Missouri-born executive whose face was memorable only for having appeared all over town for thirty years. Like a medieval mason, essential but aloof, he went wherever the construction was.

At the moment, the construction was mainly in West County, the exurban part of St. Louis County beyond the Interstate outer belt. Within the last five years Probst had built the St. Luke's West Hospital, a junior high school in the Parkway West school district, and an office-entertainment-hotel-shopping-center complex called West Port. He'd built the Ardmore West condominiums, western extensions of five county roads, and extra lanes on U.S. 40 out to the western county limits. Recently he'd begun work on Westhaven, a "comprehensive work and lifestyle environment" whose four million square feet of rental space were specifically intended to put West Port to shame.

On the third Saturday of October, a week after Singh had formulated his plans for Luisa, Probst was driving his little Lincoln home from a Municipal Growth meeting, listening to KSLX-Radio's Saturday-night jazz program. Benny Goodman was playing. The full moon had been rising five hours ago when Probst left home, but the weather had soured in the meantime. Raindrops spattered on the windshield as he drove down Lockwood Avenue. He was speeding, keeping pace with Goodman's racing clarinet.

The Municipal Growth meeting had been a bust. Hoping to build some *esprit de corps*, Probst had had the idea of scheduling a session on a Saturday night—a dinner meeting, beef Wellington for twenty-five in a private room at the Baseball Star's restaurant. It had been a terrible idea. They didn't even have a quorum until Probst called Rick Crawford and persuaded him to give up an evening at the theater. Everyone drank heavily while they waited for Crawford to arrive. The evening's discussion of city hospital care was confused and interminable. And when Probst was finally about to move for adjournment, General Norris stood up and spoke for a full forty minutes.

General Norris was the chief executive officer at General Synthetics, one of the country's foremost chemical producers and a pillar of industry in St. Louis County. His personal wealth and extreme political views were almost mythical in magnitude. What he wanted to discuss tonight, he said, was *conspiracy*. He said he found it alarming and significant that during the same week in August two women from India had assumed positions of command in St. Louis. He pointed out that India was essentially a Soviet satellite, and he invited Municipal Growth to consider what might happen now that Jammu had control of the city police and the Princess had control of the man who ran the Hammaker Brewing Company and owned many of its assets. (Fortunately for all concerned, Sidney Hammaker was among the absentees tonight.) Norris said there were strong indications that Jammu, with the help of the Princess, was engaging in a conspiracy to subvert the government of St. Louis. He urged Municipal Growth to form a special committee to monitor their actions in the city. He spoke of the FBI—

Probst suggested that the FBI had better things to do than investigate the chief of police and the wife of Sidney Hammaker.

General Norris said that he had not finished speaking.

Probst said that he had heard enough and believed that everyone else had too. He said that Jammu appeared to be doing a fine job as police chief; it was merely a coincidence that she and the Princess had come on the scene at the same time. He said that furthermore, as a matter of policy, Municipal Growth should avoid taking any action that might jeopardize its effectiveness by polarizing its membership and calling attention to itself as something other than a strictly benevolent group.

General Norris drummed his fingers on the table.

Probst noted that it was Norris himself who had stood behind Rick Jergensen's candidacy for chief of police. He noted that Jergensen's candidacy—or, rather, the strength of his backers—had been a major factor in the stalemate, and that the stalemate had led directly to Jammu's selection—

"I resent that!" General Norris leaped to his feet and pointed at Probst. "I resent that! I resent that inference!"

Probst adjourned the meeting. He knew he'd offended the General and his cronies, but he didn't stick around to patch things up. For one thing, the General had already stalked out ahead of him.

It was raining hard by the time he got home. Reluctantly he left the warm and jazz-filled privacy of his car, shut the garage door, and hurried across the lawn to the house. Wet dead leaves were in the air.

Upstairs he found Barbara asleep in bed with the latest *New Yorker* drooped over her stomach. The television was on, but the sound was turned down. He avoided the known squeaky boards underneath the carpeting.

In the bathroom, as he brushed his teeth, he noticed some gray hairs behind his right temple, a whole patch of them. They held his eyes like a running sore. Why, he wondered, should he suddenly be going gray? He was ahead of schedule on the West-haven project, somewhat short of manpower, maybe, concerned about the weather to a certain degree, but definitely ahead of schedule and not worrying about it, not worrying about anything at all, really.

Then again, he was almost fifty.

He relaxed and brushed vigorously, straining to reach the back sides of all four wisdom teeth, danger zones for cavities. Recalling that Luisa wasn't home yet, he padded down the hall to her room, which seemed colder than the rest of the house, and turned on her nightstand light and turned back her covers. He padded out into the hall and down the stairs. He unlocked the front door and switched on the outside light.

"Is that you, honey?" Barbara called from the bedroom.

Probst padded patiently up the stairs before he answered. "Yes."

Barbara had turned up the TV volume by remote control. "Do I call you 'honey'?"

Forty-second Street may not be the center of the universe but—

"How was the meeting?" she asked.

"A total bust."

And I'd tell you the whole story but we've got censors—

The picture crumpled as Probst turned off the set. Barbara frowned, briefly annoyed, and picked up her magazine. She was wearing her reading glasses and a pale blue nightgown through which he could just make out her breasts, their tangential trajectories, their dense brown aureoles. Her hair, which lately she'd been letting grow a little longer, fell in a broad S-curve across the right side of her face, shading her eyes from the reading lamp.

When he climbed into bed she listed towards the center of the mattress but kept her eyes on the page. He couldn't believe she was really concentrating this hard. Hadn't she been asleep two minutes ago? He fanned a stack of magazines on the nightstand and selected an unread *National Geographic*. On the cover was a smiling stone Buddha with sightless stone eyes. "Your brother-in-law missed the meeting," he told Barbara. "It's the kind of favor I've really come to appreciate."

Barbara shrugged. Her older sister Audrey was married to Rolf Ripley, one of St. Louis's more prominent industrialists. Neither Probst nor Barbara enjoyed Rolf's company (to put it mildly) but Barbara felt a responsibility towards Audrey, who was emotionally disaster-prone, and so Probst, in turn, was required to be civil to Rolf. They had a weekly tennis date at the old Racquet Club. They'd played this morning and Rolf had slaughtered him. He frowned. If Rolf had time for tennis, then why not Municipal Growth?

"Do you have any idea where he was? Did you talk to Audrey today?"

"Yesterday."

"And?"

"And what?"

"Did they have any plans for tonight?"

Barbara pulled off her glasses and turned to him. "Rolf is seeing another woman. Yet again. Don't ask me any more questions."

Probst looked away. He felt a curious lack of outrage. Barbara always got mad enough at Rolf for the two of them combined; he'd ceased to bother. Rolf ran the Ripleycorp electrical appliances empire (only Wismer Aeronautics had a longer payroll) and was acknowledged to be the grand financial wizard of St. Louis, but he had the habits of an idle playboy and a seedy slenderness to match. About ten years ago he'd begun to speak with a British accent. The accent grew thicker and thicker, as if with each of his affairs. He was too weird to really offend Probst.

"And here we played tennis this morning," he said. "Where's Lu?"

"I'm surprised she isn't here. I told her to be in early. Her cold's getting worse."

"She's out with Alan?"

"Good grief, Martin."

"Of course, of course, of course," he said. Luisa had terminated her relationship with Alan. "So where is she?"

"I have no idea."

"What do you mean you have no idea?"

"Just that. I don't know."

"Well didn't you *ask* her?"

"I was up here when she left. She said she wouldn't be gone long."

"When was that?"

"Around seven. Not long after you left."

"It's almost midnight."

A page turned. Rain was splashing on the windows and pouring through the gutters.

"I thought it was our policy to know where she is."

"Martin, I'm sorry. I wasn't thinking. Just let me read for a while, all right?"

"All right. All right. I've got policy coming out of my ears, I'm sorry."

Practically, in appearance, in the verifiable fact of never having sinned much, Probst had an undeniable claim to moral superiority over Rolf Ripley. From the very beginning his ambitions had kept him moving like a freight train, hurried and undeviating. By the time he was twenty, his married friends had to take steps to make sure he got out for dinner at least once a month. Chief among these early friends was Jack DuChamp, a neighbor of Probst's and a sharer of his loneliness at McKinley High. Jack had been one of those boys who from puberty onwards want nothing more than to be wise older men like their fathers. Marriage and maturity were Jack's gospel, and Probst, inevitably, was one of the first savages he tried to convert. The attempt had begun in earnest on a muggy Friday night in July, in the tiny house that Jack and his wife Elaine were renting. Jack's chest still had its matrimonial swell. All through dinner he smiled at Probst as though awaiting further congratulation. When Elaine began to clear the table, Jack opened fresh Falstaffs and led Probst onto the back porch. The sun had sunk behind the haze above the railyards beyond the DuChamps' back fence. Bugs were rising from the weeds. "Tsk," Jack clucked. "Things can be pretty nice sometimes."

Probst said nothing.

"You're going places, old buddy, I can tell," Jack continued, his voice all history-in-the-making. "Things are happening fast, and I kind of like the way they look. I just hope we can still see some of you once in a while."

"What do you mean?"

"Well." Jack pulled a fatherly smile. "I'll tell you. You've got a lot going for you, and I know for damn sure we're not the only ones who can see that. You're twenty years old, you've finally got a little money to throw around, you've got looks, brains . . ."

Probst laughed. "What are you saying?"

"I'm saying that I, personally, Jack DuChamp"—Jack pointed at himself—"kind of envy you sometimes."

Probst glanced at the kitchen window. Dishes plopped in the sink.

"Not like that," Jack said. "I'm a lucky man, and I know it. It's just we like to speculate."

"About what?"

"Well, we like to speculate—you ready?" Jack paused. "We like to speculate about your sex life, Martin."

Probst felt his face go pale. "You what?"

"Speculate. At parties. It's kind of a party game whenever you're not around. You should've heard what Dave Hepner said last Saturday. 'Satin sheets and three at a time.' Yeah, Elaine was really mad, she thought it was getting kind of dirty—"

"*Jack.*" Probst was aghast.

A moment passed. Then Jack shook his head and gripped Probst's arm. He had always been a kidder, a winker, a prankster. "No," he said, "I'm only teasing. It's just sometimes we worry you might be workin' a little *too* hard. And— well. We know a girl you might be interested in meeting. She's actually a cousin of mine. Her name's Helen Scott."

For nearly a month Probst did nothing with the number Jack had given him, but the name Helen Scott slowly gave birth to a vision of feminine splendor so compelling that he had no choice, in the end, but to call her. They made a date. He picked her up on a Sunday afternoon at the rooming house where she was living (she'd moved to the city to take a job with Bell Telephone) and drove to Sportsman's Park to watch the Browns play the Yankees. There was nothing wrong with Helen Scott. As Probst had hoped, she bore little resemblance of any kind to her cousin Jack. She had a throaty rural voice. Her hair was waved and her skirt high-waisted in accordance with the fashion of the era, which, more democratic than later fashions, at least did not detract from any woman's native looks. Probst's preconceived love kept him from apprehending her any more specifically. They sat in the bleachers. The Browns, whom the Yankees immediately jumped all over, were the perfect team to be watching on a first date, their wobbly pitching and general proneness to error giving them an innocence that the Yankees seemed wholly to lack. Probst, with a pretty girl at his side, felt a charity bordering on joy.

After the game he and Helen went to Crown Candy for sandwiches and milkshakes (here he was able to observe that she had a wide mouth and no appetite) and then they stopped in at his apartment, which was actually the basement of his Uncle George's house. There, on his daybed, with an alacrity that implied she'd been impatient with the long preliminary afternoon, Helen kissed him. As soon as he felt how she moved in his arms he knew he could have her. His head began to pound. She let him take her blouse and bra off. His uncle's footsteps, gouty and halting, depressed the floorboards above them. She unzipped her skirt and Probst kissed her ribs, and pinched her nipples, which he had heard women found intensely pleasurable.

"Don't do that."

There was pain in her voice. She drew away and they sat up on the bed, panting like swimmers. Probst thought he understood. He thought she meant he'd gone too far. And then she really did change her mind; as he sat there, mortified and uncertain, she put her clothes back on, defending herself (as he saw it) against his hurtful male hands.

He drove her back to the rooming house, where she kissed him on the forehead and ran inside. For a while he waited in the darkness, somehow hoping she might come back out. He found it too cruel that his business accomplishments had counted for nothing on the daybed, that to be a man in the world did not make him a man of the world. And either then, as he sat in the car, or in later years, as he remembered sitting in the car—the location of the moment had the shifting ambiguity, now you see it, now you don't, of a self-deception one is conscious of committing—he resolved to wait until his accomplishments were so great that he no longer needed, as the male, to make the moves. He wanted to be desired and taken. He wanted to be all object, to have that power. He wanted to be that great.

And so it happened that he was a virgin when he met Barbara and had been faithful to her ever since.

Barbara turned out her light.

"You're going to sleep?" Probst asked.

"Yes. You're not?"

He tried to make his voice sound casual. "No, I think I'll wait up for Luisa."

She kissed him. "Hope it won't be long."

"Good night."

The bedroom windows rattled in the wind. It was 12:40, but Probst wasn't worried about whether Luisa could take care of herself. He was all too certain that she could. Her control over her life was almost unnatural; the only thing that exceeded it was her control over other people's lives, over the lives of boys like Alan. When Alan would come to see her, as he had nearly every day in the spring, she would talk on the phone with other friends for as long as an hour at a time. Alan would sit in the breakfast room smiling and nodding at the funny things he could hear her saying.

Rolf is seeing another woman. Yet again.

Luisa had dropped Alan in June, on her last weekend at home before flying to France. She made the announcement at the dinner table. It had seemed a very industrial decision, as if she'd been running cost/benefit analyses all along, and Alan had finally failed one. Though Probst approved of the decision, he didn't let on. He believed that virtue grew best in an austere medium, in an atmosphere of challenging disapproval, and in Webster Groves, when one's father paid himself a comfortable $190,000 annually and employed a full-time gardener and a part-time cleaning woman, austerity and challenges were hard to come by. He therefore took it upon himself to play the role of hostile environment for Luisa. He refused to give her a car. He said no to private school. He'd made her try Girl Scouts. He did not buy her the best stereo available. He imposed curfews. (She'd already trashed her weekend curfew of midnight to the tune of forty minutes.) She received a weekly allowance, which he sometimes pretended to forget to leave on her dresser. (She would go and complain to Barbara, who always gave her whatever she needed.) He made her cry when she got a B − in social studies. He made her eat beets.

Barbara had begun to snore a little. As if he'd only been waiting for this sort of signal, Probst heaved himself out of bed. He opened his closet and put on his robe and slippers. He was tired, but he was not going to sleep before Luisa got back. She'd gone out at seven and said she'd be home soon. It was nearly one o'clock now. It was the hour of Rolf Ripley, the hour of ugly men for whom strangers unaccountably shed their inhibitions, the hour of getting it.

Was Luisa getting it? Where was she? Her regular friends knew enough not to keep her out much past her curfew, so maybe she'd gone somewhere without them. She had a will of her own. She'd inherited Probst's desires but not his disadvantages. She'd been born a girl—she was desired—and she hadn't had to earn it. She hadn't had to wait.

Downstairs, the air was cold, the weather seeping in at the windows. Mohnwirbel, the gardener, hadn't put the storms on yet. Probst imagined Luisa someplace in the rain beyond the house's walls, making it easy for some undeserving young man. He imagined himself slapping her in the face when she finally came in. "You're grounded forever." A spray of rain hit the windows in the living room. A hot rod turned off Lockwood Avenue and raced up Sherwood Drive. By the time it passed Probst it was doing at least fifty, and the blap-blap of the cylinders had become a hot moan. He felt a draft.

The front door was open. Luisa was slipping in. Turning back the knob with one hand and pressing on the weather strip with the other, she slowly eased the door shut. A hinge made a soft miaow. He heard a click. She switched off the outside light and took a cautious step towards the stairs.

"Where have you been?" he said conversationally.

He saw her jump and heard her gasp. He jumped himself, frightened by her fright.

"Daddy?"

"Who else?"

"You really scared me."

"Where have you been?" He saw himself as she did, in his full-length robe, with his arms crossed, his hair gray and mussed, his pajama cuffs breaking on his flat slippers. He saw himself as a father, and he blamed her for the vision.

"What are you doing up so late?" she said, not answering his question.

"Couldn't sleep."

"I'm sorry I'm—"

"Have a good time?" He got a strong whiff of wet hair. She was wearing black pants, a black jacket and black sneakers, all of them wet. The pants clung to the adolescent curves of her thighs and calves, the intersecting seams gleaming dully in the light from upstairs.

"Yeah." She avoided his eyes. "We went to a movie. We had some ice cream."

"We?"

She turned away and faced the banister. "You know—Stacy and everyone—. I'm going to bed now, OK?"

It was clear that she was lying. He'd made her do it, and he was satisfied. He let her go.

3

The thing was, Luisa had been bored. She'd been bored since she got back from Paris. She'd been bored in Paris, too. In Paris, people kissed on the boulevards. That was how bored they were. She'd participated in the Experiment in International Living. It had produced Negative Results. Her Experiment family, the Girauds, had apparently been specific about requesting a boy, an American boy. Luisa felt like a midlife "mistake" on the part of Mme Giraud. She'd eavesdropped on Mme Giraud in conversation with her neighbors. The neighbors had been expecting a boy.

Mme Giraud sold magazine subscriptions to her neighbors and also to strangers, by telephone. M. Giraud was vice-director of a Saab dealership. They already had two girls, Paulette (she was nineteen) and Gabrielle (she was sixteen). It was for the girls' sake that Luisa was there. She was supposed to be fun. On her second night in France, her fun American Express card had come to the attention of the sisters. Paulette had snatched the card away and held it up before Gabrielle's eyes as if it were a rare and beautiful insect. The girls smiled at each other and then at Luisa, who made goo-goo eyes and smiled back. She was trying to be friendly. When they looked away, she turned and scowled at the audience she often felt behind her.

The next day the three of them went shopping, which in

French meant Luisa plodded in and out of dressing rooms while the sisters pulled item after item off the racks. They were good salespeople. Luisa bought 2,700 francs' worth of clothes. Back at home, Mme Giraud took one look at all the boxes and suggested that Luisa go take a bath. At the top of the stairs, Luisa sniffed her armpits. Did Americans smell bad to the French? She thought she'd locked the bathroom door, but no sooner had she stripped and stepped into the tub than Mme Giraud came bustling in with a towel for her. Luisa cowered. She already had a towel. Mme Giraud told her that usually they didn't fill the tub so full. Then she told her she'd help her return all her purchases tomorrow. Then she asked her how she'd slept the night before. Did she still have zhet leg? Luisa checked her legs. Oh. Jet lag. Then Mme Giraud wanted to know whether Luisa ate liver. It was like the French Inquisition: *manges-tu le foie?* By the time she left, the water was tepid. Luisa scrubbed her pits exhaustively. At supper, over thick slices of liver, M. Giraud asked what business her father was in.

"Mon papa," she said happily, "il est un constructeur. Un grand constructeur, un—"

"Je comprends." M. Giraud pursed his lips with satisfaction. "Un charpentier."

"Non, non, non. Il bâtit ponts et chemins, il bâtit maisons et écoles et monuments—"

"Un entrepreneur!"

"Oui."

She hated France. Her mother had urged her to go. Her father had urged her to go humbly, with the Experiment. She'd got what he paid for. So she was a snob; so what? She was bored with the Girauds. She should have been sitting in cafés with guys and colored drinks. Mme Giraud wouldn't let her go out alone after dark. Paulette and Gabrielle were drafted to show her a good time, and they took her to an empty bar in the Latin Quarter where campy disco played on a jukebox. They watched her with eyes as hard and shiny as stuffed-animal eyes. Fun? Are you having fun? On Sundays the elder Girauds drove her places like St. Denis and Versailles. On weekdays she helped Mme Giraud with the garden and shopping, which was more than her own daughters ever did. Luisa even helped her with her subscriptions until M. Giraud got wind of it. She accompanied the family to a rented house in Brittany for two weeks and gained five pounds, mainly on cheese. She grew pimples in patches, little archipelagos. She missed her parents, her real ones. It rained in Brittany. In a field near the Atlantic, a sheep tried to bite her.

She was bored in August, bored in September, and bored in October now, too. It was another Friday afternoon. She walked out the high-school door into the sunlit dust raised by football practice across the street. The weather was fine because a harvest moon was coming, but Stacy Montefusco, her best friend, had been home for a week with bronchitis. Sara Perkins was getting a cold and was irritable. Marcy Coughlin had sprained her ankle in gymnastics the day before. No one felt like going birdwatching. No one felt like doing anything at all. Luisa walked home.

The kitchen radio was playing the four o'clock news when she came in. She took her mail from the table and went upstairs. The door to the sundeck was open. Her mother, around the corner on the lounger, cast a shadow across the graying rattan mat. Luisa shut her bedroom door behind her.

In her mail was a postcard of the Statue of Liberty. It was from Paulette Giraud.

> LOUISA,
> I AM IN THE UNITED-STATES! I AM COMING
> I THINK TO ST. LOUIS! OUR GROUP STAYS
> ONE NIGHT. ARE YOU HOME ON OCTOBER 20?
> I WILL CALL YOU!
>
> ALL MY LOVES,
> *Paulette*

October 20? That was tonight. She threw the card aside. Mme Giraud must have told Paulette to call. Luisa didn't want to see her. She put on some music, did a back-drop onto her bed, tuck and fall, and looked at the rest of her mail. There was another letter from Tufts and a thick packet of material from Purdue. She opened the letter from Tufts, and her mother knocked on the door. Luisa spread her arms like Jesus on the cross and stared at the ceiling. "Come in."

Her mother was wearing one of her father's white shirts, with the front tails knotted. She held her place in a book with her finger. "You're home early."

"There's no one to do anything with."

"Come again?"

Luisa raised her voice. "Everybody's sick."

"Who's the postcard from?"

"You didn't read it?"

"It wasn't addressed to me," her mother said. She had disgustingly good manners.

"It's from Paulette Giraud. She's coming to town today."

"Today?"

"That's what she says."

"We should have her over for dinner."

"I thought you and Daddy were going out."

"We were thinking of going to a movie, but it's not important."

"I don't *want* to have her over."

"All right." Her mother's interest in the conversation withered: she seemed to sigh inaudibly, her shoulders going slack. "Suit yourself." From a pile near the closet she snagged two dirty blouses. "I've got to change for tennis. Will you be home till dinner?"

"Maybe." Luisa kicked her calculus book onto the floor. "Does Daddy have any other old shirts like that?"

"Daddy has fifty other shirts like this."

Luisa turned up the stereo and waited for her mother to come back with a shirt or two. Ten minutes later she heard the BMW whirring down the driveway. No shirts. Had her mother forgotten? She went to her parents' bedroom, and there, lying folded on the bed, were three of the shirts she'd had in mind. She struggled out of her sweater and put a white one on, knotting the tails and rolling up the sleeves. In front of her mother's mirror she unbuttoned the second and third buttons and flipped back the collar. She had a good chest complexion. The shirt worked for her. She spread her hands on her hips and shook her hair back. Then she pulled down her lower eyelids and made blood-rimmed Hungarian eyes. She pulled on the corners and made Chinese eyes. She smiled at the mirror. She had nicer teeth than her mother.

At 7:30, just after her parents had sung their chorus of goodbyes, the telephone rang. A voice, Paulette's, floated above the sounds of a noisy bar or restaurant. "Louisa?"

"Bonjour, Paulette."

"Yes, yes, it is Paulette. Did you—receive my card?"

"Oui, Paulette. Aujourd'hui. *À quatre heures*. Merci beaucoup."

"Yes, yes. Em, I am on Euclid Avenue?"

"You're where?"

"Em, Euclid Avenue? It is close?"

"Um, no, that's not very close. I don't live in the city."

"I am at a bar? Yes?"

"You can speak French," Luisa said.

"This bar is called Deckstair?"

"Well, could you— Do you have any way of getting out of the city?"

"No. No. You would come to the bar, Deckstair? Yes?"

Luisa didn't remember her English being even this good. But then, they'd hardly ever spoken it.

"Yes?" Paulette repeated.

Maybe her mother had made her promise to call. But she still could have broken the promise.

"Oh, all right," Luisa said. She knew where Dexter's was. "Will you be there in twenty minutes?"

"Yes! Yes, right here. Deckstair." Paulette laughed.

Luisa tried to call Marcy Coughlin to see if she wanted to come along, but the line was busy. She tried Edgar Voss and Nancy Butterfield. Their lines were busy, too. The busy signals sounded faint, like the phone was out of order, but it obviously wasn't. She wrote a note for her parents and gave them the name of the bar.

It was almost 8:30 when she reached the Central West End, the home of a variety of up-to-the-decade bars and restaurants and specialty stores. Luisa parked the BMW in the Baskin-Robbins loading zone and crossed the alley towards Euclid Avenue. Dumpsters yawned disagreeably. In the apartment windows above her the shades were drawn down so far that they buckled and gaped.

It was strange that a tour group from Europe would want to see St. Louis. Then again, the people Luisa had met in France hadn't seemed to know what a boring place it was. Even the grownups had thought she must have a great old time living in San Louie and listening to the blues every night on a riverboat. People in Europe were convinced that St. Louis was a really hot town.

Spilling out along the front window of Dexter's was a crowd of party people, loud people in their early twenties, people who instinct told Luisa weren't professionals or good students. They clutched drinks. They laughed, their hairdos frosted flamingo pink by the glaring neon logo. Luisa looked in through the window. The place was packed. She hesitated, nervous, her hands in her pockets.

A man in a white shirt like hers had stepped out of the crowd. He had a foreign face, she almost guessed Algerian, except he was too decent-looking. He raised his eyebrows as if he knew who she was. She gave him a feeble smile. He spoke. "Are you looking—"

But her heart had jumped and she'd pushed through the doorway, hopping a little to keep her balance in the undergrowth of feet and shins. She squirmed and ducked laterally, listening for French. All she heard was English. Every word was a laugh. In every partying cluster there seemed to be one stocky woman, shorter and more flushed than the rest, who kept joking through her drink and almost spraying it. Near the blunt corner of the bar, where the crowd knotted up tightly, Luisa came to a dead stop. She wasn't tall enough for a good view of the tables and booths, and she couldn't move to reach them. And *somebody* hadn't taken a *shower* this morning. She blocked her nose from inside and inched closer to the bar. Here she recognized a face in profile, but it wasn't Paulette. It was a boy from high school. Doug? Dave? Duane. Duane Thompson. He'd graduated two years ago. He had both hands on the bar and a beer in front of him. He turned, suddenly, as if he felt her looking, and she gave him a feeble smile. His smile was even feebler.

She stuck her elbow in a fat man's midriff and forged into the sitting area. Now she could see all the tables and still no Paulette. A waitress came careening by. "Excuse me—" Luisa caught her arm. "Is there a group of French people in here?"

The waitress opened her mouth incredulously.

Luisa had that sinking stood-up feeling in her stomach. She figured it was time to go back home, and she would have left if the Algerian hadn't had his face pressed up against the front window. He was still acting like he had something in particular to say to her. As creeps went, he was handsome. She turned back to the tables, and then to the bar. Duane Thompson was staring at her. All this attention! She pushed her way to the bar, ducked under a shoulder, and faced him. "Hi," she shouted. "You're Duane Thompson."

"Yes." He nodded. "You're Luisa Probst."

"Right. I'm looking for some French people in here. Have you seen any French people?"

"I just came in a couple minutes ago."

"Oh," she shouted. She cast a futile glance into the haze. When she was a sophomore, Duane Thompson had been a senior. He'd gone out with a girl named Holly, one of those artsy liberal types who wore brocaded smocks and no bra and didn't eat lunch in the cafeteria. Duane had been blond, shaggy, thin. He'd had his hair cut since then. He was wearing a jean jacket, a preppy button-down, black Levi's and white sneakers. Luisa also noticed that he had the yellowish remains of a black eye, which made her uneasy. If you didn't see a person every day in the hall or cafeteria, you didn't know what kind of life they had, what kind of problems.

"Is there another room?" she shouted.

Duane spun around, surprised. "You're still here."

"Is there another room downstairs or something?"

"No, this is it."

"Can I stand here with you?"

He looked down his shoulder at her, smiling as he frowned. "What for?"

Insulted and unable to answer, she took a step towards the door. The Algerian was hanging just outside, watching her. She gave him a vomitous look, took a step back, and plunked her elbow down on the bar. A bartender in a shiny shirt stopped in front of her. "I can't serve you," he said.

"What about him?" Luisa cocked her head towards Duane.

"Him? He's a friend."

"You're not twenty-one, are you?" she asked Duane.

"Not exactly."

The bartender moved away. It was time for Luisa to leave. But she didn't want to go home.

"Are you waiting for somebody?" she asked Duane.

"No, not really."

"You want to walk me to my car?"

His expression grew formal. "Sure. I'll be glad to."

Outside, after all the smoke, the air tasted like pure oxygen. The Algerian had left, probably to hide in the back seat of Luisa's car. She and Duane walked in silence down Euclid. She wondered whether he was attached to someone.

"So," she said, "do you, like, live around here?"

"I have an apartment near Wash U. I just moved out of a dorm."

"You go to school there?"

"I did, but I dropped out."

He didn't look like a dropout, but she was cool enough to say only, "Recently?"

"A week ago Tuesday."

"You really dropped out?"

"I barely even matriculated." He was slowing down, perhaps wondering which of the cars parked on Euclid was hers.

"Don't you love that word?" she said.

"Yeah," he said, not sounding like he loved it. "They gave me sophomore standing for my year in Munich—I was in Munich last year."

"I just got back from Paris."

"Was it fun?"

"Oh, non-stop, non-stop." Luisa nodded him into the alley.

"This is your car?"

"Sorry, but. It's my mother's." She stuck her hands in her back pockets and looked into his face. There was a meaningful pause, but it went on too long. Duane was very cute, his eyes deep-set and blackened in the dim light. She remembered the bruise. "What'd you do to your eye?"

He touched his eye and turned away.

"Or shouldn't I ask."

"I ran into a door."

He said this as if it was a joke. Luisa didn't get it. "Well, thanks for walking me here."

"Sure, you bet."

She watched him head back up the alley. What an obtuse

person. Luisa would have jumped at the chance to jump in a car with someone like herself. She unlocked the door and got in, started the engine, gunned it. She was quite annoyed. Now she had to drive home and sit around and watch TV and be bored. She hadn't even explained what she was doing down here in the first place. Duane probably thought she'd come looking for a fun time and was going home disappointed. She drove up the alley and turned onto Euclid and pulled up towards the bar.

Duane was on the sidewalk, smoking a cigarette. Luisa pressed the button for the passenger-side window. "You need a ride someplace?" she yelled.

He reacted with such surprise that the cigarette sprang sideways from his hand and hit a building, showering orange sparks.

"You need a ride someplace?" she said again, stretching painfully to keep her foot on the brake while she leaned and opened the door.

Duane hesitated and then got in.

"You scared me," he said.

She stepped on the gas. "What are you, paranoid or something?"

"Yeah. Paranoid." He leaned back in the seat, reached out the open window, and adjusted the extra mirror. "My life's gotten kind of weird lately." He pushed the mirror every which way. "Do you know Thomas Pynchon?"

"No," Luisa said. "Do you know Stacy Montefusco?"

"Who?"

"Edgar Voss?"

"Just the name."

"Sara Perkins?"

"Nope."

"But you knew who I was?"

He stopped playing with the mirror. "I knew your name."

Well then. "I remembered you and what's-her-face." Luisa held her breath.

"Holly Cleland? That was years ago."

"Oh. Hey, where are we going?"

"Take a left at Lindell. I live right off Delmar in U-City."

So she was driving him home. They'd see about that.

"I didn't pay for my beer," Duane said.

She decided to let him live with that remark. She drove augustly, queen of the road, up Lindell. The silence crept along the floor between them. A minute went by.

"So are you still paranoid?" she said.

"Only around doors."

"What?"

"Doors."

"Oh." She wasn't following.

Duane cleared his throat. "What kinds of things are you taking?"

"Taking?" she said coolly. They were in downtown University City now, riding a wave of green lights.

He cleared his throat more strenuously. "At school."

"Are the open windows bothering you?"

"No."

"We can close them."

"No."

"I was kind of mad about the frost last week." She just tossed this out. "It destroyed most of the bugs you can catch with a net. Basically I'm a net person. I mean, when I'm collecting. I had entomology last fall, and if you're good with nets you can really prosper. But Mr. Benson started thinking I was his protégée or something. He came up to me in April and he asked me if I wanted to go collecting larval stages with him. Larvull stages. I'd hardly talked to him since first quarter. He thought it was some kind of treat. He was asking *me* to go collecting larval stages, because of my special *interest* in bugs."

Duane craned his neck.

She guessed they were passing his street. "So we go out at about six in the morning to this pond near Fenton, and the first thing I think is oh god he's going to molest me and dump me in the pond. He's kind of creepy-looking to begin with. I could just see the headlines, you know, BUGGER BUGGERS BUGGER, DROWNS HER IN LAKE."

She'd thought this up in April. Duane laughed.

"But instead he just gives me these special rubber boots that are about forty sizes too big for me, and then we start wading into this gloop with his special device for collecting larvae. He dips down in the water—I mean, it's absolute *gloop*, I think no wonder it's full of bugs. He dips down and the first thing he drags up is this disgusting little organism, I don't know, some rare gadfly larva, which he shoves in my face and says, 'Would you like to have it?' Special treat, see. I'm about to woof it. I say, *'That?'* I've probably mortally offended him, which is fine with me because it means he'll never invite me again. With larvae and me, it's no thank you. The first thing he'd said was, he'd said, 'I think this will be very interesting for you. To pursue entomology properly you have to collect *all* the stages.' I didn't have the heart to tell him that's exactly why I'll never pursue entomology."

"What about caterpillars?"

"They're larval. They squish."

The frosty glow of a Hammaker Beer sign flashed by on the right, trailing a liquor store. Luisa pulled over and braked to a hard stop by a hydrant. "Buy some wine?" she said.

Duane looked at her. "What color?"

"Blanc, s'il vous plaît. Something with a screw cap."

She turned the car around and met him across the street. In a bag in the back seat there were big paper cups. She poured some of the Gallo into two of them and handed one to Duane. He asked where they were going.

"You tell me," she said. Traffic sounds filled the car, the continuous kiss of tires and asphalt.

"My decision-making apparatus is paralyzed."

"You talk funny."

"I'm nervous."

She didn't want to hear about it. "What happened, you run into another door?"

"I'm not used to being out with people like you."

"What kind of people am I?"

"Ones who go to dances."

She blinked, unsure whether this was meant as a compliment, and put the car in gear. They'd go hit the warehouse site.

"What schools are you applying to?" Duane cleared his throat as though the question had left junk in it.

"Stanford, Yale, Princeton, Harvard, Amherst, and—what? Swarthmore. And Carlton. Carlton's my safety."

"Do you know what you'll study?"

"Biology maybe. I guess I wouldn't mind being a doctor."

"Both of my parents are doctors," Duane said. "And my brother's in med school."

"My father built the Arch."

Ulp.

"I know," Duane said.

"Did people talk about it at Webster?"

He turned to her and smiled blandly. "No."

"But you knew."

"I read the paper."

"Is that why you remembered me?"

"You just never let up, do you?"

For a second she didn't breathe. She made a right turn onto Skinker Boulevard, feeling agreeably mortified, like when her mother criticized her.

A cigarette lighter rasped.

"You shouldn't smoke," she said.

"Clearly." Duane flicked sparks out the window. "I haven't been smoking long. Like a month and a half. I came back from Germany and got grossed out by how conceited people are about their health. My family especially. I figure as soon as I've gotten Webster Groves out of my system I'll kick the habit. In the meantime it's kind of entertaining. These keep me company when I'm alone."

"Then what are you smoking one now for?"

He threw it out the window. Luisa followed an Exxon truck onto Manchester Road. To the right, ambiguous amber signals glowed along railroad tracks on an elevated grade. Four blocks further east she swerved off the road. Gravel flew up and hit the chassis of the car. She drove back between a pair of metal sheds.

"Where are we?" Duane asked.

"Construction site."

"Hey."

She cut the lights. The chalky moonlit whiteness of the area leaped into prominence. On black trailers beyond the chain-link fence, tall red letters spelled out PROBST. Duane took a small camera pouch from his jacket pocket and got out of the car. Luisa followed with her paper cup of wine. "What's the camera for?"

"I'm sort of a photographer."

"Since when?"

"Since, I don't know. Since a few weeks ago. I've been trying to sell some things to the Post-Dispatch."

"Have you had any luck?"

"No."

There was enough slack in the chain on the gate to let them slip through easily. They walked down a set of wooden steps to the warehouse skeleton, which was three hundred feet long and nearly that deep. Vertical steel members punctuated the structure every twenty feet or so, and here and there a prefabricated staircase rose pointlessly to the top plane of beams. Light bulbs were strung on posts above the foundation.

"You can't take pictures here."

"Why not?"

"We're not supposed to be here."

All around them lay hasty piles of plywood pouring forms and bundles of reinforcing rods, knobby and sagging. Duane's sneakers made soft pings on the undamped metal as he ran up a staircase. Luisa thought of her parents at the movies. They'd gone to see *Harold and Maude*. She imagined her mother laughing and her father watching stone-faced.

Through the iron parallelograms above her she could make out the W of Cassiopeia. To the south, two vertical strings of TV-tower lights competed in the night like the stations they belonged to. Trucks rumbled by on Manchester Road, and Luisa swayed in the darkness, and drank her wine, her eyes on Duane.

.

The next morning she woke up at seven o'clock. Her father was leaving for work and then tennis, his Saturday routine, and she could hear him whistling in the bathroom. The tune was familiar. It was the theme from *I Love Lucy*.

In the kitchen she found her mother reading the stock-market pages of the *Post*, her coffee cup empty. She was chewing her nails as she had every morning for the last nine years in lieu of a cigarette. "You're up early," she said.

Luisa dropped into a chair. "I'm sick."

"You have a cold?"

"What else?" She reached for a waiting glass of orange juice and coughed decrepitly.

"You were out pretty late."

"I was with this guy from school." She explained, in sentence fragments, what had happened at the bar. She rested her face on her palm, her elbow on the checkered tablecloth.

"Were you drinking?"

"This is not a hangover, Mother. This is the real thing."

"Maybe you should go back to bed."

She didn't want to. Her bed was burning hot.

"Can I make you some breakfast?"

"Yes please."

She was in her room watching *Bullwinkle* when her father returned from the courts. He was still whistling the theme from *I Love Lucy*. His face appeared at her door, pink with tennis. "Your mother tells me you're sick."

She rolled onto her back and made an effort to be friendly. "I'm feeling a little better now."

"Getting up is always the worst." Daddy was sententious.

"Uh huh. Did you win?"

He smiled. "Your uncle's a very good player." His eyes grew distant, his smile false. Uncle Rolf always beat him.

"How was the movie?" she asked.

"Oh, very funny. A good choice. Your mother loved it."

"What about you?"

"I liked the Maude character. She was very well done." He paused. "I'm going to take a shower. Will you be down for lunch?"

Sick of records and TV, she spent the early afternoon simply kneeling by the window, her chin on the cleft between her clasped fingers. The trees were in motion, and puffy white clouds were in the sky. Mr. LeMaster across the street was doing his best to rake leaves. A man in a blue van threw the weekend *Post-Dispatch* into the driveway. Luisa went down to fetch it.

Her father was on his business line in the study, ordering eighteen beef Wellingtons for some kind of meeting. Her mother was baking in the kitchen. Luisa heard the rolling pin click and the cadences of the three o'clock news.

The air outside was both warm and cold, like fever and chills. Mr. LeMaster, who thought she was spoiled, did not say hello.

She unsheathed the *Post* and left all of it at the foot of the stairs except for the big funnies and the Everyday section, which had the small funnies. These she took back up to her bedroom and lay down with. She started to turn to the small funnies, but a picture on the first page stopped her. It was a picture of a black man giving the photographer the finger. The credit read: *D. Thompson/Post-Dispatch.*

Luisa shivered. How could they print a picture like that? And so quickly? Duane had said he hadn't sold anything.

A FOREST PARK SATURDAY was the page's headline. Other pictures gave glimpses of anonymous revelers, and in the background of Duane's picture some kids were playing football on the field by the Planetarium. The lips of the man in the foreground were parted in derision. His finger was aimed at the unseen photographer. *Shirts and Skins in the Park*, the caption read. *Benjamin Brown, foreground, has been unemployed since last November. The man, right, was unidentified.*

The man, right, was a hawk-nosed Asian in a turban, a passerby. He was glancing aside so severely that his eyes were all whites. He looked like a blind man.

.

Eight hours later she and Duane were necking in the rain in Blackburn Park. When the rain got too heavy they went and necked in his mother's silver Audi, which he'd borrowed for the evening. The windows fogged up solid. People walking by on Glendale Road couldn't see a thing inside the car.

Luisa was running a temperature, maybe a hundred or a hundred one, but she didn't feel the least bit sick. It was Duane who kept asking if she had to get home. When she did get home, the house was dark; she was happy she was only an hour late. But as soon as she closed the front door her father ambushed her. First he scared her and then he was horrible to her. She couldn't understand how anyone could get so pissed off about an hour either way. Before she fell asleep she decided to keep Duane to herself for a while, even if she had to lie.

When she woke up in the morning the sun was shining and the air near her bedroom windows was much warmer than it had been the night before. After breakfast she told her mother she was going out birding with Stacy. She told her father she thought his pants were too short. Then she drove over to University City and picked up Duane, and phoned Stacy from a gas station and asked her to cover for her.

In the middle of the big field in Washington State Park she spread a blanket and lay down. Half a mile away, further up the Big River valley, smoke was uncoiling from dying fires. Campers were pouring water on the coals, packing tents into trunks. For them it was the hour of damp sleeping bags and desolation, their thoughts turning to tomorrow's practicalities while Luisa beamed in the sun. Her new boyfriend's eyes were bright. He'd slept well, he said. He'd brought a camera, a larger one, a Canon.

"Psh-psh-psh-psh-psh-psh-psh-psh-psh-psh."

"What's that?"

"Birds like it," she said. "Psh-psh-psh-psh-psh-psh-psh. Psh-psh-psh-psh-psh-psh-psh-psh."

"What birds?"

"All birds. They get curious. They wonder what it is. Look!" She pointed to a red-and-white flash in the willow grove.

"What?"

"Rufous-sided towhee. It's one of my favorites."

"How many—"

"*Sh!* Sh-shh-shh-shh-shh-shh-shh-shh."

"How many species do you know?" Duane whispered.

"I've seen a hundred twelve this year. I've got about a hundred and fifty on my lifetime list. Which isn't very many, really."

"It sounds like a lot."

"Does it?" She leaned into him and toppled him. "Does it? Does it?" Sickness and medicine made her feel spread out, a warm smothering blanket. "Does it? Does it?" She spread her arms and legs to mirror his. His hard-on pressed on her hipbone. They lay still for a long time. Luisa could see herself and how she lay and looked from a perspective that would have been impossible if her parents had known who she was with. At this very minute in Webster Groves her mother was working on dinner and her father was watching football. They expected her back before long.

"Listen!" Duane shifted beneath her.

Geese were honking. She rolled over and saw a V of Canadas heading south. She sneezed from the sun and wool dust.

"Sit up for a second," Duane said. He was screwing a stumpier lens onto the camera.

"You mean gesundheit."

He lay on his stomach and took half a dozen pictures. "What kind of geese are those?"

She turned to double-check.

"Don't look. Smile. Wipe that mustache off your face."

She smiled at the receding geese. "Am I going to be in the paper?"

"*Smile*. You're a dream. At *me*."

"At you?" She stopped smiling and looked at him. "What for?"

"So nobody gets the idea they're looking at anything but a picture. I want there to be an implied photographer."

"I guess you've got it all figured out," she said.

"I guess I do."

"Is that what you told the Post-Dispatch?"

"I didn't tell them anything. I went down there with some prints and they gave me the runaround. And then yesterday morning, like, you're putting me on the *payroll*? I thought they were going to say they'd lost my pictures."

"You're really lucky."

"I know. You're my lucky star. I can pay the rent now."

Rent? What a bizarre concept. *Pay the rent*. What a boring concept.

"Do you like me?" she said.

"What do you think?"

"Why do you like me?"

"Because you're smart and you're pretty and you came along at the right time."

"Do you want to go back to your apartment?"

"Later maybe."

"Let's go now. I have to be home at six."

4

Behind the first tee of the 18-hole Forest Park golf course, the starter emerged from his hut and called two names.

"Davis and White?"

RC White and his brother-in-law Clarence Davis rose from a bench and retrieved their cards.

"Twosome," the starter said, disapproving. He fixed his eyes on his left shoulder. He had no left arm.

"We play slow," RC averred. "We're patient men."

"Uh huh. Just wait till the kids up there hit again."

"We appreciate it," Clarence said.

Five or six groups milled behind them waiting to tee off. It was Saturday morning, the air already steamy though the sun wouldn't clear the trees for another half an hour. RC popped the tab on a can of Hammaker, sampled the contents, and tucked the can under the strap on his cart. He removed the mitten from his driver and took some colossal warm-up swings.

"You watch that," Clarence said, wiping the spray of dew and grass off his arm. He wore black chinos, a tan sport shirt, and bearded white golf shoes. RC was in jeans and sneaks and a T-shirt. He squinted down the fairway, from the various corners of which the members of a young white foursome were eyeing one another. The first green floated far and uncertain in the par-four distance, like a patch of fog that the foursome was trying to stalk and pin down.

Clarence was wagging his hips like a pro. He was RC's wife's oldest brother. He'd given RC his old set of golf clubs two Christmases ago. Now RC had to join him in a game every Saturday.

"You go on and hit," RC said.

Clarence addressed his ball and drew his driver back over his head with a studied creakiness. Everything by the book, RC thought. Clarence was like that. When he was fully wound up, he uncoiled all at once. His club whistled. He clobbered the ball and then nodded, accepting the shot like a personal compliment.

RC planted tee and ball, and without a practice swing he took a swipe. He staggered back and looked skyward. "Shit."

"Sucker's a mile high," Clarence said. "You got great elevation, say that for you."

"I got under it. *Under* it is what I got."

The ball landed sixty yards from the tee, so close that they could hear its deadened impact. They slid their drivers into their bags and strode off the tee. It turned out Clarence had caught a bunker. Good with his irons, RC reached the green in three. They had to kick sycamore leaves out of the way before they could putt. Already RC's feet were soaked. When he putted, his ball resisted with the hiss of a wet paint roller, throwing spirals of water droplets off to either side.

On the next hole they played through the kids ahead of them and took bogies. Finding a fivesome camped on the third tee, they sat down on a bench. The hole, a par three, required a long drive over a creek and up a steep, bald hill. The fivesome was pounding ball after ball into the hazard. Clarence lit a cigar and observed them with a very eloquent suppression of a smile. He had drooping, kindly eyes, skin about the color of pecan shells, and eyebrows and sideburns dusted with gray. RC admired Clarence—which was a way of saying they were different, a way of excusing the difference. Clarence owned a demolition business and had plenty of contracts. He sang in a Baptist choir, he belonged to the Urban League, he organized block parties. His wife's brother was Ronald Struthers, a city alderman who one day would be mayor; the connection didn't hurt Clarence's business any. His oldest boy, Stanly, was a star high-school halfback. His wife Kate was the prettiest lady RC knew, prettier than his own wife Annie (Clarence's kid sister) though not half as sexy. Annie was only twenty-six. In the three years since RC married her, Clarence had been "making an effort" with him. Sometimes, like when he gave RC his golf clubs, his friendliness seemed premeditated, a little too aware that RC had lost his only real brother in Vietnam. But Annie told RC not to flatter himself, because Kate would have vetoed new clubs if Clarence still had his old ones.

"Hear about Bryant Hooper?" Clarence puffed serenely on his cigar.

"What about him?"

"Got shot in the head," Clarence said. "Thursday morning."

"Aw, Jesus." Hooper was a police detective. Drug squad. "Dead?"

"No, he'll make it. Lost a cheek and teeth, ugly ugly wound, but it could've been worse. I was by the hospital last night."

"How'd it happen?"

"Oh, very routine, RC. Very routine. Some dealer dude with a weapon. Some ex-dude."

"Yeah?"

"They slaughtered him." Clarence shut his eyes. "And there was seven others in the building. This a place just north of Columbus Square. An ex-place."

"Yeah?"

"Owner requested a raid, and after Hoop got hit his buddies fired tear gas. Place burned to the ground before anyone quite noticed." Clarence turned to RC. "You wonder what the point is?"

RC shrugged.

"The point is Ronald Struthers owned that building."

"He got insurance?"

"Naturally. Good deal for him. Something for nothing."

"Sounds like an accident," RC said, finishing his beer.

"Sure. It was an accident. But part of a pattern, brother. Part of a pattern."

The group on the tee beckoned to Clarence. He laid the cigar on the bench, picked up his 7-iron, and thanked them. After a few gentle practice swings he lofted a perfect shot up onto the green.

The image of smooth Alderman Ronald Struthers in a three-piece disturbed RC's control. He shut his eyes on his downswing and—*under it, baby*—hit a line drive. But the ball cleared the hazard and bounded up the hill. Clarence sank his putt for a birdie. RC missed his first putt by a mile. He missed his second putt. He missed his third. Clarence stood with the flag pin clutched to his breast, his expression as sad and abstracted as if he were watching another man drown puppies. Members of the fivesome cleared their throats. RC felt lawless. The rising sun was in his eyes, and his beer buzz made his arms feel about eight feet long. He topped his fourth putt. Once he was on the wrong side of par, once deep in bogey country, he started rushing, pressing, choking, and he cared less and less. When Clarence got in trouble he bore down. RC just said bag it.

His ball was still two feet from the hole when Clarence said, "I'll give you that one." RC kicked it off the green.

No fewer than eight golfers were standing around on the fourth tee. Clarence led RC off behind some overgrown evergreens. "RC, man," he whispered. "You're closing your eyes."

RC closed his eyes. "I know."

"Head down, eye on the ball. That's standard."

RC spat. "I know. I just gotta settle down. You wait." With a tee, he scraped strings of hardened grass pulp out of the grooves on the face of his driver. Shouldn't *be* any grass on a driver.

"Head down. It's worth twenty strokes a round."

"So what about Struthers?" RC said.

Clarence relit his cigar and inspected it professionally. Tiny pearls of sweat hung on his sideburns. "Ronald," he said, "is much changed."

"He'll never change."

"He's changed," Clarence said. "He belongs to our new chief of police."

"Where do you get that from?"

"From the way he talk and the way he be. He's like a *robot*, RC. He's a hollow man. He's got money from somewhere. The little office on Cass? Gone. He rented a whole floor in that place by the Adventists. He's put on nine new employees since the first of October, and he ain't making no secret about it. And I say to him, Hey there, Rondo, you win somebody's lottery? And he get all stiff and say to me, It's just commissions, Clarence, I'n breakin' no laws."

RC nodded.

"That's right," Clarence said. "As if I was accusing him of something. That's OK, though. I got thick enough skin. But then I say, you know, your standard polite question: Who's buying what property? All right? And he give me this look." Clarence, demonstrating the look, squinted meanly. "And he go, Certain parties. Like I'm from the IRS, not from his own extended family. So I go, OK, Rondo, be seeing you, but he go, Wait a minute there, Clarence—and this is not the Ronald Struthers that's trying to save Homer Phillips Hospital—he go: They be razing buildings something fierce next month. I go: That so? And he go: Yep. And I go: Who's they? And he go: Folks that don't like questions. And I go: I don't like working for that kind. And he go: You'll learn to love 'em before this year is out."

"Tell him to shove it," RC said.

Clarence shut his eyes and licked his lips. "I hesitate, brother. I hesitate. I got four growing kids. And you didn't ask me about Jammu."

"Jammu." RC had had enough of this stuff. He wanted another swat at the golf ball.

"That's right. Jammu. This raid on Thursday where Hooper got it, they wouldn't never done that under Bill O'Connell. Too damned dangerous, and what's the point? But now they're taking that neighborhood lot by lot, cleaning out the junkies and the derelicts and some families too and throwing them on the street. They're fencing it all off. I knocked down some two-fams behind a ten-foot fence last week. A ten-foot fence! And no genius required on my part to see that's where these new clients of Ronald is doing their buying. Same thing's happening in those bad blocks east of Rumbold. Jammu's fighting house to house, and *somebody* is buying up the lots as she goes. Ronald is in on it, I swear to that. And somebody else, somebody named Cleon."

Cleon, RC knew, could only be Cleon Toussaint, an unabashed slumlord, an old enemy of Ronald Struthers. He went around in a wheelchair but nobody felt sorry for him. "Says who?" RC asked, fingering his driver.

"Says the city recorder. Mr. Toussaint is now proud owner of one and a quarter *miles* of frontage south of Easton that wasn't his four weeks ago. A whole neighborhood, RC. He even bought that garbage dump on Easton. And bought it all since the first of October, and doesn't care if the whole world knows."

"Where'd he get the money?"

"I was waiting for you to ask me that. Nobody knows where he got the money, not me, not anybody. What I do know is what his brother do for a living."

RC shivered in his sweat. John Toussaint, brother of the more odious Cleon, was the commander of the seventh police district, except he wasn't the commander anymore; Jammu had promoted him downtown in September.

"Not to mention the way Ronald talk about Jammu. It's almost like she's some kind of religion. She's—"

The head of a golfer appeared from behind the bushes. "You fellas want to play through?"

Clarence turned to the man, astonished. "That's very kind of you." To RC in a whisper, he said, "We'll return to this."

The men on the tee were restively shuffling the clubs in their bags, perhaps regretting their offer. Clarence teed up, spat on his palms, dug in, and whacked a moon shot across Art Hill, the fat first leg of this par five. The pond at the bottom of the hill lay as calm as an uncut jello salad. Leaves speckled it, motionless. At the top of the hill early sunlight inhabited the museum's stonework. Keeping his head down, his eye on the ball, RC hit his first clean shot of the morning. His ball bounced near Clarence's and rolled up the next hill. "Keep it," Clarence advised.

After Clarence sliced his second shot into some poplars near an arm of the pond, RC hit a blistering fairway wood over the second hill and out of sight. He walked over the crest of the hill, hoping against hope to see his ball in the vicinity of the pin. Instead he saw a multitude of sycamore leaves. They covered the green and the fairway approach. Glossy and whitish, they all looked like golf balls.

He began to search the green. Clarence's third shot sailed over his head and cracked into a sycamore trunk, ricocheting favorably.

"Lost it, huh?" Clarence was cheerful as he crossed the green, his club heads clicking in his bag. "You see mine?"

RC walked in tight circles, kicking leaves and getting dizzy; the green began to tilt. He looked into the sky and saw the negative images of a zillion leaves. Finally he had to drop a new ball in the bunker, take the penalty, and play from there.

Clarence foozled his chip, but he managed to hole out for a bogey. When he pulled the flag pin to retrieve his ball, he froze. "RC, boy." He spoke to something in the hole. "Be honest now. What ball you playing?"

RC thought. "Wilson. Three dots."

"Down in *two*." Clarence was still bent over the hole. "Double eagle. You one hell of a lucky sucker."

.

Six months after he finished high school, RC had gotten drafted and sent to Fort Leonard Wood, where sergeants taught him everything he needed to know to become good mortar fodder for gook insurgents. When the rest of his unit was shipping out, though, the higher-ups had transferred him to the uniformed infirmary staff, sparing him a long round trip. Grateful for the break, and by nature a man who left well enough alone, RC reenlisted twice. His war experience consisted of nothing more than typing histories. But when he got back to St. Louis he had a hard time readjusting. Supposedly the Army turned boys into men, but often it turned men into babies, because unlike a monastery or university or profit-making organization, the Army had no ethic. When the pressure let up, you goofed off; it was automatic. RC didn't drink often, but when he did he got plastered. The word "pussy" was major. He giggled and yukked and slept at every opportunity. It was a trash outlook. In St. Louis old friends of his stayed away from him. Potential new ones were skeptical. They'd ask him what his name was, and he'd shrug and say, "Richard, I guess." You guess? They tried Ricky, Rick, Rich, Richie, Dickie, Dick, White and White Man. They tried Ice, because he'd found a job with the Cold Ice Company on North Grand. He wasn't stupid; just uncertain. Eventually he settled on the name RC, short for Richard Craig, his first two names. He became plant manager at Cold Ice. When he was thirty he got to know a young forklift driver named Annie Davis. Four years later he and Annie had a good apartment and a three-year-old son, and then, in July, in the very month you'd least expect it, Cold Ice went out of business. Clarence quickly offered RC a job, which he quickly refused, because either Clarence would have had to lay off some otherwise OK man to make room for him, or else he would have been paying RC out of profits, out of charity.

So for three months now RC had been working as the parking-lot attendant at the downtown offices of KSLX-TV and KSLX-Radio. It was a joke of a job, but not bad for a stopgap, and not without a certain maddening challenge. KSLX had expanded its workforce by nearly one-third in the last decade without adding any area to its parking lot. RC was required to juggle a lot of cars, and to juggle them fast, especially during the two rush hours. When you parked cars four-deep, getting one out of the back row was like doing one of those sliding plastic puzzles where the object was to arrange the eight little squares among nine little spaces in various orders, but with an important difference: cars couldn't move sideways the way those little squares could. You had to keep track of exactly who wanted exactly what car at exactly what hour. And you had to keep the patterns loose. In August, Mr. Hutchinson, the station's general manager and the network's top man in the Midwest, had asked for his Lincoln four hours after he'd said he was flying to New York for three days, and RC freed the Lincoln in less than (he'd clocked it) fifty seconds by spiriting three four-door yachts into slots that he once might have thought too narrow for a ten-speed.

But on the Monday morning after he'd humbled Clarence with That Double Eagle, on the morning of the day before Halloween, a VIP asked him to perform the unperformable. This VIP, a dark-skinned foreigner, had sworn up and down that he wouldn't need his Skylark before two in the afternoon; he had business inside with top management. So RC had put him in one of the longish-term deep spaces right up front, and let Cliff Quinlan park his Alfa in front of it. Quinlan, the station's hotshot investigative reporter, had mentioned a ten o'clock rendezvous and taken his keys inside with him. This was fine with RC, seeing as two o'clock was a good four hours later than ten o'clock.

At 9:30 the VIP came out and demanded the car. Suppressing

his first impulse, which was to scream, RC urged him to be patient for one half hour.

"No my good man!" The VIP pointed at his Skylark as if it were a stick to be fetched. "You get me the car immediately."

RC rubbed the bristly backside of his head. What with his big eyebrow bones, his long ears and complicated nose, he saw fit to keep his hair short. "You have a problem," he said, "that I can't solve."

It was a gray, sultry morning in St. Louis. Passersby on Olive Street had slowed to inspect the Skylark in question. The VIP waited until they were out of earshot. Then he straightened his necktie, a shiny silver thing tied in a real potato of a knot, and said: "Know that I am from All-India Radio. I am here on a courtesy visit, and courtesy is my expectation." A horizontal palm approached RC. On it lay a fifty-dollar bill.

"Oh man. You got me wrong, man. This ain't economics. This physics."

The palm did not recede or waver.

"Well," RC mumbled, taking charge of the bill. "I ain't saying this be easy now." He squeezed past Cliff Quinlan's Alfa and climbed into the Skylark, rubbing his hands. Fifty! The guy better learn his exchange rates. RC concentrated. If he could rock this baby back and forth and move it two feet to the left, he could rev it and get the front wheels over the parking-stop, angle it around, get the back wheels over the parking-stop, brake hard, and back it down the sidewalk to the VIP.

Starting up, he wrenched the wheels hard to the left and moved forward till he touched the metal guardrail. Easy, easy. He reversed the wheel full to the right, the steering column whimpering protest, and backed up to within a millimeter of the Alfa, then reversed the wheel again and repeated the process. He did this six times, back and forth. Then came the hard part. He had to give the engine gas and, by means of the brake, leap the concrete parking-stop and stop immediately. And now Quinlan's fender, not his bumper, was at stake. RC backed up in tiny jerks, another inch, another half an inch. He was close to that fender, but he took it back a mite further, and then he heard the bump.

The impact was catastrophic.

The ground shook the car shook the building hammered in his skull. He panicked in reverse before he hit the brake. A painful deafness was fading. He heard glass and metal, large fragments, crashing into cars.

The far corner of the lot was an inferno of black smoke and orange flame. RC threw the door open, scraping it on the parking-stop, and ran to the VIP. The VIP was stretched out flat on the ground with his hands over his head. He was right on top of a grease puddle. The flames crackled and rumbled, some only visible as a wildness of air. RC could see that the inferno was none other than Mr. Hutchinson's Lincoln. The front two-thirds of it was missing. Mr. Strom's Regal lay on its side. Cars all around had lost windshields and windows.

The sirens were already coming. RC looked around. In an agony of helplessness, he jumped up and down.

The VIP stirred. RC knelt. "Man, are you all right?"

The VIP nodded. His eyes were wide open.

"Jesus, Jesus, Jesus," RC said. "What happened?"

"Nothing—"

"Nothing?"

"I *saw* nothing. It exploded."

"Jesus." RC paused to consider the man's probable religion and added, "No offense."

The air itself seemed to have generated police radio static. A fire truck pulled up. The firemen began spraying the carnage casually, men watering a giant lawn with giant hoses, before they even climbed off the truck. A squad car pulled off Olive Street and nearly ran over RC and the VIP. It braked urgently. Doors opened.

"Are you in charge here?"

RC looked up. The person who'd spoken was Jammu. "I park cars," he said.

"Is this man hurt?"

"Far's I can tell he isn't."

RC followed Jammu with his eyes as she bent down over the VIP. What a small woman she was. Smaller than she ever looked in pictures. She wore a light gray trench coat. Her hair was loose and tucked behind her ears. Though only a welterweight himself, RC stared. Such a small little woman.

The VIP struggled to his knees. The front of his suit was stamped with a large, creased grease stain.

Jammu turned to RC. "Whose car was that?"

"Mr. Hutchinson's. He's—"

"I know who he is. How did it happen?"

"No idea."

"What do you mean, no idea?"

RC sweated. "I was trying to get this guy's Skylark out of, you know, a tight spot. Next thing I know—"

He told her everything he'd seen. He hadn't seen anything. But she never took her eyes off him. He felt like he was being memorized. When he gave her his name and address she thanked him and, in leaving, brushed his wrist with her fingers. The skin burned. She walked over to the wreck, which was now smoldering and roped off by the cops. RC looked around helplessly again. He still didn't know what to do. He noticed that the VIP and squad car had disappeared.

The bad thing was, he'd put a dent in Cliff Quinlan's fender. He knew without going to check. As a job, this joke was getting old, and RC wasn't stupid. They were taking applications at the Police Academy.

·

One-fifteen in the afternoon. Jammu stood at the window of a twenty-second-floor room in the Clarion Hotel and directed a yawn at the Peabody Coal and Continental Grain installations across the Mississippi. On the near side of the river, conventioning Jaycees in paper boaters straggled along the footpaths to the Arch. Jammu looked at the reflection of her guest in the window. Karam Bhandari was sitting on the end of the double bed peeling the foil off the bottle of Mumm's between his legs. Bhandari was Jammu's mother's personal attorney and sometime spiritual advisor. Though he came from a family of Jains, he was all carnivore, his eyes lidded, his skin saurianly faceted. Jammu had never liked him, but she felt obliged to show him a good time in St. Louis. She'd let him detonate a bomb this morning.

The cork popped. Bhandari brought two stemmed plastic glasses fizzing to the window. He'd changed his grease-stained shirt but not the undershirt, and the grease was seeping through onto the pinpoint cloth. He raised his glass and showed his sharp, small teeth. "To your endeavor," he said.

Jammu returned the toast with her eyebrows and drained her glass. Bhandari had a vested interest in her endeavor. If she was sleepy today (and she was), it was the aftereffect of their meeting in her office last night. Bhandari specialized in intractable silences and bad-tempered sighs. Maman had sent him over to inspect the management of her investments, to confer with Jammu and with Asha Hammaker, and, in her phrase, "to get a sense of the situation." Maman had every right to send him, since she was dumping fourteen and a half million dollars into the St. Louis real-estate market and spending another five hundred thousand in silence money. But Bhandari was being hosted by Jammu, the very person whose judgment he had come to confirm or dispute. This made for tensions.

"It's quite impossible," he'd said at one point. "You simply must have a full-time accountant."

"I've told you," she said. "I have Singh, I have Asha's—"

"I see. May I ask why this—Mr. Singh—is not present this evening?"

"Balwan Singh, Karam. You know Balwan. He's in Illinois tonight."

"Oh. *That* Singh. He isn't to be trusted, Essie. Surely there's someone else."

"There's Asha's accountant and her attorneys, whom unfortunately she considered it unwise for you to meet. But Singh is very capable. And regardless of what Maman may have told you, he's completely trustworthy."

Bhandari had pulled a long, dull donkey face, blinking. "Surely there's someone else."

Returning now with the Mumm's bottle, Bhandari reached around her and refilled her glass. His chin lingered at her shoulder. He was in a better mood today, since she'd let him do the bomb. She gave his cheek a filial pat. "Thanks, Karam." She took a sip of champagne. "You have the transmitter?"

He stepped back and fished in his jacket pocket, produced the transmitter and set it on the windowsill. "Yes. There it is."

A pause. The sky darkened a shade.

"Is the transmitter your own work?"

"The design is."

"And you still have time to be chief of police."

Jammu smiled. "It's an old design. Standard issue."

"And the automobile?"

"It belonged to a man named Hutchinson, the station's general manager."

"And you attempt to extort, em, extort a certain— I take it this is an act of extortion?"

"No. We make no demands."

A veil of rain drifted into view from the west, applying itself to the Arch. "No demands," he repeated.

"That's right. This is senseless."

"But you wished me to make sure no one was hurt."

"We aren't hurting people yet. We want to scare them. In this case, scare Hutchinson. But we'll go as far as we need to."

"I must confess I don't see the point."

Last night, he'd failed to see the point of her strategy with North Side real estate. It was simple, she'd told him. Since even Maman didn't have enough cash to start a legitimate panic, Asha's men were buying up little lots throughout the area, from the river to the western limits, creating the impression of many parties acting on inside information. And they magnified the impression by buying only property owned by local banks. This left as much land as possible in the hands of local black businessmen—politically, this was vital—while leading the banks to believe the sum of these investments was much greater than the fourteen million dollars it actually was. Because who would suspect that someone would make a point of buying exclusively from banks?

Bhandari's fingertips floated over the stains on his shirt pocket. The real problem was his innate inability to comprehend ideas voiced by a woman; he retreated into a mental closet which seemed to grow the more asphyxiating the longer Jammu spoke. She decided to torment him further. "Formalisms," she said. "You know. Real-estate speculation is a formalism, Karam. Essentially ahistorical. Once it gets going—once we set it in motion—it works by itself and drags politics and economics along after it. Terror works

the same way. We want Hutchinson in the State. We want to strip
his world of two of its dimensions, develop a situation that over-
comes all the repressions that make him think in what the world
calls a normal way. Do you hear me, Karam? Do you hear the
words I am speaking to you?"

Bhandari refilled her glass. "Drink, drink," he said. His own
glass he brought to his lips awkwardly, as though pouring, not
sipping. Seemingly as an afterthought, he raised the glass. "To
your endeavor."

Jammu was going to have to speak with Maman. She was sure
that if Maman had known how Bhandari would behave she would
have sent a more competent spy. Or would have come herself.
Jammu raised the cuff of her cardigan. Two o'clock. The day was
evaporating. She took a deep breath, and as she let it out, Bhandari,
from behind her, inserted his hands beneath her arms and placed
them on her breasts. She jumped away.

Bhandari straightened his back, an attorney again, a trusted
family advisor. "I assume," he said, "that the proper security meas-
ures have been taken vis-à-vis our Negro liaisons."

Jammu turned back to the river with a smile. "Yes," she said.
"Boyd and Toussaint weren't any trouble. They had plenty to hide
already. But Struthers, as I said, was expensive. He was the obvious
choice—a broker and a politician too, a popular alderman, even
something of a crusader. But we managed to dig up a dirty secret,
a mistress he's been keeping for nearly a decade. It was clear that
he'd racked up a number of conflict-of-interest violations on behalf
of the woman's family, which is quite well off. So I had some
leverage when I approached him, enough to protect me if he wasn't
interested. Which he wasn't, until we came to the money part.
Maman cleared the bribes personally, by the way. We don't skimp
when my own neck's on the line."

Jammu felt Bhandari's breath on her neck. His face was sifting
through her hair, seeking skin. She twisted around in his arms and
let him kiss her throat. Over his slicked-back hair she saw the hotel
room's "luxurious" bedspread, its "contemporary" art print, the
"distinctive" roughcast ceiling. He unbuttoned the top of her
blouse, snorting intermittently. Probably the best metaphor for the
State was sexual obsession. An absorbing parallel world, a clan-

destine organizing principle. Men moved mountains for the sake of a few muscle contractions in the dark.

The phone rang.

Bhandari made no sudden motion. He was unaware that it had rung. Jammu arrested the fingers working at her bra and disengaged herself. She moved to answer the phone, but stopped, reconsidering. "You'd better take it," she said.

Bhandari stretched his neck muscles carefully and seated himself on the bed. "Hello?" He listened. "Why *yes!*"

From his condescending tone, Jammu guessed it was Princess Asha. Another postponement? She buttoned her blouse and fixed her hair. They'd be missing her at the office.

"Was it an *open* coffin?" Bhandari tittered. He'd been tittering for twenty-four hours. Late last night their talk had turned to JK Exports, Maman's wool business and her primary cash conduit between Bombay and Zurich. Bhandari had described a recent incident. "Some *Sikhs* got in one of your mother's warehouses last week." He'd made Sikhs sound like little moths.

He covered the mouthpiece of the phone and said to Jammu: "Asha can't come until this evening. Shall we make a date?"

"I'm busy tonight. Tell her after midnight. Say one o'clock."

.

KSLX general manager Jim Hutchinson rode home that night with his wife Bunny, who, as chance would have it, was downtown when the bomb went off. She was a comforting presence. When she showed up at his office, an hour after the blast, she was not the bundle of nerves another woman might have been. She looked glum, almost peeved. She wrinkled her nose. She paced. She didn't kiss him. "Good thing you weren't in the car," she said.

"Damn good thing, Bunny."

Having satisfied herself that he was unharmed, she left again to shop, returning only at 5:30 to take him home. He let her drive. As soon as they were tucked into traffic on Highway 40 she said, "Do they know who did it?" She turned on the wipers. Rain was falling from the prematurely dark sky.

"No," he said.

"Good thing we've got a police department we can trust."

"Are you talking about Jammu?"

Bunny shrugged.

"Jammu's all right," he said.

"Is that so?" A band of red lights, a lava flow, flashed on in front of them. Bunny braked.

"You may object to her nationality," Hutchinson said, remembering as he spoke that Jammu was an American, "but she's turned the entire Bomb and Arson Squad loose on the case."

"Isn't that what anybody would do?"

"That's the point, my lovely wife."

"What have they found?"

"There's not much to go on. Somebody tipped off the police at six this morning, but it wasn't much of a tip."

"Mm?"

"Are you even listening to me?"

"Somebody tipped off the police at six this morning but—"

"They didn't know what to make of it. Somebody called up and said: When it happens, that's us. The fellow at the switchboard had the presence of mind not to hang up. He asked who was calling, and the caller said, *Ow!* The fellow asked again. The caller said, *Ow!* And that was the tip."

"Some tip."

"And it's not as if I have enemies. I told the detectives it almost had to be a random thing, except—"

"Except there are a lot of cars parked downtown."

"So why ours?"

Bunny swung the car into the right lane, which seemed a little bit better lubricated. Hutchinson continued: "There were effectively no witnesses, and there was almost nothing left of the bomb. But they did figure out how it was planted. Detective I spoke with after lunch said it was one of those tape decks black kids carry around. A boom box." Now she'll start in on the blacks, he thought. But she didn't. He kept talking. "Said they found pieces of one scattered around the lot. It looks like the thing was hollowed out and filled with explosives, then shoved under the car and detonated from a distance. It wasn't dynamite, though."

"Mm?"

"It was plastic. Which is strange. It's hardly amateur."

"Oh, huh. Can you run stories on it?"

"It's news, why not? We can do whatever we want."

"Maybe Cliff Quinlan?"

"And turn up foul play in Jammu's administration? Is that the idea?"

"I've just never heard of cars being bombed in St. Louis, that's all."

Half an hour later they escaped Highway 40, exiting onto Clayton Road. Rain continued to fall. Giant plastic jack-o'-lanterns leered from windows in the older stores on Clayton.

At home their youngest daughter, Lee, was chatting in the kitchen with Queenie, their maid and cook. Two television-sized pumpkins awaited slaughter near the door. Lee toyed with a warty gourd from a basket of autumn objects. Bunny and Hutchinson washed their hands and went to sit down in the dining room, but the dinner table wasn't set. Queenie had apparently not yet finished waxing it. She'd set the table in the breakfast room. She sliced the rump roast and doused each serving with béarnaise. There was steamed yellow squash and a salad with red lettuce, scallions, and hearts of palm.

After grace, muttered by Lee, Hutchinson dug into his beef and began telling Lee the bomb story, although she'd already seen it on TV. Bunny eyed her squash disks dispiritedly. She could hear a helicopter outside. Perhaps the KSLX Trafficopter. It sounded close, though it might have been the rain or wind that carried the sound.

No. It was very close, practically on top of them. They could hear the straining motor as well as the blades. Lee leaned back in her chair and looked out the window. She couldn't see anything.

"Wonder what *this* is all about," Bunny said.

As Hutchinson shrugged, the firing began. The living-room windows went first. They shattered almost quietly beneath the screaming of the copter's metal parts. Bullets banged on the front door. They struck brass and shrieked.

As if following a script, Hutchinson dragged Lee to the floor and huddled with her under the breakfast table. Bunny dropped to her knees and joined them. She was gasping, but she stopped as soon as she threw up. Chop suey she'd eaten in bed with Cliff

Quinlan splattered in front of her. She shut her eyes. Queenie was screaming in the pantry.

The dining-room windows burst. Bullets pounded the walls. The china display in the antique breakfront hit the floor with a mild crash. The Norfolk pine near the kitchen doorway toppled off its trivet. Hutchinson clutched Lee's head.

Within seconds of the attack the first Ladue squad car pulled up. Already the street was teeming with hysterical neighbors, the Fussels, the Millers, the Coxes, the Randalls, the Jaegers, and all of their domestic help. Red lights cut the darkness. A pair of pumpers arrived, but nothing was burning. An ambulance made a disappointed U-turn and drove off. No one was hurt.

The police found the Hutchinsons' front yard dotted with flyers xeroxed on shiny paper and covered with a childish scrawl. Chief Andrews picked one up.

Free the Land!

OW = Osage Warriors = Death to Gentials

= ''' = Free the Land! = ''' =
''' = God is Red! OW! = '''

Andrews assigned two patrolmen the task of picking up all the litter and reminded them not to get their fingerprints on it. Then he radioed the St. Louis police. Chief Jammu, he was told, was already on her way.

Residents in six other communities in and around St. Louis—Rock Hill, Glendale, Webster Groves, Affton, Carondelet, and Lemay—reported hearing a low-flying chopper in the minutes following the attack. The Illinois Highway Patrol was alerted, but it was too late. The chopper had vanished in the steady rain east of the river.

·

"I'm not especially worried about the FBI. It took them years to catch those Puerto Ricans in Chicago, and even then they bungled it. This is a two-man show, Gopal and Suresh, they have no identities, their actions have no pattern, and they'd already stolen all the supplies six weeks ago. The only person who ever caught Gopal at anything was me. The FBI is out of its element. They're more in their element when it comes to what I'm doing in the city, but even if they look, which they won't, they won't find much, some transmitters maybe, but you can't trace the destination of their signals. Same with the retransmitting stations, and only a professional would even know what they are. The professionals aren't looking. Sometimes I'm tempted to shut down all the electronics anyway, but the wires do more to prevent discovery than encourage it. The people in the field—Singh, Baxti, Sarada, Usha, Kamala, Devi, Savidri, Sohan, Kashi—they need the information for their work and their own safety. Nice try, but don't bother.

"If someone stumbles onto the pattern in Asha's North Side purchases they'll find the name Hammaker. It's Maman's cash but Hammaker's bank checks. In this city, that's a real red herring. And the media like me. So do the prosecutors, all the DA's young lawyers collecting scalps. We have a rising arrest rate, and convictions bring promotions. And there's no reason to be suspicious of me. The worst police can do supposedly is beat and cheat. We don't beat people, and we don't take bribes, at least not upstairs. Does my mother squeak?

"Yes, land's expensive downtown, the city's cramped and can't annex, but what really scares off the county wealth is crime. It's a fear reinforced by racism. The city-county split is a form of discrimination. Elbow. What's surprising is that the city doesn't want reunification any more than the county does. The blacks are afraid of being outvoted in a more regional government, especially when they still don't even have control of the city. It's incredible, but St. Louis has never had a black mayor. But it's only a matter of time before it gets one, another election or two, and then no one will ever get the county and city back together.

"The industries are already established in the county, so why move? Ouch. Greed. We have tapes where you'll hear bank board members inform their friends that city land has suddenly become a red-hot commodity. This isn't just courtesy. The banks have a vested interest in land prices, and in the city's prosperity. They own the bulk of the civic bonds. Therefore the banks are already on our side.

"Maman can sell out in April for no less than thirty million. We'll take a quarter of that in taxes, but she'll still have fifty percent. Elbow! There's a law called Missouri 353 that lets the city offer long-term tax abatements to anyone who'll develop a blighted area. Blighted means anything—ten years ago they declared all of downtown blighted, so you can imagine. And our new tax plan will sweeten the deal. Do you hear what I'm saying to you?

"Of course, the police chief has no business dictating city tax policy. But how am I supposed to know that? I'm new here. And the penalty for my political activity is media exposure and personal popularity! It's completely contradictory. The reason I can take liberties with my office is the very same reason no one's afraid of me: I'm a woman, I'm foreign, I'm irrelevant. You know, the Kama Sutra enjoins you to linger."

Bhandari rolled off. The sheet clung to his damp back and followed him, exposing her right shoulder and right arm. She let her hand remain between her legs. For the moment she was a refractory adolescent again, at home with the autoerotic. She stared at the ceiling, on which the bedside lamp cast a conic section of light pierced by odd spokes of shadow, projections of the crossbars of the lampshade.

Stirring in his sleep, Bhandari brushed her flank. She was filled with the unpleasant conviction that when in Maman's house, when called upon, he made talkative and charming love.

But tomorrow Jammu would be free again, and the particles of her past, roused to flame by Bhandari, would grow cool and dim as she made her way back into the darkness, into her scheme, into the distance of St. Louis. Her shuddering came and went unnoticed.

Asha was due at 1:00. Jammu looked at her watch, her only clothing. It was 12:20. She trailed a hand along the floor, found underwear and swung her legs out of bed.

Someone knocked on the door.

She stumbled to her feet and ripped the sheet off Bhandari, who lay like a beached whale, flippers half buried in percale sand. She shoved his head. "*Up*," she said. "She's here."

He rose dreamily, gazing at her chest.

The knocking grew fierce and the doorknob rattled. This didn't sound like Asha. Jammu could hardly turn her blouse right side out. She zipped up her skirt. Bhandari was tentatively knotting the belt of his robe. "Get the goddamned door," she hissed, heading into the bathroom. After a moment she heard him shuffling to the door and unlocking it. There was a squeal, his. "What are *you* doing here?"

Jammu turned away from the sink. Singh was standing close to her in the bathroom doorway. He stared at her in blank distress, and she was pleased to see a man whom she was still capable of injuring straightforwardly. She rolled her shoulders, flaunting her dishevelment.

"Indira is dead," he said. "Shot."

"What?"

"They shot her."

"Sikhs!" Bhandari said. He had come up behind Singh, and in an anti-Sikh fury he swung his fist at the younger man. With grace, almost delicacy, Singh threw him against the wall and choked him with his forearm. He let up, and Bhandari looked around vacantly. Then he ran to the phone by the bed.

"Operator. Operator."

"I thought you'd want to know," Singh said to Jammu.

"Romesh?" Bhandari's voice shook. "Romesh, it's you? Listen to me. Listen. All files, *all* files—you're listening—*all* files marked C—C as in Chandigarh—all files marked C. Listen to me. All files—"

Something was mechanically wrong with Jammu's mouth. A hard combination of tongue and palate held it open and kept air from reaching or escaping her lungs. She felt a bullet in her spine and couldn't breathe.

5

"Barbie?"

"Hi. I was going to call you."

"Are you in the middle of something?"

"No, I haven't started yet. I have to bake a cake."

"Listen, did the package come?"

"Yeah, on Monday."

"You know, the receipt's in the box."

"She'll like it, Audrey. She saw something similar the other day at Famous that she liked."

"Oh good. Do you have any special plans for tonight?"

"Lu's going over to a friend's after dinner to spend the night."

"On a week night?"

"It's her birthday. Why would she want to stick around here?"

"I just thought. You used to do special things. I just thought— How are you feeling?"

"Well, I'm tired. My cold kept me awake last night. I could hear myself starting to snore—"

"Snore!"

"I've always snored when I've had a cold. It used to drive Martin crazy. That terrible infection I had, whenever it was, the three-month infection, I remember he'd wake me up in the middle of the night with this completely crazed look on his face and he'd say something like IF YOU DON'T STOP SNORING— Dot dot dot."

"Then what?"

"Then he'd go sleep on the couch."

"That's *funny*."

Dropping the receiver into its stirrup, disposing of Audrey for another couple of days, Barbara rested in a kitchen chair. It was the first of November, and she had a spice cake to bake before Luisa came home. Although she was going out after dinner, Luisa had a keen sense of responsibility for juvenile ritual (a willingness to use hotel swimming pools, to eat the chicken drumsticks) and she might insist on doing something traditional as soon as Martin came home, something like watching home movies of herself (there were no other home movies) or even (conceivably) playing Yahtzee. At the very least she would demand (and receive) a cocktail, and Martin would bring down the gift Barbara had bought for him to give (a typewriter) and add it to the boxes from relatives and to Barbara's own more ordinary (more motherly) contributions (socks, sweaters, tropical-colored stationery, Swiss chocolate, a silk robe, the much-discussed set of birdsong recordings, hardcover Jane Austen and, for the hell of it, softcover Wallace Stevens) which Luisa, demanding a refill (and receiving it) would unwrap. Then the three of them would make formal conversation as if Luisa were the adult which the gifts at her feet, their ready enjoyability, indicated she had not yet become. Grandparents would have helped tonight. But Barbara's parents had just left for a month's vacation in Australia and New Zealand, and even before Martin's mother died she never left Arizona for anything but funerals. Martin himself would not help tonight. He'd been on the outs with Luisa lately. On Monday night he'd come home deep in thought (about the Westhaven project, he said), and at the dinner table, still thinking, still off in his world of timetables and work crews, he'd begun to grill Luisa on what she wanted to major in at college. The grilling went on for ten minutes. "English? If somebody with a degree in English comes to me looking for a job, I just shake my head." He cut a neat rhombus of veal. "Astronomy? What do you want to do that for?" He speared a bean. Luisa stared hopelessly at the candles. Barbara said:

"Leave her alone, Martin."

He looked up from his plate. "I was just trying to be helpful."
He turned to Luisa. "Was I bothering you?"

Luisa threw her napkin in the marsala sauce and ran upstairs.
She'd lost her appetite this fall, and lost some pounds with which
(in Barbara's opinion) she could ill afford to part. At breakfast this
morning she'd looked much older than eighteen. Barbara had just
awakened from a dream where Luisa was a skeleton in a stained
white gown, and where the hands reaching to comfort her, the
mother's hands, were gray bones.

"Can I make you some waffles?"

"Can I have some coffee?"

"Yes. And waffles?"

"All right. Please."

It was painful watching her stuff waffles into her mouth. She
obviously wasn't hungry. She had a lingering cold, and though she
hadn't stooped to admit it yet, she also seemed to have a new
boyfriend, whom she'd apparently met when she'd gone to see the
French girl two weeks ago. The French girl had not shown up.
The boyfriend had taken the picture that appeared in last Saturday's
Everyday section. *D. Thompson*, the credit read, and the caption:
*Indian Summer. Luisa Probst of Webster Groves enjoys the fine weather
in Washington State Park. Behind her is a flock of Canada geese*. Martin
had bought twenty copies of the paper, and Luisa had mentioned,
rather belatedly, that Duane had been in the country with her and
Stacy. Barbara really didn't mind if Luisa tried to keep her feelings
towards Duane a secret for a while. She herself had grown up under
surveillance (the surveillance of both her mother and the Roman
Catholic Church) and she'd hated it. Besides, with Luisa still spending so much time in Stacy's company, how important could Duane
be?

Outside, it was cloudy. Two male cardinals, winter birds,
hopped from peg to peg on the feeder by the breakfast-room window. Barbara could hear a slow scraping on the south side of the
house as Mohnwirbel raked concrete. He was wearing his red wool
jacket today, his winter plumage, his cardinal colors. He lived on
the property, in the small apartment above the garage, and seemed
a more native resident of Sherwood Drive, or at least a less self-
conscious one, than Barbara could ever be.

She swallowed some aspirin with a splash of scotch and put

the glass directly in the dishwasher. She was wearing a full plaid skirt, a dark red silk sweater, slightly dated ankle boots (hand-me-ups from Luisa), a silver bangle on her wrist, and silver hoops. Every day, sick or not, she dressed well. In the spring and fall (retrospective seasons, seasons in which she married different men) she wore makeup.

As she turned on the radio, which was always tuned to KSLX ("Information Radio"), Jack Strom was introducing today's guest on the two-to-three segment of his afternoon talk show. The guest was Dr. Mickey McFarland. Physician. Professor. Disciple of Love . . . And author of the best-selling *You and Only You*. Barbara put an apron on.

"Doctor," Jack Strom was saying, "in your latest book you describe what you call the Seven Stages of Cynicism—a kind of ladder that a person climbs down on to middle-age depression— and then you discuss ways to reverse the process. Now, I'm sure it's struck many of your readers that all the examples you chose involved middle-aged men. This was obviously intentional on your part, so I wonder if you might tell us how you see women fitting into this pattern of cynicism, which I believe you once called the Challenge of the Eighties."

"Jack," McFarland rasped, "I'm glad you asked me that."

Always, always, they were glad Jack had asked.

"As you may remember, when *A Friend Indeed* came out in '79—as you may remember, it went to number one on the best-seller list—something I'll never forget. Heh. I don't know if anybody's ever said this, but your first best-seller is like your first kid— you love it to death, you know, it's always going to be your favorite. But anyway, as you may remember, in *A Friend Indeed* (in which, by the way, I spoke to the problem of feminine depression) I spoke there of the special role that women must play in meeting the Challenge of the Eighties."

"And what was that role?"

"Jack, that role was a caring one."

"A caring role."

Jack Strom was hard on best-selling authors, shaming them with his extraordinarily mellifluous voice. He'd been hosting afternoon talk shows for as long as Barbara could remember, for twenty years easily, and his voice never changed. Did one's face ever change?

". . . I'm glad you asked me that, too, Jack, because it so happens that I think the Fifth Amendment's protection of religious freedom is this country's most precious resource. I think what we're witnessing in these cults is a cry for love on a mass scale. I don't know if you've ever thought about this before, but at the center of every, and I mean every, religion, there's a doctrine of caring, be it Eastern, be it Western, I don't care. And I think—I truly believe—that there's a middle ground we're all striving to reach together."

Profound silence.

"Dr. Mickey McFarland, author of *You and Only You*. We'll get to the phone lines right after this message."

Mohnwirbel had stepped sideways into view in the back yard as he followed the ivy beds with his rake. There was enough ivy, enough property, to keep him raking all day long and the next day too. He'd had his finest hour a week ago, when photographers from *House* magazine had come to take pictures of the lawn and garden. It was the first time in eleven years that Barbara had seen Mohnwirbel agitated. He'd stood in the middle of the back yard like a dog amid angry bees, with an all-encompassing concern, menaced by squirrels that dropped sticks and trees that shed leaves.

"Hello, you're on the air."

Barbara measured butter.

"Dr. McFarland?"

"He's listening. Go right ahead."

"Doctor, my name is Sally."

". . . Do you have a question or comment for the doctor?"

"I'm listening, Sally."

She opened the sugar bin. She was struck by the—what?—of white sugar. The futility. She applied the steel scoop.

In an average week, she read four books. At the library she catalogued four hundred of them. She went out once to her exercise class, and three times to play tennis. In an average week she made six breakfasts, packed five lunches, and cooked six dinners. She put a hundred miles on the car. She stared out windows for forty-five minutes. She ate lunch in restaurants three times, once with Audrey and various fractions of twice with Jill Montgomery, Bea Meisner, Lorri Wulkowicz (her last good college friend), Bev Wismer, Bunny Hutchinson, Marilyn Weber, Biz DeMann, Jane Replogle, sundry librarians and many occasionals. She spent six hours in retail stores, one hour in the shower. She slept fifty-one hours. She watched nine hours of television. She spoke with Betsy LeMaster on the phone two times. She spoke with Audrey 3.5 times. She spoke with other friends fourteen times altogether. The radio played all day long.

"Six three three, forty-nine hundred is our number. If you're calling from Illinois it's eight four two, eleven hundred. Hello, your question or comment for Dr. McFarland?"

With the spatula she shaved smears of creamed butter off the sides of the mixing bowl. She shuttled buttermilk and eggs from the refrigerator to the counter and cracked the eggs into the smallest of the nesting bowls. Tossing the shells in the sink, she thought of Martin. He wouldn't have discarded the shells so quickly. He would have run his index finger around the inside to loosen the last, clinging globs of white. She saw him do it when he scrambled the eggs on Sundays.

In the first weeks of their marriage she'd dropped a twice-read newspaper into a wastebasket and he'd retrieved it. "These are useful," he said.

He never used them. He turned off the hot water while he soaped his hands. He put bricks in the toilet tank. The old house on Algonquin Place was lit largely by 40-watt bulbs. He burned the barbecue charcoal twice. If she threw out old *Time* magazines he sulked or raged. He pocketed matchbooks from restaurant ashtrays. When he watered the grass, he laid leaky hose joints over shrubs, not concrete, so the shrubs would get a little drink.

He conserved. But his conservatism was personal, perverse almost. When he was trying to keep his workers out of the unions twenty years ago, the city press could hardly believe that Barbara's father had decided to represent him. At the time, everyone from the Teamsters to the roofers was striking Martin, and strikes were spiraling out into sympathetic businesses. Normally her father would never have touched a case like this (one of his specialties was workmen's compensation), but it was difficult to say no to a company president who marched into paneled offices in boondockers and khaki work pants. Martin's issue with the unions was personal, not ideological. He seemed astonished to be the cause of general havoc, and seemed to think it only natural when, with her father's help, he won the suit. And when he turned up at her parents' Fourth of July party, Barbara noticed him.

She'd just graduated from college, and she had a fellowship to study physics at Washington U. In less than a year, though, she'd given it up and married Martin. She didn't need science to set her apart, not when she had Martin Probst. She liked to see him at symphony intermissions chatting with her old Mary Institute acquaintances. ("You see the trombones?" he'd ask. "I love trombones.") She liked to see him rock-and-roll dancing with her college friends. At charity balls he searched out the practicing engineers and talked about box girders and revetments and concrete piles while chiffon and silk charmeuse swept insubstantially by. She liked to be around him.

One Sunday afternoon about three years after they were married, he took Barbara on a tour of the Arch, which hadn't opened to the public yet. He unlocked two gates, a metal door, another gate, another door, and stopped by a galvanized-iron control box. He was moving with a swagger that Barbara didn't recognize, and casting disdainful glances at the work. He threw switches by the handful. In the receding triangular space above them, lights went up on stairways and cables and the inverted T's that anchored the tram tracks to the walls. Martin didn't look at her. He might have been an antebellum Southern gentleman losing his sweetness in a review of his slaves. Pulling hard on a railing, as if daring it to snap, he started up the stairs. She followed, hating him somewhat. She smelled cold grease, cold welds, thirsty concrete. Echoes lingered, buzzing, in the thin iron steps. When the stairs brought her close to the walls she ran her hand over the hard carbon steel, over drips of set concrete, over code numbers inscribed by hand, and saw a blue luster hiding in the burrs and ripples. Abruptly the stairway veered to the opposite side of the tram tracks, and veered back, adjusting to dreadful alterations of the vertical.

"Do you collect if I fall here?"

"Don't fall," he said curtly. It was an order, but she was happy to comply. Diagonal patterns—the crossties and trusses for the tracks, the guys and brackets for the stairs—were repeated at one level and then slowly gave way, element by element, to patterns more cramped and twisted. Looking down (accidentally) she could see some of the flights she'd climbed, but not nearly all of them. They zigzagged around like the spoor of a rectilinearity driven crazy by catenary logic. The colors were primitive, the rustproofing orange, the plastic wrappings a baby blue, the wirenuts red and yellow, the conduit green. Farther up, as the pace of the curve increased, she climbed long spiral staircases connected, top to bottom, by narrow gangways with flimsy rods for railings. She might have fallen if she'd stopped to think. She followed Martin. There was metal everywhere, its molten origin apparent in this sealed metallic enclosure, in the literal chill: she could see the steel's enslavement to form. Threaded, it bit itself in a death grip, bit indefinitely. Gussets like the arms of frozen courtiers held up struts, and the struts held up the gangways, and the gangways Martin. In the past his power had been a reputation, a thing for her to play with. Now, at closer range, from a greater remove (the truth is unfamiliar), she loved him very much.

Blue daylight appeared. They stepped out into the sunlit observation room. And after she'd appreciated the view east and west, after she'd selected a car driving by the Old Courthouse, a red station wagon, and followed its progress through the empty downtown streets, watched it popping in and out between buildings, and caught glimpses of it (she believed) on Olive Street all the way out to Grand Avenue; after she'd jumped on the floor to confirm its solidity; after she'd sat up on the window ledge, her back to the sun and her thighs on warm metal, after she'd kicked off her shoes and Martin had stood between her legs and kissed her: after she'd protested that people could see and he'd assured her that they couldn't, he unbuttoned her jeans and pulled them down. Then he did it to her on the floor. There were rows of chevrons on the cold steel plates. He mashed and maneuvered her while she tried again and again to sit up. Her shoulders, in spasms, resisted touching down. Did she know this man? She was almost ecstatic. The best thing was, he never smiled.

"Mickey McFarland, author of *You and Only You*. Doctor, we're glad you could stop by this afternoon, I'm sure you have a busy schedule—"

"Oh, KSLX has a special place in my heart."

"We appreciate your coming in. I'm Jack Strom. From three to four I'll be talking to Dr. Ernest Quitschak, a seismologist who's going to tell us about three of the biggest earthquakes in American history and the next big earthquake, which could happen any—day—now, right here in Missouri, KSLX-Radio, *Saint* Louis, it's—three o'clock."

Bong.

She slid the three pans onto the top rack of the oven, set the timer, and slumped into a chair. She was bushed. Her ears rang. Mohnwirbel had gone off someplace, leaving the rake in the ivy, tines down.

In New Delhi today Indian Prime Minister Rajiv Gandhi was among hundreds of thousands of—

At the news of Mrs. Gandhi's death on Monday Barbara had thought immediately of Jammu, the police chief. Jammu patterned her peremptory glamour so clearly on Mrs. Gandhi's that Barbara was sure the assassination would leave her harrowed. But when Jammu appeared on KSLX-TV last night to discuss ramifications of the murder, she spoke with her usual poise. "It's amazing the woman survived as long as she did. She didn't lack enemies." The cold smile she gave the interviewer disgusted Barbara.

"You can't judge from this," Martin said. "Who knows what she thinks in private."

Yes, there was no denying no one knew. Barbara would even grant the possibility that Martin, in private, now that his hair was turning gray, feared death. But she would never know. The guiding principle of Martin's personality, the sum of his interior existence, was the desire to be left alone. If all those years he'd sought attention, even novelty, and if he still relished them, then that was because attention proved him different and solitude begins in difference.

She remembered the election night party they'd had in their house on Algonquin Place, on the night Humphrey lost. The Animals raging in the living room, the undergraduates dancing in the front hall. Barbara had been upstairs checking on Luisa. At the bottom of the stairs she saw Martin talking with Biz DeMann's young brother-in-law Andrew, a plump law-school student in blazer and tortoiseshell glasses.

"Harvard," Martin was saying. ". . . Harvard. Somehow I thought it was a restaurant."

Young DeMann: "I can't believe you haven't heard of it."

"Listen, Andrew." Martin put his arm around Andrew's shoulders and drew him close. "There's something I've always wondered. Maybe you can help me. What does alma mater mean?"

"I don't know exactly. Something like Our Mother."

Martin frowned. "Whose mother?" He was doing his dumb act.

"Metaphorically. Like: Harvard is my alma mater."

"I see. It's your Our Mother."

Andrew smiled indulgently. "Sure. Why not."

"Why not?" Martin took Andrew by the collar and tossed him against the front door. "Because it means *nurturing mother*, you asshole!"

Barbara, turning white, dragged Martin into the dining room. "Martin, Martin, Martin—"

"I ask the kid where he went to school," he told her in a caustic whisper. "I'm pretty sure he went to Harvard, I'm just being polite. He tells me: 'Oh, a little school near Boston.' " He pulled away. "Lemme go kick his head."

"He's a *guest*, Martin."

She dragged him out to the back patio and sat him down. She realized he wasn't drunk at all. "All these people," he said. "All these people, worrying about the poor. They don't have the faintest idea what it's like to be poor . . . All these people studying. It makes me uncomfortable. It seems so . . . so *small*. I mean, how do they justify themselves? All these people. All these people. They've never in their lives had to work a job they didn't like."

All these people were Barbara's people.

If she stopped trying, she and Martin wouldn't see them anymore.

She stopped. The parties stopped. She stayed at home; she got a sinus infection. Men were circling the moon, and she sat and rested in a kitchen chair, wishing she could taste. It was the worst infection of her life. In the shower she licked the soap off her lips and found it sweet, like one of the more congenial poisons. Cooking was a chemistry lab. Heated beef turned gray, heated chicken white. Bread had low tensile strength. A liquid could be extracted from an orange, it was volume in a glass, it was 150 milliliters.

The infection continued out of February and into March, but spring was just a change in the light, a dampening of the cold, nothing more. She saw a doctor, who told her it was only viruses, she needed to sleep a lot and let it run its course. Eventually she could breathe freely, but she still couldn't taste. She started smoking again. The smoke was frosty and almost chewable, and the pain in her throat, divorced from flavor, had an electrical quality, like a leakage of current. Was it possible that people tasted what they spoke? It was possible. Words dwelt in her skull like hammerheads, falling around on their rigid claws. Martin blamed her. "What's wrong with you?" *Go to hell, I have a cold.* "You should try to get some sleep." *Go to hell.* A steak could be bent. Radishes couldn't. Every morning she licked at the soap, always hoping, and then, in April, something gave and she realized in her closet that she was smelling No-Moth. It was exactly as she remembered it. But now with each taste she rediscovered there came a sense of private ownership. Tastes and smells no longer seemed like communal stocks of which each person partook according to need and predisposition. They seemed like property. She was reading Sartre, and he hit her like a ton of bricks. She felt wild. She had insides, and at the time they weren't lonely places. Ask Martin about those years, and he'd tell you a different story. Hers was simple: she'd started to live for herself, not both of them. She'd noticed that she had a daughter.

"And how is this different from the San Andreas fault?"

"The San Andreas is on the edge of the continental plate—plates, of course, are the rigid pieces of the earth's crust that make up the continents and ocean floors . . ."

The oven was warming the kitchen, but Barbara didn't smell cake, only the heat of her sinuses. The dishes seemed a creation of the sink, which heaved them onto the counter, weird saucers, wooden spoons. In December more people from *House* magazine, including a writer named John Nissing whom Barbara had so far met only by telephone, would be coming to shoot the house's interior. They should have come today instead, she thought, and caught the house *au naturel*, caught Barbara in her chair, bowing in confusion and looking at the flour-dusted wrists in her lap. In her dream last night Luisa had had these hands, these rings, these wrinkles.

When Audrey's younger daughter Mara was Luisa's age she'd already run away from home three times. She'd been expelled from Mary Institute and arrested for shoplifting and possession. Concerned relatives, namely Barbara and her father, agreed that the Ripley household was (to say the least) doing Mara little good, and Barbara overrode Martin's objections and offered to take the girl in until she cooled off or got a diploma. Mara had always, to Barbara's discomfiture, looked up to her and liked her, as the token grown-up she could stand. She accepted the invitation, and Barbara tried to be understanding and be a good foster mother, and repair some of the damage. But after two months, on a Sunday in March, she and Martin returned from a brunch and found Luisa, who was ten, sitting in the kitchen with a frown on her face. Her indirection was elaborate.

"Sometimes," she said, "I think about rooms we don't use?" She felt sorry for the unused rooms. And all the things in them? Like in the basement. And on the third floor? It was funny how she never went up there? Did Mommy ever go up there? Wasn't there an old sewing machine with pedals? And lots of things of Daddy's? And an old sofa, sort of?

Barbara calmly cored an apple for her and sent Martin up to the third floor, where Mara (who was supposedly "outside someplace") and a boy her age were hastily dressing. Martin said Mara had to go, and Barbara agreed. She was chastened to discover that only Luisa mattered to her, that a scratch on her daughter's psyche worried her more than a festering hole in Mara's. Did Luisa know the suitcases in the front hall were the direct result of her testimony? Had she made a connection between having sex and getting thrown out? Did she know it was done on her behalf? A very peculiar sort of distrust arose in Barbara: how much are we really keeping from her? A lot, or only a little? She wished she'd been granted a mind unable to perceive so clearly the mathematics of Luisa's growth, or a body that could have given her more than one child, anything to relieve the terrible specificity of her conscience. If only it didn't matter exactly what became of Luisa, and what she became, and how it happened, through what fault and what virtues of Barbara's. If only she were like Audrey, to whom things happened unaccountably. Or like Martin, who didn't seem to care.

Upstairs she heard footsteps. The thump of books. Luisa had come in through the front door and gone straight to her room.

.

Three weeks passed. It was the day before Thanksgiving, and the high school was in turmoil. After fifth hour the clots of pep, the organizers and combatants, began to rove the halls at will. They carried orange and black threats, threw orange and black confetti, stapled orange and black crepe paper to the ceiling tiles. It was Pep Wednesday, the day before the Statesmen played the Kirkwood Pioneers. At three o'clock the Rally would be held, and then at eight o'clock the Bonfire, when five hundred of the faithful would gather at Moss Field to witness the burning, in effigy, of Kirk E. Wood. This true Pioneer would be roasted, tossing in a danse macabre, while smoke and cheers drove the school spirit to painful heights for tomorrow. Tomorrow was Turkey Day. Tomorrow was the day.

Mr. Sonnenfeld shut the door. He cast his pinkened eyes on the class before him. He stuck out his lower lip and blew air through the thin hair on his forehead. "Forty-five minutes to go," he said. "Be glad when it's all over."

The class did not look at him. They heard his words in mute boredom, as a humbling judgment on them. Yes, sir, it's just like you say. Fluorescent light filmed their tired hair, tired jeans, tired purses. They were a group as gray as the cold clouds outside. They came because Sonnenfeld would not fail anyone who attended class regularly. The boy next to Luisa in the back row was slouched so low in his seat that his knees butted the underside of his desk. His name was Archie. He was black. He was drawing on his desk with a pencil, expanding a solid gray dot into a larger dot.

Luisa rubbed the back of her hand across her nostrils. Whenever she did this she could smell Duane. Washing masked the smell, but not for long. He came from inside her. More and more his smoky human smell lodged even in her nostrils; in her brain.

Her mother had said: "What do you keep doing that for?"

"Doing what?" She'd dropped her hand, locking it between her legs. She saw how people accidentally develop disgusting nervous habits.

"Smelling your hand like that."

"I'm—not."

Mr. Sonnenfeld moistened his fingertips and walked up and down the aisles distributing copies of poems. "I've selected four poems to introduce you to the work of William Carlos Williams," he said. Luisa took her copies but was careful not to show immediate interest in them. She was only here because this course fit into her unruly schedule this quarter. She felt conspicuous. One row over, in the corner, a girl named Janice Jones was watching her. Janice was wearing loose jeans with no belt, a biker's jacket, and an embroidered Indian shirt with the top four buttons unbuttoned. She had tiny, stoned-looking eyes. Her name was scrawled on lockers and walls around the school. JANIS JONES GIVES GOOD HEAD. JJ = JOBS. Every day she stared at Luisa for no apparent reason; no malice when their eyes met, no smiles, no connection.

". . . I think when you look at these poems you'll see a lot of similarities with Ezra Pound and the other imagists we started with." Sonnenfeld's collar bit deeply into the roll of fat around his neck as he handed the mimeographs across two empty desks to Janice Jones. He nearly lost his balance. Archie sniffed. He seemed to have seen it without looking up.

"Now, first of all, has anyone ever read anything by Williams?" Sonnenfeld hopped backwards and sat on his desk. He pulled up his pants legs to relieve the stretch.

White pages turned. No one answered. This was the only class Luisa had in which she hardly knew anyone. People she knew would have said something.

"Does anyone know what Williams did for a living?"

"He's a faggot," Archie muttered.

"Archie?"

Continuing to draw his dot, Archie smiled and did not elaborate. Trouble had been brewing between him and Sonnenfeld since the quarter started two weeks ago, and the mood was dangerous today. Usually Archie was silent in class. He was loud in the halls, though, where all the black kids lost their shyness. They scared Luisa. They didn't like her, and she felt she'd never be able to relax enough to indicate neutrality, to give them even a small sign that she didn't necessarily dislike them.

Sonnenfeld put his hands on his hips and assumed a disappointed tone. "William Carlos Williams was a doctor. He lived all his life in Paterson, New Jersey. As we go on, we'll find that it's not unusual for American poets to have other full-time professions. Many have been teachers. Wallace Stevens, who's perhaps our greatest poet of this century, a very hard poet, worked for an insurance company. He was a vice president when he died. Sylvia Plath, whom I'm sure you've all heard of, was a mother and a housewife."

Vague guilt fluttered in Luisa's stomach. The Wallace Stevens book her mother had given her.

"Archie?"

Archie shook his head patiently. Luisa looked at his long, angular fingers. She thought of Duane's hands. On the palm of her own left hand his name was written in black ballpoint ink. She'd written it in Calculus, half-asleep. She'd hardly slept last night. For the third time in a month, she'd sneaked out to be with Duane. She'd gotten to the sundeck from her bedroom window, and from the sundeck she'd climbed, knees cracking, feet trembling, down the step-like quoins to the front yard. It was amazingly easy, like an open cash register and no one around. Her parents never went into her room after 11:00. The last Lockwood Avenue bus to U-City came at 12:05. She could see Duane any night she wanted to, and she liked it better at night, when she could see herself, a white semi-reflection in the bus window staring into her face and unmoved by the streetlights and neon floating through her. Duane was waiting at the bus stop, his scarf under his chin, a lock of hair above his eyebrows. He shook his head. He could never believe she was actually on the bus.

". . . Amy Lowell and Ezra Pound, who were both profound influences on Williams."

"Bow bow bow," said Archie, snatching at an imaginary bug in the air.

"Archie?" Sonnenfeld was getting mad. The pitch of his voice had risen.

Janice Jones had fallen asleep.

Luisa looked down at the copies on her desk. THE RED WHEELBARROW. *So much depends upon a red wheelbarrow glazed with water beside the white chickens.* That was easy enough. She liked short poems. She went on to the next one and, finding it just as easy, kept reading. She didn't stop until she sensed an unanswered question hanging in the air. Sonnenfeld had asked them something. She ran the preceding seconds through her memory and heard, from afar, "What was imagism?"

Without raising her hand she called out, "Free verse, strong images that appeal directly to the emotions."

"What did you say to me?"

She looked up with a start. Sonnenfeld had gotten down from his desk. He wasn't talking to her. He was talking to Archie. He hadn't even heard her answer. Archie was enlarging the gray dot, smiling.

"What did you say?"

"Fag," Archie said.

"I didn't hear you."

Luisa drove her nails into her palms and stared at her desk, the way everyone else was staring. She tried to force the blush back out of her cheeks. What an *idiot* she was. The halls had grown quiet for a moment. Sonnenfeld was walking down the aisle. She heard the unhurried scratching of Archie's pencil. Then a scuffle, the rumble of a desk's metal feet on linoleum, the plink of a pencil. She stole a glance. Sonnenfeld had grabbed Archie by the collar and was hauling him towards the door. He pushed him out and followed him. From the hall, the class heard, "What'd you call me?"

There was a murmur from Archie.

"What?"

"Fag."

"What, nigger?"

"Fag."

"Nigger!"

FAG!

NIGGER!

It stopped. It had to. Sonnenfeld was dragging Archie down to the vice-principal's office. Still feeling the pressure of attention on her, Luisa laid her cheek on her desk and shut her eyes. Outside, a pep parade was approaching to the tune of "Old Wisconsin."

On with Webster, on with Webster
Fight fight fight fight fight

The trumpeter had to slur and blurt to keep up with the singers. As the group passed the door, Luisa heard footsteps. Some of the class was deserting. She heard a match struck and raised her head. Janice Jones was lighting a cigarette.

Tonight Luisa was supposedly going to the Bonfire and then staying over at Stacy's. Actually she was going out to dinner with Duane and spending the night with him. There had been a lot of this supposedly-actually in the last three weeks. On her birthday it had gotten complicated. Stacy had even called Luisa's mother for suggestions about what kind of breakfast and what kind of presents. Stacy had a mother like Duane's, the convenient sort of parent who worked full-time and who'd believe there had been a party in her house even if there hadn't been. Luisa wasn't as much afraid of getting caught as she was sure that one of these weeks, in her tiredness, she'd forget which side of the window she was on and do something stupid at home, like French-kissing her mother or calling her father "Baby." She could feel the impatience inside her. Why don't people who like each other kiss all the time? Why do people have to lie? She was feeling more honest and acting less honest. It was a dangerous mixture, like gasoline and wine, like fever and chills. She still had a cold, sort of a permanent cold, the sense that none of the things that used to matter mattered anymore. She could do whatever she wanted. She could just say: "Give me a cigarette."

Janice Jones looked astonished. "They're menthol."

Luisa shrugged. When the match was held she inhaled lightly to keep from coughing. To her relief the smoke was mild, like a breath of mothballs. Janice Jones folded up her poems and stuffed them roughly into her purse. She looked at Luisa. "Bye," she said. It was the friendliest she'd ever been.

"See you." Drawing on the cigarette, Luisa felt almost as cool as Janice. Unfortunately the only two kids left in the room to appreciate her now were Alice Bunyan, who sketched horses during class, and Jenny Brown, who had large sad eyes and a lisp, wore overalls, and never knew the answers. Neither cared about Luisa. She closed her eyes. She felt a tiny breeze, a feathery impact on her stomach—the ash breaking loose. She opened her eyes.

Sonnenfeld.

He was leaning with both hands on the front desk in her row. He was staring at her. "May I ask what you're doing?"

She didn't answer. She dropped the cigarette and smashed it with her heel. Sonnenfeld laid a green slip on her desk. *Smokig i classmm.* "Sorry," he said coldly. "I'd expected more from you."

She gathered her books and shouldered her purse. Somehow her body couldn't believe it was leaving. The vice-principal could suspend her for three days for smoking, and barring that, a call to her parents was virtually assured. At the door she stopped and looked into the hall. There were ruptured oranges on the floor, and construction-paper artwork on the doors of lockers belonging to members of the football team. The pep club had drawn crude portraits of each member and given him a slogan. #65 WILLY FISHER "DR. MEAN GUY." The lockers looked like tombs. Luisa turned back uncertainly to Sonnenfeld.

He was seated on his desk with a book in his hand. He licked a finger, turned a page, and addressed his two remaining students. "So much—*depends*," he said.

"Just leave those spaces blank, White."

"Done. What do we say? Gateway Arch?" RC's fingers played the keys. *Gateway Arch.* "Address?"

"Forget the address."

"Shot in the leg, right?"

"Very funny. Southern leg, eastern face, hit by automatic fire."

. . . *automatic fire.* "Means?" RC said.

"High-powered automatic rifle firing steel bullets."

. . . *steel bullets.*

"Object of attack unknown. Distinctive feature: pattern of dents traced the letters O and W. Rest of that column blank."

. . . *letters O and W.* "Now, *I* know the suspects," RC said.

"Shut up, White. I'm dictating. Understand? Name unknown, sex male, height five-ten to six-two, everything else unknown."

Unknown. Unknown. Unknown.

"Bottom of the page. Three-sixteen a.m., November et cetera, Donald R. Colfax of Gateway Security Systems, 1360 DeBaliviere, telephone three three six, one one seven one—reported the sound of gunfire near the southern end of the Arch. New paragraph. Three-eighteen a.m., Officers Dominick Luzzi and Robert Driscoll—double *z-i*, White—dispatched to the scene by radio. New paragraph. Three-twenty a.m., Colfax stated that upon hearing the gunfire he hastened in that direction from his desk in the northern underground lobby of the Arch."

"*Hastened*," RC said, "in the direction of a *machine gun*?"

"Appearing at the location of the shooting, he glimpsed—"

. . . lobby of the Arch.

"—the above-described suspect fleeing through the trees to the south of the Arch. Colfax stated that the suspect was carrying—"

"Luzzi, phone!" Desk Sergeant McClintoch barked.

"Take a break, White. Appreciate the circumstances. My wife's ten months pregnant. Relax, take a break."

RC relaxed. He peered into the lunch bag Annie had filled for him. Egg salad on rye, brownies, and an apple. He was starving, but he wanted to eat late because he had a Legal Procedures class from six to eight at the Academy. Then tomorrow he had the day off. Tomorrow was Thanksgiving. The precinct-house atmosphere was pre-holiday, a little frantic.

The man at the next desk was scowling as he hunted and pecked. RC, who'd typed a million histories in the Army, was a ten-finger man. In the Army he'd trained on a machine gun, too. "*Aim, don't spray. Pick a target, five shots, next target, five shots. Atababy.*" But machine guns weren't precision instruments; you'd need damn strong arms to write something with one, even just the initials of your terrorist group. If RC ever got challenged to a duel at dawn, he'd choose a typewriter for his weapon. Rat-a-tat, rat-a-tat. The alphabet at ten paces.

He took another look at his lunch. Ten more minutes, he told himself, picking at the rip in the vinyl cushion of his chair. On the green wall two desks to his right was a 12 × 15 glossy of Chief

Jammu with Sergeant Luzzi, taken in August on the steps of the precinct house. RC himself had only talked to the Chief that one time after the explosion, before he'd signed up, and he'd only seen her in person one other time, when she gave a talk to the new recruits at the end of their first week. He couldn't remember a word of what she'd said, but it was good, whatever it was. And he had no problem with how they'd been treating him, aside from some superciliousness on the part of the younger white officers. It was a tight ship, this department, a lot more electrifying than the Cold Ice Company and a lot less dumb-assed than the Army. When they tested his gun skills here and he passed the test, they told him to stop going to the range and assigned him extra hours of office work. He put in thirty hours a week—work-study, the Chief's idea. With all this plus the classes too, he was busy. But in February he'd graduate and things would be a little easier.

Luzzi was still gabbing on the phone. Didn't look like his wife was delivering yet. It would have taken Luzzi nearly an hour (plus however long he spent on the phone) to type this report that RC could do in ten minutes. As far as RC knew he was the fourth-best typist in the whole first precinct. He'd heard officers say: "In a hurry? Take it to White there, if you don't mind his lip."

The only real ragging these days came from Clarence. "I swear to God," he said, "I never thought I'd be sorry to see you moving up. But even ice beats the heat. I hate to see you playing their game." *Their* game was the Chief's game. Lately Clarence had been hitting his golf drives too fat. He wasn't on speaking terms with Alderman Struthers, and his business was hurting. Not hurting *too* bad (this city never ran out of junk to demolish) but still hurting. RC couldn't make Clarence see that this had nothing to do with the Chief.

"Read it back, White?"

Luzzi had returned, and RC turned back to the typewriter. "Colfax," he read, "stated that the suspect was carrying . . ."

"A weapon," Luzzi said. "A weapon."

"Big surprise," RC said, and waited to be told to shut up.

At company headquarters in South St. Louis, Probst watched Bob Montgomery and Cal Markham, his vice presidents, file into his office and take chairs. They were here to plan Westhaven strategy. "Well?" Probst said.

"We get a day like this," said Cal, "it changes things. This is snow weather."

Outside the window, in an afternoon sky that was almost black, a pigeon spread its wings and decelerated, like a newspaper unfolding in the wind. They always flocked around the precinct house across the street.

"It's not snowing in Ballwin, is it?"

"No," Cal said.

Bob gave Cal a sharp glance. "Flurries."

"How'd we get into this mess?" Probst said.

"We didn't know how big the sucker was. We knew, but we didn't."

"Or how far out it was," Bob added. "Those last three miles."

"I'll tell you what it is, it's we didn't think we'd get the contract."

"Let's think a minute," Probst said.

"I've been thinking all month," Cal said.

"Let's think."

The problem was concrete: how to get 23,000 cubic yards of it mixed, transported to Westhaven and poured for foundations, all in the next four weeks. By Christmas or New Year's snow and ice would make further pouring impossible, and without foundations no further work could be done. But further work had to be done. The contract called for model units to be completed by April, the entire development by next October. And Cal was right. They'd known, but they hadn't known. They'd known it was a huge amount of acreage, they'd known it was too far out in the country (and the last three miles of road were maddeningly roundabout), they'd known they were under time pressure, but no single factor had seemed prohibitive. They'd bid high, padding every figure except the time estimates. They'd won the contract anyway, and now they were in trouble. The obvious solution—

"Sorry to disturb you, Mr. Probst," said his secretary Carmen on the intercom, "but your wife is on the phone."

"Tell her I'm in conference. I'll call her back."

The obvious solution was to subcontract. But Probst hated to subcontract, hated to spend the money, hated to give up any control over the quality of the work, hated to endanger his reputation for doing complete jobs. There was a cash problem, too. The developer, Harvey Ardmore, wasn't scheduled to pay the second 25 percent of the contract until the foundation was laid, and Ardmore was notorious for refusing to renegotiate. Probst didn't want to pay the subcontractor out of his own cash assets. And worse, it would be hard to find someone willing to buck the unions. Only Probst could buck with impunity, and not even he, really, because the other solution to the concrete problem was to hire extra shifts for a month and do the work himself. He'd need drivers. Drivers were Teamsters. Even if they did agree to work for him—

"I'm sorry, Mr. Probst," said Carmen on the intercom, "but she says—"

Probst grabbed the phone and took the call. "Is this an emergency?"

"No, not exactly," Barbara said. "Although—"

"I'll call you back, I'm sorry." He hung up. Barbara knew damned well he didn't like to have his train of thought broken, and just this morning he'd told her how tense he was . . .

The Teamsters. If they did agree to work for him—never before had he had to ask, and they'd probably refuse just to spite him—they would drive a hard bargain. They might demand the right to approach Probst's men again. At the very least, they'd drag their heels. So if Probst didn't subcontract, the only acceptable way of keeping the job in the house would be to use what manpower he had now, spend the eight weeks it would take, and risk getting stung by bad weather. Cal, the daredevil, favored this alternative. Bob preferred to subcontract. Either way, they sacrificed something, either reputation or security. The problem was the very idea of Westhaven, the grandness of the conception. It was too large a project, too far out in the western boondocks, and the market out there was too cutthroat. Harvey Ardmore set deadlines (not that you could blame him, he was racing his competitors and creditors) that Probst couldn't meet without compromising himself.

"Have you sounded out the Teamsters, Bob?"

"I have."

"And?"

Bob smiled. "I think they'd sooner haul for the devil."

From the black trees along Swon Avenue snowflakes swirled like tiny lovers, meeting and parting, falling, melting. Luisa shivered in her jacket, breathing easily in the cold outdoor air. She'd gone straight from Sonnenfeld's room to the vice-principal's office, but when she got there she found that the vice-principal had already left to supervise the Rally. The vice-principal's secretary sent her to her counselor, and her counselor accepted her ridiculously sincere apologies and said, "We'll let it go this time." She felt rescued; she'd been given special treatment; she felt all right.

She stopped in the plot of land called the Plant Memorial Wildlife Sanctuary (it was dedicated to a man, a Mr. Plant, not a kingdom) and casually looked for birds. She spotted a female cardinal and a woodpecker, but mostly there were jays and starlings. Since she met Duane, she hadn't once gone seriously birding.

A gust of snowflakes flew by. This little park had been the destination of many of the walks she took with her father when she was little. She remembered she was always surprised when he held out his hand and said, "Would you like to go for a walk with me?" Sure, she would think, but we never go for walks. But apparently they did go for walks. But there was something fake about them. Her father seemed to have some other daughter in mind.

She proceeded up Jefferson Avenue. Around Duane she'd been acting critical of her parents. She had to give him reasons why he couldn't call her at home or meet the folks, and there weren't any obvious reasons. So she talked about the way her father had treated her and Alan, his phony respect. For the purposes of mocking her, he'd acted like she and Alan might get married. He made everything seem ridiculous. It was like he couldn't bear to let Luisa forget that her friends weren't as important as he was, that nobody but he had built any Arch.

Her mother was the opposite. From the very beginning she'd felt obligated to find Alan even more interesting than Luisa did. Wasn't Alan cute and funny and sweet? And awfully smart, too? It made Luisa uncomfortable. Her mother was lonely.

With an ache in her throat she crossed Rock Hill Road, which was so deserted that the snowflakes dotted the pavement uniformly, undisturbed by tires. The reasons she came up with for keeping Duane to herself never seemed quite good enough to justify climbing out her window and missing so much sleep. The main thing was, she hadn't *felt* like sharing Duane. But now she wondered. Maybe when she got home now she should let her mother have a piece of him. Not say she'd been lying, just that she'd seen Duane a couple of times at Stacy's and really liked him. The ache faded from her throat. She was getting butterflies instead. She wasn't sure she'd have the nerve to tell her mother as soon as she walked in.

A triangle of blue sky had opened in the black clouds above her house. Mr. Mohnwirbel was digging up the brick border along the front walk. "Hi, Mr. Mohnwirbel!"

He looked up. "Hi," he said in his gruff German voice.

"Going to the game tomorrow?" she asked loudly.

He shook his head.

"Going to have a turkey dinner?" she said, even louder.

He shook his head.

"Going to take the day off?"

"I make a vacation."

"You're going to make a vacation? Wow. Where to?"

"Illinois."

"Boy." Luisa rocked on her heels. "I sure hope you have a good time."

He nodded and picked up another brick.

The butterflies were rising higher in her stomach. She marched around to the back door, gathering courage, and crashed inside.

The kitchen was dark and smelled. Her mother had been smoking. It smelled like grade-school afternoons, when she'd smoked all the time. She was sitting at the table and looking bad, all pinched and pasty. This probably wasn't the time to tell her.

"Hi," Luisa said.

Her mother gave her a baleful glance, and brushed some ashes off the table. Had her counselor called about the smoking after all?

"What's up?" Luisa said.

Her mother looked at her again. "I don't understand you."

"What?" Maybe it wasn't the smoking. Maybe— Her stomach fell a mile.

Her mother looked at the sink. "I was picking up the turkey at Straub's," she said, speaking to a nonexistent person. "I was standing in the checkout line. The woman ahead of me was looking at me. She seemed vaguely familiar. She said, You're Barbara Probst, aren't you? I said, Yes, I am. She said, I guess our daughters are good friends. I said—"

Enough. Luisa ran down the hall and locked herself in the bathroom. In the mirror she caught a glimpse of herself smelling her hand and spun away.

"*Luisa!*" Her mother's voice was harsh. "Luisa, what kind of stunt is this?"

"I have to go to the *bathroom*." She hoped the tinkling would drive her mother away. Arguing was out of the question. Anything she said would humiliate her.

She jerked up her pants and flushed the toilet. Under the cover of the rushing water, she cleared her mother's bud vases off the windowsill and parted the curtains. Snow was falling again. From the dark bathroom the sky looked light and unbounded.

The toilet fell silent.

"Luisa, I'm not going to be understanding this time. I'm sorry, but I'm not, because for one thing, I don't understand, and for another, I don't think you want me to. But if you want me to treat you like an adult you'd better come out here and start acting like one. What are you doing in there?"

Luisa hardly heard the words. It was just pathetic bleating to her. She felt evil and she wanted Duane. She was glad she'd lied. She was sorry she'd been caught.

"Imagine how I felt," her mother said. "Imagine me standing there trying to smile and hold up my end of the conversation while this woman *I don't even know* is telling me—"

She flushed the toilet a second time, for noise, and unlatched the window. Fortunately it didn't stick. She raised it and eased up the storm window. The toilet bowl gurgled as it emptied. She planted one foot on the tiled sill, squeezed through the window, and jumped into the yews outside. Her mother was still talking to her.

6

Singh was all smiles; like a boy inventor, he'd used the word "results" a dozen times in half an hour. Blinking the eternal clove smoke from his eyes, he pressed the Rewind button on the tape deck, puffed, and tapped his ash onto Jammu's office carpeting. With a lazy toe he smeared the ash to dust. He had just played, for Jammu, the scene of the arrival of Luisa Probst at the apartment of her boyfriend Duane Thompson, and then the recording of a phone call shortly following her arrival: an exchange between Thompson and Barbara Probst. "Tell her I called," Barbara had said. "She does have our number, I believe. And if you change your mind about tomorrow, just come on over. We'd like to have you."

Jammu had bitten off so much thumbnail that it seemed only a single layer of cells kept the red flesh from bleeding. Though not intense, the pain was like an itch, inviting aggravation. She pressed the rough end of the nail into the exposed flesh and felt the pressure far away, in her anus.

She'd never heard Barbara Probst's voice before, or any local voice that sounded so aware of the wiretap and so contemptuous of its presence. The voice was controlled and dispassionate, its tones unmelodious but pure, as if in the woman's throat there were a low-pass filter that eliminated the overtones, the rasp and tremor, the nasals, flutter, fear. The clarity made Jammu anxious. Not once in five months had she considered that there might be hidden elements of control in St. Louis, that behind Martin Probst there might stand not a twangy Bunny or a vapid Biz but a woman with a voice like her own. How could a voice like Barbara's restrict itself to speaking only on domestic issues? It was impossible. In the recorded conversation Jammu could hear the workings of an undercover operation dedicated to the preservation of order. The girl wouldn't come to the phone, but the mother assured the boyfriend, in phrases lulling and impersonal, that everything was fine. It was clear that St. Louis had Thought Police, and that Singh, with bizarre blitheness, had flushed out the voice of a master agent.

"Get any sleep last night?" Singh asked.

"Don't ever play that voice for me again."

The tape ran off the take-up reel. "Barbara's? You should have heard her before she—"

"Never again, do you understand?"

It was Thanksgiving morning. At three o'clock Jammu was due at the mayor's brownstone for dinner, a tête-à-tête for which she'd planned to spend these hours preparing. Already she could see that she wouldn't have time even to brush her teeth beforehand, let alone pick out clothes. No doubt she'd end up going in her stretched cardigan and a drab wool skirt.

Singh cleared his throat. "As I was about to say—"

"What's the Bonfire?"

He sighed. "Not important."

"Who's Stacy?"

"Last name Montefusco. A little friend of Luisa's. She's been lying for her."

"Where does Thompson live?"

"University City."

"How will she get to school if she stays with him?"

"Bus, I guess."

Jammu nodded. "You guess. The director of Bi-State owes me one. If you think she needs a bus line to the high school, just tell me."

"Thanks. There's a good connection. She's been taking a bus at night to sleep with him. Since the twenty-second of October they've had intercourse eleven times. On five of those occasions she was able to spend the night. Once outside during the daytime, the remaining five times in the evening, in his apartment."

"Thank you for counting, Singh. I respect your thoroughness. But why didn't she tell Barbara to begin with? If she'd told her, she wouldn't have had to sneak around, or run away. How did you manage to set it up this way?"

"How did I set it up?"

"Yes."

"The deceptions started slowly," Singh said. "There was a conversation—November eight. Evening. Luisa, and Barbara, who tried to draw her out and overdid the 'cool' bit. I could understand the girl's response."

"Which was?"

"Heavy sigh. As if it were too late to start explaining. So she lied. Only-children sometimes feel oppressed and very often they're duplicitous. They have no sibling rivals. Luisa doesn't have to worry about losing favor, so she goes ahead and takes exactly what she wants. She's also going through a typical adolescent rebellion."

"So the family is less happy than it looked." Jammu smiled wanly. "Who is Duane Thompson?"

"You don't know?"

"You haven't told me, I've been busy, how should I know?"

"But surely you've seen his pictures?"

"Don't treat me like a baby, Singh. I've seen his pictures. But who is he? How well do you know him?"

Singh rolled a chair up against Jammu's desk, sat down, and looked across the papers at her. "Not at all. Never met him. He has no connection with us—'no taint.' Luisa knew him from school. It came as a rude shock, because I'd spent an entire week setting her up to meet me—"

"For you to seduce."

"Correct."

"Good." Jammu liked to see her employees planning in accordance with their capacities. Singh was seductive, and she was glad he knew enough to exploit it.

"I lured her to a bar, and she came alone, which was gratifying. Unfortunately I'd stepped into the bathroom when she arrived. When I came out she was talking to Thompson. They stuck together. I had no chance. And forty-eight hours later they—"

"Were having intercourse, yes. Why did you step into the bathroom?"

"It was an error."

Interesting. Singh didn't usually make errors like that. He had bladder control. "I ask again," Jammu said. "Who's Thompson?"

"A youth. Unrelated to us, apart from the fact that I got him his photo job."

"When?"

"The same night they met."

"Why?"

"When a man wins a million dollars, he kisses the first person he sees."

"So I take it you weren't opposed to their liaison."

Singh smiled. "I wasn't looking forward to the mechanics. Your dictum, Chief. Nothing fancy. An affair with a local boy was clearly preferable. A matter of verisimilitude. If I take credit for the results, it's only because I did get her to the bar. And she met him there."

"If you didn't know him before that night, how did you know he had pictures to sell the Post?"

"I eavesdropped. Thompson was whining about it. I left, confirmed the story at the Post, and—forged ahead."

"Amazingly quick thinking. Will she go home again?"

"Judge for yourself. To me it sounded as if she was making plans for an extended stay."

"Are there precedents for this? Sociologically?"

"Yes and no. No, it isn't normal for 'better-class' girls, or boys, to move out of their homes while they're still in high school. Certainly Probst thinks it's abnormal. On the other hand, Barbara is at pains to accept it. Her niece—Ripley's daughter—moved out at age fifteen. She had a clinical problem, of course," Singh added, "but there is a precedent in the family."

"She'll be homesick. She'll be back in a week."

"I agree it's difficult to imagine her missing the 'holidays.' But she may very well hold out until then. She has her pride. She's been away before, in France. I'd guess a month. Thirty days. That gives us time."

"Time for what?"

"Well, assuming that the State is developing—"

"You've given me no evidence to suggest that it is."

"Well, naturally, the signs are small. But I assume they're significant, what with Probst having lost both his dog and his daughter. As early as October twenty-four—but not before, not in the September recordings—I picked up a line like this from Barbara: What's wrong with you? You haven't heard a word I've said."

"From Barbara," Jammu repeated grimly.

"And he's begun to sermonize with Luisa. It sounds a bit mad when he does it—speaks of 'opportunity' and 'self-discipline.' Masterpieces of irrelevance. He isn't paying attention. Other men talk about him—they even set him up in opposition to you, as if already there are, de facto, two camps, yours and his. And I listen to him every day, I listen for an awareness of what you're doing to the city, for a leaning one way or the other, any glimmering of historical consciousness—and there's nothing. Zero. This could be last year, or the year before that. Your name simply isn't spoken, except to tell someone else to forget about you. It isn't unreasonable to believe we're getting results."

Jammu gave Singh a long, hard look. "And how, exactly, are you planning to get him to start working for us? What is the next step you plan to take?"

"We should go for the kill right away," Singh replied. "Someone from your syndicate should approach him. Mayor Wesley, for example. Sometime before Luisa gets homesick—sometime in the next month—Wesley should hit Probst hard. To begin with, Probst is in trouble with Westhaven. Wesley can play on this, if you think he's capable. He should press urban rejuvenation, the forces that lead to new growth, new solidarity. But keep your name out of it, and nothing explicit about the city-county merger either. Let Probst draw that conclusion himself."

"So basically you're saying that Probst is in the State and will be susceptible to our suggestions."

"Basically, yes. It's a situation waiting for him to walk into. He's been sleeping on a train. You wake him up, tell him he's in Warsaw. He'll start speaking Polish."

"Assuming he knows the language." Jammu twisted in her chair to see the wall clock. It was noon. "Prepare an abstract," she said. "I'm seeing Wesley at three so I'll need it by two. Not that

I'm certain your plan is even close to being acceptable." She fed some notes to her shredder, by way of illustration. "You say Probst hardly knows my name. What do you expect me to do, congratulate you for that? You say he's vague and irrelevant when he talks to his daughter. To me it sounds like he's an ordinary father. You say that killing his dog and making his daughter run away from home hasn't bothered him. Well? Perhaps he's a thick-skinned individual. You say he lacks historical consciousness. May I ask what St. Louisan doesn't? What you have painted, Singh, is a portrait of a man in *excellent mental health*."

Singh had assumed an expression of dignified deafness that was reminiscent of Karam Bhandari. Jammu went on.

"You say Probst isn't on good terms with Barbara. But maybe that's only on the surface. She sounds like she still must be a force. Maybe she pays attention *for* him. She sounds like a bad person for him to rely on. I want him hearing my voice, the voice of what I'm doing. Not hers."

"Go see him."

"No time. Not yet. I'd need a pretext."

"Well." From his shirt pocket Singh produced an unusually fat-looking clove cigarette. He inspected it and put it back. "If Probst is by some chance not yet in the State, there's more that can be done. I can step in and get Barbara any time. The ground-work is laid. But I'd prefer to hold off until we've seen how Probst reacts to Wesley. I recommend that you brief Wesley soon, in case Probst comes to see him of his own accord. Then if he hasn't by the fourteenth, you can ask Wesley to approach him after Municipal Growth."

"All right." Jammu rose from her chair. "Bring me an abstract at home, by two."

.

Barbara returned to pulling tendons with the pliers. In the stumps of the turkey's legs there were tiny white eyes. She pressed down on the pink tissue surrounding one of them, worked the pliers into an acceptable grip, and began to tug. The phone rang. She lost her grip.

"You son of a bitch."

She took hold of the tendon again and tugged hard as the phone rang a second and third time.

"If that's Audrey . . ."

Abruptly the tendon ripped loose and slithered out, lavender and rigid like a hard-on, and trailing a maroon feather of flesh. She grabbed a dishtowel, a clean one, and rubbed the grease off her hands. She took the phone.

"Hello," she said.

There was a silence, and she knew right away who it was.

"Oh baby, hi," she said. "Where are you?"

"I'm at Duane's." The voice was very small.

"Are you all right?"

"Yes." The volume surged, as if the line had cleared. "YES. HOW ARE YOU?"

"We're fine. Daddy just left for the football game. I'm putting together the turkey. It's a big one. You and Duane want to come over?"

After a silence, Luisa said, "No." Her throat clicked.

"That's OK, you don't have to. I just thought—was I that horrible to you?"

"Doe." There was a long sniff. "Yes."

"I'm sorry, then. I'm truly sorry. Will you forgive me sometime?" Barbara listened to her daughter cry. "Oh baby, *what*? Do you want me to come over? I can come right over."

"Doe."

"No, OK. You know I worry about you."

The turkey, which had been propped against the faucet, slid with a slap to the bottom of the sink.

"Is Duane making you a nice dinner?"

"Yes. A chicken. He's stuffing it." Luisa swallowed. "In the kitchen."

"We had a really nice talk last night—"

"That's what he said."

"He was really charming, I'd love to meet him sometime. I had—"

"I'll call you back, OK?"

The line went dead.

Barbara looked around as if awakening, and it was morning,

very bright. She hoisted the turkey back up onto its rubbery wings
and found another tendon. The phone rang.

"Can I come and get some clothes tomorrow?"

Since parking promised to be a problem, Probst was walking
to the football game. From the chimneys of houses on Baker Avenue, smoke rose a few feet and hooked down, as it cooled, to
collect in bluish pools above the lawns. There was no light inside
the little stores on Big Bend Boulevard—Porter Paints, Kaegel
Drug, the sci-fi bookshop—to compete with the bright sunshine
on their windows, but Schnucks, the supermarket, was still doing
business. Probst stopped in to buy the pint of heavy cream that
Barbara had asked for. Then he joined the stream of fans issuing
from the bowels of Webster Groves.

There was a throng at the gates of Moss Field. The Visitors
bleachers were packed with red-clad Pioneer fans, and the home
stands, much larger, were also nearly full. Under the press box sat
the Webster Groves Marching Statesmen, their brass bells and
silver keys gleaming in the sun. Probst found a cozy seat near the
south end of the stands, by the southern end zone, three rows
from the top. To his right was a group of girls in tattered blue
jeans, smoking cigarettes, and to his left was a rosy-cheeked
couple in their forties, wearing orange. He felt anonymous and
secure.

"Are you for Webster?" asked the woman on his left. Mrs.
Orange.

"Yes." Probst smiled courteously.

"So are we."

He nodded in a manner indicating that he hadn't come to the
game to talk with strangers, and let the bag with the heavy cream
in it slide between his hands and knees to the tier of concrete
on which the bench rested. Up at the doors to the swimming
pool locker rooms, where the teams were suiting up, students
swarmed purposefully, as if some quality item were being handed
out for free inside. Down by the field the Statesmen cheerleaders, a dozen girls in ivory-colored skirts and sweaters, began
a cheer:

The Pi - o - neers
Think they're real - ly tall,
But the bigger they are,
The harder they fall.

Probst scanned the faces around him in search of Luisa, but he was certain she wasn't here. He wondered if she might be at the Washington U. game, sitting with Duane Thompson. Barbara made much of the fact that Duane went to Washington U.; she liked to inflate the worth of whichever boy Luisa happened at the moment to hold stock in. Probst wasn't fooled. It was clear to him that a girl who jumped out bathroom windows had a vision of her future radically different from the one he himself had entertained. As far as he was concerned, Thompson could be a total dropout.

A great roar greeted the Pioneers as they trundled, like Marines, down the stairs to the playing field. A greater roar erupted when the Statesmen followed. Mr. and Mrs. Orange leaped to their feet, fists clenched and arms outstretched. "All right!" they yelled. Everybody stood up. Probst stood up.

Kirkwood won the toss, and a Pioneer receiver, a loping black youth, took the kickoff at the 10-yard line. At the 35 one of the Statesmen tripped him from behind, sending him in a cartwheeling somersault to land, gruesomely, on his head. The ball squirted out of bounds.

"All right! All right! All right!" the Oranges yelled. There was a queasy silence in the Kirkwood stands. The trainer and coaches ran to look after the fallen runner, who writhed on his back.

"ALL RIGHT!" the Oranges bellowed. Probst gave them a critical glance. Coarse blond hair clung to their heads like wigs, and the orange Webster jerseys they were wearing heightened the impression of fakeness. The woman's cheeks were scarlet, her lips blue and retracted. The husband's head swiveled back and forth as the Statesmen cheerleaders started up a new chant—

That's all right.
That's OK.
We're going to beat you
Anyway

—an incongruous message, since the Pioneers had just lost one of their better players. The trainer and coaches were carrying him towards the sidelines on a stretcher.

After two losses and an incomplete pass, Kirkwood had to punt. The Statesmen took over at their own 20-yard line, and Probst was happy to immerse himself in the game, to count downs in his head and watch the line of scrimmage ebb and flow. He was happy not to be at home. At home, the night before, Barbara had given him the distinct impression that she expected him to take some kind of action regarding Luisa. *He was an active businessman, wasn't he?* Be firm with her! Be hurt! Go get her! Or at least comfort your wife . . . But action was impossible. Luisa made him angry like a woman, not a daughter. As he lay awake in bed a single thought monopolized his mind: I have the strength not to be selfish and deceitful while she, apparently, does not. And it was clear that Barbara, lying next to him, didn't want to hear about this. "She's only known Duane a month," she said. "I'm sure he's OK, though. I can't blame this on him. You know Luisa. She wouldn't be there if she didn't want to be . . . Oh Martin, this just tears me apart."

Probst did not know Luisa. He began to stroke Barbara's hair.

The Oranges sprang to their feet. "ALL RIGHT! ALL RIGHT!"

A referee thrust his arms in the air and the Marching Statesmen struck up the school song. A touchdown. How wonderful.

Deducing that he loved her, or overlooking his gall in desiring her if he didn't, Barbara had reached down with her cold, strong fingers and adjusted the angle of his penis, leading him in. "I'll call Lu tomorrow," he lied in a whisper. She turned her head away from him. Her mouth was opening. He increased his pressure, and then, glimpsing her teeth, he remembered a late afternoon in September. A Friday. A van with a bad muffler driving down Sherwood Drive. Dozer, his three-year-old retriever, chasing it. Dozer who never chased things. A thud and a yelp. The driver didn't stop, probably didn't even know he'd hit something. Probst knelt in the street. Dozer was dead, and his teeth, the incisors and canines and molars, were grinning in bitter laughter, and his body was hot and heavy, his splintered ribs sharp, as Probst picked him up. The embrace was terrible. He hurried to get home, pushing, pushing,

pushing, but it was too late: Dozer had become evil, staring in a crazy angle at the ground, which rose up mechanically to meet his feet. He dropped him on the grass. Eventually Barbara lost her patience, shed him roughly, and rolled away.

The Statesmen were lined up for another kickoff. Mrs. Orange clutched her husband's arm and looked around pugnaciously at Probst and the people behind him, as if they didn't deserve to live in Webster if they wouldn't even stand up for a kickoff.

Kirkwood took the touchback and started at the 20-yard line. On the very first play the stands exploded in confetti and streamers. A Statesman safety had picked off a pass and run it all the way back for a touchdown. Mrs. Orange seemed ripped by convulsions. "ALL RIGHT! ALL RIGHT! ALL RIGHT! ALL RIGHT!"

Probst decided he'd had enough. He rose determinedly. "ALL RIGHT!" He pushed past knees and elbows, hurrying. "ALL RIGHT!" The cry was fainter now. He reached the end of the row and descended to the black cinder track. There he realized, from the lightness of his hands, that he'd left the heavy cream under the bench.

"Hey Martin!"

It was Norm Hoelzer, sitting in the second row. Hoelzer was a local small-timer. Kitchens and bathrooms. "Well hi," Probst said.

"Some game, isn't it?"

"Oh. It's . . ." He didn't know what it was.

"You here with Barbara?"

How dare Hoelzer know his wife's first name?

He shook his head: no, he wasn't here with Barbara. Hoelzer's wife's name was Bonnie. Grew roses. Probst forced his way through a group of boys in letter jackets.

"Hey Martin!" A hand waved from deep in the stands. Joe Farrell. Here with what looked to be his daughter and son-in-law. "Well hi," Probst said. (At this distance Farrell of course couldn't hear him.) He kept walking. It was a tight squeeze, with the cheerleaders taking up half the track, and fans, mostly kids, lining the cable between the cheerleaders and the Statesman benches. "Hey Martin!" another voice called from the stands. Probst—well hi!—ignored it. "*Martin!*" The noise, after all, was terrific. Cheers came in sheets, like the avalanching calls of katydids. Most of the cheerleaders were idle at the moment, but a few of them did flying dutchmen out of sheer high spirits. How splendidly these girls were built. Probst followed a man in a wool coat slowly, content for once to proceed at the going speed.

"Martin!" A large hand gripped his arm. The man in the wool coat had turned around, and when Probst saw his face his heart sank. It was Jack DuChamp, his old friend from high school. Probst hadn't seen him in a good ten years.

"I *wondered* who was stepping on my heels!" Jack grabbed Probst's other arm and beamed at him.

"Well!" Probst said. He didn't know what else to say.

"I should have guessed you wouldn't miss this game," Jack said.

"I'd missed it for a couple of years in a row, actually."

Jack nodded, not hearing him. "I was going to get a Coke, but the lines were too long. Do you want to come sit with me?"

The invitation closed on Probst like a bear trap on his leg. Sitting in the stands with Jack DuChamp—reminiscing about their South Side youth, comparing their utterly divergent careers—was the last thing in the world he felt like doing.

"Well!" he said again.

"Or are you here with people?"

"No, yes, I—" The look of entreaty on Jack's face was more than Probst could stand. He'd spent too large a part of his life with Jack to be able to lie easily. "No," he said, "I came alone. Where are you sitting?"

Jack pointed towards the north end of the field and laughed. "In the three-dollar seats!"

Probst heard himself chuckle.

"Jesus, Martin, it's been a long time, hasn't it?" Jack held his arm. They were climbing into the stands.

"It must be ten years." Instantly Probst regretted having named the actual figure.

"We keep seeing your name in the paper, though . . ."

From the field Probst heard the wordless exertions of another play, the accidental grunts, rising cheers and tearing fabric. Jack DuChamp had moved his family to Webster Groves about the same time Probst and Barbara had moved there. Unfortunately, the house Jack bought was soon condemned to make room for Interstate 44, and the only houses for sale in Webster at the time were well beyond his price range. So he moved his family to Crestwood, a new town, a new school district, and Probst, whose company held the I-44 demolition contracts and did the actual razing of the houses, felt responsible. As a matter of fact, he felt guilty.

"Aren'tcha?" Jack had stopped halfway up the long stairs and was surveying the crowd to their right.

"Beg pardon?" Probst said.

"I said you're just the same."

"No."

"You always did have your head in the clouds."

"What?"

"Excuse us," Jack said. A young family in tartan stood up to let them by. Probst tried to keep his eyes on his feet, but the dark space beneath the bench reminded him uncomfortably of the heavy cream. He wondered how few minutes he could get away with staying before he left again. Would five suffice? Five minutes to atone for a decade of silence?

Jack stopped. "Martin, this is Billy Wonder, friend of mine. Bill-y, this is Martin Probst, a very old friend of mine. He, uh—"

"Sure!" A large-boned man with buck teeth sprang to his feet. "Sure. Sure! This is quite an honor!" He took Probst's hand and shook it vigorously.

"Didn't catch your name," Probst said.

"Sure! Windell, Bill Windell. Glad to know you."

Probst stared at the buck teeth.

"Can we make some room here?" Jack said. Windell pulled Probst into a narrow space on the bench. Jack sat down fussily on his right with an air of mission accomplished. Windell slapped a pocket flask in a leather case against Probst's chest. "Never touch the stuff! A ha ha ha ha ha ha ha ha ha ha!" He drove his elbow into Probst's left biceps.

"Bill's my boss," Jack explained.

"You'd never guess it to see us at work," Windell said.

"Don't you believe it." Jack reached across Probst's lap and unscrewed the cap of the pocket flask. "He's done one-forty all by himself."

"Hundred thirty maybe." Windell gave Probst a big, practiced wink, and Probst, not bothering to wonder what in hell the two of them were talking about, was filled with the certainty that Windell was a scoutmaster. His eyes, which were blue, had a milkiness that often showed up in men charged with instilling moral values. Furthermore, he had a crewcut. "So: Martin Probst." Windell sucked his teeth and nodded philosophically.

Probst had no place to put his elbows. He tilted the flask to his lips, intending to take a polite sip. He gagged. It was apricot brandy. Elbows almost knocking on his lap, he passed the flask to Jack, who shook his head. "Thanks. Too early in the day for me."

He tried to return it to Windell, but Windell said, "No, be my guest."

Probst took a long swig, wiped his mouth, and looked at Jack for the cap to the flask. Jack didn't seem to have it. Probst noticed it below him at his feet and reached down, but his legs straightened as he bent, pushing it over the edge of their tier and underneath the bleacher in front of them. He dropped into a squat, groping down.

"Don't. Here—no," Jack said. "I'll get it."

"No, no. Here." Probst stretched until his fingers reached the ground, then unexpectedly he tipped backwards, landing on his butt in the shade of the fans, who were leaping to their feet in response to something on the field. The cold penetrated his pants, but he was more comfortable down here. His hand traveled far, searching for the cap. It came upon a sneaker and backed away over the coarse, damp concrete, and then ran into something soft— an apple core. Screams rode the chafed air. The space was too narrow for him to see what he was doing. He groped further, sensing Windell's scoutmasterly gaze. Probst and Jack had been Scouts together, often tentmates, all the way up through Eagledom.

Well hi! The cap. He'd found the cap. His hand closed around it. He struggled up. "I think I'd better be going," he said.

A forlorn sound creaked out of Jack. "Nih."

"At least stay for the half," Windell said.

Probst remembered the peculiar power Jack could wield, the

whirlpool of guilt into which he could drag his more successful friend. "How much time is left?" he asked.

"Four minutes," Jack said reproachfully.

A messy running play expired in front of them. The score was still 13–0. Probst turned to Windell. "So, uh, where do you live, Bill?" He already knew roughly what Windell did, he being Jack's boss and Jack being in middle management at Sears.

"We've been living in West County for six years." Windell gave a laugh.

What was so funny about that?

"I see. Whereabouts?"

"Ballwin, Cedar Hill Drive. Not far from whatchamacallit. West—"

"Haven. Westhaven."

"That's the place. We're about a mile east of there. I'm always driving by it. See your name a lot."

"Yeah." Probst sighed.

"It looks like some project."

"The foundations alone are twenty-five acres."

"Huh." Windell stared at the field, where penalty flags had been dropped. Jack was sitting on his hands, apparently content to let Probst's presence speak for itself. His nose was red. Small brushes of straight gray hair sheltered his ears.

"But it must be a long commute for you," Probst said.

"Hm? Oh. Not too bad. It's something you get used to."

"Well, if we keep on building like this in West County, you'll be sitting pretty. Who knows, maybe Sears will move its headquarters out there."

"Sears?"

"I," Probst said. "I thought you worked for Sears."

"No. I've been with Penney since I was, God, twenty. But Jack worked for Sears. He came over to us five years ago."

Jack sniffed and swallowed. He didn't seem to be listening, but after a few seconds, without looking at them, he said, "That's right," in a loud, deep voice.

"We've—" Probst felt that he was going to pop like a balloon if he had to sit here a minute longer. "We've been pretty out of touch since Jack left Webster—"

"Oh! Way to go!" Windell shouted, interrupting him.

"What a game," Jack agreed.

This was the moment Probst had been waiting for. He stood up quickly. "That's it for me," he said. "Bill, it's nice meeting you. If you're ever by Westhaven, one of my men will be glad to show you around. And Jack, you and I—" Escape was so close he could taste it. He looked down at Jack, who had raised his chin but wouldn't meet his eyes. "We'll have to get together sometime." He clapped Jack lightly on the shoulder and started moving away.

"Martin!" Jack said suddenly. "It looks like I've got an extra ticket to the Big Red game on Sunday. Next week. Bill here's got a camp-out with his Scouts, and—"

Probst turned back, feeling his face light up. "You're a scoutmaster?"

"It's the very least an old sinner can do for the world," said Bill, who was not old, and seemed sinless.

"—the Redskins," Jack was saying. "We could catch up a little, get a bite to eat before—"

"Sure, yes, fine," Probst said, still staring at Bill.

.

Rolf Ripley liked a girl with pluck, and Devi, his latest acquisition, had it. Last night in her suite at the airport Marriott, she'd told him his nose was redder than a souse's.

"A souse's, luv? Do let's let Rolf give us a good spank."

"And you'll start to cough," she said.

"That won't happen, luv. I don't get coughs."

"No?"

"No," he said. "I've learned from decades of experimentation to sleep with my head *flat* on the *mattress*. That way, the what the devil d'you call it—the *mucus*—stays where it belongs. No cough."

Devi laughed.

"What's so funny?"

"A cold doesn't spread through mucus. It spreads through blood."

"And how do you know that?"

"I heard it on the radio."

"Then why, pray tell, do I not get coughs?"

"Your body must be as stupid as your brain!"

She was a gem, a gem. And when he wanted to change key, he simply pushed a pedal: "Take it back."

"I take it back."

He'd never had another quite like her. All the dishes in his past, the Tricias and Maudes and Amandas, the sex piglets and Dallas snobs and randy undergrads, the mute tarts, corporate wives and gold-digging salesclerks, banquet favors, cynical secretaries and door-to-door sluts: all paled before Devi. Even the few he'd had in London and New York were not the real item, but imports, farmgirls at heart, sinning venally, not mortally. Men from the capitals never shared their finest stock, and though Rolf was in all ways their superior, Fate had consigned him to Saint Louis. Oh, the Saint Louis girls! God knew, Rolf had tried his Pygmalion best to teach them; still they remained porcine and drawling. They couldn't hold a candle to Devi. She was his aesthetic fulfillment, teachable and teaching, as sharp as the glitter city Bombay and, in her docility, older than the Old World, an object to rut on and an angel to frame. In fact, he damn near loved her, and if she weren't an Indian he might have gone further and made himself her fool. But he was at pains to be careful. For not only was Devi in cahoots with S. Jammu and Princess Asha Hammaker but she was dreadfully indiscreet. Among the tidbits she had dropped were the facts that Jammu was angling for the affections of the mayor; that Asha, whose fortune was made now, was pursuing Buzz Wismer as well; and that both these South Asian lovelies were intent upon staging a real-estate panic in the ghetto. Interesting.

As for cars, he liked 'em small and fast. His Lotus whisked him home from the Marriott for a long winter's nap, and on Thanksgiving Day his Ferrari whisked him and Audreykins to the Club for civilized noontime drinks and a brief show of holiday propriety. He was a family man, after all. It wouldn't do to take Devi to the Club. There were too many stockholders at the bar, and Rolf of late had grown a tad fanatical about his stockholders. For the first time in years, his finances were iffy. If one of the club members downing toddies were to lose confidence in Rolf's good judgment, why then the next member might, too, and the next, and the next, and soon the NYSE, and Rolf might find himself producing neither toaster-ovens nor inertial guidance systems, and headquartered in neither the county nor the city, and living permanently in Barbados or Lincolnshire, not Ladue. It was better not to bring Devi. These codgers liked Audreykins, and why not?

Chester (3.7%) Murphy ambled over and confessed that Audreykins looked lovely today, as indeed she almost did, despite the fact the Armani she wore was made for a woman with a third shoulder somewhere in the vicinity of her fifth vertebra. Leaving the room to allow her and Chester to converse about Peace, Hope and Charity, Rolf placed an amorous call to Devi's suite at the Marriott. He finished by smothering the receiver, still warm from the last caller's breath, with kisses. When he returned he saw Audreykins absorbing the wise words of the Baseball Star, who was wearing a green blazer just a shade lighter than the one Rolf himself had on, and what with the Star being chums with Julian (5.5%) Woolman and Chuck (major creditor) Meisner, he found it expedient to visit the bar for a refill. Drown a fever, drown a cold. He had a nasty sensation of having inhaled water. Repeated doses of The Glenlivet were the only sure cure. His muscles ached less when steeped in spirits, though his sense of blame still throbbed. This cold was the fault of Audreykins. Two weeks ago she'd been a regular snot factory, specially diligent on the night shift, and had sniffed and sniffed and sniffled, always as though she were blubbering. Barbie, it seemed, had infected her. Rolf observed that her Armani's third shoulder had migrated into the region of her right armpit. Dear child. The Club buzzed timelessly in the afternoon sun.

"How are you feeling?" Audreykins asked an hour later, as they zipped through the cheesy business district of Webster Groves.

"Rummy, thanks," he said.

"Too bad," she said unkindly.

"Oh, it isn't the cold," he lied. "It's the thought of another meal with Martin and Barbie and the brat." Climbing into fourth gear for the big curve in Lockwood Avenue, he was gratified to see her foot press down on an imaginary brake. "I suppose," he went on, "I ought to count my bloody blessings your folks are in Pago Pago."

"I don't see why you bring this up now. We could have gone to the Club."

"Except then Martin would have said, 'Uh, how about the

Saint Louis Club instead? Uh, they've got a, uh, traditional dinner. Uh, goose, turkey, the works. Ya interested?' " Martin thought the new Saint Louis Club was the smartest place in town. Rolf did a deadly impression of Martin.

"And it's New Zealand, not Pago Pago."

"Mea culpa." He glanced to his left and caught a glimpse of Sherwood Drive, fast receding. "Dash it all, why didn't you say something?"

"Mm?" she said.

Rolf scowled. Of course she hadn't said anything. She gave him no help. "We'll just have to turn around then, won't we?" Thirty yards past the railroad bridge he swung over the left-hand curb with a well-absorbed shock. Gunning the engine, he threw the Ferrari into second gear and spurted across the median. The tires grabbed the pavement. The car tore off again under the bridge and up Sherwood Drive, while Audreykins shook like a leaf.

She fairly ran up the brick walk to the Probsts' front door. Rolf consulted his Tourneau. Twenty to four. He hadn't intended to arrive so punctually. Audreykins aimed a few girlish taps at the front door ("It's only us!") and Martin must have seen them coming, because the door swung right open. He beckoned them inside, took Audreykins's hand, and, smiling with admiration, planted a kiss on her cheek. He turned. "Rolf. Afternoon." He wore a bright red sweater and dark plaid pants.

"Good to see you, Martin." It was! Martin looked dashed bad, his eyes pinched and his hair full of lumps. Rolf felt better already.

Audreykins was speaking in a low voice to Barbie, and when Rolf saw them side by side his spirits dipped again. His wife paled when she stood beside her sister. He pushed her away and leaned to receive Barbie's kiss. "Barbara, dear." He gave her a short, strategic squeeze in the hindquarters.

"Jesus Christ!"

He straightened. "Pardon me?"

"Rolf, here, let me take your coat." Martin was pestering his shoulders, and he shrugged the coat off. Barbie was the girl with pluck. He had the wrong sister.

The women beat an effortless retreat to the kitchen. Martin was having inordinate trouble stuffing the coats into the closet, where Rolf recognized jackets dating back to the mid-sixties. One shiny gold anorak in particular caught his eye. The Martian Look. Martin the Martian. "Those old jackets do eat up the space, what?" he said meanly.

Martin gave up, leaving Rolf's coat and muffler draped broadside over the others, and hastily shut the door.

They repaired to the living room and stopped by the fireplace, where kindling crackled beneath sodden logs. A draft brushed Rolf's knees. Martin and Barbara had redecorated this room since he saw it in August, and why they hadn't gone ahead and put in carpeting was beyond his comprehension. It was as comfortable as a bloody cathedral. Martin prodded the fire with a poker. Sunlight, tinted green by encroaching ivy, showed up streaks and spatters on the row of leaded windows in the long western wall. Beneath them was a window seat with lime-colored cushions, and to Rolf's right was the piano, which Barbie could play with less precision and more feeling than Audreykins. Barbie had clearly had complete control of the redecoration. On the wall above the sofa, where Martin would have hung mail-order prints of pheasants and setters, she'd installed a series of three outsized still lifes, all by the same fellow. The paintings dominated the room. The first was a pineapple that had been split in two; the rind was gabardine, the meat a yellow tulle. In the second were bananas, fat portentous nanners on a sea of grays and whites, and in the third, a—what? A kiwi fruit. Quartered and emerald, with dark speckles, it looked like an animal from the ocean. He regarded the three paintings somberly. It was cold and glum in here. He felt unwell.

Martin clapped the dust and ashes off his hands, and Rolf closed his eyes. The man was going to ask him how business was. Invariably the crass ass inquired about business. He waited. The question didn't come. He opened his eyes and saw Martin frowning.

"Had a pleasant day?" Rolf asked, certain he hadn't.

"Went to the Webster–Kirkwood game, that's about all."

"Luisa took you?"

Martin coughed and his face grew still more sour. "No. She's gone for the weekend."

"Not coming tonight? *That's* a pity."

"What can I get you, Rolf?"

"Scotch if you have it, Martin." As if he might not.

Martin marched away and returned moments later with refreshments. He raised his glass. "Happy Thanksgiving."

"Yes indeed." Rolf turned to the dismal fireplace. One of the logs groaned. "Charming fire you have here."

"Barbara made it," Martin said, deadpan.

"Where are the girls?"

"They are in the kitchen."

"And Luisa?"

"She's spending the weekend with her boyfriend."

Rolf looked up from his glass. Martin's eyes were glassy. "I confess that I'm surprised, Martin."

"Let's go watch some football, Rolf."

"Really quite surprised."

They left the living room and watched football. Martin refused to acknowledge that Rolf was sick. Not that Rolf needed sympathy, but in the family room, while hominid Bears clashed with hominid Jets, he began to feel as though he really did belong in bed with his heating pad, a bottle of cheer, and the telly tuned in to the most explicit of the cable channels. Football was not his cup of tea. Down the hall in the kitchen the girls twittered ad nauseam, and the setting sun cast a spindly claustrophobic sort of light through the windows. All at once the light blinked out. It was night, though somehow the sky above Chicago was still glowing, the clouds still pink and violet. Had the game been taped? Rolf sank deeper and deeper into the corduroy-covered easy chair. A beastly spot of itch was developing in his chest. He coughed.

"You have a cold?" Martin was watching him severely.

He attempted a smile but saw that he was only being told to cover his mouth. "Yes." He projected a full-bellied cough in Martin's direction.

Audreykins appeared in the doorway, her third shoulder now an extra breast, and announced dinner. Rolf guessed it must be at least eight o'clock. He looked at his watch. *Five-thirty!* This house was hell.

Barbie had laid out a goodly spread, however. The turkey rested on a platter in front of Martin's chair, and on the white tablecloth were silver bowls and trays stocked with yams, peas and

hominy, mushroom-studded stuffing, steaming gravy, an uniden-
tifiable whitish something, and craggy mashed potatoes. A bottle
of superior Muscadet stood by. Rolf helped his wife into her chair,
taking care not to touch her, and took his place on the opposite
side. He rubbed his hands. "Goody!"

"Barbara made an oyster pudding for you," said Audreykins.

"For me?" He scowled. Audreykins's face was lost in candle
flames. Didn't she know he hated oysters? Surely she did. "There's
been some mistake," he said. "Not . . . plum pudding?" Which he
adored.

"You don't like oysters?" Barbie said, making oyster eyes.

"Oh, I don't *mind* them—"

"Rolf!" squeaked the candles. "Be polite, won't you. She made
it especially for you."

"Do help yourself," Barbie purred. "Take a lot."

While Martin concentrated on not severing a finger with the
carving knife, Rolf dutifully spaded up a helping of pudding and
dumped it on his plate. It would be sandy. Oysters were always
sandy.

The other bowls made the rounds, and Martin loaded each
plate with sawtoothed slices. Rolf found himself face to face with
several pounds of tradition. He coughed on it, his private blessing.
Politely, then, for Barbie, he sank his fork into the pudding and
took a bite.

Ish.

A fat oyster, and a sandy one at that.

No one else was eating. He looked up. Audreykins cleared her
throat. Dear Lord! She was going to say grace.

"Maybe we should all hold hands," she said.

He could sooner say grace than swallow this oyster. He reached
for his napkin, but they were waiting for him to join them in the
daft rite of holding hands. He extended his arms and winced as his
left hand met Martin's right, which was dangerously taut. But
Barbie's hand was small and muscley and warm.

"Dear God," Audreykins quavered. "Bless this food that we
are about to receive . . ."

He worked his fingers down between Barbara's to the sweaty
webs of skin, and tightened his grip.

"We give thanks for another harvest. For the goodness of your bounty, and the gifts around us, the blessings of family and home . . ."

She squeezed back, driving her diamond into his skin and bone. What a gem she was. He refused to loosen his grip. She loosened hers.

"Also, we remember the Pilgrims, and the first Thanksgiving, and Miles Standish, and the Indians, your loving help in times of need . . ."

This was a jolly third-grader's grace. He gave the oyster another chew, his teeth grating. He stroked Barbara's palm with his thumb. She snatched her hand away.

". . . with Mom and Dad in New Zealand, and with Luisa, and with Bill and Ellen, and in New York, in New York . . ." Inevitably, she was blubbering. "And so we pray."

His fingers crept around the gravy boat in search of Barbara's. Then, sharply and with little warning, he coughed.

"Thy kingdom come, thy will be done . . ."

He prayed they had their eyes closed. He prayed the oyster hit the plate. Good to be rid of it in any case.

"But deliver them from evil, amen."

"Amen!" Martin barked, clapping his hands. "Rolf, why don't you do the honors with the wine?"

No one said a word while he filled the glasses. The oyster had alighted in his potatoes. Audreykins sniffled and held a silent dialogue with God, who seemed to be located in her napkin. This was becoming a memorably wretched evening. Without the brat around, things got rather more hostile. "Shame Luisa couldn't be here," he said. "Delectable vino, by the way. I shouldn't have minded meeting this beau of hers."

"Stop talking like that," the candles whispered.

Barbara gave him a ghoulish non-smile. "She said she's sorry she missed seeing you."

"Did she now? Tebbly sweet of her." He flayed his slice of breast and spread the skin ornamentally over the pudding. "Young love, what?"

"Yep," Martin said. "You have enough gravy there?"

"Oodles, thanks."

Having seen to the derailment of further conversation, he turned to his dinner, filling his stomach while Martin filled the minutes with one of his fatuous technical monologues. For a topic this evening he'd chosen the obscenity known as Westhaven. Rolf repeatedly thrust his knife at him in agreement. *Yes*, it was a fabulous amount of floor space. *Yes*, it represented quite an investment on the part of the suburban banks. *Yes*, it would singlehandedly alter the economic structure of the area. *Yes*, it would be a hundred years before blight extended that far. *Yes, yes, yes*—Martin clearly had no inkling of the plans of the Hammaker coterie. It still seemed to him that the westward development of the county would have no end. Uncle Rolf, having been apprised of the impending about-face of county property values, had staked out his twelve blocks in North Saint Louis while the staking was good, and was savoring this ass's lecture on the region's economic future. As soon as Barbara moved to clear the table, however, his romantic urges surfaced. "Mind if I use your phone, Martin?"

"Sure, go right ahead." Martin nodded at the kitchen.

"Your study phone. I need to ring up my commodities man."

"On Thanksgiving?"

"Markets are open tomorrow."

"You never slow down, do you? The light's at the top of the stairs."

The study was lined with more books than Martin Probst could read in five lifetimes. There were big-bottomed chairs, a green and gold broadloom, a photo of a younger Barbara in a chrome-plated frame on the desk. The cold upstairs air sobered Rolf. Swiveling in Martin's chair, rehearsing his call, he thumbed through the papers stacked on the desk and on the floor along the bookcase. Westhaven, Westhaven, Westhaven. He picked up the phone and dialed. While it rang, he turned the key stuck in the bottom drawer and pulled the drawer open.

There were letters. He riffled them. At the back, he found three small bundles tied with gray ribbons. Love letters?

He was disappointed to recognize Barbara's handwriting, disappointed the letters hadn't come from someone else. But he selected one of the thicker missives from the middle of the pack and tucked it in his breast pocket. It might come in handy.

Devi's phone continued to ring. Where on earth could she be? He shut the drawer and dug through the papers on top of the desk. He found a stack of pages from the *Post*, a good dozen of them, with the brat's face on every one. What kind of clown would keep so many copies? Her nose was her mother's nose. He coughed unhappily.

Devi answered on about the twentieth ring.

She said she'd been in the bathroom. For twenty rings? She said she might be getting the flu. Rolf frowned. But she was already feeling better, she said, just hearing his voice, and perhaps he could drop by? Rolf assured her this would be most agreeable to him. He might even bring her a few small tokens of—

She made a kissy noise and rang off. She was obviously in a mood.

Pausing at the top of the stairs before descending, Rolf noticed a soft glow in the master bedroom and wondered if the brat might be hiding out here after all. Stealthily, he backtracked. The bedroom was empty. A lamp was burning above Barbara's vanity.

From down in the dining room he heard a gentle murmur, like the happiness of water in a fountain. He heard Audrey's voice distinctly. The murmur was repeated. They were laughing.

From the vanity he picked up one of Barbara's combs but set it down again, afraid he might weep if he smelled it. He touched her perfume bottles one by one. He noted the differing levels of the liquids in them, the witness borne to a continuum of purchases and applications, to a selection and alteration of scent unique to this woman, unique in all the world. At the back of the vanity, among bottles of lotion and jars of cream, stood a triptych of recent photos of the brat. Rolf shivered and stared, and Luisa stared back at him, fair-haired and frank, like a girl from the reserved stocks, the girl one couldn't touch. Larger than life, like the kiwi in the living room below him.

But this was silly. With a more vigorous shiver he shook off the spell and opened the bottom drawer of the vanity. It offered him a large assortment of lingerie. He selected a pair of black panties and pressed them to his face, inhaling. Would they fit Devi? Most definitely they would.

7

Monday night, the holiday over. Jammu switched on her flashers when she gained the inner lane of Highway 40. Guardrail posts lurched in the bursts of blue light. She cruised at eighty.

Her day had begun with a call from Nelson A. Nelson, the Police Board president. Nelson had just learned that since September she'd recruited 190 blacks for the force and only 35 whites. "Yes . . . ?" she said. Nelson muttered for several seconds before choking out the question: "Don't you think there's an inequality there?" Oh yes, she said. Thirty-five was too many. Whites had accounted for barely ten percent of the applications. "And why," Nelson wanted to know, "are so few whites applying?" Jammu promised a thorough inquiry. Calls from the rest of the Board followed. Even her supporters were angry, though in August they'd unanimously backed her proposal for the manpower increase. Now that she'd delivered, they treated her like a dumb broad, a naughty girl. It took a real effort to remain disingenuous. A meeting was scheduled for Wednesday.

In the afternoon the Office of Budget and Finance raised its ink-stained veils to reveal, unblushingly, a $2.4 million "oversight." The Board had transferred jurisdiction over the office to Jammu in late August. Now she saw she'd made a tactical error in assuming responsibility for finances before she'd sufficiently consolidated her control over operations. The accounting officer, Chip Osmond, one of Rick Jergensen's cronies, had grown reckless in the power vacuum. Rick Jergensen had been hoping to be named chief in July; the "oversight" had overtones of spite. The city comptroller showed up in a blaze of snideness, with budget director Randy Fitch hot on his heels. Osmond wheeled all his books into her office on a cart, and the four of them wrangled and reassessed through the dinner hour and into the evening. Finally Jammu lost her patience and stated, flatly, that the mayor would have to add the $2.4 million to her budget.

The comptroller said, "So much for your good news."

Osmond called home to his wife.

Randy Fitch giggled.

The comptroller said the mayor wouldn't do it. Jammu knew the mayor would.

Randy Fitch continued to giggle.

The men were closing their briefcases when Singh strolled into the office. "Who are you?" the comptroller asked. "The janitor," Singh replied, lighting up one of his clove things. Jammu rebuked him as soon as they were alone. His response: "Your administration lacks arrogance."

Reaching Kingshighway, she exited past Barnes Hospital. An ambulance streaked by her silently. She radioed the dispatcher. "Car One," she said. "I'm at home for the night."

"Roger, Car One."

She parked Car One in a loading zone and turned up her jacket collar. The sky was an orange urban overcast, the air metallic on her tongue. In the alley behind her apartment two gay waiters from Balaban were screaming at each other.

Inside, she sorted her mail and played her answering machine. Only Gopal had called. He spoke in Marathi confused with English code terms. He said he'd seen a trailer full of apples in a vacant lot near Soulard Market. Would the police please watch out? *Apples* meant cordite.

From the two-door refrigerator Jammu took a bottle of vodka and the drumstick left over from Thanksgiving dinner with the mayor. A loose pane in one of the bedroom windows buzzed to the beat of a television commercial upstairs. She kicked off her shoes, stretched out on the bed, and ripped open the Federal Express envelope from Burrelle's, a clipping service in New Jersey. The envelope contained a half-inch pile of clippings, an increase over last week. Fortified with a swallow of vodka, she riffled through them.

ST. LOUIS TO HOST MODEL RRERS CONVENTION
SW Bell Dividends Down
Snow Bunnies, a Musical, to Premiere in Midwest
Dip in SW Bell Dividends
Bottlers Reject Contract Offer
St. Louis Museum to Acquire Two by Degas
Changing Times at Ripleycorp
RIPLYCORP TO DIVERSIFY
Parker Will Head Cheese Commission

She unfolded a long *New York Times* article by Erik Tannenberg, who'd taken her to lunch at Anthony's ten days ago.

On the same day, Mr. Hutchinson's home in suburban Ladue was strafed by automatic fire from a circling helicopter. Two days later, KSLX's primary transmitting tower was put out of service for five hours by a third attack, this one involving hand grenades . . .

In the tense atmosphere, attention has focused on St. Louis's new police chief, S. Jammu, who in mid-July left her post as Commissioner of Police in Bombay, India, to head the St. Louis force.

Colonel Jammu, a 35-year-old woman who has maintained her U.S. citizenship, attracted widespread interest in 1975 as the architect of Bombay's "experiment in free enterprise," a police-run assault on private-sector corruption.

Initially many civic leaders here expressed skepticism that Colonel Jammu, as a woman and as one unfamiliar with American law-enforcement practices, could adapt to her new role. But with a canniness that has all but silenced such critics, she has set about reinvigorating the police department and transforming the office of chief into a political platform.

High Visibility

Colonel Jammu, who holds a master's degree in economics from Chicago University, has made high personal visibility her trademark. She has appeared regularly throughout the city and spoken on topics as diverse as family planning and handgun legislation.

In mid-September patrolmen on their beat began sporting sky-blue buttons on their caps, a reference to the "St. Louis Blues," the force's nickname, inspired by the popular television show *Hill Street Blues*. The nickname also appeared on bumper stickers donated by local businessmen and applied to squad cars . . .

Even before the attacks began, Colonel Jammu asked for and received authority to bolster the force's manpower by 30 percent. Civic leaders were astounded by the size of the projected increase, but it now appears that Colonel Jammu, for the moment at least, has won her point.

Figures for the third quarter of the year show the city's arrest rate jumping by 24 percent overall, and 38 percent for violent crimes.

The courts and prosecutor's office have promised to cooperate, pledging to streamline the justice system and to "substantially reduce" the waiting period between arrest and trial by year's end.

This has caused the American Civil Liberties Union to file a class-action suit with the Eighth U.S. Court of Appeals seeking an injunction that would freeze the average waiting period at its present rate until such time as the prosecutor can demonstrate that the right to due process is not being violated.

"We're Scared"

Charles Grady, spokesman for the local chapter of the ACLU, said that "the civil rights establishment in St. Louis is absolutely unable to cope with all that's happened since Jammu took over as police chief. We're swamped. We're scared."

Addressing a gathering of Washington Univer-

sity students last week, Mr. Grady renewed his
call for Jammu's dismissal, stressing the importance of "Indian justice for Indians, American
justice for Americans."

She stopped reading. She threw the half-eaten drumstick into her
wastebasket and drank more vodka. Two weeks ago these clippings
had still amused her and edified her; now they made her sick to
her stomach. Reporters knew too much. There were treacherous
undercurrents of knowledge in Tannenberg's tone, in the casualness
with which he'd tossed off words like "visibility" and "canniness."
Tannenberg knew her type. In New York she wouldn't be original.
The superficiality of his treatment held both her and St. Louis at
arm's length, allowing the possibility that she might dupe these
Midwesterners—it takes all kinds of cities to make a nation—while
assuring readers in New York that everything was fine, that the
nation as a whole was regulated—

A car was idling in the street. A car door had slammed. Jammu
went to the living room and depressed a slat in the blinds. Snow
was falling, seeming to climb as it fell through the streetlight and
through the headlight beams of a taxi. The taxi's wipers smeared
the melting snow. Her doorbell rang.

Lakshmi? Devi? Kamala?

She opened the door, and Devi Madan stepped in. Her hair
was tucked under the collar of a full-length red fox coat. "I have a
cab waiting," she said.

"You can send it on. The neighborhood is full of them."

"No."

"Go get rid of it."

Devi slammed the door behind her. Jammu put away the
vodka, shaking her head, and turned the gas on under the tea kettle.
Devi Madan had made one fundamental mistake in her life, when
without her parents' knowledge she'd answered an advertisement
in *The Bombayite* ("The Fun One").

GIRLS!
Are you *pretty*? Are you liberated-responsible?
Earn real good money modeling handsome USA/
Japan/France fashion for fully referenced concern.

Devi was rattling the doorknob. Jammu crossed the kitchen and let her in. "I'll take your coat," she said.

Devi hunched her shoulders. "No." She tried to shake back her hair, but it didn't move; the collar held it close against her head. Her gloved hands trembled and sought relief in touching her face, her very exquisite face, and found none.

"How are you?" Jammu said.

Devi dropped onto the sofa and dug her wet heels into the cushions. She peeled off her gloves and balled them into wads. "You know."

"You're very early." She got no answer. "Wait here."

The safe was under the counter in the kitchen. Her spare safe and the uncut heroin she'd brought from Bombay were buried in Illinois. What was here was cut to 6 percent. She punched in the lock combination, released the latch, and rolled out the drawer. The gas elements were visible through the mesh the drugs and passports rested on, ready to burn if the safe was tampered with. Sick of Devi's frequent visits, Jammu did not bother measuring out the usual amount but returned with a 50-gram bag.

The living room was chokingly perfumed. Devi snatched the bag from her fingers and locked herself in the bathroom.

While the teapot warmed, Jammu parted the curtains on the tiny kitchen window and raised the shade. Snow had collected on the outer sill. In the alley, glass clattered. A Balaban employee had dropped some bottles in a dumpster. Standing on tiptoe, he reached in after them. His shoulder jerked. Something smashed, tinkled, smashed. He was breaking the bottles on each other.

Devi came out of the bathroom with her coat over her arm and her purse in her hands. "I want to stay here tonight," she said.

Jammu sat down on the sofa and poured tea. "I get up at five-thirty."

"I can sleep on the divan. Do you have a cigarette?"

Jammu nodded at the kitchen. "On top of the refrigerator."

"Do you want one?"

"No."

Devi's youth was showing. She was twenty-two. In Bombay Jammu had been thrifty with her labor force, mothering her girls instead of just using them until they wore out. She'd regulated

Devi's habits, handled her money, given her an allowance, and paid for monthly medical checkups. Now, in St. Louis, she was trying to wean her.

Devi returned French-inhaling and swinging her hips. "These are stale."

Jammu laughed. "Where are yours?"

"I quit yesterday. I'm a Sagittarius." She flicked her ash into the rug. "What are you?"

"Leo, I suppose."

"What's your birthday?"

"August nineteenth."

"You're almost a cusp. Mine's next week. Tuesday." She saw the tea and made a face. "Do you have anything else?"

Jammu nodded again at the kitchen and gloomily regarded the cup and saucer on her lap. She wanted to be asleep. In the kitchen a beer bottle gasped. Devi came back with an Amstel Light and a cigarette in one hand, a jar of olives in the other. She drank from the bottle and Jammu winced at how close to her eye she brought the coal.

"This is ninety-five calories, but it's all carbohydrate. I was under a thousand until this." She tried to remove a boot using her other foot, stumbled for balance, and finally got it off by wedging the heel against a sofa leg. She smiled and blinked at Jammu. "I'd rather have thirty olives than a martini. It's the same amount of calories. I found out the other day how they tell how many calories food has? It's called a calorimeter. Rolf's company makes them."

She paused. Don't answer, Jammu told herself.

"They *burn* food. They burn it and they see how much extra heat it gives off." Devi propped her beer dangerously on the seat of the rocking chair and yanked off the other boot. "So I said, How do they *burn milk*? I thought I had him. He said they heat it until it boils and then they boil it until it burns. I had a picture of scientists in white coats standing around watching milk burn, and I don't know what came over me, I started laughing, and then he spanked me." She frowned at the smoked-out butt in her hand.

"Tell him to cut it out."

Through a smile, Devi mouthed a sentence.

"What?"

"I'm going to shoot his wife."

Jammu closed her eyes.

"I'm only joking."

"It isn't funny."

"I said I was only joking."

She heard Devi open the refrigerator. She looked and saw her digging in the yogurt carton with a spoon. "Right between the eyes, Audreykins!"

"Don't eat that," Jammu said.

Startled, Devi turned, her eyes wide. "Why not?"

"Because I said."

Devi stood frozen with indecision, the loaded spoon poised above the carton. Jammu set down her tea. She shut the refrigerator door, took the spoon from Devi and tapped the glistening yogurt back into the carton. "Listen," she said. "You're probably exhausted. I'm going to call you a cab, and you can go back and get lots of sleep, and I'll tell you what. We'll see if you can fly home to Bombay for your birthday."

Devi's head shook no. "He's my only friend," she said.

"He's a rotten spoiled bastard."

The slap caught Jammu off guard. She spun into the sink, and the pain sprang like an answering hand from within her cheek. She looked back with lidded eyes.

Devi had sunk to her knees. "He's in love with Barbie."

There was something wrong here. Normally Devi was a lamb after a fix. "Did you just shoot up or didn't you?"

"Please let me stay here."

"No." Jammu pulled her to her feet by the hair. A single tear had rolled a black track down her cheek. Jammu called a cab and then wiped the mascara away with a dishcloth.

Devi frowned. "What time is it?"

"Put your boots on." Jammu followed her into the living room. "You said Rolf was in love with—another woman?"

Devi nodded, pulling on her boots with underwater indolence. "Barbie."

"Barbie who?"

"You know. The sister."

Jammu felt sicker than ever to her stomach. It took a conscious effort not to run to the refrigerator and grab the vodka. "Barbara Probst?"

"We played Martin and Barbie." Devi had unzipped her corduroys and was plucking on the black fabric of her underpants. "See we—"

"Zip up your pants," Jammu said.

A car honked in the street. Devi allowed her coat to be pulled onto her. Jammu placed her purse in her hands. "Don't lose this."

Devi shook her head obediently.

"You'll be all right."

.

It was the subcontractor's fault. The concrete was like gluey oatmeal. It was the subcontractor's fault. Probst was running across the freshly poured foundation at Westhaven. He was following a trail of footprints, trying to catch the man who'd made them. (Was it the subcontractor?) A skin of rainwater covered the concrete, mirroring the blue sky, but the sky wasn't blue; it was the color of concrete. A purple bird flew across it, heckling and jeckling in its spiny tongue. Probst ran on and came to the crest of a concrete hill overlooking a concrete valley. The footprints, gouged into the slope, led to a figure far down in the basin. It was Jack DuChamp. The purple bird circled in the slaggy sky. Martin! The cry came from Jack, but it sounded like a bird. The footprints tugged Probst downwards. As he approached he saw that Jack had sunk into the concrete up to his waist, and that his eyes were crusted over with blood. They were cracked, swollen sockets. The eyeballs had been pecked out. Probst stopped, and Jack said, "Martin?" in a voice ragged with fear. Probst couldn't speak. He grasped Jack under the shoulders to lift him up, but when he raised him he saw that Jack had no legs. Probst set him down again and Jack whimpered: Am I going to die? Probst couldn't speak. He laid his hands on Jack's forehead and inadvertently brushed the crusted eyes. They were soft. They felt like breasts, and Probst began to stroke them. Nipples came to life beneath his palms.

"You can't park here, man. Nobody parks without a sticker."

He was trying to park in the KSLX parking lot downtown. For fifteen years he'd exercised weekend parking privileges here.

Jim Hutchinson had encouraged him to. The lot was generally empty, and if the attendant ever asked who he was he only had to mention Hutch's name and he could park. He set the brake. "Do you think I have a bomb in my trunk?"

"You said it, not me." The attendant had a pimply shady face, the face of a small-time counterfeiter or smut dealer. He picked his nose and molded the pickings.

"What seems to be the problem here?" A black policeman had appeared.

"Bozo thinks he can park here," the attendant said.

"Now *look*—" Probst began.

"Oh he does, does he?"

"He's making 'jokes' about bombs."

"He is, is he?" The officer brushed the attendant aside and bent down so close that Probst could smell his coffee breath. "Who are you?"

"Martin Probst, I'm a good friend of Mr. Hutch—"

"Afton Taylor, first precinct," the officer drawled, his mouth moisture clicking. "I'm very pleased to make your acquaintance, Mr. Boabst, now if you could just move your car out of this lot . . . Parking's restricted by order of the police chief, I'm sure you're aware of the circumstances."

Probst closed his eyes.

"There's plenty of public parking, Mr. Boabst. Plenty indeed. Where do you think the rest of the world parks?" Officer Taylor stepped back and motioned with his nightstick towards the street. The attendant waved a sissy good-bye with his fingers. Neither had recognized Probst, not even his name.

He'd gotten a late start this morning. He'd waited forever in line at Mr. Gas in Webster (the line at the other pumps had moved right along) after tarrying too long at home. Barbara had affected puzzlement. "You're going with Jack DuChamp?"

"Yes."

She grimaced. "Jack DuChamp?"

"Yes. I'm actually thinking it's going to be pleasant."

"It's fine with me," she said. "But I thought he'd fallen by the wayside."

"Well." He never knew what to say when she discouraged a

generous sentiment of his. "We'll see." He didn't mention the dream to her. If he had, she probably would have drawn the same conclusion he himself had reached, namely, that he felt guilty about Jack. He did feel guilty. And yet it was the memory of the breasts that lingered.

On Market Street he took a parking space in front of a hydrant, figuring he could pay the ticket. They wouldn't tow him on a Sunday.

The sky spat a few drops of rain as he approached the stadium. Jack was standing in his wool coat and beige muffler by the statue of the Baseball Star, as agreed. He was rocking on his heels, beaming amiably at the indifferent world. When he caught sight of Probst his expression didn't change in the slightest.

"I'm sorry I'm late," Probst said.

"Nooooooo problem. No problem, no problem." Jack chuckled in his salesman's baritone. "You think they'd start without us?" He handed Probst a ticket and then followed him to the gates, a quarter step behind him. The arm of a turnstile pushed across Probst's groin. "All the way up," Jack said.

Though high, the seats weren't bad. Behind them, the wind cut through the rim of the stadium, through ornamental arches modeled after the primary Arch, the top of which was looming across the field from them, dark gray and proximate. With its legs obscured, it seemed to be standing not six blocks away but on the plaza right outside the stadium, creeping up and looking down on the bluish Astroturf, where the Cardinals and Redskins were locked in combat. "Missed the kickoff," Jack said. "Second down."

Probst crossed his arms and leaned forward. The Big Red had the ball on their own 17. An auspicious beginning. The Redskins in their crimson pants and white jerseys kicked at the turf with casual confidence. They'd already clinched the Eastern Division title, whereas the Big Red—"Give it to Ottis for a change, why don't you," Jack muttered—the Big Red, for the second year running, were stalwartly defending fourth place.

"*Bumber Brarkty-Bee, Bardkdy Brarkerbark, bicking for the Brarkinals,*" the loudspeakers boomed. Acoustically these seats were inferior.

"Way to go," Jack said savagely. "Gimme a *break?*" He shook his head as the Cardinal punter lofted a good kick that bounced out of bounds at the Redskin 40. Then he turned to Probst, waited for their eyes to meet, and smiled. "How's Barbara? She come down here with you?"

The fiction was that Probst had been unable to ride down with Jack because he was going out with Barbara after the game. He was prepared for the question. "No," he said. "She decided not to. I'm going to meet her in Clayton. She—"

"What's she up to these days?"

Barbara wasn't the kind of person who was "up to" things.

"She gets around," Probst said. "How's—"

"She's doing great," Jack said. "Just great. I tell you she went back and finished her degree at St. Louis U.?"

"Really." (Elaine, of course. Elaine.)

"She liked it so much she kept right on going. She's going to get her master's in June."

"Kerking na tackle, Bumber Berky, Bork McRukkuk . . ."

"Economics. The good Lord only knows what she'll do with it. Remember we had an agreement she could go back to school soon as the kids were in high school? I'd honestly forgotten all about it, but she really got into it. She was doing homework? I've even ironed a few shirts since she started. It's done us a lot of good, a hell of a lot of good, Martin. Women these days, they really need that extra, that extra . . . that extra, I don't know, ego boost, now *that's* a play I'd like to see 'em run more often." The crowd roared significantly for the first time. "You see the right linebacker move up?"

Probst made a circular yes-no with his head.

Jack covered his square chin with his hand and studied the field. The score? Zero–zero. Probst stole a series of glances at Jack, whose next question had begun to gather like a squall, his eyes darting, shoulders rolling, fingers knotting, until it broke: "Luisa must be starting college soon."

"Forkty-rork, Dwight Eigenrarkman . . ."

"She's applying." Probst hoped he wouldn't have to mention where.

"It'd be great to see her all grown up. You know the last time I saw her she couldn't have been more than four or five. It's like yesterday, isn't it? I remember you used to take her on walks, and the time I asked her if she liked walking with her daddy? Remember what she said? 'He's too slow.' In that kind of voice. I'll never forget that. 'He's too slow.' " Jack slapped Probst's knee. "But now she's got her own share of admirers, huh?" Jack smiled at the playing field. "Yes sir." His face went serious. "She have a boyfriend?"

"She . . ."

"Ten of 'em! Ain't that the truth. And a different one every week. She'll— John-son! What in tarnation is he doing? The entire play's going *left*, what's he *doing*?"

Probst took off his coat and folded it across his lap, baring his shoulders to the wind. "Well yes," he said. To his right a quiet man and woman, both sixtyish, were carefully pouring coffee from a thermos into styrofoam cups, the woman peering down as if the cups held something more precious than coffee, her eyes brimming with a sweet purity of concern. It had been a long time since Probst saw such a pretty older woman.

Penalty flags were flying, whistles blowing. The crowd rumbled with disappointment.

"*Ladies engentlemork, the palark deparkbark has issued—*"

Silence fell in the stands.

"Laurie's been going steady with the same—"

Probst clutched Jack's arm. "Shh!"

"*. . . the stadium officials. Thurkiss nork—*"

"She's been going with—"

"Shhh!"

The stadium was holding its breath, the players in disarray, the field a jostled chessboard.

"What is it?" Jack whispered.

"*Securicle. Woorpeat. Do. Not. Panicprosurdlenerst gate.*"

It was the end. Still as death, Probst felt his body detach from his soul and billow into the sky, leaving the soul a cold lump in the pink plastic seat to await the firestorm he knew from long anticipation. Behind him a woman moaned. The stadium began to buzz. Murmurs. Voices tightening and rising. Sirens chirruped in the streets, echo on echo on echo. People were standing up. "Come on," Jack said.

Flight was pointless. Nowhere to run.

"Come *on*." Jack pulled him to his feet.

"It's a hoax," a man growled. "Just a goddamn hoax."

Probst turned to Jack. "What is it?"

"Bomb threat." He nodded down the aisle. "Let's go."

Bomb threat? Probst shut his mouth, embarrassed. He'd thought it was something worse.

"Ladies engenitoll, we rorpeat to thar palark deparkspark information concernk appossiblomp athorken reorgort the disrupture today's game between a Warninghorn Rorskins and your St. Louis Brarkinals . . . Please prosurdle the nearest hexit floor the structionork the stadium officials."

The official clock showed 7:12 remaining in the first quarter, 7:11, 7:10, 7:09. They'd neglected to stop it. On the main scoreboard a message was flashing on and off:

STAY CALM. DON'T PANIC.

A THREAT HAS BEEN COMMUNICATED.

THERE IS PLENTY OF TIME.

Fans in the aisles above and below Probst were laughing. Several imitated the explosive action of a bomb with their arms and added phlegmy sound effects.

6:54, 6:53, 6:52 . . .

If the bomb was set to go off at a specific time in the game? Silly.

On the field a few Redskins tossed footballs, made diving catches, pointed at disturbances in the stands. Whole sections had grown pink, the color of the seats, as the fans drained into the exits. The Cardinals themselves were long gone.

Through a gate behind the Visitors' end zone blue squad cars were pouring onto the field—six, eight, ten, a dozen of them, silent but flashing. Foot patrolmen brought up the rear. A halt was put to the game of catch. The Redskins trotted to the sidelines, lateraling the balls back and forth.

6:25, 6:24, 6:23 . . .

His attention on the clock, Probst walked right into the woman who'd been sitting next to him. "Excuse me," he said.

She turned. "That's all right." Her teeth were perfect, pearly, tiny. Her eyes dipped demurely. "Trudy Churchill," she said.

"Come on, come on, come on," Jack said in his ear.

Probst looked into the twinkling eyes. "Martin Probst."

Mrs. Churchill continued to smile. "I know."

He took her arm in his fingers, finding her muscles to be firm. "The line is moving," he said.

"Oh!" She glanced over her shoulder.

Something blew.

It was a sharp boom. She was in his arms, her face in his sweater. He felt the explosion in his chest cavity. His organs rattled. A flash had lit the arches in the rim of the stadium. There were crashes, distant thuds and screams. Black smoke rose in a pillar from a point outside the stadium.

"Move it, goddamn it!" a man squealed.

Awkwardly Probst stroked Mrs. Churchill's hair, his eyes on her husband, who turned, just then, and gave him a vacant look.

"Move *it*." The squeal was despairing.

There was no place to go. A sharp chin, Jack's, cracked into the back of Probst's head. He held Mrs. Churchill tight.

"Fifty thousand friggin people," Jack said, his gimme-a-break voice at Probst's ear. "And we're gonna be the last ones out."

Three helicopters descended on the stadium, darting and halting like dragonflies, the blades blurred against the low cloudbanks.

"Shit, oh, SHIT!"

People above Probst were screaming. He turned, loosening his grip on Mrs. Churchill—

5:40.

"My neck—"

A wave of bodies swept down from above him, a mass loss of balance, engulfing him and the woman he held and Jack and everyone else, and—

Uhhh—

They tumbled headlong into the seats further down. A fat leg wrapped itself crushingly around Probst's neck. His eyes bugged, and the pink plastic seats approached him swiftly, driving into his rib cage. His left pinkie got caught on an armrest. It snapped back and broke. Bodies huffed, groaned, puffed. The fat man, kicking wildly, vaulted over into the next row of seats. Through tears Probst could see the open sky above him, wisps of angry smoke and birds.

Jack was sitting upright in a seat, drawing deep breaths. Not many people had landed in this aisle. Mrs. Churchill lay next to

Probst on the Coke-spattered concrete. He started to sit up but pain in his hand forced him down. He leaned over Mrs. Churchill. Blood was gathering in a raw spot on her jaw. He put his finger on the spot. "Anything broken?" he said.

"Yes." Her voice cracked. "I think my leg."

He looked at the trim leg in plaid slacks. It lay at an unnatural angle to her hips, her ankle pinned by the seat Jack was sitting on. Behind her, the husband struggled to his feet and patted himself down with age-spotted hands.

3:47, 3:46, 3:45 . . .

The heads of other dazed fans popped up all around. The thickest clot of bodies was three rows up, where a pair of policemen waded among the scraped and bruised limbs, helping people to their feet and waving them towards the exit. The press at the exit had diminished.

"Those who can," one of the policemen shouted, "keep moving towards the gates. Keep right on moving. Please. We can take care of any injuries, so just keep right on moving."

"Shall we?" Jack said.

"This woman is hurt." Probst spread his coat over her. The husband was wiping the blood off her jaw with a napkin. "Trudy," he said. "Can you walk?"

She managed to shake her head. The husband, pale, his white hair pointing every which way, looked up at Probst and Jack. "Let's let her rest for a second. I'm going to need help." He began to work her foot free from the seat.

Overhead a helicopter approached. Probst was surprised to see the logo of KAKA-TV, KSLX's chief rival, on the side of the machine. He'd assumed it was the police. A video lens poked from the left portal.

Jack shouted something. He was pointing at the main scoreboard.

ATTENTION GENOCIDAL PIGS
GOD IS THE BIG RED
WE OW! ARE REDSKINS
WE FREE THE LAND FROM
IMPERIALIST NAZI U.S.
DEATH TO PLACENT GENTIALS

The police on the field had seen it, too. A cluster of men in blue were looking up at the scoreboard, and several ran to their cars. More than twenty cars now occupied the field, half of them circling the perimeter. Most of the stadium was pink.

2:36 . . . 2:36. The clock had stopped.

Probst stared at the glowing time. His address. 236 Sherwood.

"Let's try and move her," Mr. Churchill shouted.

Probst tried to flex his injured finger. He couldn't. Jack and Mr. Churchill slipped their arms under Mrs. Churchill's shoulders and raised her into position for a fireman's carry. She didn't make a sound. Probst's coat hung precariously from her waist. He felt useless, but his finger was killing him.

In the cavernous concession area there were radio speakers. They'd been installed to let fans buying refreshments hear KSLX's play-by-play, but Jack Strom was speaking from the studios now. His tones were low and earnest. ". . . Eighty, ninety percent of the fans have left the stadium, although there are still a good many in the immediate vicinity. The surrounding streets, particularly Broadway and Walnut, are solid masses of humanity, as the police have directed people to simply keep moving as far as possible from the threatened area. Traffic has been blocked off entirely, except on Spruce Street, which the police and fire departments are using for access to the stadium. For those of you who just joined us, there has been a bomb threat directed against the football stadium in downtown St. Louis, where a game was in progress. A small explosion has already occurred on the plaza outside the stadium. The police appear, uh, were apparently warned in advance about that blast, which was felt throughout the downtown area, and there were no serious injuries. Let me repeat that elsewhere as well there have been no serious injuries reported thus far, and the evacuation of the stadium should be complete within the next five to ten minutes. We—one moment . . . We've received confirmation that it is indeed the group known as the Osage Warriors that is responsible for the situation— We're going to switch over now to Don Daizy, who is outside the command post at police headquarters. Don?"

"Jack, it appears the situation *is* under control. I spoke moments ago with Chief Jammu, who is *at* the command post here, the explosive charges beneath the stadium *have* been located, and it *appears* that we're looking at enough explosives to do what was threatened, namely, to kill all of the fans—at—the *game*. Now, it's by no means certain the charges are in fact authentic, the Bomb and Arson Squad is at work *defusing* the charges, but the estimate I got from Chief *Jammu* is—that—the threat is *real*. There *have* been several serious disturbances in the stands, as the fans move *towards* the exits, but as you say, the police force *has* kept Spruce Street relatively clear, so it appears that ambulances *are* reaching the stadium in sufficient numbers to deal—with—the *problem*. The police were able *to* mobilize very quickly, they've done an *excellent* job so far, the evacuation has proceeded as well as could be *expected*, and . . ."

In the hot breath of the mob Probst felt his knees give way. He grabbed for the pipes beneath a drinking fountain and hit the ground, unconscious of everything but a deep unhappiness.

INFORMATION

Words crowd together single file, individuals passing singly through a single gate. The pressure is constant, the flight interminable. There is plenty of time. Born in motion, borne by syntax, stranger marrying stranger, they stream into the void . . .

Probst came to. The throng in front of him was thinning, the fans on their toes in their hurry, their fingertips resting on the shoulders of the fans ahead of them. He looked up at the rusty porcelain underside of the drinking fountain. Mineral cysts had formed at the pipe joints.

Sitting up he saw a glowing word revealed, eclipsed, and revealed again by the heads in the crowd. The word was INFORMATION. There was an information office across the hall.

"We are going to break for the two o'clock network news, we'll be back immediately following with the latest on the situation at the stadium, I'm Jack Strom, Information Radio, KSLX, St. Louis, it's—two o'clock."

"Here! You son of a gun." Jack raised a leg for balance and took a drink of water.

"I guess I passed out," Probst said, wiping a drop of water off his forehead.

"Jesus, Martin, that's a nasty gash."

Jack was looking at the back of Probst's neck. Probst reached and felt under his collar. His hand came away dripping. Now he could feel the blood pooling at the waist of his pants, but he couldn't feel the wound. "Where're the Churchills?"

"I got 'em on an elevator. But let me take a look at you. Why didn't you say something?"

Probst let him probe the back of his neck. "Yi!" Jack said. "Tsk." Probst still couldn't feel anything. His finger was throbbing, twitching. Jack's shoes gritted on the concrete. "Tsk. Oooo. Martin. Tsk.".

"What is it?"

"Tsk."

"I think we better go."

"Tsk. You have a handkerchief?"

Probst realized his handkerchief had gone the way of his coat. As had his car keys. Barbara would have to drive down with the other set. She'd have to drive down anyway. Her husband was bleeding.

Once upon a time, the land had been a hunting ground for the Cahokia people, native Americans leading lives which bore so little connection with the subsequent Caucasian experience of the eastern plains that it seemed they must have taken the very land along with them when they vanished. History lives or dies in buildings, and the Cahokians didn't build with stone. Across the river in Illinois and further down it in Missouri they did build huge earthen burial mounds, which survived to loom above the succeeding tribes like the worn peaks of a sunken Atlantis; but up here in the hills hardly a trace remained of the Cahokians, and only arrowheads marked the passage of the later Iowas and Sauks and Foxes, those Americans modern enough to be misnamed Indians.

It had taken white men to fix the land within a grid. They'd logged it over in the nineteenth century, hauling the wood five miles east to the Mississippi and floating it downstream to St. Louis, where it was chopped for steamboats or milled for houses. They had also tried to farm the land, but crops grew poorly on the rocky, uneven terrain. By the turn of the century it had fallen into the hands of creditors, who let it go to seed, as creditors will, the low land marshing over, the high ground gradually effacing the pioneer scars.

Buzz Wismer had bought up two sections in 1939 for little

more reason than his faith in real estate, which couldn't disintegrate the way his fledgling airplane business might. Ten years later, after the war had made a rich man of him once and for all, the land proved to offer security of a different sort. He had an extensive bomb shelter dug in the north face of the highest ridge here, a winter haven for the months when the prevailing winds blew from the north. His summer shelter was in the Ozarks, optimally situated to avoid fallout from both the silos and the urban centers. Unless, of course, the wind played tricks.

The land was beautiful. Secondary growth, the scrub oak and cottonwood, sycamore and sassafras, hawthorn and sumac, had crept from the safety of the ravines and vaulted, annually, ever farther into the old cornfields, converging and rising. Conifers consolidated early gains, blackberry brambles and cattails reaffirmed the swamps, the old apple orchard let down its hair, grew crazy in the sweet rot of its droppings, and no man could touch a twig of any of all of this without Buzz's permission. He'd enclosed it with an eight-foot fence topped with barbed wire and bearing strongly worded signs at the few points where it broke to let deer in and out. Within the enclosure he let the woods grow. He avoided even making paths, preferring to forge rough ones as he went, fending off thorns with his machete and his boots and gloves. Farther up, on the stonier slopes, the going was easier.

At sixteen Buzz had been a barnstorming wunderkind, touring his way out of Warren County and into the city and then cross-country from there. He'd flown the upper Midwest, Alberta, Toronto, Quebec. He'd walked wings over New England, he'd buzzed rooftops in Aurora, and with cash in his pocket and his nickname on his fuselage, he'd headed home again. At an air show in St. Charles he bailed out from six hundred feet and broke both his legs. He restructured his priorities, marrying a nurse named Nancy George and going into business. His business throve, but his Nancy, having entered his life on a flight path nearly vertical, like the VTOLs he would later build, soon took off again. She was married to an oil man now, a fellow by the name of Howard Green.

Buzz's current wife, Bev, was his third. People didn't like Bev, and although Buzz didn't either anymore, the slow revelation of the world's lack of charity had appalled him. In order to have any daytime social life at all beyond the occasional lunch with Barbara Probst, Bev was reduced to giving bridge parties for the wives of Buzz's lower-echelon engineers, wives who were honored that Wismer's wife took an interest in them. In the evenings, lacking any sort of invitations, Bev made Buzz take her to dinner at the St. Louis Club—a duty which Buzz had for many years resented and taken pains to shirk. This fall, however, evenings at the St. Louis Club had become much more agreeable, because Princess Asha Hammaker had begun to dine there regularly with her husband Sidney.

Buzz was really enthusiastic about this Indian newcomer. Jammu he could take or leave; Asha Hammaker had depth. He and Bev had shared a television with the Hammakers at the Club's election-night party. They had all shared a table at the Murphy girl's wedding reception. And finally, in the Club bar on the first Saturday in December, Buzz had had a chance to spend several minutes alone with the Princess—"Call me Asha"—while Bev freshened up and Sidney was detained by Desmond, the maître d'. With a graceful sweeping motion Asha pushed her black hair off her forehead, off her dot, and caught it in back with both hands. "I've heard a secret about you," she said, leaning closer to Buzz. "I've heard you've bought property in the city."

"Ah? Well, yes. That's true."

"So glad to hear it." She touched his wrist with two soft fingertips. "Planning to develop?"

"The property?"

"Yes."

"Oh. Maybe."

"Maybe." With a fingernail she traced a long, deliberate line down his wrist and across his palm, ending at the barrier of his wedding ring. "I'd like to discuss this with you sometime. But—" She rose abruptly from her seat. "Privately."

Buzz looked over his shoulder and saw that General Norris, whiskey in hand, cigar in mouth, was watching him. Buzz smiled, and Asha hurried off. The General ambled over and proposed a hunting trip.

All fall, with mysterious frequency, the General had been dropping into Buzz's life and standing him to drinks, talking of the agonies and ecstasies of corporate presidency, proffering cigars, and expanding endlessly on his Indian conspiracy theory. Buzz couldn't figure out why Norris was suddenly so interested in spending time with him. The General had plenty of cronies and an army of sycophants, and he always seemed to have to hold his nose around Buzz. You could hardly call them friends.

And yet here they were on Buzz's land at eleven o'clock on a Tuesday morning, preparing for a midday hunt. The two men sat on safari stools on the bungalow veranda, a hundred yards downhill from the shelter. The land was as still as a chapel on a weekday, the sky a bluish shade of white.

The General unzipped his gun case and displayed his weapon. "A big man needs a big stock," he said. He wore a red-and-black lumberjack jacket, green trousers, and gigantic swamp boots. His big thumb stroked the walnut stock. "I had this custom-made, from the barrel on up. You guess what it cost me?"

Buzz was loading the magazine of his Sako.

"Try three grand," the General said.

"That's a lot," said Buzz.

"Worth every nickel, dime, and penny of it. I show you the scope? Take a look at this field."

With an effort—the gun weighed a ton—Buzz raised the scope to his eye. It was a bright, flat field, extra wide, parallax corrected, with a crisp reticle. But a scope was a scope. "Not bad." He handed the gun back to the General.

"It fits my eye, Buzz. It fits my eye." He paused. "You got some kind of toilet out here?"

Toilet? He had thirteen hundred acres of land. "Up at the shelter."

"We'll stop there a second."

The General stepped daintily off the veranda. Buzz dropped a handful of cartridges into his jacket pocket and followed. At the shelter he opened three locks and two doors and sent Norris to the toilet, which probably hadn't been used twice in twenty years. He hoped they could kill a deer quickly so they could return to the city in time for him to eat a late lunch and work eight hours. A couple of young men from R&D had helped him write a set of programs to simulate air current tensors. He was working on weather prediction from a relativistic viewpoint, basing his model on the mutating coordinates of an individual pressure system—a new wrinkle, and it had some potential, at least in "simple" meteorological fields like the Great Plains. Around 7:00 he'd call downstairs for a Reuben sandwich, chips, pickles, and a bottle of Guinness.

Up here on the ridge the trees held their peace. Their bare crowns were studded with squirrel nests and galls and bluejays chattering at the dusty sunbeams. Today would have been perfect for just walking. Except for a short-lived inch of snow last week, there had been no precipitation since well before Thanksgiving. The land was dry. The leaves sighed and fluttered when you kicked through them, the warmth shimmering up from the red clay underneath.

Norris banged the door shut behind him and mopped his forehead and his gray-blond eyebrows with a handkerchief the size of a guest towel. "Let's go shoot us some wildlife. You got a rope?"

"Darn. I left it in the bungalow."

"We'll do without. I wanna git."

At the top of the ridge they turned and headed west at a good clip, the General striding along in visibly higher spirits and Buzz tagging after him. His machete slapped his thigh, and his high Wellingtons, not made for forced marches, bit the beginnings of blisters into his ankles. The ground was just a tawny blur. Buzz's idea of a hunt was sitting in a blind while the sun came up, drinking coffee, chatting with his son-in-law Eric and then, maybe, aiming at a deer. The General stopped. Buzz caught up with him in time to hear his question. "This Osage country?"

"Uh, not really."

The General started walking again. "I assume there was such a tribe."

"Oh yes. Yes. There were actually two tribes, and then . . . the Missouris. Who were related." Buzz drove a wedge of air into his lungs. "They were in the lower Missouri valley when the French came. The Missouris and the Little Osages, they stayed by the river. They got pretty much wiped out by smallpox, and by the Great Lakes tribes—"

"And whiskey," Norris said, staring straight ahead.

"Sure, by whiskey too. But the Big Osages, they hung on right into the twentieth century. Down in the Ozarks. Then Oklahoma. They got rich. They got rich from oil leases. Can we stop a minute?"

Norris stopped.

"At one point they were the richest Indian tribe in the world. Although maybe the new generation—"

Norris sniffed. "How do you know all this?"

"Don't you read the Post-Dispatch?"

"Savages."

"Well. They weren't all that savage."

"I haven't seen much evidence to the contrary," Norris said. "They were savages."

"Well, of course. Although that's a judgmental way of looking at it."

"Bloodthirsty, naked savages."

"They were that, yes, it's true, although—"

"There was twelve folks injured in the stadium, Buzz. Twelve serious injuries. And what do we read in the Post-Dispatch? How thankful we all should be these Warriors' bark is worse than their bite. I bet those twelve people in the hospital—"

"Thirteen, actually. Martin Probst was there—"

"Probst." The General spat and hit a sweetgum tree.

"Yeah. He got really busted up. He broke his finger and gashed open his neck. He thinks he lost about a pint of blood, and Barbara took him—"

"He have a measuring cup with him?"

"Seriously. He was right in the thick of it."

"Entertaining the ladies in the box seats."

"No, General. They had to take him to the hospital. I don't see what you have against him."

"He's a little dandified for my taste."

"I thought you were friends."

"You thought wrong."

"Aw, don't tell me you're letting that little argument at Municipal Growth stand between you two? I'm sure he's forgotten all about it. There's absolutely no—"

"A little too faggified."

"Now wait just a minute, General. Give the man a chance.

I'm on your side, don't forget, and *I* say you're taking this Indian thing too seriously. Now pardon me, but Martin Probst happens to be one of the most patriotic, generous and masculine men I know. He was at the stadium on Sunday, he was fairly badly hurt, it took twelve stitches—"

"So wait. He—*bled*?"

"That's what I just said."

"Well if he bled . . ." Norris frowned. "Maybe I've. Maybe I've. Hmmm."

Buzz owed a lot to Martin and Barbara, if only for having been kind to Bev when many of his other friends were beginning to strike her and Buzz from their dinner-party lists. He pressed on. "I don't think there's any point in spurning an ally like Martin. It doesn't make sense."

Norris fingered the muzzle of his rifle reflectively. "He bled for the cause . . ."

"If you want to put it that way."

"For the cause."

"Give him another chance, General, what do you say?"

The General set out walking, and again Buzz had to trot to keep up. The woods were growing thicker, the land sloping downhill. They'd covered half a mile. Soon the mud bank overlooking the big western meadow came in sight, and Norris hopped nimbly down the slope, planting his feet sideways. Buzz staggered after him. The dried mud, a maze of cracks, sent up dust plumes as they crossed it. The land needed rain. Buzz smelled smoke, possibly from the farmhouse just outside the northwest corner of his property. A young couple had recently bought the land and did subsistence farming. The smoke had a refreshing tang.

"Ssst!" The General beckoned urgently.

Buzz joined him on a gravelly outcropping and looked down on the meadow spread out before them. There were deer in the weeds. Four, six, eight of them. The larger of the two stags had a prizewinning set of antlers.

The General stole back up the mud bank and out of sight. Buzz watched the deer. They were leaving the meadow, bounding without hurry towards the woods on the meadow's western fringe. The larger stag hung back. If Buzz shot from a standing position he couldn't possibly hit him. But if he sat down he couldn't see. He braced himself against a maple trunk and spread his legs, shouldered the gun and followed the stag with the scope. The cross hairs wandered freely. The stag's shoulders disappeared in weeds at the edge of the meadow. Buzz unlatched the safety, stared hard, and fired.

The butt kicked him nastily. The stag, untouched, was leaping into the dense underbrush. It ducked its antlers under low branches, leaped again and lurched sideways, falling with a crash.

The shot had come from Buzz's left. A red jacket flashed farther up the slope. The General was racing down towards Buzz, who led the way.

The stag was lying on its side on a bed of oak leaves and pine needles. Blood trickled from a hole in its neck just above the shoulder blade. It wheezed. Buzz had never heard a deer breathe. It lay still, then pawed in the leaves with its horizontal front legs. Its hind legs were plainly paralyzed. The antlers tipped back and forth. Bright blood beaded on fur and glittered on the leaves. The smell of smoke, of wood smoke, hot smoke, grew stronger in Buzz's nose.

Norris was catching his breath through his teeth.

"Good shot," Buzz said.

"This baby can shoot. You wanna do the honors?"

Buzz's stomach jumped. "No. Go ahead."

Norris extended his hand like a surgeon. Buzz fumbled with the thong and placed the machete in the waiting hand. When Norris knelt Buzz shut his eyes. He heard the rip of flesh and connective tissue. He opened one eye. Blood was falling in a fat, fast, lumpy stream from the stag's opened jugular. Norris smiled. "C'mere."

Buzz shook his head.

The smile intensified. *"C'mere."*

Buzz looked blankly away. His eyes burned. The air seemed to be hazing up with smoke. He heard another long rip of flesh. The General had slit the deer's belly. He stood and put an arm around Buzz's shoulders. "Your trophy, too," he said, and led him to the carcass, and pulled him to his knees. The blood steamed, ferric, pungent. Buzz's old thighs shook and gave way. He slumped back onto his heels.

Dust speckled the deer's staring eyes.

"Feel the heart," the General said.

"What?"

"Feel it. Hotter than any Injun bitch."

Buzz watched the wave of blood sliding from the slit belly. "What are you talking about?"

"You know what I'm talking about. Feel it."

"Wait a minute."

"Feel it, Buzz." The General grabbed his wrist and thrust his hand into the animal, under the rib cage and through the ruptured peritoneum. It was hot. Buzz groped. He located the unbeating heart. It was hot and his whole body grew sick with transformation, heat barreling up through his chest into his brain, the smoke in his lungs and face, throbbing in the passages, searing skin. The animal had defecated. Everything smoked, and Buzz, unhinged by the heat, thrust his other hand in, too. IT WAS HOT.

"All right." The General was standing over him, smoking a bloody cigar. Buzz pulled away from the gore. His sleeves were crimson and sticky all the way up past the elbows. His fingers began to stiffen in the cold air. "You pass, Buzz boy," the General said. "You hang this sucker in the den, and remember this the next time she go scratching your palm."

Buzz looked up with a guilt that felt like love. He'd passed. The General, towering above him, drew heavily on the cigar and exhaled. But the smoke was invisible. The air was white. Buzz's eyes wandered.

"Oh my," he croaked.

A giant column of nimbus-gray smoke was rising in the east, from the center of his land. His land was burning.

The General turned. "Jesus."

Buzz tried to stand up, tipped back, shoved off the ground with his arms, and rose unsteadily.

The General was already running. Buzz ran after him, leaving everything behind, gun, machete, trophy. The General carried his rifle above his head like a spear. His speed was incredible for a sixty-year-old businessman. He left Buzz in the dust.

"General, wait!"

The red jacket swerved and bobbed, receding up the hill on the far side of the meadow.

"Wait!" It was pointless. Buzz stopped and coughed and retched. Big clouds tumbled across the meadow. The sun had dwindled to a hazy beige star.

Call the county fire marshal. —The closest phone?

Kids in the farmhouse. He'd seen the phone lines.

He ran for the corner of his property and fell a dozen times in two hundred yards, landing in briars. Fresh pink slashes opened on the stained skin of his hands. He reached the fence, found the deer gate, and plodded desperately down the old weeded-over road to the farm.

Faded work clothes and yellowed underwear hung on sagging lines behind the farmhouse. He rapped on the back door and looked over his shoulder. The smoke column was widening and slanting south in the gentle, seasonable wind. On a day like this a fire would spread faster than a man could walk. Buzz rapped again, tried the door, and found it unlocked. He went inside. There was a nasty smell in the kitchen that seemed to come from the sink, where the remains of a bright orange stew were floating in a pot. Buzz saw cookbooks on the windowsill. *Whole-Grain Treasures. Laurel's Kitchen. Staples of India. Deena's Guide to Cooking with the Weed.* On the wall by the stove was a phone. He dialed zero and asked for the fire marshal.

The marshal said the fire had been reported. Local departments had been notified and a man had been sent up to dust.

"A plane?" Buzz said.

"Yes sir. What's the water situation?"

"Not good. The streams are pretty low."

"Firebreaks?"

"I'm afraid not."

"We'll do our best."

The line went dead. Buzz ran out of the house and retraced his steps across the pasture and up the road. In the meadow, he stopped. The smoke had thickened, piling on in layers, shifting, settling, choking. Manpower, neighbors: he needed help with the fire, but he didn't know his neighbors. There was too much wood, not enough field, and apple trees were growing in the middle of the only roads in. It took a plane . . .

He heard it. Approaching from behind him, the plane cut into view above the trees, still high but dropping. Tufts of orange fire retardant fell from its pipes. Reverently he watched it glide overhead and dive towards the smoke. The engine quieted, and as the wings cut into the downwind fringes of the column, he heard a gunshot. He heard two more, at two-second intervals. He dropped to his knees and clutched his hair.

Another shot.

"General, *stop*!" he yelled.

Another shot.

Its engine groaning afresh, the plane banked up and away from the smoke without releasing its load. It veered off to the south at a dangerous angle. Buzz lost it in the trees, and the General, his magazine empty, ceased his fire.

.

"Martin? It's Norris."

"Oh." Probst's eyes fell shut. "Morning." Saturday morning, eight o'clock. Raindrops were inching down the windows, the gutters were creaking, and water splashed quietly in the bathroom as Barbara showered. "What can I do for you, General?"

"Martin, are you busy?"

"I was sleeping."

"Reason I'm calling so early—you mind looking out your front window?"

"Maybe you could just tell me what's out there," Probst said.

"My car. I'm speaking from my car. Are you busy?"

"I have a tennis date at eleven."

"We should be back by three or four."

"I see." Probst stretched his leg into the cool territory on Barbara's side of the bed. "Where are we going?"

"Mexico."

"Mexico. I see."

"I'll explain," the General said. "Don't worry about breakfast. I've got that under control."

"You're under the impression I'm going to Mexico with you?"

"Just come on out. I'll explain."

"Look, General. I can't go waltzing off for the entire day."

"I would've called yesterday, Martin, but the element of surprise."

"I'm surprised all right."

"Not you. Them. It won't take but a few hours. This is important."

"If it's about Jammu again—"

The General hung up. Probst kicked back the covers and rolled out of bed. His head ached. Last night they'd had hot Szechuan platters and a lot of beer with Bob and Jill Montgomery, out in Chesterfield. He strode to the bathroom and turned the doorknob.

Locked? *Locked?*

"Just a minute!" Barbara sang.

What the hell? Locked the door?

He stormed back across the room, around the corner, down the hall, and burst into the bathroom through its unlocked flank. The Vitabath-saturated steam took his breath. Barbara poked her head through the shower curtain and gave him a puzzled, smiling frown. "What?"

"I want to shave."

She frowned more deeply, hurt. "Go ahead."

"Haven't you been in there long enough?"

Her head disappeared. The water stopped. She never gave a thought to how much of it she used. "Hand me a towel."

He grabbed a towel from her rack and parted the curtains. She jumped, shuddering, to make him feel like a stranger and a brute.

"I'm sorry," he said. "General Norris is sitting in his car out in front."

She wrapped herself in the towel without drying off and left with a slam. He opened the door and called after her, "I'm sorry!"

"Whatever for?"

Things had been bad since Luisa left.

He wet his beard with an inefficient one-handed tossing motion. Water coursed down his chest to the waistband of his pajamas, and he tried to hip-check it into the sink, but it had already gained the inside of his leg, trickling down as if unzipping him. He squirted a blob of shaving cream onto his left wrist, above the curved aluminum splint, and lathered his face with his right hand. He'd always used his left hand for lathering. His face felt unfamiliar, full of inaccessible nooks and crannies.

After he'd fought his way into the clothes he'd worn the night before (they smelled like restaurant), he went down to the kitchen and had Barbara tie his laces. She double-knotted them. The General honked the horn of his Rolls long and loud.

Probst was halfway down the front walk when Barbara spoke his name. He turned back. "Call me?" she said.

The horn honked again. He smiled in her direction and nodded. The door shut, and Barbara walked into the green gloom of the living room. She watched the car, the black hearse, swallow her husband. Alone, she let her gaze travel the length of the living room and back, and wished Luisa might step out of the closet, might step out and say anything, anything at all, say, "The big bowl was too hot, the middle bowl was too cold, but the little bowl, it was ju-u-u-u-u-u-st right": Luisa, the conditional Goldilocks who'd arrived to steal the porridge and break the chair and left again to live happily ever after elsewhere, in the land of human beings. . . . Mama Bear padded through the enchanted forest to the kitchen and poured herself some coffee. She sat down at the table, and wiped her eyes, and sniffed. She would write Goldilocks another letter. Although they spoke on the phone every day, she and Goldilocks, it wasn't enough. She wrote the date on the top page of her letter pad, December 9, and smoked a Winston, reworking her addiction, doing it consciously this time, noticing how. She never begged Goldilocks to come back. Goldilocks wasn't an object, wasn't an appliance. She was a person. She was acting one way now, but someday, soon, she'd act another way. For now, it pleased Mama Bear to see Papa Bear's equilibrium upset. She wasn't going to fix his life for him. But she wasn't going to shut up, either. In an hour she'd call. For now, Dear Luisa. I've been Christmas shopping.

The smoke was bothering Probst. "Can I open a window?"

The General opened his own window and threw his cigar into the rain. It landed in the far gutter, like a roll of dog dirt. The traffic light turned green. Through the green-tinted windows it looked almost white. The engine hummed as the General accelerated up a wet empty ramp onto the Inner Belt. Probst looked again at the note he'd been given when he got in the car.

> *Don't say anything. This car*
> *is bugged. Mexico is a ruse.*
> *We'll be local. I'll explain.*

Probst slapped his thigh. "Gosh, it's been ages since I was in *Mexico*."

Norris gave him a severe look, but handed him another doughnut.

"So how's Betty?" Probst said, munching.

"Betty's well. President of the school board now."

"I guess that means textbook hearings?"

"Not if she can avoid it."

The northern extension of the Inner Belt cut between young apartment complexes and young windowless commercial facilities and brown morsels of parkland. In St. John, in the rain, Probst caught a glimpse of a tall old man in a bathrobe hanging a wreath on his balcony railing.

"Do you mind if I use your phone?" he asked.

"Go right ahead."

He punched in the Ripleys' number and got Audrey. He couldn't resist telling her: "I'm calling from a car."

"Oh really." Her voice was dull.

"Could you tell Rolf I have to cancel this morning?"

He hung up with a pleasant feeling of irresponsibility. He turned to the General, who was wearing a black raincoat and, underneath, a very fine-looking cotton shirt with broad vertical stripes, maroon and black.

"Where'd you get that shirt?"

"Neiman." The General was now driving through an industrial park somewhere east of the airport. At the rear of the park was a high fence with green plastic slats woven through its mesh and a cantilever gate at one end. He lowered his window, consulted a card, and pecked a string of numbers onto a telephone plate. The gate rose and they entered a lot in which eight or nine cars were parked. Behind the cars stood an unmarked hangar-like building with bulging Plexi-glas skylights. The pavement ran straight up to the bottom tier of its cinder-block walls without even token bordering, as if the building, like the cars, merely rested on the surface and could be moved.

Stepping out, Probst caught his bad hand on the door. His knee jerked, knocking the door into a neighboring car and making a sizable crease. The car was a green LeSabre, with rays of mud behind the wheels. He considered his responsibility to leave a note, but found himself following Norris instead. It wasn't much of a car anyway.

At the door Norris punched more numbers, the last of which caused the lock to buzz. Inside, all was carpeted and dim. Shapes near the top of a low-gradient ramp defined themselves, step by step, as a desk with chrome legs and a man in silvered wraparounds. The man sat sideways with his feet poking out to the right of the desk. "Name?" he said. He had a flattop.

"Bancroft," Norris said. "And a friend. I have a reservation, Suite 6. I'd like a different one."

"Suite 12." The man slid keys across the desk. He swiveled in his chair and faced the wall behind him. "Two lefts, follow the stairs, and another left."

The walls were unpainted cinder block, the ceilings indeterminately high. The carpeting smelled new. Halfway down the second corridor they met an Oriental girl wearing only a T-shirt, black as her triangle of pubic hair. She was going the other way. Her fingers trailed along the wall. She looked up, and Probst tried to avert his eyes. She looked right through him.

"Was she blind?" he whispered.

"They're all blind."

"That's terrible."

"This place is seedy as shit. But very private."

"What kind of thing is it?"

"Health club."

Between the corridor and suite were two doors outfitted with deadbolts and enclosing a small vestibule. The suite itself was spacious. Probst backed up to take it all in. There was a kitchenette, a Universal bodybuilder, a king-sized bed, an Exercycle, a sunken whirlpool, a tanning unit, and a number of sadistic-looking machines he couldn't identify. Near the door stood a white enamel box, roughly coffin-shaped, somewhat larger than a deep freeze. He knocked on it. "What's this?"

"Sensory deprivation."

Probst moved away from it. Warm air was pouring out of a heating vent behind him. The air smelled funny. Spiced.

"Seedy as shit," the General repeated.

Probst walked to the bed and shed his coat. He glanced at the ceiling. There was a mirror. He looked one foot tall.

"So you found—"

The General covered his mouth with a scented hand. "I couldn't even tell you what membership costs," he said loudly. "I borried Pavel Nilson's card." From his raincoat he took two black boxes with a deluxe sheen to them. He touched a button. A red light flickered and gave way to a steady green light. He touched a button on the other box. "And that'll keep us silent."

"Wouldn't it have been easier just to meet in the woods?"

"I'm sixty years old. I like comfort. I'll admit it. You?"

"Who doesn't."

The General sat down and removed his shoes. Probst shook off a tingling adulterous sensation. "You were in the woods on Tuesday, though."

"Let's not talk about that." The General laid his striped shirt on the bed and Probst continued to admire it. "I mean to take a sauna. You join me."

"Sure. Been quite a while."

"Let me just give you some answers right off the bat. Yes, I shot at that plane. Yes, it was a mistake. No, I don't regret it. No, I don't think that fire was any accident. Yes, Buzz Wismer refused to take me back to town. No, I couldn't care less. The reason you're here is that there ain't no point in conversing with Buzz Wismer."

"You smell something?" Probst said.

Norris sniffed. "Incense."

"Smells like a burning spice cake."

"I smelt a whole lot worse in here. They got promiscuous heating." Norris, now in boxer shorts, lit a cigar.

"So you found a bug." Probst began to undress. Norris reached again into his raincoat and handed him a small transparent bag. Probst had a revelation. Bugs were called bugs because that was what they looked like. This one was tiny, about the diameter of a nickel and less than twice as thick. Eight leg-like prongs protruded from one of its faces.

"That's high technology, Martin. That is very high technology."

"Where'd you find it?"

"My office."

"How?"

Norris nodded at the metal boxes. "Counter-technology. Which I will be glad to loan you."

This was too alien for Probst. He was glad when Norris dug a more humane piece of goods from his raincoat, a bottle of whiskey, something Irish. "And you found a bug in your car," he said.

"Yep. But I don't want 'em to know it. This one here, I had the custodian find it accidentally."

"What about your house?"

Norris shook his head as he walked to the kitchenette. "They got no use for my house."

" 'They' being your industrial competitors."

"Don't be dumb, Martin. You know who they is." He selected a tumbler from the cabinets and poured himself a drink of whiskey. "Can I pour you something?"

"Whatever you got," Probst quipped.

He received less than a tablespoon. This was the first time he'd ever been social and private with Norris, and he was finding him less stupid than the public General, more genteel. In the sauna they sat on opposing benches, their bodies slack in anticipation of the load of heat. Steam insinuated itself through the floorboards. Slowly it coaxed open Norris's towel and granted a view of the boneless wealth, pink and furry, between his legs. His private parts. He'd been born with them.

"Time was," he said, "I could phone a police department and get facts. But the city police won't talk to me now. Jammu ain't dealing with the Bureau much either. She's got a headlock on the stadium investigation. You could say she don't want to share the glory when she nails the terrorists. Or you could say she's trying to protect them. I say the latter. But it's still possible to find things out in this town. There were three tons of cordite in the stadium, in two batches, with a tank of nitrogen on each of them. There were eight smaller charges in the structure, enough to collapse most of the upper deck. There was also industrial chlorine, pressurized, enough to kill a battalion and blind a division. The timing devices were independent and not remote control. No receivers. The timing was coordinated and sequential, not simultaneous, with the gas last, to maximize lethality. It was set to commence at 2:25 p.m., CST. The explosion that did occur, the one that blew out the baseball statue—"

"Which I won't miss," Probst said.

"Anti-tank mine. Soviet apparently. The Bureau's not sure."

Probst leaned steeply into the wooden wall and shut his burning eyes.

"Conclusions," the General said. "First, overnight security at the stadium leaves a lot to be desired. But we knew that. Security stinks everyplace. Second, these Warriors got international connections. The Soviet mine—"

"*If* it's Soviet," Probst said.

"And more telling, the tank of N_2. That's Middle East. Born there, popularized there. Three, and this is where it gets bad, Martin, you with us?"

"I'm with us."

"Three: very pointed steps were taken to kill upwards of ten *thousand* civilians and injure thirty thousand more. I ask you for a second to imagine that kind of carnage in downtown Saint Louie."

Probst could not.

"Meanwhile a warning was communicated, to the city police, at 1:17 p.m., CST, sixty-eight minutes before the bombs were set to detonate. Now the police required four minutes to arrive at the scene, and an additional fifty-seven minutes to locate and defuse every charge. They didn't miss a one, and there weren't any accidents. So as it happened there were only seven minutes to spare. You smell some choreography in this? I do. But there's another problem—and I seen not a mention of this, I heard not a line in any of the news media: why the hell spend a fortune on some very sophisticated materiel, run substantial risks in planting it, and then give a warning? Why bomb a car with no one in it? Why fire a machine gun into the only dark windows in a house? Why bomb an unmanned transmission tower? Sure there's been some bloodshed, and I almost envy you the privilege of shedding it, Martin—"

"Thanks."

"But if you pardon my saying, it's not enough. Including that little attack on the tower, there've been four separate scenarios and no one even nicked by a bullet. To me it smells like somebody mighty squeamish is at work. Smells like a lady. It smells like Jammu."

"She hasn't struck me as particularly squeamish."

"Sure, but that's all show."

"Come on," Probst said. "You can't have it both ways. If the terrorists are squeamish, if they're just trying to disrupt things, with credible threats, then we're OK. But if they're serious, and nitrogen tanks sound pretty serious to me, then Jammu's doing a good job and they're running scared."

"That's dead wrong. That's god-*damned* wrong." The General balled up his towel, threw it into the steam, threw himself to his feet and began to pace in a tight square. "It ain't just disruption. Too much money in it, too much foreign equipment, too much know-how. But it ain't exactly serious either. It's Jammu, Martin. It's the oldest trick in the book. You create the illusion of terror, then you get credit for stamping it out; you get funds, you get power. And that's exactly what's going on. Jammu's riding high. Look at Jim Hutchinson, would you. Nobody can figure out why the Warriors went after him and his station. And nobody asks why he's still alive. It makes me weep it's so obvious. *Hutchinson backs Jammu.* He didn't two months ago. Now he's her biggest fan, and there ain't no talking to him anymore. That's why he ain't been killed. KSLX is just one editorial after another in favor of the police, in favor of the funding increases, in favor of Jammu personally, and you know as well as I do every dinkhead thinks KSLX is the voice of St. Louis. But it ain't, it's the voice of Jim Hutchinson, and look what's happened!"

"But," Probst said. The sweat was running now, a thousand shallow worms. "It seems to me that nothing much has changed. Hutch was always a liberal. Jammu's a liberal, at least partly, to read the paper. Hutch supports her now. He's still a liberal. You were thinking about conspiracies three months ago. You're still thinking about them. You knew it before it started. You haven't changed. All I see is coincidences. Indians and Indians. A princess, a policewoman, both from Bombay. The first Big Red game I've been to in years happens to be the fateful one. Coincidence, nothing else. I could make something of it, but why bother. 'God is Red.' You probably think that means communist."

"That's right."

"Well, I don't see any compelling reason for them to give hints like that. I see some reasons not to. I don't see any compelling reason for Jammu to start planting bombs when she's doing just fine the way she is. I don't think she's even capable of it. I don't think real people act that way. I don't think one person by herself— remember she's new to the force—I don't think she even has time to do much more than her job. Obviously I haven't changed either. I was saying this three months ago."

There was a pause. Dark gaps in the light steam writhed and rose, closed and opened. Then the General said, "You haven't been paying much attention, Probst."

The remark hurt. Its vagueness.

"Do you even read a newspaper?"

He was distracted by a flare of pain in his broken finger. Sweat and condensation had soaked the green sponge of the splint. "I, uh." He clenched his teeth to clear his head. "Usually."

"Know anything about North Side real estate?"

"It's—what? Doing pretty well?"

"You better find out. Know anything about the Hammaker Corporation?"

"Like what?"

"Like the announcement they'll be making on Tuesday—"

Tuesday was Probst's birthday.

"—that the City of St. Louis will own twenty-one percent of its common stock, in other words a third of the stock now in the hands of the Hammaker family."

"That's outrageous," Probst said. "What are you talking about?"

"Facts. Granted, it's a special arrangement, no voting privileges. Granted, it's hush-hush. But it's a gift. To the city. Which is heading for a financial crisis."

"They can't do that. It's not granted in the Charter."

"They can so." The General's teeth gleamed in the steam. "That paragraph they voted in when they thought they'd have to buy the Blues to keep 'em here. They can own part or all of any enterprise, I quote, that's manifestly a civic institution. And Hammaker plainly qualifies as a civic institution."

"That's outrageous," Probst repeated.

"Facts. After all, who's really running Hammaker these days? The royal bimbo, is who. The one who's also coming on to Buzz Wismer."

"Coincidence."

"Conspiracy. Now I don't mean this quite as unkind as it may sound, but. You're the chairman of Municipal Growth—you're supposed to pay attention."

"I have been paying attention, General. I've paid attention to the hospitals. I've paid attention to desegregation. To the bond renegotiations."

"Fiddling while the city burns. While the Reds hire ninety percent blacks for the city police. While a pair of bitches nationalize a private industry. While your brother-in-law double-crosses Municipal Growth. While somebody perverts your own daughter."

The sauna seemed to spin, Norris filling it centrifugally, in tangents, a bodily swastika. There was a leg in front of Probst, an arm in one corner, another against the opposite wall, trunk, neck, head vaulting over him, and dangling in the focus of his vision was a somber white-haired scrotum. "I've had enough sauna," he said.

"I haven't."

"My private life is none of your business."

"Martin, I know it ain't. But people talk. People hear things. You ought to know what people say."

"I'd rather not."

"God Almighty. I never seen so many ostriches." The voice shook with emotion. "Haven't you ever met somebody whose guts you hated but everybody else thinks she's the hottest thing this side of the sun? And you know you're right, you know you see something. How's it make you feel? Everybody cheering, and here she's putting fifty thousand innocent folks in danger. You think it's a thrill to get your legs blown off? People don't think. And Buzz Wismer? Sure, he's getting a little soft around the edges, but he still manages to keep that company in the black, year in, year out. And I see this phony Asian princess rubbing up against him, and him interested. I try to do something, all right? I see my city in trouble. I try to shore up. You and me ain't friends. Our paths wouldn't ordinarily cross. But I had this pitcher, when I heard you bled, I had this pitcher, and it got me hoping again. We're at the center of things, you and me."

Probst felt calm. The danger was past. He could handle abstractions. He raised his glass, but only a single drop reached his tongue, watery sweet.

"It ain't the blacks that get me," Norris said. "It ain't even the Reds so much. It's these Asians, the industrial Japs and these Injuns here. They got no morals, it's me me me me me. Me win, me first. You know they don't even go to movies in Japan?"

"It's funny you say that." Probst smiled. "Because that's probably what the British thought about the Americans fifty years ago. No culture, everything for business. Not playing fair. It feels bad when you're not on top anymore. We can't compete with Japanese industry. Or—or communist athletes. So we turn to finer things. Movies. Ethics."

"So you're saying sour grapes."

"Sure." He didn't mean this. He was an optimist. He tried to think of something optimistic to say. "Jammu is . . . Did you bring that bottle?"

"No."

"Jammu's tackling problems. She's doing a fine job, completely apart from the terrorist investigation. Nobody thought it was possible. She's doing it. Crime's dropping. We'll discuss the figures at the next MG meeting. I think you're jealous of her. I think we're all a little jealous."

"I don't deny that she's a ruthless cop," Norris said. "But what you can't deny is that there weren't any terrorists before Jammu came to town. I see no accidents."

"I do. Where does that leave us?"

"I'm saying grant me the possibility. Don't work against me, don't cast aspersions. I was sorry Jammu got the nod in July but this ain't personal. I didn't know nothing in July. So do me a favor. Take my signal detector and sweep your house and your office and your car. Do it today, before they know you got the technology. Then call an emergency MG meeting. Talk to Hutchinson, Hammaker, Meisner, Wesley, and for God's sake talk to Ripley. Wake up. Get the facts. We need you."

"I'm glad you think so, General."

"Sam, if you want."

"Sure. Sam."

Few men were invited to use the General's first name; it was said to be an honor.

Later, when he and Probst left the health club, everything was changed. Three inches of snow had fallen and more was coming down, whole airborne valleys, white peaks, blue forests and gray fields. It was 10:30. The car Probst had dented must have left just moments earlier. There was a black, snowless oblong on the pavement, an exhaust smudge to the rear, fresh tire tracks, and footprints. Probst stared through the falling snow at the footprints. They were nondescript.

.

"Have to beg off, old chap. Sorry, but. P'raps in January." Rolf stuck the old pegs into his trousers and zipped up. He viewed his timepiece with mock dismay. "Blast. How'd it get to be so late?"

"You insisted on another set," Martin hissed. "That's how."

"Carried away, what. Manly competition." Rolf chuckled, and donned his overcoat.

"Cut it out, Rolf," Martin said. Still in his shorts, he advanced predatorily. "You weren't in any hurry half an hour ago."

"But I was, old chap. I was. I just didn't let on. 'Twas politeness pure and simple."

"Don't give me that." Martin took another step, and Rolf was obliged to issue a cough, of high denomination, in self-defense. Martin recoiled. "Cover your mouth, why don't you."

"Came too quick."

"One hour, Rolf."

"Would if I could but I can't."

Martin's hand clutched his arm. He brushed it off, coughing, gave his scarf a jaunty flip, and turned to leave.

"Look, Rolf. I don't know what kind of lies you've been spreading—"

"Ignorance is bliss, old boy. Must run. Business calls. Cheerio!"

And away he went down the warm and paneled hallways of the Club. Only at the door did he remember the Sno. It was still falling from a tarnished afternoon sky. He plunged into it. His steps were chopping, oblique, as he fought his way up the drive to the garage. All this Sno. He liked Sno even less than he liked Petz.

Lies? What could Martin have had in mind? Surely not the little anecdote about the brat. He'd merely embellished the facts handed him by Audreykins. Scarcely much point in scampering off like this if that was all the trouble was. But probably there was more. Martin seemed frightfully queer today. First he'd rung to break their date. Then at noon he'd rung to insist they play after all. His game was queer, too. Usually he played like a robot—"Heh! Heh! Your! Point!"—but today, the broken finger perhaps ruining his backhand, he'd become a lunger. And then in the dressing room he'd charged at Rolf like a fist-shaped doggie. "I wanna tawk to yew." Seemed to have got wind of something. Tee hee. Wonder what. Tee hee.

Rolf tobogganed merrily in fourth gear up Warson Road, his shoulders hunched, his nose at the windshield. He wasn't going home; Martin might track him down there. *Thump!*

An object had struck the back window. Sno-ball?

Thump, thump! Two of them hit the car broadside. They'd come from the school, Ladue High. *Thump!* He was losing control of the car. *Thump!* Gad, he detested this substance. He slid through an intersection. There was no braking. More Sno-balls landed in the brown slush to his left.

But he reached the Marriott without further travail. He had a key to her suite, and he entered softly. She sat in underthings, a collection of rounded angles draped across an armchair, reading a magazine. She looked up. "Who is it?"

"It's Rolf." He winked.

While she changed he noted the room's untidiness, the inside-out laundry and scattered Tarot cards, the Tab cans and ashtrays. An aroma of curry. Badly out of character. Later he would have to discipline.

She came back in a green wool business suit and low-heeled shoes. "So what brings you here, on—?" She frowned a bit.

"On such a yucky day?" he prompted.

"On such a yucky day."

"I was in the neighborhood," he said. "Thought I'd stop in. Martin isn't here?"

"No, he's at a football game. Let me take your coat." She

flicked Sno off the collar. He pinched her fanny. "Oh, you *prick!*" she whispered, close to his ear, as she moved to the closet. He grabbed her hand. She dug her thumbnail into his palm and wrenched free. "How dare you?"

Suddenly he coughed, shaking his head to deny validity to the interruption.

"Pneumonia," she said.

He sighed. "Do we have to start all over again?"

"I'm sorry." She blinked. "It's such a yucky day."

"Isn't it, though. You must be lonely here."

She turned and reached up to hang the coat, and with one sharp tug he had her skirt down.

She squealed very convincingly. "Rolf Ripley!" She backed into the empty, swinging hangers, tangled her feet in the skirt, and fell against the back wall of the closet. He knelt. "At last," he said.

"Oh Rolf. Oh Rolf. Here?"

He made ready. "Here."

She took his fingers into her mouth and nibbled. She frowned. "But what if Martin—"

"He's at the game. The game just started."

She relaxed. A hanger fell, belatedly, and bounced off his shoulder. He bore down with his Eveready. She cupped the glans and began a slow, beckoning stroke with the flat of her index finger. "Oh," she said. "I've wanted you."

.

Probst was awake at dawn the next morning and frying himself breakfast by 7:15. Mormons chorused on KSLX. Barbara was still sleeping. He'd tied his laces in square knots, using his teeth.

He made phone calls, appointments, slots in the day ahead of him. He was wearing a black suit with narrow lapels, a red tie, and a white button-down with fine gray stripes. In the bathroom mirror he looked diplomatic, upper-echelon. His hair was definitely going gray, and his face was narrower than usual, more of a prominence, less of a plate. Its heat felt unvanquishable when he walked out the back door into the icy air. The engine caught at once and roared.

Driving this morning was like boating, the dips and sprays,

with every surface equally navigable. The roads were empty. Under snow the city looked nineteenth-century.

Probst was still trying to process the information the General—Sam—had given him yesterday. It took longer when he had to do it by himself, without Barbara's help. He'd come home from the health club with an almost physical need to divulge and discuss, but the need died when he saw her, the simmer of resentment in her eyes, the dark fire. Even sweeping the house gave him no joy (it didn't turn up any bugs, either) when she paid no attention. She sat reading and smoking until the den smelled like Canadian bacon.

"Entrez-vous," Chuck Meisner said, holding open the storm door. Probst entered stomping, scuffing snow into the rug. Even on a Sunday morning the Meisner living room seemed freshly vacuumed, freshly dusted, the cushions freshly plumped. Chuck was wearing shapeless country clothes, corduroy and wool.

"Can I get you something? Coffee? Bloody Mary?"

"Nothing, thanks, Chuck." His body was primed. He needed nothing.

"Is this—something you want to talk about upstairs?"

"Yes. That would be good."

Probst and Barbara had seen quite a lot of the Meisners this fall. Chuck was president of the First National Bank and a director at First Union and Centerre. If people had been withholding facts from Probst, for whatever reason, then Chuck was likely one of them. Of course in private Chuck had always been as tight-lipped about professional matters as a funeral-home owner. And Probst did all his banking at Boatmen's, the Hammaker bank, which, his regard for Chuck notwithstanding, he'd long felt was the best managed in St. Louis. He didn't believe in socializing with bankers. Pure money, like pure sexuality, was an evil demon in friendship. Other contractors in St. Louis tended to bank incestuously with brothers or brothers-in-law and they often had highly flexible credit lines, which were legal but rather unethical; Probst did not. He enjoyed seeing Chuck because Chuck was a Democrat, and Probst liked oddities, men who ran against the grain a little. A Democratic banker—it was a mild sensation, like fresh papaya.

Chuck planted himself behind the massive antique desk in his study and indicated the correct chair for Probst. Outside the window, a cloud of windborne snowflakes, marvelously tiny, a heavenly host, swirled in the sunlight. The walls creaked in the wind. Probst hoped Chuck assumed he'd come for personal advice, an investment question, a tax shelter, a sewage bond. He didn't like to mislead a friend, but the confrontation with Rolf yesterday had made him leery of stating his business prematurely. Now he was ready to come straight to the point. He began by taking a good look at his friend, and he got no further than this.

Chuck looked terrible.

He knew it, too. He met Probst's eyes expectantly, with the guilt, the sad candor, of a man detected engaging in a vice. His eyelids were puffed and folded, the whites a solid pink. There was a purple crack in his upper lip. His hair was lifeless.

"I don't look so great, do I?"

"Have you been sick?"

"I haven't had a good night's sleep in over two months."

Probst recognized the controlled fury in Chuck's voice. *Over two months*. The phrase was cruel self-propaganda, a complaint spoken silently again and again, an inner goad (You know, that den smells like Canadian bacon) until the complaint became so meaningful, so powerful, that voicing it could only lessen it, and having it was defeat.

"I don't remember you seeming that tired," Probst said.

"Sometimes I'm OK." Chuck closed his eyes. "You think you're getting by. And then one bad night." He shook his head.

"Have you seen a doctor?"

"Yes. I have pills. And amino acids. Last week I saw a hypnotist. Bea has me started with an analyst. And the result is, I slept about twenty minutes last night. On Tuesday I got six hours. The next night, zero." It seemed to tax Chuck to speak at any length. It took an ugly effort.

"Do they know what the problem is?" Probst said.

"I tried cutting out booze, coffee. I didn't eat meat for a while. I went all-protein for a while. I switched beds, which actually helped, but only for one night. I did all right at the ABA conference in San Francisco, but that was only three days, I came back, and wham. I tried meditation. Yoga, jogging, no jogging, hot baths. Warm milk, bedtime snacks, lots of Valium. I'm totally unconscious, I'm in a stupor, but the sleep part of me, Martin—" He raised his hands and, with his fingers, caged what he was describing. "The sleep part of me is wide awake."

"What do you think it is?"

"That's the thing. Everything seems like it might be important. The side of the bed I sleep on. Working too hard. Not working enough. Do I need to get angry? Or do I need to stay calm? Weekend versus week night, red wine versus white. You know? Because there's got to be a reason for this, and any part of my life, anything I do every day— There are so many variables, so many combinations. I can't pinpoint the important ones by any process of elimination. What if the reasons I can't sleep are eating sugar, going to bed too early, and watching sports on the weekend? I could never isolate that. But I lie there for hours turning over the variables. I can't remember when I *ever* slept well. As if my whole life had been this way."

Probst was stuck now. This was no time for a confrontation, no matter how friendly. He cleared his throat and remembered the box in his pocket. He lifted it out and set it on his knee.

"What's that?" Chuck said.

"A toy I got yesterday." Probst pressed the Test button. Red light. The red light! Had he damaged it?

"What is it?"

Probst rose and circled his chair. As he passed the window, the box began to squeal like a quartz alarm clock. He backed away from the window, and the squeal faltered. "I think this room is bugged," he announced. He scanned the wall to the left of the window, playing games with the squeal, to locate the center of the electronic irritation. At waist level he found a spot on the wall where the paint was a shade lighter than the rest. He tapped on the spot. Hollow. He punched his finger right through. It was stiff gauze, glued over a hole and painted to match the wall. He tore it away. The hole was an inch in diameter and half an inch deep. In the center, its legs embedded in rough plaster, was a bug. He opened his penknife and pried it free. A hair-thin wire, eight or ten inches long, peeled away from under the fresh paint. He dumped it on Chuck's desk.

"Did you know this was here?" Chuck said.

"Of course not. But I think you should know that Sam Norris found a bug identical to this one in his office."

"Oh did he?" The sharpness of Chuck's reply surprised him. "Are you sure he really found it?"

"Meaning?"

"Meaning are you sure he didn't just get it from a friend and *say* he found it?" Chuck's croaking was repellent. "Sam Norris, as you call him, has been courting the hell out of Bobby Caputo and Oscar Thorpe at the FBI. My first reaction to this thing here"—Chuck swept the bug off the desk onto the Persian rug—"is the name Hoover. Norris doesn't *trust* me anymore. My behavior is *suspect*. And since when are you on good terms with him? I thought you weren't even speaking."

"Well . . ."

"You're surprised I mention the FBI. So I don't suppose you heard Norris flew a private investigator to Bombay to dig up muck on Jammu, either. Or that he's a handshake and two signatures away from outright buying the Globe-Democrat, because nobody prints him anymore." Chuck sighed and rocked in the stationary chair. He waved his arms weakly. "So there's a bug in here. I don't imagine it's the first time. But what Norris doesn't know, what the FBI doesn't know, is that not everyone is a sneak like them. I have nothing to hide."

Except from me and Barbara, Probst thought. You hid your exhaustion. "Then tell me what's going on in North St. Louis."

"Nothing more than what's in the papers every night." Chuck raised his voice, as if many stupid people had been asking him this very question. "Nothing more than business as usual. The public invests more than just money in us, Martin. It invests its trust, and that's a pretty important thing. We've a responsibility to our investors to use that money—that trust—in the most productive way possible. We'd be negligent not to. Now, to my knowledge, there's been no excessive speculation on the North Side. Property values have risen, and the various institutions I serve have seen fit to protect their future and the future of the depositor—the little man, Martin—by making some selected and I believe wise purchases in the area. To add to what we already had. And, of course, to replace what we'd sold before we properly assessed the market's strength.

There's some very choice property down there, and it's about time the city made something of it. We're in the business of encouraging development. It's part of our public trust. I think the time is coming. We're certainly quite satisfied with the crime situation at present."

Probst, with a hypothetical wave of his fingers: "But this has no adverse effect on the overall economy of the region?"

"How can increased investment have an adverse effect?" Chuck grinned like a kindergarten teacher.

"Well, for instance, in West County."

"Oh, Martin. That particular region is still *so* healthy. So healthy. You have nothing to worry about on that score. Is that what's worrying you? Goodness! West County? Nothing to worry about, nothing at all."

·

Probst's next stop was back in Webster Groves, in Webster Park, behind the library. He kicked his way up the unshoveled walk and rang the doorbell. He waited. He hadn't heard the bell. The bell was broken? He knocked. Soon the door was opened by an unshaven man, Probst's age, wearing jeans and a green collarless surgeon's smock. "Martin Probst? Howdy." The man extended a hand and pulled Probst inside. "Rodney Thompson."

In intermingling piles along the baseboards of the Thompson living room were hundreds of magazines, mostly of the sort with text but no pictures on the cover. The air smelled strongly of dated pancakes. Plants in the windows had shed a mulch on the wooden floor, and someone had spilled a cup of coffee on the wool rug by the television set. The cup still lay on its side.

"This room doesn't get much use," Thompson said. He stuck his hands in the pockets of his jeans and walked back to the kitchen. Probst also did.

"So you're Luisa's father."

"Yes."

"I guess our wives have spoken." Thompson sat down and drank from a tall glass of orange juice and, swallowing, signaled an offer of the same to Probst, who shook his head. "And you're the man who built the Arch."

"Not singlehandedly." Standard comeback.

"Of course not. It's an achievement nonetheless. I'm very impressed. Impressed with Luisa, too. I like her."

Probst wished he could figure out a way of asking, within the context of this get-acquainted visit, just how much time the Thompsons had spent with her.

"She talks a lot about you, very positively, although I also understand you're not on such good terms at the moment, for whatever reasons."

"How often do you see her?" Probst asked.

"We've taken them to dinner a couple of times. We try to make an effort to stay in touch. These are difficult years for kids. I know Duane's going through some re-evaluations, sounding out alternatives, trying to get his act together. We stay in touch. Not that Pat and I have a lot of time these days. Pat's working, by the way, sorry she missed you. We'll all have to get together sometime, all six of us."

Thompson squinted at a nearby calendar.

"Not this weekend, though, I mean not the coming one. I guess after Christmas. January. Oh. Or February. You can all come over, we'll make a night of it. The kids really love Pat's paella. Fracture?"

"Yes." Probst exhibited his finger more completely, and then, for the twentieth time, related the stadium story. The last ten times, he'd told it identically, word for word.

Thompson nodded at every sentence. He made large swooping nods, smaller horizontal rows of nods, rotational nods of total comprehension and agreement, odd nods in angled planes, singsong windshield-wiper nods. When Probst was done, he said: "As far as Lu and Duane go, it's hard to tell how serious they are, but I think pretty. She seems very determined to assert her independence." Thompson flattened the front page of the Sunday *Post* and read a few lines. "It's really a matter of values when you get right down to it. The old story, right? There's not much I can add, personally, beyond the fact that both Pat and myself like Lu very much. What's more, we respect her." He looked at his watch.

.

It had been two weeks since Buzz Wismer had seen Martin Probst. Much had changed. Martin hadn't. He looked awake and fit when he arrived, that Sunday afternoon, at Buzz's office. Even the aluminum splint added. He looked like a brilliant soldier on leave.

"I thought," he said, "that you might be able to fill me in on what Rolf Ripley is up to these days. I'm married to his sister-in-law and I know less than nothing."

"Well," Buzz said. "There was the hoopla about his new defense electronics division. From what I hear, though, that's been in the works for quite some time."

"Stop right there," Martin said calmly. "How did you know it had been in the works?"

"Well. I guess I would know. We're in competition for engineers. My people in personnel told me back in March he was recruiting in new areas. More computer, more nuclear—"

"OK. Fine. What else?"

"Lately, you mean? Well. There are rumors he's moving some of his operations back into the city."

"But the papers print that kind of stuff all the time."

"That's true. I took this more seriously, though, because my own name was mentioned in the same connection. A lot of stockholders saw the rumor, I think even the New York Times picked up the story, and I got calls from as far away as Boston. I felt we had to ask the Post about its sources, which is like pulling teeth. To make a long story short, it appears that a highly placed officer in Ripleycorp started the relocation rumor, and he said that we were also considering a move."

"So it didn't originate with you?"

"No and yes." Buzz explained that while the rumor hadn't originated with him, it had caused him to direct Finance to look into the feasibility of a change of headquarters. Finance had advised against it but had hedged by suggesting they nevertheless purchase some property in the city before prices rose any further. Buzz had authorized the purchase. It had been routine. But he actually felt his face growing hot as he explained it to Martin, as if he were revealing a guilty secret, something primitive, because the purchase was associated with Asha.

Martin smiled wistfully. "Thanks for telling me, Buzz. Businesswise, as you're aware, I need to know what's coming next, and in some way in the past few months I've failed to pay attention.

It's bad leadership on my part, too—I feel a kind of stewardship this year as MG chairman. At the same time, I don't exactly think it's my fault. Haven't the trends around here always been visible to everyone years in advance? Like Clayton, the highways, the waterfront, West County. There used to be an openness, and I don't see it anymore. This is why I want to know what your sense of things is."

It wasn't what Martin said, Buzz thought, or even how he said it, it was the underlying honesty, the almost obtuseness. This man was whole. Evil puzzled him. He hadn't changed.

"My . . . sense of things. I think we're all right, really." Buzz blinked. "I've had a pretty upsetting week, I guess. And I tend to lose sight of . . ."

"What do you think of Asha Hammaker?" Martin asked suddenly.

For a second Buzz had the distinct suspicion that this was the only question Martin had come to ask him.

"I don't mean personally," Martin added. "I mean as a businesswoman."

"As a businesswoman I have no idea."

"Have you heard anything about a transfer of stock to the city?"

"But lest you have heard rumors," Buzz continued, unwilling to pass up this chance to confess, "I should add that it's true that Mrs. Hammaker has several times made overtures of a, em, physical character to me and perhaps to others as well, in public, so that there may be rumors to that effect which you may have heard."

Martin smiled and shook his head with rhetorical amusement. "Why don't they ever do that to me?"

Their eyes met. Buzz felt a laugh drawn out of him like a splinter.

.

It was after Probst had left the Wismer complex and turned south again, it was in the very middle of the long day he'd cut out for himself, when his breakfast was spent on the morning and remained only as metabolic by-products and a faint sourness of juice in his mouth—it was then that the weekend's burden of facts and conjectures, possibilities and risen consciousness became too much for him.

He experienced a dullness. The low midwinter sun on the land ahead of him was blindingly white, unbelievably bright, and the wet and snowy streets were a catalogue of nonsense. Chunks of every size and every shape obliterated the simple lines underneath. In the brilliance, at traffic lights, he couldn't see which of the three lights was shining, the red, the yellow, or the green. He slowed for all of them, coasting through the intersections.

And it was then, as his eyes sought relief in the rearview mirror, in the darker, cooler scenes behind him, that he began to suspect that he was being tailed. The car was a big old Chevy, a white one. He thought he remembered having seen it earlier, in Webster Park, and now it was a hundred feet behind him on Hanley Road. The windshield was a rough-edged bar of reflected sunlight.

The car followed him into Clayton, and when he made a right turn onto Maryland Avenue the car did too. He pulled into the Straub's parking lot to buy some fruit for lunch, and the car drove on past, its occupants still masked by the glare.

·

In Jim Hutchinson's living room he performed another stealthy check for bugs and got a green light. Jim returned from his study, where he'd taken a telephone call.

"I'm aware," he said, "that the General finds it suspicious that the Warriors haven't bagged me yet. On the other hand, they shoot real bullets. Have you ever been shot at? It's not an experience I'm eager to repeat. For your information, the helicopter shot out these windows to your left, because we generally eat dinner in the front room. Contrary to what you've probably been told, these windows were not dark. The curtains in the breakfast room were drawn, however, and they're also screened by trees and the house behind us. As far as the car bomb goes, I'm not sure. There are indications it detonated unexpectedly, an hour ahead of schedule. I was going out at eleven that morning. The grenade at our transmitter found its mark, and was not aimed at soft targets. Since then, I've taken more precautions. The police have also been helpful. Apparently the Warriors have changed their tactics. That's fine with me. I'd prefer not to get gunned down on the street just to set the General's mind at rest. It's also true I've changed my mind about Jammu. There's nothing to prove by stubbornness. I've met with her several times personally, and I can assure you that she's *not* a terrorist."

"How do you know?"

"Aren't you the one who's been arguing against it all fall? And anyway, I have a sense. I was a reporter for twenty years. Jammu isn't completely straight with me—she has no reason to be—but she's not that crooked, either. Not as crooked as Norris, for instance."

"Is it true he's buying the Globe?"

"He'd like to. Whether anyone will let him, I don't know."

"If he's trying to, why hasn't it been reported?"

Jim thought for a moment. "No comment. Let's just say professional courtesy. At this stage, it's nothing out of the ordinary. Anyway, I'm sure the Post will run a story by the end of the week."

"What about the Hammaker stock deal?"

"Now, that. That you'll hear about on the news—nationally, I'd guess. It's a good example of one of the ways Jammu isn't playing straight. Asha Hammaker, née Parvati Asha Umeshwari Nandaksachandra, is not just another Asian glamour girl. For one thing, she's forty-one years old—"

"Wow." Probst's head wagged. He would have guessed twenty-five.

"She has three advanced degrees, Berkeley, London School, and somewhere Indian, she spent five years working for the Tatas, rose to the equivalent of vice president, and then in 1975 underwent a political and perhaps religious conversion, completely unexplained, spent two years in jail, worked for three years in Bombay as a marxist agitator, and then, most surprising of all, embarked on yet another career, as a professional stage actress, at which again she was highly successful. Maybe you didn't hear how young Hammaker met her?"

"I didn't think anyone knew."

"She was filming in Mexico, I think her first sizable film role. Hammaker was vacationing down there. This was February or March. April at the latest." Jim paused, as if waiting for Probst to see something.

At length he did. "Jammu wasn't invited here until July. In April she wouldn't have known she was coming."

"Couldn't have known," Jim amended. "Bill O'Connell could have stayed on as chief for another fourteen months, or Jergensen could have replaced him. She couldn't have known she'd be coming here."

"Unless Asha had something to do with—"

"With both the retirement and the replacement fight? Impossible. She hadn't even moved to St. Louis, and she wasn't a Hammaker yet."

"Jim, why don't you fill the General in on some of this?"

"It's pointless. You know he isn't rational. And there are certain coincidences he could exploit if he knew about them. Evidently Jammu and Asha were well acquainted in Bombay. How do I know? I asked Jammu. If I told the General, the facts would show that not only have two extraordinarily talented women from Bombay shown up in our unremarkable St. Louis within three months of each other, but they also happen to be friends. Clearly Jammu expressed interest in the job because Asha was on her way to St. Louis already, and it's a fact of immigration that groups tend to cluster in one city. Jammu's no exception. But the coincidence remains, and I don't care to nurture the General's illusions any more than I can help it."

"So what about the stock?"

"I think Jammu and Asha engineered the deal. As far as Jammu goes, it's a power play. You help rescue a city financially, you get to ask some favors in return, and it will be interesting to see in the next few months just what kind of favors she asks. She also has a much-expanded payroll to meet, and she's very unwilling to lay off all the men she's added in the last three months. As far as the Hammakers go, this won't bankrupt them. I imagine she looks at it this way: she and Sidney are the only heirs to all those assets, there aren't any children in the offing—although if Sidney doesn't know her age he may not be aware of this—so what's the point in hanging on to assets that are irrelevant to their present lifestyle? They cut it loose, send it to the city, get all the public credit, plus they have something valuable to add to their already-monstrous marketing arsenal: Hammaker is such an institution, it's even owned by the city it's made in. They lose none of their control of the corporation, and if Asha's half as smart as she looks I bet they can take those shares back whenever they need to. Which will give new meaning to the term Indian giver. For now, the city will be putting the whole lump up immediately as collateral for a loan arranged by—"

"Chuck Meisner," Probst said.

"The Felix Rohatyn of St. Louis. Is what he wants to be. Chuck's OK, though. I think he's overextended, but that's partly because the city is overextended. I take it you've seen him recently?"

"This morning. It didn't even occur to me to ask about the Hammaker thing. He's not well, you know."

"Insomnia."

"You know everything."

"Not really."

"Well, you know more than I do. You should put out a news-letter. I'd pay a lot for a subscription."

Jim smiled. "My position never strikes me as that unusual. If you want what I've got, you have to come ask for it. The same goes for Jammu. I wish some men like you would go and see her, instead of speculating."

"I'd need a pretext," Probst said, wondering why he hadn't thought of this himself. "But tell me what you know about Rolf Ripley."

"You know more than I do. I assume he's approached you about the development he's planning—"

Probst saw black. "Development?"

"What I've heard is basically outline, North Side, twelve blocks. Executive offices, rental space, his research wing, and maybe ultimately some manufacturing as well, and of course the obligatory apartment units. No towers, I guess. What—eight, nine stories max?"

"We hadn't really discussed it yet," Probst said.

"Well." Jim glanced at him shrewdly over his glasses. "Once you've worked things out with Harvey Ardmore—"

"Ardmore?"

"Martin." Jim's voice dropped practically to a whisper. "You do know, don't you, that he's filing for bankruptcy?"

By now it must have been clear how little Probst knew.

"I hope he doesn't owe you anything," Jim added.

Ardmore, the Westhaven developer, owed Probst a quarter of the total bill. Probst had paid the subcontractors in advance, but Ardmore's payment wasn't due until this week. "Bankrupt?" Probst said.

"Very possibly. He's been making the rounds, but no one's listening. The suburban banks are all plenty strapped as it is. This boom is knocking the bottom out of West County speculation. It has the makings of by far the largest set of developments in the history of the area. Not acreage-wise, naturally. But definitely dollar-wise. And this is only a prophecy, of course, but I believe the result is going to be the re-entry of the city into the county, and on the city's terms, not the county's. You wait. Remember who said it first."

.

Probst got a phone call from Buzz soon after he'd arrived at the mayor's office. He walked the telephone to the windows and looked down at the grimy snowbanks along Tucker Boulevard, and beyond, across the Mall, to an Arch that was golden in the failing sun. "Go ahead, Buzz."

"Well," Buzz said. "Ed Smetana—you've met Ed—he was in for a while, and we had a look at your gadget. The battery and circuit are American; local, in fact. It's a General Syn Power Seed and a Ripleycorp chip, not made exactly for this function but obviously close enough. I'd guess it's something he makes for the CIA. As for the mike and housing, which are really the deftest part of the construction—I couldn't tell you. No idea. It would take a forensics lab. The only other interesting thing is that the transmitter has a maximum range of no more than three hundred meters, which would mean there's a receiver very close to where you found this."

"All right. Thanks very much, Buzz. I'll talk to you again soon."

"Do. Do, Martin."

Probst started to return to his seat, but something he'd glimpsed subliminally on Tucker brought him back to the windows. A large white Chevy was parked directly below him, idling. The driver was screened by the top of the car and shaded by City Hall.

"Something down there?" Pete Wesley asked.

"Snow," Probst replied. He went back to his seat, a leather chair with cracks. The phone had interrupted a murky monologue of Wesley's, an upbeat message as far as Probst could tell, real Chamber of Commerce talk. Probst had never cared for Wesley. It seemed to him that American mayors fell into two distinct physical classes: sprawling endomorphs with loud personalities who could roll right over any opposition, and bland men or women with small, narrow builds well adapted to wriggling out of difficulties. Pete Wesley belonged to the latter class. His face was like the face of generic *Homo sapiens* in encyclopedias.

"As I was saying, Martin, it's very gratifying to see you here."

Probst closed his eyes. Impolite. He opened them.

"Because for a man born and raised in the city, and based here—don't think I don't know your business address—dare I say we haven't been seeing enough of you lately?" Wesley paused. "Let me upshot here for a moment. Let me toss out a couple of questions. I've been thinking about your situation lately, trying to feel my way under your skin. Having been in business myself I've got a pretty good handle on the central questions. For instance: What are the limits to growth in an enterprise like yours? Have you given any thought to the theoretics here? I have, and now stop me if I'm totally off the wall— The limits to growth for you, Martin Probst, must number one be the uncertainty of the market, number two the resulting inability to go on mustering capital indefinitely, and number three the internal considerations, such as the need for tight and centralized control of operations. How'm I doing?"

Because it was abstract, Probst found himself engaged by the question. He shifted his legs. "Well, to those limits I might add that the market is finite as well as uncertain, and that unlimited growth is of far less importance to me than quality work, a fair situation for my employees, and in particular a sane workload for my executives."

Wesley nodded through this. "Right. Absolutely. The market is finite. But so is the universe! It's still very large, right? Let me give you a present-day scenario. Say suddenly a whole lot of new office buildings are going up, and to build one you've got to have a big crane. I wouldn't know for sure how many big cranes you have, but let's say two."

"One, actually. If you're talking about the derrick we—"

"One. Fine. Even better. So even if six big projects are going up simultaneously, you can still only bid on one of them. You could bid on more, but you'd have to figure in the cost of renting or financing more cranes, which could make you uncompetitive. Am I right?"

"You're not altogether wrong."

"But now let's say that tomorrow something happens that will make it a whole lot easier to finance a crane. Something—whatever, all right? And let's also say that because you're hoping to do a number of very similar projects, all in the same area, not miles apart but blocks apart, five hundred feet, you'll be able to work more efficiently, and you'll be able to knock enough off your bids so that even with extra financing costs you're still competitive. Isn't it possible that you could land all six contracts and quintuple the revenues you'd otherwise expect?"

"That would depend entirely on the terms of the financing," Probst said calmly. In the simplicity of Wesley's scenario, the feigned naïveté, he sensed the imminent proffering of an illegality, and he had always been skillful at leading men on into self-incrimination.

"Say the terms were good," Wesley replied. "Say it was in the best interests of certain extremely influential citizens to involve you, with your stature, your leadership, your whole history, to involve you in the rejuvenation of the city, in a set of projects that no matter how you look at it is in the best interests of the people of St. Louis, all of the people, all of the city. Your city."

"You're referring to the North Side."

"North Side, South Side, West End, whatever. I ask hypothetically."

"I don't care for hypotheses," Probst said with an air of cool criminality. "I like facts."

"OK. The fact is, I do know of a group of men, good men, men you've known all your life, who do match up with the picture I've drawn for you."

"Why aren't they speaking to me themselves?"

"In a sense, they are. Call me a representative."

So: an admission. "Is Rolf Ripley another representative?" Probst asked. "Because if he is, then I'm quite sure you're mistaken about their interest in involving me."

"Martin. Have you ever stopped to think what life might be like in other businesses besides contracting? In businesses that are more speculative? If you have, then I'm sure you can imagine how loath we are to widen our circle prematurely."

Circle. Ring. Clique. Something clicked in Probst and pulled him to his feet. "I have no more questions," he said.

Wesley stared as if he hardly dared to hope he'd convinced Probst without a struggle. "Surely you'd like some details."

Probst put on his coat, and now that he was standing he observed that the spools in Mayor Wesley's Dictaphone were turning. "No thanks." He looped his scarf around his neck and tugged it to a choke. "I've no use for cliques."

"Sit down, Martin." Wesley's tone was kindly. "Please. Sit down. I've obviously given you the wrong impression. This isn't a clique—God knows, I hate the very idea. This is something for everyone."

Probst checked to see that he had his glove. Yes. "Well," he said, "I guess I'll wait until I hear about it like everyone else."

Wesley shook his head at Probst's failure to grasp. "People aren't going to be interested if men like you aren't."

"Oh, I'm sure you'll find plenty who are interested. Takes all kinds. Because, Pete, if what you're saying is true, then all you have to do is bring it up at Municipal Growth. Thursday night, seven o'clock."

"I'm ex officio."

"Hammaker then. Or Ripley."

"Martin, you know damn well you're the one they'll listen to. Some of these men aren't even going to Municipal Growth anymore."

"I've noticed. I've spoken with them."

"Well, you should know they're not above resigning if the group doesn't start showing a little more relevance to their concerns."

"If they miss a third meeting they're out anyway," Probst said.

"Now, I'm going to leave, Mayor, but first, if you're so inclined, you might answer me one question: Why try to bargain? Either you need me or you don't."

"Well. I like you, Martin. There's nobody who doesn't—"

"Blah, blah, blah."

"Now wait a second. I'm telling you this for your own good. I'm doing you a favor. Do you understand? Sometimes I wonder if you're not just a little bit of a snob. The redevelopment is going through no matter what, with you or without you. There's nothing you can do to stop it. But we're your friends. We want you aboard. We want you on the team. You're a team player, and we'd miss you. The business community has stuck together under the same leadership for more than twenty years—"

"The white business community." Probst wondered where this line had come from.

"The community that counts, the people who have a real stake in St. Louis. We've stuck together, taken care of our own, and we're going to keep on doing just that. So let's not have any ugliness."

Probst strolled to the windows. The white Chevy was gone. The Arch was black. "And my bargaining power?"

"Very simple. You don't have any if you won't play ball. But if you do play, you can have just about anything you want. You'd automatically be chairman, you'd—"

"Chairman of what?"

"Whatever. You'd have constant access to the big picture. You'd have more work, and could do it more efficiently, than you ever could before."

"And if I won't play ball?"

"Don't expect many offers."

"Some friends."

Wesley stuttered. "I didn't—"

"I'm sure you didn't." Probst spun around. "Make no mistake about it, Mayor. I don't believe ten percent of what you've told me. But even hypothetically, what you're talking about is *unfair advantage*. I imagine you'll tell me it's legal, and I've heard that kind of crap all my life. Legal. But no matter how you paint it over, you're still talking about an unfair advantage for someone, either for me or for someone else. That's not my idea of good business, that's not my idea of right living. Now, Mayor," Probst realized he was close to tears, "I still have a little bit of say in how this city is run, and I can assure you right now I'm going to do everything in my power to see that this community doesn't fall into the hands of any syndicate, no matter how nice the people running it are, no matter what good friends of mine they are. As for the rest, we will discuss it later, seven p.m., Thursday, and if you're not there, you're gone, you're kicked out, you're through—I've got the votes, Pete—and we can talk about this in the presence of more than just your Dictaphone."

"Oh, for shit." Jammu peeled off her headphones and threw them on her desk. "What's he doing running the Dictaphone?"

Singh removed the other set of headphones and placed them on the desk next to hers. "He knows we're listening?"

"No." She fell heavily against the back of her chair, working herself into a brand of snit Singh recognized but hadn't seen for quite some time. "But he knows I don't need a transcript. A summary would do."

"He's dabbling in conspiracy," Singh said. "It's catching."

She stamped on the floor, slammed a drawer, stamped again.

"The Dictaphone had nothing to do with it," Singh continued in tones well crafted and soothing. "Probst was already quite 'exercised' enough—"

"Asshole. Self-righteous *asshole*."

"Calm down, hey? Why not. You must be hungry." He nudged a half-eaten blueberry muffin, the second of the two he'd brought her, into greater prominence on her desk.

She flattened it with her fist and knocked the pieces to the floor. "Get out of here, Singh. You're on my nerves. The phone's going to ring—"

"Any minute," said Singh. "And you will rush off and we will not have had our 'conference.' I'll be at a loss. Won't know what to do. Valuable hours will go wasted." He moved to the eastern windows with steps that softly stroked the carpeting. "Calm down. Why not. So Wesley misplayed him. So what. I'm not surprised."

"Wesley did fine," Jammu hissed. "It was your Probst—"

"Mm, quite. As I said. It wasn't the Dictaphone. It was my Probst. And if we'd had just a very few minutes before my Probst arrived next door, I would have told you why this was no surprise."

"Because you've wasted three entire months."

Singh gazed out the window at the silhouetted Arch. The sun was gone but the day was bright. "Could be," he said. "Although you know I've done as well as anyone could. The same goes for Wesley. My compliments. Especially his avoidance of any mention of your name. Shows dedication. A true political trooper. Now me, for example, I would have blamed you for *everything* at the first sign of resistance in Probst."

"I can't stand that bastard."

"Sure, Chief. That's natural."

"He's a disaster."

"Oh, hardly." Singh prepared a clove smoke, lit it, drew, and heard his powerful exhalation. "The informational aspect is not at all dire. I had more than enough time to silence his house. He did, I admit, surprise me when he found the mike in Meisner's study. But this is not unhelpful. Now he's convinced that his devices work. I'll rewire both devices in the next few days, and we'll be in business again. 'Green lights' only. You've said it yourself: all leaks here are self-containing. And the loss of data has been minimal. The only substantive exchange I missed was an hour he spent with Wismer. Small price to pay. And where else was he today? I sense you are about to ask me this question."

Below on Tucker, Martin Probst was unlocking his car, wrenching open the door, looking as angry as he'd sounded. Should be more careful with those doors, Singh thought. "He saw Duane Thompson's father, a short meaningless conversation, then Wismer, then Hutchinson. When I could, I took the liberty of eavesdropping with a directional mike. The sound left much to be desired, but I got the gist. You might tell Gopal, incidentally, that Bunny Hutchinson has been detected in her adultery."

"He knows," Jammu said. "He arranged the detection. Would you—"

"Of course. Busy man. How unsophisticated of me. But would I—? Yes. I will. It can now be safely said that Probst is no longer in a state of suspended animation."

"In the State, you mean. You said that was the State, you said he was in it three weeks ago. Now he isn't."

"On the contrary. He is. A textbook dialectic, really. Absolute freedom, absolute terror, the French Revolution à la Hegel. It's the proof, not the refutation."

"Would you get to the point? I have two minutes at most."

"And you'll be busy all night."

"This is a major object lesson."

"Fine," said Singh. "I believe that nothing has changed. We expected Probst to awaken at some point, and he has, by way of Norris. But to be awake is hardly the same as to be aware. Have you read my abstract of his meeting with Norris yesterday?"

"No."

"I urge you to. It's one of my best. Norris—and now Probst—knows more about the stadium incident than I ever did. But even Norris, who thinks about it constantly, cannot see the point of the warning the Warriors gave."

"I should hope not."

"He can't, and won't, though it was implicit in the entire conversation. Likewise Hutchinson. He seems to know quite a bit about Asha—"

"I helped him with his research," Jammu said. "I wanted him to know exactly when she and Hammaker met."

"He does. And I don't guess he'll figure out how—"

"Of course he won't. Nobody knows but Asha."

"Although if you have a moment—"

"I don't," Jammu said. "But what?"

"Norris's private eye?"

"The man's name is Pokorny. Bhise stung him on a whiskey violation, put him in the holding pen for sex criminals. Three days, and when the consul got him out, Birjinder set up an auto accident."

"Fatal?"

"No, but he took a taxi from the hospital to the airport."

"Pokorny. What is that—Hungarian?"

"The point, Singh. I have five seconds."

"Four, three, two, one. I'm waiting. Well. Yes, the point. No one, not even I, can judge what effect these revelations will have on Probst. But he has the facts. Hutchinson told him about Harvey Ardmore and Westhaven. When he cools down, he may reconsider much of what he's said today."

"Doubt it."

"No harm in waiting until Thursday. Municipal Growth."

"No harm, but it's four days. What if the girl comes home?"

"Won't happen. In any case, I need the time."

"For."

"Getting Barbara."

"Set it in motion tomorrow, Singh. You can always back out."

"Is what I'd planned to do. But I have your leave?"

"To get Barbara?"

Singh nodded.

"Yes, if you keep it simple. Yes, if you think it will help."

"I will, it will."

The phone rang. Singh leaned and looked down on Tucker. Probst's car was gone. It left an empty slot at the curb, the vivid absence that remains when an object has vanished between glances, blinked away: living history, the departure that precedes the connection.

The phone rang a second time. Singh turned. Jammu was already gone, the door of her outer office falling shut. Her chair was empty.

.

A white sedan appeared in Probst's mirror when he crossed the railyards on 18th Street. It followed him lazily, hugging the snowpiles in the gutters, low to the ground. Was it the same car he'd been seeing all day? Whose hoodlums would these be? Wesley's? Norris's? He eased up on the gas, hoping the green light ahead would turn yellow. He wanted the Chevy to stop right behind him. Visibility was good now. But the light didn't change. He floated on through the intersection, hardly glancing at the empty street in front of him. The Chevy was weaving from one side of its lane to the other. A week ago, two days ago, Probst would not have believed it was actually tailing him, but his credulity had stretched. They were following him, somebody interested in his movements. They thought they could do whatever they pleased. They'd spread while he slumbered, people plotting, not working, sneaking to avoid the real work, the real tests of merit, seeking to circle in together to protect their stupidity and nourish their stinking lazy greed . . .

At Chouteau Avenue a light changed for him. He stopped dead, well in advance of the stop line, surprising the Chevy, which surged and filled the mirror. Its tires screeched. He popped open the door and leaped out, and immediately he knew he'd made a mistake.

There were five youths in the car, two up front, three in back. All four doors opened. The youths had high cheeks that seemed to force their eyes half closed, red complexions and yellow crewcuts, huge arms. They held Hammaker cans.

"Hey, motherfucker," the driver said, slamming his door and advancing on Probst.

Probst backed away a step. The fifth youth, a skinny guy with thick glasses, climbed from the Chevy. Probst looked from face to face. No one said a word. No cars passed. Sunday late in a non-neighborhood, upwind from I-44: it was pretty desolate.

"Dick-in-mouth," the driver said. The other four grouped at his shoulders. They wore jean jackets, army jackets. Probst saw a tattooed Stars and Stripes. The driver hawked and spat on the Lincoln. No one knew who Probst was. Never had, never could.

The driver hit him in the ear.

He staggered into the Lincoln. "Watch that," he said huskily.

"Watch that!" Falsetto.

"Dickface."

"Fairy."

"Watch that!"

The skinny guy began to urinate on the trunk. The others whooped. The driver grabbed Probst and spun him around, and Probst, lucid at last, said:

"Here come the cops."

While everyone turned, he jerked free and jumped back in the Lincoln, locking the door. The youths began to pound on the roof and windows. Gobs of spit hit the windshield, and Probst accelerated through a red light. There was a thud on the roof and a Hammaker can skittered off to his left. Behind him the last of the four doors closed. The Chevy's windows sprouted arms, four arms, all of them giving Probst the finger.

Soon he was in the innermost lane of I-44, and the Chevy was tailgating. He could imagine them plowing right into him. His wipers smeared the spit into opaque arcs. He was doing 85. At this rate he'd be home in ten minutes. But so would they. His ear rang. He couldn't lead them home. They'd stone his house. Where were the police? For once he wished they were out prowling with their radar guns. He thought of his office, his citadel, and the precinct house across the street.

Quickly he exited. He ran a yellow but didn't shake the Chevy. Right on his tail, it barreled back up the opposite entrance ramp onto the expressway. Four hands continued to give him the finger. This was terrible. Where were the police?

The punks followed him through the 12th Street interchange and down I-55. In the gloom around him, in the gray constricted streets, blue lights darted like passenger-train windows, and there was a great silence, as of a city gone dead, as if Probst too were dying and sight and balance were the only senses he could still command. Here was the hulking smoking brewery, in the shadow of which he'd misplayed Helen Scott, here the red gleams on its smokestacks, here Broadway, all the side streets which were already dying when he'd left them thirty years ago, here Chippewa, here Gravois, funeral homes and Boatmen's Bank, here the lot where Katie Flynn's dry-goods store had stood until her retarded son played with matches, here a gypsy gambling den in what used to be a Polish grocery—

And here were the police.

Half a dozen squad cars had parked broadside in the middle of Gravois. Probst stopped. In the mirror he saw that the Chevy had been stopped farther back; it was turning and leaving. Blue lights met white lights, the sky falling and shattering in luminous shards. Sirens and radios, headlights, snow. A policeman was pointing at Probst, waving his finger, mouthing words: Turn around. Probst jumped out. He was safe now.

"Turn around," the policeman said.

"Where can I go?" Probst called.

"Road's closed." Beyond the man, others ran towards a road-block with rifles and shotguns.

"What is it?"

"Turn around."

More squad cars pulled up behind Probst, blocking his exit.

Farther back, traffic was being diverted onto Morganford. Overhead, a helicopter.

"Unit Six Unit Six," the radios squawked. "High rate of speed Kingshighway South. Unit Seven Holly Hills."

Probst got back into his car. He really was blocked in. To his left he saw another motorist likewise stranded, his rear wheels on the traffic divider.

A van with a dish antenna on top was heading the wrong way up the empty northbound lanes of Gravois. It had hardly stopped when the rear door and both side doors opened, splitting the KSLX logos in two. A cameraman jumped out, followed by a reporter Probst recognized. It was Don Daizy. Camera lights ushered him forward to the line of squad cars, and now for the first time Probst picked out the focus of all this activity: in a trench coat, leaning against one of the cars, a megaphone dangling from one hand, a car-radio microphone poised in the other, Jammu.

Don Daizy approached her with his wire-laden retinue. An officer, pistol drawn, met him and turned him back. They exchanged words. A second officer seized the cameraman and led him away to the van. Daizy donned a headset and listened, squinting and nodding. He tapped a large microphone.

Probst switched on his car radio and watched Jammu. Night had fallen. The many flashers cast a light that was almost steady, as crickets merge into a single voice. Jack Strom was speaking on KSLX. Jammu was wearing snowboots. She stood motionless by the car, staring into whatever situation lay beyond the roadblock. Two officers alongside her were staring in the same direction.

". . . following an abortive attack on a Bell Telephone installation in the southwest corner of the city. Residents in the area bounded by Chippewa, Gravois, and the River des Peres are urged to *stay indoors*. I repeat, in the area bounded by Chippewa Avenue, Gravois Avenue, and the city limits, residents—"

Probst would remember his first glimpse of her. In describing his adventure in the following weeks, he would dwell on her quiet domination of the scene, on how, by saying a few words into the radio every minute or two, by keeping almost completely still as the crisis progressed, she seemed to control every action of the men around her and of all the other men farther off in the darkness. He would remember her manner of dress, the snowboots and trench coat, the impromptu confidence, remember it even when she used her cool, cruel arguments to wring this hour—Sunday, December 10, 4:00 to 5:00 p.m.—for every last drop of its political value . . .

"Armed and dangerous. We switch now to Don Daizy, who is at the Gravois roadblock. Don?"

. . . Because the roadblocks would serve no purpose. The Osage Warriors, trapped at last, would dump their vehicle, cross the dry river, elude the sadly undermanned and unorganized local police south of it, and escape scot-free. Jammu would testify bitterly in Jefferson City: "We'd been waiting for this, we had the trap planned down to the last detail, and all of it was negated by a force not under my control." Probst would hear these words, recognize the manipulation in them, and forgive her because he'd seen her during the moment itself, seen her in person, and he knew a professional when he saw one.

"The arteries are effectively blocked off, and in the distance I can see patrol cars fanning into the streets to the south and west . . ."

Daizy was speaking into his microphone.

"Chief Jammu is standing ten yards to my left and is directing the operation in conjunction with officers in the police chopper . . ."

Daizy's voice spoke from Probst's radio.

"From what I've been able to gather, the police received indications of the whereabouts of the terrorists several hours ago, and in the last twenty minutes they've been able to follow their movements with a high degree of precision . . ."

Daizy was gesturing while he spoke to his invisible audience, his lips moving in the patchwork light while his words, in perfect sync with the lips, beat like rain against the windows of Probst's car.

Titus Klaxon and his Steamcats, local men who'd made the big time and beat it to LA, were playing an exclusive gig at Shea's Lounge on Vandeventer Avenue, an event of a must-see nature. RC and Annie left their son Robbie with Clarence and Kate's kids and let Clarence drive the four of them through a white-out winter storm and park in a vacancy whose identity and ownership (a lawn? a lot? a street?) were concealed by a foot of snow. This was the second storm in two days and still the sky was not exhausted. Passing the mute bouncer, RC watched Annie's glasses grow foggy and blind her. She removed them and smiled, and he kissed her and squeezed her shoulders. On the darkened dais somebody was playing a fast beat on the high hat, which meant the show was nowhere close to starting. Ernie Shea, a friend of Clarence's, ushered them all to a well-situated table and personally fetched a pitcher of Hammaker. The highhatter ceased. RC and Clarence, Kate and Annie all talked for a while about everything and nothing, like in the old days, a double date, except there hadn't ever been old days like this. RC was ten and Annie two when Kate and Clarence married.

Soon enough Clarence walked his chair back a couple feet for a one-on-one with RC. "So, Off-sir," he said. "How's life?"

RC reflected. The main thing in his life right now was that

he and Annie were getting squeezed out of their apartment by their landlord Sloane. There were new ordinances to keep the rent halfway reasonable, but Sloane was charging fees, doing noisy nighttime renovation in vacant apartments, and offering a tidy sum to anybody willing to move out. Already there'd been a lot of takers.

Clarence sniffed up a cigar and clamped down. "Not a hundred percent wonderful?" How bloodshot his eyes were was visible even in the low orange light and smoke. "What could be bad, Off-sir?"

"You interested, Clarence, or you just making fun of me?"

"I'm interested, Off-sir."

"Then stop calling me that." These Q&A sessions made RC nervous when Annie was right there in front of them. Clarence had an ulterior concern, as in, How's life treating my little sister? "I'm fine," RC said. "Except we're getting squeezed out of our place."

"That a fact?" Clarence puffed.

"Sloane was up on Saturday talking to Annie. He said supposedly he couldn't afford not to."

"Sloanes'll be Sloanes." Clarence's eyes looked like it hurt for them to see. "What else is new."

It wasn't a question, but RC answered it. "Annie got that job, you know. I aced my communications test."

"So you two all set to pay that nice high rent."

RC drank his beer. The players moving at the back of the dais wore fishnet shirts and tank tops, while outside it was blizzarding to kill derelicts. It was no fun, RC thought, to hang around with a pessimist who was seeing his predictions confirmed, and that was what Clarence was, exactly that. It made RC want to apologize for the world, for all the bad things in it. He could live with the troubles and expenses of his life, but watching them match up with Clarence's low expectations just killed him.

Yesterday RC had actually called up Struthers, Alderman Rondo, to ask what could be done about Sloane. Smooth, smoother, smoothest, Struthers said there was replacement housing in the works, but RC asked who'd want to live in a project if they could help it, even it was a "good" project for "good" folks, like Struthers said, which was probably a lie, one way or another, knowing projects and knowing Struthers. Struthers said the new replacement housing fund would pay three months' rent, not until February or March, but you could borrow on the chit. And RC said, "So what? We live three months in a motel. Then what? There be places to live in this city three months from now if everybody like us is in the same boat?" And Struthers said, "It'll all work out in the end, brother. Nobody's getting permanently shafted anymore." Struthers, the exact opposite of Clarence, made RC hope the worst would happen. Everything was shiny as a dime in the world of Ronald Struthers, now the richest man RC knew or had ever met.

Annie and Kate were looking at snapshots out of Kate's purse.

"We knocked down a building on Biddle on Tuesday, RC," Clarence said, putting on his anecdotal face, the narrowed eyes, the lingering cigar. "Tuesday and Wednesday. Place was stripped as they ever is, pipes, fuse boxes, hardware, doors, and a lot of the brick. Some nice old doors, I suspect. Anyway, we made sure there wasn't a thing worth taking or leaving, and we let loose with the ball, and what do you know if there ain't a little basement we overlooked. One of these real old setups, dirt floor, used to keep potatoes and pickles and coal down there, turn of the century. I mean, just a little nothing *hole*, and what should come crawling out but a family of three."

Clarence gave RC the awful smile he'd been smiling lately, that no-surprise-to-me. "Little lady not much older than Stanly, got a three-year-old, and a baby on her tit, sucking right while we talked." He paused again to assure himself of RC's attention. "These things affect me, RC. They still affect me. I backed off with the ball for a sec and talked to her. She come up in August from Mississippi, town called Carthage, never been to St. Louis for more than visits, but looking for the father of her kids. One thing leads to another, and come December she's living in a coal cellar and eating soup-line, too dumb or too shy to do any better, and living, at the present, in a coal cellar. I said I'm real sorry, little girl, but we got a job here, and where you people gonna go? She didn't know. She didn't know. Off-sir. Now, not that people *should* be living in coal cellars. It's that I was tearing down to make room for office space. It's people like this exist, and there's a winter coming on."

RC knew Clarence. "She back in Carthage?"

"I can only vouch as to her getting on the bus." Suddenly Clarence sat up straight, like a pointer. "Lookee here." He nodded, and across the room, speak of the devil, was Ronald Struthers. He was wearing turtleneck and corduroy and his gold chain with the big clenched-fist medallion, and stood talking with Ernie Shea. Both faced the dais. Behind the curtains a preliminary quiet had fallen. Points of light gleamed on the waiting trap set, on stands holding saxes and trumpets without the mouthpieces. The lounge was full and restless, the smoke so thick it would have to rain tar pretty soon.

"Ooooo," Clarence said, very unimpressed. "What's he doing here?"

"Maybe come for the music," RC answered, with sarcasm but also a little apprehension, caught as he was in a feud that was not of his making. Struthers and Shea moved towards the dais on a political assembly line, pausing at each table to let Struthers cop a handshake, grin and flatter. They ducked behind the curtains and became two lumps with feet. RC moved his chair back to the table and touched Annie's shoulder.

"Mm?" she said, smiling at a remark of Kate's.

"You see Struthers?"

"Should I want to?" She turned back to Kate.

RC filled his glass, he filled the ladies' glasses, reached and filled Clarence's too, and winked at a waitress for a fresh pitcher. He'd pay for this drinking at 6:00 tomorrow morning when he caught the bus to the Academy. Annie needed the car now. He'd be parched and shivering, and the new snow sharp as filings.

Steamcats parted the curtains, taking their places. The drummer, a bare-chested Rastafarian or Rastafarian look-alike, knocked off a few self-important fragments of rhythm, adjusted his chair, flipped a stick, and played a rustle on the snare, building to a roll. Out came Titus, fatter than ever, in a silver sequined tunic and a feathered headdress, Indian. He bobbed to the assembled guests, to scattered applause. But then, with a cautionary wink to the crowd, he stepped back and lunged behind the curtains again.

"He's the cool one," Annie whispered.

Clarence was chewing his cigar and looking ill.

Making their way through the players now were Ernie Shea

and Ronald Struthers, Ernie leading Ronald by the elbow, a guide in hostile untracked territory. They stopped at the mike and surveyed the crowd. Steamcats crossed their arms, hunched their shoulders, and stared at Struthers as if he were a white bank president. The houselights were dimming. The light retreated to the dais, coalesced in a purple bath in which the Steamcats sidled and licked their lips. Shea tapped the mike. "It's always a great pleasure," he said, "to welcome home these gentlemen who bring back such fond memories to me and I'm sure to you. Now our star just spoiled a climax by entering and withdrawing a little hastily . . ."

Laughter all around.

"But we've got all night and we'll try it again. Let's do it right this time. Ladies and gentlemen, friends, Romans, countrymen, I give you Saint Louie's own—Titus Klaxon!"

Titus came back less jaunty. Face down, he walked to Shea and Struthers and dwarfed them with his musical bulk. He stood between them. He hugged them to his sides like dolls. "Thank you," he said when the clapping began to subside. "Thank you very much."

People dying in that blizzard outside. Every blizzard, people died.

"I'd like to say a word if I may," Struthers told the mike.

Silence fast. The crowd embarrassed.

"I know we're going to give Titus the welcome he deserves," Struthers said. "I know this because I know Titus Klaxon, I know him for a man who won't forget his roots, and I know the same of every man and woman in this room . . ."

Someone snickered at RC's right shoulder; at his left, Clarence was chewing his thumb now, not the nail, the thumb itself.

"I remember when these cats were just getting started, playing the—"

CRACK. The drummer hit a rim shot and Struthers jumped. The Steamcats looked at the ceiling.

"Well." Struthers cleared his throat. "It sounds as if we're all itching to get on with it, we'll all cherish the memories tonight brings, so without further ado—" Draping an arm around Shea and an arm around Titus, he cast his smile across the room like he was fishing for photographers, and then, in a blue flash, he was photographed. Were cameras even allowed here? RC craned his neck, looking for the source of the flash. He found it. Pressed against the wall three tables over was a kid, curly-haired and white, with a camera and a girl. Young, suburban-looking. Types.

"That's the kid took the picture of Benny Brown," Clarence whispered.

Struthers had vanished and Shea was swimming through the tables to the photographer. They spoke. The girl looked worried. The kid took out a card and Shea nodded, but not happily.

While Steamcats screwed in mouthpieces and plucked strings, Titus took the mike. "My good friend Ronald Struthers here," he said, "just asked me to dedicate a song to a little lady I guess a lot of you know, and this first number's as good as any." Titus stretched his stomach and took a huge breath, as if keeping some bad food down. "This is a brand-new song. It's been a while since we saw the old streets and it may be—I want you all to consider—it may be that being an outsider now I can see things you all can't. If that's the case, I don't apologize, because I'm glad, real glad, to be with you tonight. My rule is blues is truth, and so, my men, let's show these wonderful people which blues I'm talking about." The drummer snapped to. "Here's a song for the lady in blue, it's called"—his voice dropped down to a deep bass—"'Gentrifyin' Blues.'"

•

Probst was sick. He had a bad cold, the worst in several years, complete with chills and sizzling headaches, a sore throat, and a general sense of injury and injustice. The usual drugs hardly helped. Over the weekend he had touched some surface, or some surface had touched him, and then he'd touched his eyes or nostrils and the viruses had entered. It could have been any surface. Every thing had surface, and active germs were waiting, hopping eagerly into the air, on an indeterminate number of them—on pens and seat cushions, on shoes and sidewalks, streets and floors, on tumblers and towels and parking meters. Telephones crawled with viruses. Quarters taken as change were warm, aswarm. Elevator buttons were pustules glowing with received virulence. Rolf Ripley had wiped wads of living goo on his sleeves and Probst had grasped them. There were secretions of Buzz all over his office. Hutchinson had taken Probst's coat, Dr. Thompson had shaken his hand, Meisner had had a runny nose, and the General—Sam—*had handed him doughnuts*. In retrospect he trusted no one.

It was 3:00 in the afternoon, December 12. Bundled in his overcoat, a scarf beneath his chin, he pushed through two sets of doors in Plaza Frontenac, his and Barbara's shopping center of choice. The people entering with him had empty hands and a bounce in their steps. Those leaving had packages, Saks bags swinging at shin level, wrapped books or records in the crooks of arms, the serrated tops of small paper bags poking from coat pockets. Probst stopped to orient himself. Malls were never executive-friendly, and he felt especially unwanted at this hour on a weekday afternoon. Normally even a bad cold would not have kept him from going in to the office. But he'd also come down with a birthday, which was likewise the worst he'd had in several years. He was fifty. A boy in a green loden coat chased an errant red balloon right up to his toes, and he sneezed down onto the boy's whorled blond hair.

"Gesundheit!" said the precocious voice.

"Well! Thank you."

His words left a bad taste in his mouth. People were jostling him. He took refuge at the nearest plate-glass window, behind which white torsos displayed black lingerie. Well! Well! Well! He was sounding like his father. His father had made constant recourse to the word "well," using it not as a dilatory particle but as an exclamation signifying both surprise and approval. If a customer at the Gamm's shoe store where he worked complimented the suit and tie he was wearing (he was very particular about his clothes), he began his reply with a hearty, if occasionally somewhat baffling, "Well!" When Ginny or Martin came to Gamm's to ask for money, the word expressed his delight at recalling his possession of such a pretty and vivacious young daughter, or such a serious and courteous young son. "Well!" The word put his customers on hold; these were his important young children; his children, mind you, not his grandchildren. From the store he brought home other usages, usages which did not seem at all distinctive at the time, but which forty years later were coming out of Martin's mouth with increasing frequency, as he approached the age his father had been when Martin first became conscious of him as a person weaker than himself. In recent months he'd caught himself using the word "good" as an adverb, and worse, the construction "question whether," a phrase characteristic of a man thinking aloud (there was an arrogance in thinking aloud) rather than addressing those around him. At the dinner table Ginny and Martin and their mother might have been discussing whether to replace their mutt Shannon, who one night had failed to return from his evening run; their father would sit silently with his beer while the table was cleared and freestone peaches were served in their syrup, and then, with a grunt: "Question whether it wouldn't be simpler to get a stuffed animal for Gin and a sweetheart for Martin."

In the show window, right before Probst's eyes, a white torso was coming alive. It rocked and spun as if in a frenzy over its lack of limbs; two saleswomanly hands had taken hold of it by the stump of its neck and were removing the bra from its conical alabaster breasts. He saw the saleswoman reading the size label on the bra. She turned to a customer, shook her head, and shrugged.

To his left a little girl was crying. Her mother knelt and tugged her ringlets as if adjusting the picture. She wiped the tears with her thumb, obviously not realizing that this was an excellent way to introduce viruses to her daughter's bloodstream. Probst moved on.

He'd come to buy Christmas presents for Barbara, to make sure he got at least one thing finished today. On his list were books, bath products, and diamond earrings. He planned to let Plaza Frontenac give shape to his other, more abstract gift ideas. Fortunately Barbara was the only person he ever had to go shopping for.

Yesterday evening, when he was trying to show his body who was boss by helping Mohnwirbel clear the latest eight inches of snow from the driveway, Barbara had called him inside. Jack DuChamp was on the phone. Jack hadn't called since the night of the stadium incident. He said that he and Elaine always—heh, well, for years—threw a Christmas party on the twenty-third. Sorry about the late notice, but they'd sure like to have Martin and Barbara.

Probst, under surveillance by Barbara, managed to tell Jack that it looked like they might not be able to make it, some relatives of Barbara had said they might be in town, that kind of thing, although they would definitely make an effort—

"Great, great," Jack said as Barbara, apparently satisfied, left the room. "We're really looking forward to seeing you. Be sure and bring Luisa too, it'll be a lot of families. Our kids would love seeing her."

On his way back out into the snow, Probst stuck his head in the smoky den. He said it looked as though they wouldn't have to go. Wouldn't have to go? Good grief, Martin. Of course they wouldn't go.

This morning he'd phoned in an additional order to the Florida citrus concern that provided for most of his and Barbara's out-of-town gift needs. The DuChamps would get grapefruit in wintry February; the announcement should arrive by the day of the party. Probst hoped the citrus, the formality of the payoff, would somehow have the desired effect.

Which was that Jack leave him alone.

Dodging a pair of cannonballs—squat boys in jean jackets hurtling into a video outlet—he gained the escalator, where he sneezed into his hand and then clutched the black plastic handrail for balance, infecting it. He saw the handrail race extrusively out ahead of him and round the horn into the mechanics of the operation. He saw his germs spreading out along the entire band. He turned. Ten faces looked up at him, some of them with tenuous recognition (Morton Priest . . . ?). He'd made them sick.

A shop projecting science and plenitude, a tobacconist's, caught his eye. Gallon jars with bevelled glass stoppers were labeled and stationed on shelves as in a museum of soil types, some of the tobaccos as black as Iowa, some red as Arkansas, others austere and blond, others sandy, others loamy and variegated. The store sold candy and magazines, too. An olde time shoppe. Probst went in, acknowledged the proprietor, and shook his head—just looking. Running up and down the steps of the candy display, his eyes were tripped up by triangular boxes of Toblerone. He turned one over in his hands and saw messages in German, French, and Italian, one language on each side.

No English? Well! How neat, how imported, how Swiss of these chocolatiers, to use all three languages of Switzerland. A minor mystery—why were the boxes triangular?—was clarified. He'd buy some. They came in Christmas colors.

From the periodical display he took a copy of *House* magazine. He wanted a sense of the people who on Friday would be photographing his living room, breakfast room and kitchen. The proprietor rang up the purchase. Probst asked him if he'd ordered the Toblerone straight from Switzerland.

How so?

Well, there was no English on the boxes.

The proprietor frowned and looked. "Yes there is."

Probst looked. There was English. Also German and Italian. How on earth had he mistaken the English for French?

"Yes, English, French and German," the proprietor said. Probst shrugged and made to leave, but he couldn't help seeing the man rub his nostrils with two of the fingers with which he'd just taken a five-dollar bill—

"Everything all right?"

Nodding over his shoulder, Probst found himself running into something which he grabbed to stabilize and came even closer to toppling before he saw what it was: a wooden cigar-store Indian, nearly as tall as he, rocking violently. He made it stop. The proprietor was shaking his head with annoyance and disapproval. Probst had overestimated his stamina today.

He crossed the atrium and sat down on a polished oak bench beneath a miniature tree with waxy leaves. He was in no condition to be shopping. But if he didn't shop now he'd have to come back another time. Barbara had asked how long he'd be out and he'd said at least an hour. He couldn't barge in on birthday preparations. Besides, if he went home, he'd go to bed. He hated to go to bed, on his birthday.

But what was a birthday anyway? All he could picture, when he thought of being born, was his head emerging from a hole between his mother's legs. The picture became remarkably vivid when he thought about it, as if he really had seen it on TV or in a theater and was remembering. What camera, at bed level, had captured the emergence of his head? It was a flickering old film, from an old, old camera. No history seemed more ancient.

In the days when she still fed him nice questions, Luisa had asked what his earliest memory was. That would have to have been, he said, the streetcar accident when he wasn't yet three. He remembered flying through the air and hitting a silvery bar. Yes. He'd been standing on a seat, not yet three . . .

The shoes and murmurs of shoppers passing him sounded impatient, as pedestrian movements always do to someone at rest, creating a patter so unbearable that only joining it can bring relief. Nevertheless Probst resisted. His throat was a tube of pain. He needed to sit a while longer. Then he'd shop, buy bath oil, books and earrings. He might not have the strength today to shop for bargains, but colds made him extravagant. He was sick, it was his birthday, he could do what he pleased. He could recall that for years he was haunted by the memory of propulsion, of collision with a bar, as by a nightmare undispelled by identification as such, without knowing that a thing like this had actually happened to him. People put accidents behind them, and it was only by chance that his mother, years later, had mentioned a time on the Grand Avenue line when you, Martin, were thrown and given a concussion.

He could reach back even further, into the history of his father. Carl Probst had had a farm and a house in Stillwater, he was young and unindebted and owned shares in the largest local bank, when the hard times blew into Oklahoma. His wife died, and the rain stopped falling. The banks began to foreclose on mortgages. He sold his shares in protest (so he later claimed, though undoubtedly he needed the cash, too) and sold them, moreover, in the face of what the whole town knew: there was oil in the area. By 1940 the bank was among the wealthiest in Oklahoma. By 1940 Carl Probst was in St. Louis handling the feet of strangers. If he'd hung on to his shares he'd have been not fabulously rich but not so poor that he couldn't have weathered the dust-bowl years, and leased his land, and made it. He didn't make it. Probst saw him trying to break that red brick dirt in February using two horses and his only son—Carl Jr.—to make way for seed on which no rain, or not enough, would fall, while on every horizon, on every unblacklisted tract, derricks rose. He heard him telling the young children of his young second wife that he'd done the Right Thing. And he remembered, as a child, believing him.

He popped a Sucret. Tennis shoes squeaked on the parquet floor. The feeling he had now was a feeling he'd had as a younger man sitting on benches, the feeling of being an old man sitting on a bench and able to watch the world go by. The world was Frontenac women in boots with salt stains, flitting typists who glanced at their watches, businessmen fueling one another's laughter, small children unraveling from mothers to point at the lavender elephants in the window opposite Probst, to paw from a distance. But there were parallel worlds—worlds of the invisible, of viruses, of latent behavior, of phrases of his father's. On Sunday when Wesley had made his pitch and mentioned the world "circle" and Probst had decided to leave at once, it had not actually been a decision. He had found himself below the threshold of cause and effect, following an action that came straight and swiftly from the soul of what he was, as he reenacted his father's central denial: I won't be a part of this; no matter what it costs me, I won't be a part.

An elderly woman in red rubber boots was sitting down beside him on the bench. He began to make more room between them and heard her say, quite distinctly, "Little prissy." He made it a whole yard between them.

We're at the center of things, Martin.

Probst had not stopped thinking about his morning in the sauna with the—with Sam. Sam found it important that Probst had bled at the stadium. Probst found it strange that his injuries had not been listed in the papers or on the airwaves. The more he thought about it, the more peculiar it seemed. He was Municipal Growth chairman, he'd been as seriously hurt as some of those other twelve; how much more did it take to get yourself counted? Had some police sergeant or hospital clerk refused to count a thirteenth injury for the same reason that high-rises lacked thirteenth floors? Probst didn't mind not having his name in the papers, it appeared there often enough in other contexts, but he wondered why the powers of information had seen fit, for once, to ignore him. If Trudy Churchill's name and address and broken leg were Known to them, then Probst's broken finger and blood loss must have been equally Known. A suppression had obviously occurred.

Conspiracy. Coincidence. *Conspiracy*.

Jammu controlled the police. Hutchinson, who'd spoken ominously of professional courtesy, controlled KSLX. Duane Thompson's parents were both powerful figures at Barnes, where Probst had been treated. Pete Wesley controlled the city press office. The owners of the Big Red were intimate with everyone else who mattered, with Meisner, Norris, Buzz, Ross Billerica, Harvey Ardmore.

Probst trusted no one. He had no knowledge of anyone's motives. How could he be central when he was so abysmally ill-informed? Was he uninformed *because* he was central? If so, then the conspiracy was working both ways, excluding him from the news and the news from him. He was sick. Men kept away from him. He could hear them laughing and shouting and whispering like schoolboys outside the window of his inner sickroom. He was sick, and he could no more clear his head than he could find his way back into an involvement in the city's public life, though he was nominally still at the center of it. All was treachery all of a sudden, Wesley, Meisner, Ripley, Ardmore, his own daughter, much of Municipal Growth. They wanted to use him without letting him in on the secret. He wasn't counted because the conspiracy didn't want him to count.

The thousand quiet voices of Plaza Frontenac could have been hospital visitors, mourners in a mausoleum, refugees, evacuees, late-night travelers or watchers at the scene of a crime or accident, such was the implacable unselfconsciousness of their collective voice. As Probst listened, a great waste seemed to open in the soundscape. Perceptual capillaries filled the entire indoor space, superexfoliating, dully aching, all of them translucent, and all of them Probst's own; or had the shopping center shrunk, in that sick sensation of tininess, until it fit in Probst's ear and reduced the thousand sounds to auditory dots, compressing them, in the shell of his cranium, into the pure white rushing of a lifeless ocean? The birthday feeling nagged him. His conception grew dropsical and comprehensive. What if he was the city? More than centrally located: the thing itself?

Born in the very pit of the Depression, he had groped and bullied his way into some kind of light, demolishing and steamrolling and building higher, building the Arch, building developments of the most youthful and prosperous nature, the golden years of Martin Probst. Inside, though, he was sick, and the city was sick on the inside too, choking on undigested motives, racked by lies. The conspiracy invaded the city's bloodstream while leaving the surfaces unchanged, raged around him and in him while he sat apparently unseen, uncounted, uninvolved, and it was right here, in this identity of his life with the city's life, that he could see himself disappearing. The more he was a figure, the less he was a person. The more complete the identity, the more completely it excluded him. There were two Probsts, it seemed, and always had been; who else had run the camera in the delivery room, and who else was sitting thinking on this bench right now? But the personal Probst was disappearing. As his head had appeared fifty years ago, so he was disappearing now. He was a conspirator himself, as responsible for his disappearance as anyone else was. He let a childhood friend pester him, an old struggle with Barbara wear him down, he let anything and everything distract him, and meanwhile bugs were falling out of walls, personalities collapsing in the space of weeks, and everywhere Indians—planting bombs, teasing executives, dazzling the press and transferring stock and stopping traffic, like harbingers and furies both, storming back up the trail from the old Indian Territory, from which the Osage Warriors were telling him now there was no permanent escape. *I've no use for cliques*. It was a phrase of his father's. The son should have said: *I don't have any use for*. Nothing was safe from his xenophobia now, not even his own heart, not even the heart of his own city.

He heard a splash of water.

It was the old woman in red boots. "Lit-tle Miss Know-it-all," she sang. "Lit-tle Miss Know-it-all." She was swinging her legs, her coat spread open, and in a pale splashing flood she was urinating through the slats of the bench onto the polished parquet floor, gushing urine as if she'd been punctured. Probst staggered to his feet. "Lit-tle Miss Know-it-all!" She swung her legs, still splashing when he finally got out of earshot.

He wound up in Crabtree & Evelyn, a gift box of a store wrapped in subdued colors and drenched with scents that blended in an almost caustic potpourri. Unlike Barbara, Probst seldom lost his sense of smell. He saw brushes and sponges. Soap lozenges. Pink crystals. He was shaking all over.

"Can I help you, sir?"

"Yes, I'd like to buy some bath oil."

A woman with a greenish frost was smiling, trying to help. She looked simple and good. "What sort of thing did you have in mind?"

Probst allowed himself to be shown around. Usually he wasn't so humble with sales help, but he wanted to be led. He answered questions about Barbara's preferences. He took four different bottles, ridiculously many, but they were all flavors he'd seen at one time or another on the shelf by the tub. The more bottles he took, the more solicitous the woman became. Buying, he was calming down.

"This will be plenty," he said pleasantly.

"Oh, I did want to show you one—"

"Thanks. This will be all." He accompanied her to the cash register. Payment was an agreeable business. He used American Express. The woman spoke of snow. Much, he agreed. It would melt soon enough, however. As she handed him the form to sign, the telephone rang. She excused herself.

Martin Probst

He stared at the words he had made. As always, he'd formed each letter individually, printing it. There were twelve of them, six letters in each name. The date was 12/12. Luisa was born on 11/1 and Barbara on 4/8. "Luisa" had five letters and "Barbara" had seven. Martin, born on 12/12, was both the average and the sum, and he was disappearing in the sudden blaze of schemes. Here the schemes were so perfect that there was no remainder at all, nothing left for him to do but die, his life explained.

"There you are, sir, all set." The woman with the green frost was humoring him. "Have a good day."

He tapped his card into its slot in his wallet as he left and slid the wallet into his pants as he entered the main hall. He had to get out of here. But he'd assured Barbara he wouldn't barge in. He stopped in front of the little Johnston & Murphy store, where a salesman stood like a penguin in shiny black shoes. Neiman or Saks? That was the question. Saks was larger, but the path to it led past the woman in red boots. Well then, Neiman it was. He remembered Sam Norris's striped cotton shirt.

I love you, Barbara. *I love you, Barbara.*

That was difficult, but ultimately he could manage it, because ultimately he could believe she was finite, ultimately he might see her on a stretcher and believe that she was dead.

But I am Martin Probst? *I am Martin Probst?*

There were limits—the speed of light, the moment of birth— and to pronounce his name to himself, to say it with conviction, was to pass the limit, split in two, and see himself being born. He disappeared in the crowd he saw around him. On his right was a rouged darling in sweat pants and pink running shoes and a long mink coat. On his left, two dowagers in blouses that buttoned at the neck were viewing with haughty distaste the places where they bought their gifts. Passing now, the pendular arms of a fat black man pumped affirmative glottals through his mouth. How easy it would be for a roving reporter, a Don Daizy or Cliff Quinlan, to stop these people one by one and say to each in turn, "I don't want you to tell me your name, I want you to tell yourself who you are," and for the camera to record the given face as the person did so, whatever surprise or discouragement crossed it as he or she confronted a world that was not a spherical enclosing screen on which pictures were projected, but a collection of objects to which the given person was dared to belong. It was a dreadful vision: in the mall and beyond, an infinity of carriers of latent awareness. The infection of the earth by seeing human beings.

But Probst had reached Neiman-Marcus and entered the dappled silence produced by serious shopping. He took an escalator, careful with his hands this time. He looked at the people around him in a new way: as co-conspirators. The General was right. His vision was too crude, though; he could only think in literal terms, in listening devices and docudramatic subterfuges. There weren't any bugs in Probst's house.

There were shirts galore. A line of rustic colors, woolly blends, by Ralph Lauren. Calvin Klein pastels. Outlandish Alexander Julians. Probst met the eyes of a deeply tanned man wearing frameless glasses. The eyes widened a little. There was suspicion between him and Probst. Suspicion of recognition. Probst looked for his size, which was medium in casuals and otherwise 15½–34.

There weren't any bugs. But there was worse, patterns too internal and personal to trace to a plotting human, too cohesive to be accident. It was a matter of simple arithmetic that Luisa should turn eighteen the same year Probst turned fifty. But why should this also have been the year that Jack DuChamp re-entered his life? Why not last year, or next year, or no year? Why had Barbara started smoking again after a decade of good health? Why had Dozer died? And Rolf Ripley turned suddenly the soul of malevolence, and the whole city a thing of foreignness and menace? Why was it all happening at once?

There was an answer. Silky plaids, six or eight variations on a red and yellow theme. They made him want to own them all and wear them all together, to do justice to the spectrum of the designer's inventiveness. He glanced into the face of a girl Luisa's age. She replaced the shirt she'd been feeling and glanced back. She could have been a Hatfield and he a McCoy. . . . Ugly shirts by Christian Dior which were made, as was clear on the shelf, for men with round manikin chests and wasp waists.

There was an answer: if you looked for patterns, you found them. If you didn't look, they weren't there. Probst wasn't born yesterday, after all. He knew there was no God, no conspiracy, no meaning; there was nothing whatsoever. Except shirts. By gravitation, seemingly, he'd found the shirts he wanted. They came in three colors, the maroon and black, a green and black, and a yellow and black. The latter two looked clownish, and another man already had his hands on them. The man had a mustache. *It was Harvey Ardmore.*

They scrimmaged. Angry looks and mutters of surprise and consternation. They backed off.

The man was not Harvey Ardmore. Probst turned on his heel and left Plaza Frontenac.

Substantial ramparts of snow ringed the parking lot. In the west the sun was setting, and to the south the lights were coming on in the windows of the Shriners' Hospital for Crippled Children.

After he'd stashed the packages in his study he returned to the kitchen. "I thought maybe I should go and see S. Jammu," he said.

"Jammu?" Barbara compared opposite sides of the cake she was frosting. "What for?"

Probst reinflated all the little sacs in his lungs and tried, without success, to form words with the air he blew back out. In the warm kitchen, in the persevering warmth of Barbara today, he couldn't begin to reconstruct the patterns he'd seen at Plaza Frontenac. He couldn't think in this house.

"Would you like to lick the bowl?" Barbara asked.

"I'll see."

"Did you have the radio on in the car?"

"No."

"I wondered if you'd heard about the attack."

"No."

"I think it was out in Chesterfield, at three or something. The Indians. You can turn the radio back on. I got tired of the repetitions." She spun the cake, apparently finished with it. "Somebody was hurt but nobody was killed. It was at some kind of telephone installation. Rockets. Hand-held . . . rockets. I guess I wasn't really listening."

"Huh." With a spoon Probst scraped frosting from the side of the bowl. Barbara was peeling strips of foil out from under the cake. She didn't think much of Jammu. Sometimes it seemed like she didn't think much of anyone. "I'm working on the agenda for Municipal Growth in February," he said. "I thought we might invite Jammu. She's done surprisingly well."

"Surprisingly?" Barbara licked her thumb. "You mean, 'for a woman'?"

"For anyone. But yes, especially for a woman. She's very able."

Able. It was another inherited usage, and Barbara turned to him. If he'd become self-conscious, it was largely her doing.

"By all means go and see her, then." She patted his cheek and pushed his hair off his forehead. "How are you feeling?"

"I think I'll do just that. She's remarkably communicative from what I hear."

Barbara waited a second. "Is it still in your throat?"

"I wouldn't be surprised if she goes a long way here," he continued. "She certainly shows us up a little."

"You'll probably want to shower and change," Barbara said. "We might have visitors."

"I guess she comes from a place where women do this sort of thing."

"I want to wash a few of these dishes, and then I'm going to get cleaned up myself."

"It's hard to believe she's only thirty-five."

"Martin." She pinned his cheeks between her thumb and fingers and made him look at her. "Just shut up, all right?"

He wrenched free.

"*Please* go take a shower or whatever you need to do."

He tapped the edge of a counter thoughtfully, preparing to leave the kitchen, content to let the danger pass. But it was too late. Barbara was pacing in a fury, snatching dishes and dumping them in the sink, unknotting her apron and balling it up. What was *wrong* with him? (She wondered.) He was turning into a monster. (She claimed.) She could tolerate his thick head, she could tolerate the silences, but she would *not* be insulted like this; she was sorry to act this way on his birthday, but there came a point where she couldn't help it. (She explained.) Why was he standing there? Why didn't he go change? (She asked.) Get *out* of here.

Probst frowned. "What did I say? I don't remember what I said."

"You don't remember what you said?" She moved closer. "You don't remember what you said? You *don't remember* what you said?"

Come on. He'd heard her the first time. He smiled a little, and perceived that this worked to his detriment. The style of her pacing changed. She circled the kitchen with her hands behind her back, her brows knitted, her shoulders hunched, like Peter Falk's Columbo. She stopped and stared at him. "Why do you treat me like such shit?"

"I simply said," he said, "that it might be a good idea to go and see Jammu. I don't see what's wrong with that. Just simply as a matter of civic responsibility."

"Oh jesus." She fell, sideways, into a chair.

"Now, what? I don't understand."

"Go take a shower. Go, go, go, go, go."

He was not an insensitive person. If he thought for a moment, as he was doing now, he could locate the solid logical underpinnings of his actions. When he'd praised Jammu he hadn't meant it nicely. He just didn't want to be treated like a baby, to have his face patted. Barbara was "nice" to him, so that when the explosion occurred anyway he would be the one to take the blame. He wasn't as nice as she was, but he wasn't sneaky either.

"I never asked you to spend all day in the kitchen," he said.

At this, her hands reached into the space around her, closing on invisible things. She caught something finally, and her fists dropped to her knees. "My life is in order, Martin." She paused. "Sometimes I try to do things to make people happy. I don't ask that they actually be happy, I only want a little credit for the effort, like any first-class citizen."

"I'm still not clear on what the issue here is."

"I've been saying for two months that I don't like that woman, and you come home—you're always coming home, you notice that? You come home and you act like you've just discovered her. Like the world was created on Monday, and you're the first to notice. She acts like *she's* the first one. She oh forget it. You're hopeless." Barbara's eyes scanned the kitchen table, her head faintly echoing their movement as they followed the scurrying invisible things. Outside, a dog started barking. "But you know what, Martin?" She looked up with a puzzled smile, her eyes moist and bright. "I really like myself." It was a different woman speaking now, a Barbara much younger. She smoothed her skirt across her lap, gathering the slack under her thighs. Then she sobbed. "I really love myself."

Probst no longer felt the least bit sick. When she sobbed, he got erections. "I do, too," he said.

"No you don't!" She leaped to her feet and kicked backwards, shoving the chair into a cabinet. "How dare you compare that woman to me? *How dare you compare Luisa?*"

Frightened, he pressed his back against the refrigerator. She was advancing on him with an index finger raised and her head turned to one side, as if he were flames or a bitter wind. "You better not try it again," she said. "You better watch out. You better start appreciating that girl because if you don't I'm getting out of here and I'm taking her with me. I love you, too, but—" She drew back. "Not as much."

"I'm glad we're clear on that."

"You're going to hold that one against me, aren't you? I can see it in your face. You're going to save that."

"Well, what if I do?" The volume of his voice surprised him. "You know I have a cold. I didn't come home to fight with you. I won't fight with you. You play as dirty as you say I do. You tell me to go. What, the pain is too great? Something like that. You're like your sister. It's all an act. I won't try to figure out what you pretend you mean. I won't play that game. You're just daring me to go upstairs. I'm damned if I do, damned if I don't. This *is* your fault. You were just asking for it."

"Well, for God's sake, the oracle speaks! The sphinx has spoken!"

"You cunt."

"Is this dignified?"

He stamped on the floor. "You cunt."

Something hard, a penny or an acorn, struck the outside of the window above the sink, and Barbara shrieked. She grabbed his arm and half pushed, half pulled him towards the door. "Go, go, get upstairs, go."

He resisted. "Oh, I'm interrupting something?"

Another object struck the window.

"Go upstairs, come down, and be civil, or—" She looked at her hands. "Or I'm going to stick a knife in you."

"If I don't kill you first."

They looked at each other.

"Go!"

He went. He heard her opening the back door and guessed it was Luisa, coaxed home for his birthday, maybe Duane too, and he bolted up the steps two and three at a time.

Calmer after his shower, he took his time dressing. The registers poured heat into the bedroom and carried a faint smell of childhood, of early winter evenings when he was sent upstairs before the pinochle guests arrived. He felt chastened and young.

He worked on his shoelaces. The floorboards were alive with the sound of news downstairs; he should have been watching it, to stay informed.

When he did go down he found Luisa sitting in the den watching *The $10,000 Pyramid*. From the hall, while the television filled her eyes and ears, he had a moment to observe her unobserved. She was leaning to the left on the sofa, in a shallow slouch, with her right leg partially crossed over the left, held in place by the friction of her black cotton pants, and her left arm folded up between her ribs and the cushion. She seemed to have been arrested in a fall towards the screen. If he startled her, she would assume a more comfortable position. She was wildlife, not a daughter; he was seeing in the flesh, in a natural habitat, some exotic antelope he'd hitherto known only from pictures in *National Geographic*. The studio crowd groaned. She shook her head, once, as if shaking water from her ear. Under the pressure of her unawareness, Probst cleared his throat and saw, as she turned to him, what falseness was expected of him now. He was supposed to act like Dad in a television movie, to let the seriousness show in his face when he said—the significant gesture—*Mind if I watch, too?* He stiffened. "Well!"

"Happy birthday," she said, without inflection.

"Thank you." He took the chair across the room from her. "Mind if I watch, too?"

"I was going to turn it off."

"Yes. It's a dumb show. Here." He turned it off. Barbara was blending something in the kitchen.

"Well?" Luisa said. "Are you surprised?"

"Oh, very." He smiled. "It's a nice surprise. Is, uh, Duane coming, too?"

"He's working."

"Can I get you something to drink?"

"St. Louis Magazine wants him to print some pictures. It's for their January issue and they're due tomorrow. He'll be in the darkroom all night."

"Oh really. You want a beer or something?"

Her face and bearing underwent a mild death, a loss of vitality characteristic of Barbara. "Not right now, thank you." Soon, at any moment, she would leave the room, and with an air of reproach that extended to herself, because she didn't really want to go.

"So," Dad said, "he's working, is he? That's good to hear."

She nodded. "He still doesn't make much money, though." (Money? Barbara gave her money, and she had a credit card, too.) "I guess I eat too much."

"Sure, you're still growing."

From the smile she gave him he could tell this was a good line, though he couldn't have said why. He asked her some easy questions about her grades, and calculus, and transportation, enticing questions to lure an antelope closer, to accustom her to a more domestic habitat. She gave him another smile, and he was feeling more and more like Marlin Perkins when Barbara's voice pealed in the kitchen: "Lu, you want to give me a hand here?"

She was gone like a shot.

Not as much. For eighteen years, in battles more vicious than tonight's, Barbara had managed to avoid saying that, and now, needlessly, she'd gone and done it. A sportsmanlike sympathy made him reluctant to damn her for the blunder. But she would do the same to him.

Luisa reappeared. "Mommy says we should go in the living room."

Probst followed her down the hall. When she turned east he headed north into the kitchen. Barbara was pouring frozen daiquiris. She set the pitcher down and without meeting his eyes kissed him hard, raking his neck with her nails. Into his ear she said, "I want to make love after dinner."

So did he. He always did. But he hadn't expected this, he'd expected instructions or an apology. This was a threat. This was the big gun, her attempt to save the evening. And certainly it was attractive bait.

"I wouldn't want to infect you," he said.

"Oh, I'm sure it's the same thing I had." She spun to the counter where the daiquiris stood. "Do you want to take the brie in?"

There were many presents in the living room by the fire she had made. The uppermost gift, wrapped neatly in newspaper, was obviously books. Probst claimed the last daiquiri on the tray and sat down. Luisa stood warming her back, her glass already half empty. Barbara sat on the sofa in the watchful pose she used to adopt when they played Charades at parties. The silence was made possible by Luisa, who had graduated into self-consciousness and joined them; not long ago, she would have been chattering. She sipped her tropical drink. Track-mounted lamps cast spots on the primitive still lifes. On Sherwood Drive the Probsts were in the jungle, and the flames and shadows vaulted up the walls and gave them a mystic depth. There had never been a moment like this before. The family had changed, and this could be either. Either the last of the old groupings, the last gathering, or the first of the new ones, the first of many. To Probst it seemed the room hung by a thread, and twisted slowly, the flames slanting and stretching. He was dizzy.

"SO HAPPY BIRTHDAY," Luisa said, raising her glass.

"Yes, Martin, really," Barbara loading her words with portent. He felt the concentration of her will on him, the reins of desire and threat. Her feet were on the floor. Her legs were somewhat spread.

"Thank you. Should I open these?"

They indicated that he should. He slid out a shirt box and popped the ribbon. A shirt. He thanked. Luisa went and fetched the pitcher of daiquiris, which Barbara said she'd made because she thought they would feel good on his throat.

"They do," he said. He placed the books wrapped in newspaper on his lap. "It's a pair of shoes. No, it's a lunchbox." He smiled and read the label. *To Daddy from Luisa and Duane.* Tactful indeed. He'd never even met Duane. He thought of Dr. Thompson; why wasn't his name here, too? And Pat, for that matter. To Daddy from Pat. He smelled roasting beef.

"Aren't you going to open it?" Luisa said.

He'd returned it to the pile. "I'm saving it. Best for last."

"Why don't you open it, Martin?"

He put it back on his lap. It was pleasant taking orders from her. He often imagined how he could have arranged his life differently, been more of a dog when at home, and lived from her hand. "Well! Thank you."

"What is it?" Barbara asked, suddenly smoking a cigarette.

Probst slid the books across the floor to her and slit an envelope from New York. The card fell out, a black-and-white Happy Birthday from Ginny and Hal, also Sara and Becky and Jonathan. They'd all signed, which was a nice touch. Ginny usually did things right.

"Have you read these?" Barbara asked Luisa.

"Yes," Luisa said.

Probst waved his fingers for the books. "Can I see 'em again?"

Barbara slid them back to Probst and said, "For school?"

Paterson, by William Carlos Williams. *The Winter's Tale*, by Shakespeare.

"Sort of. I'm writing my poetry paper on Paterson." Luisa glanced at Probst. "Duane recommended them."

A receipt fell out of the Shakespeare. Paul's Books, $3.95, plus $5.95, plus tax. $10.50. The waste of money hurt his throat. He put the newspaper in the fire.

"I thought Daddy would like them." She turned. "We thought you'd like them."

"I'm sure I will."

"The big box is from Audrey," Barbara said.

"Whose husband is trying to ruin me."

"What?" Luisa said, while Barbara shook her head and tried to be noticed.

"It's true," he said. "Your Uncle Rolf has been doing his best to put me out of business."

"Why?"

"You'd have to ask your mother about that." His heart was pounding. As he lifted the next package onto his lap he tried to list reasons for controlling himself. All he came up with, literally the only item, was Barbara's offer. Her whorish offer.

"So are you home for a while?" he asked Luisa. "Or is this only a visit?"

A dark hole opened across the room. It was Barbara's mouth.

"I hadn't really thought about it," Luisa said, apparently sincere.

"Of course not," Barbara said.

"Of course not? Maybe you haven't really thought about where you've been sleeping for the last three weeks either."

"I have, Daddy. You know I have."

"You know she has."

"You keep the hell out of this," he said. The command, with Luisa watching, was like a sock in Barbara's mouth, and she recoiled. "Have you considered apologizing to us?" he said. "Explaining? Promising not to do it again?"

"This isn't good and evil, Daddy. This is just what I'm doing right now, all right?"

"No. I don't know what you mean by that."

"You're just worried about how things look. You want things to look a certain way. You never called me, or anything. We've been—I've been waiting. You should apologize, too. How can I think something's wrong if you don't tell me?"

"You should know. I shouldn't have to tell you. I'm very, very, very disappointed in you."

"Well, what do you think I came home for today?"

"I have no idea."

"Because Mommy said you wanted me to. She said you loved me and you missed me. I love you and I miss you. So."

Why wasn't she crying?

"I can go if you want me to," she said. "You want me to go?"

Barbara spoke. "Don't go. It's your father who should go."

"I told you to shut up."

No answer.

He did want to leave. He was standing up. But Luisa beat him to it. She was already out in the hall, and then she was back, and to Probst's relief and satisfaction she was screaming at Barbara, her fists clenched and body bent, while Barbara simply sat there. "Why don't you make him shut up? Why don't you make him? You let him say these things. *Mommy!* You let him do these things, you let him treat you—" She kicked Barbara in the ankle, and shrank, covering her face. "Oh," she said. She ran upstairs and her bedroom door slammed.

Doors could be identified by their resonance when slammed; the latches also had specific frequencies.

There was a shriek, Luisa, probably some words overamplified. Her door opened, and after a pause a pile of magazines hit the bottom of the stairs, sliding over one another, rolling and flipping, right up to the front door. (Probst had been storing a few things in her room in her absence.) The door slammed again.

Barbara shook her head.

"I'm sorry I told you to shut up," Probst said. "But you were teaming up on me."

She continued to shake her head.

He was calm and tired. He headed upstairs to apologize. Barbara spoke:

"My fault, huh?"

He went upstairs and knocked. He knocked again.

"Who is it?"

He cleared his throat.

"I don't want to talk to you," Luisa said.

He tried the knob, but it was locked. His mouth was busy. *I'm sorry. You're my daughter. I love you. I'm sorry.* To him, the words counted. But they wouldn't come out, not without help, not when he was out alone in the hall, listening.

·

Singh had told Jammu that Probst intended to visit her. When the visit failed to materialize by Thursday night, however, it was clear that he was in less of a hurry to see her than she was to reach a decision on his fate, and that she would have to decide without having personally inspected him. She was annoyed, feeling peculiarly stood up.

The last doors and toilets in her building had fallen silent. Friday was already two hours old. In hers, the only sleepless cell, she was filing away Singh's reports on the Probsts—wicked, gloating documents—and her own notes on the mayor. She locked a drawer and put on a red down jacket, a woolen stocking cap, and "wilderness" snowboots. She looked quite American in the mirror. This wasn't her intent. Her intent was to stay warm and guard her health, although given the recent performance of her sinuses, her health was a lost cause. The few times she'd gone to bed this week, she'd gotten up again soon to pop Sinutabs.

Outside, in the bitter air, she breathed through her mouth, spitting frequently. In November they had told her that Decembers were mild in St. Louis. But this year was hers; this December was not mild. A diminished moon was setting beyond the trees in Forest Park, casting light the color of the skim milk she'd been drinking by the quart. Most of the windows in the Chase-Park Plaza shared the milkiness, but lamps still burned in a few of the rooms. The discernibility of habitation at night in the city in a compartment-alized world, where floor plans show in the faces of the buildings, here the bedroom, here the kitchen, here the bath, this correspon-dence of windows to dwellings and dwellings to dwellers, of struc-ture and humanity: this formed, tonight, a burden to Jammu.

As she crossed Kingshighway she watched a tractor-trailer starting up from the Lindell intersection. It labored interminably in first gear, interminably in second, approaching at a crawl that seemed to defeat momentum more than build it. Jumping a black bank of crud, she began to jog through the park in her boots of lead. This December wasn't mild. At 2:15 on this winter morning, when bare trees drew wind like fossil bronchi, the rock of the continent was very visible to Jammu. Resistance to her operation had developed after all, a natural and predictable counterreaction on the part of the community, and it was precisely now and here that she had lost a sense of herself. She was worn out, feeling far from her motivating hatreds, farther still from her animating de-sires. Martin Probst was in her thoughts. He'd reacted to Wesley's proposal with mindless hostility. At the Municipal Growth meeting six hours ago he'd demanded facts and assigned each of the re-maining members the task of investigating a facet of Jammu's agenda. And he hadn't come to visit her this week.

Without Martin Probst, the resistance would have had a very feeble core, consisting of Sam Norris, County Supervisor Ross Billerica, and assorted extremists. But with Probst aboard, they no longer seemed like a minority. If St. Louis public life was the court of a Mogul, then Probst was the elephants. Jammu had to steal him. But in losing herself she was also losing the capacity to view others as mere characters. Some at least were people, and the knowl-edge oppressed her. She couldn't muster the resolve to give Singh the final go-ahead for continuing the assault on the Probsts. It wasn't fear that stopped her, it was a thing more like awe, the unasked-for awe of the saboteur who, in some corporate vault, comes face to face with an instrument whose very complexity or delicacy acts as a charm against damage. In this context, any tampering at all, no matter how sophisticated, becomes an act of violence.

She ran, avoiding ice. Her running confused her, this activity of her childhood, this helter-skelter dash along a road. It did not become a chief. Her foot fell on ice—black ice.

She went flying through the air. She twisted and landed hard on her shoulder in the clean snow beyond the road. It was more than a foot deep. She realized she was warm.

She moved her arms. She flapped them, packing down the snow and making wings. Twenty-five years ago in Kashmir her mother had taken her skiing where few Indians went. They'd seen American children on their backs in the snow, and Maman, the expert on all things American, informed Jammu that they were making butterflies; but to Jammu they looked more like angels, Christian angels, with skirts and wings and halos, fallen from the sky.

The image pleased her. She felt restored to herself, indomitable again. Just after three o'clock she rang Singh out of bed and told him to go ahead with the job.

"Thanks, Chief," he said. "It'll be a piece of cake. Candy from a baby."

10

Earlier that Thursday night, Luisa and Duane had spent some quiet time in the laundromat. Luisa had woefully inadequate supplies of underwear and socks; she could wash them once in the sink, but she drew the line at twice. And sheets and towels required a machine. By nine o'clock, the last students and singles had packed up and gone, bequeathing Luisa and Duane a luxury of available dryers. Duane was reading messages on the board by the door. Luisa, her French notebook open on her lap, was looking out through the beaded window at Delmar Boulevard, closing one eye and then the other. This fall, her eyesight had gone from not-the-best to needing-correction. Duane's father had recommended an ophthalmologist, and yesterday after school she'd had her appointment, and let them dilate her pupils, and felt burdened with responsibility when Dr. Leake kept changing lenses and asking her, "Is it better this way . . . Or this? Now . . . Or now?" She finally asked him to define "better." He laughed and told her just to do her best. She told his secretary to send the bill to her parents. When she bought glasses she could use American Express. Duane gave her a hard time about the card, he called it antiseptic, but she personally didn't see anything wrong with using it.

Outside, a bus plunged past. Duane, minus both his sweaters, was copying something from the message board into his journal.

Whenever Luisa saw his journal she felt lonely. One time, right after they'd gotten together, she'd asked if she could read it. He'd said no; if he knew she was going to be reading it, he'd be too self-conscious to use it. She was hurt, but she didn't say anything more.

In the second dryer, one of their green sheets had fallen against the round window and seemed in its invertebrate way to be struggling back over the socks and towels to reach the center of the bin. They only had one set of sheets. Kelly green was the first color Luisa saw when the alarm clock rang at 6:30. She said he didn't have to, but Duane always got up and ate breakfast with her.

He sat down in the bucket chair next to hers and zipped his journal into the outer pocket of his knapsack. "How's the essay?"

"Unwritten," she said.

"You want a job? There's an ad there. It's a widow who needs her house cleaned once a week."

"I don't know how to clean houses." She shut her notebook on an unfinished sentence. "How do you know she's a widow?"

"It says. There's another ad from a retired army colonel who's selling a Nova. A 350."

She rested her hands on his shoulder and held his bare upper arm with both her hands, rubbing her cheek on his neck and taking in his smell. At close range, his ear was funny. She slung her arm around his neck, and lifted a leg and lowered it over his knee, and watched the dryers.

Cold air flooded into the laundromat. The newcomer was a thin black man in brilliant yellow pants and a red leather jacket. He tossed a duffel bag onto the nearest row of washers and looked around slowly and theatrically, aware that they were watching. He wore a ruby stud in his ear.

"Good evening," he said, bowing slightly to Duane. Then he bowed to Luisa and said it again: "Good evening." She bowed a tiny bit herself. The only thing worse than being mocked was being mocked by a person who scared you. She untangled herself from Duane.

The man unzipped his duffel and pulled out a pair of bright purple pants and a purple sweatshirt. He put them in a washer and moved to the next. That was all? He dropped in another pair of pants and another sweatshirt, both orange, and continued down the line, whipping out matched clothes, green, red, black, and blue with the flourish of a magician producing scarves, until he'd divided twelve articles among six washing machines. With spidery fingers he unscrewed a jar of blue powder and tapped a little into each machine, like a chef with salt. Then he filled the machines with quarters and started them all up. Water jets rushed in unison as he zipped the empty jar into his bag, shouldered the bag and headed for the door. He stopped. He took three quick steps to his right and snapped his fingers, explosively, right under Luisa's nose.

She squeaked. Her ears burned. He was already gone.

Duane buried his face in a book, a Simenon mystery, keeping his palm on the spine and four fingers curled over the top to hold the pages open. With his other hand he smoothed Luisa's hair and rubbed her neck.

One of the dryers stopped. She went to check. "Duane, these are soaking."

"What's it set at?" he called, turning a page.

"Argh." She turned the selector to Normal and added money. They'd be here all night. She walked around and around the core of washers, deliberately stubbing her rubber toes. "I don't like it here," she said, in passing.

"You should find a laundry service that takes Amex."

She turned. "Fuck you."

His eyes rose calmly from his book. "I beg your pardon?"

"I said it's awful here."

"Then why don't you go and get some more clothes from your house?"

She didn't have an answer. She started crying. Then she stopped. They were in a laundromat. There was nothing she could do but go out to Webster Groves and clean out her drawers. Being with Duane wasn't as much fun as she'd thought it would be—a lot of times it wasn't fun at all—but after what had happened on her father's birthday she couldn't imagine going back home.

.

The door blew open in Barbara's hand. She fell through the entering breeze towards a man prepared, it was clear at once, to catch her. The day was warm, an instance of the weakness of winter, its willingness to turn to spring. She swayed a little.

"Mrs. Probst?"

A pair of light brown eyes was appraising her figure un-ashamedly. She was too surprised to do anything but stare back.

"I'm John Nissing."

She knew, she knew. She took his hand. He nodded at the van in the driveway, where the two photographers who'd come in October were unloading aluminum cases. He let go of her hand. "We have a lot of equipment to bring in."

He strode back down the front walk, his overcoat billowing and coasting, his tweed pants wrapping muscles in his calves and thighs. Barbara had just finished her coffee. Her face looked bad, but she hadn't expected it to matter. She always held her own. She had nothing to prove, and no one to prove it to, or slay. It was too cruel, after a week of ugly strife with Martin, to meet John Nissing. Her resentment steadied her. She inhaled the sweet, dishonest air.

A case in each hand, Nissing hastened up the walk. She observed how carefully he wiped his shoes at the door. "This will take a fair portion of the day," he said, setting down his equipment. "I assume we aren't disrupting anything." He had a faint accent to match his Arab looks.

"No."

"Outstanding."

"You're not American?" she said curiously.

"Yes I am!" He swung his head and raised his eyebrows. She staggered back. "Oh yes I am! I am red, white and blue!" he said, without a trace of accent. His face relaxed again, and with a twist of each shoulder he removed his coat. "But I wasn't born here."

Barbara took the warm coat and held it.

"You've met Vince and Joshua," Nissing reminded her as Vince and Joshua marched in with more cases. "Vince, are you going to say hello?"

"Hello," said the Latin Vince.

"Nice to see you again, Mrs. Probst," said the youthful Joshua.

Nissing beamed. "Vince informs me that the kitchen gets the afternoon light."

"If it stays clear, it will," Barbara said.

"And if it gets cloudy it won't matter anyway. Perfect. Ideal. We'll begin with the living room." He leaned into the living room but didn't enter. He frowned at Barbara. "Dark!"

"Yes, it's not a light room," she said.

"Dark!" He snagged Vince, who was on his way back out. "Change the bulbs. Red wine, red roses. They've built a fire. You'll want to light it." Vince left, and Nissing addressed Barbara. "Have you had the house photographed before?"

"Just for insurance."

"We have to change the time of day. I hadn't realized the room was dark." He could have been discussing human handicaps. I hadn't realized the girl was lame. "If you're busy . . ." he said.

She shrugged and bounced on her heels. "I—no." She made an empty gesture with her hands, yielding to an impulse to cover her sense of physical inferiority with a show of youth, to act like the disconcertable girl she never was. "This is interesting. I'll enjoy watching."

"May I see the kitchen?" he said.

"Sure. You can see the whole house."

"I'd relish that."

In the dining room, where she and Martin had eaten a birthday dinner in two shifts, Nissing commented on the splendid walnut moldings, and she apologetically explained that the best woodwork on the property was in Mohnwirbel's rooms, above the garage. In the kitchen, where the radio was silent, the counters unpopulated and the windows crystalline, he described a mousse he'd prepared the night before, which caused her to shift him towards the more modern end of the sexist spectrum. In the breakfast room they watched Mohnwirbel grinding the blades of shears on a carborundum wheel at the bench he'd set up in the driveway; she pointed out the Tudor arches of his rooms. Passing the rear bathroom, the window of which Luisa had jumped from, they came to the den and cut white morning sunbeams, cast shadows on the faded-looking covers of her books. Nissing explained that his family was Iranian. In the sunroom, the repository for most of her Christmas presents, wrapped and otherwise, she took a good look at his face and decided he was significantly younger than she, possibly as young as thirty. They returned through the living room. Joshua was on his knees, blowing at a recalcitrant fire, and Vince was on a stepladder, increasing the wattage of the track lighting. Barbara's circuit with Nissing seemed to have cleansed the house, taken it off her hands. They went upstairs.

Nissing stopped to admire the guest bedroom, where Barbara

had been sleeping since Tuesday (it didn't show), and promptly asked if they'd recently had guests.

"No."

"Funny. I can usually smell if a room has been used."

She showed him Luisa's supernaturally neat bedroom, and was glad he wouldn't go in. He did go into Martin's study, taking slow steps, as if in a gallery. He asked what she did all day. She mentioned her job at the library and added, with a defensiveness ripened by time into glibness, "I read a lot. I see friends. I take care of my family."

He was staring at her. "That's nice."

"It has its drawbacks," she said.

His eyebrows were raised and his face lit up as if he expected her to say more, or as if there were a major joke in the air that he was waiting for her to get.

"Is something wrong?" she said, wishing, too late, that she'd just ignored him.

"Nope!" Suddenly his face had filled her vision. "Nothing!" He backed away, and again seemed to shake the bizarreness out of his frame. "I've just heard a lot about you." He walked into the hall and rested his hands on the stairwell railing. His skin was golden, not tanned, the native color revealed in the redness of his broad knuckles. Dark hair grew evenly on the back of his hands and fingers.

Downstairs, Vince squealed.

"This here is the master bedroom," Barbara said, nodding Nissing into it. Martin hadn't made the bed very well. Nissing went and sat on it. "Colossal bed," he said, thumping the mattress. She was now sure he knew where she and Martin had been sleeping.

"Where have you heard about me?" she said.

"I think we picked the right rooms to photograph, where have I heard about you? Well, from a woman named Binky Doolittle, and one named Bunny Hutchinson," he was counting them off on his fingers, "and one named Bea Meisner, and—hey! You're Barbara. All these B's! Is this something you've noticed? Was there some sort of advance planning involved?"

"No. Actually. Where have you been meeting these women?"

"In their homes, of course. In the homes we will feature in a sumptuous article in May. The homes of the filthy filthy rich in St. Louis. Homes like yours. I'm grateful for tips. Your home received many mentions, from these women and from others."

"Is that so?"

"It's very so. It's remarkably so. The name Probst was on the tip of everyone's tongue, at least in October."

"I had no idea our house—"

"Oh, not the house. No. That was not my impression. Or not just the house. It was the *home*. I was told that if I was in St. Louis I simply must see the Probsts' home." From the bed he glared at her. "So we added you to the list."

"Do you sleep with a lot of your subjects?" she said.

"Most of my subjects are architectural."

"But Binky? Bunny? I bet they love you."

"Possibly. But I have a living to make."

Downstairs, she watched the three of them doctor the front room. She was asked not to smoke. In a notebook Nissing took down data on the room for captions and copy. Once they started working the cameras, it was over very quickly, and she was surprised to find it noon already. Vince and Joshua began to walk tripods and cables into the kitchen. Nissing moved Barbara farther into the living room. On the spruced-up table stood a vase of roses, an open bottle of Beaujolais and two long-stemmed glasses. The vase and glasses were hers, the wine his. He poured liberally. "I'm not really a photographer," he said. "I teamed up with Vince on a freelance job, and one thing has led to another. It's easy money. I suppose I ought to have more ambition, but I've appreciated having extra time to spend with my son."

"Your son?"

He unfolded a large wallet and handed her a picture. It showed him in a white shirt and blue V-neck sweater, with his arm around a skinny boy with large dark eyes. Both were smiling, but not at the camera. Parts of a white sofa and a blond wood floor were visible. It was probably Barbara's imagination, but the lighting seemed to suggest a specifically Manhattan apartment, where high-rise living, through the proximity of a million similar apartments, became more natural and self-sufficient than it could elsewhere. She did know he came from New York.

"Who's the lucky mother?" she said.

He put away the picture. "My wife died four years ago."

"I'm sorry." She watched him take one of her cigarettes. "What's his name?"

"Terry."

"He doesn't look like a Terry." She smiled kindly, waiting for the shadow of his wife's death to pass.

"It's a good American name," he said. "We're good Americans. I was born in Teheran and spent my first six years there, but I've lived here ever since. I went to Choate and Williams. I anglicized my own name. Don't I qualify as an American?"

"Your accents are confusing."

"That's because I'm not very good at them. As you can see, my American is perfect—"

"Except for your *h*'s."

"Of course. Except for my initial *h*'s. But to the Doolittles of the world, I have to be Omar Sharif."

She was struck by the authenticity of his statement, by his awareness that in an ambitious non-American the desire to conform and the desire to be dazzling were painfully at odds. She could see how mastery of the social code might lag behind control of the American idiom. The overfamiliarity he'd been displaying was probably an accident. In her letters from Paris Luisa had complained that she couldn't seem to stop offending M. and Mme Giraud, and Barbara had easily imagined how her sarcasm, common currency at home, might have seemed presumptuous abroad. And so she gave Nissing the benefit of the doubt. She took off her shoes.

"Your husband built the Arch."

"Yes, that's right."

"Somehow I hadn't quite made the connection." He looked at her. "What do you know!"

"It's the kind of thing you get tired of hearing about after twenty years."

"But that's an incredible structure," he told her. "People who haven't seen it in person just can't imagine—"

"And this is the thing," she went on. "My husband is a general contractor. He didn't design the Arch. He had nothing to do with the design. He made use of two engineering innovations, neither of which were his own ideas, and he put the thing up. But to hear people talk, you'd think he was Saarinen."

Nissing, saying nothing, stepped back, as it were, and let her words land between them and redound to her discredit.

"It is true that his name was heavily associated with it," she said.

"There must be a reason for that."

"Well, at the time, there was."

"Uh huh." Nissing glanced over his shoulder at the back yard and then looked again at Barbara. "I like St. Louis," he said. "It's an old town. Buildings sit well here. Almost too well, if you know what I mean. The city is such a physical ramification—the brick, the hills, the open spaces, the big trees—that the architecture and landscape completely dominate. I don't say there aren't people, but for some reason they seem to get lost in the larger visuals. Perhaps it's only my outsider's perspective. I try to get in touch with the genius of places, in the old sense of the word, the unity of place and personality. The advantage of this job is that if I like a place I can go and look inside it. I do, by the way, want to see those rooms—"

The telephone was ringing. Barbara excused herself. A sudden menstrual stitch slowed her down as she left the room. To Nissing it may have looked as if her legs had gone to sleep. The mailman came up the front walk with a handful of Christmas cards. In the kitchen Joshua was buffing the sugar canister. Vince cranked a tripod.

"Barbie?"

"Hi, Audrey." She walked to the refrigerator. "Is this urgent?" She took out milk, but her pills, including her Motrin, had disappeared from their little shelf. Apparently abdominal cramps had no place in *House*.

"I'll call back," Audrey was saying. "The photographers must be there."

"They are."

"Are you OK?"

"I am."

Hanging up, she asked Vince where the pills were.

"Dining-room table," he said, intently cranking. "We'd appreciate it if you wouldn't smoke in the other room either."

She stopped. "It wasn't me."

Vince didn't answer.

Nissing was warming his back at the dying fire. "Don't mind Vince," he said. "Let's go and see those rooms. I'm a real Tudor nut."

·

Probst was jumped by Barbara before he even had his coat off. In his distraction he pulled one of the sleeves inside out.

"Martin listen," she said, wringing her hands. "We have a real problem. I don't know what to do. It's Mohnwirbel." She followed Probst to the closet. "This is just too— He has— Listen. He has pictures, photographs—big blow-ups—of *me*, he has them on the walls of his rooms."

"He what?" Probst smoothed his coat onto a hanger. The crowded closet upset him, all the more so because all the coats were his.

"In his apartment. I had to take one of the photographers up there, he wanted to see— Well, you know, the woodwork. And Mohnwirbel, I don't know where he'd gone. He was here this morning, and he's here now, but he wasn't there at lunchtime. I had to dig out our key. I was sure he wouldn't mind if we just went up and looked in. And I got the door open and I was trying to get the key out—have we ever even used it? And I sent Nissing, the photographer, I sent him in. And finally I got the key out and he was staring—oh my God, I am *so* mortified. Martin. He's a pervert or something. We have a pervert living over our garage."

"What kind of pictures?" Probst said.

"You can imagine that I did not stay to look with a stranger—"

"Clothed pictures, though," he said, trying to make her understand.

"Yes."

"Well, that's good."

"It makes no difference. It makes no difference. He's fired."

"I thought you liked him," Probst pointed out. Why she couldn't have waited a few minutes . . .

"The same as you. We didn't dislike him. What's to dislike? But he probably has corpses—"

"You're not acting like yourself."

She stepped back. "Well, I'm upset. Aren't you?"

"Naturally." But he'd meant what he said. She seemed like a different person. Even when she'd given him the news of Luisa's departure, last month, she'd completed her sentences and related the events chronologically.

"Go and look," she said. "Go and talk to him."

"You haven't spoken with him."

"Me? Jesus! Of course not."

"I see you still tolerate me when you need me."

She shook her head ominously. "You wish." And went and locked herself in the den.

Canadian bacon.

The stairs to Mohnwirbel's rooms began at the back of the garage. Probst switched on the staircase light and started up. The air was cold and flavored with the decay of exposed wood and the mold that grew in caking dust. Patches of ancient linoleum clung to the blackened stairs. It had been several years since he'd climbed these stairs. Mohnwirbel exercised autonomy. They paid him by mail.

Past the middle landing the air grew heated. The top landing was lit by leakage from under the apartment door and through the curtains on the window in it. Probst's heart beat as if he'd climbed twenty flights. He knocked, drawing footsteps. The door opened as far as the chain allowed.

"Heinrich, hi," Probst said. "Can I talk to you?"

"What do you want?"

"I want to come in."

Through the doorway came a sigh with some voice in it, and Mohnwirbel said, "You want to come in."

"I want to see the pictures of my wife."

Eyelids covered and uncovered the small black eyes. "All right."

There were many pictures, but for a moment only their existence registered in Probst, not their content. He paced along the walls of the exhibition. It was true: these were the finest rooms on the property. The ceilings were high, the woodwork extravagant, the kitchenette antiquated but adequate. Through the eastern window, the glowing windows of 236 itself could be seen, and Probst experienced a mild epiphany as he felt his way, by means of this perspective, into another life. He never saw his own house from this angle. Mohnwirbel had lived here for decades.

A second thought intruded. With Mohnwirbel out of the way, they could rent this space for at least four hundred a month.

By the bedroom door he saw a nude profile, a telephoto of Barbara in the bathroom. The guilty cameras hung on a peg near the closet where Mohnwirbel, face blank, stood watching.

Barbara was clothed in the other dozen or so pictures, her hair cut in the various styles she'd tried in the last three or four years. She'd stood twice in the kitchen, once in the sunroom, and the rest of the time outdoors. All but the kitchen shots shared the perspective Probst had now, and they looked, every one of them, like shots from the *National Enquirer* of Jackie Onassis or Brigitte Bardot on their beaches, boats, or estates. The graininess, the candidness, the flatness of the telephoto field gave Barbara glamour.

"So what's the meaning of this, Heinrich?"

"You saw them, now get out." Mohnwirbel was wearing a plaid wool woodsman's jacket and unusual pants. They were black tuxedo pants, greatly worn.

"I own these rooms," Probst said.

"In point of law, you do not. I don't rent. I have domicile."

This might be true, Probst realized. "You're fired," he said.

"I resign."

"How much will it cost me to get you out of here?"

"I don't leave. I have nowhere to go." He presented this as a fact, not a sentiment. "Perhaps I can speak with the lady of the house."

Probst went icy. "The lady of the house does not wish to speak with *you*." He tore the nude profile off the wall and into quarters. "This is filth, this is perverted, you hear me?"

"It's your wife," said Mohnwirbel.

Probst tore another picture off the wall, sending thumbtacks scattering on the sere Orientals. He reached for a third, and Mohnwirbel, seizing his elbow, levered him against the wall. "I throw you down the stairs if you touch another one, Martin Probst." His breath had a powerful ethyl stink. "I want to tell you, Martin Probst, you are the most arrogant man I ever knew. You have categories of normal and pervert, right and wrong, good bad. Like the lady's tits don't heat you up when she picks up her towel. You call that filthy and you got no God. You think she never looks at another man? Then what am I? Come on, Martin Probst. Don't say I'm pervert."

"One way or another, you're going to leave here, mister. You're going to hear from the police, you're going to hear from our attorney—"

"Sentimental, Martin Probst. You go your way, I go mine. You stand in a room of pleasure." A plaid arm swept the air inclusively. "What pleasure you got? You don't have the house, you don't have the woman, you don't have the grass on the ground." Mohnwirbel looked aside, seemingly distracted. "I don't like your daughter," he remarked.

"I'm sure she doesn't like you either." Probst broke the grip on his elbow and fell a few steps towards the windows. He looked down on the shoveled driveway.

"We see if you can put me in jail, Martin Probst."

Through the thin reaches of a dogwood he saw Barbara, in their kitchen on the telephone, with both hands on the receiver.

•

It was Luisa. She wanted to move more things out of the house. Barbara asked if she was sure. Yes, she was pretty sure. It wasn't fair to Duane not to.

That one made Barbara hyperventilate, but she stayed on the phone. She begged. She pleaded. She offered Luisa complete freedom to come and go if she returned home; offered her a car; offered to keep Martin at bay. Luisa's replies became duller and duller. Finally she made her bargain: Barbara could come and visit her whenever she wanted to, but she was in love with Duane and wanted to live with him for a while if that was OK.

She added: "I would have been leaving soon anyway."

•

The weekend had passed. Depressed, with symptoms as clinical as they'd ever been, Barbara woke up at three in the morning in the guest room. The north wind shook the northern wall. She pressed it with her fingers to still it. A full moon spent itself in the frost on the western windows. In her mind this room in the corner of the house had come unmortared and was edging out of its slot, about to fall, with the clunk of the rejected, into the bushes.

She'd recovered from the first shock of Nissing's discovery. On Saturday morning she'd spoken with Mohnwirbel and found him polite. He apologized formally, and later in the day, while Martin watched football, he came to the kitchen door with negatives and prints, dozens and dozens, in a shirt box. She asked him not to take any more, please.

He wouldn't promise. "You should be appreciated right," he said, showing perspicacity if not sanity. But Martin still wanted to prosecute or sue.

All weekend she'd felt as though she had cancer, as though she were ordering her life for a scheduled death. The shirt box of photos—which she couldn't touch, let alone open or throw away—could have held the fatal X-rays. Household objects avoided contact with her, superstitiously. It would have been nice to have Dozer back to break the spell, to wander with a jangle from room to room, sniffing, yawning, spreading his sounds. But Dozer was dead.

And yet now, on Monday, she felt better. Rain poured on the windshield and roof as she inched down Euclid Avenue and pulled into a well-situated parking space. In a busy neighborhood, a free space was an omen. She put up the hood of her rain cloak and slid across the seat and released her umbrella and stepped out, directly into a stream of meltwater. So her foot was soaked, so? She pushed quarters into the meter and ran, every second step a squish, across the street and into Balaban.

John Nissing was checking his coat.

"Wonderful!" He peeled back her hood and held her shoulders. "You're here!" He kissed her mouth as if compelled by the pure joy of seeing her again. They were given a corner table with reasonable privacy.

"I'm feeling extra specially good today," he said when the Pouilly-Fuissé was splashing into their glasses. "A parcel which has been in the mail since 1979 and which I'd assumed was lost forever was waiting for me in New York on Friday night."

He smiled complacently and waited. She waited. Suddenly he leaned towards her. "Jewelry! And jewelry, what's more, with absolutely no sentimental value." He reached into his jacket pocket. "This is for you." He handed her a velvet box. "And the rest is for Christie's."

She opened the box. It contained two earrings: diamonds, a half carat apiece, in white-gold settings. She'd been wanting diamond earrings for Christmas.

"You can keep them, too," he said. "And you don't have to worry. They aren't antiques."

"I have a hundred questions about these," she said.

Their waiter put two bowls of asparagus soup between them.

"Yes? What's number one?"

"Where do you expect me to wear these?"

"In your ears!" He half stood, and did what she hadn't thought men did, which was to remove earrings from women's pierced ears. Her hands rose defensively, but fell back onto her napkin. He dropped her hoops into the box and, tongue curling with concentration, put in the diamonds. "You can tell your husband I gave them in appreciation of the Arch."

He sat down. He looked at her soup. If she'd had anything in her stomach she might have thrown it up. But she picked up her spoon.

"And number two?" He cut into his soup with his own spoon and tasted it, his eyes connoisseurially unfocussed. With a hint of a nod, he came back. "Number two," he answered, "is what do I expect in return."

She let her eyes affirm this.

"A simple 'Thank you' will do."

"Thank you."

On the phone, he'd suggested a couple of restaurants in Clayton, but she'd asked to meet here at Balaban instead, knowing she'd feel more anonymous in the West End. In hindsight, though, she saw no reason to have avoided Clayton. People wouldn't have thought anything of spotting her with Nissing, and what did she care if they did?

"Number three?"

Forget it. She shook her head. But she reconsidered. "Why me?"

"I couldn't tell you," he said. "But it was clear to me as soon as I saw you."

"That's not really good enough. I'm afraid that won't do."

The table behind her was empty, but he lowered his voice until she could hardly hear. "I see then," he said, "that I'm required to explain my motivations while you are not, because you live in a castle and are self-explanatory, while I fly in planes and am not. I do my dance, and the lady clap a little? She is moved? She is not moved? You have a tired superiority, Barbara, and it doesn't suit you well. If I made assumptions about you the way you've made them about me, I'd go so far as to guess you've never had an affair since you were married. This makes you a prize? At forty-three? This gives you the right to demand explanations?" He glanced over her shoulder and then looked back into her eyes. "You know you don't speak like other people. Everyone around you is utterly reified. You know that. You speak a different language. You flaunt your sadness. You know damned well you'd like to fall in love with someone like yourself. Am I making myself at all clear?"

"Fairly clear, yes," she said. "But we'd better talk about something else, or I'm not going to eat any lunch."

Nissing had just paid the check, an hour later, when he mentioned that he had a plane to catch at 3:45. The news stung for a moment, but then she was glad. She was wiped out.

Outside, in a drizzle, she left him without a kiss, just a smile and a close-range wave. She didn't believe everything he'd said, but she did believe she had him on a string.

At the first traffic light she removed her earrings. She had to go home for Luisa's presents, the bulk of which she was bent on delivering this afternoon. The task looked easier in the light of that lunch, but it was a pity to drive all the way out to Webster Groves and back; Duane's apartment was less than a mile away from where she'd parked.

•

Singh rose well before dawn, performed an abridged version of his calisthenics, took a freezing shower, and shaved. On Wednesday he'd had his hair cut radically, close in back and on the sides. To change appearance was to exaggerate the passage of time, to elude past claims of ownership, to seem to own himself. He chose his clothes with a similar end. Barbara had seen him in natty woolens, so today he would wear black denim, cancel the conservative button-downs with a sea-blue collarless. He ate a bagel with butter and brushed his teeth.

Day came, melting the opacity of the skylights into a blue translucence. There wasn't much in the refrigerator. Singh threw it all away. He had an extra plate and two too many forks. He threw them away. He threw away superfluous socks and an ill-fitting shirt. He read through the Probst file and shredded ninety percent of it. He knew the essence now as he hadn't two months ago; he was narrowing in. On the top sheet of the notes he was shredding he glimpsed spent phrases: *tired superiority, in love with someone like herself.* He took the garbage to the elevator and down to the alley and came back up with the building's vacuum cleaner. He sucked what little dust there was from the green carpeting, what crumbs from the cooking zone, what hair balls from the bathroom. He telephoned Barbara, and then for a second time he listened to the conversations she'd had in the last four days, complete through the previous evening. Her composure was flawless, but that said everything; a week ago she hadn't been composed.

AR: Where were you all day?
BP: Oh, I took some presents down to Luisa.
AR: I kept calling . . .
BP: I did hear the phone once or twice. I was trying to sleep. I haven't been sleeping.
AR: I thought you might be working.
BP: No, I work all day tomorrow.

He erased the tape. Pigeons clustered. On the telephone he exchanged polysyllables with Jammu. Recently Jammu had had a mild attack of scruples, an allergic reaction to messing with lives, but she'd recovered now, and in a very few hours Singh would have the pleasure of pinning Martin Probst's wife to a mattress.

He drove a freshly rented Pontiac Reliant to his Brentwood pied-à-terre and went in to collect his portfolio. The pictures of 236 Sherwood Drive were cautious and strangely murky, like the house itself, but apparently just what the editor wanted. Singh had paid off Joshua and Vince and sent them back to Chicago. His *House* days were over. He ignited a clove cigarette but thought better of smoking it. He flushed it down the toilet and left the apartment.

The Probsts' helpful gardener was chopping ice off the front walk when Singh arrived. He returned Singh's greeting with a piercing look and silence. Singh rang the doorbell and Barbara let him in. He observed her to see how his altered appearance affected her, and he saw that she had changed her own. She'd put up her hair with a barrette and dressed in a close-fitting T-shirt and close-fitting pants, shifting the emphasis from her body's stalkiness to its maturity. Their mirrored strategies amused him. He forgot his line for a moment. He remembered. "Got some pictures for you."

"No thanks," she said, reaching up with weightless arms and kissing him. He hadn't expected this yet. His surprise showed. She pushed away. "I'm going to go lie down, all right?"

She turned and climbed three steps and paused, facing away from him.

He leaned the portfolio against the oak chest in the hallway. He considered sitting down in the living room to watch what would happen, how long it would take her to join him. Why not. Her earnest grandeur bored him. He lowered himself onto the sofa and picked up some coffee-table reading, a book of pictures of the Arch by Joel Meyerowitz. It hadn't been here last time. He thumbed. The advantage was his. In addition to her many reasons for being "unfaithful" to Martin, she had the heart of a bourgeoise and was eager to please. Less virtuous women would have hesitated when he'd called on Monday; less intelligent women would have flirted and dallied more brilliantly; Barbara, humorless, merely said yes and named a restaurant.

She appeared at the coffee table. "You came here to lay me, right?"

He filtered patience into his sigh. "I had a rough flight," he said. "Do you want to sit down with me for a while?"

She perched on the edge of the sofa.

"Relax, hey?" He slouched deeply. "Why not."

"Because it's too damn tawdry. Why don't you stop telling me what to do."

"No thanks," he said. "I had something on the plane."

Barbara pressed her knees together, her hands flat between them. "You're sweet, John. You're very sweet," she said. "But I don't want to sit and talk to you like we're dating. You're very funny, but I don't want to hear it now. You said you loved me. You knew me. So please."

She'd bought it, then.

"Let's go upstairs," she said.

"But it's such a nice sofa."

"I don't want to. He'll see."

"Oh." Singh glanced at the rear windows. "Of course."

She'd drawn the curtains in the guest room. He peeled back the bedspread and let her undress him. He looked down. Everything fine. Not that there had been much doubt. She removed her shirt and stood in her jeans and shoes, with her hands on her hips, assessing him. He felt a strain. She straddled him and pushed him onto his back, and kissed all around his mouth. The strain increased. He'd anticipated it, but still the leap had to be made. He sat up, and she followed. Here was the critical point, out of range of his charm, the point beyond which it was too dangerous to fake. He caught her wrists and focussed his eyes on the flesh lipping at the waist of her pants. It was over in a second. He loved her a little, and his chest heaved into her pinkness, ribs to ribs, stomach to stomach. His backup censor would now let almost anything past: she was soft. She was the best woman in the world. He reached and unzipped her, strained further, sliding his fingers through her slippery curls. She took off her pants and, with an exclamation that seemed to come from her whole upper body, made room for him inside. He fought her onto her back, working them up into the pillows. She made no sound. Her nails on his back spurred him into her. The work came easily to him, and though it seemed to take her an awfully long time, she finally stopped moving her hips and grew rigid. Her ribs bounced against his. She gasped and smiled with lips already mashed into asymmetry.

The phone rang itself out, remotely, twice.

The weather changed. It generally did.

He was just waking up, by and by, when she confessed to being somewhat sore. He suggested an alternative procedure. She shook her head. He let the matter drop and resumed the staple position, beginning delicately but intending this time to nail her as he'd planned to. She said he was hollowing her out. That was the idea. But he didn't want to hurt her. He let her turn with him, sideways, and as they rolled, complexly interlocked, he began to experience perceptual difficulties. He was not immune to them. He accepted them, as phenomena. The present difficulty was a TV ghost, a negative image, a woman with dark skin and dark hair and pale lips who hid in Barbara and matched her when she moved without self-consciousness, but who swerved into sight when she erred, and made the right move for her. The forms were united in the rhythm of the act and in the lathered point at which they fused with Singh, who was a fulcrum.

Who put the cash in Kashmir
Who put the jam in Jammu?

University song of his. He was losing objectivity, and spent a few minutes in no particular place. His return was purely the product of Barbara's labors. When he looked again the negative image was gone, and now he knew how complete his success had been, how impressive the results. He had her and he wouldn't let go. He had his arms across her hot back, fingers buried in her midsection, fingers jammed in her butt, teeth on her tongue, legs splinted to hers, and the remainder a great number of inches inside her, spanning cavities and crowding ridges, and he came another time, into a newfound void, what felt like gallons.

They stopped.

A look of pure, lucid wickedness popped into her face, like a jack from a box. "Bye," she said. "Glad you came."

"Bye-bye," he answered, playing along.

11

It's the night before Christmas. In the west, in a corner of the sky just blue enough yet to make treetops and chimneys silhouettes, Venus burns with utter whiteness. Perseus is dizzy at the zenith and pierced by jets; Orion is rising above television towers; the galaxy is performing its nightly condensation. Downtown, as the last stores close, the last shoppers drain quickly from the cold sidewalks into their cars. Bells toll from an empty church. Steam that smells of corroded pipes gushes from the backs of office buildings, and the boughs of the Salvation Army Tree of Light bow and tremble in the wind. In the living-room windows of apartment buildings—of Plaza Square, Mansion House, the Teamsters complex, Darst-Webbe, Cochran, Cochran Gardens—electric candles are lit, and strings of lights turn the four corners of window frames and shine like Hollywood squares. Blinds fall and curtains jerk. There's a preoccupation, an apprehension, a thing to achieve. Most people are involved, but not all. Sheraton bellhops witness the departure of well-dressed out-of-towners and drink Cokes. Two veteran newsmen, Joe Feig and Don Daizy, have stopped in at the Missouri Grill to share a pitcher of Miller and enjoy their kinship with the bartender, who is watching the waning moments of the Holiday Bowl on the house TV.

Down on the Mississippi, the steamboat *McDonald's* ("RAY

KROC, CAPTAIN") is shuttered and dead. Icicles hang from its permanent moorings, and snowmounds nestle in its plastic finials, golden arches, fluted pipes. Floes beyond it revolve and bob. Barge traffic is very light. How far this evening is from the heat and thunder of summer, when at dinnertime the sun is high and hot, and Cardinals take batting practice, and visitors rub their necks at the feet of the Arch, dripping mustard from their hotdogs, and the air smells like tar; how far this silence, these indigo depths, these cobbled plateaux. The Switzer's licorice plant has given up the ghost. On its barricaded doors a sign reads:

SWITZER'S OFFICE CENTER

FOR LEASE

OFFICE AND RETAIL SPACE

The lid from a paper cup skids on a railroad crossing, hampered by its straw. Tinsel window dressings, bleached by streetlights, could be decades old. The people who are out, by the river, are those who can't see. Even the police, Officers Taylor and Onkly, have their eyes on their watches, their minds on dinner. They get off at 9:00. The only action they'll see in three hours will involve drunks, either derelicts or drivers. They circle a block and play their searchlight on garbage cans. The static on the radio is unbroken. Earlier, the dispatcher sang two lines from a Christmas carol and then stopped with a laugh. It's the season of weariness, sentiment, and duty, except for children, and there are no children on the streets downtown.

Circle south. Past the Pet Milk building and Ralston Purina, hardy gentry relax in the rehabilitated homes of LaSalle Park and Soulard and Lafayette Square. Here, safe behind rows of double-parked cars, Andrew DeMann and his son Alex are playing with their computer while his wife Liz feeds their baby, Lindsay. Alex, growing tired, has begun to pretend that games don't have rules. Andrew gets strict and goes down to the cellar for wine. He breathes and his heart beats. He selects a bottle.

Further. On the Hill, a late-afternoon party in the home of Area I commander Lieutenant Colonel Frank Parisi is approaching the pinnacle of merriness. Chief Jammu has phoned in her best wishes. Fifty policemen and their families are packed into five small rooms. Luzzi, Waters, Scolatti and Corrigan are bellowing "God Rest Ye Merry, Gentlemen" in two-and-a-half-part harmony at the piano. Parisi is stirring fresh eggnog in the kitchen, admiring the fat swirls of rum. The card marked *Spiked* has sustained repeated dunkings. Young faces glow. The noise is perfect. More than a dozen squad cars are parked out in front, their windows ablaze with all the colored lights of the happy street, brilliant points melting halos into the snow around them on the bushes and gutters. Shouts ring out and large cars cruise. From overhead the neighborhoods look like streams of luminous plankton, twinkling in patches and encompassing dark islands of service and storage and repose. Cars speed along the sinuous drives in Forest Park. There's a danger in exposure tonight. Everyone wants to be somewhere. Just past the city limits, a dented red Nova with the lower half of a pine tree projecting from its trunk is slowing on Delmar to make a left turn. It parks. Duane Thompson jumps out and unlashes the trunk latch and hauls out the tree. They're to be had for a dollar at this hour of this day. With a spring in his step, a determined lightness, he carries the tree up the stairs to his apartment. Inside, Luisa is still on the phone. She was on the phone an hour ago when he left. She waves with her fingers. He returns to the car for the popcorn and cranberries.

Immediately to the north and east, in what the county imagination makes out to be the darkest, most crowded corner of the city, Clarence Davis sees terrible spaces and light. He was one of the last shoppers downtown. The *Messiah* plays on his radio, and the rabbit's foot hanging from the mirror jumps at every pothole. From the top of unweathered aluminum standards, electric light the color of frost falls in brittle rays and shatters his windshield again and again. Spaces open up on either side of him where houses have been punched out of rows. Block after block, the light goes on without a tinge of yellow, without a tinge of fire. It overpowers the traffic lights, brave Jamaican colors, beneath which a year ago even on Christmas boys gathered, holding bottles, looking evil, and closed in the street a little. The groups are gone. In half a mile Clarence has passed three squad cars. They're guarding nothing. No pedestrians, no businesses, just dogs and stripped vehicles. And property. High fences run along the street guarding bulldozed tracts and plywood windows. Is it such a tragedy? Not many people had to leave to make this place a desert; maybe the city can absorb those people. But Clarence is scared, scared in a mental way nothing like the gut fear of murder he once might have felt down here. It's the scope of the transformation: square *miles* fenced and boarded, not *one* man visible, not *one* family left. The hand that has cleaned this place is no American hand. No American, no Idaho supremacist, no Greensboro Klansman, could have gotten away with this. These miles are the vision of a woman's practicality. This is her solution. And she's getting away with it, and how can Clarence complain with his back seat full of gifts and these not even half of it? How can anybody complain? Only those with no voice have much to complain of. And by daylight, on a day not a holiday, these acres look different. White men and black men wearing hardhats and holding prints peer between houses, drive stakes, and confer with surveyors. Clarence has recognized faces. Brother Ronald, having trouble with his hat. Cleon Toussaint rubbing his hands. City government people pointing at future parking lots, future drinking fountains, future projects. Bigshots, the board members and figure-heads, drinking working-class coffee from thermoses. Oh, plenty of activity down here. To some eyes it must even look pretty, oh, pretty damned good. Clarence crosses the line into a neighborhood. He sees more cops, but humans, too. He presses up his street and slides the car into the garage. Stanly and Jamey are still out shooting baskets in the light from the kitchen.

The city heaves north. Flashing strings of lights become jets as they drop to plowed runways. The Lambert Airport crowd is thinning fast. Hugs happen, opening like sudden flowers, in con-courses, at gates and checkpoints, a blossoming of emotion. Flight attendants wheeling luggage are crabby. Taxis are leaving without fares. From her room the addict looks out on the air traffic with the uncritical gaze of someone viewing a nature scene, cows grazing, trees shedding leaves, jets rising, falling, banking. She lights a cigarette and sees her last one still burning in the ashtray. From a shoebox shrine she takes a long letter dated December 24, 1962, and reads it for the twentieth time while she waits for Rolf, who might, she thinks, arrive any moment.

Rolf is sleeping off a pair of drinks in his favorite chair at home. He's dreaming of sewers. Endless, spacious sewers. Upstairs, Audrey has wrapped the sweater she'll give Barbie at their parents' tomorrow. She loves Christmas. With a scissor blade she pulls a curl into each of the ribbons and, humming a little, reviews her work.

Nearly everyone lives within two miles of the Ripleys. Sam Norris, his large house full of children and grandchildren, is moving from group to group touching them with his hands, placing them, and radiating satisfaction while Betty browns meat. Three streets over, Binky Doolittle is in the bathtub talking on the telephone. Harvey Ardmore staggers across his back yard with a huge Yule log, Chet Murphy pours pink champagne, the Hutchinsons watch the CBS Evening News in separate rooms, Ross Billerica throws darts with his brother-in-law from downstate. The home of Chuck Meisner, however, is dark. Chuck is in St. Luke's West with a bleeding peptic ulcer. He's been sleeping like a baby since he was rushed here three days ago.

·

On Friday Probst worked until 8:00 in the evening, and coming home he found Barbara looking hot, in light clothes, though the house wasn't very warm. She served him dinner. While he ate it and read the notes on Christmas cards, she left the kitchen and returned. She moved along the counters and left again. She did this several times.

"What are you looking for?" he finally asked.

"What?" She seemed surprised he'd noticed her.

Distracted and small, she circulated for the rest of the evening, coming to rest only after he'd turned out his nightstand light, when she returned from her guest-room exile in a pale flannel nightgown, childishly large for her, and lay down on her side of their bed without a word of explanation. In the morning she made him French toast and juiced a quartet of blood oranges she'd picked up at a fancy new grocery in Kirkwood. The froth was pink, the coffee strong. She kept smiling at him.

"What is it?" he finally said.

"Monday's Christmas," she said.

"Don't tell me. Luisa is coming over."

"No. She isn't. Uh-uh."

"Then what?"

"Can't I smile at you?"

He shrugged. She could if she wanted.

In the afternoon they played tennis together. His finger was healing; he hardly noticed it. Barbara horsed around on the court, laughed big hooting laughs when she missed a shot. She didn't miss many. They were evenly matched, and he felt a pang when he thought of how much this little fact had meant to him over the years. But she wasn't interested in lovemaking when they got home. She wanted to eat out and see a movie.

"Sure," he said.

Halfway through dinner at the Sevens she began to give him a talking-to. It had the coherence of a prepared message, and she delivered it mainly to her broiled flounder. Luisa, she said, was eighteen now. After all. And just like some other people in the family, Luisa was stubborn. If these other people would only be a little more charitable, she'd be charitable in return, although she still might insist on living at Duane's. She was OK. She'd written outstanding essays for her applications. She would probably have her pick of colleges. She was only eighteen, for goodness' sake.

Probst was appalled by the crudity of Barbara's optimism.

After breakfast Sunday morning they trimmed the tree. She did the lights, and he, who had a fondness for certain old ornaments from his mother's collection, did the rest. For lunch there was beer, sardines, Wasa bread, cheese and deluxe Washington State apples. She played games with the paper wrappers. The sardines were Bristling at the suggestion that they opposed handgun legislation. The apples were Fancy and gave themselves to strangers for a price. Horse-radish was either a folk etymology or a false etymology, the distinction being one of those niceties Barbara had never mastered. She drained her glass and looked at Probst.

"Yes?" he said.

"I went to bed with the photographer on Friday."

He saw that suddenly her hands were shaking. "Is this something you do all the time?"

"You know it isn't, Martin."

The horseradish sauce was edged with yellow oil. The news

was true but hadn't registered in him; these were moments of free-fall, during which his words were neither under his control nor under the control of a coordinating emotion, like jealousy or rage, that would have connected his tongue to his will, his brain to his blood. "Was it fun?" he was saying.

"Yes."

"Are you going to make a habit of it?"

"No." She might have said: What if I do? He wished she had. "Are we quits?" she said.

"You've been lying to me all weekend. You've been acting."

"That's not true. I just want this to be over, I'm sick of fighting you. You've been stranger than I have. I know you're still in there. I want you to come out."

He stood. "We'll see."

"Where are you going?"

"I'm going for a walk."

"Can I come along?"

"I'd like to be alone."

"I don't want you to be alone. I want to be with you. I laaah."

"You can't say it. I can't say it."

"I love you."

She said it in room after room, at his elbow, at his throat. The more she said it, the more he pitied her. But she wouldn't leave him alone. When he put on his coat, she put on hers. She stayed within a foot of him, and finally, as they were heading up the front walk moments after heading down it, he succumbed. "All right," he said, glancing over his shoulder. George LeMaster was replacing a colored bulb on his front railing. Probst led Barbara inside and shut the door. "All right. I love you, too."

She kissed his hand, but he pulled it away. He was beginning to feel betrayed. Barbara had defected to the world at large, to its optimisms, its smooth mechanisms of love and remorse, and like everyone else now she wanted to have Probst in her camp.

"You would have done the same thing in my shoes. I know you, I know you better than anyone. I know you would have."

"So you say," he said.

"Look at me and tell me you believe in perfect faithfulness. I dare you."

Instead he went upstairs and changed his clothes, came down

and built a fire, and opened the front door. It was 3:30. Guests were arriving, all their favorite people, as if at a clap of Barbara's hands. She'd timed her announcement well. Probst had no choice but to appear himself when he let the Montgomerys in. Jill and Bob bubbled. The dining-room table was laden with interesting cookies, fruits and vegetables, tiny sandwiches of Gruyère and roast beef. Barbara popped into view with her arms full of liquor bottles. Bob made a crack, turned to Probst, and started in with a story about a flat tire he'd had at midnight on the outer belt two nights ago.

The doorbell rang again and again. Cal Markham with a new girl named Nancy, Barbara's college friend Lorri Wulkowicz, Barbara's parents, both very tan. Sally and Fred Anderson and Probst's secretary Carmen and her husband Eddie, who grinned and stammered. Peter Callahan, the widowed chief engineer, and his seventeen-year-old daughter Dana. More engineers, the Hoffingers, the Foxxes, the Waltons, the Joneses. Two of Barbara's library co-workers and their husbands. People clustered around the fire, around the laughing Barbara and the smiling Probst. Small packages accumulated on the mantelpiece. The windows darkened. Cal volunteered to fetch more firewood, and Nancy joined Probst and Dana and Lorri Wulkowicz in the chairs by the piano. Lorri in particular warmed to Probst. She still wore the little round wire-framed glasses she'd worn in the sixties. He watched her eat five Gruyère sandwiches between pulls on a bottle of Heineken. She'd recently been made chairman of her English department. It was a long time since she'd been in this house.

Good-bye and Merry Christmas. Probst retrieved coats and saw guests to the door. He kept returning to Lorri, who had gotten him started on the current political situation in the city. The phone rang. Barbara went to answer it and did not come back.

Now, towards six o'clock, only Lorri remains. Probst can hear Barbara in the kitchen on the phone. Lorri sits Indian style on the floor rolling her first cigarette of the afternoon. "That frumpy charisma," she says. "She still seems totally Third World to me. The stupidest platitudes mean something, you know, they're vital truths where she comes from. She's got the imprimatur of struggle. And the ambiguities. On the one hand she has this naïve socialism. On the other hand she's probably a closet mobster like her cousin Indira."

"Cousin?"

"Fifth? Eighth? Twelve times removed? You and *I* are cousins twelve times removed."

"People romanticize her," Probst says. "I romanticize her, too. What did you say—her charisma. A week ago I had myself completely convinced." He shakes his head.

"No, go on."

"I thought it meant something that she was an Indian, something to do with American Indians—"

"The so-called terrorists."

"But superstitiously, too." He explains.

Lorri tells him it's simply literate behavior. "You can do numerology tricks, assign a number to each letter of your name. Birthplace, birth date, sign. I'm always rationalizing attractions—"

"I'm so-o-o-o sorry," Barbara says, returning at last.

Lorri puts on her coat, which she has dropped on the floor behind a chair, kisses Probst and Barbara, and leaves with an invitation to return for dinner sometime after New Year's.

"I like her," Probst says.

"She likes you. She always has."

Silence has fallen on the used glasses and sugared plates. For the first time in eighteen Christmas Eves the Probsts can do whatever they want. The traditional activity at this hour is Luisa's opening of the gifts that come to Probst from his suppliers. "Maybe we should open some boxes," he says.

The boxes are stacked against the southern wall of the den. He turns on the TV and waits for Barbara. The lead story on the KSLX local news is a visit to a North Side soup kitchen.

Barbara comes in wiping her hands. "Luisa and Duane are going to be at Mom and Dad's tomorrow."

"And it took you all that time to persuade them."

"Yep." She sits. "You don't mind, I hope."

"Why should I mind?"

"Minnie Sanders is sixty-three. Her only child, Leroy—"

"Duane's parents are in St. Croix."

Probst sniffs. "Is it my imagination, or is there something wrong with them?"

She doesn't answer. He looks. Tears are streaming down her cheeks.

"It's not the end of the world," he says. "We'll see her tomorrow."

She shakes her head.

"You want me to call her?"

She stares at the TV, her hands on her lap, her face lined and wet. How very few tears she will have shed, Probst thinks, between growing up and dying. One cupful. Distantly the furnace comes to life.

Cliff Quinlan's face is gray. Outdoor light shows up his gash-like dimples in high relief. "I'm standing on the southern city limits of St. Louis, behind me is the River des Peres, and beyond that, a quiet residential neighborhood in what is Bella Villa. In my first report I examined the dilemmas that the regional law-enforcement community faces in dealing with threats such as the 'Osage Warriors.' It was very close to where I stand now that the group crossed the river and escaped into the county. They are still at large." Quinlan consults his text. "In my second report we saw how borders such as this one enable lawbreakers to enter and leave suburban neighborhoods with relative impunity, and how difficult it is to trace these lawbreakers in a county which is currently a hodgepodge of more than fifty independent police forces. The burglary rate in St. Louis County stands at an all-time high. However, for the last four months the city rate has been dropping steadily. Tonight: prospects for change."

Probst turns off the TV. Barbara cries. He knows what's on her mind, the whole matrix of Christmases with Luisa at eight, ten, twelve, sixteen. One girl who came in every size and every mood. He will grow sentimental and sorry for himself. On the floor between him and Barbara is a box of graphic imaginings: how she acted with John Nissing. Nissing's vulgar language, his insinuating laughter. Who touched whom when. Whether Nissing was better. How much better.

Selecting boxes from the pile at random (for Luisa, opening these gifts was a science; for him, it's a chore) he sits and slits tape with a penknife. White styrofoam roaches come swarming out of the first box, along with an envelope. Seasons Greetings from Ick-bey & Twoll, Fabricators. The roaches cling to his sweater. He brushes them off, but they stick to his fingers, eluding him, scooting around onto the back of his splinted hand, up onto his wrists. He has to pull them off one by one.

Inside the box is a clock radio. He writes *clock radio* on the card for the benefit of Carmen, who will write the thank-you's.

Seasons Greetings from Thuringer Brothers: a five-pound tin of cashews. Seasons Greetings from Joe Katz, salesman for Varia-tech: a socket wrench set. Happy Holidays from Morton Seagrave: *The Soul of the Big Band Era*, Volume XII. Peace on Earth from Fulton Electric: a two-speed drill. Merry Christmas from Zakspeks: fruitcake. Seasons Greetings from Pulasky Maintenance: fruitcake. Merry Christmas from Dick Feinberg, Caterpillar salesman: a plaid half-gallon thermos and a matching blanket. Seasons Greetings from Camp & Weston: fruitcake.

"All right, Martin."

"I think Luisa got more fun out of this than I do."

Her skin smells wet with tears and sweet with booze when he kneels at her feet and leans towards her. She comes down off the sofa and puts her mouth on his and pushes, strokes, bites. He shuts his eyes. It's last year. It's no year. He touches her ribs and shoulder blades, and feels both comforted and alarmed by the ease with which he can control his behavior, by the arbitrari-ness of attitude. When they have nothing to fight over, nothing to strain against, necessity flags. What does it matter what they've done? What does it matter what they do? The evening is free.

An hour later there's a carol outside the windows. The house transmits the tremors of footsteps from the front walk up to the bedroom. The doorbell rings. Probst kisses Barbara's hair and stays to kiss her nose and eyes and fingertips.

Downstairs all the lights are shining on the remains of some-one's party. The chorus of "O Come, All Ye Faithful" is fading, losing hope, but when he opens the door the singers take heart. He recognizes none of the faces, young and old, smiling up at him. As they break into "Santa Claus Is Coming to Town," Barbara joins him in her robe. Even the children must know what the Probsts have been doing.

·

Although the streets of Webster Groves connect with those of its neighbors, and aside from Deer Creek in the north the town has no natural boundaries, its residents experience it as an enclosure, an area where Christmas can occur in safety. It's a state of mind. A few people leave Webster Groves for the holidays, but many more come to it, by plane or train or car. And landscape recapitulates personality. There are no open fields, no high-rises or trailer parks or even shopping malls, no zones of negative potential into which spirit can drain. All houses are bright, and none stands alone. All streets interlock. Webster Acres, Webster Forest, Webster Ridge, Webster Hills, Webster Gardens, Webster Downs, Webster Woods, Webster Park, Webster Knolls, Webster Terrace, Webster Court. The air is full of woodsmoke, but the sky is clear. Born lucky, residents guess. This is a home that feels like home.

Even in the home of the Thompsons, Duane's parents, creatures are stirring. They are burglars. They empty drawers onto floors, rip mattresses off beds, shoot flashlights into closets and cupboards. They have located the silver. They have spied a VCR. A heavy coin collection has come to light.

Watson Road, né U.S. 66, is neither crowded nor empty. Oldsmobiles and other stately forms move along it at discreet intervals. Stopped at the Sappington Road intersection, by a Crestwood Plaza just lately closed for the night and tomorrow, drivers in neckties smile at other drivers in neckties, or do not, depending. As it happens, Jack DuChamp does not. He is musing. Elaine sits in the front seat with him, and Laurie and Mark and Janet are in back. They're driving to Elaine's parents' for supper. At midnight they will go to church; Laurie sings in the choir. Jack thinks how it's only a short drive down Sappington Road into Webster. He thinks it might be a nifty idea, between activities, to pay a short surprise visit to Martin, even though Martin has said they'd have family in town. The house must be full of relatives. Still, a quick surprise visit . . . The five DuChamps could act like wassailers, sing a song on the stoop: a joke. Maybe get invited in. Or did

Martin and Barbara (God bless her) open their presents on Christmas Eve and not Christmas morning? Jack can't remember. He has a great reluctance to disturb anyone opening presents.

"Green light, Dad."

Jack steps on the gas.

At this moment more than half the human bodies in St. Louis have alcohol in their bloodstream. The city/county average body temperature is 98.63°F. Lipid counts are seasonally high. Three babies have been born in the last hour (two of them will be named Noel) and five adults have died, three of natural causes.

In a West End bar called Dexter's, Singh has had two nervous drinks with a strapping young German on his way from Lübeck to Santa Barbara. Stefan is wearing a fisherman's sweater and pants with leopard spots, a purple scarf and a cowboy hat. His hair is golden and the length of Jesus's. He and Singh get acquainted in German, French, English, German; they like the rapid changes. But Singh can't concentrate effectively in a place where he is too well known. He suggests a change of scene to Stefan, who repositions his hat and says sure. They obtain hot pastrami sandwiches at the 24-hour deli around the corner, and Singh soon has Stefan in his third apartment, fed and stripped. He takes the phone off the hook. He takes off his clothes. A quarter falls from his pants pocket. He flips it, and while it flashes in the smoky lighting, falling towards the carpet, he says "Heads or tails?" and Stefan giggles.

.

Nearby, Jammu is studying assessment maps of North St. Louis. She is sick, but she has an idea. St. Louis streets are wide, and outside of downtown the blocks are small. In a six-by-one-block area the five enclosed cross streets can take up as much as 20 percent of the total acreage. As long as they provide access to individual homes, they have to be kept and maintained at considerable expense. But with larger developments replacing homes, developments like the Ripley complex and the Allied Laboratories and the Northway townhouses, the streets have in some cases become downright nuisances. The city can sell them. It stands to make millions.

Unfortunately, Jammu's eyes are not functioning as they

should. The skewed streets are parallel in her eyes, the varied densities uniform. It's an effect familiar to her from staring long and hard at something, when the mind tidies up the random patterns of reality. But now, no matter how she blinks or turns her head, no matter how close she brings her eyes to the map, all she sees are perfect crossword-puzzle grids.

It's the cold. It's the meth. It's her exhaustion. It's the dry weather, the barbed shafts shooting from her sinuses. When she inhales, her lungs crinkle and croak like waxed-paper milk cartons.

She shuts her eyes and leans back against the wall, stretching her legs until her feet are buried in the pillows. She has another dinner with the mayor tomorrow, and a meeting with Singh after that. In the meantime she has to get some sleep, to flush her mind of the hundred local faces she sees each week, faces lean, porky, greedy, lusting, humble, cold, the five hundred Americans who squeeze into a week of hers and demand a thousand answers, remedies and favors. But when she did manage to fall asleep this afternoon she immediately dreamed the phone was ringing. She opened her eyes and answered.

"Some bad news, Chief. On the surface of it."

"Tell me."

"Barbara Probst reacted negatively."

"Maybe it's temporary."

"No. She means it. I tried a variety of approaches. She won't see me again."

Singh asked Jammu to check it out for herself, and though she was tired and had vowed never again to subject herself to the voice of Barbara Probst, she hooked into the modem at the recording center and listened to segments edited through 3:00 p.m. today. Singh was right. It sounded bad. The Probsts were having a putrid, corny, weepy holiday, God and sinner reconciled, and Barbara Probst more clearly than ever an agent for the Thought Police, appealing to her husband with a calculated tremolo, wearing down his resistance with her self-help honesty and putting him to sleep with the notion that everything was fine. The instrument of repression: "love."

Jammu called Singh. "Nice going. They're happier than they've been in years."

"On the surface, yes. But I've thought it over—"

"Probst isn't even arguably in the State and it's almost January."

"As I was saying, I've thought it over and I think we're all right, because Probst will never trust her now. She pressed her luck, she mentioned me. She's still nailed."

Maybe. But with so much talent, so much investment, so much technique and theory trained on such a very few men in St. Louis, Jammu thinks it's reasonable to demand resounding victories. She owns the scalps of Meisner, Struthers, Hammaker, Murphy, Wesley, Hutchinson, and she has liens on all the rest—except Probst's.

Singh told her to cheer up. He read her a reference from a poem in *The New Yorker*:

> For Gary Carter, Frank Perdue,
> Bono Vox and S. Jammu!

Then he hung up.

Tossing aside the assessment map, she goes to the bathroom and pisses a trickle. Her urine burns her as it leaves her. On the left-hand faucet of the bathtub a roach is simulating paralysis, unmoved by the funk beat coming down the pipes.

She flushes the toilet, and she is washing her hands, she is staring straight ahead into the mirror, when suddenly all the diffuse evil in the world has puckered into a single mouth and is blowing out of the mirror at her. The face looking back is a white one, a white face made up as an Indian. An American face is showing through the mask, and it crashes into the wall as she throws open the cabinet. Her fingers close on the thermometer. She's burning up.

12

At 11:00 on Christmas morning Luisa put on the red wool dress from her mother which she'd unwrapped an hour earlier, Duane put on his previously owned pinstripe suit and an iridescent blue necktie, and the two of them drove out in the Nova to Webster Groves. When Luisa saw the little stacks of gifts her parents had just opened she wasn't exactly sad, but she did wonder what she'd been trying to prove by not coming home earlier, especially since her father had decided to be nice again. He was about as self-possessed around Duane as he'd be around the Pope. He shook Duane's hand and *bounded* through the house, doing God knew what, and returned and sat with them in the living room for three minutes, and then he *bounded* to his feet and said they should go. At her grandparents' there was a lot of drinking and casseroles. Her grandmother gave her a dirty look before pecking her on the cheek and wishing her a Merry C. Her grandfather gave her a real kiss, and she thanked him for the "present," which was the only word for a $100 bill. Auntie Audrey told her twice how nice she looked, which was agreeable. She shook hands with her cousins and allowed herself to be appraised by her great-aunt Lucy and her great-uncle Ted. Uncle Rolf had despotically occupied the bamboo chair by the fireplace, his legs crossed at the knees, his brandy glass cupped in one hand like a royal orb. He showed Luisa lots of teeth and she smiled and nodded. Then her father moved into the picture.

Technical difficulties. Please stand by. Her mother was introducing Duane to Auntie Audrey. "Yes, I *have* seen your pictures, yes." Luisa wandered over and felt excluded, as always. Duane didn't have to be *so* polite. But then he took her out into the hall and said, "Help, help." They went together to see her grandmother in the kitchen. Her grandmother said everything was under control.

On the way home Duane sat with her mother in the back seat and started telling her the story of his getting hit in the head with a baseball bat while his parents were in Aruba. Daddy, instead of listening, spoke in a low voice to Luisa. He said he may have said some things on his birthday that he didn't mean. He said he was under a lot of strain at work and Municipal Growth. He said he sincerely hoped they could see more of her and Duane, whom he liked.

"And Peter was out playing golf, so there was this unconscious eleven-year-old kid and no one knew who he belonged to, or who to call."

Her mother laughed. "So . . . ?"

"Did you have a good time today?" her father asked.

"Yeah, it was OK."

"So I woke up in the hospital, and a nurse rushed over, and the first thing she said was *What's your name?* Because none of the kids had even known my name. Somebody thought I might be 'Don.'"

"You know, your grandmother hasn't been well."

"Oh, really? I guess she did seem kind of . . ." Luisa shrugged.

"I'd given them the wrong number. They kept calling and calling, and no one answered. So finally around ten in the evening they decided to look it up in the phone book. And of course we have an unlisted number."

"Oh *no*."

"And meanwhile, Peter is losing his mind, he's so scared. He was supposed to look after me, and he has no idea, absolutely no idea—"

"And you understand that at her age she sees things rather differently from the way you or even I do. That is, I don't think you should feel hurt if she doesn't approve of your, your situation with Duane."

"It's OK, I understand."

The headlights and highway lights began to reveal falling snow.

"But by now he's not there anymore, he's down at the police station."

"Oh no, oh no."

"Will you be all right driving home in Duane's car?"

"We've got snow tires."

"You've been driving it to school?"

"Sometimes."

"And so finally it occurs to someone at the hospital to call the police—"

"What's this?" her father asked over his shoulder.

The vacation week passed slowly. Duane said he liked her parents but he liked her better. They went out once with Sara and Edgar. They went skating. They went sledding, and got mashed together when they crashed. Then on the day before New Year's Eve Duane went out to Webster to see two high-school friends of his, and Luisa stayed behind in the apartment to type up all her applications.

As soon as she saw Duane drive away she started walking back and forth through the kitchen and living room and bedroom. She'd never spent a whole day by herself in the apartment, and it was obvious that she wouldn't be working on her applications. She remembered how when her parents used to leave her alone in the house she would feel a deep pang of boredom and irresponsibility the moment they were out the door, and before she could do any of the things she'd thought she would be doing, she had to rifle their drawers, or try their liquor, or fill the bathtub to the very brim and take a bath, which her father said was criminally wasteful.

The first thing she did was smoke one of Duane's cigarettes. The next thing she did was go to the bedroom and look for his journal. Usually he left it in his knapsack with some of his camera equipment, but today the knapsack was empty. She looked through all the books along the baseboard—the notebook had a gray spine like an ordinary book—but it wasn't there either. She went through his drawers in their dresser, and then through all his prints and printing paper, and then through all the clothes in the closet. She even looked in his empty suitcases. The journal wasn't anywhere.

She had just about concluded that he'd put it in the car without her noticing, when, just to be sure, she lifted their mattress off the floor. And there it was.

The fact that he'd tried to hide it made it much more horrible and interesting that she was going to read it.

She lay down on the mattress and started looking for her name. She was immediately disappointed. The last dated entry was October 6, two weeks before she'd met him. After that there were only phrases and prices and doodles, picture ideas and sentences he'd copied down from bulletin boards and books. Her name wasn't mentioned once.

She was glad he wasn't there to see the look on her face. She was quite annoyed. Her reasons were different now, but she decided to keep reading. The first entries were from August.

> Last night we saw "A Chorus Line" at the Muny Opera and sat with 5000 giants shaking half-pint cartons of limeade and lemonade and pushing straws out of the paper wrappers. Every last one of those people looked like an American tourist.

He wrote the way he talked. Or maybe he talked the way he wrote. There was a lot of stuff about starting school at Wash U. which Luisa only skimmed.

> Connie didn't sleep alone last night.

Connie? Who was Connie? Luisa looked at the previous entry and saw that Connie was someone in his dorm.

> I heard the whole scene, all the many noises she made. Usually she speaks from her throat (when she condescends to speak to me at all) but last night the noises came from much lower down. (I don't see what's so wrong with me. I suspect she'd like me if I had a card that proved my age was 35.) The thumping went on forever. It was after midnight, the libraries closed. I went and knocked on Tex's door. Nobody home.

There were pages and pages about his parents and some neighbor of theirs, and then a very long entry from October 1.

. . . I noticed Tex (his real name is Chris) in a corner with two girls whose eye make-up made them look like hornets. I could see he was thrilling them with his rattlesnake story, or the one about the Quaalude freak at the Van Halen concert:

Curled up inside the woofer and went to sleep.

Around eleven the music improved. They played a long string of songs in minor keys, "Born Under Punches," "Computer Blue," "Guns of Brixton," plus that ten-minute Eurythmics thing. And when you're dancing to a tape & the music is so loud that it's the only sound in your ears, you wonder: *where are these voices I hear?* They aren't in anyone's throat, they aren't in the speakers, they're in your head & they sound like the voices of the dead. They make you pity yourself for being alive. They make you sad, these songs between your ears that could stop at the flip of a switch. Because the world itself could go out, like a light, at any moment. The whole world could die like a single person used to. That's what the nuclear age is: the objectification of the terror of total subjectivity. You know you can die any day. You know the world can die.

Tex tapped me on the shoulder. "You know any of these people?"

I shook my head.

"Then let's bag it."

The two girls and I followed him upstairs and out into the rain. Their names were Jill & Danielle, seniors at John Burroughs. Tex put them in the back seat of his Eldorado, me in front. We drove to a bar called Dexter's, where Jill wanted to dance, or try to & Tex obliged her. Danielle said her feet hurt, which I could believe. I saw some blood around the rim of one of her high heels. We were standing in a noisy crowd near the cash register. I told her I'd gone to school for a year in Germany. She told me she had a horse whose name was Popsy.

Does it make any sense that what I nonetheless wanted most of all was to go to bed with her? But she went off somewhere, I really don't know where, and Darshan offered to buy me a drink. I said sure. I'd never spoken to an Indian before. He was thirty maybe. When I said I was a student he said he was too. I was smoking Marlboros, he was smoking cloves & when I talked about the Phillips he understood, he knew it all, he drew my own conclusions. He *liked* me. He said: "That's the center of it, isn't it. People smoke cigarettes even though they are known to be dangerous."

When the bar closed we drove to his apartment, which was down in a bad neighborhood off Delmar. The streets in the rain were black and shiny. Inside, at the end of a long hall of closed doors, was a room with persian rugs on the floor, a rug on the wall & not much else. He went to the kitchen to make tea. I lay back on the rugs & sank into them. The radiator ticked as the heat came on. I remember concentrating on the ticking. I was fairly drunk, but the tea was good and suddenly, or maybe half an hour or an hour later, I was sinking into the rugs & my clothes were all off & the radiator was ticking again. Everything was one temperature.

Luisa skimmed a few pages, her eyes just bouncing off the words. Her heart sounded like a heavy person tromping through the apartment upstairs.

When each one ends I immediately want another. But that's not right. When each one *begins*, before I even *light it*, I'm already wanting the next one. As much as I want to see him again.

She skipped a few more pages.

. . . I left at six sharp in the rain, I went down Delmar and up two flights of stairs and knocked on the door. I saw his twinkling eyes on the back of my hand like Marley's ghost: knock knock knock (echoing the tick tick tick) but the door was unlocked. I walked right in. Six doors were wide open & every room was empty, stripped bare except for rolls of carpet. He was gone. I left the building but I hadn't gotten very far, just a block in fact, when I met two people I knew like brothers from ten years of imagining them who wanted my wallet. Well, no wallet, no camera, no $20, nothing. They laughed little bitter laughs, turned away & then turned back & hit me twice, one in the mouth, two in the eye, & left me kneeling there not thirty steps from the bus stop of epiphanous fame, so embarrassed I almost wished they'd pulled a trigger to save me from standing up. But I stood up & I was thinking ONE THING, which was: Goodness gracious, I must trot home and write about this.

Luisa put the notebook down and went and looked out the window at the street, where cars with black windows were parked crookedly between snowmounds. All the blood was draining from her head. She pictured Duane in the strong arms of a man, the dark arms of an Indian man. She could see it but she couldn't believe it. Kissing a man, rolling naked on the floor with a man. It just didn't seem like something the Duane she knew would do. But he'd done it. And that was why he'd gone to Dexter's on the night Luisa met him: he was looking for the man. Not for her, not for anybody like her: for him.

She thought about this for a while. Then she put the notebook back under the mattress and stirred some of her clothes into the blankets, and went and smoked another cigarette in the kitchen.

The telephone rang. She knocked over the chair she was sitting on, but it was only her mother. Would she and Duane like to come out and have lunch with them tomorrow?

"Sure," Luisa said. "He's out there now, but— But I'm not. So yes."

Three hours later she had the kitchen table covered with application materials. She didn't think moviemakers arranged their scenes any more carefully than she'd arranged the one that was waiting for Duane at five o'clock when he came home. She couldn't hide the fact that the applications weren't done, but she knew exactly what she was going to say she'd watched on TV if he asked what she'd been doing all day.

He didn't ask. He was surprised she'd done as much typing as she had.

For ten more minutes she moved and spoke as if all her expressions and gestures required the pulling of specific wires, wires with a lot of slack in them; her laughs were squeaks or groans and her steps were those of a bureau being walked across a room; but to Duane she was her same old boring self, and soon it wasn't a matter of pretending. She really was herself again, and so was he.

Then it was New Year's Eve. Stacy was having a party, but Luisa was mad at her for not having called during vacation until the morning of the party, and anyway, she and Duane had already made plans. They'd come back from her parents' with decent food, more of her clothes, and a week's worth of mail. Their apartment seemed tiny after 236 Sherwood Drive. The cranberries on their little tree had puckered, and the branches rained needles when she crossed the room to get the mail out of her purse. She was wearing a jean skirt and a white T-shirt.

Duane had on the Hawaiian shirt she'd given him. He was trying to slice some of her parents' salami with his Swiss Army knife. "I never use the little blade," he said, "because I want to keep it really sharp for that Special Job. But it's too short. I'm taking the tomato knife under advisement."

"How about a pair of scissors," she said, opening an envelope.

"Fittingly," he said, "this is the one holiday my parents do know how to celebrate. My father used to buy cherry bombs—"

"Brown has not received my application yet! Has not received it! They must think I'm applying or something."

An airmail envelope fell out of a glossy mailing from Baylor. The stamps were French. It was a Christmas card from the Girauds. Luisa tore it open. "This is so nice," she said. "Everything but a subscription to Elle." Mme Giraud had written a long note on the back. "But Duane—"

"Ai ai ai ai ai!" He danced and sucked his finger.

"Duane—"

"This knife isn't worth the paper it's printed on."

"Duane, Paulette Giraud, her mother says she spent this fall in England."

He looked at her, his finger in his mouth, his ears wiggling.

"Listen. Étudié depuis septembre jusqu'à décembre en Angleterre!"

"That's peculiar."

"But she called me." Luisa read the note again. Could Paulette have come to the States without her mother's knowing it? No way. Paulette was too stupid to do anything that crazy. But if she wasn't in St. Louis, then who had that been on the phone? Why would anybody want to say they were Paulette?

"Maybe Stacy faked it," Duane said.

Luisa started to shrug, but then she shook her head. "She would have told me eventually. Anybody I know would have told me, because that's when I met you. They'd want the credit."

"Hm. Right. Yeah."

"This is so weird," she said.

Duane began to clear the table, working around her.

"This is so weird."

He set out some carrots and celery. He set out rye bread, French bread, cheddar cheese, dill pickles, Doritos, dip. He set out two glasses and took the champagne out of the freezer. He wrapped it in a towel, peeled back the foil, untwisted the wire, and popped the cork.

It stuck in the ceiling.

"Hey!"

They both looked at the ceiling.

"It went right through."

"It's just paper or something up there." As soon as he'd filled the glasses, Duane got up on a chair and probed the hole the cork had made. Plaster fell in his face, and then something dropped out of the hole, not the cork, something metal. Luisa picked it up. It was a heavy, shiny slug with pinpricks on one side, like a microphone, and a wire dangling from it. "What is this?"

Duane took it from her. "Looks like a bug."

"What?"

"A bug, don't you think? The FBI or somebody. This was always a student place. Maybe there used to be some radicals here."

Luisa climbed onto the chair. The cork came loose, bouncing off her nose. "The paint's fresh," she said.

"I wonder who lived here before me."

"*We* live here now."

"I kno-o-ow we do. But we're not subversive elements."

She looked down from the chair at Duane, the homebody, who was brushing bits of plaster off the tablecloth and picking flakes of paint off the dip. Then she stepped off the chair and sat down. She'd just remembered something else. At Dexter's on the first night, the night she'd met Duane, she'd been spooked by someone she'd thought was an Algerian. But for all she knew he could have been Indian, and he was actually fairly cute. She remembered how he'd wanted to talk to her but wouldn't come inside the bar. How many Indians could there be who hung around at Dexter's?

Duane lit the candles and turned out the light. "I mean it's obviously weird," he said. "But it's also obvious that it doesn't have anything to do with me."

"What about me?"

"Or with you." He put the bug on top of the refrigerator. "We can take it apart or something after dinner."

On the refrigerator door were black-and-white pictures of Luisa that Duane had taped up before she moved in with him. She looked away from them. Someone had faked a phone call and a postcard. She wasn't making this up; there was a postcard, too. Maybe it was Duane's man. Maybe he'd wanted her and Duane to get together because he could tell that Duane needed a girl, not a man. But then why was he hanging around outside the bar? And what was the bug in the ceiling for? Did the guy get thrills from listening to her and Duane eat? She was getting confused.

"What's wrong?" Duane said.

She looked up at him. He had no idea what she knew about him, no idea what connections she was making in her mind. All at once his ignorance seemed terribly pathetic.

"Nothing." She said it with finality, and pulled her chair up to the table. "Are we going to have a toast?"

"Sure. What do you want to toast?"

"Chips. Nachos-flavored corn chips."

He raised his glass. "To chips," he said.

As soon as she raised her glass, she felt herself stop thinking. It was easy. Duane had told her once how a jetliner could lose power in two of its engines and still keep flying smoothly. Behind the curtains in the cockpit there was consternation, pilots pulling switches, yanking levers, but in the main cabin the passengers were finishing their dinners as if nothing had happened. They ate salami and compared their parents. Everything was ordinary as soon as you stopped thinking. There was no mystery about how they'd met and no magic in the candlelight on the silverware and no longer any heart-stopping difference between the sink in Duane's kitchen and the sink in her parents' kitchen. The food on the table was what people everywhere had to eat, and Duane loved her because she was smart and pretty and had come along at the right time, and she was just a girl who had lied to her parents and lied to her boyfriend and would do it all again if she needed to, the way she might sleep again and again on bloody sheets, because they were ruined. And then the plane landed safely, of course, and the passengers joined the crowds in the terminal and drove home to their ordinary houses, and never even stopped to think that just an hour earlier they'd been sitting on seats that were seven miles off the ground.

13

In the first days of the new year, a bitterly cold weather system had descended on St. Louis and established itself with a sequence of record low temperatures. The high on January 3 was zero degrees. On the fourth the high was 2. On the fifth the sky clouded and the temperature climbed into the teens to allow another half a foot of snow to fall, and then on the night of the sixth the mercury dipped to −19. For the next week, salt trucks alternated with snowplows on the streets, like gloom with anxiety. By the week of the thirteenth, more than three feet of snow was lying on the lawns of the suburbs and the urban construction sites and the levees overlooking the ice-covered Mississippi. The longer the bad weather lasted, the more aggressively it shouldered murders and politics out of the spotlight of the local news, out of the headlines, the lead-story slots. It exploited the advantage of all weather: its constant availability for comment.

Barbara had at first followed the cold spell's progress in a circus-going spirit, but eventually even she succumbed to the portents and began to believe that the reports all somehow pointed inwards, as a neighborhood's concentration of freaks and deformities might point underground, to a reservoir of toxic waste. Windchill, degree days, inches of precipitation, former records, consecutive days below x degrees, below y degrees, integers positive and negative—the numbers infected minds. There were broken pipes in warehouse sprinkler systems. Termination of gas service, and outcries. Frozen stiffs in East St. Louis. Ice-locked barges. The heart attacks of shovelers. Stalled cars abandoned on freeways. And always the search for precedents, the delight in finding none, and the feeling of specialness, the growing conviction that attendance at such a winter certified a claim to unusual fortitude and vision. The city, on the news, in the news, behaved like a witness. There was a mood. The weather oriented itself along the polar lines of the previous six months' political trends. All tendencies hung together. A peculiar watchfulness had descended on St. Louis in the first weeks of the new year.

The sixteenth brought some relief, however, in the form of temperatures only just below freezing and a breeze from the south, off the Gulf, much attenuated. It was Tuesday. Though average for January, the weather felt relatively springlike, and Barbara was cleaning. In her closet she applied the Two Year Rule, throwing onto the bed every article of clothing she hadn't worn since Christmas two years earlier. She made no exceptions, not for gifts from Martin, not even for her swankiest evening gowns. If she liked something, the rule ensured that she wore it at least once every twenty-four months. Her closet lodged no "dogs," nothing unworn or unwearable, and she was in possession of far fewer clothes than Luisa or Martin, fewer clothes, undoubtedly, than anyone she knew.

Emptied hangers stabilized on the bar. The usable skirts and blouses she slid to the left impatiently. She was looking for victims, and she found one in a foolish winter suit she'd bought four months ago. She'd never worn it.

Out it went, flapping its pleats as it flew to the bed. It was followed by a linen skirt too big in the waist, a brown dress she didn't love, and an $80 pair of shoes, accessories to a crime of impulse.

She moved to her dresser and dropped to her knees. She took a last look at the Christmas present from Audrey, the sweater. She'd worn it once, at lunch last week. Once was enough. Poor Audrey. Out it went.

Via the charitable conduit of the Congregational Church, these clothes would end up in the inner city or the Missouri Bootheel. Barbara imagined driving into some tiny town southeast of Sikeston and seeing all the decade's fashions, all of her mistakes and all of Audrey's and Martin's modeled on the dirt streets by poor black women. But the clothes could have been bound for a landfill for all she cared. She deposited an armload of gifts and badly stained underwear on the bed.

The house was quiet. Mohnwirbel had driven away after lunch and not returned. A busy bee he was. Martin had dropped the idea of suing him, and the box of unclean pictures had found its way into one of Martin's storage lairs, where it would probably stay until it molded. Barbara yearned to go beyond her strikes on his study and closets, to hit the third floor and the basement and attack those hard-core bunkers of junk. She envisioned a life untyrannized by objects, a life in which she and Martin would be free to leave at any time and so by staying prove the choice was freely made. In truth, she hoped that even death might become bearable if everything she still wanted to own when it came could fit in two suitcases; because sometimes the airlines lost your suitcases, and by the time you realized they were gone you'd reached your destination.

She added a sheaf of receipts to the piles of paper she would take downstairs to process at her desk. A little sun shone on the carpeting. Second-story branches nutated in the windows, seeking gaps in the soft assault of the southern wind, paths back to their natural positions. Squirrels paused. The house was very quiet.

As she opened her box of everyday jewelry a pair of earrings caught her eye, the earrings John had given her. She hadn't even thought to return them. With a feeling of uneasiness she glanced into the mirror. The eyes that met hers weren't her own.

She gasped. John was standing in the bathroom doorway. She stamped on the floor, trying to stamp out her fright. "How did you get in here?"

"Door's unlocked!" he said.

"I told you. Go away. I told you."

"Yes, yes." He swept into the room and sat down on the bed. "I know what you told me." He crossed his legs and looked up at her engagingly. "You persist in treating me like a substance that comes out of a faucet that you can turn off with your gentle smile or your firmness and maturity, no no, John, please. You're very sweet John but. —And yet I find you here with my little gift . . ."

"I can do the same to you," Barbara said hotly. It no longer took any effort not to like him. "I can do exactly the same to you. I can say you're a creep and a jerk. You may be articulate, but you can't make me feel comfortable around you. You can just go to hell, in fact. Get out of here. Take your damned earrings. You shouldn't walk in people's back door. Your manners are lousy. Who do you think you are?"

He sighed and put his hands in the pockets of his overcoat. "You aren't entirely wrong," he said. "But there's a fine line between effrontery and simple persistence."

"Get out." She picked up the earrings and reached and dropped them over his hand into one of his pockets. She reeled back. Her ears roared. There was a gun in his pocket. She took deliberate steps towards the bathroom.

"Stop."

She turned back and saw the gun pointing at her. He was a total stranger.

"Get down a suitcase," he said.

"Listen—"

"The middle-sized leather bag will be ideal. Take your black silk dress, the green dress with copper threads, and another winter dress. A pair of jeans, and your gray corduroys. T-shirts. You'll want T-shirts. Six changes of underwear, a swimsuit, a nightgown, and your light robe. Am I going to have to do this for you?"

"John."

"Pick three sweaters, three shirts, and a pair of decent shoes. The ones you're wearing will be adequate. Canvas shoes, too, space permitting. I have the feeling you aren't even listening to me."

She turned again to try to leave, and she heard only one footfall before he punched her in the face. He hit her in the stomach. She fell to her knees. He kicked her in the collarbone and knocked her over backwards. She felt the pressure of his heel on her throat. It was gratuitous. He was getting even.

"I'll be ever so happy to shoot you in the knees if you try to run," he said. "And in the spinal cord if you make a fuss when we're outside. You understand I mean this."

The heel went away. She heard him slide her suitcase off its shelf in the closet, and heard him packing. She heard the clink of cologne bottles, and the click of a latch.

.

What was left of Municipal Growth hardly filled the conference room at the offices of Probst & Company. Seventeen of the thirty-two active members had jumped ship without so much as offering Probst an explanation. Quentin Spiegelman, St. Louis's premier financial guardian, a man whose name appeared on the dotted lines of a thousand wills, had twice assured Probst that he wouldn't miss a meeting, and twice now he'd missed one. His lies were so childish that only an implicit hatred could explain them. Probst had not thought he was Quentin's enemy. But he was willing to think so now. He was the chairman, and felt personally betrayed.

It was seven o'clock. On the far side of the oval conference table, Rick DeMann and Rick Crawford peered over their half-glasses, ready to begin.

"Let's give Buzz another few minutes," Probst said.

He had called the meeting here at his offices to create an impression of good attendance and to ensure a businesslike atmosphere. The walls were hung with photographs of the major projects he'd worked on over the years, framed exempla of municipal growth: the Poplar Street Bridge, the 18th Street interchange, the terminal at Lambert, the county government building, the Loretto-Hilton complex, West Port, the convention center. The air smelled faintly of electricity and typewriter oil.

P. R. Nilson and Eldon Black, archconservative allies of General Norris, were conferring with Lee Royce and Jerry Pontoon, real-estate-made men. The only remaining banker in the group, John Holmes, was trying to attract the attention of County Supervisor Ross Billerica. Jim Hutchinson, still tan from a holiday vacation, was leaning way back in a chair between Bud Replogle and Neil Smith, nice men, railroad men. An awkward movement at Probst's right shoulder caused him to turn. General Norris was removing a bug detector from his jacket pocket. Green light. He put it back. "We start?" he said to Probst.

"We can wait a few more minutes."

"Righty-o." The General's head swooped closer. "Don't look

now, Martin," he said in his 30-hertz voice, "but there seem to be some interesting dishes there across the street, I said don't *look*," for Probst had turned to see out the window. "It's conceivable they have direct means of listening. Maybe casually draw the curtain, why don't you?"

Probst frowned at him.

"Just do what I say, Martin." The voice was mud—mud baked by a hot sun and cracked into tiles. "Safety's cheap."

There had always been communications dishes on the roof of the precinct house. They were antennas, not mikes. Probst shut the curtains, and a draft flattened them against the window: the outer door had opened. Carmen was letting a huffing and puffing Buzz Wismer into the room. Probst nodded to her. She could leave now.

Buzz brushed off his coat and hung it on the rack in the alcove. He took the last empty seat, to Probst's left.

"I'm glad you made it," Probst said with feeling. He gently slapped his friend's bony knee. Buzz nodded, his eyes on the floor.

A week ago Barbara had eaten lunch with Bev Wismer and come home with the news that Buzz was having an affair with Mrs. Hammaker. Probst rejected the possibility out of hand. He was sick of the whole notion of unfaithfulness, of the double standards and the way people talked. He wanted to be left alone.

"Martin," the baked voice growled.

"Yeah yeah."

"Let's go."

Probst raised his head and saw gray eyebrows, cheeks age-spotted or cold-bruised, eyeglass lenses bending the ceiling's lambent panels into bows and bars. He saw neckties in cautious colors, raked hair and bald spots, executive hands on the table with executive pens poised. Municipal Growth, waiting. A few smiles had developed like fault lines in the tension.

"I assume we all know what the big news is," Probst said. "Is there anyone who hasn't seen a paper today?"

The day before, the lower house of the Missouri General Assembly had begun to consider a bill which, if passed, would authorize a binding referendum to decide if the boundaries of St. Louis County should be redrawn to include the city again.

"We'll have a lot to say about this," Probst continued. "But for a while I'd like to stick to the agenda you received yesterday. We can't afford to spend the whole night bickering like last time. We need to get some work done."

This drew gestural responses from everyone but Buzz.

Rick Crawford delivered the first report. The city of St. Louis, he said, was living dangerously but doing well. City Hall had met its December and January payrolls by diverting moneys ordinarily spent on servicing the city's debt. It had prepared for this move by using the city's new Hammaker stock, in conjunction with the dramatic rise in the value of city-held lands, as leverage for a bond renegotiation. Its rating had improved to AA, and in essence it had taken out a second mortgage on the civic improvements of the past. This maneuver, which required neither voter approval nor tinkering with the Charter, was mainly Chuck Meisner's work. He and his friends in the city banking circles had effectively guaranteed that the refurbished bonds would find buyers. Everything had happened quickly. Leading up to the "Christmas Announcement" of municipal solvency had been a 72-hour marathon meeting attended by the mayor, the comptroller, Meisner, the budget director, Quentin Spiegelman, Asha Hammaker, Frank Jordan of Boatmen's, and S. Jammu.

"I guess that makes Chuck's position with regard to us fairly clear," Probst said.

"It also makes clear what put him in the hospital," Crawford said. "The terms of the refinancing run to more than two hundred pages, and they did the whole thing in three days."

Probst pictured the little group at work. The presence of women in it made him feel particularly excluded. It was a reminder of his high-school days, of the Saturday nights he'd spent throwing rocks in the river in the company of nobody but Jack DuChamp.

The mayor, Crawford said, had made many promises to many different constituencies, and the only cheap promise was to finance good middle-income housing for displaced families. "I needn't remind anyone how beautifully timed that transaction tax was. She—that is—well, yes, *she* got it on the November ballot and got it passed with no more than a month to spare. Imagine the resistance if she proposed it now. As for paying for the other promises, we can expect a transformation of the city's revenue-generating structure, beginning with the elimination of the sales tax and the corporate-earnings tax—"

"Oh, the bastards," Norris said. Rolling his shoulders, he disencumbered himself of his jacket. Underneath he had on black suspenders and one of those tight shirts by Christian Dior that Probst thought generally looked bad on people. It didn't on Norris. His formidable rib cage gave it shape. Probst wondered if he himself could carry off suspenders.

"—As well as continuing to waive the city income tax for city residents. This might not be as suicidal as it sounds. Property-tax revenues for the fiscal year will be up at least forty percent on the strength of the North Side boom alone. Of course, once the developments are further along, income will fall again because the city's going full steam ahead with its tax-abatement program. The way out appears to be twofold. In the first place, a bond issue—"

"To raise general revenues?" Ross Billerica interrupted. Words left his mouth as if expelled for bad behavior. "*That* will take a constitutional hamendment, Hi'm afraid."

"No, it won't," Crawford said. "They'll still have enough tax income for payroll and operating expenses. It's stretching the law a little, but even routine maintenance, if it's been postponed long enough, can be written into a bond improvement. The voters will approve and the city should find plenty of takers for the bonds. But the news today is what really counts. If the merger goes through, then the county will have to assume much of the cost of providing services, at a comparatively small cost to the city."

Crawford concluded his report speculatively. He said the history of the St. Louis area seemed to be a seesaw between the city and the county, as if this site at the confluence of rivers had never been and never would be productive enough to make both halves simultaneously viable. The city's rise and the county's fall were the same event, and it was occurring now for two simple reasons: the altered investment policies of a handful of executives, and the drastic drop in the city's crime rate.

Everyone began to speak at once, but Probst cut them short and nodded to John Holmes. Holmes bore a strong facial resemblance to FDR, but wore modern glasses. His bank had joined with Probst and Boatmen's and a dozen other creditors in a suit against

Harvey Ardmore. "You want to give us the bad news now, John?"

The bad news was county finances. Six months ago, Holmes said, only one of the area's five largest corporations had been head-quartered in the city: Hammaker. Six months from now, three of the Big Five would be there: Hammaker, Ripley, and Allied Foods. Only Wismer and General Syn would be left in the county, and only they would still be within commuting range of most of the county's newer high- and middle-income housing developments.

Men looked at Probst, who was sandwiched between these two steadfast giants. The General was staring at the ceiling, his lips closed and inflated. Buzz hadn't moved when his name was mentioned. His thighs spread like flat tires on the seat of his chair. Probst was struck by the contrast between the modesty of Buzz's figure and the power he wielded. He had direct control over thousands of lives and hundreds of millions of dollars. He had dandruff on his glasses.

Since October, Holmes continued, nineteen other firms had relocated in the city or taken steps in that direction. Eight of them employed two hundred or more people. These were Data-Rad, Syntech, Utility Software, Blanders Electric, Newpoint Systems, Hedley-Carlton, Heartland Control, and—the largest—Kelly Richardson's Compunow. In other words, the high-tech industries, the new firms, the ones with the highest median salaries. They were leading the way and clustering, as it were, around Ripley's new research division, which was already operating in temporary quarters on the North Side.

"We could have expected this from Ripley," Holmes said. "In thirty years in business in St. Louis he's never once taken a false step."

In November and December the seasonally adjusted rate of housing starts in the county had declined for the first time since the last recession, and declined by nearly 20 percent. There had also been a slew of highly visible bankruptcies, Westhaven chief among them. Real property values were in steep decline, with West County by far the hardest-hit region; this was especially cruel because the statewide reassessment, just completed in August, had left assessed valuations at an all-time high. In the many new office buildings west of I-270, occupancy was shrinking.

"From a vacancy rate of seven percent a year ago, we're already up to sixteen and it's accelerating. I'd guess the March figures will show us above twenty-five percent, and that means we're hurting, gentlemen, palpably hurting."

It was true that in many respects the county was unchanged from a year ago, with retail and service enterprises substantially unaffected. To look at Webster Groves or Ladue or Brentwood you would never guess what was going on. But the poor performance of the economic indicators was creating self-fulfilling prophecies. A front-page article in the *Wall Street Journal* had glowingly described the city's efforts to attract new business, darkly delineated the county's consequent problems, and forecast more of the same, only better, only worse.

"We've been able to count no fewer than five middle-sized firms from out of state who had planned to locate in the county, or at least were seriously considering it, but are now committed to a city location. And they're building, not renting, in the city. The city may ultimately go bust, but it's rigged things so those companies can hardly afford to pass up the inherent tax advantages in building. As for why the county didn't ever provide similar incentives, the answer is because there was never any local competition until this year."

Probst was watching the county supervisor's reaction to the report. Ross Billerica was a few years younger than Probst. His hair was Greek black and he wore it in a long crewcut, a short pompadour, with the ends of the hairs all diving for cover at once, uniformly, glistening. A lawyer by training and a millionaire by inheritance of his family's liquor-store chain, he had a (HA!) belligerency that led many people to think him highly able. But if he was so marvelous, you had to wonder why he was also (HA! TAKE THAT!) so highly dislikable, and why after twenty years of being hailed as senatorial or even presidential material, he was still just the county soup and had to campaign hard before every election.

"Stop right there, John!!!" Billerica, as if he could stand no more inaccuracy, was correcting Holmes. "For your information, we're still hrunning a neat surplus. Maybe you're forgetting that neither the tax rates nor the hassessed valuations have changed."

Holmes turned patiently to Billerica. "What I'm saying, Ross, is that with real property values and profitability making a sharp downturn—especially in your unincorporated areas, which have always been your mainstay revenue-wise—I don't see how you can avoid lowering taxes at some point. You're talking about maintaining current revenue levels. I can guarantee you that will send a number of firms either into bankruptcy or into the city. If you want to keep the default rate down—and I sure hope you do—and if you want to keep businesses in the county, I think that you and most of the municipalities are going to have to make deep cuts in services in the next year or two. In the county's case, I'd recommend as soon as possible."

Billerica smiled as if conceding a technical point.

Bud Replogle reported on hospitals. Suddenly, he said, the chief of police had become a leading advocate of improving the two city hospitals. Bud stressed the word "two" and got a round of smiles, because for twenty years the revival of City Hospital Number Two, renamed Homer G. Phillips, had been a matter of burning concern to the city's black community. For twenty years mayoral and aldermanic candidates had promised action, and for twenty years the hospital had sunk into ever worse disrepair, losing first its accreditation and then its ties with the medical schools. Municipal Growth's own study had concluded that Homer Phillips was unsavable. But now Jammu was using that very study as the basis for her own, more ambitious proposals. Foremost among them: the preservation and revitalization of Homer Phillips.

"What in God's name," Eldon Black said, "is the police chief doing in hospital planning?"

"What she's doing," Replogle answered, "is she's liquidating our assets. She's making a public show of what we've been doing privately for years."

Lee Royce's report on black politics reached a similar point: "Here for twenty years we've been cultivating a relationship with the urban blacks, and then *she* waltzes in here, with no personal affection for them, and proceeds to buy them off. They've let themselves be bought, for a new Homer Phillips, for tax concessions and a hundred favors to black property owners. For a political stake. It's a buyer-seller relationship. When they dealt with us, it was as equals."

"Emotion aside, Lee . . . ?" Probst prompted.

"We based our relationship on the fact that since the city has a large black population, a majority even, they should be given our support in every responsible effort to improve the quality of life there. They've been happy with this. It *is* their city, regardless of the color of the mayor's skin."

"Yeller, last I checked," the baked voice told Probst. "With a long streak of red."

"Jammu has worked them into a position where they'll vote pro-merger, I believe, and if she succeeds in creating a more regionally oriented government, it's the blacks who'll lose the most in terms of political say-so. But she's telling them a different story."

Rick DeMann gave his report on city schools. The prosperity of the St. Louis school district was keyed to property values, he said, and so naturally it stood to be among the boom's chief beneficiaries. "What galls me, though, what really galls me, is Jammu's attitude. It takes cash, she says, and lots of it, to improve the schools. Only good money will attract the good young teachers, reduce class size, improve discipline. And it's like, 'You ninnies. Don't you understand it takes money?' Of *course* we understand. But there was never any money until this year."

A merger of the suburbs and the city, Rick added, would render moot the touchy legal questions raised by regional desegregation. This could have serious demographic implications. "A big reason the white middle class moved out to the county is, as we all know, their desire for good schools and, more specifically, their fear of black areas. If the city comes back into the county, there won't be anyplace to run."

"Except to other cities," said Eldon Black.

"To start the next discussion—" Probst raised his voice, hastily trying to invent a new discussion topic. "I'd like to pick up on some of these questions. It seems to me, now, that, ah, we should look at this realistically." Yes. Realistically. He cleared his throat. "Realistically. Haven't we, as a group, never really been opposed to the merger of the city and county? The current layout is full of inequities. If someone had proposed a merger a year ago, we would have done everything in our power to help win voter approval for it. Because it makes sense. We stand for what makes sense. As for the supposed damage to the county economy—"

"The actual damage," John Holmes said.

"—We're not here to take sides. We're here to determine what the right thing to do is. What's right for the city and county as a whole. What makes sense."

"Martin—"

"Martin—"

"Martin," Holmes said, "it sounds to me as if you're saying we should continue doing nothing at all."

"I don't agree. I'm just trying to eliminate the sour grapes from the discussion, and to point out the strength of our pro-county bias."

"Fiddling while the city burns," the baked voice said.

Probst ignored it. "Jim," he said. "You had something to say?"

Jim Hutchinson was looking at the three-foot-tall scale model of the Arch on the rear windowsill. "Yes." He squared himself with the table. "We've been following—"

"Who's we?" P. R. Nilson immediately demanded.

Hutchinson lowered his head an inch or so, as if to let the question sail over his head, over the Arch, and out the window. "We at KSLX," he said, "have been following the development of a group called Urban Hope since its inception last month. In essence it seems to be a commercial redevelopment agency with close ties to the mayor and board of aldermen. The mayor has acknowledged privately that such a group exists, and while no one has been able to determine even approximately who's in it, my guess is that it consists of all the MG members who aren't here tonight. The ex-members, that is. Now, I thought it might be of interest if we took a straw poll here to see how many of us had been approached by a syndicate soliciting our involvement."

"Of interest to who?" Norris said, full strength.

"Much obliged, General. Of interest to all of us. Since our topic is whether or not to take sides, I thought—"

"All right," Probst said. "The mayor approached me last month and offered me some sort of role in planning and constructing some of the North Side projects. I told him to go to hell. At that point, of course, I assumed not everyone was being offered special privileges. Otherwise, heh, they wouldn't be special. Can I see a show of hands?"

All but two of the men raised their hands.

"So everybody but me and Hutch," Norris said. "What do we make of this?"

Probst was disappointed. He hadn't been the only one.

"I invite you all to review the facts," Hutchinson said. "The city now stands where Clayton stood in the early sixties. The county now stands where the city stood in 1900. Yes, I agree, the county isn't dead. But in the space of six months, a newcomer to St. Louis has reversed—reversed, not just altered—the balance of power in greater St. Louis. The reports tonight, and the show of hands, provide proof for another of the General's contentions: Jammu is at the center of this, and she's aware of our existence. Given her control of everything else, I find it highly unlikely that she isn't the motivating force behind the syndicate called Urban Hope."

"Urban Warriors, Osage Hope," Norris said.

"And yes, there are those of us who infer an involvement in the terrorist group as well. But when all her other activities—and gentlemen, I can't help saying again how remarkable it is that this woman has been here only five months—when all her other activities are both legal and extremely effective, why on earth should she be mixed up with the Osage Warriors? Now, to the fact that over half of MG appears to have left and joined a quasi-commercial syndicate, and to the fact that economic forces alone are speeding the city's rejuvenation, we add today's news that the General Assembly is about to authorize a merger referendum."

"Is about to consider authorizing, Jim."

Hutchinson looked at Probst. "Is about to authorize. We have an overwhelmingly Democratic House, a Democratic governor, and almost a Democratic majority in the Senate. If you haven't noticed the strong party flavor to what's been going on, you haven't been thinking much."

Probst narrowed his eyes.

"Because the Democratic leadership has never been more than marginally opposed to the idea of a merger, and Jammu knows how to counter what few objections they've had. They see it, and rightly so, as their chance to knock the Republicans out of power in the county. And the numbers make clear that they can do just that. Consider, further, that the mayor has gotten more attention this fall and winter than all the other prominent Democrats in Missouri combined. Consider that the attention has been 95 percent positive. Consider that this is the best thing to happen to the Missouri Democratic Party since Harry Truman. Consider that the mayor can make the merger vote out to be vital to his continued success. And then consider that the mayor owes his success entirely to one person. It started with the crime statistics. She was right there in the Christmas Announcement. And she's right there now, and she wants this merger, and consider, if nothing else, her skill as a witness at the police hearings last month. I think we'd better accept that there's going to be a special election in April."

There was a silence.

"And you love it, don't you," the General said.

Probst cleared his throat explosively. "It'll get hung up in the Senate."

"Aw, Martin," Holmes said, "not with Clark Stallhamer co-sponsoring it."

"Yeah," said Probst, a little unsteady. "What about that?"

"Stallhamer's on the same boards as Chuck Meisner," Lee Royce answered wearily. "He's never let his constituency get in his way. His wife's brother is Quentin Spiegelman. He owns a mountain of Ripley stock."

"You see, Martin," Hutchinson said (now that the form of the meeting had become Make It Comprehensible to Martin), "that's why the county Republicans are in trouble. The shift of Ripley's and Murphy's operations to the city is simply bottom-line corporate thinking. Urban Hope is not a radical group—although I imagine it gives Ross no joy to contemplate the fact that Meisner's a registered Democrat. You see what we're up against here?"

"A double whammy," Probst said.

"You got it. Someone has studied the political dynamics of eastern Missouri and seen an opportunity to form a coalition. That someone is Jammu. In the history of St. Louis there's never been a phenomenon like her, nothing even close. She's masterly."

There was another silence—Hutchinson had a newsman's flair for the dramatic—which Probst allowed to lengthen before he spoke.

"What I'd like to do now," he said, "is hear some other opinions on whether it's worth our while to try to block action in the legislature, or whether, as Jim has implied, we should concentrate on the inevitable election. I for my part—"

"Don't you think—"

The small voice checked him. It was Buzz. "Don't you think," he asked the rim of the table, "that we should determine if a merger would be so bad in the first place?" He retracted his head, and coughed a little.

"Good point," Probst said. He found his eyes drawn helplessly towards Hutchinson for more information. "I should think it depends on how—"

"What you can depend on," the General boomed, "is that the wording and effect of the referendum will, like every other action in the city since July, further the aims and power of one group, the group led by the Queen of the Blacks, the King of Toasters and the Princess of Darkness (and I mean she's a slut, Buzz boy, and we all know it)."

Here the General stood up. He hooked his thumbs in his black suspenders. "This group makes me damn impatient," he confided, "and so help me, I ain't gonna stay muzzled one second longer." He snapped the suspenders magnificently. "For two whole hours we been ignoring the main fact, and the main fact is motives. It's all very nice to talk about *what's* happening, and *how* it's happening, and through the agency of who, whom, whomever, and God knows what else it's happening, but what counts, ladies and gentlemen, is the *whys* and the *wherefores*."

He began to pace, circling close behind the ring of heads, each of which nodded forward at his approach like a daisy in a shower. "I see before me a group of human beans that's refusing to come to grips with the fact that there's a conspiracy here in St. Louis, dedicated to anarchy and socialistic propositions and the overthrow of the government and the values we all cherish deeply. I defy any man among you to prove it ain't so. The very fact of Jammu's sponsorship of this merger referendum faggotry is proof to me it stinks, proof enough."

He had stopped at the rear window, laid his hands on the model of the Arch, and lifted it from the sill. He turned with it and held it at arm's length like a man warding off a vampire with a cross. One of the tiny plastic trees at the base of the Arch shook loose, rolled across the plaster river and fell to the carpeting. The model was old and fragile. Probst was relieved when the General set it down again.

"Now, some of you still seem to need reasons to oppose this merger, and for your convenience and peace of mind I'll list me the many reasons and defy any man among you to contravene a one of 'em." He winked at Probst. Probst winked back involuntarily. "First thing, it's a power play and nothing but. We already seen from the municipalization of Hammaker that she has no respect for the sanctity of corporate structure. Your way of life and that of your workers ain't no concern of hers. The only reason she gives a damn about anybody's way of life is votes. 'Course, the way she's drawn the lines, you may see the merger as making sense, but that don't make it right. I can't stop thinking about Adolf Hitler. The way he drew the lines, total war made sense. OK, number two, it violates the spirit of St. Louis. I think you know what I'm talking about. Let me ask you this, Martin. How many times you reckon you been lied to, outright lied to, in the last four months?"

"More times than I'd care to count."

"And before that? Pick a year. 1979. How many times in a whole year in 1979 did a man you trusted lie to you?"

Probst believed he hadn't been lied to at all in 1979.

"Right. What's it tell you about the spirit of these developments? What's it tell you about the quality of the city's new leadership, this Urban Hope, when all them fellers are too yeller to show their faces here tonight? If they had a good case for the merger, or even just a honorable case, they'd be arguing it here right now. But they ain't. And then there's a practical case against it, number three." Norris was completing his circuit, reading over shoulders. He stopped at the chair of Billerica and bathed him in pity and contempt. Billerica grinned bizarrely, a dental demonstration, which seemed to throw the General. He looked at a picture on the wall, of Probst and former senator Symington shaking hands in Washington.

"Number three," he repeated. "S'posedly it's now to the county's advantage to take on the burden of the city, because s'posedly the city's going to be making more money and the county s'posedly less, and this is s'posedly the county's last chance ever to claim its fair share. All righty. Now let's forget the good chance this is all a flash in the pan. Let's forget that the reason the merger looks good now is that you all are *projecting* these rates. *If* the businesses keep moving to the city. *If* the real estate keeps falling in the county. Forget that these rates of change are based on one single solitary bit of do-daddling, namely Ripley and Murphy's move. Forget that if the trend stops in March—and, my boys, it will, it will—then the county will get plain swindled in a merger and only Jammu will come out on top. Let's us forget all this and let me ask: What the hell difference will it make to West County if we merge? Are the powers of economics so miserly and our hearts so weak and faithless that only one half the region can be on top at a time? Listen to me. Look at Martin, sitting there like the Mona Lisa smiling. Ain't he the pitcher of the average man, the common man? Our *fellow* man? He's centrally located, Martin is, he's the man to watch, and so I ask you as a fellow man here, Martin: if there isn't any merger, are you going to move out of—excuse me, uh—"

"Webster Groves."

"Out of Webster Groves? You going to start hurting for contracts? How much would a cut in county services really mean to you?"

"He may be ordinary," Billerica interposed, "but Webster Groves hisn't Valley Park. The close-in suburbs are *hnot* the problem."

"Neither are the outlying areas," Norris said. "I mean yes they is. But merging ain't going to help them much more than not merging is. The only folks really hurting is the speculators and the live-dangerous real-estate men, no offense, Lee and Jerry, I don't mean you. You understand us, Ross? We're saying merger is *bad*. The status quo is *good*."

"Hexactly my point, General. That's hexactly what I'm saying."

Fellow Man was thinking about his visit in December to Wesley, and Wesley's gall in taking him for a man of average moral means, of ordinary scruples, in even suggesting he join the fellowship of the syndicate. Fellow Man needed this parable, this clearcut arrangement of right and wrong, to cinch his decision: the merger deserved opposition. It was the right thing to do. He owed it to the loyal men around him.

"How do we stop it?" Fellow Man asked.

Hutchinson tried to give him an answer. He said he didn't share the group's abhorrence of the merger. His view was that once a good thing, always a good thing. But he was willing to act as a consultant for as long as he was welcome. Assuming the wisdom of writing off the legislative action as a foregone conclusion, he suggested that the city voters also be written off. The 1962 consolidation scheme had failed in the city too, of course, but by a smaller margin than in the county, and circumstances had changed a great deal; even the mayor hadn't supported the scheme in 1962. It would be a far wiser allocation of resources to focus on defeating the referendum in the county, and that (if you asked Hutchinson's opinion) was do-able, if not exactly easy.

"KSLX is conducting a phone survey tonight," he said, "and I think it will show the county opposed by two to one. But that stands to turn around once the issue is publicized and once the big guns—Jammu, Wesley, Stallhamer, the Hammakers—get involved in pushing it. In the case of Jammu and the Hammaker family, popularity transcends the city-county split. Jammu's popular no matter how you slice the cake. To stand a chance of defeating the referendum, I'd say it will take more than the dollar contributions of your respective companies and the Republican Party. The cause is going to require a spokesman who's widely known and absolutely trustworthy, someone to take your case before the public and give it some weight. Your side has to have a voice."

All eyes were on Fellow Man.

.

Home, and turning to drive up the driveway, he was a little surprised to see that the house was dark. Usually Barbara left at least the kitchen light on. He parked the Lincoln by her BMW and activated the garage door, ducking out ahead of it. The wind, in the time it had taken him to drive home, had turned cruel. It had the brutality of a certain kind of bleeding, not the spurt of a severed artery, but the cold seep and puddling of a mangled limb. It dragged over the neighbors' eaves and gables, rent itself on chimneys, carried sirens and a throbbing from the Mopac tracks to the north. Like a wind in Chicago or Boston, some city on open water, it brought more of an ache than a sting to his cheeks. He hurried into the house.

The kitchen was too warm.

He noticed it immediately. It was downright stifling for such a late hour. She never failed to lower the heat before she went to bed. Wasn't she home? Was she sick? Hurt? Had she gone out? Was someone hurt? Was someone dead? Had she fallen in the tub? Choked? Electrocuted? Asleep in the wrong room? Dead? The ever-latent questions coalesced. He dispelled them, but the house was too warm. They came back.

He stopped in the living room to turn down the heat (yes, 70°) and climbed the stairs. Was she home? He heard nothing, smelled neither the soap nor the toothpaste that haunted the hallway near the bathroom door at night. Still he expected to enter the bedroom and find her, the bed mussed and her body raising the blankets, to accept her presence instantly and totally.

But the bed was smooth. He'd expected this as much as he'd expected to find her. She simply couldn't sleep with the heat set this high. He bent his back, and his fingers found the switch on his nightstand lamp. Its light revealed an envelope on the pillows.

She'd cleaned the bedroom. Her sneaker prints dotted the freshly vacuumed carpeting in methodical angles. Against the wall by the television stood four paper grocery bags, from Schnucks, from Straub's, full of clothes. A note was pinned to one of them. He crossed the room and read it. CONGREGATIONAL CHURCH, it said.

Would she pin this note to remind herself? Of course not. Time itself was panic here. He'd been in the house only sixty seconds, and he was aware of the largest bite of experience he could safely swallow whole. This was just about the limit. He saw time as corporeal. He was a tube of man with a man-shaped cross-section, the one-dimensional squeezure from the kitchen to this point, where he paused in his heavy winter coat, in the heat, and then sat down on the bed. He picked up the envelope with a sportive flick of his wrist, as he might lift an envelope with happy contents: careful, it might contain a check. He played with its weight, its center of gravity, shrugged, and flipped it. Sealed. There was a trace of lipstick. She'd sealed the envelope. He slit it with his finger, sundering the BARBARA PROBST from the rest of the engraved return address.

Dear Martin,

    This will seem so sudden to you that I hardly know where to begin explaining it, or whether I should even try. I've been seeing John a lot, practically every day. That's where I was on Saturday afternoon. And most days, though you couldn't know it. I know I told you I didn't plan to make a habit of it, but it's turned into a habit anyway. Which doesn't mean you and I couldn't keep hobbling along together for the rest of our lives, but every time I sit still I hear you telling me to shut up and I hear me telling you I don't really love you, and I wonder what the point is anymore. I never intended to have a stupid life. I'm leaving for New York this afternoon. Maybe that's stupid. If I thought this would kill you, if I thought it even might mess up your life for a while, I probably wouldn't be doing it. But I don't see you having a hard time without me. That's almost reason enough for me to leave. I'm tired of taking care of you when you don't even need me. I don't want to sneak around like everyone else in this city. You hardly seemed to notice Lu was gone. You'll hardly notice me gone either. You have your work. I'll call you soon. I respect you, Martin. You deserve better than to have me meeting a lover in a hotel room. You deserve the truth, and this is it. Don't expect me back.

                                        Barbara

Probst stood up. His body leaned towards his dresser and his legs went along. He threw his wallet and keys onto it.

"Well, all right," he said.

He put his hands in the pockets of his coat and drew it tight around his waist. His chest went in and out. "OK."

After its moment of warm-up the television spewed rich laughter, the studio sounds of the *Tonight Show*. Probst turned it off just as the picture came slanting onto the screen. He turned on Barbara's nightstand light. He turned on the ceiling light. Then the small reading lamp by the rocking chair seemed to give him offense. He closed in on it and turned it on. "You—"

His mouth made words, but few had sound. In a man who'd been speaking all day long, this was illogical.

He went to the study and turned on more lights. There was a hesitancy in his pacing. He'd strike out in one direction and then draw up, bouncing on the balls of his feet, arrested by some new consideration. At each light, too, he paused and turned his head to one side, as if cocking some internal trigger. Then he turned on the light. "I respect you?" He took the picture of Barbara from his desk and threw it against the wall. "I *respect* you?"

In the living room he turned on the spotlights aimed at the three still lifes. He circled the room, and the ceiling brightened. Each new source of light showed up remnants of cobweb or the traces of a spackled crack. The dust on bulbs rarely used gave the air a burnt taint. When all the lights were on—the lamps on the end tables, the lights embedded in the mantel, the chrome tube lamp in the corner, the antique banker's lamp with the green glass shade, the sunken spots above the window seats, the small bulbs in the recessed bookcase—he left the room.

Dropping onto the sofa in the den, he dug the heels of his shoes into an embroidered pillow, but this didn't seem to satisfy him. He swung his legs onto the coffee table. A magazine slid from the stack of them. Another followed. He kicked the rest onto the floor. "*You*—" The pitch of his voice wasn't much lower than a woman's. But then, men's seldom really are. He drew his jaw back hard. Crowded by their neighbors, the middle two of his lower teeth overlapped somewhat. His skin, which had retained a taut uniformity for many years, was mottled and faulted, and covered with whiskers like dark sand, briny ocean sand which couldn't be brushed off. By themselves, his eyes were gray and gentle. Eyes hardly age; they're a window on the soul. But the face shut the window with an ugly convulsion, and Probst thanked his wife very much. The voice dropped into lower registers. "You stinking, stinking bitch," he said. He looked at the writing desk across the room from him, he looked at the cubbyholes organized for long storage, he looked at the ashtray she had washed and dried. He looked, in his overcoat and misery, like a tramp.

He went to make coffee. "I respect you, too," he said as he filled the reservoir of the device with water. He removed the lid from the coffee canister and began to open drawers, yanking them out one after another, and heaving them shut.

"Where does she keep the filters?" he whispered.

Where?

Where?

Where?

He stalked from room to room, flashing angry and cooling off in the archetypical cycle of storm and lull, with pauses for whiskey, muddy coffee, chocolate cookies, until there was light in the eastern trees. He was a man who hadn't been alone in his house, not really, for more than twenty years. His movements were driven by something more elemental than anger or grief, by the unleashing, maybe, of the self itself. At times he almost looked like he was having fun; what he did alone he alone could know. Though the temperature never fell below 65 all night, he left his coat on, kept it buttoned at the neck. It was as if sidewalks and open spaces and wind had been let inside his house.

In the morning he went to work and spent five hours at his desk, mainly barking into the telephone. Outside, the weather grew more menacing by the hour. The wind was blowing hard from the east, spraying the city with an oily coat of water which instantly congealed. Walkers clutched their heads, and squad cars leaving the precinct house and speeding west were overtaken by their own exhaust like women whose skirts billowed up under their armpits.

Traffic on I-44, normally light by six o'clock, was crawling. Probst had been downtown to sign a contract and had spent nearly an hour inching out to the black methane storage tanks at the city limits. Here the cause of the backup came into view. An eastbound semi had plowed into the double guardrail and half ripped, half flipped, to land in pieces in the westbound lanes, where at least six cars and another truck had struck it.

People had died, Probst could tell. When he passed through the one free lane he fixed his eyes on the car ahead of him, but the car braked. A stretcher moved into his vision and showed him, not six feet away, an inert body covered entirely by a blanket. The brake lights had plastic spines and vertebrae for reinforcement.

They dimmed at last. Attendants were wresting ambulance doors out of the grip of the wind, and Probst broke free into the dark, unclogged lanes.

He was in the second lane when he saw his exit, Berry Road. His hands started to turn the wheels, but some danger or paralysis, either the ice on the road or the lactic acid in his muscles, seemed to prevent him from changing lanes in time. He sailed past. He sat up straighter and looked where he was going. He was going west. He shook his head and missed the Big Bend exit, missed the Lindbergh, too. The next cloverleaf slung the Lincoln north onto I-270.

"We'll see what it looks like," he was saying half an hour later. He'd parked the car on the snow at what had been the truck entrance to Westhaven, where the mixers had left deep ruts when they came to pour concrete in December. The Lincoln rocked on its springs in the wind. Snowflakes, dry ones, skidded across the windshield.

Wired to the gate above the heavy padlock was a sheet metal sign reading, PROPERTY OF THE U.S. BANKRUPTCY COURT OF MISSOURI, EASTERN DISTRICT. TRESPASSING IS A VIOLATION OF FEDERAL LAW.

Probst slogged south from the gate, breaking the crust on the snow with his knees, until he came to the culvert that crossed under the fence. He ducked under the fence himself, in violation of federal law, and doubled back to the road. Ahead lay the foundations of Westhaven. It was a project tremendous and abandoned and now, in the winter, buried. It left a large white negative in the woods, an image of contemporary disaster, like a town bombed flat, or a pasture ostracized for harboring dioxin. The acres had been cleared and terraced, the foundations poured, and retaining walls built to separate the levels. Now the snow stuck to these walls in patches, in oval spots, in feathery ribbed fern formations, in vertical lines along the tar-sealed joints, in all the patterns of neglect. It was more desolate than a sod house on the prairie. It was a disappointment specific to the times. No project was begun with failure in mind; the spirit was eager; but the flesh was proverbial.

Trudging and resolute, Probst followed a branch of the road that curled down to the center of an excavation into what would have been—and might still somehow become?—the entrance to a parking garage. He plowed through drifts as high as his breastbone, aiming purposefully for the eastern wall. When he couldn't go any farther, he turned and raised his face. He was a speck in a bowl. From where he stood he could see only gray sky and, in angry motion, a horde of black flakes that looked radioactive but felt like snow, when they melted and ran down his cheeks.

·

It was still nighttime. Undressing, he kicked his briefs over his shoulder and caught them. He froze. An anxious look crossed his face. The briefs dropped to the floor.

He got into bed. "How you doin', hands?" he said to his hands, and grimaced. His eyes were roving the room. As if shying from something, he leaned to find a magazine to read. He heard Mohnwirbel's car in the driveway, the crunch of tires on ice as he took it around to his parking space behind the garage. The door thumped. In his head Probst heard a German voice say, *Martin Probst*. On the cover of *Time* was a drawing of missiles, missile chess, black Russian missiles, white American missiles, the face of the President on the white-king missile, the face of the Soviet premier on the black-king missile, and above them the word STALEMATE?

With a jerk, Probst turned out the light and pulled the pillow over his head.

There had been nights, in every year of their marriage, when Barbara had waked him up and told him she was scared and couldn't sleep. Her voice would be low and thick. "I've got to know when it's coming. I've got to. I can't stand it." Then he'd held her, his fearless wife, in his arms. He'd loved her, because through the skin and bone of her back he could feel her heart beating, and he felt sorry. *I respect you, Martin*. That was the point. He respected her, too. She was the woman he slept with and faced death with. He'd thought they agreed. That they were modern only to the extent of not being vitalists, of facing the future and hoping that if love was organic then it could be synthesized out of respect, out of the memory of being in love, out of pity, out of familiarity and physical attraction and the bond of the daughter they both loved as parents. That they would not leave each other. That the project mattered. He'd thought they had an agreement.

How could she have left him? He launched the question into space

· 303 ·

in a thousand directions and it hit everything but her. A magic shield protected her, something he'd never experienced before: an adamant incredulity. *She didn't. She couldn't.*

"God damn this country," Probst said.

The resonance traveled through his skull to his ears. He heard himself from the inside. He heard the country answer, the muffled booms, the thousand reports. Get with the times, Martin Probst. You think she never looked at another man? I'm always rationalizing attractions. Because there's plenty of pubic parking, Mr. Boabst. Plenty indeed. Women these days, they need that extra—I don't know. Overtures of a, em, physical character. Are we quits? That region is so healthy, Martin. My game, old chap. This isn't good and evil, Daddy.

.

He could see by the clock that it was only 12:30. He was wide awake again. He was lying on his back. His right arm was bent over his ribs, and the curve of his fingers fit the curve of his breast, covering his heart. His left hand lay flat between his legs, resting on his penis and thigh. Had he always lain with his hands in these positions? Or only now that he was alone? A peaceful feeling settled over him. Through his fingertips he felt the hair over his heart and his heart's amazing labor. He felt the ribs. Hands sent messages via nerves to the brain. He felt the crinkly hair between his legs, and the pliant genital flesh. He was dropping off, into a state woolly and primitive, because now he knew what his hands covered while he slept and the world did not and he was vulnerable.

If he was awake when the missiles fell, there was a chance he could run. He could find shelter, protect his head from falling things. But when he was asleep, his head couldn't know its importance. Asleep, he protected something else. Asleep, he was an animal. This knowledge warmed him for several waking days, while he was working to defeat the city-county referendum.

14

"My dear, dear Colonel," Rolf Ripley said. "You've surely heard the story of the chicken and the egg."

"Chicken and the egg."

"Well, which came *first*."

"Yes."

"Well? Do you get my drift?"

"Don't waste my time," Jammu said, her eyes on her wall clock. The sounds of a large and impatient crowd washed against the closed door of her office. "You wouldn't be moving to the city without everything I've done for it. I wouldn't be making a case for the merger if you and Murphy weren't moving. That's understood. But the fact is, the blacks were here before either of us. I think it's rather childish to try to wish that fact away. In any case, I don't see what you think *I* can do to help you."

Ripley raised an interruptive hand and looked at the ceiling with a kind of fondness, as if his favorite song were running through his head. His big hips filled the crook of the leather chair. "I've made a perplexing discovery, Colonel."

Jammu's intercom buzzed. "Hold on," she told it.

"It had come to the attention of my purchasing department that certain key pieces of city real estate were in the hands of colored speculators. This seemed right and proper to me until I discovered that they'd acquired most of these tracts very recently. I was quite taken aback to discover who from. It seems that Mrs. Hammaker has invested between twenty and thirty million dollars in real estate since October."

"Yes?"

"Well my dear, dear Colonel. I had no inkling she was that wealthy."

"She is from a royal family, Mr. Ripley."

"Thirty million dollars, and if you'll pardon me, she isn't an only child, and if you'll pardon me, no one puts all their eggs in one basket, and if you'll pardon me, I don't believe her estate is anywhere near as large as it would have to be for thirty million to be only a fraction of it."

"Naturally I myself have no clear idea," Jammu said.

"Mm. Naturally."

"Although I'd venture to guess the capital is largely the Hammaker family's."

"The facts would seem to show otherwise. But she's covered her tracks very well. I daresay we'll never know for certain."

"Which makes sense, since it's none of our business."

"It's entirely our business," Ripley said. "Now this will doubtless astound you—nearly everything I say astounds you—but I and the Ripley Group and Urban Hope are being blackmailed with those very tracts of land. There's scarcely a block in the entire zone where Cleon Toussaint or Carver-Boyd or Struthers Realty hasn't somehow acquired a strategically central lot or two."

"I'd think Pete Wesley could persuade the city to condemn those lots for you whenever necessary."

"The mayor is more than willing to do so. But of course you aren't aware that any project where the city condemns becomes a city project with absurd racial quotas for every construction gang from beginning to end."

"I wouldn't think the racial composition of the gangs would concern you as long as the work gets done at a fair price."

"No, of course you wouldn't. You wouldn't think it mattered to a group of businessmen if all hiring and letting of contracts on their own projects were no longer in their hands. You wouldn't think that."

"Why not just buy the lots you need?"

Ripley glared at her. "You know bloody well what they're asking. They want a black majority on Urban Hope. They want written commitments to proportional representation on our respective payrolls—if the city's sixty percent colored, in five years we'd have to employ sixty percent colored workers. And they insist on a guarantee of an ungodly percentage of colored families in Urban Hope–sponsored developments."

It was 35 percent—the figure Jammu had suggested. "Low-income families," she said.

"So-called low income."

"What, are there no poor whites in the city? Let me repeat, Mr. Ripley, that I can't be expected to intercede between you and the black leadership of the city. My role is limited. I'm in law enforcement."

"But you're so *resourceful*. There surely must be ways. Because if all I get in return is badgering from the coloreds, I shan't contribute to your merger crusade, and your support from the rest of Urban Hope will be precious tepid. And without a merger, many of us might find it pointless to stay in the city. You'll have your chance to see which came first—"

"Naturally," Jammu said, as the voices outside her door grew even louder, "I'd appreciate the aid of Urban Hope in a campaign for the common good of all St. Louisans, city and county. From informal talks with some of your fellow members I've gained the impression that the merger is viewed very kindly. Yes, the blacks want a majority membership of Urban Hope. Currently they're a minority of zero. Yes, they want a commitment to equal-opportunity hiring. Currently your own payroll is eleven percent black. Above the median income it's two percent. We're living in the 1980s, Mr. Ripley, and your corporation is now based in a city nearly two-thirds black. And yes, they want 35 percent low-income units in Urban Hope projects. Currently the plans I've seen call for levels between zero and ten percent. Meanwhile the office and luxury-housing developments your group is sponsoring are displacing black families at a rate of eight per day. Your refusal to take Mr. Struthers seriously seems less than fair. Perhaps I'm not attuned yet to your American way of thinking, but this strikes me as a golden opportunity for St. Louis businessmen to actually do substantial good for the urban black community."

Ripley was nodding and smiling at this lecture. "If I believed it," he said, "your naïveté would appall me. But I'm confident I've made my position clear." He stood up. "Cheerio." He opened the door, revealing a cluster of eager faces, and vanished in their surge.

"Wait," Jammu snapped. "Wait five minutes. Can you *wait*?"

Randy Fitch, the lead face, said, "It's—"

"Five minutes. For God's sake. Please shut the door."

The door wavered and retreated. Someone pushed on it again, but the latch had caught.

Jammu dialed a number. "Listen," she said. "I'll get this to you in writing soon, but I wanted you prepared in case you see Rolf today. He was just here making threats. Tell him I'm taking the threats very seriously. Tell him I'm scared. But I still have to make a pretense of helping out Struthers. They're making three demands of Urban Hope. Rolf should grant the first two. He'll know why I couldn't afford to tell him so myself. The black majority on Urban Hope—"

"Yes," Devi said.

"He should grant it. That's a transition group anyway, and we can replace it with a smaller board when we need to."

"And the proportional hiring?"

"That's the second one to grant. He should let Struthers pin him to the quota Struthers wants—the same percentage of blacks as are living in the city. Struthers doesn't realize this will be an all-white city in another ten years."

"You're double-crossing Struthers."

"You can suggest as much. The concessions needn't be total. Urban Hope can knock the figures down. I told Struthers to make them high and hope to compromise. Say forty percent of Urban Hope and full quotas in ten years, not five. Rolf will still have bargaining power for the housing demand. That's the key to a white city. I think Struthers will back down if Ripley tells him the projects simply won't attract financing with more than fifteen percent low-income units."

Devi repeated it all back.

"Good," Jammu said. "I really don't take his threats too seriously. His investments here started out as tax shelters, and if he pulls out now, capital gains will murder him. I think a move is unlikely. On the other hand, he hasn't made a firm commitment to the Ripley Center yet—"

"He hasn't?"

"No. Once he does, he can't pull out. So what you need to do is leave him alone on the issue—just don't ever even mention it. Let him assume I think he's committed."

"Easy enough."

"The other thing is the State. I think Rolf's Probst animus is one of the main reasons he's gotten to be so central in Urban Hope. We have to keep developing that situation. Are you still in it?"

"Very much" was the reply.

"Good. We need it, and it'll work for us as long as Probst is in charge of the resistance. You understand? Develop that situation."

"I understand."

Jammu turned the key in her desk, put her coat on, and opened the door. "Joe Feig, I'm sorry," she said. "You must hate me but we'll have to say four o'clock now. Drop in, and I'll give you what you need. Randy, talk to Suzie. I don't have time to look it over now, Suzie, but Randy needs it and I'll take your word for it. Go ahead and get the signatures. Rollie, tell Farr he's got to come and see me today. Say eight o'clock, and if I'm not here, that's his problem. Annette, is it life and death?"

"Sort of, yes. Strachey was on the front page this morning—"

"Write a memo with a guarantee. Word it strongly, and I'll check it over tonight and Pete will sign it. *No* city employees will lose jobs in a merger. Zero. At worst they might be moved to different positions. If you can work in something subtle about patronage, so much the better. And the rest of you get out of my way, I'll be back at two-thirty and free until four. My apologies to everyone, I'm eternally grateful."

The Corvette was waiting at a hydrant on Tucker Boulevard. Jammu got in with a word of apology to Asha, who peeled off her reading glasses and stepped on the gas pedal. She was wearing sable and emeralds. She dodged a U.S. Mail truck and headed up the ramp onto Highway 40. Practically, this engagement was the least important of the day for Jammu, but as she saw less and less of Singh she was coming to rely heavily on her weekly lunch with Asha.

The cars they passed looked stationary, bouncing in place on the winter-stained surface of the road. Beyond them, buildings lumbered backwards through a cold haze. Asha's hands left the wheel to rearrange her hair, and the Corvette steered itself into the innermost lane. She was at home in speed—in love with it. She was licensed to fly, she rode horses, she bet avidly. She was one of the terrible people who used speedboats on Dal Lake in Kashmir. She was speeding now, and when they passed the city limits, into the jurisdiction of other forces less willing to fix her tickets, Jammu made her slow down.

"Ripley?" Asha said.

"Yes."

"Would you have guessed in July how important he'd turn out to be?"

"Not exactly. He was a maybe. They were all maybes."

Jammu remembered July, the intimate and air-conditioned days. She'd spent her mornings with the Police Board; her early afternoons at the circulation desk of the St. Louis Library watching her book and magazine orders sucked down by the pneumatic tubes to the stacks; her late afternoons in one of the library's musty ground-floor tunnels feeding dimes to xerox machines; her evenings in motion with Asha in the county, with Asha downtown among little boats of hollandaise, with Asha and bourbon on her hotel balcony; her nights reading the day's photocopies. Would she have guessed? At the head of every discussion of civic decision-making were two words: Municipal Growth. In every list of influential locals were the names Wismer, Hutchinson, Ripley, Meisner, Probst, Murphy, Norris, Spiegelman, Hammaker . . . And Asha pumped Sidney, relayed more names to Jammu. All maybes, but the sum a sure thing. *In few American cities is fundamental policy determined by such a small and tightly knit nonpartisan group. In few American cities has the mode of policy-making survived unchallenged from the early nineteenth century to the present. Though the names have changed, the pattern of rule by a handful of established families with a romantic vision of westward progress has successfully replicated itself* . . . Political science, pregnant words, summer thoughts, engorged with possibility. Miss Jammu, we've decided, Asha, they've decided, Maman, I've decided. A city to ravish, in July.

Asha shook her coat off her shoulders. "How's Devi?"

"She's done very well. But it's rather a weakness of our approach that she's turned out to be important because Ripley has."

"Is something wrong?"

"Nothing that's visible to me. Nothing exactly wrong, I mean. She's as bright as anyone and she's too dependent on me, substance-wise and otherwise, to blow things open. But I wish we had another agent in her spot. I guess I wish you could do it all for me."

"I would if I could."

"It was easy enough to move Baxti off Probst in October. But we can't ask Ripley to switch sex partners at this stage."

"It sounds like you think something's wrong."

"I don't know. Ripley is surprisingly demanding. I feel a loss of contact. With Devi. With— Well, you're about the only one who's maintained a complete perspective."

Asha was accustomed to collecting Jammu's anxieties. She kept her eyes on the road. Brentwood spread to allow the highway through, the walls of its low square buildings as dirty as if road salt had splashed all the way up to them. Jammu saw nothing new. "Isn't this the exit?"

She was thrown forward as Asha took the Corvette what seemed like sideways across four lanes and onto the ramp. Asha's gold bracelets floated on her wrists. "Norris?" she said.

"He's warm but he isn't hot. He isn't making any new friends or converts."

"Buzz says he and Probst have gotten friendly."

"Probst doesn't have the loser's ethic it takes to believe in conspiracy. He found that bug in Meisner's place and made nothing of it. His daughter found a bug in her boyfriend's apartment and the boyfriend gave it to his landlord."

"God's on your side, Ess."

Jammu looked into the tire, deeply recessed, of a towering dump truck. All at once the Corvette seemed squashable. The dump truck was black. Written in red on the driver-side door were the words PROBST & CO. The driver, a black man in a baseball cap, glanced down at the Corvette's hood and then at Jammu. He winked. Asha passed him.

"The Warriors are doing a bridge on Sunday," Jammu said.

"What fun."

"Tell me about Buzz."

"He's cute," Asha said. "He's a genuine dear."

"So you've been saying. Is it good news or bad?"

"Indifferent. He's still one of the maybes. It's part of your random variation in moral strength. Buzz has relatively a lot of it. In principle, if not in his gut, he feels an allegiance to what's left of Municipal Growth, to the old dispensation. He's very narrow-minded on the city-county question. Or it's more than narrow-minded, it's—"

"The State. But the wrong elements hypostatized."

"Anything you say. It isn't political and it's only formally economic. What it really is is talismanic. All of a sudden he reveres Martin Probst. I find it frustrating. The more time I spend with him, the more interesting Probst becomes to him. It's hardly fair."

"Uh huh."

"On the other hand, it's personal and gets steadily more so. If you get Probst to support you, Buzz will too."

"You're sure."

"If I'm on your side and Probst is too—well, you'll have Buzz."

"You're sure. You're sure he'll move his operations to the city."

Asha rolled her shoulders. "I don't know, Ess. It's asking a lot of him. He will do something. He'd be lobbying for the merger right now if it weren't for Probst."

"I want him in the city."

"To clinch the merger?"

"Just to have him in the city. This merger is perceived more apocalyptically than it deserves to be. I mean, yes, I want it badly. But if it fails, I at least want the city and the elite. So don't lose sight of what counts."

"Getting Buzz to move."

"Yes."

"What are you going to do when you have what you want?"

Jammu smiled. "More of same."

Asha rolled down her window and took a ticket from the

electric dispenser at the parking garage at West Roads. She handed the ticket to Jammu. The time was printed in bruised purple: 1:17 p.m. They'd have an hour to eat. "You know," Asha said, as she drove up the ramp, "I've been very impressed with how keenly Singh saw the outlines of Buzz's life in September. He didn't intervene, he only listened, and he still hit every parameter on the nose, even the role of the Probsts."

"I'm hungry," Jammu said.

The hundred lights in the Junior League dining room had reflected mates in the fogged windows, and lit the fresh flowers on every table and the pollen-dry makeup on every woman's face. Glasses chimed, laughter pealed. The room smelled vaguely carbonated. A girl in a white wool skirt and a kelly-green jacket and a pink cotton blouse and a knotted plaid scarf jumped up from a table and screamed, "Asha!"

Suddenly Jammu was looking at their backs.

"I thought your phone was out of order!"

"I just love those!"

"If it's all right with Joey!"

Asha led Jammu by the elbow to a table. They sat. "The youngest of the Jaeger girls," she explained. "We're going dancing tomorrow."

"This isn't interfering with you and Buzz."

"No."

They began to speak in Hindi. The noise of the women consuming circled them, the chewing of the communal sentence, *so* nice how the cute, interesting Saturday drives to Frontenac Billblass Powell Hall, I saw small slams, I brunch divorced (Hilary Fontbonne, Ashley Chesterfield), but listen on Wednesday (touch wood), Eric sales, London Saks, cancer, curtains, Vail, six pounds.

"mere sir mem dard hai"

Every time Jammu's eyes left her friend she had to beat back invasions from neighboring tables. "Sinful" desserts on plates, caustic glances. The women were attractive and lively. She attacked her salad with a fork and said, in her hard Hindi, "Singh has kidnapped Barbara Probst."

A head turned. Ears had recognized the name, maybe.

"Let's talk about this later, Ess."

"Now," Jammu said. "We'll keep the names out of it. Eat up. Come on. Eat. In the future we won't come here. But my time is short. He kidnapped her on Tuesday."

"Where is he keeping her?"

"His place across the river."

"I don't like that." Asha touched her lips with her napkin. "I don't like that at all. Hammaker owns that building."

"I don't like the whole idea. But she doesn't know where she is. Singh has a story going in New York. He found a woman who is a reasonable facsimile of her, showed her around his apartment building, to the doorman, the neighbors. He'll do it periodically."

"But kidnapped," Asha said. "I don't understand."

"I'm glad we agree."

"You didn't approve it?"

"I approved it. Singh had a good case. P. thinks she's left him. There was nowhere to go with the operation except the kidnapping route. The State makes its peculiar demands. And B. has been the P. most opposed to me. State or no State, it's good to get her out of P.'s life."

"So she's just lying over there drugged?"

"I wish. I told him to drug her. I told him very plainly. He said it won't work in the story. He's posing as an Iranian psychopath. He needs a story because eventually, of course, he'll have to let her go."

"After the election. After P. has played his part."

"Presumably."

"But this must mean— What will he do after he's let her go?"

Jammu laid an anchovy on the side of her plate.

"You're sending him back?" Asha said.

"He's going back."

"How do you feel about that?"

Jammu, chewing, said, "I can stand it." She swallowed. "He's different these days. He has a very narrow set of concerns, and he's always sniping at me. He's too involved in the P. operation. I told him to hire a thug to kidnap B. He wouldn't. And everything in the name of doing the job right. As if trusting a chain and some locked doors to restrain B. were doing the job right."

"Why so bitter, Ess?"

Jammu shrugged. Singh was going back. By kidnapping Barbara himself he'd burned the bridges. This is America, Chief. Pretty soon you'll have to leave off with the clandestine stuff or you're going to get caught. When you stop, you won't need me. I don't like being in this country. It makes me feel bad. If I thought you wouldn't survive without me, I wouldn't kidnap her. If I even thought you might miss me a little. Every arrival is a departure, Chief. You'll find me in Bombay if you need me.

.

"It's Saturday morning. We've made savage love at dawn and I've gone off to the Midwest for the weekend to work on a story. You get up late, shower away my smell, and go out for a walk. You pick up the clothes you've had dry-cleaned. Buy a grapefruit, a couple of bagels, and a pound of fresh-ground Colombian. Yum. Smell it. You come back and eat. Have a cigarette and 'collect yourself.' It's a partly cloudy day, not too cold. We're twelve floors up, remember, and the traffic is very distant. You think about what has happened to your life. How so much has changed in five days, and what the next few months will bring. You wonder what you're going to do with yourself while I'm away. Find a job? Write a book? Be a journalist like me? Take a screen test? You're a little lonely, but it's exciting. It's a new kind of loneliness. You think about Luisa. She must have had Saturday mornings like this at Duane's, must still be having them. How new everything must seem to her. You gather your courage because you want to call her. You think about Martin's birthday party, and the scene you had with him in front of her. You think this might be the best way of explaining to her how it's happened that you've left him. You want to explain that you of all women don't have to take whatever your husband gives you. That some things are simply beyond the pale. You don't want Luisa to get the idea you've left him for purely selfish reasons. Of course, you're nervous, because you have a lot to explain to her, and because if you say any of the things I've told you not to say or if I think you're speaking in code I'm going to kill you and she's going to hear it. But you pick up the phone."

Nissing tapped the phone with the muzzle of his gun. Then he leaned back in his folding chair, and Barbara, in hers, facing him, picked up the receiver. The dial tone made her jump a little. Her eyes followed the phone cord across the carpeted floor of her cell to the locked door. The arrangement was the same as it had been the first day, when she'd called her supervisor at the library. She heard Nissing breathing, heard a cooing on the skylight above her.

"And you dial, of course. Three one four—"

She dialed the area code and paused, listening to the long-distance surf.

"You simply couldn't live with him anymore."

She dialed the rest of Duane's number.

"You lean back in my leather chair. It's already a favorite."

Duane answered.

"Hi Duane, it's Barbara's Probst."

Nissing raised his eyebrows sharply at the slip. He held a monitor plug in his ear with the index finger of his left hand. In his other hand he held the gun. The safety catch, a metal flag, was off. In five days she'd learned when it was and when it wasn't.

"She just went out," Duane was saying. "Can you call back in an hour?"

Nissing nodded.

"Yes, of course. I'll call back. How is everything?"

Nissing smiled with approval.

"Fine," Duane said. "Nothing much changes. Things are pretty good. I, uh—you're in New York?"

"Yes. I'm in New York. I guess Luisa must have spoken to her father. I—" The gun was shaking its muzzle. "I'll call you back in an hour, then. You can tell her I called."

"I will. She'll be glad."

"Thanks, Duane."

Nissing took the receiver from her hand. "You're disappointed," he said. "You'd psyched yourself. Your hand stays poised, reflectively, on the phone, and while your adrenaline is up you decide to make that call to Martin you've been dreading. If it goes well, you'll call Audrey, too. You feel sorry for Martin, not having your address. He'll want to know where not to send letters."

15

RC was cremating Clarence, he was in a groove, he was a juggernaut in gym shorts. As he took his sixth straight point with a fader in the corner, Clarence slapped his thigh and laughed: "What's happening to me?" In reply, RC served a high hard one. Clarence pivoted and stumbled, flailing at the ball, letting the score advance to 9–1. RC drilled his next serve flat off the wall and back at Clarence, who threw up his arms to protect his face. "Time! Time!" RC bounced on his feet to keep his rhythm going and watched impersonally as his opponent dropped to his knees. "Your game," Clarence gasped.

RC wasn't even winded. He ripped the Vel off the Cro of his handball gloves and stretched his punished fingers. From the other courts came grunts and rumbles, heavy shuffling, the erratic ponk! Ponk! of racquetballs, squash balls, handballs. Clarence was still kneeling and shaking his head, as if heaping abuse on himself for losing could make him a winner. He rose resignedly. "Let's get cleaned up, Off-sir."

They climbed through the little door and walked down the passageway single file to the showers. You had to pay for fresh towels here. Clarence took two from the man in the cage and gave one to RC. There were red threads in his eyes. "Played a damn fine match," he said. He turned back to the man in the cage. "My brother-in-law played a damn fine match, Corey."

RC would have sworn the look he got from Corey was dirty.

He stepped under a shower head and faced the wall, as usual, to avoid the sight of Clarence's layered back flesh and the profile of his hairy gut. As the hot water poured, he blinked and rotated his head, his vision like a movie where the cameraman dropped the camera, tumbling, blurring together glimpses of tiled floor and reaching steam, toes and elbows, a third man showering two heads over. The sound track was courtesy of Clarence, who was singing.

> . . . *All dem barges inner day*
> *Filled it lumber callin bay*
> *An ev-er-y inch of the way we go*
> *From Albany to-oo Buf-fuh-uh-lo,* OH!

Today was the fourth day of February, which would make tonight the fourth night for RC and Annie in their new apartment in University City. They'd moved on Wednesday with one of Clarence's trucks, and by now they'd emptied all the boxes except the ones with broken toys at the bottom, or summer equipment, the barbecue tools, the snorkel and fins. RC couldn't complain about the new building itself. There was a nice mix of people in it. But the footsteps above him and the voices downstairs were busy and foreign, and the rooms were just rooms. He felt like a TV actor sitting at a table that was plunked down wherever, using forks and spoons from a box of props. His actions lacked smoothness, he couldn't make things work the way they'd worked a week ago. Last night, when he and Annie were watching *Saturday Night Live* on the living-room couch, he'd reached over and taken off her glasses. Immediately the TV laughed, and Annie grabbed her glasses back and put them on crooked. She straightened them. "I can't *see*."

"What do you need to see for?" RC flopped onto the bare floor and stuck his head in the middle of the screen. "It's me," he said. "Live from U-City."

Annie leaned to one side. "Richie get out of the way."

"We have some very special guests tonight—"

"Get out of the *way*." She sat tight in the gray light, her legs folded up underneath her and her arms crossed across her sweatshirt. She'd been tired for two months, ever since she took a job with one of the new companies in the old neighborhood. She'd learned word processing. Words like: I'm fatigued, RC. There's a psychological toll. We're a two-career household now. . . . But if she was fatigued, RC was even more so. He'd come home at 10:00 after a long shift on patrol and two hours of desk work.

"So OK," he said. "OK."

"Richie don't."

"Hey, don't mind me."

He put on his coat. Annie kept watching the TV while they played games with the blame. She asked him where he was going, and he remembered that they weren't in the old neighborhood anymore. They were in U-City. He didn't know where he was going. "Walking," he said.

Annie stuck her tongue out at him, and he almost laughed, which was the idea; his mouth twitched, but the laugh came out as a cough. "You get some sleep," he said. "You get all nice and rested."

Outside, he hurried up the street. After a few blocks, as the buildings grew larger, institutional, he started seeing students. In the few lighted windows there were test tubes, blackboards, gray enamel instruments, computer screens. Girls in jeans and long wool coats pulled a little closer together when they passed him. He veered down a path among trees, away from the buildings, and cut across the snow on the big front lawn that led down to Skinker. At the top of the hill, to his right, stood the crenellated towers you could see from the golf course when the leaves were down. He reached the walk that split the lawn in two, and stopped and leaned against a tree. The shower poured on him, the water so hot it felt cold. Clarence changed key.

> Ask any mermaid you happen to see
> What's the best tuna?
> (Wah wa-wah wah-wah?)
> CHICKEN OF THE SEA.

RC was eighteen years old when he finally licked his older brother Bradley wrestling. They had a mat, a mattress they'd saved from a hide-a-bed broken by him and Bradley using it as a trampoline. It lay on the floor of the storeroom off the garage in their mother's house. Bradley was a varsity wrestler at school and used the room as his workout salon. When he dropped out of school to be assistant manager at a Kroger, he kept the salon. Besides the mat, he had a set of barbells he'd found two-thirds complete by the side of a road, and a bench press he'd bought with the part of his paycheck he didn't hand over to their mother. The room's two windows, looking into the dark garage, were filled with his beer-can collection. Under a loose floorboard was a Sterno can that never ran out of dope, and all around the baseboards ran a white dusting of DDT from a rotten cardboard can off a shelf in the garage. DD-Tox was the brand name. The dying bugs in the picture on the can were black with white eyes.

It was June. Bradley had taken to sleeping in the little room and partying there with his buddies. The transistor, always tuned to KATZ, was playing posthumous Otis Redding on the Sunday afternoon when RC crossed through their back yard, past the nasturtiums his mother tried to make grow every summer, past five kids' worth of towels and underwear, the netless hoop and Brad's Dodge, and knocked on the wall. He needed a room for the night.

"What for?" Bradley asked.

"Fiona."

"Mama won't like that."

"Mama won't know."

Bradley had a perverse reverence for certain rules. He smiled. "You can take my car keys."

"I want a room." RC was a determined kid. He had plans, images of scenes, how they should go.

"I'll rassle you for it."

"What's it to you, Brad? What's one night?"

"I'll rassle you for it."

They kicked the magazines off the mat and stripped to their underpants. RC got points for a takedown, but they weren't counting. On the mat, his fingers sought the borders of his brother's rounded muscles, any groove or bone or ligament to get a grip on. He locked the crook of his arm in the crook of Bradley's knee and pushed with all his might, his neck bending and his cheeks to Bradley's ribs and his lungs filling with the smell, scalpy and strong,

which he'd thought was Bradley's distinctive smell, the smell of
the sheets in the bunk above him, until he turned twelve and started
to smell that way himself. Bradley had never looked pretty in
wrestling meets. His style was defensive, the turtle's tactic of stomach flush with the ground and back unassailable. It didn't look like
the way a man should wrestle; the other school would murmur and
boo him until, when his opponent changed grips, Bradley exploded,
often lifting the boy clear off the mat and heaving backwards,
pinning him immediately. So RC was wary. He got Bradley to his
side and turned him around in a full circle. The mat's buttons tore
at his skin. He thought Bradley's puffing was just suppressed laughter, he thought Bradley wasn't trying, and then suddenly, for the
first time in his life, he had both his brother's shoulders on the mat
and words were coming out his mouth, four, five, SIX, SEVEN,
triumphant and surprised, as if he'd won the room purely by
chance, and he realized Bradley had been fighting after all.

Bradley giggled a frightening thin giggle, slapped the mat,
pointed. "You beat me, bro!" His eyes were beaded slashes. "You
beat me clean."

That night, while his mother and sisters slept, RC wrestled
with Fiona like a real man in a real bed. With space to roll in,
smells and liquids and limbs could intermingle. He licked yeasty,
vinegary, salty flavors off her belly (in fifteen years she'd be obese,
a teller at a Mercantile branch that RC avoided), his tongue gliding
without friction and then lodging in her navel. She scooted into
him, making noise. He closed his fingers over her mouth and bent
them backwards. Sex is in the mind, RC. Later on he watched her
fall asleep. The room was stuffy as a jar, and looking at Fiona's
rump and shoulders and neck, he saw how pretty girls, without
changing, might not be pretty anymore. Just lyin' there. It was
horrible. That these curves would stay curves but empty of meaning. That Annie could be a brittle bitch in glasses, too boring to
even fight with. He put on his shorts and went out walking in the
alleys, through ragweed and rodents. The soles of his bare feet
were thick enough to take the chips of broken glass.

Somebody's dog barked.

It was July, and the garage room was his now, Bradley gone
to war. RC smoked through the contents of the Sterno can with

new girls and took shit from the activists for not getting involved. It was September, October, November, and Bradley, without seeing action, became a number. Drowned, in ten feet of water, in an ambushed APC.

RC's own number—twenty-two—came up. In February, at Fort Leonard Wood, he overheard a conversation between lieutenants. "He's a bright kid. His brother came home in a coffin two months ago." He found himself transferred, a typist, the only black soldier on the infirmary staff. He almost took it for granted. He was a bright kid.

A pair of headlights towed a car across the lawn, approaching him over the snow. The bumper stopped a yard from his knees. White uniformed men, campus security, got out. "What can we do for you?" one of them said.

"I'm fine," RC said. "How 'bout yourself?"

"You here for any reason?"

"Just taking a walk, thank you."

"You want to get in the car?"

"I said I was fine, thank you."

"We'll give you a ride."

"Thanks but no thanks."

"Let's get in the car."

"I'm taking a walk, man. I'm a St. Louis cop."

The other man spoke. "Just get in the car, boy."

"RC, you be turning into a prune." Clarence, flushed and dripping, wound his soap-on-a-rope around his wrist. The shower room was quiet, RC's water splashing in a solitary way. He turned it off, and they went to dress.

"Something on your mind?" Clarence said.

"Nah. Just stuff. The move and everything. It's like we're some sort of refugees."

"You mean the off-sir ain't happy?"

"Cut it out."

"Never thought I'd see the day."

For three months Clarence had been saying he'd never thought he'd see the day. The day the *bright kid* complained. RC pulled his shoes off. "Are you really sorry I'm a cop?" he said.

"Me? Sorry?" Clarence went to a mirror and teased his hair.

"Sorry? Me?" With a finger he dabbed at the skin behind his ear and along his jawbone. "I'm just sorry if you're taken in by all the hoopli-do."

Sitting on the bench, RC discovered how tired he was. "No hoopli-do," he said. "I just don't see what your problem with Jammu is."

"Right. You just don't see. Neither does Ronald, which is the reason I'm so pissed with him."

"You pissed with me?"

Clarence sighed. "You don't count. It's Ronald has the mayoral aspirations. He thinks he's got a future, and in the county too, no less, just because Jammu says he does. I been feeling almost sorry for him. He's underestimated that woman, same as you've over-estimated her."

"I don't follow you."

"I mean it's the same thing. She doesn't give a damn about you or Ronald or anybody else. She's just a bomb. She's going off, and it's us who take the brunt of it, 'cause we happen to live here. Look at the hospital thing. For twenty years we been fighting for Homer G., and now we got a promise from everybody who matters, and this time it's not just one of Schoemehl's promises to do a study. They're really going to save the place, signed sealed and delivered, and now everybody says Hooray! We're gonna vote for this merger! We're gonna vote for Jammu and Wesley and Ronald! And shit, RC, *they's so blind*. Because that ain't gonna be our hospital anymore. It'll be a first-class white folks' hospital, because that'll be a first-class white folks' neighborhood. The whole city's gonna be first class, but whose it gonna be? You're already in U-City. You're already gone. You think you ever gonna make it back? You're in the county now. You think a merger's gonna do you a damn bit of good? But you're still a city cop, and I bet you, RC, I bet you, you've been thinking it be a good idea to vote yes in April, because Jammu says so and her word is law. Am I right?"

RC pulled his pants on. "You know I ain't even registered, Clarence."

Every time it looked as if they might talk about RC's life, Clarence turned it into politics. Just like the Panthers fifteen years ago, just like everybody, always. All the things that happened to him, floating into his present out of what had been the future, all the death and moving, the jobs and breaks good and bad, the turns of his life—these all had to be part of something bigger. You weren't allowed to have a life that belonged to you unless you belonged to the majority. It wasn't fair. All his life he'd known it wasn't fair, and he'd tried to ignore it, tried to play the man of independent means. Only now did he see what Clarence and the rest of them were driving at.

Get in the car, boy.

He wondered, Why me?

•

The runt month, February, half over before it started, saw the beginnings of a battle for public opinion in St. Louis. All the ingredients were at hand. There were two sides. They were committed to fight. They had the personnel. They had the materiel. They were opposed to each other. But seldom in the history of warfare had a battle been fought for a more dubious piece of ground.

What would happen if the city and county merged? The few definite answers—the Republicans would suffer, West County would be bridled and broken, Chief Jammu would eat the Missouri Democrats for breakfast, four thousand county employees for lunch, and the $200 million county budget for dinner—could not be mentioned in public argument. They required swaddling in phrases, and here the war machine really began to balk. The *Globe-Democrat* warned that a merger ("this nonsense") could unbalance the regional economy disastrously. Martin Probst warned that a merger ("unrealistic thinking") would do nothing at all, not even enough to justify the cost of a special election. Chief Jammu maintained that it ("this godsend") would rationalize local government at the expense of nothing but unfairness. Ronald Struthers, more cautious, admitted that some unfairness might linger, but promised his constituents that for once they wouldn't get the short end of the stick. Mayor Pete Wesley likewise ignored the fears of coun- tyites; he said a merger would free the city from the burden of many basic services and allow it to regain its rightful ascendancy. Ross Billerica was derisive in every direction, unable to believe that both city and county residents would run the risk of higher taxes by voting in a merger. KSLX-TV and KSLX-Radio disputed Billerica's logic and announced the ceaselessly interesting results of their weekly phone polls.

The salvos plopped in the bog, disappeared. Public Opinion, its lily pads and meandering canals, could not be taken by a frontal assault. And yet the battle affected it. Rumors bubbled to the surface after shells had fallen. Subtle forces of drainage and reflooding were at work, unseen, and at night there were flickerings and flashes in the air that looked like ghosts.

After a month of quiescence the Osage Warriors had reappeared, this time on the outskirts of the county, where open spaces grew with the square of their distance from downtown. At 3:15 a.m. on January 22, a sequence of detonations collapsed the pillars of a six-lane overpass on U.S. Highway 40 north of Queeny Park. The human toll was relatively slight. Sixteen travelers were injured when a California-bound Trailways bus overturned in braking to avoid the sudden precipice, and a motorcyclist suffered a broken spine plunging off it before the police closed the road. The blast also shattered windows up to half a mile away, injuring three more.

The real headache began the next morning, when thousands of commuters from the distant suburbs flooded narrow county roads in search of alternate routes. A heavy snowfall on the night of the twenty-second completed the disaster. Work began on a temporary overpass, but weeks would become months before the commuting situation returned to normal. West County homeowners, already facing steeper property taxes and the distant threat of mortgage foreclosures, demanded to know how the terrorists could function with impunity in what was supposedly a highly civilized district.

In the second week of February, a series of machine-gunnings terrorized isolated subdivisions along the county perimeter, in Twin Oaks, Ellisville, Fenton, St. Charles, and Bellefontaine. As usual the Warriors showed a curiously high regard for human life, firing their guns into dark windows and tool sheds, and as usual they were prompt in claiming credit for the attacks. In response, state and county police staged frequent roadblocks, but they had only the sketchiest physical descriptions of the terrorists, could only guess at their numbers, and were able to cover only a fraction of the vast network of county roads. The roadblocks did, however, compound the traffic tie-ups.

West County was slipping, a little, in public opinion.

Meanwhile Chief Jammu was rising. Even though she'd been in the news for months, she hadn't really been a phenomenon. Like so much of the ephemera of American popular culture, from funk rhythms to rollerskates, her popularity began to blossom only after sinking roots in the inner-city black community. It was in the ghetto that the first tank tops stenciled with the Chief's image were marketed. It was in the Delmar paraphernalia shops that the first Jammu posters were sold (she was fully clad), in the windowless unisex hair salons on Jefferson Avenue that kinks were straightened and bangs pulled back to form the stark, easy-care "Jammuji," and in the studios of KATZ-Radio that Titus Klaxon's irreverent "Gentrifyin' Blues" began its climb to the top of local charts.

But the Jammusiasm spread. It spread through the young people, the high-school and college kids. Somehow the Chief always found time to play to yet another crowd of young people. She spoke at concerts and basketball tournaments, at science fairs and Boy Scout expositions, at student art shows and Washington University debates. Her messages were contingent on the circumstances. Science is important, she would seem to say. Sports are important. Boy Scouts are important. Chess is important. Civil rights are important . . . Wherever she went there were cameras and reporters, and it was they who sent her message to the youths: I am important.

The rest of the city, the upper two-thirds of the demographic pyramid, respected and admired its youthful underpinnings. Youth got around. Youth knew the score. Youth was beauty, and beauty youth. That was all that mature St. Louisans needed to know before joining the parade. Jammu became the star of a hitherto glamourless city. Earlier, the city's "stars" had been talented older men or married female politicians; following their nightly movements hardly thrilled. But Jammu was a nova, a solid-gold personality, as bright (in the eyes of St. Louis) as a Katharine Hepburn, a Peggy Fleming, a Jackie or a Di. She wasn't pretty, but she was always where the action was. The typical middle-aged man of the suburbs could hardly help loving her.

This man was Jack DuChamp.

Jack's idea, propounded mainly during coffee breaks, was that Jammu would win the Democratic nomination for the U.S. Senate as soon as she was eligible, and would handily beat whatever Republican opposed her. He said it made sense. She was a good cop, but she was obviously more than that. He said he wasn't sure he'd vote for her, in the eventuality. But darn it. He might.

If he did, it would be a million-dollar vote. Jack DuChamp possessed a God-given aptitude for calling elections. If you checked the results of all the state, local and national elections of the thirty years Jack had been voting, and if you read the voting histories of all St. Louis County residents, and if you hunted for the closest correlation, Jack's was it. With an instinctive jerk he'd yanked the Kennedy lever in 1960. After a last-minute struggle with himself he'd gone Republican in the very close '84 senatorial election. Bond issues, special propositions, referenda, Crestwood city-council votes—in every case his ballot turned out to be the list of winners.

He knew his record was good. He bragged about it, sometimes even staked small sums of money on the strength of it. What he didn't realize was that it was perfect. Perfect, that is, in every election in which he'd bothered to vote. And the frequency with which he'd voted (rather less than half the time) bore a suspicious resemblance to the average voter turnout for the average election over the years.

On the merger issue, Jack was undecided. He figured he still had a few months to weigh the options. If the vote had been held on Valentine's Day he supposed he would have voted for the merger, although now that Martin Probst was on TV opposing it he knew he had to do some serious thinking. As the typical voter, he faced this task with little relish.

·

Sam Norris had no patience with public opinion. Constitutional processes were all very fine when only policy was at stake. But fire had to be fought with fire.

There were three orders of actualization.

Traffic regulations, in the lowest order, you trusted to the police. This was the province of modular rationality, of right and wrong, granted the requisite fudge factors of "yellow light" and so forth at the upper limits, at the blurring of law and a more rarefied authority.

This authority warred, in the second order, with its counterpart—call it politics, call it self-interest, call it clouds, call it what you would—and floated in the atmosphere. Public opinion had its place in this mezzanine.

In the highest order, planetary law and playful airborne strife were subsumed and transcended. Call it power, call it plasma, call it cryogenic circuitry. Agencies, in any event, no longer obeyed grim constitutional dictates or the inertial tuggings of the policy dynamic, but flowed without resistance, the energy of reason but a corollary of the deeper quantum-mechanical numen and free to run backwards in time. A button was pushed and twenty million dead people unburned themselves, stood up, stopped, and went on living.

In short, Sam Norris smelled it. Conspiracy. He'd smelled it from Day One, he'd sniffed it: something was up. But no one else could smell it. Even Black and Nilson were unenthusiastic, and the rest were even more obtuse. Good-hearted people, they trusted the Soviets, they trusted the Sandinistas, and they trusted Jammu. They wanted to believe in niceness. Prime example was Martin Probst, and Norris was not without affection for the boy. He was a classic man-woman, a champion of the hearth and so of all those lovely side effects to which Norris returned after a long day at the center of the universe. But the universe would be a mighty poor place if every man were Martin Probst. It would grind to a stand-still. Smell the flowers. Watch a sunset. Read a book.

There was a conspiracy, but it was difficult. The fact consoled Norris. All great ideas were difficult. All great ideas were also simple, as this conspiracy was simple: Jammu had St. Louis by the balls and she wouldn't let go. This fact was true. And yet it was difficult.

1. Jammu was not acting communist. (Here was further proof of the philosophical insufficiency of public life.) Asha Hammaker did not act communist either. The one was a tough cop and moderate Democrat, the other had a solid non-socialistic profile, even taking into account her transfer of stock to the city.

2. Asha's engagement to Hammaker predated Jammu's arrival, and the marriage would sustain no causal connection with Jammu's rise to power. (Here was proof of the insufficiency of cause and effect.)

3. The elaborate bomb scare at the stadium, the expense of it, made no sense whatsoever. (Proof of the insufficiency of ordinary human reason.)

4. The FBI would not investigate. They claimed to have no evidence of wrongdoing or subversion, and no orders from the police or from Washington. (Proof of the insufficiency of the ways of the mezzanine.)

5. St. Louis lacked the international strategic value that would make it a likely target of the evil empire. In October Norris, on a hunch, had pulled strings and persuaded the DOD to audit the protection of defense secrets at Ripleycorp and Wismer, and the auditors had given both companies high marks. Assistant Undersecretary Borges had said he wished all his contractors protected national security type secrets as well as the St. Louis firms did. It was possible that Jammu was waiting until she had control of those companies and could simply crack the Classified seals herself, but Norris knew the politics of espionage. If her employers were after secrets, they would expect at least a few small payments before continuing to finance the operation. There was no evidence of espionage, none. The mystery remained: why St. Louis? (Proof of the irrelevance of Newtonian space-time.)

6. Why Ripley and Meisner and Murphy and the other traitors to Civic Progress had done what they'd done was inexplicable—apart from the fact that they were bastards. They were still businessmen. Could money itself (that noble gas) be subject to the bio-logic of this day and age?

7. The conspiracy had taken off too quickly. It was in the air on the day Jammu took office. Norris had performed an extremely thorough inquiry into the Police Board—or rather, into those members who didn't owe him fealty—and found no evidence of foul play. Jammu's selection had not been rigged from outside. She must have been at least somewhat surprised. But the conspiracy sprang to life as soon as she arrived. *It must have existed beforehand*. This confirmed an axiom of Nor-

ris's alchemy of the spirit: individuals were vectors, not origins. But it left the question: Who had planted the seeds? Ripley? Wesley?

It made no sense. The conspiracy was a substanceless region of pungency, maddening him. It had no flanks, no promising point of entry, promised nothing within. But it was instinct that had won Norris his silver stars in the war, and instinct told him how to pursue his theory now.

Working his federal connections to the bone, he got his hands on the USIA's list of Indian visa recipients and other India-originated entries to the U.S. since June 1. It came on a diskette, delivered by messenger.

His private investigator, Herb Pokorny, specialized in detective telecommunications. Pokorny lisped as badly as platypuses would if they could talk, he'd run into all sorts of legal and linguistic obstacles while snooping in Bombay, but when he was working in St. Louis he was a good man. He tapped into airline ticketing records, into hotel reservations, car rentals, credit card and telephone and utility accounts. What emerged was a list of 3,700 Indians now living in the St. Louis area who hadn't been there eight months ago. Even after children under eighteen were eliminated, the list had 1,400 entries. But Pokorny didn't despair. Ordinary foreign immigrants left a signature on the records entirely different from the signature of spies, and while a few conspiring individuals might slip through his net, most wouldn't. By mid-February the list contained fewer than a hundred names.

Pokorny's operatives began a program of systematic surveillance. Prime targets were Jammu, Ripley, Wesley, Hammaker and Meisner. They paid especially close attention to Jammu's office and apartment. (The apartment, they discovered, had an anti-break-in system for which Jammu appeared to change the magnetic card combinations daily. The good news was, she had something to hide. The bad news was, she was hiding it well.) All visitors to the parties under surveillance were identified and catalogued.

A net of connections began to emerge. The beast which Norris had been smelling for months began to take on shape.

Deft fieldwork by Pokorny turned up the source of the cordite used in the stadium bomb scare. The theft had occurred on August

7 in the warehouse of a blasting company based in Eureka, Missouri. The timing pointed plainly, for a change, to Jammu.

Then on February 15 Pokorny solved the mystery of Asha Hammaker's early engagement. Speaking by phone with his brother Albert, who ran a detective bureau in New Orleans, Pokorny happened to bring up the mystery, how she'd already been engaged by the previous April. Albert chuckled and said: shrewd lady; in that very same April she'd been engaged to Potter Rutherford, the reigning sultan of securities in New Orleans. Immediately Pokorny got on the horn to all his nephews and cousins and uncles at their respective agencies across the country. By mid-evening, five of them had called back with corroborative evidence.

Pokorny phoned Norris, lisping liberally. "We've cracked it, Mythter Norrith. Asha got herthelf engaged to the motht eligible thun of a bitch in every town from Bothton to Theeattle."

Norris clenched his fist in triumph. So that was it! But the fist came unclenched, his cosmic triumph giving way to injured local pride: if Jammu had been willing to go anywhere, then chance alone had brought her to St. Louis.

16

Probst was glad to have landed in the thick of the anti-merger crusade, but he wasn't glad enough to be willing to act as director of Vote No, Inc. Directing a campaign was an endless, thankless job. John Holmes had directed the Prop One fight a few years back, and towards the end he was putting in more than sixty hours a week as he attended to the last-minute minutiae singlehandedly (he did the voice-overs for television ads, personally fetched the Kentucky Fried dinners for phone-a-thon volunteers), because when the heat was on no responsible director could delegate responsibility, or even find anyone to delegate it to. The failure of Prop One had brought Holmes many pats on the back, many dewy-eyed shows of gratitude. ("You deserve a month of R and R in Acapulco, old buddy.") A week later, his work was utterly forgotten. In the partisan world, dedication earned a man a salary, and success a sinecure. In the nonpartisan world, the world of Municipal Growth and its causes, the sole reward was the opportunity to run the next campaign. This was what happened to John Holmes. Probst made him the executive director of Vote No, Inc.

Even so Probst wasn't safe. When the campaign grew more demanding and the volunteers quit, he'd still be around and would probably get touched for some particularly odious job, such as recruiting new volunteers. Caution dictated that he determine the boundaries of his role right away. He decided to see himself as a costly and essentially immobile fixture. He saw himself as an elephant.

Elephants weren't very articulate. Probst did not participate in strategy sessions at Vote No, Inc. Elephants didn't zip around, didn't retrieve shotgunned ducks; Probst would not run errands for Holmes. Elephants were heavy, however, and Probst agreed to trample whatever influentials needed trampling. When practicable, he did this by telephone, in the evenings, from his choice desk at Vote No headquarters on Bonhomme Avenue in Clayton. Often, though, he would rise majestically from his desk, nod across the room to Holmes (if Holmes wondered where he was going, he had to stand up and follow and ask, because Probst would not stop) and drive, at low speeds, to the home of the mayor of Richmond Heights, or the chancellor of Washington University, or the president of Seven-Up.

Since the night in January when Municipal Growth decided to fight it, Probst had become much more convinced of the wrongness of the merger. The driving economic force behind it—speculation— offended him profoundly. The North Side boom was built on paper, on being in the middle, on buying low and hoping, later, to sell high. The spirit of the renaissance was the spirit of the eighties: office *space*, luxury *space*, parking *space*, planned not by master builders but by financial analysts. Probst knew the kind of thing. And now that Westhaven had failed he could criticize.

He'd always spoken well when facing microphones, and he was at his best when he was angry. He alone, of all the faces on television, dared to mention the party aspects of the referendum. He alone employed elementary arguments. He described in calm detail the syndicate in which he'd chosen not to participate. (Grudgingly, the day after his statement, Mayor Wesley confirmed Urban Hope's existence.) He stated that the referendum had been drafted far too hastily to allow a realistic assessment of its consequences. What was the rush? Why not postpone the election until a thorough study had been conducted? He stated that countyites should not trust the word of popular political figures. Did they believe that Jammu and Wesley cared personally about the quality of their lives? If so, where was the evidence? It was the Deplorable Question, the charm that silenced politics. There was nothing the reporters could do but change the subject.

Afterwards, while showering or eating, Probst would feel his heart leap a little: he was an anarchist!

John Holmes didn't complain about his approach. The phone polls revealed a steady swing of public opinion towards the Vote No camp, and since it was too early for anything besides Probst's appearances to have made an impact, too early for massive advertising and door-to-dooring to have begun, the swing could be attributed only to Probst. Still, Probst did not feel loved. He was something apart, the self-styled elephant. He didn't fraternize with the volunteers as he once might have done, never made late-evening doughnut runs. He sat at his choice desk and read *Time* and *Engineering News-Record* and the city papers. The polls had proved his value and he was learning—it was never too late to learn—to ask for what he wanted (a choice desk and no responsibilities), to claim the rewards of his unique position and not feel so damn guilty about it.

He was glad to have two full-time concerns. His days he spent at his office, his dinners he ate at Miss Hulling's or First National Frank & Crust, often with his vice president Cal Markham, and his evenings he spent in the rented space on Bonhomme Avenue. The Sherwood Drive house—he thought of it as the Sherwood Drive house now, as if he'd lost custody of it and only visited to sleep—was nearly always empty. His days were full. Barbara had judged rightly. He didn't really miss her, not after the first week. When people asked about her, he said she was on vacation in New York and let them wonder. It was in her absence that he'd learned to follow her example and say no to what he didn't want and to wear his crown unabashedly. He could have done without her weekly phone calls.

SHE: You're home.

HE: ???

SHE: I called earlier and there was no answer.

HE: I wasn't home.

SHE: That's what I said. You weren't home.

HE: No.

SHE: You're still angry, aren't you?

HE: What's to be angry about?

SHE: Well, I mean is there any point in my calling?

HE: I wonder that myself. But it's pretty quiet around here.

SHE: Do you see Luisa?

HE: We ate dinner on Thursday. She's healthy. She's into Stanford.

SHE: I know. It's funny to think. Have you spoken with Audrey?

HE: They're incommunicado, or whatever the expression. Rolf gets to her first. It's very complicated.

SHE: So he's still trying to screw you? Well of course why wouldn't he be.

HE: It's very complicated.

SHE: This is strange, Martin.

HE: It's very strange.

SHE: I mean talking like this. Isn't it strange?

HE: Strange is the word all right.

Transcontinental hiss

SHE: Are you in the middle of something? It sounds like I'm interrupting—

HE: No. No. Very quiet around here.

But it was less quiet when he'd hung up, when he could talk to himself again. It was Saturday. Noon shadows cupped the potted plants on the kitchen windowsill. They were dying from the roots up. He'd directed Emerald to take care of them and she appeared to have overwatered.

He ate a large even number of Fig Newtons and two bananas. Then he drove to Clayton and sat at his desk, from which he had a view of Bonhomme Avenue to his right and a Formica partition at his back, screening him from the activities of the rank and file. There was no activity this afternoon. A male volunteer sat on the desk of a female volunteer, a paid secretary waited for the phones to ring. Probst worked through the messages that had accumulated since Thursday.

At 4:00 he drove to Eldon Black's home in Ladue to beg another donation. At 4:30 Black wrote him a check.

By 5:00 he was back at the Sherwood Drive house and dressing. Earlier in the week he'd finally procured a black-and-red-striped shirt of Egyptian cotton, like the General's, and while he was waiting for his receipt from the Neiman salesgirl, a pair of prewashed black denim jeans attracted him. They completed the ensemble. They fit him well, hugging his butt and thighs as no pants of his had for years. The difference was remarkable. He looked forty. Thirty-nine, even.

But he had no shoes to match. Lunging, on his hands and knees, he pulled dusty shoes off the back of the rack in his closet. Everything was leisure or oxford or rubber-toed or tasseled.

He went down to the cardboard carton in the basement and burrowed through sixty pairs of footwear, shoes, fins, skates, rubbers, thongs, mukluks. They smelled like a condemned house. Green mildew had erupted on the leather. Many of the soles had holes.

He climbed three flights of stairs to one of the storage closets on the top floor. He had to clear magazines and business gifts out of the way, but at length he found what he wanted: the Exotic Shoe Collection. There were white espadrilles from Spain, embroidered Oriental mules, painted shoes from Holland, the three sets of clogs he'd bought for the family in Sweden, moccasins from the Sioux Veneer store in South Dakota, straw sandals from Mexico, alligator shoes from some Caribbean stopover, ballet slippers he'd never set eyes on before, and, just as he'd remembered, a pair of suede desert boots from Italy. Perfect.

In the car, the fashionable clothes surrounded him with a thin layer of self-awareness, like a cushion of air that reduced both the friction and the precision of his movements. The boots insisted on depressing the gas pedal further than necessary. Soon he was approaching the Arena, and the vapor plumes above it, white against the deepening twilight, were blotting out an ever larger arc of sky. He parked. The vapor came from a long column of grills set up outside the Arena's rear entrance. The grills were 55-gallon drums split in two and mounted on sawhorses. He read the plastic words on the marquee: FIRST ANNUAL GREATER ST. LOUIS LIONS CLUB BARBECUE AND FISH FRY.

Elephant, he told himself.

Tricolor bunting hung from the Arena's rafters and the railings at the base of the seats. A portrait of a lion had replaced the scoreboard, and beneath it stretched a banner reading L I O N S, each letter a capital with a lower-case tail, iberty, ntelligence, ur, ation's, afety. On the floor, where Blues had lately skated, children and their parents sat eating at aluminum tables with white paper tablecloths. Well-barbered, well-shaven, well-fed men in dirty aprons moved back and forth through the rear doors like executive coolies, the inbound toting tubs heaped with brown food, the outbound holding empty tubs on their hips or thighs. LEMONADE, a banner at the serving tables declared. SOFT DRINKS. SLAW. At the foot of the podium beneath the giant lion a crowd of perhaps a thousand legs swished and mingled. Probst saw orange-and-yellow paper cups and a smattering of ceremonial hats. The noise was oddly subdued.

He checked his coat, laid a twenty on the ticket seller's desk and walked away without waiting for his change. He wondered why the Lions hadn't held their functions separately in their respective towns. There couldn't possibly be many Chesterfielders willing to make the long trip in, especially with Route 40 out. It didn't make sense.

It made sense. He was passing through the fringe of the standing group when he saw the reason: Jammu was here. She was sitting in the middle of a crescent of folding chairs occupied by Ronald Struthers, Rick Jergensen, Quentin Spiegelman, some men in uniform and some Lions in hats. Probst recognized Norm Hoelzer, president of the Webster Groves chapter.

Turning away, he searched the crowd around him for a friendly face and found one in Tina Moriarty, the press secretary at Vote No. His palms moistened. Tina stood embracing a clipboard and craning her neck. She was a dark, pretty woman in her late twenties, somewhat prone to an anchorwomanly glibness, perhaps, but humanized by her paid efforts on behalf of Vote

No (the underdog) and by her knees. It didn't show when she walked or wore pants, but when she wore a skirt and stood still, her kneecaps became concavities and the backs projected. She approached Probst sideways and began to speak without looking at him.

"You're here," she said. "For a while I thought I'd be the only damn one. You see Jammu beat us here. It's going to make things more difficult. You haven't met her, have you? I just did. I'll never wash this hand again. John was supposed to come at five and I haven't seen him. Literally, I thought I'd be the only damn one. These affairs are obsolete, Mart. I swear they don't affect the standings. This is not the press. This is not the public. This is the *Lions*. Goes to show how much I know, I thought the Lions were a carnival. Ringling Brothers, literally, a carnival. You understand my confusion. This is where the circuses come when they come, the Arena, formerly the Checkerdome, formerly the Arena. I guess maybe I saw one at some stadium once, the Shriners. At Wash U., the field there. That's a nice shirt."

"What are we going to do?" Probst said. After criticizing Jammu on TV he was more reluctant than ever to meet her.

"Press some flesh," Tina said. "Wait, wait." She held his shirtsleeve. "Don't go anywhere yet. I don't want to lose you. Oscar's here somewhere, but I lost him. He's got his equipment, so at least we'll get some pix out of this. Butch Abernathy, he's the organizer. President of the Hazelwood chapter? He was sitting with Jammu but he isn't now. Be forewarned about the food, by the way. They're heavy-handed in terms of salt. It's a wonder these women aren't literally blimps if they eat like this all the time. Let me write your name down, I'm getting paid for this. Probst. I love monosyllables for names. East meets west. At least you dress better than she does. But my hand, my God, I'll never wash it. The weird thing is there's nothing wrong with them. People talk about double-jointedness, but the word has no meaning. I've asked. It means literally nothing. This is one extreme within the range of normal. What you see is a hundred ninety degrees. Most are a hundred seventy. It's a natural variation."

A large hand gripped Probst's left deltoid and drew his head towards Tina's. Ross Billerica stuck his face between them and kissed her cheek. After scanning the crowd he inclined his head confidentially. "We've got our work cut out for us, kiddos."

"Evening, Ross."

"Ross, for a while there I thought Mart and I'd be the only damn ones."

"I said five," Billerica said.

"It's six," Probst said.

"Horseshoes and handgernades. Tina, I've booked spots at Abernathy's table for you and I with some other chapter presidents, Hoelzer, Herbert, Manning, DeNutto, Kresch, et cetera, et cetera. Martin, Hi'd sug-jahest you work the crowd a little and get yourself photographed."

"That sounds fine, but maybe Tina should stay with me."

"Go fish," Billerica said.

"We're missing John, we're missing Rick, we're missing Larry. This is yesteryear. This is a twilight zone, I mean it, I swear. I don't know whose idea this was."

"Habernathy's sitting down." Billerica led Tina away by the wrist, weaving through the crowd towards the food. Tina wandered back and forth like a towed sled as she followed.

Probst looked at his desert boots. He bit down on his cheeks.

Martin! Dave, sure, Dave Hepner. Yer looking real good. You too. I want you to meet Edna Hamilton, Martin Probst. I thought, no offense, I thought you were dead. (Through a window in the sport coats and pants suits Probst glimpsed Jammu in the midst of laughing faces, her cheeks flushed with the pleasure of a successful joke.) The Arch is growing on me. Me too, uh. Dave Nance, Shrewsbury. Super people really, super-duper. I'm sorry, I. Martin, pardon a sec, I'm sorry Dave, Martin, I wanted you to say hello to my son and his squirrel— Dave, this is Martin Probst. Of course. The Bison Patrol . . .

A local hush had fallen. Probst turned. Jammu was extending a hand, which he automatically took and shook. In her other hand she held the hand of a little girl no older than five. The girl was drawing on a drinking straw with all of her attention, dredging the ice in a cup. "Well!" Probst said.

"I'm S. Jammu, I'm glad to finally meet you, Mr. Probst."

"Likewise, likewise." He dropped her hand. "Who's the little girl?"

"Her name's Lisa. Quentin Spiegelman's granddaughter. Lisa, you want to say hi to Mr. Probst?"

The girl's cheeks collapsed around her straw. She seemed to be glaring.

"Nice crowd," Probst said.

"Re-arc-shun-ary," Lisa said.

"Kids." Jammu smiled and took the cup and straw away from the girl. She was wearing a plain beige dress, lavender stockings, and black pumps. Probst felt underdressed. He felt a little dangerous. Jammu had the best of two worlds, the old pol trick of baby-kissing and the old female trick of caring for a child while a man stood waiting. He cleared his throat. "Well."

"Don't lose it, Mart," said a voice, Tina's, in his ear. "Oscar's coming."

Jammu looked up, and Probst put his arm around Tina. It was his turn. He put his nose in Tina's hair. "I'm just about ready to write this one off," he whispered.

"You're Barbara?" Jammu asked Tina.

"Christina Moriarty. We just met."

"Say," Probst said. "Where's Quentin? I'd like to *talk* to him."

"I think he's in line," Jammu said.

"Re-arc-shun-ary."

"Likewise, likewise." Probst had no desire to confront Spiegelman. He turned Tina around by the clipboard and hustled her through the crowd. He had only one desire, and it was primal.

"Uh, Mart?"

"My name's Martin, all right?" The desire was to get out. "You have a coat?" he asked, claiming his.

"Shouldn't we head back? I left Ross holding my plate when I saw Oscar at the brownies."

Probst frowned at her. "You need your coat because we're leaving," he said. "We're going to go have dinner together."

"You lost me somewhere." She took her claim check from her purse and handed it to him as if she couldn't make heads or tails of it. She offered no further resistance.

For restaurants, of course, it was the busiest hour of the week. The Old Spaghetti Factory was mobbed. Probst and Tina each finished a pair of strawberry daiquiris in one of the Factory's catacombs before the wall speakers brought the words, "Moriarty, party of two, Moriarty." The hostess gave them a table next to a child's birthday celebration. Probst objected, but Tina overruled him. She made him sing along when the child's cake arrived.

Outside again, on the cobblestones of Laclede's Landing, he paused to plan the next stage of his campaign. Tina leaned back against a lamppost patiently, like a painting on an auction block. "Where to?" she said.

He considered. He knew he could never say the words, any of the words, that might seduce her. An elephant couldn't speak. But if he simply drove to Sherwood Drive, she would have to come along. "Let's go get the car," he said.

In the narrow streets they passed laughing young couples with faces smudged by drinking. Warm eddies of spring air mingled with the hot burgery exhaust of local grills. "I've discovered," Tina said, "that the only thing I can stomach on top of a dinner like that is straight Pernod on ice. Trouble is—" She skittered a little, and Probst decided not to put his arm around her. "It makes me ramble. I mean really ramble. I suggest you take me to a bar and buy me a straight Pernod with ice and then cut me off. Take me by the shoulders and say, No, Tina, no. Billerica has a drinking problem. You can file that away in that silent head of yours. The difference between you and her, incidentally, is that she's still at the Arena. She'll stick it out, speak the speeches. I'm in love with her. I think we all are. Just shut me up when you get sick of this. I pretend I don't know I'm doing it but actually I do. I've been told, literally to my face, to shut up. So you're not the first, just so you know."

"Feel free to shut up," Probst said, stopping at the trunk of the Lincoln.

"The thing is, I try, and then I think of all the things I'm not saying. On the other hand, I never talk to myself when I'm alone. Am I to understand that we're to have a relationship?"

He closed his eyes and opened them. "Is it convenient for you?"

Tina's lips rolled tightly under one another, and her black eyes sparkled. A waning moon the shape of a football was rising above Illinois. Its light rubbed off on the nap of the fabric of her coat and lost itself inside it where it parted. Probst held his breath. Barbara had actually left him. He was actually free to do whatever he chose.

"To tell you the truth, Mart—"

His heart sank.

"I just don't really feel like it."

·

The room was evasive. On the first morning, Barbara had awakened from the drugging she'd received in the car to find herself on a standard-sized mattress, on a fitted bottom sheet with the kitty-litter smell of package-fresh linens, her face aching where he'd hit her, and her ankle bound. This was New York.

Or so she assumed. It could have been anywhere. The skylight diffused a light that seemed to fall, not shine, powdery and pure, free light, unreflected by a landscape. Her ankle was locked in a fetter, an iron ring attached by a ¼-inch cable to a tremendous eyebolt anchored in the wall. At the foot of the bed was a camping toilet, which she used, and then retched over, bringing up nothing.

When she awoke a second time she believed the light had changed, but only because that was the nature of light (to change) and the brain (to expect it). The carpeting had the color and texture of moss that hadn't been rained on for a while. Her suitcase stood across the room from her, by the only door, in the center of which was a peephole. A small framed portrait of the dead Shah of Iran hung on one of the walls adjacent to hers. The fourth wall was bare. That was the catalogue of her medium-sized rectangular room, the sum of its contents and features. With anything more, it might have had a personality; with anything less, it would have been bare, and bareness, too, was a kind of personality. She could only assume that Nissing was insane.

But when he opened the door and said, "Breakfast of astronauts!" she began to wonder. He handed her a tray bearing raspberry Pop-Tarts and a tall glass of Tang. His pistol was stuck under the waist of his bluejeans, half buried in his shirt. Through the door, which he'd left ajar, she saw that a black curtain completely filled the outer door frame. She asked where she was. Captive, he said. What was he going to do with her? They'd see.

He brought her three meals a day, breakfast always Pop-Tarts and Tang with seconds and even thirds if she asked; lunches lukewarm soup and Saltines; dinners TV-dinners. He watched her eat, which didn't really bother her. At 236 Sherwood Drive, in the bedroom, he'd had to drag her to her feet by her hair. But when he'd drugged her, in his car, her instincts of flight and resistance had gone to sleep, and they had not reawakened. The pain in her bedroom had been terrible to her. Nissing's physical dominance was complete, monolithic. She was happy to believe that further resistance would only feed his sadism, because she didn't want to feel that pain again.

For a while she lived by natural light and natural time. When darkness fell she sat or lay or did exercises in darkness. She asked for a lamp and a clock. He said no. But when she asked for books and he brought them, new Penguin paperbacks, he brought a reading lamp, too. She asked for magazines, a newspaper. He said no. She asked to take a bath or a shower, and on the third night, a few hours after darkness fell, he came in, unlocked the fetter, and tied a black hood over her head. He led her through two rooms that she could tell were empty from the way his voice twanged in the corners. He unhooded her in a newly redone bathroom and sat on the toilet, gun in hand, while she undressed, showered, and put on clean clothes. He led her back and refastened her fetter. She was allowed to do this every three days. Every two days, after she complained about the smell of the porta-potty, Nissing took it away and returned it clean. Eventually she realized it was more than clean; each time, it was brand-new.

"We're at Sardi's, a 'whim' of yours, a kind of tourist thing. Those peas you're eating are escargots in garlic butter. I'm savoring pâté with toast points. Three tables over, you can see Wallace Shawn waving his fork over a plate of spaghetti and talking with his mouth full. It's Valentine's Day. You spent the afternoon at the Modern on a bench facing a Mondrian. On your lap was a spiral notebook. In your hand was a black felt-tip pen. Everyone wants to be an artist. The thought was on your mind and it paralyzed you, the problem of originality, of individuality qua commodity. You'd thought you could start small, start concrete, describe a painting on a wall in the museum. You were thinking about the roots of modern writing, both literature and the other sort, my sort. Liberated men and women confronting the new art and learning new methods of vision. But the only thing you were able to write was the letter T. A capital T. At the top of the page. You didn't dare scratch it out, but what would it become? This? The? They? Today? Tomorrow? You felt the problem. You were thinking about me and my sort of writing, my facile typewriting in the study, in that favorite chair of yours. I was the problem. *I* had liberated you. You hadn't done it yourself. An hour passed. In a stupor you watched the postures and paces of the visitors. A guard told you a little-known fact about that particular Mondrian and walked on. Now that a guard had spoken to you, you couldn't stay."

"This is very clever, John, but I'm trying to eat."

"Is it my fault your story isn't new? That piece of fried chicken is your prime rib. The last time you had prime rib—it must have been January fourth at the Port of St. Louis."

All his statements about her were true. From the very first moments of their new relationship, when he'd given her a type-written letter to Martin for her to copy onto her stationery, he'd displayed—flaunted—a criminal familiarity with her private life. He knew exactly what had happened on Martin's birthday, three days before she'd even met him. She asked him how he knew. He reminded her that since they'd seen each other nearly every day in early January, she'd had plenty of time to tell him the story of her life. She asked again: how did he know what had happened on Martin's birthday? He reminded her that they'd met in October when he came to photograph the garden. He reminded her that they'd necked and petted like schoolchildren in the leaves behind the garage.

"After the waiter takes our plates, I reach across the table with a velvet box for you. You think of your first lunch with me, my first gift. I say Happy Valentine's Day. This time, you're gracious. You open the box. This time, it's a watch, a Cartier, with a silver band."

He dropped a silver watch on her lap. The hands showed ten of two, the jeweler's magic hour. She put it on her wrist.

"This time, you're gracious, and you're prepared. You give me a black silk tie you bought secondhand on East Eighth Street. We order champagne. We are the paragons of ostensible romance.

But we're ruthless, almost trembling with cynicism as we go through the motions of an extramarital affair, the motions that every modern man and woman craves. Self-expression. Individuality. The youth that hasn't seen or read it all before. The dousing of the fires of doubt with bucket after bucket of dollars. We're united in pain—"

"This watch doesn't work."

"Dead? Dead? Dead?"

Nissing leaped to his feet and fired. Barbara saw black, smelled smoke, felt a peppery burn on her neck, and sound returned; she heard the bang. Nissing had shot the wall behind her head. She touched the hole in the plaster. It was hot.

"Back at the apartment, we make savage love."

He couldn't fool her. She saw how all his sudden pirouettes and shouting, the Hamletesque free associations, were merely steps towards madness and not at all the thing itself. She'd taken those kinds of steps herself when she was younger and feeling "crazy" and trying to impress her friends with her complexity and danger. His steps were the same, only a little larger. Obviously no one could formulate an airtight definition of sanity, but he met all of her intuitive requirements. So why had he stalked her and kidnapped her? The question might never have come up if he'd kept his mouth shut. But he opened it and she heard a mind like her own. The question clung. She nursed it. She tried to keep her mind clear. It was the perfect time, she joked, for her to read *The Faerie Queene* and *Moby-Dick*. Then John came in and fed her and told her what they'd done that day in New York. If she got bored, she began her evening sit-ups and leg-lifts before he finished.

She found it impossible to think about Martin. He was locked in their past, rattling the bars of conditions that now never got an update, pacing between walls of activities and scenes that aged like inorganic matter, fading rather than changing. Their weekly conversations confirmed this. It was the conclusion reached by some students of the supernatural: you could speak to the dead, but they had nothing to say.

At first she'd believed that captivity couldn't alter her if she developed a routine and kept her mind active. But it altered her. Towards the end of the first week she noticed she'd begun to wring her hands in the darkness. She was shocked. And increasingly often she fell into a deep confusion, in the small light of her lamp, about the time of day. Was it early morning or was it late evening? She couldn't remember. But how could a person not remember what she'd been doing one hour earlier? And then the spatial disorientations. Nissing freed her ankle only on the nights she showered. The cable, about six feet long, allowed her some play but not enough to move far from the mattress or reverse herself on it. She therefore slept and read and ate always with her head closer to the wall with the Shah's portrait. She'd come to associate this wall with East. Suddenly it would be West, when all she'd done was turn a page. The frightening thing was that she cared which way was East. Trying to jostle her internal compass needle back to its correct setting, she'd pinch herself, blink, bang her head on the wall, kick her legs in a frenzy.

"Sunday morning," Nissing said, entering with the telephone and folding chairs. "I'm out for my morning run in the park. You haven't talked to Luisa for a while."

"And I don't feel like it this morning. I just wrote her a letter."

"I'm afraid that letter was lost in the mail."

She threw aside her book. *"What the hell was wrong with that letter?"*

Nissing blinked. "Nothing!"

"Then why did it get lost in the mail?"

He unfolded the chairs. "I don't control the mails, my darling. That's the postmaster's job. I'm sure if you asked him he'd tell you that a certain percentage of articles, a low percentage of course, do get lost, inevitably, in the mail. Perhaps a machine tore the address off. Perhaps the letter blew into a sewer while the postal service employee was emptying the box on Fifth Avenue, honey, where you mailed it."

"You just never get tired of yourself, do you?"

"Our first quarrel!"

"FUCK YOU. FUCK YOU."

"It's becoming inescapable that you call Luisa. After a fight like this? You get tired of my steady talking, my steady self-confidence, and we quarrel. I lose my cool a bit. Yes, I do. I shout. Why don't you go back to your husband, someone you can subjugate? And then I slam the door and go out running. You think of me and my concern with bodily perfection, the joyous agony on my face as I enter the fourth mile of my run. You're heaving. Sunday morning. February 18."

"I asked you a question." She stood and wrung her hands. "I asked you what was wrong with that letter."

"Don't try to reason with a madman, honey."

"You aren't any madman."

"Oh yes I am!" He shoved her into the wall. "Oh yes I am! I'm madder than the arms race!" His free hand reached out of space and closed below her jaw and squeezed. She smelled clove smoke on his fingers. They tightened on her throat. She couldn't swallow, and then he squeezed harder. "You're a piece of meat. I'd kill you right now and enjoy it but not as much as I will when you're fat and ripe and I beat the life out of you and you're mooing for more."

Her certitude wavered, but she held on to the words of the assertion in her head. "No you won't," she squeaked. " 'Cause you're not."

He let go. She fell, coughing, to her knees.

" 'Cause you have to work these things up," she said. "You have to do exercises. You have to find the impulse 'cause it isn't in you. I know you. You cannot be. Credit me with some sense. Of human personality."

"Oh, credit you. You think I have to stand here and argue with you?"

"Yes." She coughed. "I think that. You're doing it. Aren't you."

"Do your gagging and then speak normally."

She looked up at him. "You can't prove—"

"Because when you're dead, dear, when you're a pile of garbage, you won't be around to have it proved to. You don't know what goes on behind that door, what goes on in me. You may think otherwise, because I am pleasant, to a degree, in this room with you, you may have a 'sense' of me, a 'gut feel' for my sanity, but you only get what I give you on this side of the door."

His eyes were black and tan, his skin tanned deeper, from underneath, from a brightness inside him. He looked like a well-read Mediterranean beach bum. If she could prove him rational then she could begin to figure out why he'd done this. She remembered Dostoevsky, and the willed wildness of students. She thought of the Iranian students. But was he even Iranian? The picture of the Shah had been seeming more and more like a joke. John was a nihilist, not a royalist. Could he have dared himself to kidnap her? As an experiment in evil? In revolution? Oh! This was the worst pain of all, that the world seethed with motives she could never grasp. Even if this captivity were clearly political she still wouldn't understand it, how a political demon or even ordinary pragmatism could lead a person to take risks like this. And politics stood for all the other motives she couldn't grasp.

"Why did you single me out?" she said.

"Out of all the women I've met? I guess it's natural you think you're the first."

And the small mystery—it was large to her but small in the larger scheme—merely stood for the larger mystery, the unconditional ignorance: why had she been born?

"Time for a phone call."

"No."

"Aw honey. Will you promise to do it later?"

He was trying to look drowningly pathetic. But he couldn't make his face as wild as his words, which didn't count as proof of insanity, because anyone could learn to speak wildly. And what did he care, anyway, whether she believed him insane? The question led into briars.

"Be nice to me, John," she said.

"It isn't me, it's the postal service. Soon this becomes a motto of our home. We make up and we make love, savage love."

"Be nice to me."

17

She was clean again, odorless, a spiritual wife. At the bathroom mirror, in a robe that came untied and fell farther and farther open the longer her hands were raised, she was sharpening the edges. "Ow, damn it," she said, because it hurt. But then maintaining appearances always hurt. "Ow, damn it." She allowed herself an oath for every pluck. Rolf had called her plucky. On the bottom shelf of the medicine chest, in a bed of crud composed of dust and baby powder and leaked creams and the white flakes from the mouth of the Colgate tube, there were Q-Tips, a medical thermometer, hypos in their aseptic sleeves, the various therapies. "Ow, damn it." She wasn't exactly healthy, of course, but Rolf, without knowing it, had taught her that three martinis would relieve most afternoon flu symptoms, and though the flu still hurt a little, the pluck proved her a respectable woman. Already, after only ten weeks of economizing (Mamaji used to say that men couldn't economize because they were made in the true image of profligate gods), she had tucked away more than an ounce of prevention for the future. "Ow, damn it." She had faith in a divine closed-circuit television which monitored her every move, her every economy and respectable impulse, and which Mamaji would one day find time to view. She was a witness to maya but kept faith. Jammu gave her small credit for self-respect, but she was no addict, no fallen creature, as much as she might have seemed that way at certain times. "Ow, damn it." Jammu held her down, didn't care about her but gave her a pound of cure every week which she did use half of, because the lot of woman was hard. All women did things in the bathroom that no one knew anything about. All women. And Jammu was especially easy to fool because she was busy and she thought the very worst of Devi, believing Devi depended on her. But the other she would have her revenge, except it wouldn't be revenge, just something for Rolf (and one day maybe Mamaji) to see. "Ow, damn it." She practiced her accent for the day the scales fell and she stepped forth with Rolf to be his. All that remained was to prove to him that she could manage, could manage a household with independent means and economize.

It was finished. She checked her work and smoothed the raw skin with isopropyl on a cotton swab which smarted, and rinsed the little hairs down the drain. She was coming down with the afternoon flu. A sudden horrid chill made her hands tremble and drop the eye-shadow box in the sink and it got wet and its plastic lid fell off. It gummed up her fingers, made them all gray. She sat down on the toilet lid to recover, thinking it was horrible how the robe kept falling open. She could tie it tight but the silk knots loosened inopportunely unless they were square, and square knots broke nails. She wasn't frowsy. The button on the bathroom door was a navel, locked. Press me. A fine way to demonstrate her capacity to manage, to sit here in the bathroom with gray fingers and tiny pricks of blood ("Accent") pricks of blood above her eyes, and shaking. Rolf never said so but sometimes, more and more, he refused to see that there were two of her. She wanted to explain, The rent's too high here! and, It isn't my job to clean up, I'm supposed to manage! She was running a fever not a home. But good managers didn't make alibis. She had to try very hard to be good a little longer, possibly even clean things up herself, until there were, if possible, two ounces of prevention. Then she could pay her own way. Pay her own way! But it hurt, because skimping was almost worse than starving, and she didn't want to smell like martinis every time Rolf came.

·

With 41 percent of the corporation under his direct control, Buzz Wismer was, on paper, one of the twenty wealthiest men in the country. But Wismer had never diversified in the classical sense, since aerospace was already sufficiently diversified to adapt to a changing market, and the company's cash assets, though comfortable, were relatively small. A high proportion of its other assets took the form of accounts receivable, primarily from the airlines. Buzz's wealth was therefore not the wealth of the speculator or oil tycoon who spent in panics. It was tied up in the firm, and he'd tailored his tastes accordingly. He liked good company, virgin land, peace and quiet. Salty foods, cool drinks. He came from a large heartland family in rural Missouri. One of the pities of his life was that he'd never become the head of such a family. His three marriages had brought him two daughters, one of whom would probably remain in therapy for life. Unlike Martin Probst, Buzz had been too busy and too constitutionally flawed to enjoy ordinary family pleasures. The older he grew, the more acutely he experienced the lack. After the fire on his land, he threw himself obsessively into his computer work. Like a splayed beetle clinging to a great globe of wealth and importance, he tried to hang on. Then the globe began to roll.

·

"Deviiiii?" The hinge squealed slowly. Uncle Rolf eased his head past the jamb and the key from the door. "Dev—iiii?" He crept in on tippy-toe.

Something clattered behind the bathroom door, but whatever sounds followed were lost in the thunder of a rising jet. It was frightfully loud; he saw she'd left a window open. The room felt and smelt like a train platform. Crossing to close the window, Rolf glimpsed a face reflected from the telly. The face was Martin's, in a flock of microphones. The thunder exhausted itself in the time it took Rolf to reach the set.

"... I'm not saying we've ruled it out, but it is indicative of their entire approach. Debates don't resolve issues, they never have. They're personality contests, and that's precisely the kind of confusion about the referendum I'm interested in seeing eliminated."

"Oh it is, is it?" Rolf smeared Martin's face with his palm. The screen was hot. "Poophead! Fart!"

"We'll have a definite answer on Thursday."

"Can't wait, y'old turdbrain."

Rolf had never much liked Martin Probst, but he'd never known until this winter how deep a revulsion lay buried in his bosom. Tittering, he zapped him off the screen.

As he leaned to shut the casement it caught a gust of wind and swung out of reach. He braced himself on the sill and stretched after it. Above him, on a shelf cut into the exterior wall above the window, he noticed a small box wrapped in plastic. He closed the window and latched it. He stroked his mustache. Small box. Hm. Wrapped in plastic. He opened the window again and leaned out— but best not to inquire, eh? An uninspected pet was the only kind worth having. He shut the window just as she emerged from the bathroom.

"Evening, Rolf," she said with coy flatness.

"Good evening, my love."

She was wearing new glasses modeled after Barbie's reading specs, flat black mules to play down her height, blue Levi's, and a large white shirt. Rolf hadn't seen the genuine article in more than two months, not since the holidays, and his blood pressure rose. Five months into the relationship she could still reduce him to a knock-kneed juvenile. Her hands approached. He stood fascinated as they slowly closed in, nudging aside the lapels of his jacket, brushing along the sweater beneath his arms, and the rest of her following, to begin an embrace in slowest motion. He lived for this. He coughed.

The look crossed her face. He pushed her roughly aside and gagged on another cough, his ears popping.

"I'm sorry." She went limp on the sofa.

He saw the little band-aid on her forearm, the dry makeup. He didn't care what she did when she was by herself, but when her control lapsed in his presence . . .

"Why did you call me?" he said.

She looked up and made him love her again with the perfect half-ironic smile. "Rolf," she said, "I'm totally dependent on you. I can't survive a day without hearing your voice. After all these years, every day counts, every minute. Don't you see? We've waited so long for each other."

He cupped his hand and pushed a small cough into it.

"Don't be angry with me, Rolf. I'm a weak woman, but things will be better soon, just the way you want them to be. I've left Martin. The whole world knows it. Oh, the years I wasted with him! Just waiting. I was missing something, I knew I was missing what other women had, and, well, I've left him now. And the way he yelled at me I couldn't ever go back."

"Accent."

"The *way* he *yelled* at me I could *never go back*. And you complain when I call you at the office." She curled her lip. The likeness was uncanny. Rolf dropped to his knees and pressed his cheek against her chest, and bit with his lips, like a toothless baby. Sweat filled his eyes.

"Just think," she said, "if Martin could see you doing this to me."

·

Began to roll on Christmas Eve when Buzz was toiling at his office and the lobby guard called to inform him that Mrs. Sidney Hammaker would like to see him. "Send her up," Buzz said. While he waited, he ran a systems check on himself and found red alert lights flashing in every sector, his moral processor spewing error messages across the screen—FLOATING POINT DIVISION BY ZERO AT 14000822057G—broken ventilators in the power regulator, a board out in the vocalization unit, and his whole program TERMINATED BY A SUPERIOR PROCESS, FATAL AOS ERROR, DO YOU WISH A SYSTEM DUMP? He unplugged the telephone and checked his hair in the green plotting screen, the convexity of which doubled the scale of his double-barreled nose and oval mouth and made his head outrageously round. He was a green-faced monster.

Asha tapped on the open door. She hoped she wasn't disturbing him. He said heck no, Christmas Eve, shouldn't be working anyway. She perched on the table by his console. The dot on her forehead seemed suspended somewhere just beneath the surface of her clear, cool skin, like the decimal point in an LCD.

In the minutes and hours that followed her arrival, her skirt began to creep upwards with a life of its own, a pace independent of their conversation. It revealed more and more of her legs, steadily raising the line at which shadows deepened the color of her sheer charcoal nylons from gray to black. The skirt would halt its upward journey and camp for half an hour, forty-five minutes, as if it planned positively to go no farther. Then Buzz would look and another inch of thigh had come to light.

Asha, it turned out, knew her way around tensor analysis. She listened actively to Buzz's presentation of his iterative method, and as the December sun went down on the North County snowfields, she spotted a redundancy in his tensor, a hidden symmetry, and suggested he collapse it and add new variables. She was trying, she said, to bring Hammaker into line with the times. Only the cola companies could rival Hammaker's success and originality in marketing, but even Hammaker hadn't, so far, faced up to the most fundamental mystery of the day: did advertising work? Sales proved little. Market testing—pools of randomly selected TV-viewing drinkers surveyed in soundproofed conference rooms—was pure shamanism. Asha shuddered at the terrific overkill implicit in blanket advertising, the shameful waste of resources. She longed to attain a god's-eye perspective from which she would see at a glance the formula that would make Hammaker the beer of everyone's choice, not the choice of 37 percent or 43 percent or even 65 percent, but of everyone. The formula would have to consist of more than a single slogan or tactic, of course, because those would inevitably be copied by Hammaker's two major rivals. It would be an infinite series which took into dialectical account all counterattacks, and overcame them automatically. This was where Buzz came in. Asha had read his papers on n-variable tensor simulation of meteorodynamics. She wanted to apply his method to selling beer.

"Instead of passively viewing this pressure system on your plotter," she licked her lips, "imagine a war game. Imagine the system in the hands not of random global climatic patterns but of you yourself, and your mission is to create temperate low-humidity conditions in St. Louis 365 days a year, with, let's say, a single drenching rain every six days from six to eight in the evening." And Buzz said, "You're describing a monopoly." And the Princess said, "Nine tasters in ten can't distinguish us from our competitors.

Competition only encourages saturation marketing, which adds a dollar a six to our product." And Buzz said, "Psychological laws are notoriously unabsolute." And she said, "You'd be surprised. They may be a lot more absolute than you think." The room was dark, the screen's hatchmarked toroids so green and bright they seemed to dance, and as she leaned to switch on a lamp, her elbow on the table, Buzz caught a brief white glimpse of lace under her skirt.

.

Audreykins was playing cards at the antiqued writing table in her boudoir. She wore a pink ribbed robe. Before he spoke, Rolf paused for a moment and watched her indulgently. She held the club 7, her hand hovering as if she were trying to present her Platinum Card to a distracted salesclerk. She placed the club on the heart 8, then snatched it back. She looked up over her shoulder, blank-eyed, a female clown in cold cream.

"You're up late," Rolf said.

She absorbed this and turned her attention to the game. She laid the club firmly on the heart, dealt another card, a diamond queen, and transferred a number of cards in rapid, intricate fashion.

"Coming out nicely for you, what?"

Again the merest twitch of acknowledgment. Her head moved back and forth in search of further plays. Rolf chewed the in-growing whiskers at the corners of his mouth. Particularly mellow after the evening's intercourse, he gave it another go.

"Couldn't sleep, I guess?"

"Spade ten," she murmured.

A few moments such as these were enough to make Rolf regard more seriously Devi's prattling about a rearrangement of legal ties. Almost immediately, however, he remembered the old logic—joint trusts, half the stock, both the houses, half the bonds, the lots in Arizona, Oregon, St. Thomas, Jesus Christ, at least twenty million dollars—which of course was no logic at all. Never marry a lawyer's daughter.

"Probably worried sick about Barbie, what? No sooner does your little head hit your little pillow than you think of her spreading for a handsome stranger."

She pinched a card from the discard pile.

"You shouldn't cheat, Audrey, honestly it takes all the fun out of it. Not to mention the eight hundredth commandment, thou shalt not cheat at solitaire. I've no doubt Father Warner would be most distressed to hear of it."

He found a pair of bird-beak shears on her vanity and tidied up a bit at the corners of his mouth. In the mirror he saw her not looking at him. Heat began to rustle in the register above her bed.

"Very comfy in here, incidentimente. Let's remember Martin for a moment. Shall we bow our heads? Think of him *all* alone, in that *big* house, with those *lovely* furnishings, and nobody to talk to. Think of it." Rolf saw jolly Martin kicking the furniture in voiceless cuckolded rage, or playing solitaire in the middle of his bed. Because the brat had left him, too! Mr. Right had been caught at last with his pants down, losing his virtuous girls and making a perfect ass of himself campaigning against a foregone referendum.

Audreykins had turned. Her expression was frank but cordial. He smiled. "Hm?"

"You're insane, Rolf," she said. "You've gone out of your mind."

·

Buzz's work began to suffer and he rationalized it. No one could expect him to be producing original ideas at his age, so anything he did manage to do, even if it was less than what he'd been accomplishing a few months earlier, was still pure, untaxed pudding. The work provided a pretext, too. Every day he instructed his secretary not to disturb him for any reason. At night he interposed an answering machine between the world and his inner sanctum. His weather research, he informed Bev, had entered a stage demanding his full powers of concentration. She didn't believe him. He didn't expect her to.

Leaving the inner sanctum uninhabited, he rode the spacious freight elevator down to the ground floor. While his employees in the service hindquarters of headquarters lifted boxes or pushed brooms, he briefly passed the time of day and always mentioned that it was imperative that no one know of his comings and goings. He dropped dark hints of supersecret high-level business dealings. He shouldered open the heavy rear doors and stepped off the loading dock. Asha was waiting in her Corvette, in the afternoon or in the night, usually the night.

It was she who placed the bets at Cahokia Downs, ate the chili at the 70–40 Truckstop, and drank the coffee in the urban diners. Buzz just accompanied her. He was amazed that all the hick locales she led him through, the pageant of spavined waitresses and dowdy bettors and cakes and pies revolving in slices, had survived the forty years since he was young and something of a hick himself. Even the roads could surprise him. Asha drove miles and miles north on state highways he'd never seen although he'd spent his whole life in eastern Missouri. After midnight on weekdays all traffic fled the roads to leave a ghostly undisturbed extinctness, suggesting neutron bombing. She'd top a hundred miles an hour on the flats.

But the custodial pool couldn't keep a secret. Bev told Buzz that the husbands of her friends believed that he and Asha really were carrying on supersecret business discussions. The wives themselves, including Bev, believed they were simply carrying on.

Buzz was more or less innocent on both counts. He respected Asha too much and depended too heavily on her companionship to risk a physical involvement. And apparently the possibility never even occurred to her. They were just friends who occasionally chatted about business—a subject that Buzz would have been happy to avoid entirely. Whenever Asha tried to encourage him to develop his property on the North Side, he got confused. The responsibility for soundly managing Wismer Aeronautics devolved upon him personally. But he, personally, could no longer imagine life without Asha Hammaker. In the word "personally" two inimical curves jumped an asymptote. The result was chaos.

As February slid into March, his thoughts turned increasingly to Martin Probst, the other friend he believed in. Martin stabilized the curves, re-establishing the boundary conditions. Loyalty to Martin meant loyalty to Buzz's reputation, to the honorable, gentle man the world had always considered him. Again and again Buzz telephoned him. "Listen," he said, "anything you've heard about me and Mrs. Hammaker—I know there are rumors—it's not like it seems. It's purely social. Sidney might as well be there, or Bev, if she'd ever agree to come. There's nothing shabby or fiscal— physical—or—"

Martin said he understood.

"And you've got to believe I'm on your side with the referendum. I know I haven't been able to spare the time to help out with more than my pocketbook, but I'm firmly committed to the way things are. No merger for me, no sir. No sir. It makes no profit sense for me to move headquarters—you see, again, I don't know what yort of, what sort of, rumors. I do feel some—well, some pressure to move just the headquarters—as I told you, we do have the land, have had it—but I've found it to be true that it's vital to keep management close to the technical center, and I certainly couldn't move that—"

"Buzz, really. Don't bother. You've told me what your plans are. I trust you."

"No! I want you to believe what I'm saying, specifically."

"Sure. It makes perfect sense. That's why I'm involved in this campaign. The technical center, it makes perfect sense. I believe you."

.

Rolf dallied at the mirror, teasing his hair with a silver comb. Insane indeed. His chest hair, clean and fluffy, buoyed a golden chain which rose and dipped over the individual tufts like exquisite roller-coaster tracks, disappearing, at his neck, in the collar of his ruby red robe. Craggy, rugged, his face was quite unlike all the Charlie Brown mugs of the rest of the St. Louis crowd. He wiggled Captain Caterpillar, the name which Mara as a wee lass had given to his mustache. The memory of the make-believe pinned her to her years of innocence.

He went to the door and opened it. Across the hall, honey-toned light flowed through the chinks around Audreykins's door. *Combing her tresses.* Every time he happened to look across the hall at night, no matter how late the hour, he saw light, and the phrase wandered into his mind. Imagination was a wonderful thing. *Combing her tresses.*

He tore the late Telex printouts from the printer by his laundry hamper, poured himself a snifter of The Glenlivet, and went to bed. The time, half past one, nearly lost itself in his Gübelin's maze of gilt.

In the morning he would oversleep himself a bit, tool over to

Lambert, and fly to San Antonio to confer with the president of Gelatron, a plastics concern he was in the process of acquiring. He walked his fingers down the closing quotations his broker had forwarded.

Gelatrn   7   2061   8¼   6⅝   8¼   +1⅝

So the cat was out of the bag, and the response was favorable, a solid vote of confidence in Ripleycorp. In a few months San Antone would be losing a few jobs, as Gelatron pulled up stakes and headed for the north side of Saint Louis. Wholly owned subsidiary. The words, in combination with the whiskey, added warmth to Rolf's post-acquisitional glow. He reached for his cordless for a chat with his favorite wholly owned subsidiary, but corrected himself in time. He called her far too often. His indiscreet little wholly owned . . .

He made his last trip to the jerry. The stillness on Audreykins's side of the hall seemed a tribute to him. He was at the top of his game now. Never again would he fear a Probst, never again endure an evening with them, nor would Audreykins find refuge in the kitchen with Barbie. For a moment, as the tinkling started in the bowl, he found himself believing, unaccountably, that Barbie was dead. It didn't disturb him. He had Devi, and Martin had no one. The best man had won. He flushed. In the window a pane vibrated with the drone of a late-night small plane.

.

"Don't you think we should have had some, uh, radio contact?"

Past Ladue now, Asha closed the throttle and took the Cherokee into a shallow dive, straightening her out at 1,800 feet over University City. "At this hour I think it's safe not to," she said. "Visibility's excellent. I like flying without a flight plan once in a while. It's like skinny-dipping."

She was taking them due east into the city. In New York or Chicago they would have been scraping high-rises, but St. Louis lay low, and desolate, its street intersections strange laneless crosses the color of bone. Lone cars pushed pale pools of light along in front of them. If this were a bombing mission . . . Night flight brought out a special proneness in American cities, or so it seemed to Buzz, who was thinking how America, St. Louis, had never been bombed and now never would be by anything short of nuclear warheads. The lack of an intermediate experience sharpened his feel for the frailty of the continent, whose population had no cultural memory of black plagues or air raids. A splendid illusion, this North America, gave rise to the most pitiful dread, the dread of a man who, like Buzz, had never so much as spent a night in a hospital but who, unlike him, now faced a certain, grisly death.

"Heading right over downtown, eh?"

"I thought we'd have a look," Asha said.

"It's kind of eerie this late. I'm getting to like this sort of thing."

"I know you are. It's exciting for me, too. The shapes are still so alien to me. That a city looks like this. Could find reasons to look like this."

Losing altitude, they followed the Daniel Boone Expressway east. Like all the major roads, it led to the waterfront, to the Arch. It was the Arch that made St. Louis lie down. Buzz watched it with naïve fascination, an unthinking delight in its unlikely size, its reaching three-dimensionality, its steady sweep along the Illinois horizon. It stood nearly as high as they were flying. It transformed the downtown area into an indoor space, and Buzz and Asha into birds, wheeling through it. *Martin!* To be above the city but also in it: Buzz felt suddenly his kinship with his other friend, in whose speech and carriage and stature all the plasticity of the actual St. Louis found expression. Then he heard the engine grow quiet. He saw Asha pull the control column back and realized what was about to happen.

"Asha, don't," he said.

A city ordinance prohibited flying through the Arch. Asha concentrated. The colorful stadium opened up black and white beneath them.

It was already happening. Undangerously, with a speed proportional to theirs, the Arch spread its legs to permit them. Wharf Street was a gutter into which they were falling. For an instant Buzz could almost have touched the sharp steel inner angle. Then they were through. Asha pulled them into a steep climb.

I couldn't, he told himself. I'm firmly committed to the way things are. No merger for me, no sir, no sir. It makes no profit sense for me to move I've found it's vital close to the technical center much that—

"You saying prayers?" Asha said.

"Was I—?"

"I can't quite hear you."

Below them the Mississippi receded, swung down with East St. Louis, where Buzz glimpsed the yellow flares of tiny fires.

18

Probst was just sitting down to breakfast on the first Sunday in March when he noticed a pair of trespassers in his back yard.

One was Sam Norris, a lesser yeti in a blue loden coat. The other was a stranger, a short man in a green parka with the fur-lined hood thrown back. Probst saw Mohnwirbel plodding out of the garage, the legs of his pajamas bunched between his overcoat and the tops of his black rubber boots, and making his way stiffly across the snow to Norris and his companion. Words were exchanged. Probst took a bite of sticky bun. Norris pointed at something in a bank of leafless azaleas. Mohnwirbel shook his head and made emphatic little karate chops. Norris smiled and looked directly at Probst without a trace of recognition.

Mohnwirbel returned to the garage. Arms akimbo, Norris and the short man squinted and stamped. Probst could see himself finishing breakfast and reading the paper and never bothering to find out what was going on out there. But now Norris was beckoning impatiently.

He went out in shirtsleeves. "Morning, Sam. What brings you here?"

"Herb," the General said, "Martin Probst. Martin, like you to meet Herb Pokorny."

The little man folded his arms behind his back. He wore a

thin helmet of blond, wet-looking hair. His nose was flat and small, his skin pockmarked like weathered stone, his eyes shallow-set and practically lashless, and his lips the same beige color as the rest of his face. He reminded Probst of the famous sphinx whose nose Napoleon's soldiers had shot off.

"Glad to meet you," Probst said.

Pokorny looked at Norris.

"Looks like a tasty breakfast you have there," Norris said. "Herb and myself were just talking about a little hole here in your yard, Herb, you show him the little hole?"

Pokorny took a step and pointed with a duck-booted toe at a patch of snowless, freshly turned earth between two azalea bushes.

"You want to show him the footprint?"

Pokorny pointed out a footprint in the snow to the left of the azaleas.

"That your foot, Martin?"

Several smart cracks occurred to him, but he said, simply, "No."

"It ain't your gardener's either."

Probst looked into the slowly churning sky. Four crows launched themselves from a hickory tree, their wingbeats wrenching out caws.

"You been using that detector like I told you, Martin?"

"I can't say I have," Probst said. "The novelty wore off after the first few months."

Pokorny scowled at this mild joke.

"When's the last time you swept your house?" Norris said.

"Maybe three weeks ago," he lied.

"That's very interesting. Because there's been a receiver-transmitter buried in this here hole until last night about two-thirty a.m."

"We heard the thignalth."

"Oh really," Probst said.

"Yep. Digitized and coded, or we'd have been able to tell you what exactly they picked up. Not that we can't guess."

"So there was a transmitter in what you're calling this hole. It was transmitting coded messages. Now it's gone."

"We only tuned in yesterday. They had one hell of a little

processor buried there." Norris nodded at the loose dirt. "Received signals from your house, digitized 'em, compressed 'em by a factor of a hundred or so, and sent 'em off in a burst every two hundred seconds at a variety of very high frequencies—that is, when it was active. Not a peep until you came home, I'd guess voice-actuated. So give Herb some credit. That ain't a easy thing to discover."

"Very impressive," Probst told Pokorny. "But then someone came in the night, dug it up, left one single footprint, and ran away."

"Bingo."

"You'll pardon me if I don't believe any of this."

"Show him the list, Herb."

Pokorny knelt in the snow and opened a cracked leather satchel. He handed Norris a folder from which Norris took a pair of dot matrix printouts, stapled together. He gave them to Probst.

> .
> .
> .

    Ahmadi, Daud Ibrahim
* Asarpota, Mulchand
    Atterjee, T. Ras
* Baxti, V. L.
    Benni, Raju
* Bhandari, Karam Parmanand

"Yes?" Probst said.

"Suspects."

He yawned. "I see. What kind of suspects?"

"All persons of Indian origin and Type Q profile known to have been in St. Louis between July 1 and—how up-to-date are we, Herb?"

"Tuethday."

"Tuesday the, uh, twenty-seventh of February."

"What do the stars mean?"

"They're the ones that either we or reliable witnesses have seen meeting with Jammu. Now, have you—"

"You'll pardon me if this makes me a little ill, Sam."

The General's eyelids twitched. "What do you mean?"

"I've raised no objections to your looking into something illegal like the stadium bombs, but this is something else entirely. Some kind of McCarthyesque stunt, if you ask me. This is guilt by association, by place of birth."

"You can spare us the editorial. I want you to read through this and tell me if you heard of or know of any of the persons on it. Do me that favor?"

       .
       :
       .

    * Nand, Lakshmi
    * Nandaksachandra (Hammaker), Parvati Asha Umeshwari
      Nanjee, Dr. B. K.
    * Nissing, John
      Noor, Fatma
      Patel, S. Mohan
      Pavri, Vijay

Probst gave the printout back to Norris. "Apart from Mrs. Hammaker, I can't help you."

"You sure?"

"Yes."

Norris exchanged a glance with Pokorny. "Well now, that's interesting. Because from what I understand this one here—John Nissing—took some pitchers of your house."

"Oh did he." Probst could see that Norris knew Barbara had left him. But how much more did he know? Had Pokorny seen her with Nissing? Snooped in New York? Probst saw no reason to discuss his private life here in the back yard with Pokorny making faces at him. "I never met the photographers," he said truthfully. "Barbara dealt with, uh, them."

"And how is Barbie?"

Norris knew. The whole world knew. Probst's eyes wandered across the twig-strewn snow, up the walls of the garage to Mohnwirbel's windows. "Fine. She's in New York."

"Oh yes?"

"With relatives."

A wind whispered in the azaleas. Probst's arches were cramping in his tennis shoes, in the snow.

"Okey-doke," Norris said. Pokorny nodded, snapped his satchel shut and walked to the driveway. "I suppose I'm a little sorry about this, Martin."

"Sam—" Probst's voice cracked; he realized he was angry. "Sam, I'd say that if you want to mess around with this kind of thing you're going to get what you deserve."

"But don't moralize with me."

"Private investigators deal in dirt. You give them enough time and money—"

"Damn it, Martin, don't moralize with me."

"I've been as good a listener as you've got. When you want help with a legitimate project, you know where to come. But an episode like this is what I'd call an abuse of—"

"You do me a disservice. I apologize for disturbing you, but you do me a disservice. I already told you I could care less what goes on in your family. I told you that and—"

"I want that little weasel off my property."

"I'll let that pass. I'll let that pass. Now listen. I've apologized for any embarrassment. Will you accept my apology."

Norris's fingers dug almost desperately into Probst's elbow. He couldn't help feeling flattered. "All right."

"Thank you. Now just two things before you eat your breakfast and spend your day in Clayton, just two things. Will you listen?" Probst sighed.

"One. You got to believe there was a device buried in your yard here. This ain't conjecture, I can play you our tape if you like. Now I don't guess you'd allow Herb—he'd do a neat job, of course—and it'd be very beneficial if he could do a search in your house right now—"

"Not a chance."

"But you do believe me about the device."

"I suppose. I believe there's a South Pole. I haven't seen it and I don't care, but I believe it's there."

"You oughta work on your attitude—but but but but. The second thing is, just a simple yes or no. Was Mrs. Hammaker honest to God the only element on the list you've heard of?"

"Quite frankly," Probst said, wondering what he'd say. He found he didn't care. "Yes, she was."

"All right. Sorry to bother you." Norris walked to the driveway and kicked his feet clean of snow pellets. He turned. "You understand I believe what you say. You understand that." Then he was gone.

Probst went inside, finished his cold breakfast, and paced the kitchen trying to walk away his shaking, as he had over the years in the wake of various Sunday morning quarrels. He placed his cup and saucer on the Rubbermaid mat in the sink. A few days ago he'd turned over the mat to discover yellow patches of slime, clouded like the chicken fat in cooling soup.

He went upstairs to his study, heaved a pyramid of second-class mail off his chair, and began to work through the three-inch stack of résumés his personnel director Dale Winer had given him. There were applicants for four new positions, one managerial, three clerical. His practiced eye homed in on misspellings, patterns of instability, overqualification, North Side high-school diplomas (affirmative-action-wise, they could really use two black women), wanton preening, irrelevant experience. Not that most of these applicants couldn't have handled the jobs. But you had to pick and choose.

The telephone rang.

It was Jack DuChamp. Just checkin' in, Jack said. Now that Laurie was confirmed she didn't go to Sunday school, so he and Elaine and Laurie had started going to late church instead of early church because the kids were turning into late sleepers on the weekend. Elaine liked to sleep in too sometimes. Mark was taking a semester off from college, trying to get his act together, practice-teaching deaf children, enjoying it. But it was funny to have the extra hour or two on Sunday morning, funny to see new faces at late church, and Jack and Elaine had both made New Year's resolutions to try to do something worthwhile in the extra time, which wasn't really extra since late church meant coming home later too, but anyways, to try to improve life in little ways, as best they could, on Sunday mornings. Which explained why Jack was calling.

"Yes," Probst said.

Laurie worked thirty hours a week now at the Crestwood

Cinema on top of high school and rehearsals for *Brigadoon*, the spring musical, and— Did Luisa work?

"She—"

All the more time for her schoolwork. And it showed on the report cards, Jack was sorry to say, although he thought colleges these days were interested in more than just grades, that maturity and independence must count for a lot, and if they didn't, then that said something about the college, didn't it? Anyways, with Laurie working and Elaine with a light course load this semester, the two of them had been rediscovering their evenings and they wondered if Probst and Barbara—just the four of them—some night this week—maybe a restaurant so no one had to cook?

Helping deaf children, Probst thought. Helping deaf children. Helping deaf children.

Or next week, if this wasn't enough notice.

"Jack," Probst said. "Barbara and I are separated."

Oh.

It was the first time Probst had used the word "separated," even in his thoughts, and the word rang in his head as if he were practicing it after the fact. Jack said some more things to which, unlistening, he replied that it was OK, it was OK. And as soon as they'd recovered, Jack said maybe a Blues game, the two of them, Saturday night. The Canucks.

Then Luisa called. Duane was showing pictures at a gallery and the opening was Friday night. Could Daddy come? Daddy would love to come, he said. He sensed that she hadn't called to chat, but he made her chat anyway. He cast out snare after snare, heard about her college choices, her grades, her eyes, her latest cold, her conversations with Barbara, Duane's dealings with the gallery, Duane's car's new exhaust system. By the time they said good-bye it was 10:30.

The phone rang again immediately. It was a woman, Carol Hill, calling from the *West County Journal* to confirm the quotes he'd given her the day before.

". . . The last one is, Ultimately we have to look at this in terms of democracy taxation without representation is a very old issue in this country and it's a valuable perspective to keep in mind will the merger create a more or a less representative government for the residents of the county and I think the answer is pretty clearly no."

"Yes. That's fine. I appreciate your checking this with me, Carol."

"No problem. Thank *you*." Her voice became a dial tone.

Probst looked into the hickory tree outside the window and cried, "Wait! It's less! The answer is clearly *less*!" He shook his head.

MARY ELIZABETH O'KEEFE. Born 6/16/59.

The phone rang.

He tossed the receiver onto his shoulder, pinned it with his ear, and heard Barbara's voice. He spoke. She spoke. He spoke. She spoke. ". . . Maybe make this more formal," she said.

"What do you mean?"

"Well, this is sort of an uncomfortable situation for both of us. I've been asked at parties and I don't even know how to refer to it." *Parties.* She was really ruthless. "Not to bring up a sore point, but if we could agree to call it—"

"A separation," he said. "I've been referring to it as a separation when people ask."

"That's probably adequate."

Adequate: the term "separation" adequate on its own strength to induce them to hate each other where they otherwise might not have.

"Look," he said. "Do you want to divorce me?"

There was a silence on her end of the line. But the silence was not complete, for Probst heard the vowelly edges of at least one murmured sentence. Nissing was in the same damn room with her! While they talked! She and Nissing discussing it! She spoke again. "It's kind of—"

"Because I don't care if I ever see you again this side of hell."

"Martin. Please."

"Are you alone?" he said.

Her silence hummed with pictures, the frantic glances at her lover, the hand waving him from the room, Nissing taking his time. "I—no, and you're right. You're right. This isn't the time to be discussing this. Can I call back?"

"Take your time."

"Don't say that."

He swiveled in his chair. "I don't want to see you, I don't want to talk to you, I just, don't, want, any of this. I'm sitting in my chair. I'm just trying to sit here. I'm."

Out of the receiver came the words "Martin, I love you," and she hung up.

I love you? What was that supposed to mean?

All at once Probst had doubts. Her haste, the consultations. It was possible, he realized, that Nissing was somehow keeping her in New York against her will. That Nissing was a criminal or conspirator, that there really had been a transmitter in the back yard. That Probst as Municipal Growth chairman had been singled out for psychological torture in order to influence his decisions, that Jammu was behind it, that Norris was right about something damned peculiar happening to the local leadership and that Probst, since Luisa left—since Dozer was hit by a van!—had been a target, that the ongoing crisis in his family was not the inevitable product of its history, but a condition imposed from without: that Barbara did love him.

Hastily he dug through the papers on his desk and found the number she'd given him. He'd never used it. He dialed the 212 and the other seven alien digits, and after a pause that seemed unusually long to him, the connection went through. "Hello!" said a plangent male voice.

"This is Martin Probst. I'd like to speak to my wife."

"It's your husband," Nissing said. Probst heard Barbara laugh. "Yes?" she said.

"It's me. Are you alone?"

He heard her say, "Get out of here, please," and the rest muffled except for a laugh from Nissing. He heard her lips return to the phone. She was breathless. "I thought you didn't want to talk to me."

"I don't. Believe me. But I'd like to see you for a little while and get some things straightened out. Do you think you could manage to fly here for a day this week?" He thought to add, on the chance of its hurting: "I'd pay."

She sighed. "As I was about to explain when I called, John and I are flying to Paris for a week and a half, we're leaving tomorrow. We'll be back on the fifteenth. So maybe then, if you think it would help."

"I don't know. You see what I mean about not wanting to get into it. It's not as if I don't have plenty to do myself."

"After your election, how about. I told Lu I'd like to see her on my birthday. Maybe then. Early April. Time's been going very fast, at least for me."

Probst cleared his throat. "All right." A headache was developing behind his eyes. "Why did you hang up on me?"

After a pause she said: "Use your imagination, Martin. Picture a small apartment, all right?"

She didn't sound like his wife. She sounded like a different woman. Maybe the woman she'd always wanted to be. Maybe that was the idea.

As soon as he'd hung up, the phone rang yet again.

"Probst," he said.

"Hello. Mr. Probst. George Snell. *Newsweek*. Sorry to bother you at home on a Sunday. Like to see if we can arrange an interview for tomorrow or Tuesday. Your press secretary indicated you'd be agreeable."

"Well!" Probst said. "Certainly. My schedule's plenty packed, but I'm sure we can arrange something."

"Glad to hear you say that. Tomorrow?"

"We'd better say Tuesday. Breakfast time? Lunch time? After hours? It's up to you."

"Could you give me an hour in the middle of the day?"

Probst reached and parted résumés to find his appointment book. His recollection was that Tuesday was wide open, but—

A woman broke into the conversation. "This is the operator, I have an emergency call for 962–6605."

"That's me," Probst said.

"Fine," said George Snell. "If I don't catch up with you, we're listed. *Newsweek*."

"Thanks, uh. George."

He broke the connection and waited for the next call. It was John Holmes.

"Martin, I'm sorry. I've been trying to reach you all morning. I've got some very bad news."

"What."

"Well, I'll tell you. Ross is dead."

Probst stared at Tuesday. "I see. An accident?"

"No. He was shot in his home last night, late last night. It looks like he interrupted a burglary."

He wrote NEWSWEEK between noon and one o'clock as though this were his last chance ever to do so. "I can't believe this, John."

"None of us can."

No one had witnessed it, but the house was half ransacked. A single shot had been fired, through Billerica's throat, and this was all it took to make Probst love a man he'd never been able to stand, his death revealing all his faults and effronteries as mere symbols for the final, forgivable weakness. Billerica's parents were handling the arrangements, but Holmes wanted Probst at Vote No headquarters. He wanted everyone there.

.

It began in August, in living color. He was looking out of a swimming pool into the face of an obese and idiot-eyed tabby whose paws rested on the pool's concrete lip and whose tail lay flat and parallel to a single leg, a woman's, on a lounger in the background. Two grade-school boys opened their lunchboxes on raised knees and showed him their contents, the apples red, the Twinkies orange. The faces were bleached to nostriled spectres with dried eyes and checkered teeth. And the city turned black and white. All was hilltop or valley now, the horizons, no matter how broken, falling away at the margins of his vision as if, out of sight, the remaining world were gathering like a storm. A black man gestured obscenely, an Indian tried to grope out from under the scope of what was seen, and distant boys played football, their feet planted in earth that seemed no more stable than a tilt-o-whirl. Luisa, in high contrast, smiled. Geese flew like happy thoughts at her shoulder. Under her shirt her breasts fell away from each other, rolling towards her locked elbows. Why was there danger in the smile she gave him? Three golfers, marked by their serene grayness and puffiness as retired, posed and mugged while a fourth golfer appeared, in the flatness of the vision, to swing his driver into their heads. The city lurked in the trees beyond the tee. In November the days fell thick and fast. Ghetto ten-year-olds straddled a chain-link fence as the cable of a wrecking ball went slack with the ball's impact and a tenement teetered into the sky. The women were haggard. They looked like miniatures of themselves, three feet tall, package-laden and well-to-do. One was speaking to him, tossing him words with a flick of her head. The Plaza Frontenac parking lot died behind them at the edge of a flash, and neither the sky nor the windows of Shriners' Hospital were lighted. He looked at a young policeman and saw nothing but face; above the bill of his cap, beyond his large pale ears, south of his receding chin, in the darkness behind his metal front tooth, in the material underneath the rays of his eyeballs, lay terra incognita. Ronald Struthers's cheeks ballooned when he saw him, and his arms hung limp as a scarecrow's over larger figures, one a balding apoplectic, the other a sad man in a lamé tunic and paisley robes. What was happening to the city? He saw Luisa's naked back and paid as little attention to it as if it were a bathroom door; the funny ripples and blades turned livid as his stare lengthened in time and the snow falling outside the window faintly scuffed the nighttime. She was an object. This was what was happening. At the top of the Arch he captured the chubby hand of a baby stopped, by glass, from touching St. Louis. Chief Jammu and Asha Hammaker linked arms outside the Junior League, gl'amour, gl'amour, and Binky Doolittle, emerging through the door, sealed their union with a dirty look. A volunteer youth displayed a fistful of Vote No bumperstickers while a man in Fortrel climbed into a Cougar, hurriedly, to escape being pasted.

Probst was impressed. He lingered in the front corner of the gallery, alone behind the flats on which the pictures hung. Beyond the flats, coffee splashed, the guests of honor and assorted friends pattered, and Joanne, the gallery owner, dropped her *r*'s. Probst didn't look forward to sitting in a folding chair with no place to put his elbows. He glanced at the work of the young woman with whom Duane was sharing the gallery space. Duane was better, he decided.

It sounded like several new visitors had come in while Probst was behind the flats. "They're the first thing I look for when I open the paper," he heard a familiar voice say. He stepped into the area behind the last flat. The voice was Jammu's.

"Do you mind if I ask how old you are?" She was sitting in a trench coat between Duane and Luisa, both of whom were twisting napkins on their laps.

"I'm twenty," Duane said.

Luisa saw Probst peeking. He had to step out. "What do you think?" she said.

Jammu and Duane looked up.

"They're excellent," he told Duane. "I can see a lot of hard work." To Jammu he said, "Hello."

"I've just had the pleasure of meeting your daughter."

Luisa turned away. Her dress was silk, dark purple and dark green, with tassels on the hem and cuffs. It looked secondhand. What was she doing with the money he sent?

"I think I'll have a look." Jammu touched Duane's knee. "If you'll excuse me." Probst stepped aside to let her past, but with a jerk of her head she made him follow. "I'd like to talk to you."

He gave Luisa and Duane a smile of distaste: business. Jammu had folded her coat over her arm. She was wearing a gray knit dress, surprisingly well cut for a woman he'd considered couturially drab, and a string of pearls. "Yes?" he said.

"As I mentioned the last time we met," she said in a very low voice, "I think it's ridiculous that in seven months we haven't managed to speak to each other."

"Yes, scandalous," Probst replied. "We should be ashamed of ourselves." She'd charmed the city and most of its leaders. She wouldn't charm him.

"But I mean it," she said. "I think we should talk."

"Oh, certainly." He turned his gaze to Duane's pictures, encouraging her to do likewise so he could look at her. She was small, he saw, much smaller than news photos or television let on. Her body had an unusual prepubescence, as if she were a girl wearing adult clothes from a costume bin, and so her face, though normal for a thirty-five-year-old, looked sick with age. Casually, he predicted she'd be dead in ten years.

The gallery door opened, and Duane's parents, Dr. Rodney and Dr. Pat, hurried in. Luisa sprang to her feet to greet them. Duane stayed with the cookies and drinks. His nose disappeared in a styrofoam cup. Rodney kissed Luisa. Pat hugged Luisa. Probst blamed them. Luisa handed Pat coffee and stood with her hands on her hips, shaking her hair back at regular intervals. When had she learned to act so at ease?

Jammu had proceeded without Probst to the last of the pictures. "You know," he said, joining her, "I'm not really doing anything later on—"

"Tonight?" Jammu looked at her watch. "I have a visit to pay at Barnes Hospital. You're welcome to come along, of course, but if you'll be here a while, I should drop in again. I live just around the corner anyway. We could have a drink or something. You're here alone?"

"Yes. My wife's out of town."

Rodney and Pat had taken center stage between Luisa and Joanne, forcing Duane to come to them. Luisa turned and looked through Probst.

"I'll come along," he told Jammu.

·

She left him standing on the second floor of Barnes while she consulted at the information desk. The Wishing Well, the hospital gift shop, was fully lit, but the security portcullis had been lowered. In the lobby carpeting a flesh color predominated, a background for abstract organs of pale blue and ochre and pale yellow connected by mazes of red arteries and deep blue veins.

Jammu was autographing a page of a notebook for a high-school-aged boy. Probst heard the boy thank her. He hoped that sometime, once, before he retired, someone would approach him for an autograph.

"We only have a few minutes," Jammu told him.

The room was on the fourth floor. In the bed nearer the door, amid potted mums and a small forest of Norfolk pines, lay the officer. Bandages circled his head, winding from his ears on up. He had no pillow. His whiskers had been growing for at least a week. A white sheet was draped across his chest and legs too neatly, the even lines of the hems on either side of the bed testifying to an inability to move. From the IV tube rising from his hand his arm seemed to have contracted a terminal slenderness.

Probst hung in the doorway while Jammu moved along the

side of the bed until she could look straight down into the officer's open eyes. The head rolled a few degrees towards her.

"How's it going, Morris?" she said levelly.

"Awr," said the officer.

Probst read the clipboard. PHELPS, Morris K.

"You're looking good," Jammu said. With a tiny fierce movement of her head she forced Probst to join her at the bedside. "I was at your home today. I spoke with your wife. I understand she's been spending almost all her time here with you."

Probst looked down and felt paralyzed. The eyes were on him but in a line perpendicular to that of his own. No meeting was possible. He didn't dare turn his head sideways to meet the eyes for fear of seeming to condescend. "Sheerft," the mouth said. "Nadir."

"I understand," Jammu said. "But she seems to be holding up very well. You have some great kids."

A nurse appeared behind them in the doorway and raised a monitory finger. She didn't leave. It was still fifteen minutes before 9:00. Probst wished it was one minute before 9:00.

"This is Martin Probst."

Phelps released a breath. "Huh."

Probst felt himself imploding around the lack of words to speak. "Hello," he attempted. Why had she taken him here? Or not warned him not to come? He wanted to hit her. The nurse came a step closer to them.

"Adit ove," Phelps said. "Dunsim."

"I know you would have. You're a good man, Morris. They'll have you up and around in no time."

The nurse put an end to it. In the hall, Probst asked what the prognosis was.

"Probably full-time care for the rest of his life," Jammu said. "From the neck down he has the muscles of an ox. But one little bullet in the head . . ."

They were crossing the lobby downstairs, heading for the street, when Probst veered into the men's room.

·

Earlier that evening, before he'd driven to the gallery, he'd read an editorial in the *Post-Dispatch*.

. . . The public has not been well served by the discussion thus far. Jammu's case for a merger would be far stronger if she were willing to discuss the referendum's impact on the county. We believe the facts will show a moderately negative impact far outweighed by the benefits to the region's truly needy, its collective economic health, and its deteriorating infrastructure. Jammu has no reason to fear the facts.

We can only speculate why Probst, while correct in pointing up the need for careful study, has steadfastly refused to enter into a responsible discussion with Jammu. An attempt to deny legitimacy to the pro-merger forces is surely beneath him.

Probst claims that the proposed debate would focus too heavily on personalities. The claim has merit. But with the public starving for input, he must be faulted for overfastidiousness. He is hiding behind his scruples. Must the present confusion persist merely because one man refuses to lower his sights a little?

Let Jammu acknowledge the need for study. Let Probst come down to earth. Let the final month of the campaign be a model of spirited, informed discourse.

The piece had delighted him, and not just because he enjoyed ignoring the advice of editors. It was another example of the magical capacity of public life to magnify his person faithfully. Vote No ran a clean campaign. It stuck to the facts. If he had any doubts about whether he was a stickler when it came to ethics, he only had to open the newspaper. There they said it: Martin Probst is a stickler when it comes to ethics.

He and Jammu went straight from the hospital to the Palm Beach Café, a restaurant peopled by the generation of St. Louisans halfway behind Probst and Barbara's. They ordered drinks, and after a very awkward silence Jammu looked up at him.

"Why don't you tell me in one sentence," she said, making no effort to clear the hoarseness from her throat, "what you have against the merger. We can debate in private, can't we? Our personalities aren't swaying anyone here."

"One sentence," Probst said. "Given that I and the rest of Municipal Growth used to advocate city-county consolidation ourselves." He thought a moment, looking for other bases to cover. "Given that the referendum was drafted in response to the county's own fear of missing the boat. Given that the context is a free political market and the question is whether the market will bear a merger—"

"You haven't touched on any of this in your statements."

"Didn't need to, with you hammering away at it. I'm simply trying to show you I've mastered your arguments. And what it comes down to, then, is that my intuitive distrust of this referendum—since everything indicates that I should favor it—my intuitive distrust means a lot."

Jammu's eyes widened. "That's your argument?"

"And to articulate this, then," he said, "the first thing is the knee-jerk quality of what's been going on. The voters can't vote intelligently, and you have to be afraid of drastic change, an unregulated marketplace of ideas, just like you have to be afraid of new toys that could maybe hurt children. Now, I trust *you*—" He tried to engage Jammu visually, but she was playing with her drink. "And I'd like to mention that that's what I've been telling Municipal Growth all along. But in the case of Urban Hope, it's as if Municipal Growth had suddenly begun to make policy recommendations based purely on the profit motives of its member chief executives. Rolf Ripley wants it to pass for trickle-down welfare, supply-side progress, which is what I myself practice at work, except that I'm employing men while Ripley is making real-estate killings. Plus the fact that he's allied himself with populist public-sector Democrats like the mayor! Somewhere, somebody isn't telling the real story."

"None of this makes the merger a bad idea," Jammu said.

"The thing is, we don't know. Aren't your convictions pretty intuitive, too? Taxes won't fall. The city payroll won't shrink, it might even expand. But you see this all somehow transmuting into an urban utopia. All of today's sinecure holders out in droves tomorrow clearing weeds from railroad tracks on the South Side. The North Side blacks happily filling the pockets of the Rolf Ripleys. This is what I mean by unrealistic. And it's far worse in the county. You're trying to hook people intuitively yourself. With your vision of a united greater St. Louis."

"What you're saying is that we're in conflict over the potential for positive change. You're pessimistic. I'm optimistic."

Probst didn't like how this sounded. He'd thought it was the other way around. He sanguine and St. Louisan, she dour and tired. She (in the words of Barbara's friend Lorri Wulkowicz) unconcealably Third World. At closer range everything she wore—her fine pearls, her fine dress, her fine makeup—seemed cheapened by her face and figure. She looked (Probst couldn't have said exactly why) like she needed a bath. He watched her swallow a pill with her wine. "Antihistamine," she explained, snapping her purse. The purse was a black clutch. Like someone determined to pay for the drinks, she kept it ready on her lap.

"Who are you?" Probst asked.

She coughed. "What do you mean?"

"Well, for example, what's your first name?"

"Colonel." She smiled.

"No. What is it?"

"I don't like my first name. It isn't 'me.' I would have changed it if people hadn't got used to calling me by my first initial, which is S. I don't mind S. You can call me Ess. That's what my mother calls me, that and Essie. Can I call you Martin?"

"Your mother," he said conversationally. "Where is she?"

"She lives in Bombay. You can read all about it in the Post on Sunday. Everything you always wanted to know about my private life but were too bored to ask."

He paused to admire how this blocked further questions. Then he said, "I'm not bored, and I don't trust what I read in the paper. And anyway—"

"And anyway, I should be more polite. I'm sorry. Rough day."

Another deft block. He tried an end run. "Why did you leave India? Does anyone ever ask you that?"

"Well, all the reporters do."

He gave up. Soft light still bathed the tables, the piano still appealed to moods, but to him the room now had the ambience it must have had at 10:00 in the morning when the extra lights were on and the vacuum cleaner was run. Some tables, some chairs. He looked around Jammu to catch the waiter's attention, and it was then that he noticed that the couple at the next table were speaking to each other but facing him and Jammu. Other faces at other tables, too. People were watching them. He hunched his shoulders and retracted his head.

"It was a typical midlife career change," Jammu said. "I had the opportunity to come and work here, and I took it. I like this country—I've said as much to the reporters, only it sounded bad in print."

Probst nodded. "How did it happen that you didn't forfeit your U.S. citizenship by holding public office in India?"

"They bent the rule for me."

"You mean they broke it."

She looked at the piano. "Unwittingly, though. They could have revoked my passport, but my mother took care of the renewals. She never mentioned that I worked for the police service, and the INS never asked. Now I don't hold office in India, so there's nothing they can do."

"Didn't the Police Board wonder?"

"They said if I could prove my eligibility they wanted to have me. It was up to me."

"But if the INS had been awake you wouldn't have had citizenship in July."

"I suppose not. Why are you asking me these questions?"

"I'm still trying to tell you what I have against the merger."

"Go ahead, then."

"How did you win the war on crime? What's happened to all the muggers and heroin addicts? And the Mafia. I can't believe they're all in jail, and, pessimist that I am, I know they haven't reformed. Are the crime figures for real?"

"They're for real. And you know I've come under very close scrutiny because of it. We've had police chiefs from all the major cities here asking the same question. We've had the ACLU breathing down our necks. We've had the media looking for a scandal. And as you'll have noticed, we've had no serious complaints. Why not? Mainly I'd say that for once the small size of St. Louis has worked in its favor. It simply isn't large enough to produce an endless supply of places for crime to breed. What in other cities would be just a major rejuvenation here amounts to something nearly total. The North Side redevelopment currently covers about fourteen square miles. That's one-fourth of the entire city. In a city like Philadelphia or Los Angeles or Chicago it would be about five percent. Here a large percentage of the city land has become so valuable that the owners themselves do most of the policing. On property worth a hundred fifty dollars a square foot, you don't see much crime, apart from the white-collar variety. So the rate drops."

"But the people who engage in it. Where are they now?"

"That really isn't my concern. They're spread much more evenly over the rest of the population in Missouri and Illinois. The crime rate has risen in places like University City and Webster Groves, but the local forces can easily handle the work. And if some poor families have moved to the county, then the county welfare apparatus now has a somewhat heavier caseload to process. This doesn't sound nice. But you must admit it's more efficient and more fair than having the entire region's underside concentrated in the city. Doesn't this make sense to you?"

It made sense. But Probst didn't see where all the frightening black young men of North St. Louis had vanished to. He'd seen their faces. He knew that none of them had ended up in Webster Groves or in any of the other nice county towns. Where were they? Somehow the reality had gone underground.

"How come everyone likes you?" he asked.

"Not everyone does."

"Most seem to. I'm talking about the fact that you're the political linchpin in St. Louis now, and you only got here seven months ago. What have you done for both the black politicians and the Quentin Spiegelmans that they're so willing to work for you?"

"They aren't working for me. They just need me."

"Why you?"

"You mean, what have I got that other people haven't?"

"Yes."

"I don't know. Ambition. Luck."

"Loads of people have ambition. Are you saying you're in the position you're in just because you're lucky?"

"No."

"Where are your enemies? Where are the people whose toes you've stepped on? The people you've offended."

"There are plenty—"

"There aren't. You know there aren't. There's only the right-wing Republicans and some old women and they only hate you out of principle. And because they're jealous. The thing is, Colonel—"

"Ess."

"The thing is, I can understand why Ripley and Meisner get along with you now, given the decisions they've made, and I can see why the situation is stable now, why the only people against you are criminals or crackpots, and I can see how the war on crime and the war on blight work hand in hand now, I can even see the motives behind the union of Democrats and industrialists. We're at point B. You hand it to me. It's a fait accompli. It makes sense. But I don't see how you got here from point A. I don't understand what possessed so many of my acquaintances to desert Municipal Growth. I don't understand how you knew enough and where you found the leverage to plan and execute this complete, this bizarre reversal of the city's fortunes. I refuse to believe a total stranger, no matter how lucky and ambitious, can come to an American city and change its face in less than a year. I don't know what I expect you to say in reply, but I find there's a huge gap between the person I'm sitting here with and the person who's done all the things she's done. I wonder how you see yourself."

"I don't know, I just did it."

"Well, you can see why I wonder who you really are."

"I don't know. Who do you think I am?"

"I don't know."

They stared at each other. The problem had become impersonal.

"I don't ask," she said. "I just do things. I wanted the city to go places. I did everything I could. Why don't you understand? You've been rather successful here yourself."

"I was born here. I skipped college." Probst's voice trembled at the drama of his life. "I worked fourteen-hour days for ten years, and I didn't change anything. I just made do with what was already there."

"And it sounds to me as if you therefore feel a necessary attachment to what was already here. You're a little bit in love with troubles. Isn't it so? Isn't that what's behind these questions? A bankrupt, crime-ridden inner city is fundamental to your outlook as an old St. Louisan, and you don't *want* it to change."

"I don't think that's true."

"I don't mean to imply that you're heartless. You're just a pessimist, that's all. You give to UNICEF, but you don't believe it will stop African governments from letting their children starve. You build these bridges in St. Louis but not because you think it will make the people who drive their cars over them any less odious to you—"

"Or to you."

"Am I right? Isn't this how you feel?"

"You *are* saying I'm selfish."

"Only insofar as you deny the validity of what I've done for the city. If you'd just accept that things have changed, you'd support the referendum. I can see you on television saying, Yes, I, Martin Probst, have changed my mind. I believe this can be a great city if everyone works together. If we all share the burden, the burden disappears."

She was sitting up straight, her eyes questing for the good, the brave, and the true. Probst was embarrassed for her.

"Who's John Nissing?" he said abruptly.

"John—" She frowned. "Nissing. The writer."

"You know him, then."

"Yes. He wrote the article for Sunday's PD Magazine, which he'd hoped the New York Times Magazine would take but didn't. I haven't seen the piece, but it should be everything you wanted— oh, you know. All that crap about my mother and the sweltering streets of Bombay. I gave him too many interviews earlier in the year."

"He's from India?"

"No. I hadn't heard that. Not American, but I don't believe Indian. But he'd been to Bombay and bombarded me with facts. A real cosmopolitan, independently wealthy. A snob and a know-it-all. He kept weaving in all the places he'd seen, Antarctica, the Ryukyus, Uganda, that sort of thing." Jammu bit her thumbnail. "And forty-six of the fifty states. Why do you ask?"

"Just wondered. He photographed my house for an architectural magazine." A snob and a know-it-all: exactly Barbara's type. "He looked Indian," Probst added recklessly.

"I'd say more like Arab."

Later that night he watched her take off her clothes. Her hair hung over her face in ebony blades as she supervised her fingers, her short square hands, which were fighting with the catch on her puckered bra. The blinds were raised. Snow fell outside. Probst couldn't believe he was going to see it all now. She was even thinner than she looked in clothes, and when she lowered her underpants, the fabric taut between her fingers like a string game, his jaw felt as if it were dropping open down to his waist. There was no hair between her legs. There was just a crater with a plumped rim, a second navel. She was a virgin. She looked at him. "This is it," she said. Where the bullet entered.

Probst was the bullet.

The room was full of moonlight. He'd been dreaming on his back, half sitting, propped on both the pillows, his and Barbara's. The moon was full. He couldn't remember its ever having filled the room this way. Its light flooded in through the western windows so brightly that it made the room seem small and portable. The bed extended nearly to the walls on all sides. Probst shut his eyes and tried to return to where he'd been, to the dream, to Jammu, and deflower her.

He opened them again. There was something on his lap, under the blankets and bedspread. He peeled them back and felt a claw, a tiny claw, and the weight of something warm on his pajamas at his hip.

It was a kitten. There was a kitten in his bed. Furry and imploring, its small paw reached up towards his face.

This time he really woke up. He was lying on his stomach, his eyes shielded by pillows. He'd ejaculated in his sleep. Nudging aside a pillow, he saw moonlight, in the eastern window, not the western, slipping in below the bottom of the heavy shade, which he hadn't quite pulled down all the way. It was different from the moonlight he'd dreamed. It was hard and modest, just a bluish glare on the sill.

·

When he went to work at Vote No in the morning, the fun was gone. As usual, the volunteers brewing coffee offered him a share of the first pot. While he waited, he savored his mild hangover, the vestige of the long evening that seemed, now, to have leeched the wicked pleasure from his elephant act. Holmes and the others had made him the repository of the cause's rightness and purity, and he despised them for it. He waved away his coffee when it came.

Feathered shafts of tobacco smoke pierced the air. At the high-rise Holiday Inn across the street the revolving doors worked like ventricles, admitting tubby travelers with baggage, ushering out others with showered hair and pink faces and baggage less sleek. The spectacle had decadence. The participants in the purchasable pleasures of hotel stays, room service and ice machines, a pool on the roof, were interchangeable. The doors revolved.

To fly on a jet was a nice thing. (Millions thought so.) To stay in a hotel was a nice thing. To dine out was a nice thing. (Not many citizens of India dined out.) Vote No had assigned Probst the task of fashioning sentiments to sway the great plane-taking, hotel-utilizing, restaurant-going middle classes. To vote no was a nice thing. To vote yes was a nice thing. Did it really matter? Both arguments ran like tops. (To own a Buick was a nice thing.) This was decadence.

Sometimes Probst thought immediate action must be taken to rid the world of nuclear arms lest a war accidentally start. At other times he thought the only path to safety lay in constructing more arms, a deterrent so frightening that neither side dare accidentally start something. He only knew he was frightened. He could argue both sides. He didn't want to argue. He found it ludicrous and burdensome that the *Post-Dispatch* and maybe thousands of other people cared what he thought. Those people adored Jammu, and he had been with her. People had stared in the Palm Beach Café. She cast a silver light on him. In his mind she was a silver chain he couldn't stop pouring back and forth between his hands. Barbara had her cosmopolitan lover and her new, liberated version of herself. Luisa had her malleable artiste boyfriend. Probst had something coming to him, too.

Excitedly the volunteers were heading from the main office

room into the conference room. Holmes was showing a red-hot video, a series of two-minute campaign ads they'd be running on prime time over the next three weeks. Tina tapped Probst on the shoulder. "Showtime, Mart." He gave her a look devoid of expression. She turned on her heel. (To get laid was a nice thing.) What a state he was in.

19

"There's a man."

"No."

"I can hear it in your voice, Essie. A mother can tell."

"You've been getting the money, haven't you?"

"It's Singh again. Isn't it."

"I hardly see Singh."

"Well. It's your life."

"I said I hardly see him. I don't know what your problem is."

"You can tell me. I've reconciled myself."

"I asked if you'd been getting the money."

"Some money, yes."

"What's that supposed to mean? You've been clearing a hundred twenty percent and the rate is climbing. He sends you photocopies of every—"

"Photocopies, yes."

"Send Karam back here if you don't believe me."

"I will. You can be sure I will. And I do hope you're more civil to him this time."

"Ho. I wasn't civil."

"Karam isn't one to complain, but I had the impression. His feelings were hurt. He's a sensitive man, Essie. Very tender where you're concerned. Like a father. I understand that Singh was violent. I'm not surprised. But you're thirty-five years old now. There comes a time."

"It's over between Singh and me, Maman. He's leaving in a month and I doubt I'll ever see him again."

"All the more reason to watch him. I was given to understand a hundred percent was a minimum figure. I was sure you'd do better."

"Singh isn't stealing your money. No one cares about your money. No one's as greedy as you are."

"Nor as naïve as you. Think about that."

"You make two-twenty on every dollar you spent in September. The exchange rates are good. As for the taxes, well, I warned you. Don't think you're the only one getting taxed. I'm having enough trouble with—"

"Karam will be with you next week. If you warn Singh he's coming I'll be very unhappy with you. But not surprised. A mother can tell."

"I will remind you I've known Singh for nineteen years."

"A mother can tell."

Who's Singh? Norris asked.

Dunno. Dozen Thingbth on our litht and fifty aliathes.

What's the money?

Thupposedly Asha's, actually the mother's.

Anything we can nail her for?

Not yet.

Jammu left the lights on in her office, ducked into the bathroom, and changed into long pants and a leather patrolman's jacket. She pinned her hair and put on a cap, pulling down the bill. Operatives of Pokorny had been following her movements—General Norris had enough wealth to fund an army of spies—and she had to be more careful now. She crossed the walkbridge to the Police Academy, exited onto Spruce, and got in the unmarked Plymouth that Rollie Smith had left at the curb for her. It was a good thing she didn't need to make surprise inspections often. She drove for twenty minutes before she was sure she wasn't being tailed. Then she crossed the Mississippi on the MLK Bridge and entered East St. Louis, Illinois.

East St. Louis was a small-scale version of the South Bronx, of Watts, of North Philly. These cratered streets three miles east of the Arch would have been a menace or a social issue for people in St. Louis if they weren't protected by a wide river and a state line. Singh had done well to imprison Barbara Probst in his loft here. The town was a black hole in the local cosmos, a place so poor and vicious that even organized crime stayed away. No one would expect a finicky psychopath like John Nissing to take his pretty hostage to an area where stepping out of one's car—where even letting up on the gas pedal—invited death. Jammu parked by the rear loading dock of the warehouse and walked quickly to the door. Asha had given her a set of keys. On the top floor she unlocked a steel door and, to make sure Singh didn't shoot her by mistake, whistled a fragment of an old drinking song:

Who put the doxy in orthodoxy,
Who put the sad in saddhu?

Then she went in.

Singh did not look up from the papers spread around him on the floor. He was punching with a single finger, rustically, on the keyboard of a calculator. "What a pleasant surprise," he said.

"My mother thinks you're skimming some of her profits."

"How is the dear old woman?"

"Bhandari's coming to do another audit next week."

"Interesting that you warn me."

She sighed. "I appreciate your doing all this for me."

"Not at all, not at all." He drew a red line through a column of figures and stood. "You came to view the merchandise?"

"Yes."

He opened a door and they passed through an empty room. "The word is mum," he whispered. He parted a set of curtains to reveal the door. Jammu looked up at the peephole, which was set near the top. Singh went away. He returned with a small stepladder with pads of grooved black rubber. She climbed it and peered into the last room.

It was also empty, or nearly so, its walls and floor and ceiling curving together in the peephole's optics like the skin of a bubble. The woman and the mattress appeared to cling, suspended, to the floor. She lay on her stomach reading in the light of a dim lamp. Her hair hung loose and overgrown and shaded the rest of her body from the light. Jammu could just barely make out the legs extending to the foot of the bed, the cable connecting her ankle to the wall. But the face was unmistakable. This was Martin's wife. Jammu had heard her and heard about her as a free person moving through St. Louis. Now she might have been a butterfly tickling Jammu's palms. Jammu wanted to crush her. Your husband doesn't love you. Your daughter doesn't need you. Your Nissing's an old fairy. She couldn't remember why she'd objected to the kidnapping. She hated to think of letting Barbara go, of throwing away a thing bought at such a price. She didn't see how she could survive without moments such as this, without total control. *Who are you?* This was Martin's question. When she was with him she forgot the answer, but she remembered now. Barbara glanced up from her book and gazed at the door.

Satisfied, Jammu stepped off the ladder and crossed the room again. Singh followed. "Exactly as advertised," he said, shutting the second door. "Safe and sound."

"I know she's safe. As long as the release goes smoothly."

"Quite." He hovered at the outside door, waiting for her to leave.

"It will go smoothly."

"Should."

"You're still a psychopath."

"Uh huh."

"I'm not ready to leave, you know."

"Oh." He walked to the middle of the room and sat down on the floor. "You make it with Probst yet?"

Jammu entered the kitchenette. "What do you have to drink here?"

"Tap water. Tang."

"Aren't we pure these days." She put one of his clove cigarettes between her lips and leaned over the gas stove. "Do you find him attractive, Singh?" she said in a conciliatory voice, dragging.

"No, ma'am. You ought to know by now."

"I can't always tell."

"As a rule—"

"You've been slack with your abstracts lately," she said. "I don't want to see any itineraries. I want it all digested."

"What's to digest? Use a plate for the ashes, please. It's become rather Heisenbergian. The more we take away from Probst, the fewer gauges we have of what's happening. He talks to almost no one. He has no friends. Except you, of course, as I'm sure you are aware and will exploit. But since we've yanked most of the bugs, it's probably just as well. The phone taps help, but the quality has been terrible since I cut the amperage. This Pokorny needs to have another accident arranged. Bombay would have been the ideal place for it. It was a mistake not to have Bhise follow through. Have you considered—"

"Not this close to Billerica. Anyway, Pokorny's replaceable."

"Your choice."

"You still have Barbara calling him."

"That also doesn't help much. In fact, she tried to arouse his suspicions, on the fourth, when he'd suggested a divorce. Told him she loved him and then hung up. The only thing that saved us, apart from my fist, was that he treats her so badly that she really does, for the most part, detest him. Thank you, I know. It's because I developed a situation already nascent. With a tip of the hat to your theories."

The cigarette was making Jammu's sense of the vertical swim. She'd have treated Barbara badly too if they were married.

"The tone of his pronouncements has changed," Singh said. "His attitude in the last six days amounts to a declaration of neutrality. If I were John Holmes I'd be scared."

"So it looks like I'm getting the message across to him."

"Not to worry, Chief. He likes you. He thinks you're cute."

"Enough."

"He moons about the house."

"I said enough."

"I'm sure you're wishing we didn't have to release the little wife. That I could check her as baggage when I fly home."

She put out the cigarette and licked the sugar from its paper off her lips.

"But you'd like him to go all the way with you," Singh said.

"To support the merger."

"That's what I *meant*." He paused. "Dear Miss Singh. I think my boyfriend really digs me but he has cold feet. I'm ready to go all the way. What can I do? Dear Lovelorn. This is the moment for objective correlatives. Contrary to Baxti's expectations, we haven't aged him by accelerating the process of loss. His habits and orientation have become youthful and shockingly selfish, which is fortunate because yours—if you'll pardon my saying it—is a youthful, selfish appeal. I have two ideas and a suggestion."

"Which I wouldn't have heard if I'd left just now."

"The envelope, please." Singh took a white envelope from the inner pocket of his jacket and tore it open. He scanned the abstract it contained, and read aloud: "One. Urge him to file for the election to fill the county supervisor seat vacated by Billerica." He looked at Jammu.

"Maybe."

"Two. He has never served as the Veiled Prophet. Have him selected."

"Maybe. The VP organization is mainly a city affair, and that means a lot of its members aren't happy with Probst at the moment."

"Egon Blanders? You got him that Easton site. He should owe you favors."

"He does."

"Well then. Probst is still popular no matter how he stands on the merger question. He should be the Veiled Prophet this year. And the county supervisor. In the fall he 'mused' a lot about his 'semi-retirement,' which is how he referred to a five-day work week. If you were the one to bring him tidings of a larger role in the public sector . . . Which brings me to my suggestion. Flatter his vanity. You've done well with his physical vanity. But the State, which at this point is little more than a quasi-youthful chaos, needs to be solidified. My suggestion is destiny. He already half believes he's destined to play a vital role in the history of St. Louis, he's been told so often. He should believe additionally that he was destined to team up with you—that his family was destined to leave him to achieve this very end. And you don't care if this turns out to be bunk on the day after the election. Do you. More important yet is the correlative, which is that the city and the county are destined to be rejoined. That the merger isn't a violence but a necessity. It was destined to happen. The task should be easy for you, because you yourself believe in historical necessity, in your own quaint way. And the symbolism—you the city, he the county—should help reinforce the personal attraction. City of symbols, recall. So 'go for it.' "

Jammu said nothing. She felt she'd outgrown Singh. Probst wasn't glib, and he had a position of authority. She admired him for his hesitations, his scrupled observations, for the doors to truth he opened with his careful picking.

"How will you keep the Ripley dynamic active," Singh said, "if Probst ends up on his side?"

"Ripley can't back out now."

"And Devi?"

"I still use her. But she has a bag packed. Pokorny and Norris would like to get me any way they can."

"You're very patient with the General."

"You underestimate his value. His theories have kept him busy. He's done almost nothing practical to oppose me. And he's been a walking worst-case scenario. Having kept one step ahead of him, we've been two steps ahead of everyone else. The thing is, Singh, it all fits together so neatly. Gopal bagged Hutchinson for us, he publicized the inadequacy of the county police forces, he damaged West County's popularity, he contributed to the atmosphere of fear, *and* he did a few things like the stadium trick. Pokorny still has a man trying to figure out where all the equipment came from and what it was for if we weren't going to use it. It was for him. For the knowledgeable few, for the informational elite. For Norris, who will never figure out that he shouldn't have wasted time trying to figure it out."

Singh stood up with a grunt. "What goes on in your head, friend? You must know you always sound like this when you've talked to her."

"Like what?" Jammu wanted to know. What had he heard in what she'd said? Sometimes he just made these things up.

"In ten years the two of you will be indistinguishable."

She sat with her legs crossed and her arms crossed, in blue serge and black leather; at least she'd never be as formal as her mother. Who as a young woman had changed her name and run off with an American and had a child by him in Los Angeles, very possibly believing the same thing.

·

Winter came early in Kashmir, late in October when the valley sloshed humidity into the mountains to tumble back as cloud, gothic mist to intrigue in the avenues of Srinagar, in liaison with wood-smoke, in a pre-modern smog. Night began with the unseen dropping of the sun behind unseen peaks, at four o'clock. Balwan Singh entered a bungalow on the city outskirts, threw his coat on a peg, and approached the hunched and red-eyed members of the Marxist Students Reading Group, speaking before he reached them, before they could greet him.

"Classically," he said, "the revolution proceeds at the most general level along dialectical lines between theory and praxis, praxis and theory. Lenin's perception of his historicity became Lenin's stewardship of the Bolshevik actions, which actions, their practical successes and failures, led to a refinement of his theory, specifically in the concepts of imperialism and the Communist state. As long as Lenin lived, this dialectic closely matched its counterpart, that of man as participant and man as percipient, as subject and as object. But the death of Lenin, the emerging imperfections of the early state, and above all the rise of Stalin created a crisis in the dialectic: praxis dictated that theory, in the short run, be its apologist."

His comrades squatted on the floor, leaned against walls, chewing *paan* or smoking, like a congregation of ruminant boatmen a generation older. Most of them were sons of well-heeled Hindus, their eyes Brahmanically mournful, and they'd adhered to the Indian pattern by which youths become men early. Textbook materialism had exalted them. They filibustered in classrooms. They got themselves expelled. They laughed at jokes that were correct.

Singh, whose jokes were always correct, never laughed. He paced back and forth before them, standing at the center of an asterisk of shadows cast from his legs by the lanterns, his strut as always part professorial, part firebrand, and mainly Heinrich Heine—and he began to sense that he was not being heard. His comrades' shoulders bucked and dipped as if they felt a draft. They did. It was a newcomer, behind them, a girl, a very young girl with a boyish body and a boy's short hair, sitting cross-legged in slacks on the floor near the wood stove. Singh interrupted himself to ask for her name.

"Jammu," she said.

He welcomed her stiffly and, by example, led the group to ignore her for the duration of his lecture. When the meeting broke up she slipped out of the bungalow like a shrug embodied, like a self containable in one small word. He followed her, with a glance over his shoulder to make sure no comrades saw.

She said she came from Bombay. She said she was sixteen. She was studying in Srinagar against her will. She told Singh it wasn't a good university. Her mother wanted her to marry a certain forty-three-year-old Kashmiri landowner because she was a bastard and the landowner had asked. She was studying electrical science. She spoke no Kashmiri. Her mother wanted to manufacture transistor radios in Ahmadabad and wanted her to run the company. She wanted to go to London or Paris and be a writer and not marry. She'd seen one of the Reading Group's handbills. Her mother had told her her religion was neosocialism. In the cellar of their house, in Bombay, she had watched a cat in a window well push five wet babies out of its body. The cat became angry and tried to escape but was too weak to climb out of the window well. The kittens were squirming like living excrement on the dead leaves. The cat lay down again and ate the sac. She asked Singh who Trotsky was.

She would have fallen to the first man unscrupulous enough to claim her, would have become, at someone's arbitrary urging, a fascist or an industrialist or a criminal, would have put out for the most tertiary member of the Reading Group. (And then would have included him in a biting *roman à clef* and left it unfinished in a footlocker.) She was preternaturally innocent, like the simple brain of a time bomb. She was incapable of love but acted wed, directing Singh's life ("You can't afford those boots") and viewing other men with airtight indifference. She went where no women had gone, did what few girls were doing, and so it didn't matter what she said. If you were Jammu, it didn't matter. The Reading Group, soon recast as the Kashmiri Alternative Socialist Front and thence as the People's Reading Group, believed her to be doctrinaire. So did Singh. He promoted her to a position of command. He forsook all others in bed. He and she dressed identically.

When she went to Chicago (under a false impression of that city's political climate; it was 1968 and she thought it was a hotbed; hers was, Singh came to see, a peculiarly Indian blunder) he departed for Moscow to study mechanical engineering. He had a room in the largest freestanding structure in all of Eurasia, the MGU on the Lenin Hills, a monument to Stalin's conviction that More Is More. One day he went to the thirty-fifth floor and found a neglected rock collection and a door to a tiny elevator, an elevator with space for only two people squeezed tightly together, so that when he'd ridden it up as far as it went and the door had opened, his face was a matter of inches from a steel fence and a sign which commanded in Russian DO NOT TOUCH and which was marked with a skull and crossbones and a bolt of lightning piercing the skull's eyesockets. He took the elevator back down to the rock collection. He had a fling with a young engineering student named Grigor who worked part-time in the Soviet patent office and who claimed, when drunk on vodka, to have the task of copying patents from Western nations into Russian and dating them to appear to have been issued in Moscow several years before the originals. Then he would weep and claim he was lying. From Chicago Jammu sent Singh a postcard that read in its entirety, "Miss you." Back in Bombay he found that, out of his sight, she had entered the Indian Police Service. He didn't mind. She was still his favorite, his first and only woman to date, and in reminding him that he could go both ways she made him feel universal and powerful. He performed his historical function religiously—if religion implies the submission of the autonomous mind to ritual. As the most erudite Catholic theologians take communion and are confessed, in Bombay Singh never stopped recruiting, inciting, discussing. For several years he lived in Mahul, in the shadow of the Burmah Shell refinery. Every morning he would leave his rooms to ply the streets or wait tables at the Lady Naik Hotel or burn time in a tea room with his leftist pals, and on the steps of his building he would stop in front of a deformed little cigarette seller and drop coins on his outspread scarf and take a package of genuine Pall Malls. For arms the man had two ebony hemispheres protruding from his shoulders, arrested in utero thirty years earlier, shining in the red morning light as though varnished. The deformity wanted to shame the concept of arms, or perhaps reproduced in Singh the man's longing to have them. The man was an avatar of Jammu.

Frequently in those early years Singh visited her mother's house on Mount Pleasant Road. Shanti Jammu hosted nightly showings of the creations of her Pathan chef and of her own conversational effulgence. Shanti fancied herself a marxist of the gradualist school. "Ours is a country of caste divisions, Balwan," she would twinkle, as if this were news to him. "Not class divisions. The Petits against the Patels. The tinkers and the tailors. Sikhs and Hindus, and vice versa of course. How can this be changed? Who's to break the traditions? Who's to build the slums and run them on the Western model? A very wise man I once knew spoke of dehumanizing this generation in order to humanize the next one. So I'm a capitalist roader. A ruling-class dog. Just fulfilling . . . my historical telos!"

"Your dharma."

"Come, come, let's be modern."

"That's my point. You aren't transcending the superstructure. You're still a Brahman squeezing Harijans in the name of wisdom and racial privilege."

"And you're still a superior Sikh. That's *my* point. You and your Russians! They were nothing but Frenchmen in sable. Germans with samovars. We're still Indians. We won't shed our Oriental souls overnight. If we look west, it's to England. Dignified, class-conscious sentimental old England."

"Home of Marx and still the only Labour government in post-war Western Europe."

"Do have some beef, Essie. You too, Balwan. You're looking peaked. Where is the working class in 'socialist' India? Where is the Industrial Revolution? It's a generation down the line."

"Not in Bombay, Poona, Delhi, Bhopal. And it's the urban centers that matter, because that's where the organs of repression are concentrated. Russia itself was a feudalistic agrarian state in 1917."

"Well goodness gracious, then be my guest. Foment! Ignite the slums! Only drop me a line on the eve of your revolution." She touched his arm, and winked at her daughter. "I'll want to pack. I'm sure the canaille won't grasp that I've been working in their best interest. Will they?"

"Does a chicken have lips?"

"But it will all be in the family. Essie keeps you out of jail. You'll keep us off the guillotine."

Jammu kept him civil. She said she shared his contempt for her mother, saw the egregiousness, knew all about it, so why bring it up? She had no other family in the world. So Singh held off, and by and by Shanti banned him from the house. Both he and she made believe, for Essie's sake, that their enmity was rooted in politics. It wouldn't have done to let Jammu know that there was simply bad blood between her only two loved ones, that their antipathy could not be rationalized. It was a measure of her dictatorial potential that people close to her felt compelled to shield her from unpleasant facts.

In Bombay Singh gained a reputation for irresponsibility because he was forever dropping out of sight, abandoning his cohorts. In thirteen years they never even trusted him enough to make him a section leader. The truth was that he was responsible to Jammu, the rising star of the Bombay police. He made sure he stayed available in case she needed a job done. He made sure she believed the nights they spent alone together meant a great deal to him. Perhaps they did. And perhaps her career would mean more to the future of India than any amount of marxist agitation. It was this possibility that kept him in her service. The margin of hope in Bombay ran very thin. Jammu was an anomaly, foreign to the culture, and Singh knew that change had always been forced on India from outside, by the Aryans, the Moguls, the British. Even Gandhi had come from across the ocean. If you were Indian and socially responsible, it was your obligation to leave India, literally, intellectually, or both.

When the call came, he was ready to leave. The destination— St. Louis, Missouri—hardly seemed to meet the requirements of an Archimedean fulcrum. But Jammu said the specifics shouldn't make any difference. (Especially when it was clear that no matter what she did, stay or leave, the Bombay police would be rioting by mid-autumn.) She said that in every social entity, even a quiet mid-American city, there were inequalities that could be parlayed into subversion. (Subversion! Constantly, in her innocence, she took corruption for subversion.) She said she was impatient with India. She wanted to leave her mark on a place, on a culture, and she knew it wouldn't be Bombay. It had taken her nearly fifteen years with the Bombay police to reach this conclusion, which Shanti had been drawing for her all along. Of course she maintained she'd planned from the beginning to use her police work merely to launch her to America. That was a lie. She said she was bored and restless. This, Singh believed. He followed her. He was interested in attacking the United States.

But the operation had turned out to be a repeat of her performance in Bombay, where, as a member of the People's Reading Group, she'd infiltrated the Indian Police Service and penetrated to the depths of its bureaucracy, becoming the police commissioner in India's largest city and receiving along the way the active financial support of Indira and her party, and then turned her back on the entire country. She'd sold her work, all her chances, for a job in St. Louis. And here again she'd ridden history at a velocity that seemed miraculous to the unthinking. And here again velocity undid her. She loved it for its own sake, obsessively, with a modern desperation that tied her progress to the ghetto, which was also modern and obsessed with speed. The sudden trends, the sudden deaths. And where she'd had perhaps the only opportunity ever to arise in latter-day St. Louis to bring a small revolution to its black residents, she'd subverted subversion instead. She was on the wrong side of the law. Poverty, poor education, discrimination and institutionalized criminality were not modern. They were Indian problems, sustaining an ideology of separateness, of meaningful suffering, of despairing pride. In the ghetto, just as in the Indian ghettos of caste, consciousness would come slowly and painfully. Jammu had no patience. She'd hauled the big industrial guns into the inner city and called it a solution, because ultimately it was far easier to change the thinking of a rich white fifty-year-old or to deflect the course of his eighteen-year-old daughter than it was to give a black child fifteen years of decent education. Jammu had lied to the blacks, swindled them out of their homes, bribed and cajoled their own advocates into betraying them, and all in the name of speed. Of appearing to solve the problem quickly. Of seizing power while it could still be seized.

Still, Singh had no ready-made category for her. She was too self-conscious, too protean, too amateur and peculiar for him to dismiss her. But at least he could see now that she and her methods weren't what he'd hoped, her methods not the fuse of any revolution anywhere, and she not the entelechy he'd imagined he'd beheld when she was sixteen and wanted to have intercourse on gravel and in boats and to make people obey her laws. He could see now. America was the seat of her atavism. She was just like her mother. All the subtle countertrends that had nagged him from the first days in Srinagar—her lack of direction, her indifference to suffering, the patness of her utterances—had culminated in St. Louis. Senseless St. Louis. She would stick here, permanently associated, her methods sound enough to vanquish the locals but too fancy to take her further. She'd use Probst because she thought she cared for him and then discard him soon enough, for behaving like a human being. Singh was glad to have seen the changes she'd wrought, the spectacle of speed, and to have achieved momentary fulfillment in his handling of the living Probsts. He'd enjoyed the ride, and he'd be glad in a month when he was gone.

·

ELIGIBLE NO MORE? Chief Jammu, the world's most eligible police officer, has been seen of late on the streets of St. Louis in the company of wealthy contractor Martin Probst (glimpsed here climbing into the Chief's private squad car). The match-up is rumored to have estranged Probst from his wife of twenty years. But, insists Jammu, "we're only friends."

When Barbara had studied the picture to Singh's satisfaction he took the copy of *People* away from her. "It was idle," he said, moving his chair close to her mattress. "You were in the check-out line at the tiny A&P and paging through the magazine rack. You just happened to see the picture and the caption. But it sends you reeling, if that's not too strong a phrase. First his talk of divorce, and now this. He's anticipating you. You can hardly stand it. He's chipping away at the trenchancy and originality of what you've done. You were never in control and you still aren't in control."

She lay back on her pillows. The eye he'd blackened on the fourth had healed. It no longer stared out autonomously. "My husband is weak, John. But he usually manages to redeem himself."

"You think, with condescension. When hatred ceases to suffice, you can always condescend. Anything to prove you special, to give you purpose, to show yourself the only thing you've ever lacked is appreciation. You push open the doors of our building and take the elevator up and for the first time, honey, for the first time, you see our love nest as it really is. You wonder about the furniture. Is it fashionable? And if it is, then whose fashion? Which year's? Time has never been less on your side. You notice the smell, the smell of all high-rise apartments with low ceilings and climate control, from the odd pockets of organic things that cross-ventilation can't reach. You see the photograph of my pretty dead wife and you begin to remember how, when you first met me, before I swept you off your feet and taught you the true nature of sexual love, how you pitied me. You see the blank notebook from that afternoon at the Modern. Still just a *T* in there. Estranged wife. His wife of twenty years. It's a dark Sunday night. I've been away all weekend, since we got back from Paris. You put the few groceries in the refrigerator and sniff. The box of baking soda isn't really doing its job anymore. The tandoori chicken left over from our night out before our vacation is red and blue like a tropical fish. You throw it away, and roaches dive for cover in the trash can. Cars honk outside. You glance at the Van Gogh weekly desk calendar on our kitchen table. It's the eighteenth. You've been away for two months."

"Get to the crazy stuff," she said loudly. "You know that's what I live for."

"You mean those nightmares you were having the first few weeks you slept here? That I was a psychopath? The Great Unknown? You're good at dreams, you know those were just drama, psychic ways around the plain old-fashioned ordinariness of what I am."

She laughed. "Oh, that's real good." She reached for the cigarettes he'd brought her.

"You stand bitterly in the kitchen, smoking. *Your* husband and that arrogant new bitch of a police chief! And—"

"Why not believe her? Maybe they're only friends. He certainly thinks highly enough of her."

"You say that aloud and hear the jealousy. Of course they're more than friends. Your husband's weak and Jammu is strong. And no one will guess, because your husband is the man. You picture them together. Laughing. Strolling. Smooching. Holding hands. The darlings of your hometown. While you and I hang on in the eastern provinces, trying only to uphold each other's sanity. But you love me. You do love me, Barbara, like you never loved him."

She scraped ash on the hem of her jeans and rubbed it in.

"Because what have you done with your life? How did you reach forty-three without noticing your delusion in following him? He never appreciated what he had in you for twenty years. What's worse, he never will. What happened at the side of your cradle or behind the scenes at your Catholic confirmation that doomed you to live in the shadow of a powerful man you respected and admired and found amusing and condescended to but never loved? How were you damaged? That you'll live your whole life as his victim. His sacrificial victim. That you could appear in the pages of *People* as the wife from whom his affair with Jammu had estranged him. It's you you feel sorry for in me. I'm out grubbing up another story, another check to pay another month's rent. Except I'm not. You hear a noise in the hall and you turn, and it's me. I say, Surprise! You jump a little, and I kiss you."

Singh dropped to his knees and kissed her mouth, his eyes on the lengthening ash. Her lips didn't move beneath his. "Like that," he said through a frog in his throat, and rose.

"You're too strange," she said. She turned her head away from him to bring her lips to the stained filter. "I mean that seriously."

"So we aren't in the mood." He sat down again. "We're in the mood for soul-baring and stories. We sit down at the table and I tell you one. I tell you I was born in the hills. I grew up in the hills and I went to school in the hills. I was a radical student—"

"In India."

"Of course. In Kashmir. I was a radical student, and there came a time when it was important to me to establish my credentials. I rode up into the hills—"

"On a horse?"

"On a motor scooter, with a young female radical student also on a motor scooter. We were nearly at the border when we came to a game preserve overlooked in the far distance by a charming little castle. We parked our scooters and walked deep into the preserve. We found a broad meadow surrounded by fir trees and sat down in it. We sat there for four days. We slept, and ate pakoras. Otherwise we mortified the flesh. The owner of the preserve wasn't a prince or a nobleman, but he owned all sorts of land and his tenants suffered greatly. As you may have heard, non-princes seldom feel a bond with their tenants. At least this one didn't.

"After four days, we heard horses, as my companion knew we would. I stood behind a tree while she waited in the hot alpine sun. Into the meadow rode the landowner and his bodyguard. He felt the need for a bodyguard, you see. The men dismounted and spoke to her as if they knew her. The bodyguard helped her to her feet, and she stuck a knife in his throat. I stepped out from behind the tree, and with a bayonet—just the simple bayonet, a family heirloom, you understand, a metal symbol—I cut open the landowner's abdomen. I had to use both hands, but the blade was sharp. He doubled over, and I lost my hold on the blade. I pushed him into the grass, and my companion bent over him and smiled and said, 'We're the People's revenge.' He was so terrified that I couldn't look at his face. But she could. She could. He tried to double over again by sitting up, and I pulled the bayonet out and pushed it in again further up his chest, this time towards the heart. There was a fair amount of resistance, about like cutting up a raw chicken. His head fell back, and blood and also clear mucus came out of his mouth and ran into his nostrils. I remember wanting to blow my nose. In fact I sniffled the whole time we were riding our scooters back down to where we lived. I feel strongly about many ethical issues, as you know, but existence and nonexistence aren't among them. You don't deserve to live and you don't deserve to die. This landowner had lived forty-three years—about the average for his tenants, though of course below average for his own family. He didn't deserve to die. It was merely that a lifetime of his actions had begged a violent response. And on our side of the Danube you see a great many violent responses. You become inured, but that isn't the right word for it. You become a little less afraid, or a little more jungly, and if you really thought about this you might decide that by your standards, though I now lead a civilized life in Manhattan, I'm insane after all. As I might decide you are passively insane because you're unable to look down at your body, at your belly, which has swelled to allow Luisa but never been cut open, and at your breasts, which I'd venture to guess you've always felt were rather OK as breasts go, and at your legs, which like the Third World you can't seem to devote much serious consideration to—you can't look down on this and see it entirely as yourself. Maybe, I don't know, if people's heads were where their feet are, they would respect the body more, looking up to it. You're amazed that you contain hot blood in quantity, organs, flesh, gray brains— you can imagine Luisa after a car accident, imagine her pretty head split in two but not your own, and so you think I'm a little too strange to be loved. A little too—honest? Crude?"

"Tiresome."

"If you talked more I'd talk less."

20

Probst had been black and white the last time he'd appeared in *Time* magazine; his lapels and necktie were narrow, and his hair was as short as an astronaut's. For a caption the editors had paraphrased a line from the article: *more than a monument*. The St. Louis skyline then consisted of an Arch rising from a bald, bleached riverfront, a handful of high-rises surviving from the 1930s, and some low apartment buildings, dull fugues on a theme by Mies van der Rohe. The city looked to have awakened from the darker part of the century to find the hour not dawn but midday, with the Missouri sun beating mercilessly on the vacated areas, whiting out the faces of its structures. Under its crewcut and all around, the city's scalp was pale.

Twenty years later, in the space of twelve months, the city had undergone a contemporary styling, become a shopper's mecca and a commercial force rising and expanding in steel and stone. Color was making a comeback, and this apparently was pleasing to *Time*; it had chosen St. Louis as its cover-story subject for its April 2 issue.

With his electric Remington Probst shaved the evening shadows off his cheeks and neck. Red patches of irritation formed immediately. A *Time* reporter, Brett Stone, was coming to interview him at eight o'clock, which was less than an hour away. Stone hadn't mentioned a photographer, but Probst expected one. He leaned close to the bathroom mirror, craning his neck and examining the line of his jaw with his fingers. Downstairs, the stereo boomed out a major-league symphony. He hadn't had the stereo on since Barbara left, and the classical sounds that came out of its speakers now seemed to be picking up where they'd left off two months ago, when she had listened. Stringed instruments were sawing all over the house, cellos rumbling in the rafters, trumpets leading a charge up the stairs into the bathroom. Beethoven, if that was who it was, could make washing your face feel like a momentous act.

He dressed to the second movement, adagio, and descended the stairs under a full escort of minor chords and worried glissandi. Turning the music off, he inspected the living room. He moved the latest issue of *Time* to the top of the coffee-table reading pile but reconsidered, burying it again. He sat down on the sofa. He sprang to his feet energetically. He went to the kitchen and drank some bourbon. He went upstairs and brushed his teeth, came back down and had another drink and said, "To hell with it." Brett Stone wasn't going to write about how his breath smelled.

He'd been giving dozens of interviews, passing time with gentlemen and ladies from *The New York Times*, *Newsweek*, *U.S. News*, the *Christian Science Monitor* and all the lesser publications, but he hadn't been this nervous since Christmas Day, when Luisa had brought Duane over for the first time. St. Louis was about to hit the cover of the magazine that had reserved the right to name the Man of the Year. Probst wanted to make the best possible impression. And, as always now, Jammu was on his mind. He hadn't really enjoyed a calm moment in any of the eighteen days during which they'd socialized. The nervousness arose from the strain of waiting, each day, to see how long he would hold out without making contact with her. That he would make contact was inevitable. It was merely a matter of prolonging the suspense.

He sat down at the breakfast-room table and put his feet up on a neighboring chair, reached over his shoulder to the telephone, and dialed her number.

"Jammu."

"Probst," he said. "Do you want to have dinner?"

"I thought you were busy."

"I should definitely be done by ten. I'll make sure I'm done by ten. I have my lines all memorized."

" 'It's just not realistic.' "

"That's right." He smiled. She made these jokes without a trace of malice; they were even fortifying. "And I'd say the answer is emphatically less. And who stands to gain by this."

"Seriously, Martin, you can say whatever you want about me. I won't hold it against you if you feel you can't contradict what you've said in the past."

"That's very generous of you. Considering you're going to be the cover girl."

She coughed. "Touché."

The receiver was shaking in his right hand. He switched it to his left, which for some reason was rock steady. "Why is this such an event?" he said. "What is it about Time that makes this seem so important?"

"I think it's the red border on their cover."

"The—? Oh. Uh huh."

"Congratulations, by the way, on your selection."

"You're not supposed to know about that."

"It's Chet Murphy who can't keep a secret. But it is true, isn't it?"

"Yes. I get to wear the veil and the crown, hold the scepter and ride in a convertible and review the debs. And make predictions, I guess, if I'm a Prophet. But it's so unexpected. Most of the organization isn't speaking to me. I haven't even been going to the meetings."

"It sounds like they want to make you feel guilty and change your tune on the merger."

"They should know me better than that." His right hand, recovered, took the receiver back. "Ess?"

"What."

"Nothing." He was just testing to see if her name worked. "I'm watching the second hand go around on the kitchen clock. We got four pages in Newsweek but not a cover. This will really do it for St. Louis. People are going to invest here like never before."

"It's interesting to see you appropriating my optimism. It's just what your campaign needs, less defense, more offense. But I do wish you were on my side."

"You want me to change my mind?" He asked because he had a peculiar feeling she didn't. "You want me to make Stone's day?"

"Yes."

"No you don't."

"Yes I do."

"You don't sound like you mean it."

"I just don't want you *giving* me anything. But I say yes to be honest with you, because I don't think you'd have had anything to do with me if your heart were really in the merger fight. And it's been at least a week since you told me about your, quote, intuitive distrusts."

For a while he'd been careful to keep in mind why he was seeing her: not to become friends with her, but to continue sounding her out, testing her story. But her story had passed the acid test. It was clear that if he'd been she he would have done almost exactly the same things in St. Louis. It made sense. And meanwhile, in a rush of mutual infatuation, they'd gotten to be friends.

"You could be county supervisor, Martin."

"I've told you why that's out."

"Not very persuasively. And if you were supervisor, or even if you were plain Martin Probst, and if you'd thrown your weight behind the referendum, and if it became law, then the region would be reunited in more ways than one. Admit you'd like to see that happen."

"I admit it. But what if I stick to my guns?"

"You know that won't matter either."

"Why not."

"Because you're special to me."

He rested his head on the hard back of the chair and released the controls in his head, let it throb. The ceiling was a solid white but consisted of an infinity of points; without betraying their individuality, all of them began to glow. "What about dinner?" he said, with effort.

"Call me when you're through with Stone. I'll be here."

It was somewhere between fifteen and ten before 8:00, a crooked time, the minute hand marking a fractional. Probst stood up and ate a handful of salted peanuts from a blue Planter's can. He reached for the liquor cabinet but didn't venture in. He understood her. She was in no more hurry to see him abandon John Holmes and Vote No than he was to see her undressed: all in good time.

Of course he didn't trust her. He wasn't born yesterday. He suspected that Quentin Spiegelman had been told he was special to her, that Ronald Struthers had been told he was special to her, and before that, Pete Wesley. That was how coalitions were formed. But now at least he had a sound alternative to General Norris's theory of conspiracy. Jammu didn't need to plant bugs or bomb cars when there was a handier point of access: she made people love her.

He could smell his peanut breath. Up the stairs he went again to brush his teeth. His gums were sore, it was ridiculous. Then again, an aura of peanut butter might easily have undermined his credibility with Brett Stone. He didn't plan to get into a discussion of Jammu. He did, however, plan to hint that he wouldn't actually be all that disappointed if the merger went through. He'd recently come up with a good new twist on his American Revolution analogy, just the sort of thing *Time* would go for. The doorbell was ringing as he came down the stairs.

On the doorstep stood a rosy-cheeked thirty-year-old whose head came up as far as Probst's shoulders. The photographer? Wisps of vapor trailed away from his nose; the night was cold and wet. Probst didn't see anyone else.

"Come in. You're—"

"Brett Stone." Nodding, Stone stepped inside. The hand he put out for Probst to shake had short black hairs on the knuckles, and puckered white palms. Apparently he hadn't brought a photographer.

"Shall we get right to it?" Probst said.

"Sure." Stone led him into the living room, nodding.

"Can I get you something?"

"Thanks, no." Stone's watch pipped eight o'clock. He had curly hair the color of motor oil, and pale green eyes. His nodding was rapid and barely perceptible, as though residual from some big bang earlier in his day or life.

Probst was fascinated. "Any trouble finding me?"

"Nope!" Stone had opened his briefcase on his knee and placed a microcassette recorder on the coffee table. Probst stationed himself at the fireplace, and Stone began to ask him questions. Why had Westhaven gone bankrupt? Of Municipal Growth's members of a year ago, how many were still active in the group? Was Probst making any effort to expand it now? Apart from being a chief executive, what other criteria were there for membership? Had Probst been asked to join Urban Hope?

Probst fielded the questions thoughtfully, crafting his sentences with an eye to the tape recorder, and threw in as many interesting sidelights as he could before the next question arrived. Soon he was sweating with concentration. Yet there remained in his head a whispering voice. You're special to me, Martin. You're special to me . . .

At 8:25 Stone finished the lead-off factual questions and put away his pen and clipboard. Probst took a seat in the wing chair by the sofa, threw one leg over the other, and turned to Stone. It was time to get into the meaty issues. Stone stood up and said, "Thank you, Mr. Probst."

"That's all?"

"Sure." Stone nodded. "Appreciate it. You've been very helpful." He turned off the tape recorder. "Unless there's something you'd like to add."

"Well—no. No. I do have some thoughts on the city-county—"

"They're well documented." Stone locked his briefcase and spun the combination wheels. "*And* I had a very productive talk with John Holmes this afternoon. We hate to take your time when there's already so much on the record. You've been very eloquent in the past."

Very eloquent. Rabbits know instinctively the meaning of the shadow of a hawk; Probst felt the shadow of New York.

Stone was waiting for him to stand up. "But if there's anything else you think might help us—"

"I had a question, actually." He didn't stand up.

Stone looked down at him patiently. "Sure."

"What kind of story is this you're writing?"

"*Well.*" Stone hitched his pants up over his hips. "You'd be surprised how many people have mentioned that CBS documentary 'Sixteen in Webster Groves.' I think CBS really traumatized this area. Everyone's afraid we're going to smear you. Don't worry. None of the media are, not this time around. I myself have been uniformly impressed here."

"That's not exactly what I mean." Probst made himself comfortable in his chair. "I mean more specifically. How you're going to fill up the pages."

"Sure." Stone buried his hands in his pockets. "You never know what the editors will do, so I can't really give you a point-by-point rundown, but you can expect to see, oh, the political dynamics of the region. Chief Jammu, of course, in many different contexts. The downtown redevelopment and the philosophy behind it. Crime, welfare, the new federalism. Possibly Municipal Growth, its demise. And you can't run a story on St. Louis without the Arch. Within the rubric of St. Louis we'll also do a spread on other up-and-comers. Knoxville, Winston-Salem, Salt Lake, Tampa."

The Arch? Probst had built the Arch. Perhaps Stone was unaware of this. George Snell of *Newsweek* had been aware of it. He'd interviewed Probst for ninety minutes and cited him liberally in the article, calling attention to the key role he played in shaping public opinion.

Stone's watch pipped again.

Probst stalled. "The special election?"

"The referendum, the Baltimore situation. Sure. It's interesting. We'll treat it. But at this point it's mainly news because it's divided the region, not because it's united it. And what we're interested in is the forces of unity."

Probst stood up and walked to the fireplace. He was so in love with her he couldn't see straight, but he could see how generous she'd been on the phone, talking like he mattered. "You want a scoop?" he said.

"A what?"

He raised his voice. "Do you want me to tell you something?"

Stone was listing slightly to the left, as if his nodding would eventually topple him. He grinned. "Sure."

"I'm calling a press conference tomorrow." Probst wet his lips. "I'm quitting Vote No and supporting the merger."

"Really. That's very interesting. Because of course you've been instrumental in opposing it."

"Yes."

"If it wasn't clinched before, this should certainly do it."

"Yes."

"Can I ask if you're planning to divorce your wife?"

"No comment."

When Stone had gone, Probst began to pace the dining room and living room. *Chief Jammu, of course.* He could still renege. He could still vote no. If he didn't follow through, *Time* wouldn't tell. But having made his little declaration of love in Stone's presence, as if by a slip of the tongue, a guilty blush, he was much less inclined to back out than to go on and shout the same declaration from every street corner in St. Louis County, so good did it feel to have the secret shared at last. *In many different contexts.* She was all over the living room. He threw himself onto the sofa and saw her in all the places she hadn't ever been, stretched out on the window seat, leaning on the mantelpiece, standing on the arm of the sofa to inspect the three still lifes above him. She outnumbered him. He was very small. He let the telephone ring a long time before trudging to the kitchen to answer it.

"Hello," he said.

"Martin."

"What," he said.

"Is Stone still with you?"

"Ah, no." It was no accident she was calling now. She knew he couldn't have called her himself. "Mr. Stone left. I didn't have much to say to him, and he didn't need much that he didn't already have. Something like that."

"The same thing happened to me. He took some quotes and a picture."

"Oh really."

"Yes."

"If you lie to me," he said, "I don't know what I'm going to do. Stone spent three hours with you if he spent half a minute."

After a long, wounded pause, she said, "What's the matter?"

"Read the paper on Friday."

"What did you say about me?"

"You know what the matter is."

"You changed your mind?"

"For the last time, Ess, *don't pretend*. Of course I changed my mind."

"And how, may I ask, was I supposed to know that?"

He sighed. She was still pretending. "How thrilled you sound," he said.

"Just wait a minute. Let it register. This changes things."

"No it doesn't." He began to speak with some authority, to save his pride. "If I quit Vote No tomorrow, I do it because I want to and because I think it's right. I like you, but I would certainly never let a thing like that affect my decisions. I want that understood. The merger wasn't the only obstacle between us. I'm also married. I have a wife. And I've changed my mind about dinner. It's the price you pay. A lot of people love you, but not many of them trust you. I'd have to count myself among the majority there."

Excessively pleased with having said he loved her without having to say it, he looked at the clock. For a moment he believed it was 9:00 in the morning. Jammu was speaking.

"My name is Susan, Martin. Susan Jammu. And I haven't changed my mind about dinner. I know you aren't going to work for the referendum on account of me. I thought that sort of thing was understood between us. I thought we respected each other more than you make it out we do. I know you're married. I wish I didn't have to be saying this on the telephone. If I don't sound shocked that you're planning to sell out John Holmes and the rest of them, it's because I felt you never belonged there in the first place. Obviously it isn't an easy thing to do, what you've done. I'll understand if you want to cool it for a while, cool it for as long as you want, but I think you owe me a dinner, tonight of all nights."

Susan. It was pathetic. A name was such a tiny thing—so tiny that she couldn't have expected him to be impressed if she weren't impressed herself already. She must have considered it her big secret, her ace in the hole. Probst felt sorry for her. "I'll be there in twenty minutes," he said.

The cabdriver tried to give her forty dollars back from her fifty, but she slammed the door and let him keep it as a tip. Maybe it was too big a tip. Was it too big? Her shoe heels conveyed the force of the ground pleasurably into the center of her foot heels as she ran up the pink sidewalk to the entrance of Rolf's headquarters. It was noon. The lobby was empty. Was it too big? Four hundred percent! That was much too big. But no one would find out, and next time she'd make it up by not tipping at all. The lobby guard, who knew her, didn't smile this time. He looked at her as men look at women who can't manage money. The elevator came and she got on, but she had to get off because people wanted out. She got on. On the phone Rolf had called her—and then he'd called her Devi, but they'd quarreled before, but then the maid had said— and then the desk had said the bill wouldn't be paid after 2:00 p.m., and then she'd hit an artery, and then Jammu had called and reasoned with her and told her the flight number and the gate number and the airline desk to get her ticket at, and she'd reasoned with Jammu. Everything was happening at once. Everything was the same when she went to bed and different in the morning. Jammu said Martin was on Rolf's side. She said that wasn't possible. Jammu said pack. The elevator door opened. Four hundred percent. That was four times everything! She ran down the hall and pushed open the glass doors.

"May I help you?"

She ran past the typewriter and the red nails of the woman's outstretched hands and into his office and closed the door. She kneeled.

"Now, Devi—"

He didn't understand. She couldn't reason with him.

"I told you on the phone, now. You can't deny I've been dashed square with you. Be a big girl."

He pulled her to her feet. He pulled her to the door, and she said one last—

"All over, Devi."

He didn't understand. One last— Give me one last—

"The game is over. Wash your face, and do try and get that silly color out of your hair. You'll feel ever so much better."

One last— She was wearing his first present, and she guided his hand down under and then inside, using her nails to make sure he didn't leave until he felt. The maid was nice. The maid asked about her things. The maid listened and said chippying, which meant economizing. She wished!

She locked the door with her other hand and went down to the floor. Martin always said Rolf was a prick. Rolf told her he always did. She could see it now. She hated it. She'd go back to Martin and apologize to him. Martin would be madder than ever when he found out that prick had done this to her on the floor even though its mind was made up and she knew it would call the police because it had said so on the phone. Its teeth unclenched.

"That was it, now. Happy?"

Yes happy. Good-bye forever! (She couldn't wait to count it.) When she ran through the glass doors again the woman was gone and her red nails with her. It was still noon. This time she ran down the stairs. She lost a heel. She stopped to break the other heel and knock it off and ran the rest of the flights flatfooted. The guard said, You'll never learn to manage. You should learn to drive your own car. His telephone rang as she revolved through the doors onto the pink sidewalk. She began to run.

"Stop right there, young lady!"

She heard the guard running, and she ran floating like a deer. The credit cards were perishable. He was gaining on her, and she didn't see any cabs on the circular drive. For forty dollars he at least could have waited three minutes! Fortunately a white car pulled over and a back door opened. She got in and turned around in time to see the guard draw up and stick his hands on his hips and his chest heave and his cheeks scarlet and his mouth say, hoo boy, hoo boy. She knew the driver in the front seat. He had a friend she hadn't met.

"We stopped and picked up your bags."

He said in a foreign language she understood, catching her breath. They were driving her to the airport. Jammu had said. She hadn't expected the royal service and she wouldn't tip them. They drove on the freeway. They didn't say anything except the friend was coming along with her. She looked in the wallet still warm from the seat of the only one besides Martin she'd done it with. In the front seat they were eating pills and they gave her one which she noticed was different from theirs. She smiled and put it in her mouth and took the can of Crush.

"Dramamine for your flight."

"You'll feel calmer."

She put her compact up to her face to work on her personality and dropped the wet, crumbling pill in the compact. She snapped it shut. At the airport the driver and his friend got out and set her bags on the sidewalk. She got out. Her feet were flat! The driver tried to take her purse away from her, and somehow the strap broke and people were looking. The two friends looked at each other and tried to reason her back into the car for a minute.

"Do you know theeth men, young lady?"

One man was very interested. The two friends jumped in the car. She told the man they were harassing her, which was funny because the car drove away.

"Can I give you a lift thumplace?"

She read the chrome words COUNTRY SQUIRE. His car was older, a station wagon with weathered plastic wood siding. The Country Squire smiled and held the passenger door for her. They left the airport. The Squire was driving awfully fast.

"What'th your name?"

She wasn't sure right now. She hadn't ever met the Squire, and she was coming down with the afternoon flu. Wait a second. She opened her purse, zipped the wallet into a pocket and arranged things for the cure. On her right the Marriott disappeared. People didn't understand Barbara, and when they gave her no credit there was no one left to turn to except Martin. She didn't believe Martin was really on Rolf's side.

Trying to reason with her the whole way, the Squire took her downtown. Was she cold? No, she said she only thought she might be coming down with something for the moment. He finally stopped for a light. His mouth widened, a smiling prick. She sprayed Mace in his face and kept spraying until the car behind them honked at the green light. She got out of the car and looked up the street for another cab. Get well soon! she told herself, hopeful even in her chills.

·

In the first light of Friday, before the city rose, Probst climbed the central staircase at his South Side headquarters. At two or three o'clock he'd stopped trying to sleep. At five he'd stopped trying to keep his eyes closed. He was behind even with his personal tasks at the office, and he knew that the phones at every place where he could conceivably be reached would start ringing at eight. He also felt he owed it to Cal and Bob, who of late had effectively been running the company for him, to come in and work some early mornings in the name of the team.

Mike Mansky, at his desk in Engineering, nodded to him and in the same motion leaned forward to kill a cigarette in the ashtray on his blotter. They had a night crew out rebuilding a bridge on Route 21, otherwise Mansky wouldn't be here.

Probst negotiated the dark, windowless corridor to his office and opened the door. Carmen's battened-down desk and typewriter were gray in the light of the new day. The same gray of imminence dwelt temporarily in walls soon to be white, carpeting soon to be blue, file cabinets soon to be more indigenously gray. Already some color was coming out—a spot of red enamel in the corner, a small electric coffeepot. Carmen liked a cup of instant soup on cold afternoons.

The door to his inner sanctum stood ajar, its polished surface reflecting the light rectangle of one of his windows. He pushed it open and walked in.

General Norris was sitting at his desk. He was reading some sort of large-format technical journal. He flipped it onto the desk and looked at Probst. Probst looked at the floor, but the General's features, the grooves on his forehead, at his eyes and around his mouth, his disappointment, had left an imprint on his retinas. He sighed. "You have a thing about showing up on other people's property, don't you?"

"You mind?"

"No-o-o—" Probst set his briefcase on the floor. He wasn't used to being received in his own office. He did mind that.

"You probably got work you want to do," Norris said. "I won't keep you. I just wanted to ask why you done what you done."

Probst looked out the window at the stark precinct house. "I think the papers will state my case pretty clearly."

"Oh, your case, yes. Yes indeed. You've always got a case. You know something, Martin? I never seen anybody like you before. I've seen a lot of self-interest and a lot of cynicism and a lot of weakness, but you—you're the feller with the finger in the dike who somebody offers you a sandwich and you take your finger out to eat it. And you know the water's gonna drown you too. You're really something."

"Was there anything else?"

"Yes, there was. Like to give you a piece of good advice." The General stood and rolled his magazine into a tube. "Call it a sixth sense, but I ain't giving up on you just yet. I'd like you to stay in one piece for what's gonna happen pretty soon."

"The advice."

"Don't be snippy with me. I'm civil, you be civil. My advice is, do whatever you have to in private with that woman but don't make it public."

"Uh huh."

"Don't make it public." With his magazine Norris tapped a black plastic binder on Probst's desk. "I'm leaving you a copy of the interim report we sent the IRS and FBI yesterday, and you can judge for yourself. Maybe you'll get the idea of handing it over to her. I hope you don't. But I can tell you we'll find out if you do and it won't hurt the investigation any but it'll sure as hell hurt you. Don't be any stupider than you been already."

The General left.

Probst read the label on the binder. *Preliminary Report on the Indian Presence in St. Louis. Commissioned by S. S. Norris. H. B. Pokorny & Sons.* He riffled through the pages and saw lists, transcripts, financial breakdowns, in all about 250 pages, a bulk that scared him. If this was all make-believe, their imaginations must have been working in very high gear. He decided to read one page. He opened to what looked like a *Who's Who* section.

MADAN, Bhikubai Devi, born 12/12/61, Bombay. Prostitute. Residing Airport Marriott Hotel, St. Louis, 9/19–present. Visa #3310984067 (tourist) exprd 11/14. Indian psprt #7826212M. Documented encounters: Jammu, 10/8, 10/22, 10/24, 11/6 (am & pm), 11/14, 11/24, 11/27, 12/2, 12/12, 12/14, 12/29, 1/17,

1/21, 2/20, 2/27, 3/15 (see chronology, Appendix C). Ripley, 50+encounters beginning 9/19 through present. A probable heroin addict, Madan would appear to be the primary and perhaps sole liaison between Jammu and Ripley. (See Transcript 14, Appendix B.) Justiciable offenses: possession of Class 1 narcotics, violation of visa (Sec. 221 [c], Act of 1952, 8 U.S.C. [c]), prostitution. Criminal record in India: not available.

The phone was ringing, and he read no more. He could guess who was calling.

•

"It takes guts to do what Martin did," Buzz Wismer said.

Friday had passed without Martin's having backed away at all from the severe pro-merger stance he'd adopted on Thursday. It was Saturday now, and Martin had been selected at the eleventh hour to deliver the keynote speech at the pro-merger rally to be held on the Mall downtown at three o'clock.

"It takes real guts," Buzz repeated. With a spoon he depressed the cheese skin on the French onion soup Bev had taken out of the oven. He wanted lunch, but lunch was molten and dangerous. The single-serving earthenware crock was too hot to touch. "Yes sir," he said, pinching his napkin in hungry frustration. "It takes real guts."

Bev cut the cheese strands out from under her raised spoon with a stoned-wheat cracker and took her first bite. Her mouth slackened at the corners. He heard the unwillingness in her swallow. She coughed, explosively, and gagged. Something in her throat. He leaned across the table to slap her on the back but she waved him away, coughing and shaking her head. When she'd recovered, she picked up her crock with a pot holder and set it in the sink. She sat down and broke a cracker in two.

"You shouldn't have made yourself any if you weren't going to eat it," Buzz said.

"It takes guts all right," she said. "Now that he's done it, you can do it too. Right? Now that he's done the hard part. You can follow suit. It would take guts *not* to. Wouldn't it." She'd broken each half cracker into halves. Four equal squares lay on her placemat. She took another cracker from the basket. "You can follow suit. If he leads clubs, you play a club. Just follow suit. Except for the fun part. Barbara made that easier for him. Didn't she."

She swept the eight squares of cracker into a cupped hand and went and dropped them in the wastebasket. Buzz managed a bite of soup, shuttling it around inside his mouth before it could burn anything too badly. He took a gulp of Guinness. Bev sat. "I'd like to help you, Buzz, I honestly would. I'm your helpmeet. But there's no one in sight to take me off your hands. Not for miles around."

"Maybe you should lie down."

"I just got up."

"Oh."

Once he'd emptied the crock, he got hers from the sink and ate most of her soup, too. She served him a large slice of Grand Marnier–impregnated Bundt cake for dessert. (Her cooking was too rich for him, but it gave her something to do, measuring the substantial pounds of butter, the substantial cupfuls of grated cheese.) He put the crocks in the dishwasher, making a mental note to check after the dishwasher had run to see if it had actually cleaned the crusted cheese from the rims. (Their latest maid had quit after six days.) It was one o'clock. He gargled with Listerine and put on a leather jacket and called to Bev that he was leaving for the office. She came to the front door with a glass of sherry on ice.

"I guess I'll see you when I see you," she said. "Guess I'll be seeing you around. Be seeing you. See you later."

He smiled. "I won't be gone that long."

There was no practical reason for Buzz to copy Martin and make public statements in support of the referendum. The campaign had for all intents and purposes come to an end at noon on Thursday. It was now just a matter of waiting another nine days until it was official. Nevertheless, Buzz wanted to do something. In the first place, it never hurt one's public image and executive credibility to be on the winning side. In the second place, Martin had done a brave thing, and Buzz felt that giving him his full support was the least he could do to make it up to him ("it" was a litany of shadowy, late-night offenses). In the third place, there was Asha. As he drove up the road to headquarters he saw a cream-colored Rolls-Royce idling in the middle of the vast empty parking lot, and as he coasted up to it he could almost hear the news: Edmund "Buzz" Wismer, chairman of the board of Wismer Aeronautics, today stunned the city by announcing his intention to move his operations, based for the last forty years in suburban St. Louis County, to downtown St. Louis. The announcement, following on the heels of a related announcement by Wismer's longtime friend and confidant Martin Probst, comes at a time when Asha was growing impatient with him. Her engine was running, after all, and he wondered whether if he'd come a few minutes later she still would have been here. From the smile on her internationally renowned face, however, Wismer can tell she was glad she'd waited.

.

The countdown to Election Day had entered the single figures. On the whole, Probst's former allies at Municipal Growth and Vote No had shown commendable understanding and patience with him, at least to judge by their silence. Partly, no doubt, they were recalling his refusal to sully himself with the practicalities of the campaign. They wouldn't miss his labors, and he'd made himself so unlikable (he knew this) that not many would miss him personally either. Beyond that, St. Louisans naturally respected well-reasoned changes of heart, even surprising and hurtful changes, and perhaps especially in the case of a man with a reputation so unimpeachable. People were used to Probst by now. Their latest reaction, as he imagined it, amounted to an Oh jeez, Martin Probst, he's done it again. As usual, events had conspired to keep his actions in character.

By Sunday night there remained only one last unpleasant task. He had to clean out his desk at Vote No headquarters and turn in his keys. He'd put it off as long as was seemly, and then a little longer still; it was midnight by the time he left the house on Sherwood Drive.

The night was warm. He pulled on a switch to lower all four of the Lincoln's windows, allowing in air that had risen off soft, recuperating lawns and banks of daffodils and jonquils and snowdrops. Spring had come all at once and in full force, having sent no red herrings in February or January. This spring, the city had earned.

Probst had read Pokorny's document cover to cover, and he hadn't been afraid to test Jammu on every point. These were serious charges. She understood that she had to answer them, and she did, over IHOP pancakes Friday morning, over a dinner at Tony's on Saturday. He studied her for the least sign of vagueness or bluff. He observed none.

"You have to understand the context, Martin. Devi Madan is a twenty-three-year-old who had the misfortune, sometime in September, of falling into the hands of a very experienced and unscrupulous abuser of young women. The first thing Ripley did was take away her passport, supposedly for safekeeping. He installed her in the Airport Marriott, and he left her there. Even after her passport stamp expired he wouldn't let her go home to Bombay. That's where I came in. As Joe Feig pointed out in his feature last month, a good many Indians have immigrated to St. Louis, and one of the reasons they're coming here appears to be me. Families that want to leave India for America find out that St. Louis has welcomed at least one Indian, namely me, in a big way. So then they come here and immediately they find themselves in all sorts of trouble, some of it with the law but most of it with the customs and language and institutions and impersonality of the place. And in India there's a very old tradition of intercession. At any agency you go to in Bombay you'll find mediators who for a fee which is sometimes reasonable but usually not will fix things for you with the bureaucrats inside. That's not how it works in St. Louis, though, so to all these Indians here, especially the ones like Devi who really are in bad shape, I've been the next best thing to a paid mediator. Not to compare myself to Mrs. Gandhi, but she also used to devote time every week to hearing the grievances of ordinary people. It was a Mogul tradition she reactivated, in her regal way. Devi certainly isn't the only one I've had to take care of, although she is one of the ones I've seen the most of, up until a few weeks ago. I suppose Pokorny doesn't mention that she's finally been able to fly home to Bombay, after I did everything but have Ripley arrested as a thief."

"Including blackmailing him?"

She took the question seriously. "I'm not a blackmailer, Martin. On the other hand I'm not as pure as you are. I can tell you exactly to what extent Devi figured in some of the moves Ripley made."

"Save it."

In deference to Norris, he hadn't let her see the actual report. (Not that she'd shown any interest in seeing it.) He'd sliced it in two, lengthwise, with Carmen's paper cutter, and disposed of the halves in two trash cans, one at work and one at home.

There were no lights in the windows of the office on Bonhomme Avenue. Probst parked, took the elevator, and let himself in, turning on the lights. The place was dead. It looked deserted for more than just the night.

He began to load sheaves of yellow legal-sized paper into his briefcase, the drafts of his old speeches. As souvenirs he took some Vote No pencils, an SX-70 snapshot of him at his desk (working hard, his head bowed), and a copy of every document he'd had a hand in writing. He took down the picture of Luisa Duane had given him. He left all the drawers half open as a sign. Then he sat down to write John Holmes a note to leave with the keys.

Dear John,

"Don't bother."

Probst jumped in his chair and turned to see Holmes himself, unshaven, in shirtsleeves, standing at his shoulder.

"Sorry if I scared you."

"It's all right," Probst said. "I—"

"Yeah. I went out for a drink." Holmes took a seat on his desk, leaving one foot on the floor. "Pretty quiet here, isn't it?"

"It's late."

"A week ago there were still plenty of people around after midnight, even on a Sunday." Holmes smiled. "We've lost a lot of volunteers in the last three days."

"My fault?"

"Your fault. Evidently." He shook his head. "I don't want to lay any guilt trip on you. But in some way you might be pleased to know it meant a lot to have you in our corner here."

"Thanks, John."

"And for purely selfish reasons, I'm loath to complain. You and I are both off the hook now."

"How so?"

"This should be the last campaign I'll be asked to run, and the last one you'll be asked to work for."

Grateful for the joke, Probst said, "You think anyone suspects we planned it this way?"

Holmes looked into the fluorescent lights. "I'll take your keys now, Martin."

.

Soft snores made their way into Rolf's ears from under the pillows to his right. An unfamiliar clock radio was blinking at him, and a framed photo of middle-aged parents cast its benignancy upon the bed. He'd surfaced suddenly, his blue somnolence vanishing like liquid oxygen as he shed it. He was wide awake. A divan and a love seat loomed beyond the bunched bedspread and its lacy fringe, in the living end of this living room-cum-bedroom. It was too dark to make out the words on the piece of embroidery hanging by the kitchenette door, but he remembered its message: Today Is the First Day of the Rest of Your Life. That was the kind of girl Tammy was. Rolf had revealed to her that the feminine orgasm was a mere figment of fashion-magazine editors' imaginations. True, perhaps a certain sort of woman did feel something like . . . Tammy wasn't that sort of girl. She'd believed him. She'd found it to be true.

The air of the room tasted clear and clean. All things considered, Rolf was well pleased with his condition. Gelatron, and now Houstonics as well, were his. And the level of indebtedness was so low it made him blush. The Texas immovables of Gelatron and Houstonics had been sold in a highly favorable tax context, while the companies moved into Ripley-owned property in Saint Louis, thus avoiding any need to sell out in Saint Louis and take the tax punishment there. The corporation had grown painlessly. Even Martin Probst's conversion to the pro-city point of view could not diminish Rolf's pleasure in the maneuvers—because all at once, as if he'd awakened from deep sleep, Rolf didn't care a jot about what Martin did. He could have his Barbie back now (if he could find her, tee hee). Rolf was well pleased. It was not just any man who could fund a sexual theme park and sample the wares of the man down the street. Nor could just any man have cut his losses so neatly when at length he grew sick of it and shut it down. Rolf was even more admired for his timely bailouts than for his shrewd acquisitions. Devi had left his life—at a cost to the contingencies fund of nothing but a few hundred dollars in cash and ten minutes of his secretary's time spent reporting the theft of his plastic. And for once Jammu had been a dashed good sport about things, informing him on Wednesday that Devi was addicted to drugs and reminding him that as an illegal alien she had no rights. It was a likely thing, of course, that Jammu had finally realized Devi was stealing her secrets. Jammu wasn't one to perform selfless favors.

Now Tammy, on the other hand . . . She stirred, rolling onto her side. A delectable boobie looked Rolf in the eye. She was a stewardess with Ozark. One of Rolf's goals in life was to take a girl in the bathroom of a commercial airliner at 30,000 feet, and he was sure that he could now look forward to fulfilling that goal. There was much to look forward to in life, and little to regret. Ripleycorp today stood on the firmest financial footing it had known in twenty years, footing that would only get firmer in the future, now that Ripley had replaced Wismer and General Syn as the pacesetting industrial giant in Saint Louis. His profit motive had lost none of its potency. In fact, if he didn't fall asleep soon he'd have to wake Tammy up; she'd be too impressed to be cranky.

The most splendid thing about making money, of course, was the leverage it gave a chap playing the morality market. Devi had lived high on the hog off Rolf's munificence, and she knew it. He'd bought her many fine things. She could scarcely have done better, and ever so easily have done worse. It was a general phenomenon. When he looked back on all the dears he'd shared bliss with in forty years, he could say to himself, in full candor, that he'd been square with every one of them.

.

"Jack. How are you."

"Pretty dang good." It was Thursday evening, a week since Probst's announcement. "Just got back from the Maundy Thursday service at our church. *Beautiful* service. The new choirmaster has a real sense of taste, you should come sometime. I was never much of a church booster really, but I tell you, in the last few years— Do you still go to that little Lutheran church there on—where was it?"

"No," Probst said. "Not since I stopped living with my parents."

"Oh, long time. *Long* time. Huh. Well, listen. You're going to say here I go again with this late-notice business, but—do you have any Easter plans yet?"

"Ah."

"See, Elaine and I were thinking you might be all alone there, or you and Luisa, and. Well, I don't know, it's a family holiday. It's a quiet holiday. Let me just tell you what we're thinking of. We *are* going to go to early church, darn it—*if* we can get the kids out of *bed*—and vee have vays, heh—which would get us home by 10:30 or so. Dinner would be around two, and in the meantime, heh, we're going to have the old egg hunt on the lawn. Elaine and I, we tell the kids they're getting way too old for it, but every year they insist on having it. It's more of a game now, of course. Well, like bridge. They take it real seriously, and I'm usually out there half the night hiding eggs. There's a strategy, you know, whether you're going to psych 'em out by using some of the old standard places, or not. Anyway, if you think this is something Luisa would enjoy, she could—"

"I don't know, Jack—"

"She could come early. Or both of you. Otherwise, about 12:30."

Probst crossed his eyes until they hurt. "I probably should have stopped you sooner, Jack, because unfortunately I do have some—"

"Oh, OK," Jack readily agreed.

Anger leapt in Probst. "I do have some plans. I'm having Chief Jammu here for dinner."

"Hey! From the cover of Time magazine to the table of Martin Probst."

Was Jack insulting him?

"I mean, that's great! Two people like you with such a lot on

· 426 ·

the ball, it's great to think about. We saw your name in that article, by the way. Still doin' the old neighborhood proud. And it's pretty neat, you abandoning ship like that at the last minute. Heckuva surprise. I think you did the right thing, getting on the winning side. I call it the winning side because—remember how I used to be pretty good at calling elections?"

"Yes," Probst said. He had no memory of it.

"I've gotten even better in the last few years. Ninety, ninety-five percent accurate. Anyways, this referention looks like a cinch."

"That's what the surveys would indicate."

"Yep, and you know what made my mind up? I and Elaine always look for you on TV, and we listen to what you say. I thought you had some good arguments—that's Martin, we always say—but what you said on Thursday or whenever. I really liked that."

"Thanks, Jack. I hope you're not the only one."

There was a pause. Probst still had to do the grocery shopping for Sunday before the last stores closed, because it didn't look like his schedule would allow him any time for it in the next two days. "Well," he said.

"You doing anything right now?" Jack said.

"Right now?"

"Sure. We were going to have some coffee and cake."

"Unfortunately—" Probst felt his knees weakening. With sudden resolve, he said, "Listen, Jack. Have you noticed that I haven't had time to accept a single one of your invitations this year?"

"No, Martin." The reply came in a new, sarcastic package. "I hadn't noticed."

They could turn vicious on you, just like that. Jack had done it as a teenager, too, flashed the bitter superiority of the less advantaged.

"I'm just trying to be honest with you," Probst said. "I don't want to waste your time."

"Didn't seem wasted."

"Well, I guess then I don't want you to waste mine."

"OK."

I'm Martin Probst. I'm chairman of Municipal Growth. I'm the builder of the Arch. I'm the friend of Jammu, I'm the Veiled Prophet, and I might just be the new county supervisor if I feel like it. "I'm sorry, Jack. I just think it might be better for both of us. It's no reflection on—"

A dial tone.

"Bastard!" Probst slammed the receiver onto its hook. He collected his keys, coat and shopping list and fled the house before the phone could ring again. You try to be the least bit nice and—

They know what the score is, and still they—

And Barbara thought him spineless, patted him on the cheek. He was going to make her damn sorry she left him. He was in good shape. He was in very good shape.

He was going to broil lamb chops, bake potatoes, make a green salad and use the bottle of balsamic vinegar he'd discovered a week ago in a silver-colored box in the cupboard. It was what his salads lacked which Barbara's hadn't. In the last few weeks he'd begun to eat salads again. His steady diet of restaurant food had been adding a pound to his weight every five or six days, and suddenly he'd run out of places to hide the extra pounds.

He pulled into the Schnucks parking lot, took a cart from the queue outside, and entered the temple of light. He'd been coming here so often that he could now arrange his shopping lists sequentially, according to the aisles in which the foods were shelved. Vegetables fruits deli coffee cereals sauces dressings meat. Was it too early to buy the lamb? Not at all! Meat was tenderized by aging, and besides, by Saturday night Schnucks might have run out. He chose two packages of the best. He thought of the irony of slaughtering innocent lambs to celebrate Easter. He remembered when he'd known Jammu so casually he'd been afraid she was a vegetarian.

The lines at the only two checkout lanes still open curved around an extensive candy display. Probst put a large, hollow chocolate egg in his cart, edible bric-a-brac for Jammu's appreciation. (But who would be fooled by these hollow eggs? Kids, that was who. Kids were fooled. The economy was fueled by the stupidity of kids.) As usual, he'd gotten in the slower of the two lines. (That bastard Jack.) He took a closer look at the graphics in the candy display. The chocolate bunnies came in flimsy cardboard cartons, brightly colored, wrapped in cellophane. Somewhere on every box were the words *hollow milk chocolate* and a list of enes and benzos and phosphos and lactos. But these weren't ordinary bunnies. They were individualized, the box illustrations picking up on the creations within. A bunny on a chocolate motorcycle was identified as Chopper Hopper. A bunny with a magnifying glass carried the moniker Inspector Hector. There was a Jollie Chollie and, with a tennis racket, a Willie Wacket. Manning a chocolate fire engine was a group of bunnies collectively known as Binksville Fire Control; its higher price reflected its greater net weight. There was a Rolly Roller on skates. ("Excuse me!") Super Bunny with a cast brown cape. Busy Bigby. Peter Rabbit—so they remembered Peter Rabbit, did they? And they sold these things to children and did not go to jail. Little Traveler. Parsnip Pete. Horace H. Heffelflopper. ("Excuse me!") McGregor, simply. Mr. Buttons. . . . Probst was pawing through the cartons, seeking out fresh slaps in the face. He found yet another: Timid Timmy. (We are the greatest nation on earth.)

"Excuse me!"

Probst turned towards the voice, which seemed to be addressing him. He saw no one. He looked down and saw a little boy, nine or ten years old. "Yes?" he said.

"Excuse me," the boy said, "are you Mr. Probst?"

"Yes?"

The boy pushed a curling cash register receipt into his hands. "Can I have your autograph?"

Probst groped in his coat pocket for a pen.

21

It had been a hot day, the hotter end of a long warming trend. Downtown, Jammu twisted in her weary swivel chair, trying to shift some of her weight off the calluses that eight months of desk work had inscribed on her ass. She had a backache that neither standing up nor lying down nor even, she imagined, traction could relieve. At night now she was too tired to sleep or to get a kick from any sort of pills, stimulant, narcotic, or depressant. She could feel the chemicals turning and slipping, as if they were bolts and she a nut whose threads were stripped.

But she could function. She was running, at the moment, on the six hours of sleep she'd stolen on Wednesday night. She'd had Martin over to her apartment for fried chicken. As soon as her stomach was full her eyes had closed. She told Martin she had to lie down for a few minutes. She awoke three hours later, a little after midnight, to find him twisting the knob on her television set. She wasn't sick, but she felt as if she'd been sweating out a fever while he sat by her side. Too weak to be embarrassed, she sent him home and slept another three hours, as long as the faint protective smell of his visit lasted. She dressed at 4:00, her heart pounding. There was so much work to do.

She wanted to sleep with him again, just sleep.

The soft air lolling in through the open windows carried with it some of the heat the streets had trapped during the day. Traffic was sparse for a Friday, engines passing singly down below, not in packs. The latest issue of *Time* lay on the floor to her right. Cover headline: THE NEW SPIRIT OF ST. LOUIS. Beneath the headline was a picture of her. Her lips were tight and her eyebrows raised; *Time* gave bizarre expressions to figures it considered bizarre.

> Adroit as Jammu has been in dissociating herself from her Subcontinental origins, a wave of immigrants from the urban centers of Bombay, New Delhi and Madras has washed ashore on the banks of the Mississippi in seeming pursuit of her. The ensuing slew of curry joints, saris, saffron robes, and especially the parade of exotics spotted in the company of Jammu have produced pangs of paranoia in many St. Louisans, including Samuel Norris, the fiery sovereign of St. Louis-based General Synthetics. "There's nothing more dangerous than a political leader who pretends she's not political," says Norris. "Jammu is animated by a deep-seated and foreign socialism, and I see no reason to apologize for being concerned about a non-St. Louisan calling the shots around here."
> Jammu, for her part, sees no reason to apologize . . .

She imagined Brett Stone interviewing Norris for hour after hour, ripening him until at last he yielded one quote mature enough to meet the presses. She could remember when she'd felt a deep-seated and foreign animosity towards journalists. She could remember being a committed socialist, being passionate about a variety of intellectual issues, as Singh still was. She could see that as an adult she still bore the scars of a younger anger, could remember a time when this *Time* article would have delighted her, infuriated her, called up a flood of critical insights. It didn't now. She'd read it twice and thrown it aside. She only wanted to finish her operation. Her unideological, unscientific, inconclusive, wholly personal operation.

.

"We would have been a normal family, I think, if there had been more of us. None of my father's siblings survived adolescence, and my mother had only one sister, my maiden aunt, who was blind. The Army moved my father around until he retired and we settled in Kashmir. By then there was no extended family left at all—and no more Sikhs than there'd ever been in Kashmir. I had a younger brother who died when I was four. My older brother had no thought apart from becoming an officer, the fifth generation of the family to do so, and the last. He was gung-ho. He was sent to a military academy in Delhi while I went to school in town, so I was an only child of sorts. I weighed seventy-eight pounds on my fourteenth birthday. My diet was very rich in butterfat, but it didn't help. My mother worried. I started at the university in 1960, and within three years there'd been martial law in Kashmir and a dismal war with China. My father never left the house. He wore a silk jacket with sleeves he had to roll up half a dozen times. When they were unrolled it looked like a straitjacket waiting to be tied. My brother became a cadet. I hardly remember if there were summers. The streets were cold, winter always seemed to be coming on, troops always freezing in their insufficient bedding up in Ladakh. And I would go home to see my parents and I would be wearing perfectly ordinary clothes, and my mother would chide me.

"Balwan, she would say, it's cold out there. How long have you been clearing your throat like that? Ibraim Masood's second son has tuberculosis of the spine, and you in nothing but flannel. The son spent himself with low women, and now instead of inheriting the rug business he'll be lucky to see his twenty-first birthday. He's been in bed since he lost the use of his legs, and they tried to move him and he bent in two, backwards, Balwan, like a rotten banana. It ruptured his lower bowel, which had to be removed, and now they have him on a plastic bag. And they consider themselves lucky to have that plastic bag! I heard him on Tuesday, twelve degrees of frost and he with his window open shouting to the boys in the street: Don't make the same mistake I did! Don't spend yourself with low women!

"To which I would have to reply, Are you sure this is TB, Motherji?

"And she would say: That lump in your father's abdomen is growing, I feel it every night when he's snoring, and I can tell.

The worst mistake I ever made in my life was sending him to that Anglo doctor Smythe. He wrote a ten-page report on your father's health and it was all just words. But now your father has something to use against me, he waves that silly report in my face and says Smythe gave him a clean bill of health. And meanwhile, whatever it is he has in his stomach is only getting larger. I can feel it. I'm not stupid, no matter what your father says to you and I'm sure he says the worst. That man is very sick. And then there's your brother's growth.

"I would smile and say, Growth?

"In his mouth, she would say. He's always had canker sores, you know, but this is something else. He wouldn't open his mouth the last time I saw him because he doesn't want to face the truth. Some fine, brave officer! He won't even open his mouth for his mother. It's the suicidal business that hurts me, Balwan. They refuse to take their problems seriously, and look what happened to Ibraim Masood's son.

"But I didn't spend myself with low women. My health has always been excellent. As has hers. She's fading now, in the bitterness of justified fears, in the luxury of a fat Army pension. Her health remains good. My brother's was also good, until a sniper shot him in Dacca in 1971. I believe he did have a benign form of herpes. My father's tumor was benign. And still it killed him, in 1964, it hemorrhaged. The magic of suggestion, eh? Which could be your own Webster Groves, your own family. When there are no problems, the problems must be invented. I'm pleased to think my mother talked my father to death. I know she didn't like him."

.

She reached for the telephone, precognitively, grasped the receiver and raised it so quickly that she heard only one grain of its granular ring. "Jammu," she said. The needle of the wiretap detector she'd installed on Monday rested calmly on the zero.

"Can I talk?"

"Yes, Kamala."

"Well, there isn't any sign of her. But I wondered about the house in St. Charles."

"Gopal goes there regularly."

"I have no more ideas then."

"It's not your concern. We'll find her. You catch your plane."

"I hate to go when—"

"Catch your plane."

"Yes, all right."

"And go see my mother when you're back, first thing."

"Yes."

"Good-bye, Kamala."

"Bye, Jammuji."

And so the book on Allied Foods chairman Chester Murphy, opened in September, was closed at last. A visit from a Punjabi trade representative. A doctored X-ray at Barnes. A forged intra-hospital memo and two herbal poisons. And, finally, a desertion of Municipal Growth and the panicked purchase of South Side riverfront property. A neat job, to which Jammu had scarcely needed to pay attention.

Devi, on the other hand, had made a mess of her job. She'd called Jammu on Wednesday, spoken indirectly of blackmail, and hung up before Jammu could even think of having the call traced. She hadn't called again. Jammu lacked the manpower to search every hotel and flophouse in greater St. Louis. She could only ask all her agents to keep their eyes open in the hope that Devi would turn up at one of the meeting places. Gopal periodically checked on the safe houses and the communications warehouse, and Suresh was slowly working through the more promising hotels. But their primary responsibility was to avoid capture themselves. Their caution slowed them down.

It was Singh who should have been hunting for Devi. But even though Martin had become Jammu's ally, Singh continued to devote all his time to Barbara. He'd drawn a distinction between Jammu and the operation and declared his allegiance to the latter. He said Barbara posed a graver threat than Devi did. He said extreme care had to be taken in preparing Barbara for her release. (Jammu wondered what the fuck he was up to over there.) He seldom left that apartment now. He said the operation must cul-minate cleanly, he said Jammu's assumption of power must be seamless. He said they could learn more from Martin's reintro-duction to Barbara than from anything else they'd done in St. Louis. He said all of this easily; his neck wasn't on the line.

Jammu didn't want Barbara reintroduced to Martin. She wanted Barbara to disappear and never return.

This was what Martin wanted, too.

But he might change his mind. He'd changed it once already.

All week Jammu had teetered on the brink of picking up the phone and giving Singh the order. It was true, of course, that America could change one's perspective. In a sparsely populated country the individuality of the victim glared, as did the extremity of the sentence, since death seemed almost an anomaly here. But Jammu had long ago shed her scruples. The old murders hadn't kept her from playing the enlightened leader of St. Louis, and a new one wouldn't keep her from continuing to play the desirable woman Martin felt her to be. She was only afraid that if she gave the order, Singh would not obey.

She couldn't quite see herself doing the job with her own hands. Her role was to stay at her desk, the constant center of the operation. Singh and only Singh had the time, information and imagination to plan an unsuspicious death. But Singh wouldn't do it. Barbara had taken him away. Next Wednesday he would set her free. Then she'd take away Martin as well, and Singh would return to India, and Martin would return to his old life.

"Who cares?" Singh disingenuous. "You have him now, and after Tuesday it won't matter whether you do or don't. Trying to keep him, in fact, is one sure way to guarantee that Barbara makes the connection between you and me."

He gloated. See how neatly it works out? How the operation prohibits selfish deviations? When Jammu was with Martin she was forever thinking: I can't control Singh.

Who cared?

She did. She wanted Martin Probst, the genius of the place to which chance had brought her. She wanted his love and fealty. Martin still couldn't see how she belonged in St. Louis, how she had the right and the means to make a place for herself. He was the key he couldn't see. When he saw himself, if she could make him, then Barbara would be dead to him anyway.

•

Luisa slammed the door behind her, slammed it again to make the bolt catch, and ran down the stairs to the street. Music was blaring in the building next door. Through a set of second-floor windows she could see a big party in progress, a crowd of people older than she but not much older, dancing with beer bottles. She walked up towards Delmar.

Her fight with Duane hadn't lasted long. For a while, in the cold part of the winter, the arguments had gone on for hours, from kitchen to bedroom to hallway; one time she'd had to sleep on the floor in the living room, under coats. Now the fights were short again, like they'd been in the first month or so when she was afraid a single yell would mean going back to her parents. Now a single yell was about all she could stand to invest.

Tonight Duane thought he'd found the answer (he was always thinking he'd found some answer) to how to fight fascism (he didn't know what fascism was; she'd asked him) in extrapolitical (he liked to make up words that weren't in the dictionary) institutions like organized religion, because only a cultural extremism could combat the bourgeois (she told him he'd better stick to foreign languages he could pronounce) liberalism that could, if left unchecked, develop into the kind of nationalistic myopia that developed in Germany (*what??* Suddenly he was talking about Germany in 1933, as if she knew all about it) and took the form of Nazism. She said she didn't understand. He said it was no wonder when she kept interrupting him.

The fight had started because it was Good Friday and he'd decided to give her a religious quiz after dinner. He felt he had the right to give her these quizzes because he was older and more learned. It was the Socratic Method. (He never exactly called himself her mentor, but whenever she wanted to whip up her dislike of him she'd repeat the word in her head: MEN-TOR, MEN-TOR, MENTORMENTORMENT.) Did she believe in God?

"Give me a break, Duane."

Did she believe in the sanctity of human life?

"Yes."

Why?

"Because I'm alive and I like myself."

But that didn't satisfy him. He hemmed and hawed and tried a different approach to making her say what he wanted to hear. (He wanted to hear her be an example of all the things wrong with boozh-wah Webster Groves.) And about three questions into the abortion quiz (it was going to turn out to be somehow hypocritical to be pro-choice) she threw a glass of milk at him. He sat there nodding, indulgent and furious, while she put her sweatshirt on.

She went into Streetside Records. An oldie was playing on the store stereo ("Jackie Blue"?), and graying men in beards and army jackets were pawing through the bins. There used to be about twenty groups and singers whose records Luisa would check on whenever she went to record stores, to see if anything new or pirated or live had arrived. Now there were only about fifteen. She stayed away from the Rolling Stones because Duane admired their honesty and the integrity of their sound. She stayed away from the Talking Heads because Duane had interpreted all their lyrics for her, and from The Clash because whenever Duane played them he made her be quiet. She stayed away from the Eurythmics just because Duane liked them.

Having picked out the new Elvis Costello record (in Duane's opinion Elvis had gone seriously down the tubes) she decided she didn't want to lug it around. She put it back and left the store and headed up Delmar in the good direction, towards Clayton. It was a night almost warm enough for a prom. She thought of the mini-quiz Duane had conducted on the topic of deodorant use. She gave a little laugh. She took a Marlboro Light out of her purse and gave another little laugh. The laughs were really just twitches, something slipping, in her chest.

Why couldn't she have held out just a tiny bit longer?

If she hadn't started to smoke after Christmas, when the cigarettes were around, she wouldn't be doing it now; in a moment of health consciousness one day in February, Duane himself had quit. She could probably quit now, too, but she didn't feel like it as long as she lived with him, and she wasn't positive she'd feel like it afterwards either. She'd started because everything made her nervous, the fights, the whole situation. She was even more nervous now.

In six months she'd be living in Stanford, California. If she hadn't met Duane, if she'd only managed to negotiate her last year in high school without him, she'd be looking forward to college. Now she couldn't. Duane had spoiled the mystique, spoiled it as surely as he'd be writing his own applications in the fall, ready to go have himself a good college experience or a good art school experience, as he'd probably never really doubted he would. He was flexible. He quit smoking and didn't cheat. While he and Luisa were being sad and lonely together, he was also assembling an exhibition of photographs that everybody loved. He had attention left over to watch out for himself. He was strong because his family was supposedly happy and well adjusted (it didn't matter that he and she both knew it was actually scary and diseased).

While he was at it, he'd also guaranteed that Luisa wouldn't find her dream man at college. She'd never find him. She didn't believe in him anymore. And now that she'd lived on her own, in an apartment, that adventure was spoiled, too.

Who would drive her to college? She'd probably take a plane.

And no one in the world would understand. She didn't rule out the possibility that someday she might be happy and successful, maybe even married, though right now she couldn't begin to imagine how that would happen. But no one could ever know how different things might have been if she'd held out a tiny bit longer. She couldn't even put her finger on what she'd had which was lost now. It had something to do with her parents, with her mother who'd trusted her, and with her father who'd tried in his own way to warn her about Duane. Her parents were separated now. Her mother had left town and seemed to have no intention of returning.

I'm very, very, very disappointed in you.

She threw the remains of the cigarette into a sewer. The world had changed, and it wasn't just Duane's spoiling of it. Suddenly she was living in a new world made for people like him, for people who could despise it and succeed in it anyway, and for people who could use computers (all the classes at school except the seniors were learning to use them; she'd probably learn at Stanford, but all her life she'd carry the knowledge that she'd learned late and that once upon a time computer-lovers were gross) and for people who couldn't remember that downtown St. Louis had ever been anything but a place to shop and eat lunch, who didn't care that once there'd only been an Arch which her father had built, for people who didn't care enough to have fights.

Somehow it was she who'd spoiled things.

She could see the stoplight at the intersection with Big Bend, the road to Webster Groves. She wanted to go home. She'd changed her mind. But there was no home to go to. Her own parents had defected to the newness of it all. Her mother's letters and phone calls were gay and uncritical. Her father had a harder time acting modern, but he was doing his best. She'd seen him leave the gallery with Chief Jammu, and the next thing she heard was newscasters talking about the new Martin Probst. She hated the smiles on his face. She hated everything the world seemed to love. She wished her father would yell at her again and let her cry.

.

What interested Barbara, as she lay awake missing her putative lover, was how very little was different. She'd exchanged one prison for another. She was still far from her daughter. John still loved her, and she still didn't love him, not even after the conversion to honesty and ordinariness he'd undergone for her sake. She remained, yours painfully, Barbara. If ever there had been such a thing as kindred souls, then John was hers. So she liked him, for the likeness, not loving him, as she loved Martin, seldom liking him. Between heart and mind was a fracture not even sex, especially not sex, the push of cunt and cock, could mend.

It would disappoint John. He seemed to be working under a self-imposed deadline, increasing the tempo of his disclosures and narratives almost hourly. Or maybe it wasn't a deadline but a sense of dramatic climax which he believed she could share. She remembered how Martin used to work so conscientiously to make her come. He'd increase his speed, increasing it more when he thought she was almost there. If she was, it helped. If she wasn't, it only hurt, as if nerves had no function beyond reporting contact and pain, heat and cold, pressure. She wanted to come, she had no earthly reason not to. But she couldn't.

22

The national press arrived in a stream that widened from a trickle on Thursday to a flood on Saturday, in numbers hitherto seen only in Octobers when the Cards had reached the World Series. CBS, NBC, ABC, CNN and NPR had sent big names. All the nation's major papers found reporters to spare for St. Louis that weekend, and many minor papers did, too. The Wichita *Eagle-Beacon* and the Toledo *Blade*, the Little Rock *Gazette* and the Youngstown *Vindicator*. Internationally, the Toronto *Star* and *L'Express* of Paris had correspondents on hand, and a German crew from Norddeutscher Rundfunk stopped in long enough to be counted and, laughing, to unpack a video camera at one of the baggage-claim carrousels in Lambert Airport.

The network crews were hosted and herded by their local affiliates. The men and women from the large-circulation dailies, all of whom had covered events in St. Louis before, claimed the interviews they'd reserved in advance and set about writing stories from premeditated angles.

The lesser newspeople weren't sure what to do. They'd been assigned to cover the goings-on in St. Louis. But what was going on? All anyone could say for sure was that the police chief was a female of Indian extraction named S. Jammu.

Cradling this knowledge and hoping for a chance to talk to

her, small units of reporters began to appear in the dim cubical vestibule of police headquarters, where the guard, austerely denying them entry to the elevator, directed them to the information officer down the dim hall to their right. After the first twenty inquiries, it dawned on this officer that special circumstances were the order of the weekend; he phoned upstairs and received instructions to send the visitors across the street to the PR director's office at City Hall. There they helped themselves to stacks of press releases and three-color brochures on glossy paper, free coffee and doughnuts, a twenty-minute documentary film on the reorganization and current practices of the St. Louis Police Department, unlimited access to Jammu's right-hand officer Rollie Smith, and lottery blanks for the drawing to be held on Sunday morning to determine which thirty-six reporters, in groups of twelve, would be granted twenty-minute interviews on Monday morning with the great lady herself.

As a consolation prize the others would get passes to the press conference she was holding on Monday evening.

The PR director, noting what a marvelously vital and multi-faceted place St. Louis had become, urged the out-of-towners to wander about, acquaint themselves with the city's layout, and sample such pleasures and edifications as appealed to them. Interested parties were told which bars and restaurants the local press corps frequented. To the younger female reporters the word was dropped that senior *Post-Dispatch* editor Joe Feig was throwing a Tex-Mex fiesta on Saturday night in his Webster Groves home, nothing formal, come as you are, byob, strictly private, but feel free to crash.

The real newshounds could refer to a three-page list of special events scheduled for the upcoming days and plan to cover whatever they considered most newsworthy. The list included the grand opening of a string of boutiques and bistros in the exciting Laclede's Landing area; a nonstop Lasarium program at the Planetarium entitled "The City and the Stars"; a pops concert in the fine all-purpose Stadium featuring music by Missouri composers; the maiden voyage on Sunday of the completely rebuilt *Admiral*, St. Louis's unique and enormous aluminum-plated Mississippi-cruising pleasure palace; the third and final referendum debate between Mayor Peter

D. Wesley and Citizen John Holmes; the opening at 3:00 p.m. Tuesday of an Election Information Center at Kiel Auditorium, free admission to all holders of press cards; and, finally, St. Louis Night.

St. Louis Night was a gala extravaganza to be held from 6:00 until midnight on Tuesday. All of downtown St. Louis would be lit up in celebration of itself. Three soundstages would provide continuous live music and laughter, including appearances by Bob Hope, Dionne Warwick, and the pop group Crosby, Stills & Nash. A dixieland band and an oompah band would rove the streets, spreading good cheer. Favorite sports personalities from the Cardinals, Blues and Big Red would hold autograph sessions. Fifteen of the city's top restaurants would open sidewalk cafés and also booths at which their wares could be sampled by the spoon or by the cup. At midnight a Grucci family fireworks display would cap the festivities. St. Louis Night would unfold regardless of the outcome of the special election. In the event of rain, tents would be erected on the Mall.

Highlights, tabulations and analyses of the special election would become available in printed form at the Election Information Center at 10:00 a.m. on Wednesday.

Insiders could hardly fail to see the thinking behind all these activities. Tuesday's election promised to be a laugher. The most conservative local pollsters projected that the merger would pass in the city by a four-to-one margin, and in the county by three to one or better, depending on which way the many undecideds went. At this stage of the game, only a public-relations catastrophe of the first order could alter the outcome.

Yet an idle brain is the Devil's workshop. Within hours of arriving, every reporter had fired off to his or her editors a story about the St. Louis equivalent of Amsterdam's brothels or Berlin's Wall. *Chief Jammu is a woman driven* and *Chief Jammu is a woman with a vision* were the two most common lead-paragraph disclosures greeting readers the next day, and as substantiation the reporter would offer his or her top choices from the sayings and confessions of Jammu collected in Handout #24 at City Hall. But after they'd cashed in this journalistic blue chip, the more bored reporters might have sent out feelers of their own, might have spoken with disgruntled cubs and searched back issues of the local papers for dissenting voices. Naturally, if the man from the Fresno *Bee* were to find anything, the news wouldn't reach many ears. But if Erik Tannenberg of *The New York Times*, for example, began turning over large stones and discovered something ugly or even simply peculiar underneath one of them, the consequences for Jammu, the pro-merger campaign, and the city as a whole could be most painful.

There was the little matter of the nine black families illegally occupying a pair of four-bedroom homes in Chesterfield. A removal agency in the employ of Urban Hope had displaced the families from their North Side homes without finesse or compassion. As restless and downtrodden Americans have been doing for two centuries, the families headed west. Construction on the Chesterfield homes had proceeded to the point of drywalling before the builder went bankrupt. Ownership had passed, by default, into the hands of a bank of which Chuck Meisner was director. Happily, the homes were situated in a remote corner of West County accessible only by way of Fern Hill Drive, the new street. Since no one yet lived on Fern Hill Drive, and since Meisner had financed the hasty installation of an eight-foot fence around the entire construction area, the families' presence had not become public knowledge. They'd boarded up the windows and barricaded the doors. They appeared to have enough water to hold out for several weeks. They had plenty of food as well, in the form of the sacks of flour and rice which the Allied Food Corporation had quietly been selling in East St. Louis at a large discount because of unacceptable levels of ethylene dibromide. Armed with shotguns, carbines and a small cannon, the squatters were being held under discreet siege by Missouri state troopers and St. Louis city police, the involvement of the latter rendered legal by direct orders from Missouri's governor. Negotiations had proved fruitless. The families were offered first-class housing in a public project, immunity from prosecution, and a sizable cash damages award. Incredibly, they declined. Their leader turned out to be Benjamin Brown, perennial 21st Ward aldermanic candidate on the Socialist Workers Party ticket. Brown refused to resume negotiations until he'd been given a chance to speak to the media. The siege force requested time to mull this over. It appeared likely that no decision would be reached before Wednesday. Meisner spent the weekend arranging new conduits for the inconveniently large campaign donations his banks wished to make to fund the last-minute pro-merger television blitz.

There was also the little matter of East St. Louis, Illinois. The crime situation on that side of the river had gotten out of hand. It was, to be sure, common knowledge that under Jammu's administration the city of St. Louis had grown markedly less hospitable to bookies, pimps, narcotics dealers and their victims, and that some of these individuals had moved east. The *Globe-Democrat* had printed an editorial lamenting the deterioration of law and order in East St. Louis (not that law and order had ever been that municipality's long suit) and expressing the hope that those people might at last find the courage to face up to their very real problems. But no *Globe* reporter had actually seen the situation firsthand. Nor had any other reporters. People who went to East St. Louis often got shot, and this was a risk that members of the Missouri journalistic community were in no special hurry to take. Illinois was a totally different state, after all. An investigation could wait until after the election on the western side of the river had been covered and analyzed.

There were other matters. Acting on a tip from a Washington University professor of law, a researcher at KSLX-TV had turned up a slight constitutional hitch in the real-estate transactions tax approved by city voters in November. The law apparently could, if challenged, be struck down by an unsympathetic court—for instance, by the conservative Missouri State Supreme Court. But no KSLX reporters were willing to write the information into a story. And when the researcher thereupon wrote it up herself, station executives close to general manager James Hutchinson delayed its airing for more than a week, penciling it in for broadcast on Tuesday, after the polls closed.

Rumor also had it that a private detective agency was compiling a massive dossier on Chief Jammu and her allies, with evidence suggesting that the Chief's rise to power owed less to her popularity and more to crass horsetrading than was generally supposed.

Barroom cynics maintained that the incorruptible Martin Probst had switched sides on the referendum solely in exchange for sexual favors from a certain somebody in whose cruiser he had been seen to ride.

And then there were the Osage Warriors, those local terrorists who had made the national news repeatedly in the fall and winter. Now their attacks had simply ceased, and investigations by the police and the FBI had turned up no substantial leads. If their sudden appearance had been surprising, their disappearance was even more so. What had it all meant? County conservatives were beginning to wonder why an armed revolutionary group should have tailored its battle plan to suit so neatly the political needs of Jammu and the pro-merger forces.

But the fourth estate heard none of this. It was Saturday, March 31, and the only sounds in the city were the applause and calliopes of special events and the clamor of the fêtes to which the major media representatives had been treated.

Late Saturday afternoon a hostage situation developed at a Pizza Hut in Dallas. Many of the reporters decamped for Texas. But many remained. There was nothing to do but see the sights and praise them. On the streets, in the seductive spring twilight, phrases whispered provocatively. *The new spirit of St. Louis . . . Farewell to the blues . . . Arch-rivals no more . . . A great Indian chief . . . A classic example of wise urban planning . . . The cardinal virtues . . . Delightful mix of old and new . . . First truly modern city in the Midwest . . .* And then from a hundred hotel rooms, later in the evening, came the impassioned sounds of typing. A new city, a new national image, was being conceived in the night.

Why us?

Those who might once have asked the question, in the rubble of their late great city, now saw the prospect of a more satisfactory fate, the elimination of the political split which for over a century had halted St. Louis's progress towards greatness. St. Louis had stepped into the limelight. It had cured its ills. Against the odds and contrary to expectations, it was making something of itself.

The local prophets were in twenty-seventh heaven.

But the city? Its self-pitying, self-exalting essence? That part of the place which would not forget and which had asked, Why us?

It was dead. Prosperity, Jammu, and national attention had

killed it. St. Louis was just another success story now, happy in the one-dimensional way that all thriving cities are. If it had ever had anything extraordinary to tell the country, anything admonishing or inspiring, it would say it no more.

Oh, St. Louis. Did you ever really believe that Memphis had no history? That citizens of Omaha considered themselves unexceptional? Were you ever really so vain that you hoped New York might one day concede that, for all its splendor, it could never match your tragic glory?

How could you have thought the world might care what became of you?

.

Herb Pokorny had laid off all his extra help and driven his family out for a weekend of relaxation at Lake St. Louis. He didn't stay there. Sam Norris had gone to Lambert with a briefcase chained to his wrist and caught a plane to Washington. He, likewise, didn't stay there. By noon on Saturday they were both in St. Louis, with all the pertinent files and instruments stored in the back of Herb's souped-up station wagon, the color and plates of which had been changed on Friday night.

Herb had cracked the last nut, the mystery of where all the Indians were concealing themselves, their weapons, their receivers and their records. The break had come very late, by process of elimination. After wasting upwards of four hundred man-hours engaging in surveillance on the residences of all the likely aliens and tailing the likeliest ones to see where they'd lead, he'd realized that once again Asha Hammaker was the key. The Indians could only be hiding in Hammaker-owned properties.

Sam and Herb now had a complete catalogue of those properties. The list was long, but not too long. In three days, four days max, they'd be able to scout and search every one of them.

Sam gave no thought to sleep. Every hour counted, what with Jammu already beginning to bail out. To date, she'd sent home five of her operatives and had tried to send a sixth, the girl, Devi Madan.

Herb had photographs of the two men with Madan at the airport, and would have had the girl herself if she hadn't, as he told Sam, pulled a gun on him.

So Sam knew Jammu was sending them home. But he also

knew his quarry's psychology. She wasn't secure enough to let go of everyone and all her tools. Maybe on Wednesday she would be. But on Wednesday the game would be up. They'd have worked through the list of properties.

On Saturday afternoon they scored on item one, an eleven-acre tract along the Meramec River in Jefferson County. Searching the wooded ground methodically, they turned up the trace of an old road. Fifty yards from the river, by the side of the trace, they found three crates of cordite and a box of caps under a heavy tarpaulin. The explosives matched the description of those used in the stadium scare. It was a cold scent, but a scent nonetheless. Herb figured there might be other evidence on the property, but it would have to wait.

The next stop was in St. Charles County. Four and a half acres. Developed. This turned out to mean a secluded farmhouse set into a hill off a gravel county road. Dusk fell while they watched it. In an hour, one vehicle came by on the road, an old man on a tractor. They moved in. Sam had a heavy outer heart, his pistol in its shoulder holster.

They observed fresh tire tracks on the driveway, but the garage was empty. They broke into the house and found a smell of fried onions and cumin. The only furnishings in the place were mattresses and blankets. The refrigerator was running. Vegetables in it. Herb pulled open the fruit drawer and let out an uncharacteristic gasp. There was a machine pistol in the parsley.

A car was coming up the driveway, flashing blue lights in the kitchen windows. Too late, Sam and Herb noticed the blinking red eye in the living-room thermostat and realized the place was burglar-proofed.

It took them two hours to talk themselves out of the St. Charles police station, with a Thursday court date. A St. Charles squad car escorted them to the county limits. But it was only a small delay. When the squad car turned around, they doubled back to the house on the hill, found it unguarded, clipped the power line where it entered on the side, and went back in.

·

Probst hadn't slept well. Upset by the humid, changing weather, he'd tossed in the grip of a dream that felt like awakeness, interminable variations on the concept of opinion polls in which each part of his body had a percentage attached to it, meaninglessly, his legs 80 percent and stiff, his back a knotted 49 percent, his swollen eyes coming in at 22 percent each, and so on through the unraveling of the night.

At sunrise the bells at Mary Queen of Peace had rung in Easter and proceeded, all morning, to repeat the announcement. Trees were budding in a green fog. It was also April Fools' Day. The blasphemy of the coincidence had been shooting little spitball-like jokes into Probst's head. The tomb is empty? Oh. April Fools'.

He wasn't a churchgoer, of course, but he'd long allowed the Resurrection a certain margin of credence, maybe 37 percent in a random sampling of his mind's constituents. Faith was a ticket, and he split his. An event like the creation of Eden scored a zero, while the parting of the Red Sea polled a solid 60 percent, carrying easily. The sea had parted for Moses but swallowed the chariots. The idea of a people being Chosen had the ring of truth, as did the entire Old Testament, whereas the New had the flat clank of the robotic young men and women with leaflets who bothered people on the streets downtown. Probst didn't believe in God. Fortunately a comfortable silence on the matter had surrounded him for all his adult life. Men might discuss politics at Probst & Company, but never religion. At home, Barbara was the warden of the silence. "God?" she wouldn't say. "Don't be silly," she wouldn't add.

He heard the toilet flush and the bathroom door open. Jammu appeared in the kitchen doorway, stopping before she entered. For half an hour she'd been hanging in doorways and sticking close to walls, like a small animal that shuns open spaces for fear of predators. She was shy today, and rather pretty, in new jeans, a lavender cashmere cardigan with mother-of-pearl buttons, and only a bra underneath, the straps of which raised faint boundaries fencing the meadows of her back from the slopes of her shoulders and sides. She flipped through the scraps and cards on the refrigerator door, neither idle nor overcurious. Probst, soaping his hands at the sink, didn't worry about what she'd see. He'd removed the more visible evidence of Barbara from all the downstairs rooms. And from the bedroom.

"Do you need some help?" Jammu said.

He pushed the pan of lamb chops under the broiler element and noted the time: 2:38. Even on holidays he didn't like to eat dinner this early, but Jammu had functions to attend in the evening. "No," he said. "Thank you. You can sit down."

She strolled into the breakfast room, changing it as she went, shedding a light whose wavelength only Probst was equipped to see, revealing force vectors in the furniture and a saturation in the blueness of the curtains' piping. He joined her at the windows. In the driveway, losing its sheen to the mist, stood the unmarked car she'd driven. Mohnwirbel had gone to Illinois for the holiday. Probst suspected there was some woman he saw over there.

"We bought the house for the yard," he said. "In another couple of weeks you'll see why."

Jammu gazed coolly at the flower bed where Norris and Pokorny had appeared a month earlier. A gap in the daffodils marked the spot. Staring out into the static yard, Probst remembered the one or two lucky Sunday afternoons a year when Ginny and his parents had all happened to be out and he, as a teenager, had had their small house completely to himself. The sky and world lapped against it. He stood looking out window after window in an expectancy larger than boredom, more mysterious, and needing an object. Was this how Barbara had felt every weekday of her married life? Was this where John Nissing came in?

Jammu's arm brushed his. A clean coconutty shampoo smell rose from her hair. She looked up at him just as he leaned, without strain, and slipped his arms under hers. She shook her hair back and looked past him in the last second before he placed his lips on hers and realized he was finally kissing her.

She turned her head back and forth, presenting her nose, her forehead and her eyes to his lips, and her fingers combed through his hair, pulling him down to kiss her harder. The cashmere was warm and shifted on her skin, bunching at her straps. Her breasts flattened softly, through cashmere, against his chest while her mouth, a busy metaphor of hunger, opened and closed. He raised one of his hands and filled it with her hair, her personal hair. He drew her head away from his to see her face. She swallowed and released a breath, coming up for air, and something popped. It was the lamb under the broiler. Probst pulled away.

Jammu laughed voicelessly, bending over a little. "I'm very hungry." She laughed again. It was an aspirated smile. "And I've brought you something."

He made his way back to the oven. "What is it?"

"A surprise. You'll see."

He turned the chops and opened the refrigerator for the salad. He tried to hand the teakwood bowl to Jammu, but she stepped around it, pressing him into the refrigerator. Its light, which smelled like pickles, glared down into his eyes. Her tongue opened his lips and brought the sweet tastelessness of her mouth into his. Did she want to do it right here on the floor while the ketchup and mayonnaise watched? He was willing. But she backed away, with a glance at the oven. "You're going to have a fire in here."

They ate in the dining room. The food tasted good, but not as good as the feeling of power he had now: she wouldn't escape the house without making love. She knew it, too. Their forks clattered in a chaste somberness. Separated by a corner of the table, their bodies couldn't feel what their minds knew for certain, where their love would lead them as soon as they touched again.

She told him how she would bring economics to bear on the close-in suburbs of Maplewood, Affton, Richmond Heights and University City, Ferguson, Bellefontaine Neighbors, Jennings and others to force them to accept outright annexation by St. Louis, once the merger had paved the way. "Because the referendum per se does nothing to relieve the city's lack of land," she said. "The shortage is already critical."

"So you're going to make Webster Groves a semi-autonomous part of St. Louis." Probst filled her wineglass. "The Family of St. Louis." He grimaced. "I can already hear Pete Wesley with a slogan like that in his mouth."

"You really don't like him, do you?"

"I can't stand him."

Jammu nodded ambiguously.

"What kind of terms are the two of you on?" he asked.

She turned to the windows. "You mean, what kind of woman am I?"

"Not exactly . . ."

"Wesley didn't consider me attractive."

"More fool he."

"But if he had, and if I needed to, I'd have slept with him."

Probst was appalled.

She seemed to observe this with satisfaction. "I told you I wasn't pure."

His voice grew chalky. "So who've you done it with?"

"No one. But that was mere chance."

Probst set his fork down and stared at the peppery pools of juice on his plate.

"Don't be dramatic, Martin. I'm not the married one here."

"You want me to drag my wife into this."

"Of course."

"You want me to divorce her."

"Don't you want to?"

"Yes."

She tipped her chair onto two legs. "Oh, I know. This is horribly unbecoming of me."

"No, it's natural."

"Well. Where is she?"

"In New York," he recited. "With someone you've met. Remember John Nissing?"

She frowned. "Who?"

"John Nissing, the cosmopolitan. Of PD Magazine fame."

"Yes, yes." She was squinting at something unpleasant. "But you didn't mention that."

"Can you blame me? We'd only just— What is it?"

Her frown was deepening. Outside, a car passed on the wet street. "Nissing is a homosexual," she said.

Probst couldn't help chuckling. "I doubt it."

"You haven't been out to dinner with him and his gay lover."

"What?"

"Are you in communication with her? Does she call? Have you seen her with him?"

"Yes," he said. "We talk. She seems happy. Happy and busy."

Jammu shrugged. "Well. You never know. But from everything I saw of the man I'd be very surprised if this turns out to be a long-term understanding." She shook her head, puzzled. "It's strange. I don't often misjudge people this badly."

"Maybe we're talking about two different Nissings."

"Maybe. Or two different sides of him."

Probst didn't believe Barbara was in trouble, but he begrudged her the very possibility. He didn't want a disaster to complicate his life, and he didn't want Barbara pathetic and remorseful and returning home to make him feel guilty about throwing her over, which was what he was going to do no matter what. He was through with guilt. He'd forgiven her. He'd removed her from his life.

Jammu was twirling her glass sadly by its stem. Probst wished there were some way to assure her he wouldn't renege on his commitment to her. But there was no way. He couldn't prove it until the time came. He reached and raised her chin with his thumb, something he'd seen done in movies. "You can sound so tough," he said.

"I am tough." She smiled startlingly, at a wall. "I'm just out of my element here. I've never—oh."

"Never what," he fished.

"I feel great, Martin. I do feel great."

Her tone would not have been much different if she'd said she felt sick, Martin, she did feel sick. But he felt a little sick himself. The surrender to love, at his age, pulled certain muscles in the stomach and the neck, muscles connecting the will to the frame, because there was another, more final surrender which they'd already contracted to resist.

He cleared the table. In the kitchen he turned on the coffee maker and took the chocolate egg out of a cabinet. He brought it back to the table.

"Happy Easter," he said.

"Happy Easter yourself." She pushed a large brown envelope across the table to him. She tested the egg's weight.

"Real imitation milk chocolate," he said, raising the envelope. It wasn't sealed. "This is the surprise?"

"Yes."

He peered in and saw signatures, hundreds of signatures, and his name in capital letters.

"They're yours if you want them," she said. "The filing deadline is Friday noon. I think you should run."

He was swept up in a rush of passion, pure transparent happy passion, as he drew the petitions from the envelope and read the hundreds of names in hundreds of handwritings, and one name, his own, at the top of every page. FOR THE OFFICE OF SUPERVISOR, ST. LOUIS COUNTY. The woman in the lavender cardigan was peeling foil off the egg. He drank her in small sips. He would run. With her helping him, he'd win. He'd marry her. And then see what Brett Stone had to say.

But after her second cup of coffee Jammu stood up and, leaving the dining room, said she had to go.

It was four o'clock. Rain was ticking on the storm windows.

"I can't, Martin," she was saying. "I really shouldn't. You know the kind of schedule I have."

She was fetching her trench coat from the closet for herself. She was putting it on. She was in the living room, speaking loudly for some reason. Probst hadn't left the table. Each of his fifty years of unblemished right living hung from his limbs, his shoulders and his hands. This was how it felt to sit on heavy Jupiter. Where was the woman who would let him shed the weight?

She was bending over to kiss him good-bye.

·

At six, in a booth against which rain pelted steadily, Jammu placed a call. "It's me," she said.

"Yes."

"Did you hear?"

"No. I told you it's been no use listening. That mike has a range of two meters."

"Well: forget the subjective correlative."

"Poor you."

"I'm only calling because I thought you wanted to know. For reasons of science. He switched on the merger, but not on Barbara. He's running for supervisor but he won't touch me."

"You must not have tried very hard."

"I tried hard enough. So now you know. It's only a question of her release."

"Yes. Tuesday after sundown. I'm driving her to New York. The world should begin hearing from her sometime Thursday morning."

"Poor you."

Jammu hung up. Martin's semen was falling into her under-wear. Cars wallowed by on Manchester Road, their taillights smearing in the glass of the booth. The plan was laid. She'd decided to do it herself. She was giving Singh the best reason he'd ever had for fleeing a country. And maybe it was the scientific sin of falsifying his data on the Probsts, or maybe her sudden betrayal of her lifelong partner in crime; but to look at her standing in the phone booth, twisting her hair and trembling, one might almost have thought she'd never killed anyone before.

23

Tuesday morning, eight o'clock. RC sat on the living-room sofa watching *Today* and eating Cheerios. Annie came out of the kitchen in a yellow rain slicker. Robbie wore a red Big Red poncho. They kissed RC good-bye.

   Today was reporting live from St. Louis, from Webster Groves, no less. It focussed on a boxy Lincoln joining a line of parked cars in the playground of a red brick school. An umbrella got out of the car, followed by Martin Probst. *Today* zoomed in. Around Probst large cardboard yes's and no's bobbed on sticks. He seemed to recognize *Today* and went out of his way to meet it. Lesser men and women with cameras fell away behind him, the pros and cons craned their wooden necks, and out of *Today* came an all-weather microphone held by a hand with raw skin and purple knuckles. Probst made a joke. Smiles opened in the rain. And what about that rain? Probst didn't think it would be much of a factor in the election. He excused himself; he had to perform his patriotic duty. The crowd parted for him and his umbrella, and *Today*'s gaze lingered on him before shifting, by way of a short and zany interlude of visual static, to a nationally known face. The black Arch behind her had lost its crown in low clouds. What about that rain? The Chief's joke was even funnier than Probst's. And now back to New York.

RC turned off the set and stared at the screen, trying to shake the desolation of *Today*. He'd been feeling lonely and stunned on and off for two weeks now, ever since Clarence and Kate and the boys had left St. Louis. After more than forty years, they'd pulled up their roots and moved to Minneapolis, just like that. Clarence's cousin Jerome had invited him to move north and buy into his contracting firm, and before he had a chance to say no or maybe not, the Gallo Company, his main South Side competition, offered to buy him out completely on advantageous terms. After six hours on the market his four-bedroom house was sold to a white family of three, and on the day between the third and fourth quarters he pulled the boys out of the St. Louis school district and whisked them north to suburban Edina. That rhymed with China. RC still couldn't believe they were really gone for good.

He got up and washed the dishes, cleaned his revolver, got dressed and ate a strip of raw bacon (bad, bad habit of his) with some Townhouse crackers. Then he left to vote. He had an appointment at two o'clock to have a mole taken off his back, and then at three his patrol shift started. On the sidewalk in front of his building he passed a blond kid with a camera who looked vaguely familiar. RC got halfway through the word "Hello" before the kid's swift "How's it going?" cut him off.

.

All Sunday, all Monday, picking locks and scaling walls, they ran into the same phenomenon at every turn: a fresh scent, but the quarry vanished. They took fingerprints, but they'd never nail Jammu on fingerprints alone. They turned up weapons, food, clothing, hair dye, gas masks, burglar tools, traces of controlled substances, boxes of radio guts, a miniature forging kit, and some phony IDs: one hundred percent diddly-twat. They killed half of Sunday night staking out a ranch-style house on Highway 141 where lights went on and off behind the curtains and a television flickered, and when they finally broke in, the sum total of the house's contents turned out to be timed lights and a television. *The people had been there.* But the people were gone, as surely as if they'd been warned of the imminence of Sam and Herb's arrival. It didn't seem to matter that Herb's car was clean. It didn't seem to matter that they were working through their catalogue randomly, doubling back and forth across three counties, taking twice as much evasive action as they had to, approaching some of the properties on foot from strange directions, changing course abruptly and returning to places they'd already raided. Despite all these precautions, the Indians were eluding them.

At dawn on Monday they busted into a condo in Brentwood which contained a darkroom rigged for printing microfilm, a bed with sheets still warm under the blankets, and utterly no evidence of a specific and compelling nature. If they'd raided this place on Saturday instead of the place in St. Charles, or on Sunday instead of four homes and two office buildings in neighboring towns, or if they'd raided it even just one hour earlier, they could easily have hit pay dirt. How were the Indians dodging them? How could the conspiracy be closing down with such infernal timing? How could it be closing down, period, when they were dealing with a woman who for eight whole months hadn't gotten through a single day without recourse to her agents? It was driving Sam crazy. He shouldn't ever have listened to Herb. They should have sent every man they had into all the properties in the catalogue at the same hour on Saturday. But it was too late now. They had to keep going.

By Tuesday morning their stock of unhit targets had dwindled to three commercial properties, two in the county and one across the river. The printout listed the first one as undeveloped, but when they got there they saw a two-story warehouse behind a fence off a Mopac spur and some rusty sidings. Gray, cracking sheets of plywood had warped away from the nails fastening them to the building's doors and windows; on the roof, aluminum and brazen, stood three brand spanking new radio antennas. Herb looked at Sam. Sam looked at Herb. This was the communications center they'd been hunting for.

.

Buzz Wismer arrived at his headquarters late in the morning and found his employees curiously transformed. He said good morning to the pretty lobby receptionist and she smiled weakly. He said good morning to a pair of voluble custodians who traded glances in sudden silence as if a ghost had passed through the room.

In the elevator he tried out a few pleasantries on his friend Ed Smetana, and Ed punched the button for the Accounting floor, where he almost never had business. Buzz said good morning to his secretary, and she dove under her desk, groping around near the Dictaphone pedal. He stopped in his private washroom and inspected his face. Same old Buzz. His nose was a little red from the wet wind outside, but then, it usually tended towards the red. He went into his office. A big blue-and-orange Federal Express envelope was lying on his desk. It held a single sheet of paper.

TO: Edmund C. Wismer, Chairman
FROM: Steven Howard Bennett, et al., Stockholders

Buzz skimmed.
Resolved April 2 extraordinary meeting those present included proxies registered mail March 26 54% with deep regret long history of service recent pattern of decisions move of headquarters questionable judgment unfeasible fiscally unrealistic without consulting violation Chapter 25 Corporation bylaws relinquish duties Friday April 6 plenum proxies April 16 to select new chairman and officers . . .

Sinking into his chair, Buzz was young again, skydiving and poor, and he felt the abrupt tug of a golden parachute, the crush of straps across his chest. His secretary was bringing him a glass of water.

.

The trail was so fresh that the rain hadn't even blurred the tire tracks or washed away the muddy footprints on the loading dock. Once again, the footprints were feminine. Herb photographed them and spoke into his pocket recorder. "Eleven-fifteen a.m., now twenty-theven hourth thince we thaw a fresh thet of male printh, the loading-dock door wide open but apparently it'th been clothed judging from the concrete. We enter with flashlighth . . ."

His running commentary was getting on Sam's nerves. More and more Sam questioned whether he'd hired the best St. Louis had to offer.

Whoever had left the footprints had made sure the warehouse

was emptied. In the second-floor office, coaxial antenna cables dangled from the ceiling, pointing obliquely at two flats of Orange Crush cans, yellow junk-food crumbs, a pile of Maxell and Memorex reel-to-reel tape cartons and floppy-disk boxes, a set of fold-up aluminum tables, and some tubular lawn chairs.

"I don't underthtand it."

Sam aimed a gratuitous kick at the sody cans, scattering them across the room. "Well," he said. "I suspect if the materiel ain't here it ain't anyplace. But we got two more properties to try. See if we can't still catch us a couple of personnel."

.

Jammu was at home in her apartment changing out of her smelly interview clothes. She put on a white linen skirt and a white blouse to match her mood, which was bright. She'd even slept a few hours; Devi Madan was out of the country.

Gopal's man Suresh had located her on Sunday afternoon. Registered as Barbara Probst, she'd been staying at the Ramada Inn on I-44 near Peerless Park, out by Weiss Airport. She wasn't in her room when Gopal arrived, so he and Suresh waited in the bathroom for her. Eventually she drove up in a rented car. She entered the motel lobby and then hastened back out. Through the bathroom window Gopal fired at her tires with a silenced automatic, but the angle was wrong and the car was moving. When they followed her, the holiday traffic on I-270 prevented them from forcing her off the road. She reversed her direction on a cloverleaf, drove south ten miles, reversed again, and again, ending up at Lambert just in time to pass through the document checks at the international gate and board a British Airways jet before it took off for London. Under orders to follow her wherever she went, Gopal and Suresh flew to Washington, lucked into a Concorde flight, and reached London just thirty-five minutes after her plane had landed. This morning she was still in England. Gopal and Suresh would kill her when they found her and return directly to Bombay.

The operation was closing like a wound miraculously healed. Of the twenty-one men and women who had followed Jammu's orders in St. Louis, only Singh and Asha remained, and Asha was staying. For the last three days she and her personal maid had been collecting hardware and printed matter from the houses and relay stations and storage facilities. At this moment they were driving south in a borrowed Pevely milk truck to detonate the operation's more damaging side effects in an abandoned lead mine in the Ozarks. Asha was accustomed to manual labor; she'd been running guns when Jammu got to know her in Bombay.

Jammu straightened her white cuffs and parted the curtains on her bedroom window. Singh was due here with a carton of financial records, the only written vestiges of the operation not yet in her apartment. All the paper and magnetic tape now fit easily into two four-drawer file cabinets. You threw away the preparations for an overtaken future.

A fat man in sunglasses was toiling up the alley with a soggy cardboard box. Jammu went to the door.

Singh entered her front door glaring at her, panting, dripping. He'd put on three jackets and two pairs of pants, tucking them neatly under a set of overlarge clothes, and it looked like he'd stuffed a pillow under his shirts as well. Dried spit had caked in the corners of his mouth: the suffering man.

Jammu took the box from him and set it on the floor. "You're going back now to close up that apartment?"

"It's nearly closed," he said. "I've changed a few things."

"In the apartment?"

"In the plan as well. I'm no longer psychopathic or Iranian. I couldn't sustain it."

"*Now* you tell me." Jammu turned in a full circle on her heel. "How long has this been going on?"

"Quite a while. She thinks I'm straight with her now. She feels an allegiance—"

"An affection, an attraction, a tenderness—"

"She won't tell Probst the real story when she gets out. She'll say she's been living in New York with John Nissing. She's that proud. And yes, there's affection."

Jammu stared into his sunglasses. He was crazy to think a plan like this was good enough for her. She'd never met Barbara, but she knew her. She'd ruin everything. The solution was more obvious than ever.

"It made all the more sense," Singh continued, "as soon as

Probst refused to get involved with you sexually. There's no other woman in his life, nothing to make her angry, and certainly no Indian woman to make her suspicious."

"I don't like it."

"I guarantee you this was the only way to play her."

"I don't like it."

"Then you shouldn't have left Bombay."

"You shouldn't have snatched her."

"You might not be winning this election if J hadn't."

"All right." There was nothing more to say. Jammu raised her hands for some kind of farewell contact with him, an embrace or a handshake, but he left her standing. He limped down the stairs, wheezing and obese.

.

Probst was spending the day at the office to keep his mind off the election and to let the company know he was still its president and guiding spirit. He was revising timetables for his first, cautious entry into the downtown building spree, a pair of North Side office projects on which ground would be broken in May. Carmen typed speedily at her desk.

It pleased him to spot in the timetables a number of redundancies and avoidable delays which even Cal Markham had overlooked; it demonstrated that he still had a function in the company and it drove home the reason: he had great intelligence and experience. How easily a man could lose sight of this. How easily, when his home and milieu fell apart, he could disdain the consolations of pure activity, pure work, the advancement of physical and organizational order.

Of course, he could also see that for thirty years he'd worked too hard, could see himself in hindsight as a monstrosity with arms and hands the size of Volkswagens, legs folded like the treads of a bulldozer, and his head, the true temple of the soul, a tiny black raisin on top of it all. He'd failed as a father and husband. But if anyone had ever tried to tell him this he would have shouted them down, since the love he felt for Barbara and Luisa at the office had never waned. He had a heart. All the things he'd been unable to throw away, all the memorabilia and useful spares and fixable wares, these objects and annals of childhood and honeymoon, early and later parenthood—he'd saved them all in the hope of one day finding time to participate more fully in the stages they represented.

But he wouldn't change. He loved Jammu because she accomplished things. With her he'd start afresh, wise enough never to expect the opportunity to resurrect the past. A year from now they'd be living together, not in a house (what did he really care about gardens?) but in a spacious modern condominium on Hanley Road or Kingshighway to which they would both return late in the evening, and in which there would be no junk.

.

All women were equal in the eyes of the airlines, except maybe those with babies or wheelchairs. Floating above the earth, flight attendants brought her pillows, blankets, drinks. The only problem was between flights, when she couldn't tilt her seat back and the ground made her knees wiggle. But all it took to get back in the air was cash, and cash had been as simple as selling most of her strength to the boyfriend of the maid at the Marriott, until suddenly she found herself in Edinburgh with only enough to last through the coming weekend and too few pounds and two silly friends who were trying to kill her. They'd all been flying and flying in a huge misunderstanding. She flew for the pleasure and the dinners in their comprehensible plastic trays, while her friends believed it was a chase. As far as she was concerned, their intent to kill her had merely provided an itinerary.

Now she was home again, bewildering the immigration officer by brushing through the gate and running away and disappointing the cabdriver because she had no suitcase to tip him extra for. There had been bewilderment and disappointment in her friend's eyes in the Edinburgh ladies' room when he'd opened the stall where she'd left her tall boots standing and turned around right into the blade which she, in bare feet, stood holding against his neck. He'd pulled the trigger anyway, and she couldn't be blamed for the gurgling in his windpipe, or for the funny pop the gun made when the other friend came in afterwards and fell to the floor, which was dirty. They were terrorists. If Rolf could have seen her saving her life like that, her cool practicality, he would have been so proud and would have knelt and kissed her hands. But logically she knew she was losing everything. When she shot up she dozed without sleeping, and though they didn't bother her, that gurgle and that pop never left her. They were waiting for her strength to fail. How much misery could a living woman deaden before she stopped wanting to? She remembered when Devi was thirteen on an exciting vacation with her parents when they visited a beauty consultant in Paris and the Alhambra in Spain and the pyramids in Egypt. She'd never seen anything as heavy as the great chops, built by slaves. Now the cabdriver was stopping to let her try her luck with her signature at Webster Groves Trust, where she hoped she had an account and people knew her or at least were trusting. That was all she really wanted, for people to treat her right. Because no one did. Everything was the great chops turned upside down with its point pressing into her.

. . .

Five stories below the windows of Buzz's office, on the drive outside the main entrance, reporters laughed in groups of three and four, making a social event of their siege. Buzz had tried to reach Asha at all the numbers she'd given him. Nobody knew where she was. In his one hour of greatest need she was unavailable. He grew desperate and indiscriminate and tried calling Bev. She didn't answer, though she'd indicated she'd be at home all day, as Miriam Smetana had canceled their luncheon date for reasons unclear at the time. Perhaps the media had been pestering Bev as well and she'd simply unplugged the phone.

. . .

"We'll have to continue this on Thursday," Jammu told her district commanders. Stiffly, the nine majors returned the narrow chairs to their places against the walls and took their leave singly, clogging the doorway like marbles in a funnel.

As she'd expected, Singh was close to the phone in his place across the river. "What now," he said.

"Gopal just called from London. Devi's taken care of, but they got her to talk first, and it sounded like she'd sent a letter to Probst before she left. Probst was fine this morning, but I'm afraid the letter's in his mailbox in Webster Groves."

She waited. In the silence on the line she could feel Singh

thinking, weighing her story and deciding whether to believe her.

"What do you think she said?"

"Any letter at all is bad," Jammu said. "The only way your release of Barbara works is if there's no hitch, no suspicion of any kind."

"This is the last thing I'm doing for you."

"Thanking you in advance, then. But call me at three."

In her purse was a hammer for the deed, and also a revolver in case Singh hadn't really bought the story and hadn't left the apartment. She stopped and told Mrs. Peabody that she was going to lunch with Mrs. Hammaker. Mrs. Peabody told her she must be starving. She went out into the drizzle, unlocked Car One, and drove south to the brewery, where Asha had left a Sentra for her without knowing the reason. Once in the Sentra, she put on a curly red wig. The disguise was token; Singh's building stood on a block where, day or night, she'd never seen another soul.

•

At 2:45 Sam and Herb arrived in East St. Louis. Five minutes later they located the last item in their catalogue, a fireproof storage warehouse. It had no windows, but it did have skylights, in which, from a block away, against rainclouds, they could see light.

As they pulled closer, they saw someone enter.

"That's him!" Sam said. "That's Nissing. They're in there."

Herb parked the station wagon behind a deserted filling station across the street and down a hundred yards. It was the only cover for blocks around, clear out to the surrounding expressways. He and Sam forced entry to the office with a wrecking bar, bringing gray light to bear on plaster rubble, fallen ceiling tiles, roaches, glass daggers, Fram and STP stickers, a 1977 Pennzoil calendar. They carried in two folding chairs. They set up the video camera and the infrared source, aiming both through a chink in the boards on the glassless windows, and while Herb went back out for the thermos and field telephone, Sam peered up the street at the target, a tall and slender building, a castle in this barbarian wilderness. He focussed the camera and settled in to wait. There was no place left to go.

After a late lunch at the local grill with Bob Montgomery, Probst was at his office with the rest of the company, with the draftsmen, clerks and secretaries who were beginning the last leg of their day, their afternoon coffee breaks behind them. He was letting everyone leave thirty minutes early today to give them a jump on the evening rush at the polls, and to judge from the absence of laughter or even conversation leaking into the hall outside his office, they were returning the favor with special diligence. Metal drawers rumbled in the silence as Carmen filed. Probst was proofreading and signing her morning production of letters. Typewriter bells rang faintly in the hall, the patter of rain and keys blending. Someone in narrow heels was walking briskly towards him. The heels reached the carpeting of the outer office and fell silent.

"Oh, Mrs. Probst," Carmen said.

Probst's arms went numb. He stared through the open door to the outer office and saw her shadow, the back of a familiar skirt.

"Hi, is he here?"

"Yes, go right in. Mr. Probst—?" Carmen sang.

"Thank you," Barbara said.

He spun in his chair to the window, and reflected in the glass he saw his wife shut the door behind her, rest a closed umbrella against the wall and stand looking at him, her hands at her sides. "Martin?"

Her real voice was different from her phone voice, more nasal and clipped. He'd forgotten her. He'd been wrong to think she'd have no power over him when she returned.

"Martin, help me."

He spun around.

It wasn't Barbara. It was a woman with Barbara's light hair, her body, her clothes, her hairstyle and posture and something like her fair skin, except where raindrops had eaten it away. Her hands were dark.

She smiled at him hopefully. "I'm back," she said, tossing her raincoat on the coatrack. He shrank away. She sat down on his lap sideways and put her arms around his neck. The arms were damaged, purple and black, with scabs and ulcers and long fingers of green beneath the dark skin. She smelled of rotten perspiration. Her lips touched his like ice. She was Barbara's corpse.

"Who are you?" He tried to stand, dumping her off his lap. She landed in a crouch.

"I'll be yours," she said.

"Out, get out."

"I've been with Rolf," she explained.

Clumsily he put on his coat. Devi Madan. He opened the door and marched past Carmen, and Devi Madan followed.

"Where are we going?" She slipped her arm around his waist.

.

Jammu made her first pass around Singh's building and saw that his car wasn't in the fenced-in lot. He'd gone to Webster Groves. Could he have taken Barbara with him? Hardly likely. She was inside this building, unprotected, and Jammu had time to circle the block once more, to let the criminal pressure build up in her, and to rehearse the scene again. She would give Barbara a chance to speak. One sentence, a few words, enough to fill her killer's ears with the slick, vulnerable intelligence she so hated, and then it was a Beatles song. Bang, bang—

No.

A Country Squire, repainted but inevitably Pokorny's, was parked behind a low boarded-up building across the street. Jammu stepped on the gas, shifting up. She would have done it, but she wouldn't now. She went back to her desk on Clark Avenue.

.

"Don't touch me."

"Martin."

"*Don't touch me.*"

They squared off in the parking lot, on the white football grid of the spaces reserved for Probst's project managers, who were all still out on the job. Devi Madan leaned forward, her eyes wide and more hopeful than ever, with the overexcitement of a friendly dog about to lose control and yelp, and bite. "*Martin.*"

Rain was falling on the outer layer of his hair and draining onto his scalp. He didn't know what to do, but he had to do it quick. The reality of this Indian girl's presence pelted him, sought gaps in his protection, tried to get inside and drench him. He turned away and unlocked his car.

She ran around to the passenger side. "Where are we going?"

"Go away."

"What do you mean?"

"Go anywhere," he said. "You can't be here."

It was too late. Each word they exchanged confirmed her right to speak to him and make demands. He couldn't even tell her to leave without implicating himself. She was in his life.

She looked angrily at the sky, up into the rain pouring down on her eyeglasses. "I'm getting kind of wet." She was so familiar. She's insane, he thought. It made no difference.

"Use your umbrella," he said.

"I left it in your office."

His was in his office, too.

"Hurry up," she said. "Get in."

She knew him. She knew him as surely as if a Hyde-like second Probst had been leading a life with her unbeknownst to the first. He got in the car and leaned across the front seat to raise the lock button on her door. She jumped in and shivered. "Where to?"

Wet clothes, wet skin. Perfume and sweat and cold automotive plastic. Wet exhaust from passing cars. He leaned back and closed his eyes, only dimly aware that he'd made a mistake in letting her into the car. She curled one hand around his neck, laid the other on his leg, and put her mouth to his. Would he kiss her? He was already doing it. The taste of a new mouth didn't surprise him now. Barbara, Barbara, Barbara, Barbara.

In the street a car door opened.

It was the police. Barbara pulled away from Probst, and through the windshield the two of them watched a patrolman cross the street to the precinct house. His companion remained in the squad car and rested his eyes on them uncuriously. Probst gave him a dumb smile. Barbara's face had assumed the blankness of a reasonably law-abiding citizen's. The cop looked away.

Jammu had said Devi Madan was an innocent girl who'd returned to Bombay several weeks ago. Jammu had lied. But Probst loved Jammu. He would be calm. He'd try to help.

He started the engine, backed out, and made a right turn onto Gravois. Two blocks up the street he pulled in alongside the taxi stand outside the National. Old women were wheeling caged groceries away from the automatic doors. He set the brake. "You need money."

"Yes."

He opened his wallet and counted bills. "Here's two hundred twenty." This wasn't enough. He took out his checkbook. She was folding up the bills and tucking them in her purse: just another domestic transaction.

"There's a Boatmen's right over there," he said. "Will a thousand be enough?"

She nodded.

He wrote out the sum in numerals and then in words. He paused. After Barbara had moved out, he'd stopped using their joint account. "Who should I make this out to?"

She was watching a taxi drive away. She didn't bother answering. He penned in the words *Barbara Probst*.

·

Singh had not driven to Webster Groves. He'd merely moved his car to a lot near the river and returned to his apartment on foot. He hadn't for a moment believed there was a letter in Probst's mailbox. Jammu, he expected, would come to East St. Louis and see that his car was gone. She would enter the building planning to murder Barbara and pin the blame on him.

But Jammu had not arrived. He was beginning to wonder if he'd given her too little credit, if perhaps she had no objection to the experiment of releasing Barbara as he'd arranged. Perhaps Devi had sent a letter after all. Then his telephone rang.

"It's me."

"I called at three o'clock," Singh said.

"I was over at your building. Do you have the letter?"

"There wasn't any letter."

"Did you notice who's watching your building?"

"Sure." Singh took a guess: "Our favorite detective."

"You know what this means, don't you?"

"It means it will be trickier getting Barbara out."

"No. It means you kill her."

Singh laughed lightly. "Oh, does it?"

"Yes. How do you think you're going to get her out?"

"The back door, late tonight."

"No way, Singh. Sorry. They'll have the entire area bathed in infrared and a pair of men watching the back side of the building. They know you're in there. They'll stop you if you try to leave with anything more than the shirt on your back. The only way out is empty-handed."

"They'll tail me anyway."

"You think you can't shake them? Don't be modest."

Singh swallowed. Had she known in advance that Pokorny had found out about this building? No. She wouldn't have come over here herself if she'd known Pokorny would be here. Clearly the only thing she'd known for sure was that she wanted Barbara dead.

"This is great," he said.

"Do you think I wanted Pokorny on our ass like this? Do you think I want that woman's body turning up over there? Two miles from my office? I'm telling you, this is the only way to save both our necks—"

Yours and Probst's, Singh thought.

"—You do the job, you take the fall, you get out of the country."

"I could just release her over here."

"Are you serious? Your plan was bad enough without letting her know she'd been in East St. Louis all this time. You can't let her out alive anyplace but New York. And that won't work now."

"Death is messy, Susan. You'll regret it."

•

As she walked up the long driveway she saw a gaunt and red-faced man in the window of a garage in the back yard, on the second floor. He gave her a wave and a friendly smile. She waved back. A friendly smile! She felt better, but she went to the side door of the house so he wouldn't see her. She punched her gloved hand through the window in the door. The flying glass surprised her, which was silly considering that was why she'd punched it. She reached through and turned the bolt. They had a fence to keep out burglars, but they left the gate wide open. One of these days she'd have to fix that.

.

Probst drove aimlessly, following the path of least resistance—straight through green lights, right at red ones, left when he found a left-turn lane empty—while he waited for the turmoil in his head to condense into thought and resolution. The defroster circulated strange perfume through the car. A feeling of deep evil had descended on him as soon as he'd written his wife's name on the check. The feeling intensified his longing for Jammu. He was her accomplice, and he missed her. He loved that she had lied to him about Devi Madan, because it meant she shared the evil. At the same time he wondered if she'd really lied. Maybe she hadn't realized the extent to which Rolf had perverted the girl. Yes. That was it. Rolf had perverted the girl. Yes. And if Jammu was innocent, Probst would love her for that, too. Her childlike purity.

Way up north, on Riverview Drive, where rain blew like blue sand off the flat Mississippi and collected in puddles on the empty bicycle path, he turned on the radio. The many voices of the city urged him south again. He was guilty. He'd betrayed his city. Jack DuChamp had been right to hang up on him on Maundy Thursday. Now at last he felt that it was necessary to go to Jack's house, to pay that long-deferred visit, to hear Jack's judgment on him and see if it was final. He almost hoped that Jack could not forgive him.

.

A woman's place was in the home. A gray Tuesday afternoon, the gutters gulping quietly, swallowing rain. Cigarettes burned in several ashtrays. A cookbook fell open to a cake recipe, everything in its place. Martin would be home, upset, at dinnertime. Men spent half their lives thinking women were a nuisance and the other half thinking they were special. Right now she had to bake him a special treat. The rest of dinner would come in good time. Men liked to come home and smell something baking and hear little splashes upstairs, a sensuous woman in the tub.

She opened all the cabinets and took out the spices and the

silver teaspoons and tablespoons and a colander for sifting. She found a bag of potatoes. They were covered with big white sprouts. Just like men, they couldn't help it—they were *supposed* to act that way—but it could still be disgusting. She looked in every cabinet for the flour. Would wheat germ be OK? She unscrewed the lid and sniffed it and saw some tiny beige worms in the germ. Germs made you sick. She put the jar back and looked everywhere. What did flour come in? Every minute counted if she wanted the cake baking when he came home.

She ran down to the basement, where it seemed she kept many extras, but all the coffee cans were empty. There were piles of boxes spilling onto rows of plastic bags, metal wardrobes, wooden filing cabinets. Spiders grew on the walls, unmoving, like mildew. So many things to digest!

She opened a flat box of pictures in which she looked rather stern. She frowned sternly. The pictures were a manual on how to act if you lived in Webster Groves. How to hold your head when you got out of the car. How to kneel when you cut fresh roses from the garden. How to be a perfect wife. How to take a bath! How to frown in concentration when you baked a cake! How to smoke cigarettes. She had to practice right away. She ran upstairs and came back down with a package. She shook all the cigarettes out and looked into a nearby mirror.

.

When school let out, Luisa saw her friends Edgar Voss and Sara Perkins walking south on Selma, the way they did every day. She hurried to catch up with them. She was going to Clark School to vote.

"Wow, that's right," Sara said. "You're old."

Sara and Edgar were still seventeen, and to prove their irresponsibility they started grilling each other. Sara asked what Afghanistan was. Edgar said it was a territory in Risk, sort of an olive green. He asked her who the state senator from Webster Groves was. She couldn't even make an educated guess. Edgar didn't know either. Luisa didn't know. But a ninth-grader in copper-framed glasses who was passing them on the sidewalk said, "Joyce Freehan," and hiked up his books in embarrassment.

This sounded correct. "He's her son," Edgar told Luisa in a stage whisper. The kid jogged a few steps to put some space between them.

They wanted Luisa to come along with them to Edgar's house to watch *Gilligan's Island* and drink lime Kool-Aid, two activities that seemed to have come into vogue since she stopped spending time with them. She wondered what else was in vogue. Group sex? Riflery? They gave no hint of disappointment when they turned up a side street off Glendale Road and she kept on towards Clark. She watched them shoving each other, playing chicken with the puddles, and not looking back at her. It was just like the day before, when no one at school would comment on her hair, not even Stacy. In a bleak mood on Saturday she'd had it cut very short, shorter than she'd ever worn it before. She was positive everyone had noticed—she looked like a punk where three days earlier she'd looked like Stanford material—and it hurt her that they should be so freaked out they couldn't say anything at all. Maybe they were being delicate because they thought she had emotional problems. But she couldn't have had emotional problems if she tried.

Wet weather didn't stop cigarettes from burning. In war footage soldiers smoked through the muddiest of battle scenes. Luisa wondered if anyone passing in a car now, any of her mother's friends, would recognize her with her glasses and her hair like this, and the cigarette. It wasn't really her friends who hurt her. She herself, when she got home on Saturday and locked herself in the bathroom, had almost cried at the sight. Her scalp showed white all over. Her lenses were coated with soapy light. She looked so strange and old and unhappy. But what really hurt was that the new style matched the inside of her. This was how she'd look on the inside, too, if anyone could see in there.

Worst of all was that Duane had come home with his cameras and said she looked great. She more or less agreed. She wasn't stupid. She wouldn't get a haircut that destroyed her looks. It just seemed unfair that the person who sympathized with her the most was someone she didn't even get along with anymore.

.

"Light rain is falling," Nissing said to Barbara in a calm, accessible voice. "We sit in this room like two lifelong friends, having this last conversation."

Last? She raised herself onto two elbows. "What's going on?"

"I'll tell you, but you should know by now. Can't you feel? In this room that could be anywhere in the world when the rain falls and the afternoon is dark? You've said it yourself. You're still as lonely as you were when you left your husband. Some things can't be changed, and it seems that you are one of them. It was a happy dream for a while, when you'd broken free and everything was new, living in Manhattan or wherever it was, living with a man who understood you. It was fun while it lasted, until the problem of originality put an end to it and you became, conceptually, what you'd actually been all along: just another forty-three-year-old woman who'd left her home for a younger man and a life of more complete self-expression. Just another victim of the age, with too little youth remaining in you to dismiss your entire past as a prelude and then fashion another life. Maybe other women are braver than you, maybe their stories at this point are the stories of looking bravely to an uncertain and difficult future. But other women aren't Barbara Probst, and you don't want to be those other women. And if nothing else you've recognized that the apparent novelty of taking up with me and leaving Webster Groves hasn't been novel at all. The emancipation will begin when you go home. You're telling me, as we sit here, that you've decided to return to St. Louis. Admit it. That's what you've wanted to do all along."

"But not for any reasons like this."

He slowed his words even more. "Are you saying you don't miss your husband and daughter?"

She shook her head. "I hate this game. But if I'd been doing all the things you say I have, I don't think I'd be making this decision."

"While I'm saying it's the easiest decision you've ever made."

"Because you're making it for me."

"Leave me out of this. These are thoughts you might think. If my presentation isn't perfect you should blame it on my not being in your head. I don't believe I'm that far off the mark." He

· 473 ·

stood up and fished in the pocket of his sport coat. He came up with a syringe and a glass bottle with a silver cap.

"What's that," she said dully.

"It is immaterial. We continue to talk in our quiet room." He knelt by her bed and laid the syringe and bottle on the carpeting. He ripped open a small packet, grasped her left forearm, and wiped a patch of skin with an antiseptic swab. She didn't resist—but she did remember that if anyone had tried to shoot something foreign into her before she'd done time in this cell she would have gone down biting and kicking. Hadn't she tried to run from him when he kidnapped her? Hadn't she screamed when he drugged her?

Had she?

"Everyone has secrets," he said, plunging the needle into the bottle's cap. "They're good for the soul. They're a form of nourishment for the grimmer days. I have a feeling that for the sake of your pride you will recall only the brighter days we've spent together, and let Martin believe you've had the best time a woman could have had."

She felt the needle enter. "You're letting me go?"

"That's right." He held her hand ominously. "I'm giving you your freedom, though it hurts us both. There's no place like home. A funny notion. There's no place like home. You say it."

Her blood ran cold. "What are you doing to me?"

"There's no place like home."

Already the room was turning. There's no place like home. He was speaking from the other side, and a pounding heart moves poisons all the faster. This was her last thought.

·

". . . Jack Strom. We're very pleased to have as our guest Dr. Carl Sagan on the topic of nuclear winter. We have time for just a few more calls from our listeners. Hello, you're on the air—"

"Thank you, Jack. I wonder if I could ask Dr. Sagan whether he thinks that publicizing this issue might not force the U.S. and Russia to invest more heavily in weapons like the, the neutron bomb. That is, instead of making war unthinkable, whether your research might actually be putting even more stress on destroying soft targets instead of on weapons that would, you know, start fires. Uh?"

"Thank you very much. Doctor?"

"Well. In the first place—"

"An overnight low down around forty. Tomorrow should be mostly sunny and much warmer, with highs in the low to mid sixties. The outlook for Thursday and the weekend calls for—"

"K-A-K-A, Music Radio, closing in on four o'clock on a dur-*reary* Tuesday afternoon, the Moody Blues with a song by the same name. We have a traffic report coming up at a little after four, and Kash Kallers remember the number one *thousand*, six hundred and three dollars and eighteen cents, that's one *thousand*—"

"Cannot simultaneously reduce the number of warheads in the arsenal and introduce a new doctrine like the one the caller—"

"Jesus didn't turn his *back* on these people. Jesus said—"

·

The gym was miniature. In the entryway, on either side of the inner doors, a volleyball pole stood on an inverted metal dish with a bite taken out for a pair of wheels. The pole on the left had the net wrapped around it, the one on the right just a rope. Luisa wiped her feet on the rubber mat.

The American flag was planted in a weighted wooden base which had reminded her, when she went here, of one of the disks in her Tinkertoy set. There were curtained voting machines against the stage, against the low trellised doors that swung open to let barges laden with folding chairs roll out. The pollwatchers sat at tables from the cafeteria, doll tables. Thick climbing ropes looped from rafter to rafter at a height no longer dizzying; wires attached to the cranks on the gym's pale green walls held the knotted ends aloft.

The clerks smiled when Luisa stepped up to their tables. She was the only citizen voting in the gym. When they paged through the rolls and found her name, she could see that her father had been checked off as voting while her mother, of course, had not.

·

Cakes could be confusing. The directions called for cream, but there wasn't any in the list of ingredients or in the refrigerator. And she couldn't see how to mix the sticks of butter in with the sugar and spices and wheat germ. She decided to melt them, leaving them in their paper so they wouldn't drip into the stove element. She wasn't really thinking clearly. She was starting to care again. She needed to make a trip to the ladies' room. She needed to step out for a minute. She needed to excuse herself for just one sec. She had to make a call. She could use a breath of fresh air. She had to fix her face. She required a moment to compose herself. The directions called for cream, but there wasn't any in the list of ingredients or in the refrigerator. She went upstairs.

All through the house something rustled like dogs in autumn leaves. She opened her purse and looked for a vein, and started to regret undertaking a cake, if only because the smoke was so bad. But in a minute she'd forget all about it. She'd take a luxurious bath. Splash, splash. When Martin came home. Splash, splash. The many bottles of colorful fluids suggested their own scents, orange blossom, musk, and nature's pure honey. The sensuous woman knew how to please her husband when he came home from work. She'd seen it in a book. A peignoir could be very sexy.

.

When Jack DuChamp came home from work, Elaine was studying in the living room. "Did you vote?" she asked.

"No."

"Oh, for pete's sake."

"It's too crowded at the polls."

"It sure wasn't crowded when I went," she said. "You better go."

Jack opened the closet door and smiled bitterly. "You mean for Martin's sake?"

"Jack," Elaine said. "How come everything always has to be so personal?"

.

Singh left Barbara lying in the corner while he carried the dresser and chairs into the room and arranged her clothing and jewelry. He'd patched and repainted the bullet hole in the wall a month ago. He'd taken the lock and peephole off the door a week ago. All that remained was the cable by the bed. With a screwdriver he removed the cable anchor from the electrical box to which it had been bolted, and replaced the original outlet, wiring it nervously, as blue sparks popped on the tips of the live wires. He raised his pants leg and fastened the fetter around his calf; it was the only article besides the needle kit that he had to take with him. The cable he left coiled tightly in the cupboard with the household tools.

He reflected on how fortunate Jammu was. He doubted there were five thousand people in the entire world conscientious enough to have prepared the apartment for evacuation as he'd prepared it.

Taking Barbara on a slow trip through the three rooms and the kitchen, he applied her fingerprints to walls, dishes, fixtures, ashtrays, handles. He plucked hairs from her head and distributed them. Using her extra shoes he dotted the carpeting with footprints. A bachelor pad nevermore. He was just putting her back to bed, along with his own pillow, when Indira called him. "Well?" she said.

"Throttled. Clearly at the hands of a strong and passionate man."

He heard a sigh of relief.

·

The fire had begun in the basement when a forgotten cigarette, losing its ash, lost its balance and fell into the excelsior in which a Christmas fruitcake had been packed. The pine shavings and wrapping paper burned fiercely, igniting adjacent boxes. They were good sturdy boxes. Some of them were more than ten years old.

Strengthened by a diet of magazines, books and clothing, the fire had climbed up the paneled walls and burned out a window, venting smoke on the front side of the house. Given fresh air, the flames sprawled in all directions, consuming the stairs and within minutes the ceiling above them, rupturing into the staircase between the first and second floors and developing, then, an intense circular draft which carried them on up to the third-story rooms. At this juncture it still seemed a peculiarly selective fire, having started in the first of Probst's storage areas and traveled by the shortest route to the second. Box after box of unlabeled Kodak slides fed the flames. His collection of restaurant menus from around the world, from each of the countries he'd had the privilege of visiting, sets of towels and linen given as gifts and worn out but not thrown away, board games and books that Luisa had outgrown, World Series and World's Fair ticket stubs, twenty sets of anniversary cards, small Halloween costumes, Salvation Army paper roses, it was the thin organic matter that was burning, the ephemera.

But at approximately the same time Betsy LeMaster called the fire department, the blaze became a storm, indiscriminate and unstoppable. Probst's passport burned in an instant. Flames engulfed Luisa's bed, eating the dust ruffle and searing the mattress with a wolfing sound. Barbara's letters to Probst disappeared in a yellow flash. Portraits of the family continued to smile up until the last moment, when a wave of ash-in-progress crossed their faces. Oil paintings blistered like marshmallows, blanched, and hung until the wires tore loose from their burning frames. Luisa's old orthodontic retainers melted into pink plastic pools which boiled and took fire, the wires within them white hot. Barbara's underwear burned, Probst's favorite pajamas, Luisa's two formal dresses, the toilet paper in the bathroom, the toothbrushes and bath mats, *Paterson* and *The Winter's Tale*, the book of erotic verse hidden and forgotten in Luisa's nightstand, the ribbons in the family typewriters, the pasta in the kitchen, the gum wrappers and sales slips beneath the sofa cushions. In a third-floor window, an Indian woman screamed in a low unnatural voice, a contralto, a word that began but didn't end. Mohnwirbel staggered, drunk, from the garage and thought he saw Barbara.

·

Luisa heard the sirens as she was walking down Rock Hill Road to catch the bus. By the time she crossed the Frisco tracks they were coming from every direction. She'd never heard so many all at once. They mounted from behind the horizon and rang from every house, in jarring keys and rhythms, punctuated by the difficult speeding of fire trucks. Two pumpers roared past her and headed down Baker.

·

To the right of the front door was a grooved oblong button. Probst pressed it, hoping he'd found the right house. He hadn't been here in nearly fifteen years.

The door was opened by a woman with silvering hair and tiny burst capillaries in her cheeks. He identified her tentatively as Elaine DuChamp. "Martin?" He was dawning on her. "Why, come in!"

They clasped hands and brushed cheeks, a form of greeting for which they'd both grown old enough in fifteen years. Probst caught a glimpse of a girl running down the hall to the bedrooms. A door closed sharply. Ground beef and onions were cooking in the kitchen, imparting a mildly nauseating atmosphere to the living room, where notebooks and notecards were spread out on the floor. Elaine sidled away from him, untying her apron in back. "This is sure a surprise," she said, not unkindly. She dropped to her knees and with a few swift strokes gathered the notes into a pile.

"I was in the neighborhood," Probst said. "I thought I'd stop in and see Jack—see all of you. I've had to pass up your invitations lately, but the campaign's over, the—"

"He'll be thrilled." Elaine tucked the pile of notes into a niche in the wall unit. "He forgot to vote, but he's just around the corner. Can I offer you something?"

"No, thanks."

She left to attend to matters in the kitchen, and Probst, dumped on the sofa as if by time machine, scratched his head and looked around. The furniture had new slipcovers, but the shapes of the major pieces, of the couch and the three larger chairs, hadn't changed since the last time he'd sat in the DuChamp living room. The closest thing in sight to plant life was a giant blown-glass snifter half filled with waxy plastic fruit. Little joysticks from a computer game protruded at cocky angles from the shelf above the television.

He turned and studied the three pastel portraits in brass frames on the wall behind him. They must have been done at least seven years ago, because the younger girl didn't look any older than ten. A spot of white chalk in each eye made her radiant. The boy had sat for the artist in a blue blazer, a white shirt, and a red necktie, each of which unraveled into squiggling chalkstrokes at the bottom of the portrait, above the artist's black initials. The older girl had worn a pale pink dress with a high lace collar; she'd already had some chest, seven years ago, and the sheen on her lipstick was yellow-orange. Probst recalled that once upon a time the major department stores like Sears had hired portraitists who gave appointments at the various branches on a rotating basis and turned out drawings at very reasonable prices. It seemed to him that these itinerant artists had rendered something essential, that these three children would always live as they looked here, forever happy.

.

"This has been one hell of a pincer movement. One half a pincer and nobody to pinch."

"At leatht we got Nithing trapped."

Herb's brother Roy was parked on the far side of the target, ready to spot any and all action on that side and to follow anyone who tried to leave. In case things were still hopping in Missouri, Herb had also assigned three operatives to cover the Indian outposts that had looked the most heavily used. He'd assigned a fourth to keep an eye on Jammu.

"Sure," Sam said, peering down into the mirrored depths of the thermos. "After we give the rest of 'em four whole days to ditch their equipment and fly home to Katmandu."

"I'm thorry, Tham. You're free to dithcontinue our relationship."

"Oh, never mind me." Sam patted the small detective on the back. "We got a good enough shot at nailing Jammu if we quit right now. But I can just see 'em in there with their shredders."

"You're free to terminate."

"No need to cry, Herb. You reckon there's an open liquor store in these parts?"

"Shhh!"

Sam heard the zoom of Herb's video camera. "What is it?"

"Nithing!"

Eagerly Sam pressed his eyes to the chink. Nissing was standing on the street under a red and white golf umbrella, looking left and right as though checking to see if the coast was clear. Sam raised the telephoto lens to the chink, aimed through the viewfinder, and depressed the shutter release, letting the auto-advance motor whiz while Nissing walked purposefully west towards the river. In his mind he was already writing the caption for the photos: *John Nissing, close Jammu associate, leaving property owned by Hammaker. Property contains—* What did it contain? Sam looked at his watch;

it was 5:15. A swarm of heavily armed aliens? Regardless, in another four hours he and Herb were going in.

.

It was bound to happen one of these years. The chief executive of a publicly held corporation couldn't expect to continue running things forever. Buzz regretted only that he hadn't stepped down before they forced him to. His failing grasp of the concept of profit should have tipped him off. How could he ever have made the mistake of letting his feelings for Asha and Martin influence his policy decisions? What had he been *thinking* this spring? At the time, to be sure, his actions had made sense. And now they didn't matter. He was retiring on Friday. Of course, as the major stock-holder, he'd surely be allowed to continue whatever personal projects he chose. If need be, he could liquidate a few assets and fund the research out of his own pocket. He looked forward to having more time for his dear friends, and better yet, in a way, to having time to devote to the queer assemblage that was his family. When the top priority ceased to obtain, all the lower priorities moved up a notch.

He escaped headquarters in a company car without being accosted by the press. Rain was spattering the ground with forsythia petals. He'd long envisioned himself being retired on a different sort of day, a crisp and blue Novembery day, with a warm fire and brandy at the end of it. Spring was more the time of year when great men died.

He drove first to the Hammaker complex to inquire after Asha. She hadn't been seen at the office all day. He called the Hammaker estate once more, spoke with the same vague servant he'd been speaking with since 9:00 in the morning, who said that no, Asha wasn't there yet either. She'd gone out with her maid. Shopping? Buzz drove home.

Finding Bev's Cadillac parked by the gatehouse, he smiled a small smile of gratitude, his lips joining like a fortune cookie. When all else failed, he could count on Bev. He went inside, called to her, went upstairs, and saw her lying on the bed. On her nightstand stood an empty Seconal bottle and an empty fifth of Harvey's Bristol Cream.

As soon as she saw that her father's car wasn't in the garage, Luisa lost interest. She inched back through the crowd. In the bad light, none of the neighbors recognized her, not even Mrs. LeMaster. Though she saw something familiar and significant in Luisa's face, though she stared, screwing up her eyes until it seemed she might cry, Mrs. LeMaster was so unsure of her identification that she couldn't bring herself to collar a cop and say: that's no towhee, that's Luisa Probst, she used to live here. Luisa turned and walked back up Baker. It wasn't her mess.

She thanked her luck that she'd moved all her favorite things into Duane's apartment before this happened. She thought of various dresses and purses in her closet that were better off burned. She wondered what it would be like to move to another city and introduce herself using a different name. Her first name would be McArthur. Her last name would be Smith. She tried to imagine what kind of job she could get, and then for some reason she thought of her father's *National Geographic*s.

She stopped on the sidewalk and set down her purse, turned to an oak tree and socked the trunk as hard as she could. She bit her lip and looked at her knuckles. Shreds of white skin were bunched up and hanging ragged from the edge of pits into which blood was starting to seep. She hit the tree again with the same hand. It stung more but overall hurt less. She hit the tree two more times, and with each blow she could feel how solid it was, how its roots went deep enough to hold it powerfully vertical. The smell of burned wood was strong in her nose.

On Lockwood she sat waiting for a bus while cars rolled by, the commuting men shadowy in their interiors. Car after car, man after man, always one driver, starting up from the Rock Hill intersection. If you put together all the men in Webster Groves in the darkness of their cars at five o'clock, it added up to a mystery with the power of a crowd, but divided and more secret, a mystery like the business section of the newspaper and its esoteric concepts, like futures and options, which every day the men were privately assimilating. Did they understand it? In libraries Luisa had looked into just about every kind of field at least once, a psychotherapists' journal, the bulletin of the Missouri Historical Society, invertebrate morphology, the works, and the only kind of thinking she couldn't begin to follow was the kind the men with their loosened neckties in their expensive cars were presumably involved in as she watched.

The bus came. She threw a new cigarette into a puddle—you grew up to be a litterer—and got on, dropping her quarters into the box. She sat down across from the rear doors and looked forward at the black cleaning women sitting in the seats for the handicapped and elderly, returning home to their families. One of them leaned forward, her chin and hands propped on the handle of her umbrella, and spoke in a low voice to the others, who sat with their heads bowed to the no-slip floor and the collapsed umbrellas lying at their feet like drenched, docile pets. Lights in store windows on Big Bend drifted by, solitary and painful, burning in the greater darkness.

.

Three hundred officers had been assigned to patrol on foot to ensure that St. Louis Night proceeded in an orderly manner, as a crowd in excess of 500,000 was expected to pour into the downtown area for the festivities. Sidewalk duty wouldn't have been too bad if the weather was nice, but the rain was still coming down and a mean wind was kicking up. RC and Sergeant Dom Luzzi sat snug and lucky in their squad car, listening to the radio and skirting the main event, the authorized forklifts and vans plowing back and forth between the reserve parking zones and festival sites, the white tents on the Mall, the canopied booths and tables. The St. Louis skyline was lit up in sections, the floors like illuminated aquariums on shelves in a dark room. But where were the fish?

At 5:25 RC and Luzzi responded to a call from the offices of KSLX, where a group of street people were harassing employees as they left for home. Luzzi pulled the car around the police line blocking the inbound lanes of Olive Street and sped to the scene. Their arrival scattered the street people. They saw the soles of shoes flying up the alleys. A crowd of KSLX employees, many of whom RC recognized, dispersed and headed for the parking lot. Whoever was working the lot would have his hands full for a couple of minutes. RC craned his neck and saw they now had a woman there doing the parking.

Luzzi spoke with the security guard and got back in the car. "Something about a Benjamin Brown," he said.

"Huh."

"Are you familiar with the individual?"

"It's a name you hear."

"If these people stick around and make trouble in the crowd tonight, they'll be picked up separately. They aren't local."

"No, sir?"

Luzzi shook his head and jotted on his pad. "East St. Louis."

"The root of all evil."

"We've had enough of your humor, White."

•

When Gopal failed to make his scheduled call at 4:00 and another hour passed without her phone ringing, Jammu began to worry, routinely. She wondered what had been going on in England in the last twenty-four hours. She wondered what was going on in St. Louis. If her phone didn't ring she had no way of knowing. She called the Hammaker residence and found out nothing, called Singh's place and got no answer. She tried Martin at his office.

"No," his secretary said. "He left a while ago with Mrs. Probst."

It took Jammu a moment to find her voice. "When was this?"

"Oh, three o'clock or so."

"All right, thank you."

Things had been too quiet.

Either Singh had released Barbara to destroy the operation, or else Devi had returned. Knowing Devi to be resourceful, Gopal to be punctual, and Singh to be loyal if not to her then at least to the operation, Jammu concluded that Mrs. Probst was Devi and that Gopal, her strong arm, quite possibly was dead.

Where was her authority now?

•

Jack came in the front door shaking his umbrella. His coat was a woolen carapace, a tall gray bell without tucks or flaps. Probst looked up from the sofa with a smile, aware that his presence here was surprising. But Jack only nodded. "Hello Martin." The pitch of his voice rose on the last syllable. A hint of angry tears.

Probst crossed the room and extended a hand. "Hi, Jack."

"Good to see you." Jack's grip was weak. "What's the occasion?"

"No occasion. Just thought I'd drop in."

Jack wouldn't look at him. "Great. Excuse me a second." He swung around, and with a nonchalance undermined by little hitches in his stride, like the grabbing of a wet chamois on a windshield, he walked to the kitchen. He was obviously nursing a grudge. But perhaps he would abandon it. Probst sat down on the sofa again. He didn't mind waiting. Waiting rooms were places in which it was impossible to think.

In the kitchen, where melted cheese had joined the hamburger and onions, there were murmured consultations. Probst had already accepted Elaine's invitation to stay for dinner, and her murmurs were placating. Jack's were upbraiding. Then hers became more heated, and Jack's more resigned. He returned to the living room composing his hair and adjusting the cuffs of his baby blue sweater. "Do you want a beer, Martin?"

Again his voice rose as he spoke and cracked on the last syllable.

"Sure, thanks," Probst said. "I'm not interrupting anything?"

Jack didn't answer. He went to the kitchen and returned with a can of Hammaker, set it on the coffee table in front of Probst, turned on the television, and marched back to the kitchen. Probst was amazed. He never got the silent treatment from anyone but Barbara and Luisa.

"Oh, for pete's sake, Jack." Elaine was angry.

". . . tonight as fire fighters from three communities continue to pour water on his three-story house, which burned to the ground late this afternoon. Cliff Quinlan has a live mini-cam report."

"Don, no one knows how the fire started, Webster Groves fire chief Kirk McGraw has said it's too early to speculate on the possibility of arson, I don't think anyone here really thinks the blaze was in any way related to Probst's recent political activities, but this has been a deadly fire. When Webster Groves fire fighters arrived, they witnessed a man believed to be Probst's, ah, gardener entering the house. He did not come out again. The intensity of the heat has made recovery of the body impossible thus far, and it may be another one to three hours before it's determined whether any other persons were in the house at the time of the blaze. The one known victim is the, ah, gardener, who lived on the property and has not been seen. However, neighbors say that Probst's car is not on the property, so it appears unlikely that he himself was in the house. I've asked Chief McGraw how a fire could burn out of control for as long as it did in this residential neighborhood."

"Well, Cliff, first I'd have to point up the secluded nature of the residence, you see the hedges and the fence, the residence is set well back from the street, and at the period of time in question, namely the late afternoon, with visibility being what it was—"

Telephones rang throughout the house.

"Yes, he is," Jack said in the kitchen. He appeared in the doorway. "Martin, it's for you." He pointed—jabbed—a finger at the phone on the console in the hall. Then he withdrew again to the kitchen.

Probst retrieved his coat from the closet and walked out the front door into the rain. He'd hardly recognized the Webster Groves scene on the news. But he could identify the phone call with certainty. It was the summons he'd been waiting for. Only Jammu would have thought to look for him here. He'd mentioned Jack to her once, and once, he was learning, was all she needed.

·

She woke up with a headache and some grogginess, but basically the substance he'd given her had treated her as gently as he himself had. For a while she lay breathing experimentally, accustoming herself to consciousness, expecting dinner. But when she shifted her legs and opened her eyes she saw that everything had changed. The fetter was gone, the sheets were clean, a big lamp with a shade stood on a dresser by a chair on which her clothes—

She'd nearly fainted. On her next try, she stood up in increments, raising her head gradually, as if placing it atop the statue of her body. She crossed the room and opened the door. The lock she'd heard turn so many times was gone. And now, where for all the weeks she'd been led to the bathroom she'd heard the unmistakable echoes of vacancy, she was walking through an apartment very much like the New York apartment John had been forcing her to imagine.

Books of hers lay on the arms of Scandinavian chairs. She'd hung lingerie up to dry in the bathroom. On a desk in the dining room, above a pack of her Winstons and a dirty ashtray, she'd filed away her letters from Luisa and Audrey in a set of modular shelves. She'd stocked the refrigerator with her preferred brands of yogurt, diet chocolate soda, martini olives. (She was starving for real food, but she didn't touch anything.) She'd written a grocery list and left it on the counter. On the floor near the outer door she found a scrap of white paper.

> Bhimrao Ambedkar
> Barrister at Law
> Chowpatty, Bombay

.

The nurses, orderlies and candy stripers gave Buzz a wide berth. In the waiting area on the ICU floor at Barnes he sat hunched and trembling, a small, hungry old man. He hadn't eaten anything since his Reuben sandwich at noon. What the intercoms were saying he didn't understand. A nurse manipulated jumbo file cards and a telephone pealed electronically. A thin, even layer of scar tissue covered the walls and floors, the residue of the artificial light that had been falling twenty-four hours a day for twenty years.

The chief neurologist had told Buzz that any brain damage would not become evident until Bev regained consciousness, but that he should begin to prepare himself for a long and arduous recovery period. Asha had told him, when he finally got in touch with her, that she wouldn't be able to see him tonight because she'd made a commitment to appear at the election festivities downtown. And Martin's phone wasn't working.

Strain was building in his throat and behind his nose when he heard a familiar voice. He stifled a sob, looked up and saw his urologist strolling with another doctor at a conversational pace. Both of them peeled off green caps and massaged their scalps. Buzz raised his head further and uncrossed his arms to let himself be recognized and spoken to. They didn't speak to him. Dr. Thompson said, "Kids get side-aches."

The other doctor said, "Kids eat candy."

Dr. Thompson said, "Candy causes side-aches."

Both men laughed and walked onto the elevator, which had opened for them as they approached it.

.

Tired of driving but not of moving, Probst parked the Lincoln in one of the Convention Center garages, counted five other cars on the entire Lemon level, and set out from there on foot. It was nine o'clock. He'd spent two hours at the police station in Webster Groves, speaking to Allstate, thanking firemen, accepting coffee and condolences from Chief Harrison, and giving information to a series of lesser officers who transferred his statements onto dotted lines. He was told there would soon be a body to identify. He was left by himself in a corridor to wait, gratefully, on a carved walnut bench. Then an officer called his name: he was wanted on the telephone. It was the second summons, and again he walked away, got in his car, drove east.

Rock music, so loud it could only be live, reverberated inside the Convention Center and through the walls across the plaza. The song's chorus seemed to go, *You love you won you win.* Maybe the Center was packed with young people dancing and waving their arms above their heads, but maybe not; the plaza and surrounding streets were barren of stragglers. Pairs of policemen in mackintoshes turned their heads back and forth with an air of defensiveness. They stamped their feet and blew on their hands. Probst crossed Washington Street in the middle of a block and didn't see a car coming in either direction. The downtown streets, of course, were off limits to private cars tonight. Pedestrians were expected to carry the party into every square yard of the area. But there were fewer pedestrians in sight than on an ordinary Tuesday night.

A dixieland band was playing beneath a plastic awning in front of the Mercantile Tower, next to the chromium sculpture, which gleamed cheaply, a household knickknack grossly enlarged. Three teens in ski jackets stood listening to the music. The washboard player took a short solo, hunkering down and giving a vigorous rub to the slats of his instrument. He winked at the kids.

At the empty sidewalk cafés on 8th Street, waiters sat smoking, dozing, playing cards. Rain pelted the canopies, which shivered in each gust of wind like dogs that had evacuated. Probst stepped up to the sampling booth for Jardin des Plantes and ordered a slice of quiche from a short man with a bullet-shaped head.

"Five."

"Five dollars?"

"It's a benefit."

He bolted the quiche before it got too cold to stomach, crunching the bean sprouts and miniature shrimps embedded in it, squeezing the oils through his mouth and down his throat.

In another booth, above a tank of water, in a seat connected by springs to a bull's-eye at which passersby could pay to throw tennis balls, Sal Russo sat reading the *Post-Dispatch*. Sal was a city alderman from the ward in which Probst & Company were located. He looked quite toasty, his hair dry and styled, between a pair of radiant heaters. "Hey, Martin."

"Hi, Sal." Probst turned to the attendant. "How much?"

The attendant pointed to a sign. "Five bucks a throw. Sir. Or ten for three. It's a benefit."

He bought six balls, and then six more. Before Sal could surface in the tank, Probst had hastened around the corner onto Market Street. Here he stopped in his tracks, shocked by the Arch.

Colored lights were playing on the stainless steel, mottling it garishly. They shifted, the reds and greens and yellows intermingling on the flat integral sections. It wasn't Probst's Arch anymore. It was the National Park Service's.

Games and German sausages, clowns and unicyclists, raffles, accordionists, and elected representatives waited for a throng of visitors who, since they hadn't come by 9:00 in the evening, would surely not come at all. Probst himself had come only to seek necessity, to let himself be guided to Jammu. The Arch blushed as red lights rose and deepened to purple. He walked east, down the center of the Mall, under the eyes of lone policemen with billies.

Beneath the largest tent on the Mall, Bob Hope was speaking to a meager gathering with a peculiar demographic profile. It consisted entirely of youngish men. Probst couldn't find a single woman in it, nor any man under twenty or over forty. Two hundred rather small young men in London Fogs and Burberrys, in white shirts with tab collars and neckties of median width, in brown walking shoes with crepe soles, laughed on cue. Pete Wesley and Quentin Spiegelman and other dignitaries stood in a phalanx on the stage behind Hope, who was saying, "No, seriously, folks, I think it's just great to see what's been done in St. Louis. When you think what it looked like thirty years ago—of course, I only know from pictures. I was still a teenager in California."

The youngish men erupted in laughter, clapped their hands and nodded to each other.

"You know, I was in Washington the other day—"

•

Barbara hadn't meant to leave. She'd picked up the Bombay address from the floor and stepped into the hall, intending to explore the building, find a window and figure out where she was, and then return to the apartment and try some numbers besides her old one, which seemed to be out of order. She had to know the address before anyone could come and get her. But the apartment door had fallen shut behind her, locking.

There were no windows in the hall, only brick and steel, the brick painted gray and the steel a ferric orange, all lit by bulbs in cages. She boarded an elevator, stamping nervously on its worn wooden floor, descended to the ground floor and entered a hallway identical to the one on the top floor. The air was chilly and stale, the building completely silent. She walked to one end of the hallway and pushed open a heavy door, hanging at the threshold and looking out.

Beyond a wet empty street was an elevated highway. Trucks with small amber lamps around the margins of their trailers were passing in the rain. Clouds beyond the highway captured the bright lights of a city, but whatever skyline loomed there was obscured.

She shivered in her pants and sweater as the flavorless air blew in. On the floor lay a fragment of cinder block. She kicked it onto the threshold, against the jamb, stepped outside and carefully eased the door back against the cinder block. She looked up and down the street. It was a Hiroshima neighborhood in the spring of '46, so flat and lifeless that it seemed almost to promise safe passage. She saw distant streetlights, traffic lights, vehicle lights, some very distant office lights, but not one sign of commerce, no light in the shape of letters. She could find an entrance to the highway and flag someone down. But she hesitated. Somewhere in the warehouse there might be another telephone, or at least some tool with which she could force her way back into the apartment. She'd call the operator and have the call traced. She didn't want to leave.

A hundred yards away from her a thin man in a dark coat without luster crossed the street on a diagonal. He approached her steadily, implacably, with the hypnotic steps of a frog-gigger who'd "fixed" his prey. She stepped away from the doorway, wringing her hands. It was a matter of balance. She broke in the direction she'd been leaning—away from the door. The man walked faster and she fled along the front of the building, away from the city lights. The pace of his steps matched hers. She began to run. He began to run.

"Myth Madan!" he shouted.

Her sneakers slapped the broken pavement, bending around irregularities to average them and overcome them. She was stretching muscles she hadn't used since January. She kept running even when she heard the man stop, far behind her, with a scrabble of leather soles. Looking back, she saw him heading towards the warehouse. She ran between two sets of pillars beneath the highway, through a very black space, and suddenly into light.

The light came from fires, from flames licking out of barrels and from bonfires built on the pavement of a narrow street, flames oppressed by the rain but not subdued, sprouting sideways, clinging to the square-edged boards that fed them. At the far end of the street a single filament shone on an intersection with what appeared to be a similar street. In between, in tents and under lean-tos on the sidewalk, in the hulks of four-door cars and vans without tires, leaning from frameless windows of blackened buildings, were many more people than Barbara could count. There were hundreds.

She heard a few isolated voices, but for the most part the people sat and stood quiescent, crossing a leg here, raising an arm there, as if deep in thought. She looked back towards the warehouse. A pair of headlights had appeared in the gloom, expressionless disks of luminance, the distance between them slowly increasing as the car moved swiftly closer. She entered the street in front of her, and

with a relief she tasted in her mouth and felt in her chest she realized
that most of the people were women. She turned to the nearest
group, a threesome on the corner, but the car was almost upon
her. It was a station wagon. She ducked into an alley where more
women stood warming their hands at a barrel. The smoke lacked
the green aromatic complexity of nature; it smelled of old wood,
of lumber, not logs. The women were lost in their clothing. They
wore fishnet tights, platform heels of lacquered glitter, boots of
licorice leather that hugged ankles and calves, leather mini-skirts
and polyester hot pants, and short, padded jackets. Their faces,
some black, some white, peered out from between mounded hair
and fake fur collars. Two by two their eyes were coming to rest
on Barbara. She pressed against a brick wall, catching her breath,
as the station wagon passed in the street.

Closed shop, sister!

The laughter was loud and hit her like stones, fell dead on the
ground. Two women threw cigarettes into the barrel, ritually. They
were all looking at her.

"Where am I?" she asked.

You in Jammuville.

There was no laughter.

She was beginning to breathe normally. "I mean what state
am I in?"

Same state we's in!

You lookin for work?

Closed shop, closed shop.

They fell silent.

"I'm looking for the police," she said.

The police? She lookin for the po-lice? Oh ho.

One of them pointed.

See dat highway? You just follow it over the bridge.

They laughed again. Somewhere deeper in Jammuville a gun
was fired. Barbara headed up a cross street even more populated
than the one she'd just left. Puppets paced the sidewalks, their
seductions creaky in the cold, their turnings stiff and grindings
labored, while male eyes gleamed in the shadows. Not a word was
spoken. Barbara passed sore-looking breasts bared to the weather,
ecstasies in which only the agony wasn't simulated, a skirt raised

above a meaningless vulva framed by black straps. She stepped off the curb into the street, where automobiles were cruising in a steady stream, almost bumper to bumper. One of them drew even with her. Through the open driver-side window she saw a jowly white man in a red blazer with an unlit cigar between his teeth. He removed the cigar and looked her over.

"Listen," she said, "I'm—"

He shook his head. *"Tits."* The word was final, the voice prophetic. "I need mammoth tits." He had a vision of them. "Monster tits."

The next car honked her out of the way, but the one after that stopped, and she rapped on the window with her knuckles. The meek-eyed man inside frowned and shook his head. She looked down into his lap. He followed with his eyes, smiling modestly at his exposure.

Near the end of the street she saw the city. It was St. Louis. The Arch stood huge and stationary against a backdrop of brightly colored mists. It was St. Louis. It was the city in which her dreams had taken place all her life, all through the last two and a half months, the city which whenever John left the room she peopled with her family and her friends, the city she'd never stopped trying to remember and imagine: this was the city itself, and it was completely different from the city in her head though identical in detail, completely itself, the quality of reality overpowering all the more specific landmarks. But even now she couldn't shake the feeling— didn't want to—that she was about to wake up in John's arms.

.

Beneath the Arch, Probst faced the river and the unconstellated urban stars that twinkled in Illinois. A northbound barge spanned invisibly the four hundred yards between its lighted cabin and its lighted bow. Cars were moving at sixty miles an hour across the Poplar Street Bridge, but their progress looked painfully slow. In the depths of downtown a metallic man barked to muted cheers.

Piercing the seawall and leading down to Wharf Street was a long, wide set of concrete stairs. Probst sat down on the top step. He watched a familiar sedan travel along the street, halt, and back into a parking space between him and the *Huck Finn* and *Tom*

Sawyer, both of which were moored at their docks. The car door opened. Jammu stepped out.

On Easter she'd lain on top of him, hipbones on hipbones, knees on knees, and he'd held his arms around her narrow body trying less to stop her shaking than to make it match his own. The shaking was steady, unprogressive, Brownian. They smiled to acknowledge it, but it didn't stop. It excluded them, reduced them, made them equal in their mutual submission, and this was ideal, because in the ideal bed, in the twilight that came peculiarly to bedrooms, one wanted only to submit.

Don't tell me this is just a midlife infatuation. Don't tell me the lights are shining anyplace but here.

Halfway up the stairs Jammu stopped and sat down on the retaining wall on the right side of the landing. Probst felt the rainwater seeping through the seat of his pants. She drew the flaps of her trench coat together, crossed her arms, and put her hand to her mouth. He watched her chew her thumbnail. There was nothing left to want but her. And he could see how the year had happened, how a man in his prime, the envy of a state, could lose everything without even putting up a fight along the way: he hadn't believed in what he had. Something had always been missing, or interposed, between possession and glory, a question: Why me?

Maybe if he'd known that all the things around him that he loved could vanish like this, he might have succeeded in controlling himself, in making himself love them, or in losing control, in letting himself believe. But how could any man know when the end was coming?

What remained was a room in his mind, all around which the world had fallen away to a whistling galactic distance. The eye of the camera had shifted from a December delivery room to a Main Street location a week after the bomb had dropped, beholding now the rubble in which the living Martin and Susan had vaporized, and beaming the image back to the room, where the world, in them, made love. He might wander through the remembered forms of a city, but the only future that would happen would happen in this room.

·

She was going to wait for him to come down the stairs. She would never have won him in the first place, even for one afternoon, without some basic readiness on his part, some identity between her planned and executed destruction of his life and his acceptance of each stage of the destruction. In its purest realization the State was an exhaustive sense of fate. But she, who'd ordered Barbara killed, who'd arranged this one minor violation, couldn't share it. She'd thought she would be climbing these stairs all the way to the top and embracing him. But that wasn't how it worked.

Election Tuesday, the underwater throbbing of tug engines, the river's shallow sucking at the banks, the shrill of trucks, the sighing of tires in the sky, the vapid mutterings of St. Louis Night all lacked the volume to drown out the creature growing inside her, a creature glimpsed occasionally in mirrors or heard in fevers, a small, sad child. The child spoke aloud in her labors, able only, like Jammu, to plan and speak and work, to construct a life. Who of the two was the terror? Clearly the woman had fabricated the child as much as the child the woman. Both were cheap Taiwanese goods like everything else she'd ever thought or had a hand in, but the child, at least, had a name: Susan.

Gathering strings of lint from the inner folds of her coat pockets, glancing up at Martin, who sat like Patience at the top of the stairs, beneath the Arch, she began to cry. She pitied the child. She lacked the capacity, the basic instrumentation, the hardware, to love Martin as he loved her. But although the artifices had forever displaced the emotions, the child was making plans—*I had no idea Devi was back in the country, she'd sent me a letter from Bombay, very self-dramatizing, you must believe me, you do believe me, I can see*—only because she hadn't yet learned the emotions.

•

Somehow Probst had imagined that obeying her summons and meeting her here, meeting her eyes and accepting with her the lovely evil of caring only about each other, would be as easy as facing her in bed had been, as uninhibited by shame and selfconsciousness, as purely a matter of compulsion. But when he saw that she was crying and that specific and ordinary words of comfort were required, he knew the affair was over.

He became impatient. The wind off the river was picking up again, and he noticed that his hands were cold, his feet wet, his butt sore, his bladder full. He noticed where he was. He raised his face to the shape above him, to the beams of yellow, blue and violet light streaming into it and cut, terminated, in the form of the great black curve. It merely stood. Raindrops fell on his eyes. While in the room in his head the pleasure could not relent, because if it did it would beg the question of what became of it when it was over. Sex wasn't a life-prolonging satisfaction like food, and at their age the idea of reproduction couldn't rationalize the pleasure. Only repetition could. After all, in that room on the edge of space, he and she weren't just sitting around. They were eternally fucking. In an Eastern room, in a mode of existence in which the present life, the persistent problem of identity, was skirted by reference to past and future incarnations. But in Missouri you lived only once.

He stood up, finding in the stiffness of his shoulders an indication that he was ultimately not an evil person. His body was able to distract him. He was capable of growing impatient. He was not compelled. Actions emptied of meaning, feelings ceased to matter. The story of his life could not be all exclamation marks. He needed to find a bathroom or at least some secluded weeds, and it was with this practical haste that he shouted at the woman below him, who was slumped on the retaining wall, her posture shattered as if she'd fallen from the sky and landed in a heap: "Good bye!"

Without looking up she waved an arm at him, throwing an invisible stone.

.

Fear was getting the better of Barbara as tires squealed in the streets around her and people argued in the dark buildings. She wanted to walk briskly, purposefully, confidently, but walking required muscle control to maintain momentum. She started to jog. Relative to the warehouse she'd started from she was totally lost, but she could hold the Arch and part of the St. Louis skyline in view and she kept moving towards it. Only when she came to a block where there were men she didn't like the looks of did she change direction and run tangentially, south. Jammuville. She waited in vain for a police car to pass or a police station to rise out of the darkness.

If she could have figured out where the warehouse was she would have run there more eagerly than she was running to St. Louis. For more than two months she'd lived there in safety, a safety she appreciated now that she saw what lay all around. There was no place like home. John brought her meals. Oh, she was crazy, but she couldn't help it. She was lost in the place of her nightmares, of the nightmares of every citizen of Webster Groves, in a skeletal maze where every kid had a gun and every woman a knife, and a white female face was a ticket to gang rape after she'd been bludgeoned if she'd let them know she was afraid. Barbara was a good-hearted person and had never allowed herself to believe this. Who would hurt a defenseless woman without a purse? But the threat was physical and it surrounded her.

Still clutching the soggy slip of paper with John's new address, she jogged towards the Interstate, through one block and into another, thinking, *Get back, get back home.* She jogged almost to the end of the street, close enough to see the bright green sign with its arrow pointing to ST. LOUIS, she came within a hundred steps of the chain-link fence she would climb to reach the shoulder from which she would flag down a car, before she spotted the four loitering black men. *Keep running right past them.* She couldn't. She was making the Mistake but she couldn't help it. She was turning around and running away from them, showing her fear, and she heard the reports on concrete of their feet as they skipped to keep up.

"Hey there—"

"Hey—"

A rattling black Continental was passing through the intersection. She ran right in front of its headlights. It swerved and screeched. She let herself glance back. The four men were standing in a line, their faces inexpressive as they looked at her. The car started to drive away, but she grabbed the mirror on the driver's side. The window unrolled. A pair of white men in polyester jackets and pastel sport shirts were sitting in the front seat. The driver looked out the window at the men behind her. "Need a lift, honey?" The voice was sedated, confident.

"Yes. Please."

The driver consulted his companion, who gave her the once-over, shrugged, and unlocked the back door. As Barbara got in she saw a station wagon slowing to a stop halfway up the block behind the car. It was the same station wagon that had followed her away from John's building. The four men crossed the intersection, waving through the rear window, receding swiftly.

"Where to?" the driver said.

Nashville music whispered in the stereo speakers behind her. "Anywhere," she panted. "I'm lost. Police station."

"I don't know about that. How about our place instead?"

"Nigs givin' you shit?" his companion asked her.

"I was just scared," she murmured. The air smelled of after-shave and engine heat. At her feet were Burger King bags and two aluminum suitcases. To make room for her legs she started to move one of them aside.

"Don't touch," the companion said.

The driver turned the steering wheel hand over hand, languidly, and looked back over the headrest. "We're nice boys, honey, but fair's fair. I reckon you owe us one gratis. Those nigs wouldn't of been gentle."

He returned his attention to the road. They were driving fast, but Barbara closed her fingers around the door handle anyway. The side of the driver's hand slammed down on the button of the lock, his fingertips trailing on the window. His companion was kneeling on the front seat, smoothing back his straight hair with both hands. He grabbed Barbara's wrist as she lunged for the other door. He started to climb into the back seat but dropped his head to peer out the rear window. He frowned. "That company we got?"

The driver turned around to look. His face hardened. "You bitch, what is this?"

"I don't know. I don't know. Just let me out."

Red light filled the car. She turned. The station wagon was still following her. On the roof, above the driver's window, a flasher had appeared.

·

The Lufthansa woman in Chicago rested her fingers on the computer keyboard. "Mit Film oder ohne, Herr St. John?"

"Was für ein Film?"

Your attention, ladies and gentlemen, Flight 619 nonstop service to Frankfurt will begin boarding in—

"Ein Clint Eastwood."

"Ohne."

"Ja, dann haben Sie mehr Ruhe. Gepäck?"

"Die Aktentasche nur."

.

RC and Sergeant Luzzi had chosen to spend the last half hour of their shift parked under the I-70 overpass at the head of the Martin Luther King Bridge, while they listened to the force's own account of this St. Louis Night. A grill fire at one of the booths on Chestnut. Disorderly parties trying to crash the invitation-only Election Night Ball. An escort for Bob Hope's limo. A detail to keep spectators away from the fireworks barge in case spectators showed up.

The big display would be starting in twenty minutes, and RC and Luzzi would have a primo view out over Laclede's Landing and Eads Bridge. RC couldn't figure out, though, why there weren't more people heading for the waterfront. On the Fourth of July this intersection always swarmed with pedestrians, all tromping to the Arch. Tonight the traffic, what there was of it, was confined to cars, mainly VIPs arriving for the Ball. They'd seen Ronald Struthers drive up Broadway in a Caddy decorated for a wedding getaway, with crepe paper and tin cans and the words *Just Hitched* on a soggy cardboard plaque, meaning city and county. RC guessed the Chief was already at the Ball, playing hostess. Luzzi had dryly predicted she wouldn't be with the force much longer, to which RC had replied that that might be so but she'd never forget where she got her start. When it came to Jammu, even RC and Luzzi could be civil to each other.

Out over the Mississippi on the MLK a couple of cars were heading towards them. One of them had a flasher, which probably meant it was the East St. Louis force, since the dispatcher hadn't mentioned any chases, and anyway not too many of them lasted across the river and back. RC turned to Luzzi, who'd already switched on their flashers and made contact with the dispatcher. ". . . Over the MLK. We'll take appropriate action to stop the vehicle."

They pulled square across the exit lane and looked at each other in the light of the Seagram's billboard by the Embassy Suites.

"Better draw," Luzzi said. He took the rifle and got out of the cruiser, crouching behind the left front fender. RC unholstered his revolver. All at once this looked like action as real as any he'd been through yet. The lead car on the bridge had picked them up and was weaving in its lane as if trying to make up its mind. But the tail car had slowed down, stopping in the middle of the bridge. A station wagon. There were no official markings on it.

The lead car hit. It squealed and jumped the curb onto the lane divider, right in front of RC. Luzzi was standing up. A muzzle flashed twice as the car skidded sideways across the length of the divider.

"Tires, hit the tires," Luzzi shouted, diving back inside. He'd taken a bullet in the right shoulder. RC got out and scrambled up to the right front fender. The car had stopped moving not more than twenty feet from him. There were three people in it, two of them struggling in the back seat. RC fired twice at the rear tire and hit the hubcap twice. Luzzi's voice crackled over the loudspeaker. "Come out with your hands high."

Tires bit pavement. RC took aim again, raising the gun and bringing it down as the car gained speed and distance, twenty, thirty, fifty feet, heading up Third Street. The back door opened and a female jumped out headlong just as he pulled the trigger. He plainly saw her head jerk as the bullet entered. Luzzi was shouting incoherently. RC dropped his revolver and howled.

.

Leaving the Arch, turning off Lucas, Jammu heard Luzzi's voice on her radio. She wheeled around the corner and saw traffic piling up on Third Street. A black officer knelt clutching his head. Luzzi leaned against Cruiser 217 with his arms crossed, one hand pressing on his wounded shoulder, the other hand holding a microphone on the end of a stretched spiral cord. In the middle of Third Street, all alone, a woman lay in faint headlight beams.

Jammu heard herself walking. Her knees bent into view beneath her as she crouched by the woman, whose eyes were wide open. A crumpled slip of paper had fallen from her open hand, and from a flaring oval hole where her nostrils had been, blood fanned down her cheek and collected, orange and oily, on the weathered white paint of a lane line. A crowd was gathering around her at a respectful distance. Press badges were pinned to most of the lapels and purses. "Oh God," a woman said. Behind her Jammu heard the sobbing of the black officer, evidently the one who'd fired. He'd just guaranteed himself a series of promotions. She pocketed the slip of paper. With her index finger she touched the warm blood streaming from the woman's nose. "Stand aside," she told the reporters. Fresh officers were arriving from every direction. They pushed back the crowd, and no one noticed when Jammu, turning to confer with them, put her bleeding finger in her mouth and drew it out clean.

24

After midnight, as the merrymakers gravitated towards the seventy-inch television screen off the ballroom proper, the character of their drinking began to change, to cross the line between lubrication and anesthesia. Mixers were omitted. Whole bottles of champagne were hogged. Men danced with men, and women with their drinks. Peripheral guests and out-of-town celebrities departed discreetly, leaving the hard core of the pro-merger campaign, the Struthers-Meisner-Wesley axis, to shake their fists at the silver screen, wrangling with it, until the channel was changed to *His Girl Friday*, the late-night movie on KPLR.

The referendum had needed to carry both city and county by simple majorities. In the city, where less than 17 percent of registered voters had cast ballots, it was failing narrowly. In the county, with voter turnout barely 14 percent, it was missing by a four-to-one margin. Overall, the merger was receiving just over 20 percent of the vote. But even Vote No declined to term its victory a landslide. When little better than one eligible adult in seven had bothered to go to the polls, the only thing anybody could say had carried by a landslide was apathy.

Apathy? The analysts frowned. After all, the campaign had generated extraordinary publicity. Both sides had put forth cogent arguments, and neither had shied from unleashing the more vicious incentives, the racism and jealousy and greed, that tended to flush voters out in droves. The brightest lights in the St. Louis sky, the Jammus and Probsts, the Wesleys and the Hammakers, had guided the campaign. No one who paid the slightest attention to local news could have failed to grasp the importance of deciding whether the city and county should be reunited in a single new county. And yet no one, in effect, had voted.

It was a night when men and women paid to face the public would have paid to stay home in bed. The election was a Comet Kohoutek, a Super Bowl XVIII. Commenting on the returns as they came in, apparently still believing themselves to be heard at one and two in the morning, the local newspeople sensed their responsibility for the excess hype and did everything but apologize. Their eyes scurried back and forth like panicked mountaineers on Rushmore faces, appealing to their associates for help, coming to rest again on the camera only after they'd succeeded in obtaining it.

Don, uh, you wanna try and explain this?

Take a crack at this, Mary?

Bill. What would you say?

To the media, with their ethos of combat, St. Louis looked suddenly and inexplicably craven. Threatened with the prospect of thinking and deciding, the body politic had surrendered. It embarrassed the commentators—but only because they failed to place the election within the larger context. Their shame was a measure of their obsolescence. They did not understand that America was outgrowing the age of action.

With a maturity gained by bitter experience, the new America knew that certain struggles would not have the happy endings once dreamed of, but were doomed to perpetuate themselves, metamorphically foiling all attempts to resolve them. No matter how a region was structured, well-to-do white people were never going to permit their children to attend schools with dangerous black children. In any system devisable by mortals under lobbying pressure, taxes were bound to hit the unprivileged harder than the privileged, the exact nature of the unfairness depending only on who happened to be privileged at any given moment. The world would either end in a nuclear holocaust, or else not end in a nuclear holocaust. Washington would uphold repressive regimes overseas unless it decided not to, in which case communism would spread, unless it didn't. And so on. All political platforms were identical in their inadequacy, their inability to alter the cosmic order.

Enlightened Americans accepted the world as it came. They were willing to pay a high price for the food they ate—dense buttery ice creams, fresh pastas, chocolate truffles, boneless chicken breasts—because high-quality foods went down easily, leaving the mind free for more philosophical pursuits. By the same token, sexual promiscuity was passing out of fashion. The threat of AIDS ensured that the spirit would no longer be a slave to the passions. Instead of making love, instead of making war, young people were mastering their base instincts and going to professional schools. The national economy played to perfection its role in this trend. It also came to the aid of investors uncertain about how best to spend their money, as times of instability called for greater inwardness, for devotion to arbitrage and tax-free bonds and leveraged buy-outs, to profits devolving from mathematics itself, the music of the spheres. Entrepreneurship was spiritually and financially polluting. Americans seeking purity wisely left the toxic wastes and consumer complaints and labor unrest and bankruptcies to other nations, or to the remnants of the original merchant caste. The path to enlightenment led through the perception that all communal difficulties are illusions born of caring and desire. It led through non-action, non-involvement, and individual retirement accounts. The new generation had renounced the world in return for simplicity and self-sufficiency. Nirvana beckoned.

.

At dawn the brain trust gathered in Jammu's office for damage assessment. Seasoned campaigners, familiar with setbacks, they took the long view, eschewing childish outbursts. They paced in shirtsleeves. They smoked cigarettes. They gazed out the eastern windows at the gray streets and the fog-locked Arch. Only in their solicitude towards Jammu did they betray their awareness of the magnitude of the catastrophe.

Pete Wesley had brewed coffee, stepping back from the 30-cup pot and scowling at its controls, forcing proficiency in a field of endeavor with which he was not that well acquainted. He brought steaming conical cups in plastic zarfs, two by two, to the craving, sobering hands all around him. He pointed at Jammu. "Do you, ah," he swallowed, nearly garbling his question, "want coffee?"

She shook her head.

The men milled with their cups, drinking. Each time one of them stopped at the big pot for a refill he glanced at Jammu. Coffee?

She shook her head.

Her foreignness and gender heightened the innate pathos of the moment, complicating, with paternal tenderness, the unwanted superiority most underlings feel when their commander has met defeat. Because it was her first American election, and she was bound to have seen it as a referendum on her personally, they were afraid she might be taking all the blame. But they were even more afraid of trying to forestall this, since in their circle the intimacy of alibis and consolation was considered bad form. They waited for her to come around, to remember again that up until the last minute the opinion polls had continued to show both city and county residents giving her very high approval ratings. If every resident had been *compelled* to vote, or if the sun had done them a favor by shining on Tuesday, or if the campaign had induced less boredom and more grass-roots participation, the merger would have carried easily, for the simple reason that she supported it. In the practical sense, too, the election hadn't constituted a referendum on her, because her strength had never depended on her effectiveness in getting out the vote. The merger's failure took nothing away from the motives her various followers had for remaining in her camp. She still formed the nexus between the industrialists like Chet Murphy and the Democrats like Wesley, between the bankers like Spiegelman and the informationalists like Jim Hutchinson, between the planners and the blacks: between private maneuvering and public opinion. In September she'd had only an aging ex-lover named Singh to comfort her in her early-morning depressions. Now she had the cream of the St. Louis elite, doting on her, trying to keep one another tactful for as long as she was gloomy, and she was still the kind of woman, brooding and brilliant, grand, who merited these attentions. The great wouldn't have become great if they were easily satisfied with themselves.

"Hey." Ronald Struthers stopped in the middle of the room and spread his arms, facing her. "Only thirteen more years."

The others looked away. She raised her head. "Thirteen more years?"

"Until you're eligible to run for the office of U.S. President."

Her weary smile deepened the lines dividing her mouth, her soft beak, from her cheeks. The others squirmed, wishing Struthers hadn't tried.

Then Asha Hammaker breezed in, kissed Jammu, and set a large waxed-paper bag of croissants and pains au chocolat on her desk. Wesley dumped the grounds and made a second pot of coffee with greatly enhanced self-confidence. The party grew lively, its participants finding their second wind as the light of the new day filled the office. They chatted around Jammu. Asha had left a smear of lipstick on the Chief's forehead, a small red feather. This morning the graying zone above her left ear reached further back around her head than it had on mornings in the past.

She began to test inappropriate facial expressions, to wince, widen her eyes, stretch her lips taut across her mouth, frown deeply, balloon her cheeks and cross her eyes, all in a manner acutely reminiscent of her mother, who often, when conferring with lawyers or entertaining legislators, could not help making faces which had utterly no bearing on the matter at hand. It was a sleepy heedlessness, but also a senility, the open contempt shown for the world by people with few years remaining in it. Her friends tried not to notice.

"It's the county's loss, not ours."

"Where's Ripley?"

"We'll just buy some of those towns. Out and out buy them."

"Start with the county-level police force, by July, the whole thing step by step."

"He left with his wife, I think around eleven."

"I'd like to see some of those town councils politicized."

"Careful, careful."

"We've got the momentum."

"You say that this morning?"

"You hear about Probst's house?"

"The second quarter will make believers out of them."

"From the roof, the finale."

"Coffee, Ess?"

"This hardly qualifies as a democracy anymore."

"Like a baby, Jim."

"What?"

"Burnt my tongue."

"I need a hot shower, first and foremost."

"They're better in France."

They all began to sing the Marseillaise. Only Asha knew the words. The rest filled in the lyric slots with dums and doos, covering their hearts with their hands, simulating Frenchmen. Jammu rose and left the room. Singing, they looked after her and realized they might have gone a little too far. She was opening a cabinet in the outer office. She took out a black leather jacket, her holster, and a folded pair of blue serge pants. Could she be planning to do a day's work as police chief? She never let up.

She stopped in the bathroom, pumped on the metal button above the sink until the spigot produced a pink ooze, and began to wash her hands.

She was clean. Barbara and Devi were dead, the wound of the operation was closed and the scar was only faintly visible. Jammu had made a few mistakes, perhaps. At the very least she should have ordered Singh to move Barbara from his building. Her failure to do so had resulted in a less than perfect murder. But in terms of the operation the murder was harmless. At her request, the East St. Louis police had already performed a warranted search of the building and informed her that they'd found nothing out of the ordinary, just a loft apartment in which a man and woman appeared to have been living on an irregular basis. Nothing pointed to duress, everything to normal urban life. Singh had left open the possibility of the story that would now be used: Barbara had occasionally been accompanying Nissing on his trips to St. Louis, staying in the apartment without telling her husband. One evening while Nissing was away she came out and got spooked, got in trouble, and ran. She'd certainly behaved peculiarly, of course, but as Jammu had warned Probst, Nissing was a peculiar man. It didn't matter that the story was full of holes. With no one left to dispute it, the police had no reason to scrutinize it. The parties actually involved in the murder were in custody. The officer who'd fired the fatal shot would be given a short leave of absence for any counseling he might need, and Brian Deere and Bobby Dean Judd, the two small-time narcotics dealers who'd picked Barbara up, would be charged with second-degree murder under the principle of reasonable force. As long as there was some explanation for Barbara's presence in East St. Louis, any explanation at all, the detectives would not be forced to use their imagination. The same went for Devi Madan's presence in Probst's house when it burned. Here, Rolf Ripley was the explanation. And Ripley wouldn't be called to testify in any criminal proceeding, because there would be no criminal proceeding, because the firebug herself was dead. Jammu also believed that Probst would let sleeping dogs lie and not attempt to initiate any civil action or public crusade against her. To forge a comprehensible case, he'd have to acknowledge that he and she had had sexual relations and then advance the more or less fantastical hypothesis that she'd arranged the shooting of his wife for personal reasons. Either that, or make reference to the full story of the operation, a story she'd now placed immovably within the realm of fiction.

The operation's concrete appurtenances had been destroyed. So had every financial record to which American investigators might have obtained access. All of Jammu's agents were either dead or in India, where, if their emotional loyalty ever waned, they could easily be bribed into silence. The evidence Pokorny and Norris had gathered was purely circumstantial—the circumstances were, to be sure, sometimes rather damning on the surface, but Jammu had at her disposal a complete array of plausible justifications for everything from her meetings with Devi to the real-estate transactions her mother had made through Asha, and more important, she knew how to play a paranoid public inquiry to her own advantage by raising the spectres of McCarthyism and sexism and racial prejudice and such. What worried her more at the moment was the publicity that Barbara's death would bring to bear on East St. Louis. Theoretically a city with an exceptional police force could not be faulted for having diverted unwanted elements into a neighboring community. But Jammu had staked much of her reputation as a problem-solver on her apparent ability to make street crime simply disappear. The real story would soil her in the eyes of the public. She was ready, naturally, to present a new aspect of her personality, the aspect of a woman calm under fire and willing to accept all the responsibility she bore, however indirectly, for Barbara's death and for the situation as a whole in Illinois. A small scandal would humanize her; already, as of this morning, she'd lost her aura of invincibility. Public life required that popular figures sometimes play the sacrificial victim. It was a part she could handle and survive. Hadn't Indira bounced back strong after the Emergency? As for the defeat of the merger and the squatters in Chesterfield and all the other minor bitches—well, as police chief, she of course could not be expected to take the blame in any way. She might even be allowed to accumulate political capital as the voice of moderation in these and other crises. No one would stop her from using her office like this, from venturing out to solve problems far afield and then retreating to her humble official position in the face of difficulties, so long as she was deft enough to avoid charges of hypocrisy and opportunism, and successful enough to reap the region's love and appreciation for her efforts . . .

The voice in her, the pressure of justification, the apology, went on and on. She pulled two paper towels from the dispenser and dried her hands. Then she changed her clothes, looking repeatedly at the mirror, at the face within the face.

. . . When the reporters came, she would present the facts surrounding the shooting death of Barbara, explain how the prosecution of Deere and Judd would work, and personally take the lead in exposing the crime problem in East St. Louis. She'd make an example of Barbara and, without explicitly mentioning it, allow her audience to recall how close she and Barbara's husband had become, how personal a tragedy this was for her. And then, donning a new mood, she'd make a brave joke about the outcome of the election. But first, before she could face them, she'd need a glass of vodka and a nap. She absolutely had to get some rest this morning. Mrs. Peabody would cheerfully inform the reporters that she was sleeping. The idea would charm them—Chief Jammu is sleeping—children sleep—sweet, innocent sleep—

The shot ate its way into the walls and stalls and vanished, leaving only blood. Where one moment two individuals had faced each other in the mirror, the next moment there was no one. Wesley and the others threw down their pastries. They came running.

·

Two months before they were due to be married, on a warm April Sunday afternoon, Probst and Barbara had gone out driving in his silver Valiant into the western sun on Big Bend Road, through Twin Oaks, Valley Park and Fern Glen, where the lawns tumbled down shaggily to the mailboxes at the shoulder and a passing car was an event of some note for the natives, and the roads wore their original concrete topping, unreplaced since the transition from dirt to pavement twenty and thirty years earlier. Barbara sat sideways in the passenger seat with her back against the door and the fingers of one hand out the half-open window, letting the wind smoke her cigarette. Her knee was braced against the glove compartment to stabilize her as the car bounced right and left at a disruptive frequency, a bit faster than breathing, a bit slower than heartbeats, when the tires hit the swollen joints between the slabs; the jolts, like skipped frames in a movie, created the impression of excessive speed, and she slowed her own movements accordingly. She was wearing a white blouse under a gray crew-neck sweater, blue dungarees with the cuffs rolled up to the tops of her argyle socks. The strip of tint on the windshield dyed her forehead green. One of her stockinged feet rested on Probst's right thigh, and through his pants, through the difference in humidity, he could just feel the sweatiness of her sole. Her toes wiggled languidly, of their own volition, the reflex of a foot accustomed to shoes.

She always wanted to go driving that year. Looking back, he was inclined to see in the impulse a scientific method of filling up their time together, as they hadn't yet developed that body of mutual friends whose weaknesses, in later years, would provide the staple of their conversational diet, and as they'd begun to tiptoe around the engineering lessons which made her face go blank, and the French literature and German science to which he tiresomely responded with comic ignorance or earnest distrust because he didn't yet dare ask to be educated. To a couple separated by age and background and not in the mood to buy entertainment, almost any alternative to silly games or love talk, any cruising or walking or sex, was welcome. But at the time, her proposals of drives they might take had seemed more positively motivated. They seemed to spring from a hunger which he himself lacked. They were promises—as though, whenever she proposed a destination, she had been there already and could attest to its beauty or interest and then, when they arrived, she were vouchsafing him glimpses of the twenty-two years hidden inside her, in the fall foliage at the Algonquin Country Club, the Creve Coeur lake that was indeed frozen and could be skated on, the fritters and ham hocks at the all-Negro restaurant off North Jefferson Avenue. The world she promised was latent in how she looked, three-dimensional and life-sized, sinking into the seat cushion and dimpling its plaid upholstery as she said planets dimpled outer space, a woman in his car brought through the agency of something like grace, as if it were the exception, not the rule, that young people fell in love and went out together and he, Probst, were specially blessed. It was because she betrayed no consciousness of being his reward. She didn't smile unnecessarily, didn't comment on the route they were taking out to Rockwood Reservation, but sat in his car neutrally, as she might have sat in her father's car, occupying herself without relation to him, intense only in anticipation of arriving. Hers was the indifference of a foreign country to a new immigrant: he was allowed to stay, but the rest was up to him. Nor could he imagine becoming used to her, although, in the universal and destructive ambition of fresh love, he wanted to know everything about her. He looked forward to fighting with her, to seeing the pink cords of her will exposed.

Winding and braking, skirting a small Ozark spread with budding oaks, they came to the intersection with Route 109, the road to Rockwood. Probst looked both ways before making his left turn. On his right, in the lane he was about to enter, he saw a pickup truck approaching fast, but for reasons he'd never understand he did not really see it. He pulled out into the intersection, aware enough of making a mistake that he floored the gas pedal. The truck was heading straight for the passenger-side door. Barbara gasped. The horn blew. Probst braced himself, accelerating. The truck swerved and slammed into the rear fender and trunk, and careened into the opposite lanes. The Valiant, half demolished, landed in the ditch. Barbara split her lip and broke a tooth on the dashboard.

After the police had come and the wrecker had towed away the Valiant and Barbara's brother had come out to pick them up and they'd stopped at the hospital and left and had a couple of drinks, Probst asked her not to marry him. And for a while that night two distinct personalities had wrestled visibly in her, one assuring him, with the haste that grips a shy woman when a fellow diner has spilled gravy on her dress, that everything was fine and nothing had changed, and the other, like a girl too young to be mindful of any obligations but to herself, regarding him with revulsion and thinking how close this man just came to killing me.

He saw that sometime in the last twenty years the county had installed a traffic light at the intersection. The morning sun was shining on long pools of water in the ditches, on the silver propane tanks outside the houses in the distance, on his left shoulder as he drove south on 109. The asphalt was seamless. He'd been driving all night except for the two or three hours he'd spent parked in front of a Schnucks after hearing the news on the KSLX midnight roundup. He'd thought his mother's death four years ago had demonstrated once and for all that he wasn't a man to cry in anything but anger. But he hadn't been married to his mother. But the intervals between the contractions of grief in him had gradually increased as the individual memories that triggered the contractions melted together into a more general history, a sad book that was closing. By the time he'd watched the sun rise over the Chrysler assembly plant on I-44 he felt he'd be strong enough to function through the day—but felt it with a dread, the fear of soberness, because when the grief ended the questions began.

Highways didn't help. The landscapes offended the eye passively, by disappointing it, leaving unfulfilled the traveler's hope that the opening of the country might, as roads actually did in England or Africa, reveal significant traces of the indwelling spirit. There were, for instance, the zinc-plated standards of exit signs and mileage signs—upright I-beams whose burrs and pits reflected low-cost fabrication, wide tolerances, U.S. government specifications. The structure of each sign was sturdy enough and the design pleasing enough that it teased travelers with the possibility of being appreciated as a less literal sign of place. But its impersonal adequacy denied that possibility, at least to any native. Maybe if foreign travelers passed one of these signs they might find the name "Fenton" as exotic and indicative as Probst had found "Oberammergau" and "Oaxaca" when he'd toured them, or they might have been delighted by the mile as an outsized unit of distance, or by the greeny green of the sign as it contrasted with the yellow or white signs of home, or even by the stocky proportions of the upright I-beams. But maybe not.

Having had thoughtful road experiences in other countries and in his youth, Probst wanted to have them still, longed to be foreign again—as Jammu, in relation to the city, had made him. To be young, to live in the world as opposed to merely inhabiting it, a man had to stay foreign. But in the country there were only hillsides scarred with driveways and pastures, billboards for inexpensive ryes and inexpensive motels and inexpensive restaurants at the pinnacle of whose menus stood New York strip steak and batter-fried jumbo shrimp with cocktail sauce, the prices working down from there. License plates bore unhelpful combinations of characters, with too few letters to play word games, too few numbers to hunt for patterns. The rivers were muddy. Nothing raised or lowered the horizon by more than a few degrees. All the cars had four wheels, all the trucks had mud flaps behind the tires, all curves in the road translated into a single mechanism, the turning of the steering wheel. The interesting architecture—new churches with derricklike campaniles or nautical profiles, corporate headquarters with nonrectilinear floor plans or geodesic atria—was ugly. The uninteresting architecture was uninteresting. Distance diluted the color of flowers. If glamorous women or criminal men drove on the highways, the windows of their cars were smoked, or else it didn't matter, as it didn't matter if a truck was loaded with unusual cargo like poisonous chlorine or sheep, because everything hurried past. Probst wasn't an aesthete. There was no cause for hatred. But as he approached the city, the countryside filled him with a sense of betrayal, a pain intense enough to counterbalance his fear and begin to answer the questions. He was alive. Sadly, angrily, in a world he was only now realizing he didn't like, he was alive.

Outside a convenience store on Big Bend he put a quarter in a telephone.

Audrey's voice was chiding, practical. "Where have you been?"

"I've been driving."

"Well, you'd better come over. Luisa's here. Everyone's here."

Probst said nothing. A Hostess truck pulled up beside the booth, and out of the telephone receiver came flooding the interior of the Ripleys' house—the smell of the cold fireplace, the clatter of cups in the kitchen and the rhythmic sucking of the coffeepot, the voices subdued in every room including the one in which the dead woman's husband might already have been sitting, the Probst whose face the relatives, between sips, consulted like a template. Their expectations would not let him be. They pulled at his features, restoring the grieving contortions of the night before, voiding the experience and forcing a repetition—the rooms filled the phone booth, and Probst rose swiftly from the sofa, hurried down the hall past Audrey and her tray of cups, and reached the bathroom just in time to shut the door before the paroxysms overcame him.

"Martin?"

A man with pink Snoballs debouched from the Hostess truck.

"You're coming?" Audrey said.

He swallowed. "Yes."

At Central Hardware the orange-coated experts were opening the main doors. Nine o'clock. Probst turned north on Lindbergh, and fifteen minutes later he was pulling to a stop in front of the Ripley residence, where he recognized Barbara's parents' Volvo and Duane's Nova. All the curtains in the big house were drawn. The eastern chimney dribbled white woodsmoke into the pale blue sky.

Behind the glaze of light on the storm door, whose mild concavity gathered the reflected trees into a single star-like tree with radiating branches, the front door opened and a figure looked out from the shadows inside. There was a reprimand in its indistinctness, in its seeing him without being seen. Then the storm door opened and a tall young woman in glasses stepped out. She hesitated before, looking aside, still reluctant, she made up her mind to come down the front walk to meet him. That it was Luisa brought joy to his recognition: she was a stranger to him.

.

When Singh had boarded in Chicago he'd scanned the central compartment of the fully booked 747 to find his seat, which, he'd been told, was situated on an aisle. Passengers were stowing their last belongings and sinking into their seats, testing them to make sure all the comforts for which they'd paid were operational, and making immediate yawning preparations for sleep. Well before Singh had edged through the roil and found his row, he was certain that a particular aisle seat in the distance was his, because a small infant in the throes of a diaper change was lying on it.

"Excuse me."

The mother, a young Southerner with an intricately layered coiffure, hastened to wrap up the infant and remove it. She confided to Singh that she had sort of hoped his seat would be empty.

The infant was flying to be with its father, a lieutenant at the U.S. base outside Frankfurt. Apparently the anticipation ruled out the possibility of sleep, although the mother, under the influence of a split of Moselle, went out like a light after the late dinner was served. The infant lunged and knocked aside Singh's eyeglasses and pushed into his left eye a fist covered with clear mucus. Singh awakened the mother. She collected the arms and legs into a bundle and went back to sleep. Singh reclined deeply. He opened one eye to ward off violations of his territorial limits and saw the infant staring at him, drooling through a smile, its eyebrows raised. Singh showed teeth. The infant shrieked with laughter. He shut his eyes but the laughter continued. He opened them. Reading lights were blinking on all around him. The mother, unbelievably, snored. A weary businessman leaned across the aisle to ask if the infant belonged to Singh (had sprung from his loins, was the fruit of his seed). He shook his head and awakened the mother again. She took the infant on a tour of the plane, returned, and went to sleep. The infant began to cry. The mother awoke and proffered a bottle. The infant took a deep draught, turned to Singh, and sprayed him.

"*Clifford.*"

A smell of decay arose, prompting another trip for Clifford, who, on departure, took a last swipe at Singh's glasses, which were already well spattered with juice.

Over Newfoundland Clifford vomited onto the knee of Singh's wool trousers. Over England, with a precision that presaged a future in the artillery, Clifford threw a glistening wad of scrambled egg through Singh's open shirt collar. The egg dropped all the way down to his belt. Determined to spend the remainder of the flight away from his seat, he rose and repaired to the lavatory. He removed his shirt, deposited the egg in the toilet, and while he was brushing yellow morsels out of his chest hair the jet encountered turbulence, causing him to lose his balance. One of the cuffs of his white Pierre Cardin dress shirt swooped into the blue liquid in the toilet. On the loudspeakers the flight attendants were advising all passengers to return to their seats and fasten their safety belts. He soaked the soiled cuff in the sink and wrung it out. The next jolt of turbulence, in combination with the slick floor of the lavatory, threw him over backwards. He extended an arm to break his fall and brought his hand down directly into the center of the toilet, onto the steel plate on which the blue liquid rested. The plate was hinged; at the pressure of his hand, it opened, activating the flush mechanism.

By the time he emerged, smelling strongly of the candy-scented toilet fluid, the plane had entered more orderly German skies and was preparing to land at Frankfurt. The pilot, a relaxed and ped-agogical captain, narrated the final moments of the descent.

"Ten meters . . .

"Fife meters . . .

"We are over se runway now . . .

"Two meters. One meter. We lend every second now . . .

"*Ser.*"

In the Frankfurt mega-terminal Singh changed fifty dollars and bought a new shirt. His comrades would jibe him, make him pay for every hour he'd wasted in America with at least a minute of embarrassment, but they would also be disappointed if he failed to come home looking dapper, their well-traveled brother in struggle.

By noon, local time, he was in the air again on a direct flight to Bombay. From his window seat he watched the refueling op-erations at Istanbul and fell asleep. When he awoke he was over the Indian Ocean, an hour west of Bombay.

And then he was there, in a motor cab leaving Santa Cruz and passing bicyclists on Jawaharlal Nehru Road, tooting aside the short spindly men in turbans and dhotis who loomed up in the morning dust, and tailing, at ten miles an hour, a gray lorry on the rear gate of which three teenagers sat and kicked their legs. It was spring, Singh noticed. The old was new. He made the cabbie stop and pressed a purple 100-rupee note into his hands. In his slippery oxfords he sprinted to catch up with the lorry. One of the youths, a round-eyed schoolboy in a University of Wisconsin sweatshirt and copper-colored bellbottoms, inched aside to make room for him on the gate. He jumped, turned in midair, and landed seated, looking back into the empty western sky as the lorry carried him east to set him free among the other thirty million Indians named Singh.

Jonathan Franzen

The Corrections

THE INTERNATIONAL NUMBER ONE BESTSELLER
AND WINNER OF THE NATIONAL BOOK AWARD

The Lamberts – Enid and Alfred and their three grown-up
children – are a troubled family living in a troubled age.
Alfred is slowly losing his mind to Parkinson's disease. As his
condition worsens, and the Lamberts are forced to face the
secrets and failures that haunt them, Enid sets her heart on
gathering everyone together for one last family Christmas.

'A book which is funny, moving, generous, brutal and intelligent, and which poses the ultimate question, what life is for
– and that is as much as anyone could ask.'
Blake Morrison, *Guardian*

'A novel as alive to the pressures of the present moment as any
I can think of; a book in which memorable setpieces
and under-your-skin characters tumble over one another to
compete for attention. Like the greatest fiction, for all its
edgy satire and laugh-out-loud comedy, this novel is, above
all, an exercise in generosity.'
Tim Adams, *Observer*

'A wonderful book. Every page simmers with wit, close observation and intelligence.'
John Burnside, *Scotsman*

'A novel of outstanding sympathy, wit, moral intelligence and
pathos, a family saga told with stylistic brio and psychological and political insight. No British novelist is currently writing
at this pitch.'
Jeremy Treglown, *Financial Times*

All Fourth Estate books are available from
your local bookshop.

For a monthy update on Fourth Estate's
latest releases, with interviews, extracts,
competitions and special offers visit
www.4thestate.com

Or visit
www.4thestate.com/readingroom
for the very latest reading guides on our
bestselling authors, including Michael Chabon,
Annie Proulx, Lorna Sage, Carol Shields.

London and *New York*